LIMINALITY

TJ NICHOLS

LIMINALITY

Like everyone in the Dark City, Elliot Brand never has enough coin for anything. There is never time for more than survival. He does everything he can to make sure he and his brother, Dayne, have a place to live. But when his brother goes missing, Elliot suspects the worst—that he has been taken by the Kin.

The Kin live in a castle on the lake that only appears at night. They trade with the rich up the hill. In exchange for giving the rich the orbs that light the city and healing nectar, the Kin are permitted to hunt humans in the Dark City.

Elliot swore on his mother's death bed that he wouldn't let harm come to Dayne, so he makes a plan to go to the castle and get his brother back. Dazzled by the wealth and the attentions of Umbra, a Kin with their own plans, Elliot gets caught up in machinations far beyond his wildest dreams.

But Dayne has tasted Kin blood and become one of the devoured. Elliot's plans quickly unravel. If Elliot and Umbra are to survive, they'll need one another.

PART I
BLOOD

CHAPTER 1

*E*lliot Brand drew in a breath. The sweet smoke burned the back of his throat, but he held it in his lungs for as long as he could before blowing the cloud out of his mouth. This close to the lake edge after sunset, he wasn't taking any chances. The cigarette crackled in his fingers, smoke coiling upwards. He took another drag, the paper and marshmallow leaf burning fast and almost singeing his fingers before he dropped the butt on the gritty shore. He exhaled again. Hopefully there'd be enough poison in his blood that the Kin wouldn't see him as supper.

He squinted into the dusk waiting for the mist to gather and the castle to appear like a ghost intent on consuming the living, but the surface of the lake remained stubbornly empty. It was safer to be well away from the lake before the castle appeared. One never knew when the Kin would ride out to hunt.

The inky water lapped at the shore, hiding its secrets. It was said that at night, there were monsters in the lake that ate boats. Maybe the monsters were all that stopped the devoured from swimming to the castle.

He ground his heel on the butt of his cigarette and walked along the shore, past the bonfires that marked the camps of the devoured.

He scanned the thin faces, searching for his brother's the same way he had every night for the past month.

The devoured played music and danced all night, hoping to lure the Kin into appearing and taking them once again.

Fools.

They should have never gotten themselves taken in the first place.

But not everyone danced in search of ecstasy. Some lay on the ground, gaunt and shivering. Starving because all they could think of was Kin blood, not the food that would sustain them. They forgot the troubles of the world and danced until they died.

They weren't living...but did they realize they were suffering?

A woman reached out to him, begging with mumbled words and split, dry lips. He stepped back.

Dayne wasn't here.

Relief and worry intertwined. If his brother wasn't here, he must be *there.* His gaze skittered toward the mist eddying over the lake.

People didn't vanish, no matter what the marshal said as he'd shrugged and tried to get Elliot out the door as fast as possible. People from the dark part of the city didn't go in asking for help, they were usually the ones being arrested. Dayne hadn't skipped town to avoid arrest. Nah, it was far more likely he'd been arrested on some minor charge and offered to the Kin.

His stomach turned, refusing to think of what the Kin were doing to his younger brother. Born only eighteen months apart, it had been Elliot's job to look after his brother. He'd well and truly fucked up this time. At least his parents weren't alive to see it.

A vibration filled the air, a rumble in his lungs that made it hard to breathe. The devoured whooped with joy and turned to the lake. Elliot spun. Where there had been only empty sky over water was now a shadowy building that pierced the sky with its turrets.

He fumbled in his woolen coat for his cigarettes. Only two left. He couldn't afford more until Fourteenday when he got paid. That would mean three nights without protection while he searched the beach for Dayne. He couldn't skip a night.

The vibration became a rumble as the bone beasts held together by magic and ridden by the Kin spilled out of the castle and onto the lake.

He fumbled with the cigarette, dropped it, and picked it up. His hands shook as he struck flint to get a spark. The leaf and paper lit. The lake rippled, spilling silver starlight over the inkiness. Shadows flew across the surface. Elliot hunkered down near the boulders that had once been part of a wall supposed to keep the Kin out; it had failed long ago. He sucked in the smoke, hoping it would be enough to keep him safe.

The rumble grew louder, like the growling of wild animals. From his hiding place, he watched as the shadows took shape. Moonlight caught on the white bones of the beasts, and the dark leather coats of the Kin flapped. They were a glorious flock of beautiful monsters with bright hair streaming behind them.

Like any idiot he was transfixed, mesmerized by the pretty riders.

The swarm raced past, ignoring the devoured who offered their bodies and blood so they could taste the magic in the Kin blood— enough magic to drive a man mad. The Kin rode toward the city. If they went up the hill, it was to trade with the rich; if they turned toward the dark, it was to hunt.

Elliot sighed out smoke, unable to hold his breath any longer, and the last rider's head turned. Pink eyes locked with his for a moment, and then they were gone, their brown coat and braided pink hair streaming behind.

He stayed hidden, expecting the rider to turn back and snatch him off the ground. He finished his cigarette with shaking hands. He was alive. It was several more breaths before he was able to convince himself to get up.

The devoured wailed, crying like it was the end of the world. The Kin didn't want withered bodies, the ones that had already been sucked dry and tossed aside like a bone that had nothing left to offer even the thinnest soup. Elliot shuddered. It would be kinder if Dayne were dead.

Elliot turned toward the city and trudged home. The red lights of the Lit City up the hill were too far away to offer any kind of useful light, but he had the stars and walked this road often enough over the last month that—

Something lay by the road. Discarded clothes? Elliot wasn't above picking through to see what would fit. Turning on the lights up the hill each night was a job that barely paid the rent and fed him.

He squatted down, but it wasn't a pile of clothes. A man. Cautiously, he turned the body over. Not Dayne. Elliot sagged. The man was alive, if this could be called living. His eyes were wide and lit with the fever of a bite addict. His neck was a bruised mess, and his arms would be the same.

What favor had this man needed from the Kin?

Or had he offered himself to pay for some crime?

Or had he simply been snatched off the street?

Elliot glanced up the track. He didn't want to be out while the Kin were still riding. They'd dumped this man here, and Elliot should leave him. It wasn't his business. Never get involved in Kin business.

But he was already involved. The Kin had no right to take people. He and Dayne should've left. They'd talked about saving up and going inland where there were no Kin—he'd heard the stories. But he'd also heard the marshals didn't let folk leave, and that the Kin were every-where like fleas on a dog.

The truth could be anything, but they'd figured the only way to find out was to go.

Elliot put his arm under the man and helped him to his feet. He'd get him to the fires where he'd at least be warm and wouldn't die overnight.

The man stumbled, barely able to walk. "Did you see it? Oh, it shines. Where is my wine? I want to dance again." He took a few steps and pulled Elliot into a clumsy twirl. Elliot had no talent for dancing, and no time to learn.

"Come on." He tugged the man toward the bonfires. He could reminisce with the other devoured until he either wasted away or found something else to live for. Some woke from the craving and carved out a new life. Most didn't.

They reached the edge of the pebbly beach and the first bonfire.

Sparks wafted up into the night sky and heat bathed Elliot's skin. The gaunt faces of the devoured stared at him as if they knew he didn't belong. He was too well fed when compared to them. What a joke.

"There you go." He helped the man sit by the fire. Elliot was almost sure he wouldn't last the night, he was too wounded, but there was nothing to be done. He sighed and turned away, then stopped. "Hey, did you see a man called Dayne there? Little taller than me, same dark eyes?"

The man stared up at him, eyes wide but unfocussed. "The pets are lucky."

Elliot squatted down, the hem of his coat in the sand. "My brother, Dayne, he's missing."

"Or he doesn't want to be found." The man grinned.

They'd sucked his brains out along with his blood.

"Screw you." He blamed the smoke for the stinging of his eyes as he stamped away. He shoved his hands in his pockets and hurried down the road. He wouldn't stop to help any more of the devoured. He should know better. All they cared about were the Kin.

And all the Kin cared about were themselves.

He made his way to the room he called home. It was big enough for a family; it had been home to his family. Then his father was arrested and had disappeared. A few years later, when Elliot was fifteen, Mama had started coughing—a side effect of smoking the leaves. Dayne had taken Mama's place at the factory, processing the marshmallow when she'd gotten too sick. A year later, she'd died.

With Dayne missing, Elliot had taken his place as well as doing his own job.

The room was cold and dark, but he didn't light a candle. No point when it was only him and he knew where everything was. He stripped off his boots and pants in the dark and fell into bed, only remembering at the last moment to wind his clock so he'd wake up before dawn and turn off the lights.

*F*og rolled down the streets, the red of the lights barely breaking through. It was always colder in the morning. Elliot pulled his snood up over his nose so it didn't freeze and fall off. Today, he was gritty and tired. He wasn't getting enough sleep. No chance to nap during the day when he was at the processing plant holding Dayne's job for him. He'd need to try and steal a little leaf today, assuming the foreman wasn't watching him. He couldn't afford to lose the job.

But he couldn't keep going either. He was barely keeping it together. He tripped over a cobble, stumbled, and kept walking. With numb fingers, he shoved the last piece of bread into his mouth. It wasn't much of a breakfast, but it would do. A couple more nights until he got paid. He was used to being hungry the last day. The whole of the Dark City rumbled, waiting for coin.

He was still chewing the heel of the bread when he reached the workshop. Or what had been the workshop. The walls looked like they were going to fall over, and the roof had a massive hole in it. Elliot stood there blinking like a landed fish.

One of the marshal's men in an official bright green coat stepped out, looking like he wanted to hang someone. And Elliot happened to be standing there. "Oi, what are you staring at?"

He swallowed the last bit of bread; it caught in his throat like a rock before it went down. "I work here…I'm a lightman." Where was Fife? "What happened?"

"Someone tried to steal the orbs, and it looks like the Kin took offense to someone taking what's theirs." The man stared at him a little harder, his lips curled into a snarl.

The Kin wouldn't have done anything. The orbs were fragile and temperamental and had to be handled with care. That was the first thing Fife had taught him. The workshop was mostly for fixing the actual lights and storing the orbs so that the old ones could be collected and new ones handed over. Fife and Elliot never did the handover. Elliot didn't mind, he didn't want to deal with the Kin or the rich up the hill.

Elliot crossed the road. The acrid scent of damaged Kin orbs filled the air.

The same red pulse and glow that lived in the ribs of the Kin's beasts and gave them life also lit the city. All of the lights were paid with the blood of those in the Dark City.

Between the Kin and the rich, the poor had very little blood left. The marshals were the vice in charge of getting every drop. If he thought it would get Dayne back, he'd offer to cut his own vein.

"Where's Fife?" Was he in there, hurt? He was always there first.

"Dunno. I'd like to talk to him, too." The man stepped aside. "You better get to work. Don't want to waste the light."

Elliot stepped into the workshop. His gaze skimmed over the upturned table and the mess on the floor. The shelves had tumbled under the weight of the fallen roof. Elliot peered up. The pink stained sky was visible through the hole that was as big as the table. The thief had taken the fresh orbs—or had tried to take them. The case was open, and all six orbs were missing. The floor was stained blood red and littered with delicate shards of glass.

Blood and Bother.

He forced a breath out and it whistled through the wide gap between his front two teeth. They needed those orbs to fix the broken lights. He couldn't afford to lose pay.

He closed his eyes. Willing himself to go on instead of crumpling. He'd find Dayne, everything would go back to how it was, and they'd be fine, scraping by together.

He scrabbled around in the mess until he found his tool bag. Most of the time he could fix the light—if it wasn't an orb problem. Sometimes they had to replace them and bring the old one here. On the undamaged side of the workshop were the glass boxes the orbs were placed in for protection. All of them were waiting to be repaired, their glass broken, or maybe they didn't lock, or the connections no longer held the orb stable, or they'd been damaged in a brawl. It didn't matter why the light no longer worked. The result was the same: less pay.

With his bag slung over his shoulder, Elliot stepped out of the workshop. Fife had arrived and was chatting with the marshal. The tension that had been smothering Elliot melted away. Fife was alive, and Elliot wanted to hug the man. Fife probably wouldn't appreciate the gesture even though he'd been like a father to Elliot.

Fife gave him a nod, but his face was a mask, not his usual smile but something else Elliot didn't like. It was only when the marshal left Fife grinned. "You're going to stay and help me clean up, right?"

He should. He would've happily stayed before. "I have to get to the plant."

"You need to think about what you're doing. I can't keep picking up your slack. The workshop is full."

Elliot glared at him. "I'm sorry. I need to keep his job open for when he comes back."

Fife shook his head. "Elliot, what you're doing is a kind thing, but—"

"But nothing. Please, a little longer. He's all I have left."

"I know…and I took you on as a favor to your mother. May the Kin never touch her." He crossed his fingers. "But I ain't getting any younger, and my girls won't do this. They want nothing to do with Kin and their magic."

Elliot stared at the ground and his scuffed brown boots. This was a good job, the best someone like him could hope for. The pay was better than the marshmallow leaf processing plant, though not by much. Those that lived in the Dark City never got jobs that paid above the bare essentials, and sometimes not even enough to cover them.

"I'll give you until the equinox. About three fortnight. If you ain't found Dayne by then, he's dead or wishing he was."

Three fortnight. Dayne had already been missing for two. He'd be returned by then if he was in the castle. The hollow eyes of the devoured haunted Elliot's sleep. He nodded. Three fortnight. He could do both jobs for another forty-two nights and still look for Dayne.

And then what?

His brother would be back, that's what, and life would go back to how it had been, with Dayne courting the girl across the hallway and Elliot going to the smoke-filled bar where men who liked other men could get a drink and more while killing a few hours before bed. The man he had been seeing frequently had probably moved on in the four weeks Elliot had been absent.

"Fine," Elliot said, not sure he'd actually stop in three fortnights even though he couldn't do this forever. What was he supposed to do? Give up?

Fife reached into his pocket and pulled out a small cigarette. "Figured you'd be needing that to get you through to pay day."

Elliot wanted to reach out and take it. If he was going to the lake, he should be smoking to be safe. But he didn't want to take from Fife, so he lied. "I'm good. Been rationing my supply better."

He'd run out the first fortnight Dayne had been missing. He had tried to ration better this time but had failed. A tin of marshmallow leaf wasn't meant to last a fortnight, but he couldn't afford a tin every sennight, and he hadn't realized how much Dayne had been pinching from the processing plant.

"Have it your way. You're courting danger going down there all the time." Fife walked into the workshop and put the cigarette on the work bench, then turned around to find his bag. He didn't seem at all perturbed by the mess.

"Why were you late?" Fife was always at the workshop before him.

"Gracie's sick."

The youngest of Fife's three girls. The cold made it hard for her to breath. She'd been sick for years, struggling every winter, and Fife didn't have the coin or the nectar to heal her.

"I hope it passes." Elliot stared at the cigarette, and then at Fife's back. He needed it. He hesitated, then leaned over and snatched up the cigarette and put it in his pocket. He'd be safe for another night.

Fife grunted. "If you can't help me clean up, you able to come in on your day off and do some fixin'?"

He was exhausted and the sun was barely risen. A couple more nights, then he'd get paid, and he'd get the day off from the plant. The promise of a day off was all that had kept him stumbling through. But he nodded. "I'll come in on the fourteenth day."

No day off.

The laundry would have to wait. So would sleep.

The landlord was waiting by Elliot's door when he got home, his fingers smelling like the sweet marshmallow leaf and his feet aching from standing since dawn, then turning off the lights. All he wanted to do was fall onto his bed and sleep until his alarm woke him, early so he could check the beach before getting up to turn off the lights. He didn't even care about dinner. There was almost nothing left to eat anyway, and he didn't want to chat.

"Rent's doubling, kid."

Elliot halted like he'd hit a wall. "What?"

"I got a waitlist for that family room and since it's only you." He shrugged and sipped his tea. "Supply and demand."

Double. Elliot ran the sums but couldn't make them work. "You can't do that."

"Sure I can, you're in a family room, and I don't see a family. Now I was nice in letting you and your brother be called a family, seeing as how you've lived there since you were knee high, but I can't have a single man taking up a room for four or more."

This had been his home for as long as he could remember. He shook his head. "My brother's coming back."

"Kid—"

"I'm not a bloody kid." He was twenty-two. Half his mother's age when she'd died.

The landlord's face hardened. "If you want to stay, it's double. Otherwise there's a single man's room upstairs for half what you're paying."

"The attic room where Sydney hanged himself?"

Dead Man's Room. Sydney was just the most recent. Two other men had killed themselves up there. There was a rumor one had been snatched out of his bed by the Kin. Dead Man's Room wasn't home. It wouldn't be safe.

"It's a nice room, biggest single room I have. Got a view of the lake and all."

That didn't make it a nice room at all, but at least he'd still be in the same building. The cheaper room was tempting. How long would it take to make it a home so the Kin wouldn't be able to cross the threshold?

No. He wasn't moving up there. This was his home. This is where Dayne would look for him. "I'll get you double."

The landlord waived his tin cup at Elliot. "You aren't thinking right. You're like one of the devoured."

"I'm not."

"Your brother isn't coming back."

"You'll get your coin." Elliot unlocked the door and opened it. "That's all that matters, right?"

Even if he gave everything and ate nothing, he'd still come up short. But there were other ways to make money.

"Just take the single room. If your brother comes back, there's room for him up there."

Elliot closed his eyes. "Maybe next week."

"It might be gone."

"That room's been empty since you took the rope down."

Elliot shut the door. He leaned against it, wanting to feel as solid as the wood. Instead, he was falling apart like dried marshmallow. One breath, and he'd disintegrate.

CHAPTER 2

*E*lliot tipped out the tin where he kept his coins. There were two halves. He'd gone through all of Dayne's pockets hoping for scraps of leaf or half a coin, but there'd been nothing. He bit his lip and stared at the coins.

He had Fife's cigarette in his pocket and enough coin to buy a bit of bread to get him through to pay day. Even with Dayne's pay from the plant and his pay, there wouldn't be enough for double the rent, and that was before he thought about eating or buying oil for the light —which hadn't had oil since last pay, and the final candle was shorter than his thumb. It would only last a few more nights.

He glanced around the room and then pulled back all the curtains to stare at the two beds. He was wearing the coat that had once been his father's. The cuffs were frayed but it had been good once. It had also been a nice shade of green—not marshal bright green—if the underside of collar were to be believed. Now it was more of a gray-green, like dried beans. There'd been a time when his parents hadn't lived like this, but he didn't remember living anywhere but the Dark City. No well-heeled relative had ever stopped to offer Elliot and Dayne a hand up after their mother's death.

His mother's clothes had already been sold. His father's shoes they'd kept because Dayne was still growing and would probably need them next year. His own feet hadn't grown in a while, and he was never going to fill his father's shoes.

He stared at the shoes tucked neatly under the bed a little longer. It would cost far more to get a new pair when Dayne needed them than what he'd get if he sold them. He forced out a breath and turned away.

There was nothing more to sell.

He clenched his fingers, unable to do anything else. He was too tired to find the solution. He hadn't found Dayne, and he wasn't ready to believe the truth. He just had to keep going. Fife had given him a deadline of the equinox. And after that?

Would he move upstairs then?

Maybe the Kin would take him from his bed, and he wouldn't even care.

There were marks on the floor where Dayne and he had scored a grid to play a game with pebbles and chips of wood. Mama had made the curtains. This was the only home he remembered. It was the only home Dayne had ever had.

He wasn't giving it up. There was one more thing he could sell.

Himself.

If he went up the hill a bit to the places where men paid for fun, he'd be able to get the extra coins. He hadn't done that since Mama was sick. He'd had to pay for the doctor, and that had been his only option. The doctor hadn't helped her though, just drugged her so the pain went away. If they were rich, he'd have been able to get some of the nectar the Kin had. He'd heard tales of how no one up the hill died.

After paying the doctor, he'd sworn never again. He'd sworn plenty of things though and had broken every one. He'd promised Da he'd take care of Mama. She'd died anyway. He hadn't been able to keep Dayne safe either. What was one more broken promise?

It would mean less sleep, but he'd have enough coin for food and candles and rent.

He flexed his fingers. His stomach grumbled. He wasn't getting any sleep anyway, so he might as well eat and keep his home.

15

Decision made, he boiled water, stripped, and scrubbed in a basin. They'd need more soap soon. He did his best with his hair and considered cutting it all off like he had when Mama had died, but he liked his hair. Even if his clothes were falling apart, he could at least look good naked.

Shivering, he dried off and dressed in clothes that were clean and passed for his best. The kind of thing one wore to a funeral or a wedding or a town hall meeting where it didn't pay to look like you were as poor as the rats in the roof.

He tugged his still damp curls out of his face and figured he looked as good as he was going to. One day he'd like to have one of those fine shirts with all the small buttons down the front and a pair of boots that buttoned up the side. The closest he'd ever come to those items of clothing was when helping a customer take them off.

He put on his coat and snood and jammed his hands in his pockets for the walk up the hill to where the rich folk played.

The lights he'd turned on earlier burned brightly, casting their red glow over the cobbles. Every step took him further from the lake and the shore. He was spending almost as much time down there as one of the devoured. He shoved the thought away. If he didn't pay the rent, everything he owned would be tossed out of the room, and then Dayne would have nowhere to come home to. No home meant they'd be easy prey for the ever-hungry Kin.

He yawned, knowing he needed sleep but unable to find the time. All he could do was grit his teeth and push through. A day at the processing plant after little sleep, separating the root from the leaf so it could be dried and sold, wouldn't be so bad. Maybe the boss wouldn't notice if he was extra clumsy or slow.

Elliot turned down one of the laneways. There were no lights on this street, but cheap and smoky oil lanterns hung out the front of the buildings that were open for business. Nothing much had changed since he'd been here last; he recognized some of the signs even though he couldn't read them. Hopefully one of the clubs would be in need of extra flesh. He went around the back—people like him didn't go through the front—and rapped on the door of a club he'd worked at before. A few had good reputations, but there were plenty he'd avoid. Some people thought money bought them more than what was for sale.

The window in the door slid open. The man gave him a quick once over with narrow hard eyes. "What do you want?"

"Just wondering if you needed anyone extra."

"What do you do?"

Elliot had run this conversation through his mind on the way over. He couldn't afford to be fussy. "Whatever you need."

"Like to be ploughed?"

Liked it well enough when he clutched a cold coin in his palm. "Yes."

The man shut the window and opened up the door, ushering Elliot in. He drew in a breath of cold night air before stepping into the heat. The walls were still a pale apricot with gold trim tracing the edges of the ceiling. Laughter spilled from the front of the building where drinks were served and deals were made.

"Leave your coat and snood in here." The man threw open the door to the cloakroom. His wasn't the best coat by far. "Leave your shirt, too."

Elliot removed that and his boots.

The man laughed. "Not your first time."

Elliot didn't join in. His hands had shook the first time. Dayne had begged him not to go out and leave him with Mama, but they'd needed the medicine. His brother hadn't needed to know how he was getting the coin.

"You can either try your luck on the floor or take a room and I'll send up clients."

The floor was nicer—if he didn't like the look of someone he moved on—but it didn't pay as well as the sure thing. He swallowed, torn between speed and pretending he was there for his own enjoyment. "I get more for the room, right, even after you deduct expenses?"

"Yes." The man stared at him. "I know you. Never forget a face. You were popular. Why'd you stop?"

"Death in the family."

"Why're you back?"

He couldn't tell the truth. "Need to make the rent."

"Lot of that going around. 'Course, we don't let just anyone in." The man gripped his chin and turned his face to the light.

He knew he was still young and pretty enough for this place. He forced a smile. "I know. That's why I came back."

"You're taking the room? How many?"

"What's the price?"

The man smiled, two teeth missing at the side. "You look healthy... I'll give you two fulls for each after expenses."

Two fulls, shiny and fat like the moon. The smaller halves were bronze. He'd never seen a golden sun in his life.

Elliot nodded. He could earn the whole rent in a night. "Four."

The man considered him. "No. Two. Don't want a squealing mess."

"I was doing this when I was fifteen, I'll be fine."

The man considered him for a moment, probably already assigning clients. "It's your ass."

Not for the rest of the night it wasn't.

~

He wasted money buying himself a hot supper before leaving the lit part of the city, but he bloody well deserved it. And he'd loved every bite of the meaty pastry. The pie had been scalding, and he'd even paid extra to shove a bit of cheese in the top. His mouth watered at the memory as he wandered through the Dark City toward the lake.

There were no shops open this late in the dark. Everyone was shut up tight in case the Kin came hunting. Even if the shops were open, it would've been cheap cold meat cuts, bread, and cheese that wasn't aged and tasty, but soft and creamy. He liked the harder cheese and the way it melted in hot pies; he had expensive tastes.

He lit the cigarette and blew out the smoke, pretending for a few moments that life was grand. His belly was full, and he had coins in his pocket, and he'd enjoyed himself well enough.

He was doing the wrong job. If he worked on his knees, he'd have plenty of coin. While he'd get a few good years, he'd seen what happened to those who looked too old; they were in the line outside the plant hoping to take the place of someone who didn't show. But earning coin that didn't have him working every waking moment—and some sleeping ones—was so tempting.

If he worked a few more nights or maybe even one a fortnight, he wouldn't be scrabbling like a rat in a trap. With all the pays combined, he had enough for rent, even the double rent, and food and oil for the next fortnight. Maybe a bit left over so he could save for some newish clothes.

But he didn't want to pretend to like men who'd sell him to the Kin without a thought if it would better their situation. He tolerated them because the money was good, but he'd much rather go to the Moss and Mallow where money never changed hands.

He made his rounds of the bonfires, searching the hollow faces for Dayne. Tonight, the devoured were dancing like the Kin were visiting. Elliot hadn't seen them ride over; had they crossed the lake while he'd been on his belly?

Hope and dread entwined so tightly he wasn't sure which made his heart beat faster and his hands shake. His body was wrecked. He needed sleep. More than the little he'd get between now and waking to turn on the lights.

He rubbed at his eyes, unable to clear the grit. He blinked and stared at the castle. That's where Dayne was. Or his brother was dead, and Elliot was well on the road to killing himself. He was wearing away like an over-washed shirt that couldn't afford to be replaced. Threadbare and the holes were growing.

What if he skipped a night and didn't search?

He squeezed his eyes closed. No. He wouldn't let Dayne lie on the beach, devoured and dying for another taste of Kin blood. And when he came home? Elliot didn't know. His plan didn't go beyond getting Dayne back. He couldn't think that far ahead.

He turned away from the beach and stumbled home. His breath clouded in front of him, and he wasn't even sure why he was going home when he'd have to be up in a few hours to turn the lights off. His thoughts jumbled. He wanted to lie down where he stood. He couldn't keep doing this.

Fife was right.

The landlord was right.

Despair made his eyes prickle with hot tears. How could he have been so careless as to have lost his brother?

One more day and night, then he could sleep. Fuck the laundry and buying food. Fuck Fife and broken lights. He'd stay in bed all day. He hunched his shoulders and buried his face deeper into his snood to stop the cold from biting.

Usually at this time of night, the world was silent like it was dead. He liked it, because he owned the streets. But tonight, footsteps darted through the dark. Laughter and cries echoed off the tightly packed buildings.

Elliot froze. The devoured were excited because the Kin *had* crossed. He shoved his hand into his pocket, but he'd already smoked his last cigarette.

Were the Kin looking for their stolen orbs or hunting?

It didn't matter what they wanted; he wanted to sleep for a bit until he had to be up again. He rubbed his eyes and stifled a yawn, walking quicker, determined to reach the safety of home. Every scrape became the Kin creeping after him and every whisper became a warning.

Just rats.

His heart hammered in his throat, and he gave in to fear and ran. His boot scuffed the uneven pavement, and he tripped.

Hands caught him and dragged him into the shadows, one covering his mouth.

"Do not even breathe." The words were a silken charm in his ear that stilled his breath if not his heartbeat. The hand was cold on his lips. Not human.

Kin.

His heart exploded and sleep fled, but he didn't breathe. He didn't move. Out of the shadows came antlers, tall and multi-pronged. They tilted as though the owner was listening, then melted away. Few of the Kin had such a fine set; he'd love to hang them on his bloody wall and use them to dry his socks.

It was several more heartbeats before Elliot drew in a breath through his nose. Another few before the hand on his mouth eased but didn't leave completely.

The Kin whispered in his ear. "Vermillion is hunting. Not a good night to be about unless you want to be dinner."

Elliot's stomach tightened at the name. Vermillion had a grand set of antlers and had been the leader of the Kin for a while, since Elliot was a child at least, and no one had a good thing to say about them—most folk didn't have a good thing to say about any of the Kin, but Vermillion was considered exceptionally cruel.

He might have dodged Vermillion, but he wasn't any safer in this Kin's hands. Is this how it happened? Was he going to be dragged away and taken to the island?

He didn't want to be bitten and left for dead. He dragged up every shred of energy he had to fight. He wriggled, trying to slip free.

Arms locked tight around him. "I'm not your enemy tonight."

The Kin's breath was cold behind his ear. Their tongue tasted the side of his neck, and Elliot closed his eyes expecting the press of teeth in his skin. He'd be drained and left dead, crumpled in the street. Someone would take his clothes and boots, and he'd be found naked and frozen in the dawn. For a moment, that didn't seem like a bad option. At least he wouldn't be tired and hungry.

Teeth pressed against his skin, drawing a shudder, but the bite didn't come. The Kin released him and stepped back. "Flee home and be glad I'm not hungry tonight."

Elliot spun to look at his captor and savior. It was the Kin with pink hair from the back of the pack. This Kin's antlers were small, barely hand sized, meaning they were young. Their eyes were deep pink, as though the sky were burning. It was impossible to tell if they were male or female by looking at their face. The Kin could change, their bodies weren't fixed like humans, and it was best not to make assumptions. He glanced down, but the leather coat and shadows hid everything.

When he lifted his gaze, the Kin smiled and revealed their pointed fangs. Elliot's heart raced again, like it had somewhere pressing to be. "Why?"

"Why not?"

He was talking to a Kin. What was wrong with him? *Run.* But his feet wouldn't move.

"Go," the Kin said.

Elliot took a step away, then stopped. Not sure which he'd regret more, asking or not, he decided the latter. "My brother...is he on the island?"

"There are many humans on the island."

"Dayne. His name is Dayne."

The Kin's eyebrows lowered. "Maybe it's better he is there."

"He belongs here."

"He belongs to us." There was a blade in the words. "Go before I change my mind and deliver you to Vermillion myself."

Elliot didn't move.

"I have your scent...I can find you." The Kin grinned. It wasn't the wolfish grin Elliot had expected from a predator, but something else.

He nodded and fled. But even when he later lay beneath the covers, his sleep was broken, and he startled awake at every sound outside that could be the Kin who had his scent.

CHAPTER 3

*U*mbra lingered in the shadow of the wooden building until the man disappeared from sight. Their palm cooled, the heat of the human's breath long gone. The fear in his eyes lingered, souring the memory.

Since arriving a few nights ago, fear was all Umbra had seen from humans—unless they'd already tasted Abyr blood.

Umbra listened carefully to the night sounds before sliding through the dark, away from where Vermillion was hunting either for food or pets to add to their collection. It was too close. They shouldn't have stepped in…but they knew the man, had seen him before and didn't want him to fall into Vermillion's hands.

No one deserved that fate.

They shouldn't care about a human with poison in his blood when their own life was on a precarious edge. They'd gone from being prime, heir to the border castle where they'd been raised, to being nothing.

Worse than nothing.

The Abyr who guarded the border were expected to change because it made them better fighters. Unlike the other Abyr of this castle, Umbra hadn't fed on human blood and was still unchanged like the Kin of the heartland.

They'd argued with their parents and fled into the heartland, hoping to disappear and become a bard. Instead they'd been hauled back, whipped, and starved. Their sire had then offered a human which Umbra refused to taste. With the scars still healing, they'd been sent to Vermillion. Vermillion also expected them to feed and change and worse…become their mate.

Until tonight, Umbra had never felt the urge to bite someone so thoroughly. If not for the hint of poison, they would've sunk their fangs into that man. *Maybe.* But once blood had been tasted and the Abyr's body changed, there was no way to go back. There was only the choice to be male or female.

Umbra didn't want to be male or female in the way humans were; they wanted to remain unchanged.

Saving the human man tonight had been a simple act of defiance against Vermillion. Umbra smiled, not entirely sure if it was because they'd cheated Vermillion of a meal or because of the way the man's skin had tasted. The bitter poison in his system lingered beneath his scent, but there was something else that appealed. The hot iron and earth of his blood, the beat of his heart in an unmistakable rhythm.

If that weren't enough, he'd fought back. He'd questioned them.

Umbra's tongue ran over their fangs. For a moment they could still feel the heat of the man's skin on their lips.

Their steps faltered. They could, but to bite without permission… to take a human who didn't want to be taken… That wasn't how it was done where they'd been raised. Under Vermillion's rule, it was the norm.

Umbra glanced back, knowing they could follow the scent to the man, and while his blood was toxic, it would clear in a few nights. And a man's blood would shatter the plans that had been made for them by Vermillion and their sire. But they should want blood and to change for a better reason than ruining plans.

Their mouth tasted of the man's skin. Maybe his blood would be as pleasant as his skin and it wouldn't be all bad to be stronger and faster...

They made their way back to where the beasts were guarded. The beasts vibrated with energy, their bones white and their hearts red and pulsing. But where an animal should have legs, they had hide covered wheels. A concoction of magic and bones that was almost alive.

Umbra sat in the shadows and waited. There would be trouble again because they'd failed to capture a pet. They couldn't keep on like this.

The man's face was clear in their mind as they unraveled and rebraided their hair, save for the side freshly shaved, a punishment enacted before they'd come here to make their shame obvious to all. They ran their fingers over it, the smoothness like the softest flower petal. It would be a long time before they could hide the short strands with clever braids.

Their hands stilled.

The human wanted his brother. Umbra wanted to live their own life.

One wasn't possible, but thwarting plans was a close second.

The edges of an idea formed. Their sire wanted them to prove leadership and strength. Very well, they would do that, but it would be on their terms. Which were sure to please no one. Not even them as it would mean changing.

Blood scented the air, but not human blood. Umbra got to their feet, serrated knife in hand, ready to defend. They had no problem killing if attacked. Fair play. When they chose a human to feed on, they would get a choice and a chance.

Would the man he'd saved tonight offer himself, or would he fight back? Umbra was sure they'd enjoy either option. It would be a shame to let him go if he didn't want to be bitten.

Xanthin staggered toward the beasts, dark blood staining their leather coat and dripping off their fingers. Their antlers on one side were broken.

"What happened?" Umbra held the knife loose and ready.

Xanthin glanced their way. "We were attacked, fool. The humans will pay for this insult."

Umbra didn't respond. After a few nights under Vermillion's rule, they knew anything other than what Vermillion said was wrong. Sooner rather than later, Umbra would have to comply and feed. There were no unchanged in this castle, and fleeing to the heartlands where the unchanged lived wasn't an option. They knew that now and wouldn't make the same mistake twice.

They were stuck here. Their sire had given them to Vermillion for a year and a day. They'd survived the first few days but weren't sure they could survive much longer as an unchanged.

Other Abyr poured into the street where the beasts waited. It should've been a simple orb drop and feed. Instead, there were wounded Abyr, and they dragged equally wounded humans with them.

Vermillion strode through the street, antlers gleaming, green braids spilling over their shoulders like venomous snakes. Their gaze landed on the knife in Umbra's hand. "You killed and fed?"

Umbra should lie, but it would have been obvious in a few days. Their body would betray them with the lack of changes. "No."

"Weakling. We need to be strong. These humans exist because we allow it."

The humans exist because this is where they live.

On this side, the Abyr were the intruders, seeking food and offering magic in exchange. Umbra knew the bard tales. The ones of peace, times when human and Abyr traded before leaders like Vermillion wanted to prove their strength. The new tales told of battles and blood.

Vermillion hauled two humans toward them, both women. "Choose one to make your pet and kill the other."

Umbra froze. They did not want to be female and bear Vermillion's child, no matter what was expected. The other Abyr stared, their gazes hard and assessing.

"You weaken us, when we must be strong against their growing resistance." Vermillion pushed the women to their knees. They had already been fed on; their collars were stained dark with blood. "Choose, or you will be left here, tied so every human can take their fury out on you."

Umbra glanced at Vermillion. They'd admitted the humans were angry with the Abyr.

"Perhaps if you didn't take so many humans, they would be less vengeful," they said in a soft voice, meant for just the two of them.

Vermillion's hand whipped out so fast Umbra barely saw it, but they felt the sting across their cheek. Their head snapped back and blood filled their mouth. They straightened and glared at Vermillion.

They'd chosen who to kill.

CHAPTER 4

*E*lliot's alarm went off with a screech. He lay in the gray predawn, refusing to believe he had to get up already and not sure he could force himself out of bed. He reached out and shut the clock up before the neighbor thumped on the wall.

If he closed his eyes he'd go back to sleep—if it could be called sleep. He'd woken easily at every noise and dreamed of the Kin with pink hair.

It was almost dawn, so it would be safe to go out. Go turn off the lights and survey the damage, then go to the plant, then turn on the lights, then go to the lake. Then he could sleep.

A day off tomorrow. He could do this.

But could he do it for another fortnight, and another?

He'd have to work another night on his belly to pay the increased rent.

Before despair could press him firmly to the bed and make living impossible, he forced himself up. He shoved his boots on; he hadn't bothered to undress, and he didn't care that he looked like a sack of shit. Actually, a sack of shit had more prospects than him. Being a sack of shit would be a step up.

In the cupboard, he rummaged around until he found something to make tea with. He tossed in willow bark and dried ginger root to wake him up and washed his face with icy water while he waited for the kettle to boil. He'd need to get wood…either buy it or find it. Did he spend his day off scavenging? The temptation to do a second night was there. He'd have spare coin for a change.

He moved around the room like the last dried pea in the bag.

Or he could move and go upstairs to the dead man's room.

He knew the stories. Two suicides and a murder had happened up there. Cheapest room in the building. Cold all year and said to be haunted. He'd never seen a ghost and wasn't sure he believed in them. If ghosts were real wouldn't the city be crawling with them, every room filled to bursting?

In the polished tin mirror, his eyes were blood shot. He needed to shave; had it been three or four days ago? On the side of his neck, almost hidden by his shoulder length dark hair, were two small, silvery dots. He scrubbed at them, but they didn't come off.

A shiver like water was in his veins traced through him. That was where…

He was a marked man.

Bloody great. Just what I fucking need.

He closed his eyes and leaned on the counter. The water boiled.

He drew in several breaths. He should quit trying. What was the point when the Kin would come for him?

At least when they did, he'd find Dayne. They could become devoured together and die cold and bony on the beach oblivious to anything but the craving for the bite.

No. He opened his eyes and shoved away.

He arranged his coat collar and snood so the mark wasn't visible, then made his tea. It was bitter and stale, but he didn't care. He'd buy fresh when he got paid. He could take a little out of what he'd earned and buy something decent to eat on his way to work.

He did the math, adding up the pay to come in, taking out the docked pay for broken lights, wood and oil and food and leaf. He couldn't live off street food. If he didn't buy lamp oil and he went to the store, he could make it through another fortnight. He didn't need a light at home; he was never there.

If he moved upstairs, there'd be room for Dayne when he came back. More importantly, he'd have money left over and he wouldn't need the extra work. He finished his tea, rinsed the cup with the rest of the boiled water, then left the cup in the sink. He chucked the water he'd washed in down the drain and turned the oven down low. There wasn't enough wood to keep it lit for the day, but it would keep the chill off the room. He'd be needing to light it from cold after he bought wood. By tomorrow, the room would be like a day-old corpse.

He wanted to wilt to the floor and stay there until someone made everything all right. Before Dayne had vanished, they'd been getting by. A bit of coin leftover to have some fun at the end of each fortnight, but nothing ever saved. The rent increase was killing him, and he hadn't even paid it yet.

Elliot checked his key was in his pocket and trudged to the door. He locked it behind him and made his way downstairs. The landlord was standing by the main door to the house door, sipping what smelled like fresh mint tea.

"Kid." The landlord nodded.

"You'll get your money on rent day."

"It's not about the money. I have a family that needs the room. You aren't going to last another sennight the way you're going. Not even the Kin'll touch you then."

Well, then at least he'd save on leaf. That was how he felt; too dead even for the Kin. Is that why he hadn't been taken last night?

"That room's my home." All the memories of his parents were contained there, the good and the bad.

The landlord sipped his tea. "I know, kid, but I got to make sure that the room is fair. You taking a family room on your own isn't. You want parents and kids sleeping on the street?"

Were they really sleeping on the streets? There were other rooms for rent, though this end of town tended to be rather crowded because of the low price. No one wanted to live this close to the lake if they could help it. "They really on the street?"

"They were. Mother's just got a job, and they can afford a roof. I'm not tossing you out, I wouldn't do that. I've let you and your brother stay in that room, but it's time to move."

"I've got the money." But the fight had gone out of his words. He'd be dead before the next rent was due if he kept this up, and they both knew it.

"I don't wanna know how you got it, kid." He shook his head. "Get yourself some hot food. If you kill yourself, I'll have to find a new lodger, and at least you aren't no trouble. You can move tomorrow."

His mouth was bitter with defeat and old willow bark. He stared at the scuffed toes of his boots. The hems of his good pants were frayed, and the knees were wearing through. The landlord was right. If he moved, he wouldn't have to choose between oil and leaf and food. A family would be off the street and into his nice room.

He sniffed, knowing what he had to do. "Yeah. I can move upstairs tomorrow."

"Smart choice. I'll send my mister to the store for you. Make sure you start the next fortnight right?"

It didn't feel like the smart choice. Just another failure. How long until he was the newest dead man haunting the attic room?

He was being offered help, and he knew he should be grateful, but it burned like poison. The landlord's mister worked at one of the gin slingers. Nice enough man; he'd helped arrange Mama's funeral. There were worse buildings to live in. Landlords who didn't give a shit about the people who lived under the roof, selling rooms to the highest bidder. The tenants here were pretty consistent, and there was never any trouble.

Elliot nodded. His tongue too thick to make words.

The landlord clapped him on the shoulder. "Go and spend your ill-gotten coins. Live a little. You shouldn't look as old as me."

The craggy face and rosy nose of the landlord wasn't appealing. Elliot didn't look that bad. Maybe he would, if he could afford gin instead of watered-down ale.

*R*ed lights and predawn silence filled the streets. Fog rolled up from the lake in swirling clouds and ever shifting shapes. Elliot had never minded the mornings. There was no danger from the Kin, and no one else was out. For these few moments the city was his.

There'd been mornings when he'd ran to work, taking the long way to see as much as possible, no mama to watch and no master to tell him to walk. Running these days was entirely too much effort, but he still savored the emptiness.

This was preferable to the noise and chatter in the plant. The monotony of sorting leaf and root or spreading the leaf to dry. He didn't know how Dayne did it. But it was that or nothing. Jobs didn't grow like marshmallow plants.

He rounded the corner. Halfway through the market square, he stopped. Beneath his feet, the cobbles were streaked dark. Bundles lay in the street or against the walls. His mouth dried. The fog eddied around him as he turned, looking for stray Kin, but they wouldn't risk the sunlight.

No one else was there. Just him and the dead.

Their blood stained the cobbles, and their bodies waited for collection.

He should ring the bell, let everyone know that there'd been an attack. Why had no one rung it last night? Where were the marshals? If he rang the bell, he'd be questioned and he'd miss his shift.

Or he could go to work and leave this for another to find. His fingers curled in his pockets. He should at least check the bodies to see if there was anything of value he could use. He hesitated. No. He didn't have time, nor did he want to be caught. People would be on the street soon.

Carefully, he lowered his gaze and kept walking. The fog reached for him, like the dead were judging his callousness. That could've been him. He rubbed his neck, imagining he could feel the mark where the Kin had tasted his skin and pressed their fangs to his flesh. A shiver traced through him.

Everywhere he looked, there were signs of a fight. Blood streaked the walls. A smear on a black lamppost. This wasn't the Kin's usual hunting ground. It was too far from the lake and too close to the lit part of the city. The folk who lived up here would pitch a fit.

A cruel smiled curved Elliot's lips. It was about time they knew what it was like to live in fear of the Kin going hunting. Bet those up the hill would be better tasting. They could afford three meals a day and they didn't break their backs working. Those up the hill owned the boarding houses, the plants, and farms where everyone else worked. The rich would be like fattened up geese, ripe for eating instead of the scrawny chooks that pecked around the yards of the boarding houses.

He made it to the workshop, thinking he was on time, but Fife was already there. Elliot grabbed his bag and checked over his tools. "Did we get replacement orbs?"

"No."

"But the Kin—"

"If they delivered, we didn't get."

Someone had covered the hole in the roof and put boards up in the windows. The mayor would have to arrange the repair...and who knew when that would happen?

"But we'll lose pay over it."

Fife nodded. "Punishment because the orbs were taken."

"But that wasn't our fault."

Fife grunted. "Clean up a bit in here, then we'll head out."

Elliot stared at the floor. "There was some trouble last night. I didn't ring it out."

Fife looked up from the dull orb he was fiddling with. "Neither did I."

"What are you doing?" They weren't supposed to fiddle. They just replaced them, turned them on and off. It wasn't a hard job.

"You don't wonder how they work?" He held it up as though it were an apple. The red oil inside sloshed and swirled.

"Course I do." But that didn't mean he wanted to touch them more than he had to. The orbs were dangerous.

33

"What if we could make them work, relight them without the Kin?"

Elliot shrugged. "What if we could? There's other magics the Kin give the rich." In exchange, the rich gave the lives of the poor.

"We don't need the Kin to survive. They need us."

"They heal the rich."

"They do, and they take their payment in our blood. What if it wasn't that way?"

What other way could it be? "Like the cities without Kin?"

"Or if the rich stopped treating us like crops for the Kin to harvest."

Elliot laughed, but it was cold and hollow. That was never going to change. Best way not to get taken was to keep your head down and work hard. The more trouble one created, the more likely the marshals would hand you over to the Kin.

But Fife didn't laugh. He wasn't smiling either.

Elliot stared at him. "What are you talking about?"

"People aren't happy. And we hold something powerful."

The explosion in the workshop yesterday…Fife being late…Elliot didn't want to know. Knowing some things brought trouble. He wanted no part in Fife's dealings.

"We'd best be getting the lights off." Elliot started toward the door.

"No one cares if they're left on a bit late."

"They don't like seeing us in their streets. And I have to get to the plant after." He couldn't linger the way he once had.

Fife put the orb in its case and locked it up. He slung his bag over his shoulder. "There'll be extra repairs from the trouble last night."

"I can't come in like I said I could. I have to move tomorrow." He needed the time off. His bones ached like every step he took was uphill.

Fife shook his head. "You're needed here."

"You gave me three more fortnights." But he should stay back and help Fife fix the busted lights, instead of going to the plant.

"I didn't think you'd take them." Fife pressed his lips together and stared at Elliot. "If Dayne comes back, he won't be fit for working."

Elliot bit his lip. He knew that. The devoured couldn't keep a job. They got distracted by thoughts of the Kin and the bite. When he moved, he wouldn't need the extra coin from Dayne's job, and Dayne wouldn't be able to work at the plant anyway. He rubbed his neck.

He couldn't tell Fife about his run in with the Kin.

A bell tolled, announcing someone had seen the mess in the square.

"We'd best be on our way." Fife strode out the door. He locked it behind Elliot.

Fife led them straight to the square, even though it wasn't where they started their route. The fog had rolled back, exposing the full horror. Dark human blood and brighter Kin blood was everywhere. There were no Kin bodies, only half naked humans, already stripped of their useful clothing. The Kin must have taken their dead and almost dead.

"We shouldn't be here." Elliot hadn't told Fife where the trouble had been. And Fife shouldn't have walked through the square to get to the workshop.

"There's two lights busted on the other side. We'll come back at the end for them."

They weren't the only shattered lights on their route. Smashed glass littered the streets, orbs were missing or dropped on the ground. Some were cold and gray, others still glowed red. He put back what he could, but the amount of work to get everything fixed would be more than he and Fife could handle.

"What happened? Did you hear anything?" Fife lived close to the Lit City.

Fife shrugged. "It looks like people fought back."

It looked like they lost. "The Kin will retaliate."

They'd come hunting. His neck throbbed.

Or they'd demand a higher payment—which meant the prison would be emptied and the people inside handed over to the Kin. The marshals would round up extra people on piss-weak charges to make up the numbers.

"Maybe…but there's more of us than them. You ever heard of the venerie?"

Elliot's gaze snapped to Fife. Dayne had mentioned that name.

Fife grinned. "You have. It's not a rumor."

"That's a hanging offence." No one attacked the Kin and lived.

"Nah…that's a ten-cut lake offence."

Ten cuts to the arms and forced to walk into the lake. Didn't sound so bad in daylight. People fished at the southern end where the water entered. But sometimes at night, the lake roiled with something else. Like the Kin, whatever lived there didn't exist in daylight.

"Were the venerie fighting the Kin last night?"

"Wouldn't be surprised." Fife turned. "What? You thought the Kin rode in and took what they wanted, and no one lifted a finger to stop them?"

Elliot didn't want to answer that.

Fife shook his head. "This one's all munted." He held up the twisted light he'd removed. The metal that held the orb and the glass box that surrounded it were splayed out like petals. "Orb must have gone off."

"Exploded?"

"'Cept they don't explode. Not really. They kind of flash and throw out heat then go dull."

"So one didn't explode in the workshop." Elliot examined what was left of the light. "What happened to the orb?"

"Stolen most like."

"By the venerie?"

"By anyone. Some folk are desperate enough to steal them and offer them back to the Kin."

If he'd known he could return orbs to the Kin for favors, he'd have bought their healing magic for his mama. "Does it work?"

"Depends on who they offer them to. Don't be getting any ideas."

"No ideas." He didn't have time for ideas.

Would he be able to buy his brother back?

～

*W*ith his pay and his brother's in his hand, Elliot bought bread and cheese and sugary nuts on a stick that were still hot in their paper wrapping as he handed the landlord the rent for the next fortnight. Dead man's room. Cheap, much cheaper than the family room. The noose around his neck was looser.

He ate the nuts, enjoying the burn on his tongue and the rush of sugar. Nothing had ever been as sweet. The treat almost erased the bitterness of having to move. He tried not to think of it as failure, but as doing the right thing so a new family could enjoy the room.

There wasn't much to pack. If he did some tonight, there'd be less to do tomorrow. Day off. He wanted to spend it sleeping late, then going to the lake to talk to the devoured. Someone must know something about Dayne.

He carried up a bundle of his parent's things first. The key was stiff in the lock and the room was like ice. His breath clouded in front of him. This didn't feel like home; it was dark and there was a smell that he didn't want to think too much about.

A small stack of logs and a bundle of kindling sat by the stove. A bag of beans, a block of cooking oil, and a few other essentials were stacked on a shelf. The landlord's mister had been shopping as promised. All this place needed was some heat and light to make it home.

He set the fire and struck his flint to get it going. The flames crackled, and he warmed his hands before shutting the door but leaving the air vent open. He checked the flue was open, then stepped back. The kitchen was comprised of the oven and a small countertop. Less cupboards. The table he was used to eating at was too big to fit up here. He could sell it to the new family.

He drew back the curtain that divided the kitchen from the beds, aware that it was attached to the beam where the body had been found hanging. The sleeping area wasn't too bad. There was an awkward slant to the roof, but more than enough room for both of them.

It wasn't a bad room.

It warmed up quickly, and the smell would go with time—he'd open the window tomorrow and let the fresh air in. He walked over and peered through the glass. The city was dark, no light until the stars reflected on the lake surface.

From here, it was beautiful. He was far enough away the danger couldn't reach out and grab him. He pulled a cigarette out of his pocket and lit it on the stove. The sweet smoke filled his lungs, and the heat tickled the back of his throat. He coughed and grinned. Maybe not everything was shit.

He stared at the lake as he smoked his silent *fuck you* to the Kin who'd marked him, the marshmallow poisoning his blood with every breath.

CHAPTER 5

*U*mbra leaned on the stone railing and stared over the lake at the human city beyond the beach and the fires lit by the hopeful. From the dark, neat lines of red lights ran up the hill. Today, there were new dark areas in the city.

Umbra's gaze swung back to where the Abyr usually hunted. The disaster of last night had been about Vermillion flexing their power and had resulted in two Abyr deaths. How the humans had gotten hold of antler, Umbra didn't know. But the humans knew how to kill them, and now they had more, having snapped Xanthin's antlers.

Umbra's skin prickled in warning, and they turned. Lapis stood several paces away, their orange hair braided elaborately. Too elaborately for their bloodline.

Umbra should've ignored them; now they had to acknowledge Lapis. However, it was better not to keep one's back to the enemy. And everyone was the enemy, a supporter of Vermillion, and because Umbra wasn't obeying, they were suspicious.

"Ver wants to see you."

Umbra glanced at the city. In the darkness was the human whose taste now lingered in their mouth. "I'm sure they do." The demands wouldn't have changed. Feed. Change. Obey. It had been easier to ignore the hunger before they'd marked the man. Now the taste of the human was on their tongue, and there was an edge in their blood they couldn't deny. "How goes your change?"

"Slowly. Too many decades spent feeding on exclusively males."

Once changed, there was no returning to the unchanged. They sighed. If not for their sire dragging them back to the border, they could've explored the heartlands. There were unchanged who tended the old ones, those whose antlers were so big they could no longer lift their heads. A forest grew out of them, complete with birds and animals, if the old bard tales were to be believed.

They'd never have gotten that deep into the heartland anyway. Too much human blood flowed in their bloodline. They didn't look like the unchanged Abyr who lived in the heartland. But maybe they could've been a bard in the border castles.

They bit back a sigh. Or they could accept that they were born to be prime, change with grace, and protect the border. All this resistance was a childish rebellion and nothing more. Their sire was right; they needed to prove themselves and take control of their fate.

But that didn't mean giving into it and becoming Vermillion's.

"Don't keep Ver waiting." Lapis stalked away, leather coat flapping behind them.

Umbra wished they could keep Vermillion waiting until the end of time.

They glanced up at the ink black sky and the burning orange sun that never disappeared. The only time they saw the moon was when they'd crossed the lake to the human city. The brief jaunt into the heartland had given them the chance to see moonrise in their land.

They went inside and paused to draw up strength. Below in the hall, there was music and dancing. Humans joined in. Did they realize they were the entertainment and the food? Or were they so entranced by the bite and blood they didn't care?

When the humans died, they'd be tossed into the lake. But if the Abyr got bored, the humans would be returned to the shore. It was no different to their birther's domain in that regard.

Umbra made their way down the winding stone staircase. From

one of the tables they picked up a glass of the nectar. The idea of taking a beast and fleeing, again, had filled their spare time. In the human world, they'd be hunted and killed for what little antler they possessed; in the heartland, they'd be unwelcome. Vermillion would hunt them down and the penalty would be far worse than the whipping their sire had delivered. There was no escape.

And if there was no escape, Umbra had to find a way to live.

They drained the goblet and made their way to Vermillion's private rooms, took a moment, and then knocked.

"Enter."

Umbra pushed open the door and shut it behind them. Vermillion sat in a chair, a half-played game of ossic in front of them. A human pet rested his head on their thigh.

Vermillion considered Umbra, their fingers running through the human's dark hair. Not a caress, but something more calculated. The curve of the man's lips was familiar, but his dark eyes were empty, as though he were already dead and simply going through the motions of living. Yes...that was a common problem here.

Umbra's gaze lifted to Vermillion's antlers. Not big enough to slow them down. There was a tale Vermillion had charged another Abyr and impaled them. That would explain the broken tang. Though that didn't make the tale true. Their own antlers weren't big enough to take on anyone. The young were expected to obey the elders.

Blindly.

Umbra was several decades older than the human man on the floor. Vermillion could be close to one hundred. They had at least another couple of hundred years before their antlers were too heavy for their head. Few lived to be old on the border. Most were killed.

And now the humans were arming themselves. There would be war soon if changes weren't made. Did Vermillion fear an uprising, or was he sure of his power?

"Several hunts, and here you are, still unchanged. Still refusing my hospitality and mateship and shaming your parents."

Was it hospitality when they were as much a prisoner as the human? Their sire should be full of shame, forcing their child to follow a life they didn't want. That Umbra didn't know what they wanted wasn't the point; it would've been nice to at least see what was available beyond border security. Nectar gathering in the heartland might have been nice.

Anything other than terrorizing humans would've been better.

"I don't want to rush," Umbra said truthfully.

"Forty-three winters; you are hardly rushing." Vermillion yanked on the hair of the human, exposing the veins stained silver on his throat. "We have standards and rules, and you will conform."

"Or what? You'll send me away?" *Yes, please do that. Send me to the farms, to the old ones...anywhere but here.*

Vermillion smiled and didn't ease their hold on the human. Pain flickered across his features, but he didn't make a sound. "No, I would not offend your birther so."

Umbra kept quiet. Their birther didn't care; their sire had arranged this. But their birther had the reputation that bards sung about.

Umbra wouldn't be fast enough to snap off antler and ram it through Vermillion's chest. And even if they were, what then? Would Lapis step up? Would there be a battle for who would run this border castle?

There was a chance they could slip away during the upheaval, but a greater chance they'd be thrown in the lake for the leviathans. Or worse, left on the shore to burn in the sunlight.

"But deaths happen, and the humans are brave at the moment." Vermillion shoved the human to the floor and stood. They were taller, but only because of their antlers.

Umbra held their gaze, cool and unblinking, as though they didn't care what Vermillion said next.

Abyr on the border were trained to fight and feed and be strong, something different to the heartland Abyr. The human blood changed them, changed their children, and generations of it had left their mark. Taller and heavier than their heartland cousins, the border Abyr were also more prone to violence.

Vermillion's hand neared his knife.

"If you want to kill me, make an attempt." Umbra knew how to fight. They may not have started drinking blood, but Vermillion would be a fool to underestimate them.

Vermillion laughed. "We should be friends. Your birther is to be much envied. You stand to inherit should you do well here."

Inheriting Cerulean's castle was the last thing Umbra wanted.

Vermillion stepped closer. "I will have you held down and pour the blood down your throat myself." They put their hand on Umbra's shoulder and pressed their forehead hard against Umbra's. "You will change, and you will obey me, or I will leave you to the humans for a day. Think you can find somewhere to hide? Think they will protect you? They will cut off your antlers and put you on a stake to burn in their center square." Their grip hardened. "So when I ask you to join me in a drink tonight, you will. You will bite and drink, and I will see your tongue stained red."

Umbra pushed back, even though their antlers were smaller. Talking to Vermillion had failed. It was time to try another way to buy a few more days. They drew their knife and pressed it to Vermillion's ribs. "I would rather be left in the city than drink with you."

Vermillion leaned into the blade so it bit the leather of his waist-coat. "You do have some of your birther's blood in you. The violence is in your eyes, and I can smell the hunger. You want to feed."

They hadn't before coming here. The hunger had been something they could ignore. Ever since marking the human all they wanted was to bite. Did those in the heartland ever feel the urge or were they content to feed on nectar?

"When I do, it will be my choice, and I will choose which human to take as my pet." Umbra sheathed their knife.

Vermillion stepped back and ran their fingers over Umbra's jaw. "You will feed tonight and start the change. You will come to my bed when I ask."

"I will not."

Vermillion grabbed Umbra by the throat and shoved them against the wall before they had time to react. Age and blood made them fast.

Umbra's toes barely touched the ground. They brought their forearms down breaking the grip and dropped to the floor.

Vermillion backhanded Umbra into the door. Their head smacked the wood. "You are insolent."

Umbra stood. "One of my better qualities." They didn't bother to wipe the blood from their face. Vermillion was no different to their sire; it was easy to see why they were friends. This was no worse than anything Umbra had received before. If Vermillion only respected violence, that's what they'd get.

Vermillion lifted their hand to strike again.

Umbra lifted theirs as well. "I may not be changed, but do not think I am subservient or will obey like a pet. I was raised as prime, and I will not be knocked around by you. I was sent here to learn, and I will. In my time."

Following orders hadn't worked, perhaps demanding would.

"You were sent here to be my mate." Vermillion lowered their hand and their smile returned. "I will have a human female sent to your room. I expect you to feed."

"I have already marked a human." Vermillion didn't need to know it was a man. They would feed and change, not because they wanted it but because it would destroy Vermillion's plans.

The smile flattened into a line.

Umbra cupped Vermillion's jaw. "Hit me again, and you will learn the violence of my birther's blood." They leaned in close, lips almost brushing Vermillion's. "Your wooing skills need work. Perhaps if you had been nice, I'd have considered you a mate. Instead, you bullied me from night one."

Vermillion had been unimpressed to find Umbra unchanged that first night. No changed would pursue an unchanged in bed as that was a taboo no one broke, not even Vermillion. It had been humiliating but a blessing as Vermillion sent them away. Since then it had been the consistent pressure to feed. Diplomacy and pleading to be left alone had failed. Now they had a plan.

Vermillion gripped Umbra's hand and bit their thumb. Their fangs sank deep, drawing bright blood. Vermillion wiped the blood from their lip. "You are mine. I want an heir with a good bloodline. Bring your human here. Take your place at my side."

Umbra pulled their hand away and wiped their bleeding thumb on their trousers. "You will not kill my pet?"

"You have my word."

But not the word of every Abyr who follows you.

CHAPTER 6

By the end of fourteenday, dead man's room felt a little more like home. Elliot had bought more firewood, oil for the lantern, and tallow candles. He'd sold the table and chairs to the family—who were paying in installments—so he actually had spare coins.

It had taken him a while to find a decent place to store them, but above the window there was a loose wood panel. He'd hung a little bag of coins there and then put a few in the tin in the kitchen. While dinner cooked, he rolled some cigarettes. Dinner was lavish by recent standards. He had beef and beans and vegetables. The rest of his salted beef was in a small box by the window where it was coldest.

He was trying very hard to be positive about the move. It had been easier after seeing the family with three small kids. He didn't even regret selling himself for one night as he was rich by Dark City standards. No scraping through this sennight and then starving the second sennight until he got paid.

He checked the beans had softened and deemed them done, and then he didn't bother with a bowl. He ate them straight out of the pot, sitting on the windowsill. He was going to have to buy a couple of stools. Next fortnight, that's what he'd do on his day off. Maybe

Dayne would be back and they could do it together. If Dayne didn't like the room, they could talk about moving. Though in truth, Elliot didn't want to leave the familiarity of this house.

He washed the pot and spoon. The pipes rattled and the water was only a trickle, but he had running water. The privy was downstairs, as was the bathroom.

He lit his cigarette on the stove and shrugged into his coat. It would be full dark soon and he needed to get to the lake. One of the cuffs had started to unravel. He tied off the thread, knowing he'd need to fix it soon, before it all came undone. Then he put on his snood and curled it over his head, locked up and half slid, half ran down the stairs.

Coins in his pocket and a full stomach…for today life was grand.

He left the city, puffing clouds of marshmallow into the night. Tonight, he noticed the lean-tos on the side of the road that lead to the lake. The family who took his old home had been living in one of them while the parents were between jobs. He might have lacked coins, but he was young and single and had ways of making ends meet. Some people didn't have that option—or didn't want that option. If he'd ever had scruples, they'd scuttled away years ago.

Scruples were expensive to tend, and he preferred having a roof and food.

Maybe after going to the lake, he could go to the Moss and Mallow and press his luck further. Maybe Killian hadn't moved on, but even if he had, there'd be others.

Elliot's steps slowed as he reached the shore. There were fewer fires than usual. Fewer devoured.

"What happened? Did the Kin take them back?" he asked the first person he met, a woman with eyes so glazed with bite hunger she could barely focus.

"Dead."

"Dead?"

She smiled and snapped, "They got their last bite. Their patience was rewarded. Why didn't I get bitten?" She pawed at his clothing.

Elliot stepped back, and she crumpled to the ground, sobbing.

Bodies lay on the shore, not sleeping, but dead. Their fires had been left to go out. The Kin had come to feast on those that were close instead of coming to the Dark City. He should be glad. Relieved. But he was only numb. There was always death.

"When, last night? Tonight?"

"All nights are the same." She grabbed Elliot's ankle. "I'm next, not you."

Not him. He didn't want to be next.

"I'm looking for my brother."

Was he lying on the shore? Had he missed him somehow?

Elliot freed himself and went to the next fire, checking the bodies that lay cold on the ground. The living warming their bony frames watched him but made no move to help. Did they not care they were surrounded by the dead?

"Have you seen my brother, Dayne?" he asked the way he had every night. "He looks like me." In that way siblings resembled each other. They shared their mama's coloring, but Dayne was much more like their father, taller and heavier even though he was younger. Elliot's feet became numb from the cold; his toe stuck through a hole in his sock he hadn't had time to mend. "I'm looking for my brother."

At every fire that was lit, he asked the same thing.

The same as he'd done so many nights before.

Of those that answered, no one had seen him. But a man couldn't vanish into fog.

He stared across the lake as the castle became visible. Wreathed in mist, it looked as insubstantial as smoke. While he'd been searching, the night had closed in. The last traces of sunset were long gone, and the moon hung overhead like an unspent coin. The surface of the lake heaved as the things that lived there woke. One long tendril reached out and grabbed the closest body, dragging it into the cold inky water.

He closed his eyes and drew in a breath to stop his stomach from turning and tossing out dinner. There was nothing for him here, but he'd be back tomorrow. Had to be.

Where had Dayne been when the Kin had taken him? He should've been safe at home. Kin couldn't enter a house without permission.

There were rules.

Weren't there?

He'd seen the blood on the cobbles; there'd been no rules then.

Something vibrated in his chest. A warning and a longing. The skin on his neck warmed. His eyes snapped open, but he didn't wait to see what was happening.

He ran.

～

The heat of the Moss and Mallow was a welcome slap to the face. Elliot undid his coat, but left his snood on, not wanting to reveal the mark on his neck. He ordered the cheapest ale he could—which would be well watered, but he didn't care. He was indoors, and not alone. He wasn't ready to go back to dead man's room and sleep the night there.

"Elli!" Killian slung his arm around his shoulder and kissed his cheek. "We were starting to wonder what had happened to you. Thought you'd ended up by the lake."

But none had looked for him or asked after him. When people vanished, most sensible folk accepted it and moved on. Was he being a fool? Killing himself when he should be living his life?

He wasn't ready to admit Dayne was gone. Not yet.

"My brother's missing. Been working his job and looking for him." He lifted his glass and took a drink. The ale was weak, but the sharp medicinal undertone was one he liked. He never added honey the way some did.

"That's rough." Killian sat and smiled at him as though nothing had changed.

Elliot shrugged. It was what it was. All he could do was keep things going until Dayne came back...or didn't. The thought was a knife in his gut that twisted each time he gave the thought room to move.

"You have the night off too?"

Elliot nodded. "Got to start before dawn."

"You have the shittest job."

The hours weren't great, but he didn't mind it. He liked cutting the glass and repairing the lights. Handling the orbs was something he'd gotten used to.

Having seen the damage they did when they…flashed, he wondered how they could be made to flash and burn. Nothing he'd ever done had caused that, and he'd dropped one more than once.

"At least I'm not emptying the shitters of the rich."

Killian tapped his glass to Elliot's. "My pay's better."

No amount of coin would tempt Elliot to even consider that. "You been doing much?"

"Nah." Killian nudged him and smiled at him again. "I knew you'd be back."

"Why's that?" He wanted to slip into the easy banter and pretend Killian cared.

"Some folk get taken but others, they're too bloody slippery to get caught. You got more street smarts than everyone in this room."

Elliot grinned and wished that were true. He'd made one mistake, because he hadn't been sleeping, and now he was marked. It was only a matter of time before the Kin came. All he could do was make sure his blood was poison. "You trying to flatter me into bed?"

"Would it be quicker if I bought you something other than that swill?" A smile curled Killian's lips, his eyes bright in the lantern light. Herb smoke other than marshmallow coiled along the ceiling.

"Buy me a drink, and I'll let you know."

Killian signaled the bartender and ordered two of the darker brew he was drinking. When Killian brushed the hair from Elliot's face and tucked it behind his ear, Elliot didn't pull away. It was nice to be wanted, the tavern was warm, and Killian knew what to do with his pretty mouth. There were worse ways to spend the night.

The chatter in the room increased, someone started playing a set of panpipes, and another started to sing. Out there, nothing was fine, and they all knew it. The Kin were hunting more often, humans were killing the Kin, people were barely scraping by. But in here, they were warm and safe and could have a little fun. As he drank the brew in front of him, his blood warmed and a real smile formed.

Killian put a hand on Elliot's thigh, and Elliot didn't nudge him away. He leaned in closer until his lips almost brushed Elliot's ear. "I've been waiting for you to come back."

Elliot closed his eyes. They didn't have that kind of thing. He didn't want that kind of thing. He didn't have the time. And while Killian was nice enough...there was something about him that Elliot didn't trust.

"You couldn't find another to plough your field?"

"Not like you."

Elliot lifted an eyebrow. What were people saying about him? He could count a handful of men in the room that he'd fucked either in their bed or out in the back of the tavern in warmer months. "Is that so?" And he flipped for coin, so maybe he should charge for both...or not. Some things he liked to keep for himself.

Killian blushed. "I've been fallow."

"I don't believe that."

Killian put a hand over his heart. "You should. My job puts most off."

"I figure you clean up before going out." Elliot glanced at Killian's hands; his nails were clean. His gaze traveled back up to Killian's freshly shaven jaw. Definitely worse ways to waste the evening. It wasn't a relationship, but it was easy.

Killian nodded and finished his brew. "I'm only down the street. Be nicer than out the back."

"That's closer than me." Elliot drained his glass; the dregs were almost too sweet. But he wasn't so graceless as to whine about a free drink.

Elliot followed Killian out into the cold. The night had settled, and the fog was creeping up from the lake. He didn't bother buttoning his coat because he'd be out of it soon enough. Killian grabbed his hand and drew him swiftly up the road. Elliot spun Killian toward him and kissed him. It wasn't necessary, but he wanted to taste him. He hadn't kissed in too long.

Killian's lips moved against his. His breath was warm on his lips. They made it up the road to Killian's boarding house, and upstairs to his room with only a few more breathless pauses to kiss and fumble. Killian opened the door, and they stumbled in. They shed clothes in a hurry and slid beneath the blankets to hide from the cold.

It was only in the dark that Elliot remembered the mark on his neck. But Killian was kissing and stroking and sliding down to lick and taste, and Elliot wasn't sure Killian would care if he did notice. He rocked his hips, thrusting into Killian's mouth, knowing he'd need to stop soon to give Killian what he wanted. All he wanted was to do was spill on Killian's tongue. Another time. Reluctantly, Elliot pushed him off.

Killian dragged him close and kissed him hard and hungry.

"There's no rush."

"I know." But his hands betrayed his words. They were all over Elliot.

"You got something so it's not rough?"

"Yeah." Killian reached over to the nightstand. A hard lump of cooking fat rested on a scrap of paper. He'd been looking. If Elliot hadn't stumbled in, he'd have sated his hunger with another. "That's all I got."

"It's fine." He cupped the block in his hands to warm it up while Killian worked his fingers over Elliot's length. When his hands were good and greasy he put the lump down.

Killian lay back and bent his knees. The ambient light in the room was enough for Elliot to see what he was doing as he ran his oiled fingers over Killian's hole. His other hand stroked his own length, making sure it was slick. Carefully he eased one finger in, wanting to take his time.

"Come on. I'm ready." Killian hooked his leg around Elliot's hip.

Elliot gave in, making each thrust deeper until he was buried to the hilt. A quiver of lust traced down his spine. It may not be quite what he wanted, but it was what he needed.

Killian rolled his hips. "You ain't going to break me."

Elliot grinned. He pressed forward so he could kiss Killian and drive in harder. "You breaking yet?"

"Not even close." But his words were breathy.

Elliot laid into him hard. "Better?"

The bed creaked its protest, and Killian groaned. "Yeah."

He gripped Killian's shaft and stroked. Killian threw his head back as he came, slicking Elliot's hand. Elliot let himself fall over the edge, thrusting a few more times to draw out the pleasure before resting over Killian. He kissed him again. It was so tempting to rollover and stay the night in the warm bed. To not be alone. But he needed his alarm to drag himself out of bed before dawn. This time, he groaned for all the wrong reasons.

"You're not going to stay for more are you?"

"I can't." He wanted to.

Killian ruffled Elliot's hair. "Another time?"

"I'd like that."

"So would I." Killian shoved him off, and Elliot took the hint.

He pulled on his clothes, his skin cooling fast, and then tossed Killian a smile. "See you at the Moss."

～

*T*he streets weren't quite deserted as he made his way home, down the Eighth and round the corner onto Dyers lane. His feet were light over the dirt streets. Too late, he felt rather than saw the person closing in on him. He turned, but the Kin was on him, pressing him to the wall, hand over his mouth.

His heart stopped and restarted, then he lifted his knee, hoping to collect whatever the Kin had in their pants. The Kin grunted and thumped Elliot's head against the wall before following up with an elbow to the gut. Pain exploded in the back of his skull, and embers formed at the edges of his vision.

"I'm not going to kill you. I want to talk."

Elliot glared at the pink haired Kin. He didn't really have a choice. He had no weapon, and the Kin was stronger than he was. He nodded as much as he could, his skull resenting the movement. If the Kin wanted to kill him, they could've done so already. Did the Kin talk to their victims?

Or did they know something about his brother?

The Kin removed their hand but didn't step back. They kept their body pressed to Elliot's, holding him against the wall.

"What do you want?" Elliot muttered. Where were the venerie now?

"I need a pet."

"Sod off and find someone else."

The Kin moved closer, sniffed his skin, and kissed the place he'd marked before. Elliot drew in a breath and held still the way he would if a stray dog was too close and he wasn't sure if it was friendly or furious.

"You've poisoned your blood."

"You're welcome."

"Fool." The Kin stepped back. "You make it easier for the Abyr to kill you."

"Why do they want to kill me?" *Why not me?* The Kin killed all the time, hunting in the Dark City. They were the cats and people like him, the rats. Those up the hill with their lit roads paid in blood for the magic and luxury, but not *their* blood. Never their blood.

"Because I marked you."

"So I'm dead because of something you did." He should be showing more respect. He should be begging for his life. "Undo it."

"I can't…" The Kin glanced down. "I shouldn't have, but I liked the way you smelled, and I couldn't help it. Now I need you."

Elliot wanted to make a smart reply, but he had nothing. He didn't want to be needed by the Kin. "Thanks for the warning. I'm going to get some sleep, because some of us have work." He pushed past.

The Kin slammed him into the wall again. The breath left Elliot's lungs and he forgot how to inhale. Pinkie would kill him before the others got to him. He kicked the Kin's shin, but they didn't move. However, their feature's hardened as though they at least felt pain.

"You think we don't work? We are the guards that stop you invading."

"Invading what?"

The Kin shook their head. "I need your help, and you need mine if you want to live."

"Why do you need me?"

"I need a pet, to feed, to change."

"I don't give a fuck." He pushed back, trying to get free, and failed. The Kin was too fast and too strong.

"Your brother is Vermillion's pet."

The ground fell away, and Elliot stopped struggling. "You found Dayne?"

The Kin nodded. "I'll help you, but you must help me."

"I don't want to be one of the devoured."

The Kin stared at him. "The what?"

"On the shore."

"Oh the hopeful...they've tasted Kin blood." Pinkie shrugged as though it were nothing. "I will not ask you to swear obedience and sup my blood."

"I don't want any part of this. I just want my brother."

The Kin blinked. Their eyes were the same pink as their hair, like summer wildflowers, deepening to purple around the pupil. Elliot blinked and looked away. The mark on his neck was cold as though the Kin were pressing their lips to his skin.

"And I need a pet."

Elliot shook his head.

"I was sent here to bear Vermillion's child. I do not want that. I do not want to feed and change, yet I must. I will have your blood."

"If you don't like it, leave." He wished he'd done more than talk about leaving with Dayne.

"You don't understand." And he didn't want to. The Kin released him, but this time Elliot didn't try to escape. His body ached, and he wouldn't make the same mistake a third time. "Humans are born one or the other, you never experience being neither."

"Some are Kin-touched. The parents not sure if they are male or female, or they know their body doesn't match who they are."

"Your bodies change?"

"No." How much did Kin bodies actually change?

55

Elliot frowned trying to pull together his thoughts while the ache in his head bloomed into something solid. "Your leader wants you to drink female blood, to become female and have their babies? And to avoid that, you'll drink male blood and become male? It doesn't need to be mine."

He didn't want anyone drinking his blood. And he definitely didn't want to be caught up in Kin politics.

"I don't have to help you get your brother before Vermillion tires of him, and I don't have to stop Vermillion from sending Abyr to kill you." They smiled; the tips of their fangs visible.

Blood and bother. He did need this Kin to get his brother back.

"And if I were to agree to…" He swallowed and the mark on this neck throbbed in a very unsettling way. "If I let you have some blood…how does it work? Would you visit each night?"

"No. For the first moon, it is best if the blood is from the same person. From a pet. You would need to live in the castle."

"And make it easier for the Kin to kill me? No."

"A pet has protection. Here you have none."

He was not considering this. Not at all. He was not a stray dog looking for a home. He couldn't leave. He had a job, and his brother's job, and rent to pay.

And his brother was a prisoner in the Kin's castle.

The Kin watched, their face sharp planes that could be male or female depending on the light. Their long leather coat masked their body.

This seemed like a really bad idea, but if he walked away then Dayne would stay as Vermillion's pet, and Vermillion would kill him eventually. "We'd have an alliance?"

"Yes. We both need something."

"Or Vermillion orders us both to be killed."

The corner of the Kin's lips curved up in a crooked smile that on another face might have made Elliot's heart skip a beat. "Possibly."

If this Kin hadn't marked him, hadn't saved him the first time they'd met, none of this would be happening. He'd already be dead. "How do I know you're telling the truth about my brother?"

The Kin's smile widened, and they inclined their head. "Humans are smarter than many Abyr say. What proof would you like?"

"Ask him…" What would only Dayne know? The last few years their paths had barely crossed with Dayne working days and Elliot working nights. "Ask him where I hide my coins."

"And if the answer is acceptable, you will come with me tomorrow."

Elliot's toes curled in his boots. "I will be able to leave with my brother?"

"After the moon completes its change."

"You swear?" His heart was banging so hard on his ribs he could hardly hear.

The Kin placed a hand over their heart. "By the forest of the old ones. But you must stop poisoning your blood."

Elliot licked his lip. He'd sold himself before, and this was no different. His blood instead of his ass.

He glanced up at the moon; it was almost gone. Tomorrow night, there'd be nothing left. His mouth was dry.

"Okay."

He took a step away, and then another, and the Kin let him leave. He shoved his hands into his pockets. The tingle in his skin let him know that the Kin stalked him until he was home. He climbed the stairs to dead man's room.

The room was stuffy, the stove throwing out too much heat for the small space. He banked it and opened the window a crack. On the roof of another building, the pink haired Kin crouched against a chimney. Beyond the houses was the lake, the castle shrouded in mist.

Below were the dark cobbles. He'd never thought about jumping, but there was an appeal in those few breaths. No more scrabbling to get by. No more dodging the Kin. He lifted his gaze, and Pinkie was gone.

He pulled a cigarette out of his pocket and lit it on the stove, before sitting on the windowsill. The paper burned and the leaf crack-led, but he didn't bring it to his lips even though he wanted the sweetness on his tongue. If he was going to save Dayne, he had to stop poisoning his blood.

He closed his eyes. It was only for a lunar cycle. Twenty-eight days. He'd spent more days face down in the brothel getting coin for Mama's medicine. It was only blood. Blood for blood.

He opened his eyes and let the butt fall from his fingers, the ember extinguished before it hit the ground.

CHAPTER 7

$\mathcal{U}$mbra watched their pet until he was safely indoors, then moved away. There were few Kin hunting tonight. They'd ridden out together, over the lake and into the city. Umbra had been followed as expected and it had taken time for them to lose the follower and find their pet. There'd be blood when it was revealed their pet was a man.

From the roofs, Umbra watched as other Kin scoured the streets searching for unpoisoned prey; it was getting harder to find them. They'd heard the grumbles, that they had to wait for the humans to hand over those they no longer wanted.

For tonight their pet was safe. Tomorrow, a new danger would happen.

No Abyr should kill another's pet, but it had happened before. As Vermillion had said, accidents happened. Their pet would have to fake the docile obedience of the blood fed.

This was a fool's game, and to what end?

If they wanted to remain unchanged, they were losing. But they were losing on their terms,so was that not better?

Umbra cursed their sire and their birther. Perhaps they could pretend to feed from their pet and thus remain unchanged. But changing would give them extra strength and speed. Without those things, surviving Vermillion's rule would be impossible. Without those things, they'd never be respected as prime; they'd always be the unchanged runt, regardless of their bloodline.

Vermillion wasn't respected as prime...feared, yes. But that was a very different thing.

They ran their tongue over their fangs. They'd been tempted to bite their pet tonight. His scent was alluring, the way he'd fought back more so. No fear in his eyes, just a fight that warmed their blood and made them wish they had a lover in the castle so they could rub away the hard edges of desire.

They drew in a breath and exhaled slowly. It would be best to return and speak with the brother before Vermillion got in the way.

They slithered off the roof and landed where the beasts were parked. Their bones gleamed white in the starlight and they hummed with magic. Umbra got on their beast and the vibration intensified, a pleasing rumble between their thighs. Skeletons given wheels and life, they were a pleasure to ride.

The Abyr who'd stayed behind to guard the beasts from human attack stepped forward. "Where are you going?"

"Home."

"You will wait." The guard put their hand on Umbra's beast.

"Am I free or a prisoner of Vermillion?"

The guard didn't answer.

Umbra ignored their request and wheeled away, racing the beast down deserted streets toward the shore. A few moments alone were all they needed to take the first step in their rebellion.

The bonfires tossed sparks into the night and the hopeful turned to look at them. They'd never travelled this path alone. Many eyes watched, wanting to be chosen. Their desperation wasn't appealing. It never had been.

All of Umbra's life, other Abyr had wanted them for who they were: prime of Octadine. Their pet was no different. Everyone wanted something from them. What they wanted didn't matter.

They edged the beast away from the main path and slowed at the next bonfire. They scanned the thin faces, seeking a man for the first taste. Traditionally, the blood should be from the same human for the first month as it was said to make the first change easier. None of this was easy, but it was the way it had to be if they wanted to survive instead of breaking.

If Vermillion forced female blood into them first, it would be too late. A moon of blood starvation had to happen before switching. Umbra's arrival had upset Lapis's plans to carry Vermillion's child, but Lapis was welcome to that role.

Umbra beckoned to a human with a beard.

He rushed forward and dropped to his knees in pathetic abasement. "I am yours, do with me as you will."

Umbra considered him for several heartbeats. If there hadn't been poison in his pet's blood, this wouldn't be necessary. The change would've have already started, and the taste of their pet's blood would be on their tongue. "Stand."

The man obeyed.

While many Abyr expected obedience, it was dull. Umbra would never feed a pet their blood. They would much rather fight—they blamed their birther's blood for that. Their tendency to resist and disobey is what had gotten them sent here in the first place. Sent away to learn how to behave and rule.

Had this man been someone's pet before being discarded? Or had he simply been brought across for fun before being returned and abandoned only to long for a return to favor in the castle?

Umbra glanced up the hill to where the wealthy resided. Those humans were as bankrupt as Vermillion. The corruption fed on both peoples.

"You have tasted Kin blood?"

"Yes. It's not something easily forgotten."

"If you are my eyes and ears, then you may taste it again."

The man bowed. "I'm your servant. Whatever you need."

"I need blood."

The man pulled aside his coat collar and stepped closer. There was a line of dirt that revealed the extent of his washing. He smelled nothing like their pet. He wouldn't taste like him either. But they were luxuries that hadn't been granted tonight.

Umbra drew him close and hesitated for a heartbeat—this wasn't something that could be undone—then bit him. It took more pressure than they'd expected to break the skin, but then their mouth flooded with the hot juice that coursed through humans. It was nothing like the sweet nectar they'd grown up on; blood was sharp and hot. The man became liquid in his arms, and a groan escaped his lips. Umbra drew away, gagging on the sticky texture.

Was that enough or did they need more?

Blood trickled down the man's neck. Umbra watched the line disappear into the man's coat, then they took a second taste. Instead of waiting for the blood to spill into their mouth they sucked, drawing more in and swallowing. It was easier the second time, but they stopped after a couple of swallows, not wanting to take too much.

They helped the man to stand and made sure he was steady on his feet, before cutting open their thumb and offering it to the man.

He lapped the spilled blood with a greedy tongue. "You'll take me with you?"

"No, you will stay here and keep me informed. Tell me who comes and goes." He took his thumb away. "Your information will be rewarded."

"Your offer is most generous." He bowed, his eyes bright in the firelight.

The taste of blood coated their tongue, but Umbra didn't feel any different. They had expected something rather more dramatic given the way the change was talked about. They swallowed and wanted nothing more than to scrub their tongue and wretch until their stomach was empty because even though there was no sudden blood thirst or change, something would be happening.

*T*he castle was never quiet, but tonight it was subdued. Vermillion gambled with their friends, dice rolled and bets placed. Umbra didn't want to join in, but they had to start playing the hand they'd been dealt. They had to appear as though they were complying, albeit reluctantly.

Glass vessels of nectar were cradled in copper wire and hung from chains. Dangling beneath on hooks were goblets. Umbra filled a goblet, hoping to wash the taste of blood from their mouth. They drank deeply, but the taste wasn't what they craved. It was too sweet at the back of their throat.

For the first few days, there had been no nectar for them to consume as Vermillion tried to force Umbra to drink blood. The nectar had been brought out when it was clear Umbra would rather die.

Yet here they were, very much alive.

Vermilion lifted their gaze and nodded. Their pet watched from the floor, his dark eyes glazed. Would he be able to answer the question his brother had asked?

Umbra took another sip of nectar and meandered closer to the game, so it was clear their obedience was barely there. Vermillion noticed; there was a twitch to their lip that only occurred when they were annoyed.

It would be Umbra's mission to ensure Vermillion's lip never rested.

"Still sipping nectar?" Vermillion said with a snap.

Umbra glanced at the glass in their hand as though that were obvious and didn't bother to answer. With Vermillion's attention on the game, Umbra studied the pet. There was a resemblance in the eyes and the set of the man's mouth, but there was no fight in him. There was nothing in there at all.

That was not their problem. Their problem was getting close enough to ask the question. *Where are your brother's coins kept?*

"Join the game." It was an order not an invitation.

Umbra sat on the vacated chair. They needed to make an effort to be at these games. They were supposed to be Vermillion's mate, and as appalling as that idea was, appearing to accept that role would elevate their status—at least until it was noticed that Umbra was not changing as Vermillion desired.

"What is the wager?" There was always a wager.

"For you...I want to see you drink blood if I win." Vermillion's smile was as cold as the moon over the human city.

"And if I win?"

"You get to delay another day."

Umbra sipped the nectar. "So all I have to do is win every night to remain unchanged?"

Vermillion shot them a glare. "Those stakes will get old fast. Tonight, they will do."

The bard settled with their harp and started to sing Vermillion's favorite tale of war. And Vermillion started the game, rolling the seven seven-sided dice, each decorated with a unique set of symbols. They were a nice set made of polished black stone, and Umbra had no doubt they were weighted just so, if one knew how to throw them.

Umbra picked up the dice and held them for a moment. "Any word from my parents?"

"None, and I have sent none either. Do not give me reason to."

Umbra let the dice fall. They rerolled only two, though they could've rerolled them all. Not a winning hand, but a middling score that might keep them safe for tonight.

Back and forth the game went with Vermillion edging a little ahead with each hand. If they were cheating, it was subtle. The tension that had been a small discomfort intensified, gripping Umbra's stomach.

Vermillion's grin widened with each throw. "You will be mine. Is this what you wanted, a better wooing?"

None of this was what they wanted.

"No quest? No captured kingdom?" They wanted a prime to court them and offer them a castle. Not an upstart who took over through underhanded means.

"You've listened to too many of the old tales. I know your sire loves them."

"I have listened to many tales. If you expect someone to change and bear your child, you need to offer more than brute force."

"Perhaps, but it is efficient." Vermillion made their last roll. They picked up three of the dice, not the ones Umbra would've chosen to re-roll. The odds of making this a good hand were long...but if Vermillion succeeded, Umbra would need something even better.

The dice hit the table, spun, and turned. They landed as Umbra had thought they would. And now they knew which dice were weighted even if they didn't know which way to throw them. There would be time to figure that out later.

Few here would be able to read the hands and feel the dice the way they could. Their birther had taught them young that all battle was a gamble and the smallest detail could make or break a victory.

They'd been able to cheat with unweighted dice before they were twenty.

Umbra threw the dice. They fell badly. Carefully, Umbra picked up two dice, one of which was weighted. They held them, getting the feel for which way the weighted one needed to be thrown. They didn't need that symbol; they needed the one on the opposite side. And even then they wouldn't be able to produce a winning hand. They rolled the dice and they fell as planned.

Vermillion tallied the final score, and their lips curved. "We are done with games. You concede?"

Umbra held their gaze. "Never. But you have won today."

Annoyance flared in Vermillion's green eyes. Where Umbra relished the fight, Vermillion resented the rebellion to their rule. It was a bruise Umbra would press on until the skin broke, until the bone beneath shattered and Vermillion begged to be released.

"We could be friends."

They could've been, had Vermillion been anything other than themselves. "You started the animosity. You need to be kind first."

Their lip twitched. Vermillion's pet watched the interaction. He wasn't totally dead inside.

Vermillion reached across the table and put their hand over Umbra's. Umbra let the gesture lie, for the moment. "Do not push. You were prime in your birther's castle, but you aren't prime here."

"I was born to rule. You expect me to gratefully bow?"

"You should. This is a good match."

For you.

It was common for young primes to be sent away, offered up to strengthen bloodlines and ties, but usually it was done after the prime had changed. Their sire had grown impatient. Or had Vermillion pressed old friendships and offered new threats? That Vermillion had become male and chosen to remain male instead of changing to female to birth their own prime and second was odd, but there must be a reason.

When Umbra didn't answer, Vermillion signaled to one of their generals. There were four who were closest to Vermillion and obeyed everything they said. Weld was one of them, a tall well-antlered male form Abyr with dark blue hair. Pretty, but not to Umbra's taste, and probably of no use to them either. Everyone had to be weighed by their allegiance.

After a hushed conversation, Weld left.

Umbra spun their goblet. "Do I not get a choice?"

"I know you." Vermillion pointed a finger. "You would choose none."

Vermillion didn't know them at all. They'd already chosen.

A woman was brought forward. "The pet I selected for you, since you have not brought one."

"I will, when I'm ready."

"Well, when you finally do, they will be welcome. Until then." Vermillion gestured to the woman. "Please have your first bite."

"It's not my first." In truth, the man on the beach was a pet, though Umbra would never call him that. There was none of the care or affection that the term implied. The other man, the one he wanted to bite, would never be a true pet because he didn't want to taste Umbra's blood. Umbra gave Vermillion a small smile.

"Then it won't be a problem will it?" Their voice hardened.

Vermillion reached out and cut the woman's arm. Blood splashed on the table before pouring into Umbra's half-drunk glass of nectar. The blood and nectar didn't mix but swirled uneasily together, gold and red.

Vermillion pressed the wound closed until the blood stopped. The woman hadn't even whimpered. "Drink, *mate*."

Umbra's stomach turned. They were mixing male and female blood. Their body would be a mess.

Vermillion stood and grabbed Umbra's face. "You lost the bet."

They brought the glass to Umbra's lips. When Umbra didn't open their mouth willingly, Vermillion squeezed their jaw, forcing their mouth open, and poured the blood mix in. It was vile, but Umbra swallowed a little while the rest spilled down the front of their shirt and waistcoat.

Vermillion slammed the goblet down, shattering the glass. Blood and nectar spilled. "You disgust me. Show some grace in defeat." They stalked away, leaving their pet leashed to the throne.

Weld glared at Umbra. "You shouldn't anger Ver. They can be kind."

Umbra stared sullenly at Weld until they led the woman away, rewarding her with a little of their blood.

With nothing more to watch, any Abyr that had been lingering moved away. Umbra let their gaze come to rest on Vermillion's pet. "Dayne?"

The human looked up with something more than hopelessness in their eyes.

"Don't look at me, but answer."

Dayne lowered their gaze and shifted a little closer.

"Where does your brother keep his coins?"

Dayne stared at the floor for several heartbeats before speaking. "He doesn't keep coins. He spends them at the Moss."

What kind of an answer was that? Moss was a plant. Was it something he ate? Why ask where he kept it if he didn't. Ohh... Umbra smiled. Their pet was indeed smart. He would be trouble. Bringing him here would create chaos.

And it would be most delightful.

Umbra stood, then bent to retie their boot. "Stop drinking Abyr blood, pet."

Dayne looked up. "Says the Kin who was forced to drink human blood."

"We're all fighting a war. Pick your battle. Now I have somewhere to be." They desperately needed to empty their stomach.

CHAPTER 8

$\mathcal{I}$t was dark when Elliot woke. His alarm hadn't gone off. For a few moments, he listened to the creaking of the building and wondered why he was awake with his heart beating too fast. Then the events of the night before bubbled up in quick succession.

He sat up, clutching the sheets too tightly. He'd agreed to go to the castle for a month. To let Pinkie feed off him. He didn't know that much about the Kin, except they fed off humans, and they changed depending on who they were feeding on. It had seemed like a good deal last night, a bit of blood for his brother.

This morning it was madness—and he couldn't even blame the Kin. It was his own desperation. If he didn't do it, Dayne would remain Vermillion's. Everyone knew who ran the pack of Kin and who the main players were. Their hair made them easy to spot.

Pinkie was new.

And helping him.

A trap? Or part of something bigger?

He glanced at the time. There was no point in trying to go back to sleep, and he wouldn't find it even if he searched. He threw off the blankets, lit the lantern, washed in icy water, and dressed. He sat quietly and mended his coat and socks, not knowing when he'd get the chance again. Then he gathered up the perishable food into a bag to give to the family in his old apartment; they could give the landlord the rest of the money for the table.

But then he checked his coins; he was short for a month's rent. He'd known he'd be short. Even if he hadn't gone to the Moss last night, he wouldn't have had enough. Even with the family paying off the table, there wasn't enough. He'd have to offer the food to the land-lord and beg for leniency. Though how he'd pay for the room after, he had no idea. He wouldn't have a job, and neither would Dayne. He hung his head.

That was, of course, assuming he was coming back.

That all this mattered.

Maybe it didn't. His parents had scrabbled for everything, and he and Dayne had done the same. Always running, always tired, always keeping an eye out for the Kin when they hunted. It wasn't right. Not when those up the hill had everything.

His alarm rattled on the side table. He got up and turned it off, but not before the person below thumped on the wall. The room went silent, the sky turning gray. The sun would rise, and the castle would disappear. Where did it go?

Where would he go?

He slipped on his coat and snood, buckled up his boots, and gath-ered up all his coins and food that would spoil, then made his way downstairs. The landlord was sipping his tea and staring out at the street. Why people got up early when they could stay in bed, Elliot didn't know. If he had the chance, he'd lie in bed all day.

"I need to pay up in advance."

The landlord considered him. "I thought you were going to sort yourself out."

"I am. I'm going to get my brother." When spoken aloud, it didn't sound like a smart thing to do, even though it was the right thing.

"From where?"

"The Kin's castle." Now his plan, Pinkie's plan, sounded downright dumb.

"That's not how it works with the Kin, kid."

"I know. But I have to try. I almost have a month's worth of rent." He held out the food and coins.

The landlord sighed and shook his head.

Elliot's heart sank. He needed a place to come back to. "Please."

"I told your mother I'd watch out for you. This is foolish. Brave, but foolish. You need to think about you and forget about your brother. He'll be devoured, if he's still alive."

Dayne was alive. He was sure of it.

"I need to get Dayne."

"What are you going to do? Walk over the lake?"

"I don't know." He'd work that out when the time came. "I'll be leaving soon, maybe tonight." Would Pinkie return with the proof that fast?

"So you want to put your affairs in order, kid?"

"Dead man's room was empty for over a month before I moved in, so what have you got to lose? You have the rent for a month, and when I come back with Dayne, there'll be two of us to pay it."

"Those that leave the island end up on the shore. They don't come back to the city."

"If I don't come back, you can sell my things and rent out the room. No loss to you." He doubted the landlord would throw out his things while he was away.

"One month. Pretty specific." The landlord watched him with narrowed eyes as he sipped his tea.

Elliot shrugged. "No moon tonight. Seemed like an omen or something."

He wasn't about to share what had happened. He couldn't tell anyone. No one would believe him for a start, and if they did, they might try to sell the info. Then Vermillion would hear and that would ruin everything.

"Fine, kid. But I think you're throwing away a perfectly good life on a wisp of a wish." He put his hand out, and Elliot handed over all his coins and the food.

This wasn't a perfectly good life, it was getting by and hoping that

71

he didn't get the wasting cough from smoking marshmallow. It was hoping that the marshals didn't pick him up for something small and send him to the Kin as punishment. It was knowing that he was one payday away from being tossed out. Sure, the landlord had promised to look out for him, but that didn't extend to doing anything. The landlord had a business to run, and Elliot didn't begrudge him that.

For a day, Elliot had enjoyed the illusion of having money. Maybe that was all people like him got. And if he wanted to throw it all away…well, there wasn't that much to re-gather to rebuild was there?

"If your mister was taken by the Kin, what would you do?"

The landlord smiled. "We're too old for the Kin to bother with us." The smile faded. "But when I was young, I didn't do anything. The Kin take what they want, and we go on. That's how it is. You get him back, what do you think will happen? They'll want him back. You can't take from them and win." He turned and walked inside.

Elliot swallowed hard. He hadn't thought about what happened after. It was hard to think that far ahead.

The sky was lighter now, and he was going to be late. Again. He ran through the streets, uphill to the workshop, and breathlessly let himself in.

Fife had this bag over his shoulder. "Didn't think you were coming."

"Here now. I'll stay today. Cut the glass and so on." He picked up his bag and slung it on.

"Given up on your brother?"

"No. I'm going to the castle to get him."

Fife stopped halfway to the door. "What?"

"I'm not going to be here for the rest of the month." Was he quitting? This wasn't the kind of job that could be held open. Fife would take another apprentice; the city would make him. Elliot's job would be gone.

He'd be back to selling his ass until he found something else. Even if he begged the officials, they'd never let him be a lightman again. Apprentices were cheap, and he would've proven himself untrustworthy by not showing up.

"And how are you getting to the castle? You going to walk on water like the Kin?"

"I'm going with one."

Fife frowned. "You've made some kind of deal."

"I'm getting my brother back."

Fife nodded. "I understand that bit. You ever stop to think about why he's there?"

"He was captured by the Kin." Elliot had gone to the Moss after turning on the lights that night. If he'd gone home, maybe he could've stopped Dayne from going out. Or they could've gone out together.

"He was caught by the marshals and turned over to the Kin because he had antler."

"Why'd he have antler?" Everyone knew an antler to the heart would kill a Kin, that's why it was banned. Stab a Kin with anything else, and they shook it off like it was a bee sting. "He attacked a Kin?"

Fife licked his lip. "Your brother was venerie."

Elliot stared at the man who'd been his master. "How would you know that? Why would you say that? He's a kid. He worked at the plant sorting leaf."

"He's nineteen and knew his own mind."

"But…" Elliot shook his head. "How did the venerie find him?"

"We're everywhere if you know where to look and what to say."

Elliot blinked. "You never said anything to me."

"You've always been happy with the way things are."

"I have not."

"Okay, maybe happy isn't the right word, but you weren't ready to fight for a change." Fife lifted his hands. "Not saying that's a bad thing. You were making a go of surviving. But Dayne watched you and wanted more than getting by and making do."

"He never said." Did he even know his brother?

"Why would he? You raised him and kept a roof over both your heads."

But that hadn't been enough for Dayne.

Elliot sagged onto a stool at the work bench. Pieces of glass waited to be cut, metal waited to be soldered, strips of lead lay on

73

shelves. Everything needed to make replacement containers for the orbs.

"You're…one of them."

"I watch and report."

"You recruited him."

"No." Fife shook his head. "But I know he wouldn't want you tearing off to the island to free him."

"How could you know that? He's my brother." Of course Elliot was going to save him. Dayne would be waiting for him. Expecting him.

"We all know what we do is dangerous, that we might get caught, and we know no one is coming for us."

"Well, he didn't tell me that, and I'm going to get him."

"Don't be a fool. It won't be Dayne. He'll be devoured."

"He wouldn't drink Kin blood."

"He won't have a choice," Fife snapped, but then lowered his voice. "The Kin aren't like you and me. They're immortal. Violence means nothing because their injuries heal by magic. They'll break you apart. Make you forget who you are until you only live to serve."

The lump on the back of Elliot's head was a reminder of the Kin's violence. Pinkie had thought nothing of slamming him into a wall. By the lake, he'd seen how broken the devoured could be. But Dayne wouldn't be like that. Elliot would get him home, and he'd be fine. "People do recover."

Fife lowered his gaze. "They do…but you ain't got the coin to pay the marshal to get the medicine. Only those on the hill have that."

He'd make sure that Dayne got the medicine; he wasn't going to fail again. "You can't talk me out of it."

"And what? You're going to walk into their castle and take your brother?"

"Something like that."

*E*lliot spent the day in the workshop making boxes to hold the orbs. Shards of glass glittered on the workbenches, and the metallic scent of solder hung in the air. His hand shook as he finished the one he was working on. He hadn't managed to eat all day, and his stomach was a small, hard knot.

Fife returned at dusk to turn on the lights. He put a small package on the table. "Not much, but all that that could be given."

Elliot picked it up and turned it over. "What is it?"

"Open it and have a look."

A small knife, like the kind fancy folk up the hill carried to cut up their meals, fell onto the table. The blade was as long as his finger and wouldn't scare a Kin. Elliot lifted an eyebrow. "How's that going to help?"

"It's not just a knife." Fife gave the handle a twist and it came off, revealing a second pointed object. He handed it to Elliot. The point wasn't metal…it looked like bone. Antler.

He dropped the knife. Even holding antler was a crime.

"Be careful with that. Cost more than your pay for the month." He put the handle back on. "You need to be armed."

"I don't want to be killed."

Fife laughed. "What do you think is going to happen over there? That they'll welcome you with open arms? They're going to eat you and make you like it."

"They'll definitely kill me if I carry this." He doubted Pinkie would see the wearing of antler as an act of good faith.

"They'll kill you without it, too. Besides, how will they know? It's just a knife, right?" He handed it back to Elliot. "Welcome to the venerie."

CHAPTER 9

*E*lliot made his way home after turning on the lights. A simmering rage filled his belly as he walked past the houses of the wealthy. He'd met plenty when earning extra for his mama's medicine; they'd bought him drinks as they'd talked about what they wanted from him. Back then, he hadn't realized that the Dark City was theirs for the plucking. They could pay the lightmen better wages, they could grow more marshmallow, or remove the fines for people who grew their own. They could do something about the Kin. But they did nothing.

Dayne had complained, but Elliot laughed it off. What could they do? They worked thirteen days out of fourteen and had little spare coin. There was no saving up and getting a better job.

There were no better jobs.

Tanning, dyeing, even being a lightman were the good jobs for people in the Dark City. And he still couldn't do more than scrape by without selling himself.

Fife had reminded him of all that when trying to talk him out of going. It had only reinforced the deal he'd made with the Kin. He might not be able to do much, but he could get his brother back. And he could create a little havoc while on the island.

As for the venerie...he'd make sure Dayne didn't have anything to do with them again. They'd leave town, go somewhere away from the Kin. There must be places. The mountains maybe. He blew out a breath that streamed like fog before him. That was too many steps ahead.

Every scuffle in the shadows made his heart leap, the knife was heavy in his pocket. He tried not to glance over his shoulder but failed too often. Were the Kin hunting under the moonless night, or were they trading up on the hill?

Why yes you can kill three of the poor so that my wife can be healed.

One life per orb you say? Seems fair, as long as you only take from down there.

How did the rich sleep at night?

They were as bad as the Kin. No. The rich were worse. The Kin needed human blood the way a cat needed mice. The rich on the hill, they didn't need Kin magic or light; they were simply greedy.

The tall wooden building of home loomed in front of him. He cast his gaze around, but there was no one watching him or following him. Pinkie wasn't lurking on the roof like an oversized, brightly colored crow.

Elliot unlocked the door and slipped inside, careful to relock it. Then he made his way to the top, hating the extra two flights of stairs when he was already corpse tired.

Maybe Pinkie wouldn't come for him tonight.

Maybe his brother wasn't really there, and Pinkie was trying to come up with a convincing lie. Or maybe Elliot was telling himself stories.

The room was warm, the smaller space holding the heat much better than the big family room even though the stove hadn't been banked all day. He sat on the bed and unbuckled his boots.

He had no coins to go to the Moss, and while he was sure Killian would buy him an ale on the promise of another romp, he didn't want that between them. Not every part of him was for sale...just most parts. His affection couldn't be bought or bribed. That was all he had. That was all anyone had in this part of the city.

He took off his coat and lay on the bed. If Pinkie didn't bloody come, he was skint and with no food until pay day...which wasn't that different to normal. A dark laugh escaped. He'd have lost the job at the plant by not showing up today. They'd have filled his spot on the line before piss break time. There was always a queue outside waiting for no shows so they could claim the job. The owner didn't really care as long as the work got done.

Elliot peeled himself off the bed. There was yesterday's bread, dried meat, a little cheese, and an apple—he hadn't gotten rid of everything, but this was a pathetic last meal if Pinkie did show. He made up a plate, and got some water boiling for tea, and then sat on the windowsill to eat. With his shirt sleeve, he cleared the condensation off the glass.

The cold night pressed against the glass as he chewed the coarse bread.

The skin along his arm prickled, and he glanced out the window. There on the roof was Pinkie, crouched and waiting.

Elliot ate the last piece of bread and cheese. He chewed thoroughly, not rushing his dinner. The bread stuck to the roof of his suddenly dry mouth. When his plate was empty, he licked his fingers and opened the window in invitation. Pinkie didn't climb down.

Elliot wasn't going over. He couldn't scale buildings.

He busied himself making tea and trying not to glance out the window. Something landed on the roof above him, with a thump and a skid. His stomach hollowed, and he lifted his gaze as Pinkie filled the window.

"You don't hide your coins, you spend them at the Moss. Or should that be on moss?" The Kin tilted their head.

"At the Moss. It's a tavern I like to go to." It was the place he could go and pretend that everything was fine for a little while. Like everyone else who went there after scrounging up a few coins for a drink, he wanted nothing more than to put aside the day and talk and kiss and dance and maybe find more. No one there had ever talked about revolt or killing Kin.

Were there other places where that was discussed?

"Will you let me in?" Pinkie perched on the outside sill, their hands above their head gripping the window frame. They didn't appear at all concerned about falling.

Dead man's room was his home. If he let the Kin in, then they would always be able to enter, and he'd have no safe space. But having a Kin sit outside his window would attract attention.

"Other people live in this building." They hadn't been desperate enough to make a deal with a Kin.

"I know. Their homes will still be protected."

The Kin hadn't lied so far. Dayne was on the island.

"How will I leave the castle, with my brother, after the month is up?"

"Ride on the cusp of day so that we may not chase you and the leviathan in the lake doesn't eat you."

"You've thought about it."

"I think about a lot of things. Mostly how my life isn't truly mine."

Elliot frowned. "What do you mean?"

"Exactly that. No one is free to live as they choose, but we can all make choices within those boundaries."

"You're Kin. You have a city to feast on, what problem…" He remembered what Pinkie said about being expected to feed on a woman and have Vermillion's child. There was nothing maternal about this Kin, but Elliot knew nothing about Kin children as he'd never seen one. Given that the Kin could change from male to female, did they even have families the way he understood families to work?

"Politics is always a problem. Being prime makes it worse."

Shouting from the street made Pinkie glance back. If Elliot pushed, would they fall to their death? If he pushed, any chance of getting his brother was gone.

"You may enter." The words were barely off his tongue before Pinkie was in his room.

The tips of Pinkie's small antlers almost grazed the ceiling. They looked around, and from the pinched look on their face, found nothing to their liking.

For a moment, Elliot stood there, not sure what to do. His mother had always said to offer a guest something to drink. So that's what he did. "Tea? The water's freshly boiled."

The cold night air sucked the warmth out of the room.

"No."

"It's not poison."

Pinkie tilted their head as though not convinced. "I don't need to drink or eat your food."

"Can I have another cup before leaving?" He wasn't ready. He'd never be ready.

Pinkie nodded and sat on the edge of the bed, perching as though not comfortable. "What's your name?"

"Elliot. You?" He put some dried herbs into the cup and poured the hot water over. His hand shook as he poured. When he picked up the cup, he held it with both hands, but that didn't stop the tremor.

"Umbra." They drew in a breath. "It will be dangerous in the castle for you."

"You said I'd have protection as a pet." The word rankled. He'd kept a mouse they'd trapped as a pet once until it chewed its way out of the box and into the barley. Mama had not been impressed.

"No one else will feed on you, but pets usually drink the blood of their Abyr."

Elliot suppressed the shudder at the use of the Kin's true name. No one ever called them that. To do so would summon them. It was a little too late to worry about that, though.

He shook his head; he'd never drink Kin blood.

"You will have to feign obedience. Watch the other pets and mimic."

"Mimic what?"

Umbra considered him with bright pink eyes, pretty but unnatural. Unnatural for humans, not Kin. "They seek only the attention of their Abyr. They do not carry the tension you have. It will not take long for others to notice you are the brother of Vermillion's pet."

Elliot nodded. "You noticed."

"I knew the moment I saved you."

He was nothing but a token to be risked. "Is it true my brother was venerie?"

"I don't know. Are you?" He smiled as though he found the idea appealing.

Elliot sipped his tea.

"If your brother was, he is no longer. His mind is clouded by Vermillion's blood."

He didn't want to imagine his brother as a devoured, craving only a bite and a taste of Kin blood. "Can he be fixed?"

"Some would argue he has been. He is no longer a threat." Umbra stood, and their leather coat fell around them. This close, Elliot could see the detail in the leather, the tooled pattern and the rubbed-in color. Their waistcoat carried the same detail, but with a different pattern and different color. They were the kind of clothes Elliot would never be able to afford.

"Am I a threat?"

"Not to me, because I can help you. To others, maybe." That smile again.

It wasn't only Elliot's blood they wanted. "You want me to kill someone."

Umbra drew in a breath. "Kill is such a blunt word. Let us see if you can survive three nights first. Then we can talk about grander plans."

Elliot drained his cup, rinsed it, and set the stove so it would die during the night. He checked his door was locked and put on his coat and snood. "If you want someone dead, why don't you do it?"

"I am a guest of Vermillion. If I break the rules of hospitality, there will be trouble." They moved toward the window and flung it open. "Good, they are riding across."

"Hunting," Elliot spat.

"Trading. We don't eat human blood as often as you think."

"You said you need it every day."

"When changing, yes."

"You were sent to be Vermillion's mate. Does that make you their equal?"

Umbra turned sharply. "I'm a prime."

"What does that mean?"

They looked back out the window. "Leader's first child. My birther rules another border castle. Meet me at the shore." Umbra climbed out the window and paused. "You should be safe because they'll be heading up the hill."

"Why can't I follow you now?"

"Because they'll know I'm missing and be looking for me. I can't ride around the city with a human." They launched up. There was a thump on the roof, and then they were gone.

Elliot closed the window and locked it, then drew the sheet across.

Blood and bother, he'd landed himself in the middle of Kin politics. Umbra was nothing but a rich child traded for parental benefit.

CHAPTER 10

*U*mbra made their way to the shore. The Abyr trading party had passed and the hopeful were agitated. They weren't spread along the shore at their fires like they usually were but instead gathered in one large group, shuffling and singing or muttering the war songs the bards told. Those words should never form on human lips.

Umbra's skin prickled. While they had taken care to avoid the trading party—they'd offer the humans up the hill baubles to placate them—there was a beast near the water.

Where was its rider?

They scanned the lake, but the water was still and inky. Had the hopeful finally turned on their masters, the love they'd once had replaced with hate?

Umbra wouldn't be surprised at all if that were the case.

But they'd sent Elliot into this mess, and even though there was no blood between them, yet, there was a measure of protection. They needed Elliot far more than Elliot needed them. The human didn't realize that...or maybe he did. He was smart and would be trouble. That was something to look forward to.

They eased the beast onto the pebbly shore. Heads turned.

There were about twenty. Gaunt and hungry with lank thin hair. The human hopefuls didn't look after themselves. They thought only of the return of their masters, and a return to grace that would never come. It would've been kinder for the Abyr to kill them instead of returning them, but some liked the ego trip of knowing they were wanted.

Orange hair gleamed in the moonlight as Lapis stepped forward from the waiting crowd, coat flapping around their ankles, lips twisted into a grin as they blocked the causeway. "You snuck out early."

"Things to do. Leaving is no crime." They were free to come and go as they pleased so long as they did not hunt and feed except on the nights it was approved. Technically Umbra had broken that rule by feeding on one of the hopeful but many broke that rule on the lake shore. The hopeful didn't count; they were already considered lost.

"What were you doing?" Lapis stood as though rooted to the spot, the humans eddying around them like a tide that was uncertain about which way to flow. First closer, then to the left. then closer again. The humans moved as one.

"Preparing my pet." They'd warned Elliot of the dangers and the expectations. Lapis getting the wrong idea wasn't their fault. "What are you doing?"

"Making friends."

From what Umbra had seen, Lapis didn't have friends. They had conquests and people who owed them favors. Lapis wanted Vermillion's respect and more, given their change. Unfortunately Vermillion was obsessed with bloodlines, and Lapis didn't come from one of note. While ruling a border castle was hereditary, that didn't mean it couldn't be snatched away by a more ambitious or brutal Abyr. Umbra was starting to understand why their sire was so adamant they be sent away to grow up. Running a castle wasn't only about protecting the heartland from the humans, it was about keeping the Abyr in line.

Blood changed more than Abyr bodies.

Umbra glanced along the shore. If Elliot was there, he was remaining hidden, which was safest. Lapis would bleed him dry and break his neck.

They shouldn't be enemies; Lapis was welcome to Vermillion.

"And what do your friends want?" Umbra knew the answer without asking. There was only one thing the hopeful wanted: Abyr blood.

Lapis grinned. "You."

"I have broken no rules of hospitality." Their grip on the beast tightened.

"And I have broken none either." Lapis shrugged. "Pets."

Umbra glanced at the humans as they stumbled closer. They didn't want to ride their beast through the hopeful and risk killing them. "This will be considered an attack on family."

"Only if you live."

The tide of humans surged.

"What would Ver say?" They used Lapis's nickname for their leader.

Lapis stiffened. "Nothing. You're a thorn in their side. Disobedient and willful."

"Thank you." Umbra gave a shallow bow from the seat of their beast. "You can have Ver; I don't want them."

"Ver wants you." The words were an animalistic snarl. Lapis spun away and stalked toward their beast, leaving Umbra with a tide of hopeful humans who would tear them apart to get blood. Why they'd never gathered together and done that before, Umbra didn't know. Perhaps because the hopeful loved their old masters too much.

Umbra glanced at the humans, then Lapis who was now by the shore on their beast and ready to flee.

If this was sanctioned by Vermillion, living would really annoy them. And if it wasn't, living would give Umbra a chance for revenge on Lapis. Dying wouldn't provide any benefits.

Umbra accelerated, hoping to swerve past the humans and onto the causeway, but the tide turned quicker than they'd thought possible. The humans grabbed the beast and hung on, getting dragged along until the beast toppled. Umbra scrambled free to avoid being crushed by the bones. The beast grumbled unhappily on its side, wheels spinning.

What had been a problem was now dire.

The humans were going to rip their arms and legs off to get blood. He'd have to give it freely. Umbra drew a knife, the serrated edge like teeth in the starlight. That stopped the humans for a heartbeat, maybe two.

Then the man he'd fed on stepped in front of the tide. "Wait."

"That one owes us blood," someone else said

"I don't owe you anything. I'm new here," Umbra said. "The ones who cast you off after promising to care for you owe you." A pet was for life, unless they committed some heinous act of betrayal. There was little need to hunt when pets were kept.

Umbra's birther was many things—brutal in battle and known for running a very strict castle—but careless with blood and life wasn't one of them. Vermillion, however, treated humans like disposable treats, something to be enjoyed then put aside. It had only taken Umbra one night to see that. The odor of fear and the disregard for the human's in the castle had been a shock to them.

"Give us blood." A woman reached for Umbra.

The man Umbra had fed on tried to push her away, but their pathetic scuffle didn't deter the tide. The hopeful wanted blood. They could have blood, but it would only prolong their agony. Their craving would never leave. There was only one cure, and Umbra had no doubt Vermillion never handed out nectar to ex-pets.

Umbra pushed up a sleeve and cut their arm. They hissed as the blade tore skin, then bright blood spilled. They held out their arm for the humans to taste. They all stared transfixed at the blood, then lunged for him, getting their fingers wet and licking them clean. But after so long without, they were greedy, and Umbra didn't want to die to satisfy their hunger. Already, the wound had started to heal, the stream of blood lessened to a trickle, and the edges of the wound drew tight. Umbra needed nectar to replenish what was lost...but really craved blood.

The first change was already happening.

Umbra yanked their arm away.

"More," they pleaded. The humans tugged at their coat and licked their hand hoping for another drop.

Elliot pushed through the throng of people, wrestling the beast. The beast was making this extra difficult by trying to wrest it's horns out of Elliot's hands. Beasts didn't like humans; some had been known to deliberately throw them off. If the tales of the bards were to be believed—and not all of them could be—beasts had once been animals of flesh and blood before some dark magic had twisted them into their current form.

"Get on," Elliot ordered.

Given that the hopeful had pulled them off, Umbra didn't think that getting on would be a wise move. They'd just get pulled off again. But the tide was holding back, watching Elliot.

"Be off, you've had your feed. If you wanted more, you should've taken it from the Kin with orange hair," Elliot shouted.

"They have an addiction." Umbra got on the beast. He pulled Elliot in front of him, not wanting the beast to dislodge him.

"And whose fault is that?" Elliot muttered for their ears.

Umbra gripped the horns of the beast. "Let's go before they change what's left of their minds."

They steered the beast along the beach away from the hopeful, Elliot's hands on the beast's horns near his.

"How does this work?"

"The beast? You have to steer and think fast." Umbra nudged the beast faster, urging it home.

"Think fast?"

"Yes. It probably won't work."

"Because I'm not Kin."

"Why do you call us that?" Umbra steered toward the causeway. The castle rose before them, tall and gray and wreathed in fog, the green of the roof barely breaking through.

"Because to say your true name is to draw you to our house and death with it."

Umbra had never stopped to think about the way humans felt. Obviously, they had lives and hopes and dreams. But it had never been a concern before. Where they'd grown up becoming a pet was a choice. "You don't think being a pet is an honor."

"No."

Umbra willed the beast faster. Crossing the causeway slowly was never a good idea in case there were trapped leviathans in the lake.

Elliot gasped as the beast shot forward into the water. His knuckles whitened.

The gray rock of the causeway became visible through the inky water, wide enough for two beasts. On either side was the bottomless black of the lake. Elliot swore and put his feet out as though to stop the beast. The beast obeyed, slowing. Water lapped at the wheels. "What about the thing in the lake?"

"If we're moving, we'll be fine."

"You don't sound convinced." He glanced at Umbra, his eyes as dark as the lake.

"The longer we sit here like bait, the less convinced I'll be."

Elliot hesitated. His heart beat a fast and beautiful melody. Then he lifted his feet. "Think fast?"

Umbra smiled, liking Elliot more than they should for a temporary pet. But they didn't leave the speed to Elliot's human thoughts. The beast leaped forward as though it knew it was going home. Three quarters of the way over, the lake surged, and a tentacle thrust up as though to taste the air.

Umbra pushed the beast faster. The beast might be immortal, but an eternity in a leviathan's stomach was no way to live. It surged forward, kicking up water and spraying their clothing.

The narrow causeway widened as they approached the gate. In the dark, it was hard to tell if it was open or shut until it was almost too late. If Lapis had ordered it shut, Umbra was going to peel them like a fruit and drop them in the lake. The blood thirsty thought jolted their concentration, but the beast didn't slow.

The gate was mercifully open, and they sped though.

Umbra exhaled. "Left is the stable."

But the beast was already slowing and heading in that direction.

It was only then Elliot lifted his gaze from the ground and eased his grip on the horns to look up at the castle.

CHAPTER 11

The gray walls of the castle rose into an inky blue sky. Even though Elliot's feet were on the ground, for a moment it felt as though the earth had betrayed him and left him hanging. There was nothing for him to grasp onto. He tilted back, unbalanced. Umbra steadied him, drawing him close. It was enough to break the spell.

Elliot blinked and shook his head to clear the beauty from his eyes. For all the delicate spires capped in green and the intricate arches, this place was the home of the Kin. He was a rat in a vipers' nest.

He took his hands off the horns of the beast…a living thing that at times had seemed to know where it was going. It had known where the causeway was—whenever he saw the Kin ride across the lake, he'd know it for the illusion it was. Now, the bone creature meandered through a set of arches that were intricately carved and into the stable.

Was this thing truly alive or something the Kin had created with dark magic?

There were others in the stable, their glowing hearts like half shuttered lights, and their bones casting shadows on the walls and floors. They didn't move when the one he was on stopped. There was no greeting that one would expect from animals. But the rumble that had filled the thing while it was moving became little more than a hum.

Behind him, Umbra got off.

Elliot did the same. His legs and back aching from the ride. "Are they alive?"

"That depends on your definition."

Elliot turned, but Umbra was already leaving the stable, so he followed. He didn't want to be wandering alone. There was a pervasive unsettledness that made him glance about, seeking an attack even though they hadn't seen anyone.

The orange haired Kin would be here. He'd watched them talk to the humans, and whatever they'd said had caused the devoured to turn on Umbra. It had been tempting to remain hidden and not get involved, but he needed Umbra to get his brother.

He'd saved a Kin. Many would hate him for that. Plenty would hate him for making a deal.

Umbra led them up a flight of stairs that coiled and twisted ever higher.

"Where's Dayne?"

"Probably in Vermillion's quarters, which are unfortunately too close to mine."

Because Umbra was supposed to be Vermillion's bride. Did the Kin have weddings?

"How annoyed are they going to be?"

Umbra stopped and looked at him. "I'll deal with that."

It was very noble, but if Umbra was killed, then Elliot was royally fucked. And Umbra and Vermillion seemed to be what passed for royalty. He had to survive twenty-eight days. Two fortnights, four sennights... Not that long, not really. It had been a month since Dayne was taken, and it already felt like forever.

"Maybe I shouldn't have come." Every fiber of his being wanted to get Dayne and leave. "You could've brought Dayne to me."

"I can't steal another's pet. We have rules. You need to be here where I can protect you. Though I will not be announcing your presence until I have to. Which is why we're going up the back stairs."

"How am I supposed to know which stairs we are using?"

"You don't, so follow and keep quiet, pet." Umbra started walking again.

As much as Elliot wanted to argue that he wasn't a pet and that he had a name, being on the stairs where they could pass other Kin wasn't the place for it. He had to act the part of a pet, and pets didn't argue.

They looped around, following a walkway. Small windows revealed slivers of the world beyond. The shore and bonfires. The lake. The lake with something large moving beneath. He frowned. Land.

He stared out the window. The castle was on an island in the middle of the lake. But here, the castle wasn't on an island. He jogged back to the previous window. The castle was on a spit of land.

"Come on," Umbra beckoned.

"It's not an island."

"No, of course not. It's an outpost."

But the land he was seeing wasn't what was on the other side of the lake when he stood on the shore. There should be farms, rust colored cattle with horns that spread wide—like the horns on the beasts, gray shaggy sheep waiting for the weather to turn and their coats to be shorn. None of that was out there. "But where's the rest of the lake?"

Umbra grasped his hand, his touch cool. "You can stare out at your missing lake from my chambers."

He wasn't allowed to stop and stare again. Umbra hustled him up more stairs and along another walkway, this one more open. Finally, they stopped. Umbra motioned him to stay. Really, where was he going to go? He didn't even know where he was.

His stomach was a tight knot, and nothing made sense. How did half a lake vanish?

"Move quickly. You can gawk another night." They entered a corridor that was lit with the red orbs he was familiar with, but they were tiny, hanging in ornamental clusters and dripping from chains. He wanted to stop and stare at the lights, the floor, and the details carved into the walls, but didn't. This was where the Kin lived. He expected one to pounce with every footstep.

Umbra opened a door and stepped in, and Elliot breathed a sigh of relief as he entered. He leaned against the wall and raked his fingers through his hair as he took in Umbra's chamber.

It was far bigger than the room he'd grown up in. There was a dining table and sofas to recline on. Maybe to sleep on?

"Come through." Umbra opened another door. "This is my private room. No one comes in here without my permission. The outer room, anyone can enter, though I've locked the door for the moment."

Elliot glanced back at the first room they'd been in, and then at the bedroom. The bed was bigger than anything he'd slept in—or been in. There was a small table with some kind of game set up in the center and two chairs. A wooden closet hung open, revealing enough clothes for an entire family.

"This is all yours?"

"No, I left a lot of things at my parent's castle. I never planned on staying long." They forced out a breath. "Sending me here was my sire's idea."

"Your father?"

Umbra looked at him. "You could call them that, though they haven't always been male."

"And your mother?"

"My birther...they have always been female and terrifyingly so. They are very well respected, and their castle is to be envied."

"Then why were you sent here?"

"Vermillion is a friend of my sire's. They were sent to the same castle to finish their education, and since my sire was responsible for sorting out the children, and I am the prime, I was given this *honor*." Umbra's lips twisted into a bitter smile.

Elliot wanted to touch the blanket on the bed and feel the fine wool. He wanted to run his fingers over everything. Nothing looked secondhand or worn out. The colors were bright, and the fabrics fine.

"There's a washroom through here." Umbra opened another door that was almost invisible, a part of the wood paneling and nothing more. But it led through to a room the size of dead man's room. There was a large bath in one corner and a screened area—a privvy he was guessing. Where did the night soil go? Killian didn't come and clean out the castle.

"Who do you share with?"

"No one."

All of this for one person? He knew the rich up the hill had fancy houses and wore clothing of a better quality, but he'd never thought the Kin would be the same. Elliot couldn't resist touching the edge of the stone bath and tracing the engraved lip. It seemed to be some kind of plant, but parts had been rubbed away after years of use. The stone was warm beneath his fingers. It would take a long time to fill. When he was young, Mama had boiled many pots of water so Dayne and he could have a bath in the wash tub.

"Do you want a bath?"

Elliot shook his head. "That'll take half a day to fill. And where does the water get boiled?" He didn't have the time to sit around wait. Then he remembered he no longer had a job. What was he going to do all day?

Umbra tilted their head. "Nowhere near that long. I've had breakfasts that took longer than the bath does to fill."

They turned a knob, and three holes opened up. Water tumbled down the wall and into the bath. They put a stone stopper in the hole in the bottom, and the bath started to fill. Steam rose off the water.

He was beginning to understand why people wanted to be pets and why the devoured wanted to come back. What was a little blood loss when the Kin had chambers that could house three families, maybe four, and they had a private bathroom with hot running water?

"You wanted to see what was outside?"

Elliot tore his gaze from the bath. "Yes."

They left the bath to fill, and Umbra tugged aside a heavy curtain. A furnished balcony was on the other side of an ornate window that depicted a Kin with lilac hair holding a raised sword. Umbra opened the glass door and immediately sat in the chair that was suspended from the ceiling. The other chair seemed to be made for napping, as it was reclined and covered in cushions.

"This is my balcony. It's mostly private." They'd lowered their voice. They touched their ears. "Mostly."

They could be heard but not seen.

Elliot nodded and walked to the edge. The stone railing was as intricate as everything else he'd seen so far. Beyond the railing weren't human farms like there should be but rolling hills. There was a town in the distance that he could just make out in the eerie light. He glanced up at the dark sky and the not-a-moon. It looked more like a sun, a deep orange sun that seemed far too close.

This wasn't Fotyna. He knew the Kin disappeared during the day, and while he'd wondered where they went, it was more of a sigh of relief and a hope they wouldn't come back. The causeway…would that be there in daylight or would that vanish, too? He'd need to know before he left.

"Where are we?"

"Quinteck. An outpost on the border with Sanguise—where you live."

"Do we disappear in daylight?"

"This is not night…the sky doesn't change. The sun moves in an oblong through the sky, but it never sets."

"The lake and Fotyna is always there?"

"No, your sun makes your city vanish."

"And what takes our place? There should be human farms." He pointed at the road and the hills and the town in the distance.

"Your city is replaced with open water. Leviathans sometimes get caught when the sun sets and sometimes they like to try their luck at an easy meal."

Elliot scowled. What Umbra was saying didn't make sense. "How can there be water where there should be a city?"

"My world interacts with yours at the edges. The outposts are liminal. They exist but not always."

"So we don't exist?" He felt real enough. The stone of the railing was solid and cool against his palm.

"Oh no, the castle remains very much real to us. The world changes around us depending on your sun. You can see the ocean tomorrow." They stood. "The bath should be full. Would you like something to drink while you're in there?"

He wanted to flee. He knew what to expect in the city. The world didn't move and change. It might have been three parts drudge another part shite, but it was at least constant with its shittiness.

"Sure...but I don't know what you have."

"Whatever you want."

Elliot stared at him. There was the ale he could afford, well-watered and as weak as piss. The spirits he'd been plied with when he was younger were beyond the stretch of his coins—not that he wanted to drink them now even if he could afford them.

"How about a goblet of warm mead?" Umbra suggested.

He was about to nod but stopped. "What will eating your food do to me?"

"Nothing. It's our blood that will get you into trouble, and we have agreed that is off the menu."

"You have food?"

"Of course we do." A look of disgust flickered over their face for half a heartbeat. "I'll have something sent up. Soup? Bread and cheese? We don't have much at hand unless there is to be a banquet."

"Bread and cheese is fine." He was being asked to pick something when he didn't know what was on offer. But bread was bread and cheese was cheese, so that would be fine. He should be saying thank you, but he was a captive and not really a guest.

Umbra put their hands on Elliot's shoulders. "It's okay to like it."

"Is it?"

"We aren't monsters."

Aren't you? The words were on the tip of his tongue, but they didn't fall off.

He looked away. "I should turn the water off. You've gone to too much trouble already." He didn't want to be further indebted to the Kin.

"You're my pet; it would be poor of me to not put in effort. My birther would string me up by my guts as punishment."

The horror must have shown on Elliot's face.

"They'd take me down again and heal me, but the point would've been well made." Umbra pressed their lips together. "Go, bathe." They gave Elliot a nudge toward the bathroom.

Elliot went in and closed the door. The bath was almost full, so he turned the knob and shut off the water. Steam coiled lazily off the surface. On one of the edges was a bar of creamy yellow soap. He touched it, and it was the way he thought silk might feel, slippery and soft. It was nothing like the course ash and lye soap he was used to. He glanced at the door, then back at the bath.

If he didn't use it, it would be wasted. Maybe there were people behind the walls boiling and pouring water. He should wash before it went cold.

Hurriedly, he undressed. He took off his boots, aware that his socks were wearing through. He shucked his pants to reveal under-shorts that were clean but threadbare. His coat was well mended, and while warm, it was not fitted like Umbra's. Finally he pulled off his shirt. It was missing two buttons, but he'd sewed it up the middle, so it was more of a tunic. Now he had spare buttons if more fell off.

Naked, he stepped over the lip and into the bath. The heat of the water cooked his toes. It was delightful. He'd forgotten what a hot bath was like and was hard pressed to remember the last time he'd made the effort. He must have had one since Mama's funeral. Had he really made do with washes in a basin or a swim in the lake over summer?

He sat, and the water lapped at his chin, then he drew in a breath and went all the way under. The heat sunk into his bones, and they ached as though they'd forgotten what it was like not to be chewed on by the cold every day. His lungs burned, and he had to surface.

But he didn't have to get out.

The soap beckoned, and he picked up the soft bar. It squirmed away into the bath. It took a few moments and a few waves splashing over the side before he got ahold of it. When he did, he never wanted to let it go. It lathered and felt like cream, the really good cream that was skimmed off the milk long before it was sold in the markets at his end of town. He washed his hair and went under again. Perhaps he'd never leave the bath. He'd spend twenty-eight days in the warm water. Maybe he'd turn into a fish.

He lay back, resting his head on the edge, and stared up at the light. Red again. Always red. This light was three fist-sized orbs that hung off one silver chain.

The door opened, and Umbra came in with a very large glass of liquid gold.

Elliot sat up, aware of the splashed water everywhere like he was a child. His cheeks heated. "I'll clean up the mess."

He shouldn't have gotten so carried away, but the bath was almost a lake, and it was hot, and he didn't want to get out and put his clothes back on. Maybe he should wash his clothes after so the water didn't go to waste.

Umbra shrugged. "Someone will clean up if I ask. Here." They held out a goblet. "It's spiced and hot."

The goblet in Umbra's hand contained a paler liquid. "You aren't having any?"

"I'm going to have some nectar."

Nectar…the same as the medicine he hadn't been able to afford for Mama? "You sell that to the people up the hill?"

Umbra gave a careful nod. "That is Vermillion's current deal."

"Trade with them, eat in the dark." He tried to keep the bitterness out of his voice and failed.

They opened their mouth.

"Let me guess. It wasn't like that where you grew up?" What would it be like to grow up in a castle where hot baths and plentiful food were everyday occurrences?

"Well, it wasn't."

"Tell me what it was like then. Tell me how much the humans loved having you as nighttime neighbors." Elliot picked up the goblet and took a swig of the mead, expecting it to be like warm ale.

It wasn't.

It was sweet and heady and bloomed like fire in his stomach then rushed along his spine to settle in his head and groin.

Umbra sat on the lip of the bath, not caring that it was wet. "Fine." They took a sip from their nectar-filled goblet. "I grew up in Octadine."

CHAPTER 12

*U*mbra glanced at their goblet even though they wanted to look at the naked man in the bath. The pulse of his heart was a tempting rhythm, pleading for them to dance. As much as they liked to dance, they had never danced with anyone besides other unchanged. But they were no longer unchanged, and there had never been rules about associating with humans.

They took another swallow of nectar, hoping to drown the new cravings. While it was still sweet on their tongue, and the warmth healed any aches, it was no longer filling the way it had been. They would need to eat food and blood. For a heartbeat, they let themselves mourn the loss of no longer being unchanged, but that was all, as they could feel Elliot watching them. Waiting.

"Octadine is a liminal castle, at the edge of the world like this place. Our history is written in blood. There's been war between our kinds for centuries…longer if the bards sing the truth." They smiled. "It's hard to tell with bards where the embellishment starts and the truth ends."

"War between Kin and human?" Elliot sipped his mead. Umbra knew he shouldn't watch the way his lips moved or the way his throat flexed as he swallowed.

"Yes. Your kind wants nectar, mine blood, and so we fight about it. Octadine was invaded, Abyr slaughtered, and the humans made it to the nearby town. They took barrels of nectar." They paused. "This all happened before I was born, maybe fifty years ago? My birther, Cerulean, took over the castle and put down the rebellion. Blood flowed down the streets. We secured our border, and Cerulean gained their reputation—although to be fair the bards do sing of their previous battle victories. But then Cerulean tried something new. They set up trade."

"Blood for nectar."

"That has always existed. It exists here."

"No, it doesn't. You give the nectar to the rich, and you feed off the poor. I'd have given my blood to get nectar for my mama but couldn't. I didn't even know what it was called. Only that the rich had something that could cure her, and I could never earn enough coin to buy some." The bitter edge was back in Elliot's voice.

"You'd have given your life for it in this castle." They shook their head. "We've always had pets. I've heard of some Abyr having several. Keeping them is a sign of status. But my birther set up something different. If people wanted nectar, they had to offer their own blood. There would be no on-selling and only willing humans could become pets."

"Did the humans know about all this?" Elliot lifted his hand then let it fall back into the water. "Before agreeing to be pets?"

Umbra nodded. "Some people will never give up their freedom. Some will never offer their blood. Humans still try to steal the nectar and accuse us of hording it, not realizing that it is also our food. Abyr still try to steal humans, there have been some who've killed because they were so blood hungry, but Cerulean runs the castle firmly, and all transgressions are punished. There will always be friction between our kinds, but at Octadine, there has been no all-out fighting in my lifetime. Here, there seems to be a flare up every ten years. Sometimes more often. The city is boiling and ready to spill again."

"The Dark City is always simmering, but survival is time consuming." Elliot finished his mead. He looked at his hands, the skin wrinkled like drying fruit. "I should get out."

Umbra stood. "I'll get you a cloth."

They put the glasses on the table in the bedroom and pulled a thick cloth from the wardrobe. The softly woven fabric was absorbent and warm—no one liked to get out of a bath and be cold.

Elliot's head was tilted back, his eyes closed, but he didn't look peaceful. There was tension around his eyes, and his mouth was a hard, thin line. Umbra's gaze drifted over his face and the stubble that darkened his jaw, then down his neck to where his pulse beat too close to the skin. Beneath the water were glimpses of what Umbra's body would change to.

They reminded themselves that even if they had fled to the heartland again, they would never have fitted in. Too many generations before them had fed on human blood for Umbra to be seen as anything but a warrior only suited to keeping the border secure. That was the dice that had been cast, but like any good game, they could take a reroll and make a few changes. A smile curved their lips.

"I know you're watching me," Elliot said, but he didn't open his eyes.

"Thinking mostly." They opened the towel. "Come on. I'll find you something clean to wear."

He opened his eyes and glanced up. "I'll wash my clothes. They'll be fine."

Umbra shook their head. "I'll arrange for them to be cleaned." They gave the coat a kick and the knife fell out. "Did you want to put that lethal thing somewhere safe? I'd hate for another Abyr to find it and think you were here to kill us."

Elliot's eyes widened, and Umbra heard his heartbeat quicken.

"I felt it when we were on the beast. Antler has a particular vibration."

"It was given to me."

"And who were you told to kill?" Depending on who it was, they might even help.

"No one. It was for protection. My friend thought I was a fool to agree to this arrangement."

"Some would say the same to me." If they'd been smart, they'd have followed the plan set out by their sire and ruled with Vermillion. The thought turned their stomach.

Elliot got his feet under him, then promptly toppled onto his ass and went under, sending a tidal wave over the edge of the bath. He came up spluttering and rested his forearms on the edge of the bath. "What was in that mead?"

Umbra suppressed a laugh and held out the towel like it was a shield. "Mead. Pull the plug while you're there."

Elliot obeyed and this time moved more carefully. He was like a milk drunk kitten attempting to walk. Umbra tried not to smile and failed. They offered their hand, so he didn't slip and crack his head, thus spoiling all the plans they were weaving. Elliot glared, but took the offered help. His grip was strong even if he was unsteady.

"Perhaps next time, I'll have it watered for you."

Elliot shot him another glare. "I was fine until I tried to stand."

"I have that effect on people, but it's usually the morning after."

While his cheeks flushed, Elliot was too busy trying to get out of the bath to comment. He carefully stepped over the lip, but his back leg didn't quite make it over, and he stumbled into Umbra.

Umbra wrapped him in the towel and held him steady. "I would recommend not drinking so much in the hall. Maybe don't drink at all."

They fully expected Elliot to pull away, but he didn't. He let himself be held for several heartbeats before he seemed to shake off whatever weakness had been momentarily revealed. Umbra felt the moment the armor went back on, and Elliot drew away. There was something in his dark eyes that was safer not to question.

"Shall we eat? You could use the food." He was too thin, all muscle and sinew as though wound tight and ready to fight.

"Soak up some of the liquor." Elliot shuffled to the bedroom, wrapped in the cloth that covered him from shoulder to knee.

Umbra made sure he didn't fall or otherwise injure himself, but truthfully, it was an opportunity to touch him.

Elliot stopped. "I thought it was just bread and cheese."

The tray was in the middle of the bed where they'd placed it for after. It was a simple spread. "It is. Two different breads, four cheeses, and some nuts and fruit."

"Four different cheeses?" He shook his head, drips falling from the ends of the dark curls. "I can't do this. It's all..." He waved his hand around, and the towel slipped. "It's too much and not right. People would kill to be here instead of working and dying in the dark. I'm here, and when I go back, I'll have no job, and I'll be thinking of all of this, and I'll never be able to forget that you have four different cheeses in one meal. I know there are different cheeses, I've seen them, but I've never tasted them. And I don't belong here. And I don't know how I'm going to go back. I don't even have a bath in my room. Your bathroom is bigger than my room." The words tumbled off his tongue like nectar from a tipped goblet.

"I know. I was there." They tore off a small piece of bread and smeared a little of the soft creamy cheese on it.

"And now I can't live there because I've invited you in, and you can come in anytime."

"And bring you cheese." They offered the bread and cheese to Elliot, holding it near his lips so all he had to do was lean forward and take the morsel.

His shoulders dropped but his gaze remained on the cheese. "It's not about cheese."

"I know. Do you know why we have these nice things at the border? It's payment for giving up all the other things we could've done or been. For keeping the heartland safe. They send us food and drink and nectar because we stop humans from invading."

"No one has ever talked of an invasion."

Umbra nodded. "It happened at Octadine. I'll have the bards sing you that tale."

Elliot took the bread from their fingers and shoved it into his mouth. He wanted to hate it, that was clear on his face. He closed his eyes and lost his balance, so Umbra sat him on the edge of the bed.

They grabbed Elliot's hands. "Enjoy what I can offer."

He swallowed. "You must think I'm so rude. I haven't thanked you."

"We made a deal. I'm upholding my end. No thanks are required."

Elliot leveled his slightly unfocussed gaze at them. "And when do I need to start upholding mine?"

Umbra lifted his hand and sniffed the skin of his wrist where the blood was close to the surface. "Tomorrow, when the poison is out of your blood."

"This is the first time I've sold my blood." He picked up a piece of fruit. The cloth was coming loose, sliding off his shoulders.

Umbra tracked the slipping towel for several breaths, then tore their gaze away. They got up and rifled through their shirts until they pulled out a pale green one that would look nice on Elliot.

"But it can't be that different to selling anything else. Will it hurt?"

They held the shirt and stared at the man on their bed, the cloth now barely covering anything. Umbra wasn't sure if it was lust or hunger in their veins. Either way it was uncomfortable, and they weren't sure they liked the sharp edges.

They exhaled. They were going to have to get used to it.

"I'll make sure it doesn't hurt. Some like it." They walked over. "What else have you sold?" What use did humans have for blood or other body parts?

"You know…" He turned and slapped his ass cheek. "I figured that was part of the deal? Right? You bought me for the month." His gaze dropped to Umbra's groin. "Unless you like to be ploughed." Elliot gave them a sly grin. "I'd have done that for free."

It took several heartbeats for Umbra to understand what Elliot was implying. Humans traded for sex. They weren't sure if the idea was horrifying or intriguing; it wasn't something the Abyr did.

"The agreement was for blood only. Put this on." They handed over the shirt.

Elliot slipped it over his head and sighed. His gaze had lost all focus, and he lay back on the bed. "I am so wrecked." But he rolled onto his side and reached for more bread and cheese. "This is really good. Maybe I'm already dead, and this is the afterlife. Alcohol, bread and cheese and baths like lakes."

He smiled and ate some more. His legs were stretched over the bed, the shirt reaching only to mid-thigh. Those legs would look very nice in a pair of well fitted leather trousers…or wrapped around their hips.

They tugged on the towel until Elliot moved off, revealing a little more than Umbra wanted to see. The edges in their blood sharpened the longer they looked. They wanted to explore what was under the shirt. This was one of those things that wasn't discussed in detail among the unchanged and those that had changed took it for granted that everyone knew what would happen. They gathered the towel and tossed it on the bathroom floor, then took several breaths before turning around. Elliot hadn't moved.

This was not blood hunger in their veins.

"You keep calling yourself unchanged…what does that mean?" Elliot popped another piece of bread into his mouth, then licked the cheese off his finger. "Whatever this one is, I think it's my favorite."

"Herb and mushroom. It means I haven't fed on a human." Umbra paused. They should tell the truth. "Though I am not unchanged anymore. I fed on one of the humans on the shore."

Elliot sat up. He hadn't done up the buttons on the front of the shirt, so it slipped off his shoulder, but covered more of his legs. Dark spots formed on the fabric where his hair still dripped. "You said it had to be one person."

"I said it was supposed to be, by tradition." And possibly because if it were the same person, the whole process would be smoother. Theirs was going to be a mess given that Vermillion had made them drink female blood. "A pet is also status."

"So you didn't *really* need me."

"I do." They were going to be blood siblings with Vermillion because Vermillion had Dayne. Umbra sat on the bed and picked at the food. They would have to get used to eating, they supposed.

Elliot moved closer with a small smile. The kind Umbra was used to seeing on a lover's lips. "You just *wanted* me."

His hand trailed over Umbra's calf. The leather of their pants not thick enough to protect them from the heat of Elliot's touch.

They put their hand over Elliot's. "What are you doing?"

The heat in Elliot's eyes was far too tempting. They could have some fun licking and grinding and…well, they had no idea what humans did. But Elliot was also quite drunk, and when he sobered up, this would create other problems and they had more than enough already.

Elliot lifted his eyebrows. "Being a good pet?"

This had seemed like such a good idea—much better than the alternative—but now Elliot was on their bed they were having doubts.

"Blood only." But they weren't sure if that was a reminder for Elliot or themselves.

It was going to be best if Elliot didn't drink again. For both their sakes.

CHAPTER 13

*E*lliot's mouth tasted like a sock, and his head was thumping. He hadn't had a night like that in a long time, couldn't afford to.

He forced his eyes open. The room was barely lit, the red orbs made shadows like blood, and there was a blanket over him. His arm prickled from being slept on. He sat up a little more.

He was in the castle, on Umbra's bed, but Umbra wasn't in the bed. He lay back down. His head weighed too much, and he was dying. He was sure of it. As much as he wanted to lie there unmoving, he needed to go to the bathroom, and there'd be no pot under the bed. Curse the Kin with their fancy baths and private bathrooms.

He lay there for a couple more heartbeats, then threw back the blanket, expecting the cold to wrap around him like it did at home. But there was no cold to creep under the shirt, and Umbra's shirt was all he was wearing. He paused and tried to think if anything had happened and was only reasonably sure it hadn't. Though he was certain he'd suggested or offered or otherwise made a fool of himself.

One night done, twenty-seven to go.

No more mead.

He slid off the bed and padded across the floor. There was no one else in the room, and Umbra wasn't in the bathroom either. His clothes were no longer on the floor. The knife was also gone, but he was going to have to solve that later when his thoughts didn't hurt.

He stepped behind the screen and pissed into the hole. As he was finishing, a door opened and closed.

He froze.

Soft footsteps paced through the chamber. "Elliot?"

He exhaled. "Here."

He washed his hands in the basin, wondering if it would be bad manners to drink some. He cupped his hands and took a little. It tasted fine, so he drank some more. While it alleviated his thirst, the thumping in his head was becoming stronger with every heartbeat.

When he turned, Umbra was in the doorway, holding a goblet of something that was sure to do him in. "I thought you might need this."

He shook his head and regretted it.

"It's nectar. Have a little, and it will fix what ails you."

He stared at the goblet, not sure he could bring himself to drink something that could save lives when all he had was a headache.

"I've put your clothes away."

"Well, I can't go anywhere without pants." He wanted to ask if anything had happened but figured if he couldn't remember, it hadn't been memorable, so it was probably best to move on.

"No need to, for the moment you are to stay in my rooms." Umbra smiled. "But I'll give you some trousers."

Elliot frowned. "I have to stay here for the whole month?"

He wanted to see Dayne and let him know that he'd be home and safe soon.

"A sennight. By then, my changes will be clear, and I'll take you around the castle."

"What will I do for a sennight?" He'd never sat around and done nothing.

"You can read, or draw, or learn some of our games."

"I can't read." There was no need. No one where he lived could read. There were free schools, but uniforms and books still cost coin. If a shop had signs with letters, the odds were he couldn't afford to step foot in it. People like him got hauled off by the marshals for sticking their noses in places they didn't belong.

"What do you like to do when not working?"

Elliot stared at the pink-haired Kin. "It doesn't matter what I like. I do what has to be done to survive." He reached for the goblet as he brushed past, but Umbra grabbed his wrist.

"I would show you the castle now, but I don't want to rush. The longer Vermillion knows about you, the more dangerous it will be. I know you want to see your brother, and you will. He is alive, but I dare not tell him you're here in case he tells Vermillion."

"He wouldn't." Elliot tried to pull away.

Umbra's grip tightened. "He isn't the man you knew. He's been drinking Abyr blood."

Elliot closed his eyes. "This nectar cures everything, right? Will it cure him?"

"It heals, but there is nothing to heal in him. It can dull the craving for more, though."

And he was never going to be able to afford it. His brother was lost, and he was on a fool's mission.

Umbra touched his cheek, and he opened his eyes. "He will not last in Vermillion's care. You're doing the right thing."

He'd wanted to get his brother back so badly, he hadn't stopped to think about what had happened to him. But Umbra was right; Dayne couldn't stay here. He nodded, and Umbra released the goblet.

His stomach rebelled as he brought it to his lips, but there was none of the sharpness of liquor. Nectar smelled like flowers and ran like hot honey. He took a sip, enjoying the sweetness on his tongue, and waited for an instantaneous cure. It didn't happen, so he took another sip.

Umbra took the goblet away. "That's plenty."

"What happens if I drink too much?"

"Nothing pleasant. Today isn't the day to find out." They took a sip themselves. "This will also clear the rest of the poison from your blood."

"Of course it will." He coughed, his lungs too tight. The headache receded with each breath, and he thought he might be feeling better. Hungry even. "Is there leftover bread?"

"There are fresh pastries. I brought them up for you."

"Where'd you go?" Even as he spoke, he knew Umbra couldn't stay with him all the time.

"I can't hide in my chambers. I have to be seen, or people will suspect something is going on."

"The extra food won't give it away?"

"Let's hope not."

Elliot followed Umbra into the bedroom. The pastries were on the table with more fruit. He wanted to sit and eat but it wouldn't be polite to put his bare ass on the chair.

Umbra opened their wardrobe and pulled out a pair of cream pants. "Will these do?"

They looked like they'd fit. Unlike the leather pants that Umbra wore, these were made of a soft cloth like the shirt, and they had a drawstring in the waist to keep them up. Elliot pulled them on. They were a little long, but not by much.

"I usually wear them to sleep in." Umbra said with a smile, the tips of their fangs visible.

Elliot's heart bounced hard. Knowing he was wearing Umbra's sleepwear made it somehow more intimate than just wearing their clothes. That Umbra had defined sleepwear and didn't wear the shirt that was too ratty to be worn in public was another revelation.

He didn't know what he'd do if he had all these clothes…or all this space. But he had twenty-seven nights to find out.

He pulled on the pants and tied up the waist. The hems scuffed the floor, but he didn't care. He didn't even need to put socks on; the floor was warm beneath his toes. It was like those perfect spring days before summer became baking hot and filled with midges that wanted to empty his body of blood.

He glanced at Umbra. Maybe it was summer, and he hadn't realized. His gaze drifted to the pastries. He'd seen something similar in bakery windows up the hill. He'd smelled them in the mornings when he was turning off the lights. The day before payday his stomach usually growled so hard it hurt. "May I?"

"They're for you. I don't need to eat much, yet."

"But you will." He picked up and then bit into the fluffy sweet pastry. It was filled with a tangy purple fruit. It would be far too easy to devour the whole plate. His headache had gone, and he was feeling...not at all tired or worried. He should be worried. Dayne, their room back home, that he was here. But the worries were a minor thing, not something to be lugged around like a cart full of shit.

That nectar was powerful. Would those two sips have been enough to cure Mama? He'd taken all the coins he'd earned on his stomach up the hill to the marshal to buy what he could. The marshal had looked at him and his coins and laughed. Told him it wasn't for the likes of him and that he didn't have enough anyway. The marshal had then kept a third for inconvenience. Elliot had spent the rest on paying the doctor who couldn't do more than keep Mama drugged up and out of pain. She slept but didn't eat, and one morning, when he'd slunk back after a night working, Elliot had discovered she'd drunk the whole bottle.

That night's coins had paid for her funeral, and he hadn't gone back.

"Plenty of people in the dark would give you blood for nectar. We can't afford what the rich charge."

"That's not the agreement Vermillion has."

"Why can't you break it?"

"I'm a guest, they are the host. If I break the rules of hospitality first, they can retaliate. They have to be the first to break." They nibbled on a pastry as they walked toward the balcony and stared out. "You'll see how it all pieces together soon."

"What if I break a rule?"

"Just act obedient and follow me around."

Elliot rolled his eyes and shoved more pastry into his mouth so he didn't make a comment that would prove the plan was sure to fail. As long as his mouth was full, he'd be fine.

Beyond the glass, the landscape hadn't changed. The weird orange sun and deep blue sky was still there. "How do you know when to sleep if the sun never sets?" Or had it set and was now in the same place? No, he hadn't slept that long.

"It does set, but not this close to the border. Here, it's always daylight. Thus, the curtains."

"Then how do you tell when day and night is? You're only ever in Fotyna at night." The rest of the time the castle didn't exist.

"We can feel it. Your sun has set, and the moon is rising. I'll have to leave soon, but I'll lock the door."

"And then you will sleep during my day."

"For some, there is no choice." Umbra glanced out the door again. The light from the odd sun shone through the colored glass and stained the floor. "The older the Abyr, and the more blood they've consumed, the less they can resist the urge to sleep when the sun rises."

"And if caught in town, you burn."

"I'm sure Abyr have hidden in town before, but to be caught in daylight is bad." Their face became pinched as though their pastry was filled with maggots not fruit.

"You're immune to the sun at the moment."

"Not immune, but I won't go up in flames. I'm too young and have barely drunk blood."

Elliot tried to marry all this new knowledge up with what he knew from the warnings and tales. They weren't the hungry monsters he'd been warned about, they were soldiers protecting their lands from humans who wanted nectar. He didn't blame the Kin or the humans for wanting the miracle cure.

He joined Umbra in looking outside, but he wasn't seeing past the glass. The intricate leading and fine solder work was far more complex than what he did. He was lightman not an artist; he wouldn't know what picture to create even if he had the colored glass.

He shifted his focus to the land beyond. "You don't need blood to survive...the Kin out there don't drink it. Why at the border?"

"It makes us stronger, more prone to violence and less toward art." They touched the glass. "The Abyr who built this place centuries ago hadn't yet become blood drinkers. But they would. And then once sampled, it becomes a craving."

Their fingers swept Elliot's hair behind his ear, exposing his neck. Umbra's cool fingers trailed over his pulse. Their hand fell away and curled into a fist.

Elliot didn't move. He was prey and the cat was toying with him. "Just bite. I've already agreed."

"I should, before I go down to the hall. Vermillion might try to force me to drink female blood again."

"They did that? Isn't that wrong?"

"Yes. No one should be forced to drink blood, and everyone is free to choose whose blood they drink. Vermillion is a coward who rules by fear, and since I stopped being meek, they've started lashing out."

It might be best to spend the whole twenty-seven nights in Umbra's chamber.

Umbra sat in one of the chairs. "Join me." But they patted their lap, indicating where they expected Elliot to sit. "I don't want you to faint and hurt yourself."

He was more likely to hurt himself sitting on Umbra, but he walked over with his best swagger and sat sideways like they were about to discuss wants and prices. He slung his arm around Umbra's neck and leaned against them. "Like this?"

Umbra's eyes widened, and it took a moment for them to find words. "That'll be fine."

Elliot breathed a sigh of relief. This was weird already. He didn't want it to be weirder.

"Shall I..." Their hand was on Elliot's thigh, holding him close.

"Yes, just get it done." He then quickly leaned away. "Wait. I'm not going to turn into a devoured, am I?"

"No, you have to taste my blood for that. I swear."

Elliot moved back in close and tilted his head, so his neck was exposed.

"I was going to bite your wrist, but since you insist."

Elliot didn't have time to think it through before Umbra's lips were on his neck, kissing and tasting in a way that created gooseflesh on his arms even though his blood had suddenly become too hot. Umbra's grip on his leg tightened, and their fingers threaded into Elliot's hair. He didn't move, could barely breathe.

A pop and a sting, then heat. He closed his eyes, not sure he should be liking it as much as he was. When Umbra pulled away, he couldn't help but gasp at the loss.

Umbra licked his neck and slowly eased their hold on his hair and thigh. "Did that hurt?"

"Not really." He didn't know how to describe it. He shivered, and the odd sensation was gone replaced by something much more familiar that settled low in his gut. Getting bitten shouldn't get him hard.

"Good." Umbra smiled.

Elliot became aware of something pressing into his hip. At least he wasn't the only one affected. "You like the taste?"

"Yes...very nice."

"Great." Elliot stood up. He ruffled his hair and then grabbed a pastry so he had something else to focus on.

"I'm going to go." Umbra fiddled with their braids and glanced at the door. "I'll bring up some food for dinner. There's a few books and games. I'll sort something out today." They grabbed their coat and fled.

The door clicked. He was locked in.

He rubbed his neck, expecting blood, but his fingers came away clean.

His gaze landed on the wardrobe and all the finely made clothes. He really shouldn't...but he had all day to fill. He put the pastry in his mouth, drawing the shirt off as he walked toward the wardrobe.

CHAPTER 14

$\mathcal{U}$mbra made it to the stairs before the attack came. They sensed Lapis before they saw them and were already twisting away, but Lapis managed to grab their shirt. Cloth tore.

Lapis shoved them against a wall. "You survived."

"Have you forgotten who I am? Or that I'm a guest?" They brought their arm down, breaking the hold, and followed through with an elbow to the jaw that left Lapis shaking their head to dispel the stars that would've formed.

"I was merely expressing concern, after seeing you become swarmed last night. I left to get help." Lapis grinned, but their eyes remain cold and dead.

"Of course you did." Umbra smoothed their clothes. They weren't going back into their chambers to get changed. If they did, they might want another taste of Elliot. Three nights ago, drinking blood had turned their stomach. Now, it was something they enjoyed despite the metallic taste and thickness on their tongue.

They didn't want to like the taste, but they had definitely enjoyed the way Elliot bared his neck so readily. The frustration still simmered. A need they weren't going to be able to fulfill now that they could no longer pass time with the unchanged in the castle—those not associated with Vermillion's pack.

How many days until the changes became noticeable to all?

Maybe they were only seeing change because they were searching, not because anything had happened.

"Is there anything else I can help you with, Lapis?"

Lapis stared at Umbra for several heartbeats then leaned close. "You're playing at something. When I find out, you'll be stripped and whipped and staked in the sun, and I'm sure you'll suffer more than a mild case of sunburn."

Umbra whispered in their ear. "That is why I'm here. To change." They drew back. "Remember, I'm a guest. I'm also Cerulean's prime, and unless you want their wrath brought down upon your beloved Ver, back the fuck off."

Umbra turned and stalked downstairs. They checked their room key was still in their pocket and ignored the sweat beading on their back. That was new and unpleasant.

Spending the day locked in their room with Elliot was already more appealing than spending the day placating the ego of Vermillion.

~

The sun was rising as Umbra made their way upstairs. They hadn't meant to stay away the whole night, but it had been too hard to slip away. Lapis watched them too intently. Vermillion had retired a while ago, taking Dayne with them. Dayne seemed fine, though Vermillion took no chances with their pet and forced the human to taste their blood.

There'd been a different set of dice, weighted a different way. Umbra had gotten the feel for them and listened to Vermillion talk about plans if the humans invaded. Vermillion had talked about the last uprising ten years ago and how the dead Abyr had been stripped of their antlers, their bodies left in the street to burn in the sun. They talked about how they'd quashed the humans' spirit, but they could

117

feel it rising again. The humans needed to be reminded of their place, he said.

Umbra unlocked the door and slid in, locking it behind them. The outer chamber was empty, and so was the bedroom. Was Elliot in the bath again? No, they wouldn't torture themselves by going in while he was naked and wet. Then they turned and saw him in the hanging chair, one foot on the ground, rocking himself, the other tucked up. He glanced up from the book that was in his lap and smiled as though he were happy to see them.

Umbra couldn't help but smile back.

Elliot's smile faded as Umbra walked closer. "What happened?"

Their shirt was torn, and dark blood stains marked the front of their clothes. They'd deliberately lost at dice again, and Vermillion was enjoying what they thought was a show of power. "Nothing to worry about."

Elliot's expression shuttered.

Umbra went to sit on the other chair. The rising sun in Elliot's world was making them foggy. They were tired, and while they could resist more easily than the older Abyr, they were still affected. But the other chair was draped in Elliot's frayed and patched clothing. He'd found them and had clearly kept himself busy by washing them.

"Sorry." He went to get up, putting aside the book.

"Stay. It's fine. I shouldn't sit anyway, or I'll end up sleeping out here." There were worse places to sleep.

"Is it daylight?"

Umbra nodded, and their gaze fixed on the pulse in Elliot's throat. They could hear his heart. They forced themselves to look away. But they should taste him and wash away any remnants of the female blood Vermillion had forced down their throat.

"Did you need to…" Elliot lifted his wrist. "They made you drink again, didn't they?"

They wanted to say no, to refuse the offer. But couldn't. "Yes. I would like to, but I'll clean up first."

They walked back in and saw the empty plate. They hadn't brought food up. They bit back the curse, but they didn't have the energy or time to get to the kitchen and back. "I won't bite you. I forgot food."

"It's fine. I ate all of the pastries, and I've done nothing all day."

"You're my responsibility."

"I'm an adult, and I said it's fine. It wouldn't be the first meal I've missed. And I'm sure it won't be the last."

"Thank you." Umbra couldn't look at him, though. They grabbed a cloth and went into the bathroom to wash. Tomorrow, they'd bathe. All they wanted now was to get the blood off their skin and the taste of Vermillion's hard kiss from their mouth.

When they came out wrapped in the cloth, Elliot had brought in his clothes and folded them up. The book he'd been looking at was on the table. They went to the wardrobe to grab clean pants to sleep in and stopped. Nothing was out of place...but everything was wrong. They lifted the sleeve of their favorite blue coat, with the orange suns down the front, and inhaled. It smelled like Elliot.

If they sniffed the other clothes, would they all carry his scent? How long until everything they owned, their bed, smelled of their pet? How long until others noticed?

They didn't care what others thought. They liked it. They released the sleeve, wishing they had seen Elliot wearing the coat.

"You were well occupied today?" They pulled out pants and slid them on, letting the cloth fall to the floor.

"I napped, looked at the books—well, the ones with pictures—and did laundry. A very lazy day."

Umbra glanced at him, not sure if he was being serious or not. It appeared he was. "I'll find some other things for you to do until it's safe to take you around the castle. I'll show you the solo version of ossic, but it will have to be when I wake."

The goblet of nectar was half full and untouched. That surprised them. Humans were meant to be very greedy about the stuff, not realizing they didn't need much.

They watched their human as he got ready for bed, brushed his teeth, and ran his fingers through his hair. He'd offered, but they still didn't feel right about walking over and taking a bite. Elliot glanced at them in the mirror, a polished disk of silvered glass.

"I'll need to get you a razor."

He shrugged. "It can grow for a bit. Will you get a beard?"

"Not for a long time." But they couldn't help but touch their jaw. That took months of drinking male blood. They had no intention of being that committed to the change. They just wanted to escape Vermillion's clutches. After that, they'd drink only when they had to.

Vermillion was growing a beard. No doubt they'd be ordering the slaughter of animals for a fertility feast, too. They were looking forward to spoiling that party.

"Come." They extended their hand. Sleep was already dragging them under and keeping their eyes open was difficult. They sat in the chair and drew Elliot close. He straddled their lap and faced them, making this far too intimate. They'd thought the chair safer than the bed, but they'd been wrong.

"Will your voice change? Is this like puberty?"

"A little, and no. I went through that over twenty years ago as normal." They touched their antlers. "Children don't have them."

They ran their fingers over Elliot's jaw enjoying the scratch on their fingertips. They wanted to rub their cheek against his, inhale his scent, and bite his neck as they pressed their hips closer. They swallowed.

Elliot waited with one arm slung over Umbra's shoulder. "You really don't like biting." He leaned in and rested his forehead against theirs, a move that from another Abyr was pure aggression.

"Don't do that." Umbra pushed him back.

He opened his mouth to speak, but Umbra sank their teeth into his wrist. Keep it impersonal, pleasurable. They had to do it, but they didn't have to like it. And yet, every time they drank blood it tasted better.

Elliot gasped. There'd been no lick to prepare the skin, they'd been too rough, but Elliot wasn't pushing them away. When Umbra lifted their gaze, Elliot was watching. They looked down, but that was no safer. The front of Elliot's borrowed pants tented forward. Umbra was never going to be able to wear those pants again.

They licked the trickle of blood off his skin and offered Elliot the nectar. "To heal the wound and make up for no dinner." And to take away the pain. "I'll be more careful next time."

Elliot ran his fingertips over the two tiny punctures. A faint silver shimmer traced the vein beneath his skin. "I know why people crave the bite."

Those words would not give Umbra peaceful dreams.

CHAPTER 15

*E*lliot lay in bed wide awake when he should be sleeping. With nothing to do during the day, he'd had another bath and a nap. He'd expected Umbra to join him in bed, but the Kin was in the chair, legs stretched out as though sleep had claimed them before they could get up. He sat up, then got out of bed. He opened the curtains to stare at the fat orange sun in its inky sky. Umbra didn't stir.

All the Kin were asleep. They couldn't resist because it was daylight across the lake.

If he left the chambers, he should be fine. He wouldn't go far. Maybe if he did some walking around, he'd feel sleepy. Usually, he fell into bed exhausted. This not being tired was odd, and he wasn't sure he liked it. He didn't think he'd be able to survive another twenty-six nights of doing nothing.

The key was in the lock of the outer door.

It was safe in Umbra's chambers, no one could get him…but there was no one to get him because they were all asleep. The only people who might be up were other humans, like him. Like his brother.

He unlocked the door and paused, breath held. Umbra didn't wake.

The door that had seemed silent when Umbra came and went, now creaked a warning. Elliot opened it far enough for him to slip out and no more. Then he took careful note of where he was and the carvings on the door and door frame. Even then, he only crept as far as the next door. The carvings were different. A little grander?

He touched the door. Were Vermillion's chambers on the other side. Was his brother? If he opened the door, would Dayne be awake? His breathing came in hard pants as though he were running for his life, his fingers curled as though to open the door, but he made himself step back.

He had to wait. He needed Umbra to be able to fight for him, and there hadn't been enough blood consumed to turn them into a warrior—assuming his understanding of the change was correct.

As he'd poured over Umbra's books with their neat lettering, he wished he was able to read. Not that the letters matched the kind he was used to seeing. There were far too many circles making the shapes in the books that Umbra had and not enough straight lines.

He turned away from the door. Even if Vermillion was sleeping, creeping into their chambers wasn't wise. Still, the need to see Dayne crawled through his veins like a dozen roaches.

He crept further along the walkway. Below was a huge hall set with several long tables. Great chandeliers of red orbs in different sizes hung from the ceiling. They were beautiful, like drops of blood spilling but never hitting the floor. In the hall, some people slept curled up on chairs or on the floor. But some people moved around, clearing the tables of food and wiping them down. He watched for a little, torn between remaining hidden the way Umbra wanted and the need to speak to other people.

Who was willing and who had been captured? Who else had been desperate enough to make a deal with a Kin? Or had they decided any life was better than the life they had over the lake? Was being a servant in such a grand place better than scavenging in the Dark City and scraping up enough coin to last another fortnight?

The beds were better, and it wasn't so bloody cold. The rent was paid in blood, something he had plenty of. He shivered as a trail of heat ran down his spine, and he rubbed at the silvery mark on his wrist. The two holes had healed in moments.

He changed direction, determined to retrace the route they'd taken from the stables. If he needed to get out, that was where he'd need to go. Get a beast and ride at dawn so the Kin couldn't follow. That had been Umbra's plan. And as far as Elliot could tell, it seemed like a good one.

His fingers trailed along the wall, tracing over the carvings, as he walked. He peered out the windows in the walkway, but there was no lake or city. The sun had risen in Fotyna, and it had vanished. While he'd never seen an ocean before, this endless body of water had to be one. Out there were the tentacled leviathans that sometimes got trapped in the lake when the sun set.

Down the stairs and into the courtyard, on the other side, were the stables. He'd remembered correctly, but he didn't breathe a sigh of relief. He lingered in the shadows, waiting to see who was about, half expecting to see one of the Kin on guard. It seemed too easy that they were all sleeping, giving the humans the run of the castle. Across the cobbled courtyard was a set of grand doors that must lead to the dining hall. He lifted his gaze to the great stained-glass window, an orange sun in one half and a clear moon in the other.

If his family had coin or he'd been born in a better part of town, he might have had the chance to become an artisan. He could've made pretty glass things or clothes or furniture, things that the folk up the hill would buy. His brother wouldn't have been prey for the Kin, and he wouldn't be here either.

Some people married up. If he hung out at a different tavern or made the effort to be in the places where the artisans went, then maybe... He lowered his gaze. Was there nothing he wouldn't sell? Put his heart on a plate and offer it to the highest bidder. *No.* There was a reason he hadn't done any of that. He couldn't. It was possible that someone from the artisan class would love him, but the chance was small. Smaller now he had no job.

The hair on his arms prickled, and he became aware of someone watching him from the stable side of the courtyard. He froze, not sure if he should slink away or if he should greet them. He needed a friend. An ally.

He drew in a breath and stepped out of the shadow. The human on the other side stepped back and vanished into the darkness. For a heartbeat, he considered giving chase, but if he was creeping about and not wanting to be caught, that meant others were doing the same. For the hours, the Kin slept, and the humans ran through the castle like mice with no fear of cats.

A smile curved his lips.

He'd map a few more routes, watch the main hall, and see if he could find the kitchen. While he was okay with skipping dinner, this was food he didn't have to pay for.

It took a while, and he had to go down below the level of the main hall, but he found the kitchen. There were a few humans scrubbing pots, and two Kin sleeping by the fire in small beds. Their antlers were smaller than Umbra's so they must be younger.

There were several platters of leftover food on the center work-table. Large blobs of dough rose half hidden under a rainbow of cloths. There were barrels of something and cheeses under glass domes. Herbs hung from the ceiling, and baskets of fruit were placed along one wall. A piece of fruit and some leftover bread would be fine.

He stepped into the kitchen, half expecting the Kin to wake, but they slept like the dead.

The woman stopped scrubbing the pot. "What do you want?" Her voice was low, and her face fixed in a scowl.

"A bit of bread." He pointed at the platters of leftover food. It was more food than he saw in a week and it was probably going to waste.

"Take some and go. If they were up, they wouldn't let ya." She jerked her chin at the sleeping Kin.

"Thank you." Elliot grabbed a few things off the platter, including some of the sweet dried fruit that was far more delicious than it looked. He was about to leave when the man stopped chopping fruit to study him.

"Have I seen you before?"

Did they think he was Dayne? Should he agree or admit that he was new?

"Maybe?" He shrugged and scampered, taking his meal to eat on the walkway where he could watch the ocean even though its vastness made him dizzy. He stayed until a fog rolled in. It was then he realized he'd been up far too long. If the lake appeared, the sun was setting, and Umbra would be waking.

He ran back up to the room, opened the door as swiftly as he dared, and locked it behind him. The click echoed through the room. He froze, waiting. One breath, two breath, three. Nothing, so he crept into the bedroom and slid between the sheets. It was only then he let himself glance at Umbra, still sprawled in the chair, head back, eyes closed, lips parted.

Elliot smiled. He'd taken his first look at the castle and gotten himself dinner. All without arousing suspicion.

CHAPTER 16

$\mathcal{U}$mbra made their way up the stairs, a plate of sweet and savory pies in one hand and a glass pot of tea in the other. Elliot had been sleeping when they'd risen, and Umbra had thought it best to get up and be seen before returning with breakfast. A substantial though late breakfast, to make up for forgetting dinner.

Vermillion leaned against Umbra's door, arms folded, lips pressed into a narrow line which wasn't an improvement on his usual smirk. "You're eating."

"Yes." They'd had too much blood to avoid eating food. Their stomach cramped when hungry, and nectar no longer sufficed. Not that they'd avoided eating when unchanged—some things were delicious and should be eaten—but they hadn't needed to eat. But there was rather too much in their hands for just them.

"Or are you hiding something from me?" Vermillion stepped forward and grabbed Umbra's arms, pressing them against the door. Pies slid off the plate, and hot tea sloshed over their arm. Umbra hissed. "What have you brought into my castle?"

Umbra knocked the pot into Vermillion's arm, breaking their hold. Vermillion retaliated by smashing Umbra's hand against the wall until they dropped the pot. It shattered and sent hot tea and shards of glass spinning across the floor. Umbra struggled against the much stronger and older Abyr.

Vermillion's hand roamed up their chest. "Still flat like an unchanged. You need more blood."

Umbra kneed them in the groin. When Elliot had done it to them, it had been uncomfortable, but they knew why Elliot had done it now. Vermillion crumpled. "Keep your hands off me. You have no right until the change is complete."

"I have every right. You're my mate." Vermillion said through clenched teeth.

They would see about that. There would be blood spilled when the truth came out.

"I'm your guest until I'm your mate. You would do well to remember that and remind your minions. The next time Lapis threatens me, I may not be so forgiving. Nor will my letter home be so gracious."

They straightened, fury in their green eyes. "You cannot threaten me."

Vermillion leaned forward, and Umbra met them midway, their foreheads crashing together, antlers locking. There was no way Umbra could get the upper hand or defeat Vermillion, but they wouldn't back down either. There was an anger in their body, a tension, a rage that flooded them and stripped thought.

They knew it was caused by the blood drinking but couldn't step away from the edge.

"I can defend myself, though I shouldn't need to, *mate*," Umbra spat the word.

"And I can defend my castle from intruders." They shoved, and Umbra's back hit the door. Their foot slipped on the spilled tea.

"What intruders?"

"My pet was seen roaming last night, but that's impossible because he was chained to my bed. Was your pet?" Umbra opened their mouth, but Vermillion grasped their jaw so they couldn't speak. "I do not want your lies. Unlock the door."

Fuck.

When Umbra didn't move, Vermillion's hands pawed over them again. They batted them away and retrieved the key, their pulse so loud it drowned out all other noise.

They fumbled with the door lock before it clicked open, and Vermillion pushed past to enter. They didn't remain in the receiving room like they should have but strode through to the bedroom like they had a right to be there.

Umbra's heart was in their throat, but Elliot wasn't in the bed. Where was he? They resisted the urge to look wildly around and instead breathed and tried to listen for the now familiar beat of his heart.

The balcony.

Umbra threw open the bathroom door as a distraction. "Satisfied?"

"Where is your pet?"

"Not here." The lie fell surprisingly easily from their tongue.

"You will bring them to the castle so I can meet them."

"And your intruder?"

Vermillion gave them an icy glare. "I will take care of it, do not bother yourself, mate." They pressed a hard and hateful kiss to Umbra's mouth. Umbra let them then wiped it off as soon as Vermillion's back was turned. They strode out of Umbra's chambers, kicking the plate away from the door. Umbra counted to three, then retrieved the key from the outside of the door, and locked Elliot and themselves in.

The anger hadn't slipped away.

They shoved open the balcony door and hauled Elliot out of his hiding place behind the lounge chair where his clothes had dried yesterday. If Vermillion had come much further into the room, he'd have been seen.

"What did you do?" Umbra kept their voice low; they could be heard out here. They grabbed Elliot's collar and thrust him inside, shutting the glass door after them. Elliot stumbled back.

Umbra lunged after him throwing him to the bed. Elliot twisted and squirmed out the shirt and out of their grip, but he wasn't getting away so easily. Umbra grabbed his arms, pinning him to the bed before he could slither off like a snake. Elliot's feet were on the floor, back arched. Umbra loomed over him. "What did you do while I slept?"

He lowered his forehead to Elliot's, their antlers close to Elliot's face. Elliot's arm muscles flexed beneath their fingers as he tried to wriggle free.

"Nothing."

"What did you do? The truth, or I will offer you to Vermillion myself," they snarled, knowing it was a threat they couldn't follow through with.

"I got dinner. I wanted to see the castle, and you said it was safe."

"I said no such thing."

Elliot bent his elbow and grasped Umbra's antler, forcing them to pull their head away.

"Release me." The fury solidified into something else. Elliot's heart beat fast, and the scent of fear clung to his skin. They wanted to taste it.

"Let go of me," Elliot countered.

Neither of them moved. Elliot watched him with wide dark eyes.

"You were seen, and it was reported. You look too much like your brother."

"Like that's my fault." His grip on their antler eased, though he didn't let go.

He didn't need to.

Umbra lifted the arm they'd been pinning down and brought it to their mouth, unable to resist the call of Elliot's blood any longer and needing to remind him he was a pet, not free to roam. Their fangs sank into the soft flesh at the crook of his elbow. He cried out at the rough bite, releasing Umbra's antler.

Then he curled, and his knee collided with Umbra's cheek breaking the bite. Blood spilled across the sheet. Despite the blood, Elliot sprung away, putting distance between them.

The anger that had been boiling within them swelled again, driven by the fresh blood and prey in their room. This wasn't right. This wasn't who they were.

They leaped off the bed, needing more distance. In the bathroom, they closed the door. Their hands shook and rage vibrated through them like a leviathan lashing out and seeking prey.

It was the change, that was all. But knowing what was causing this wasn't reassuring. They should be able to control themselves. They touched the split skin over their cheekbone and tried to find some calm and logic.

They couldn't stay in the bathroom; the bite was open, and Elliot was bleeding. Their breathing was still too fast, and their body was full off odd edges that they didn't know how to smooth. They grabbed a cloth that had been hung over the bath and swung open the door.

Elliot was sitting on the floor, holding the green shirt to the wound. He scuttled back, until his back hit the bed.

Umbra deliberately walked past him and picked up the nectar. He splashed some on the cloth then walked back and knelt. "Here, this will heal it."

Elliot snatched the cloth and pressed it to the ragged wound. He sucked in a breath. Umbra was familiar with the sting of healing wounds. Their back had been a mess after their escape attempt.

They sat opposite Elliot, back against the wardrobe.

"This isn't working. You bite me like that again, and I will kill you in your sleep."

"You leave this room while I'm sleeping, and Vermillion will have you killed." They scrubbed their hand over their face. "I trusted you."

Elliot lifted his wounded arm. "And I you."

And now that was all gone.

"Your arm will be fine."

He peeled away the cloth and sure enough, where there had been torn flesh there was only a smear of blood. Elliot pressed his skin as though to be sure. "That doesn't make it right."

"I'm sorry."

"You need to fix your face." He tossed the cloth to Umbra.

They caught it and pressed the nectar-soaked cloth to their cheek. The heat of healing skin was a welcome pain.

"I heard the fight at the door. I knew I was in trouble."

Umbra nodded. "I had pies and tea for you. And I was going to teach you how to play ossic."

"That would've been nice." His gaze didn't leave Umbra. It was cool and level.

"And impractical." Learning how to play a game wouldn't save Elliot's life if he needed to fight.

"I need to see other humans. I need allies."

"You need to survive. If you're going to walk around you need to carry a knife—not the one you came with. You can take mine."

"So now I'm allowed to walk around without you?"

"I could chain you to the bed like the others do with their pets, but I don't want to. You need to get your brother and…"

"And what? You need me for more than my blood."

"Vermillion is planning something. They want a fight."

"And you don't." Elliot pushed himself up and sat on the bed.

Umbra remained sitting on the floor. "It's a side effect of the blood. There's a reason only the border Abyr drink it. It makes us violent, makes us stronger."

"Well, you need to get that under control. Or I'll rip your antlers off."

"You do not touch antlers. Ever."

"And you don't tear at me when I give it to you willingly."

Umbra glanced away. "I don't want to like it, but when you sit on me and act…like you want more…I do like it. I don't like any of this. I don't know who I am."

"I was treating you like any client. Giving you what you paid for."

They stared up at the human man sitting on their bed. They wanted, and they craved, and they didn't like any of the wild sensations ricocheting through their body.

Elliot leaned forward and rested his elbows on his knees. He studied Umbra like a bug. "We need rules if this is going to work."

"We do."

"I won't touch your antlers or do the forehead thing."

"I will be gentle with the bite. But no more sidling up and looking at me like that." Elliot smiled, and his expression changed. "That, no more of that."

"I think you're supposed to like biting; it's what the Kin do. I shouldn't like it...I didn't like that." He touched his elbow.

"But if I'm gentle, you like it?"

"Yeah, and I can deal with that. The bite is weird, but it wouldn't be the first time I've enjoyed myself while getting paid. You're going to have to sort yourself out."

"It's part of the change. I don't know what I can do."

"Would it be different with female blood? Perhaps I'm not what your body wants."

Umbra didn't want any blood, but the sun had risen on that tide. "It's said female blood is stronger."

They were both silent for a little while, Umbra dwelling on the fact that this was the new them, or at least they were becoming the new them. They were going to have to get used to it because while they could eventually leave this castle, they couldn't escape themself.

"Are you sure you don't want to make peace with Vermillion? They seem like a bad Kin to annoy," Elliot finally said.

Umbra lifted their gaze. "I want them dead."

"Okay, that's a no." Elliot held their gaze. "You want me to kill him? I could walk in there while they're asleep—"

"No, they have human guards. You're lucky you didn't go into their room last night."

"Why don't the guards do it?"

"You're not the only one to make a deal."

"But not all will be loyal; some will be resentful. Not everyone here will love Vermilion's leadership style."

Umbra smiled. "No, but the next in line is Lapis, and they are just as bad."

"What about you? You're prime."

"I can't take over a castle."

"Why not?"

"Can you take over a city?"

Elliot laughed. "I'd need an army."

133

"So, you'll go back to your hovel after this and be happy?"

"That's my home."

"You don't want more?"

Hunger flared in Elliot's eyes for a moment before being shuttered. "Of course I do, but I was born in the dark and I'll die in the dark...or here." He shrugged, but that carelessness was gone as though he were thinking.

"If I were to take over, I'd need an army, too."

"You have one, on the shore. The devoured would do anything to get back here. Then you could break the trade deals and feast on the rich instead of the poor."

"You can't break trade deals. That's how wars start. Vermillion wants a war; I don't. But there must be more in the dark than up the hill."

If Elliot could take over the city and they took over the castle...

"You think this hasn't been whispered about before in the taverns, on people's day off, with their lover as they fall asleep? We don't work, we lose our jobs, and there's always someone hungrier who'll do it. I'm not going to have work when I get back." He glanced up at the orbs. "Well, not the job I want, but there's always work if you ask in the right places."

"Doing what?"

Elliot gave them *that* look, the one where his eyes softened and his lips almost curved, his tongue darted over his lip as though he were looking at something delicious.

"Don't do that." They didn't like the way their body responded. They liked sex, but that had been before.

"Are you sure you've been bedded?"

"Yes. How about I twist your body into something new and I see how you like it?" They stood and pulled their knife out of the wardrobe. It was sheathed, and they tossed it to Elliot. "I can't stop you from creeping around, but I can at least do my best to keep you safe."

Elliot held the knife as though he didn't know which was the pointy end.

"You know how to fight?" Umbra touched their cheek. Elliot had twisted and turned and didn't fight like an Abyr at all. They liked that.

"Not with a weapon."

"But you were carrying a knife."

"That had been given to me. I couldn't afford a weapon. As a child, I fought with sticks."

"You did?" They pulled out their staff. It was shoulder height and each end was tipped with a glass point. "Would you prefer this?" Umbra spun it, so the glass tips glinted red in the light.

"What? No. Not that kind of stick…just ones that fell off trees."

"I'll get some more pies, and then I'll teach you to fight with the knife."

"I don't think that's a good idea. I've experienced what happens when you get hyped up." He placed the knife next to him. "I don't want to get hurt, even though you can fix it."

It was clear nectar hadn't fixed the wound. They shouldn't have bitten Elliot in anger or given into the temptation. "It's a craving, clawing at me. I can hear your heart beating. It's how I knew where you were hiding."

"So, drink more."

"Then you need to eat and be strong. You've got a city to take over."

Elliot laughed.

Umbra didn't.

The smile fell off Elliot's lips. "You're serious."

CHAPTER 17

*E*lliot remained sitting on the bed after Umbra left, the sheathed knife by his side. He ran his fingers over the fresh silvery scar on the inside of his elbow and shuddered. The fight replayed through his mind. He thought he'd been fighting for his life…but he hadn't been, or he'd be dead.

The Kin were too strong and too quick.

He raked his fingers through his hair. When he'd heard the scuffle at the door, the slamming of someone, probably Umbra, against the wood, he'd hidden. He hadn't thought to grab a weapon. If Vermillion had hauled him out from behind the chair, would a knife have mattered? Would there have been time to pull the blade free, or would Vermillion have tossed him over the edge of the balcony and been done with it?

If he'd gone into Vermillion's chambers last night, he'd already be dead.

He forced out a breath, knowing he needed to move, but unable to find the will. There was blood splashed on the floor, the brighter Kin blood and his darker human blood. It was on the sheets too. But he remained sitting. Somehow, he'd thought Umbra was different, a reasonable Kin.

The feral hunger in their eyes had been terrifying.

He picked up the knife and unsheathed it. It curved like a sliver of moon, smooth and sharp on the outer edge, toothed on the inner curve. He ran his thumb over the blade, and it whispered over his skin. It was only after that he saw the faint mark, then blood welled from the cut. He stuck his thumb in his mouth.

The door unlocked, and he startled, grabbing the knife as though he knew how to use it. Umbra came in holding a tray which they balanced while locking the door. Elliot didn't move. His thumb bled on his tongue.

Umbra put the tray on the table and looked at him, then the knife. "It's sharp."

He took his thumb out of his mouth. "I know." Blood trickled over his skin. Umbra watched. "Want it?"

Desire flickered through Umbra's eyes even as they shook their head.

"I think you should stop fighting the need. Your body wants it." He knew that raw hunger when he ate something, anything, to stop his stomach from hurting.

Umbra shot him a glare. Then they walked over and sucked on Elliot thumb. If being bitten and licking it weird, this was even stranger. Their tongue moved against his skin and a shiver of goose-flesh trailed down his arm. The glare softened, and the grip on his hand became gentler. Elliot pulled his hand away.

The cut gleamed silver but had stopped bleeding.

Umbra licked their lower lip and considered him for a moment before stepping back. "Eat. I'll sort out this mess. Then I'll teach you to use the knife."

The pies smelled delicious, each one no bigger than the palm of his hand. "What's in them?"

"Fruit." Umbra pulled the stained sheet off the bed and used it to wipe the floor before tossing it in a pile with the other dirty clothes.

"No meat?"

Their head snapped up. "No. Why would there be?"

"Because it's nice...and I can't afford it very often, so I thought...

never mind." He picked up a pie and took a bite. He shouldn't be getting used to living here.

Umbra studied him. "The Abyr only eat meat when they want to be fertile."

It was his turn to stare. "So you change but...what about the unchanged?"

"You don't have to be changed to make a baby. The changed are the aberrations, the ones living at the fringes. The warriors who are never accepted back into the heartland. Generations of human blood flows through my veins, and because of that I am taller and stronger than other unchanged. Those of us who were born on the border can never go back. I tried."

"To leave here?"

"My parent's castle. I wanted to see the forest of old ones, to travel and be something other than a warrior. Quite clearly, I failed."

He hadn't realized how badly Umbra didn't want to be part of this. "If you take over this castle you'll be—"

"Trapped in the life I never wanted. In a body I don't even recognize."

Elliot's gaze skimmed over Umbra but he couldn't see anything different. He wanted to ask but kept eating instead. Talking about their body was a prickly subject. "What other options do you have?"

"Why do you care?"

"Maybe I'm making polite conversation because this isn't exactly fun for me." Except he was liking the luxury a little too much.

"I have no options. If I flee and return home, I'll be punished for shaming my blood line. My birther would not be so forgiving a second time, and even though we can only be killed with antler, that doesn't mean we can't be hurt and kept alive and unhealed for far too long." There was an edge to their words that was sharper than the knife.

"Do they not care what you want?" Elliot's life had been rough and missing plenty of things, but his family had loved him and wanted him to find some happiness.

They sighed. "What I want is impossible. Even when I was unchanged."

Elliot took a sip of the nectar. He was getting used to the sweetness and the way it warmed his chest. "You need a new plan."

"I'm making one."

"That's right, we're going to take over the city." He scoffed. That was never going to happen. No one would listen to him. He was a nothing from the Dark City, little more than Kin food. The possibility was a wild thought he refused to chase.

"First, you have to survive." Umbra handed him the unsheathed knife hilt first. They immediately corrected his grip. "You aren't buttering bread."

"I won't be cutting many Kin either. You move too fast."

Umbra glanced at him. "If you're creeping while I sleep, you'll be fighting humans. Do not go after your brother. I'll help you when the time comes."

"I'm not a fool." And he didn't want to die.

Umbra pulled the heavy padded leather waistcoat out of the wardrobe and slipped it on. "You didn't try this one on."

Elliot startled then smoothed his expression. "You knew?"

"Course I did. I can smell you on everything."

That wasn't odd at all. His heartbeat quickened. Umbra could probably hear that too.

"I don't want to get stabbed while teaching you." They crossed the front flaps and laced it closed. The leather hung almost to mid-thigh with slits up the side.

He'd wondered what that ugly piece of clothing was for.

That was highly unlikely. The knife was strange in his hand. "What do I do?"

"Slash and hook." Umbra moved Elliot's hand directing the cut across their belly.

He'd seen the butchers at work early in the morning, cutting out the guts and selling the offal to those who couldn't afford more. He couldn't do the same to a person.

Umbra cupped his chin. "You can fight. You struggled and wormed even though you say I'm stronger."

"You are, but I'm not going to lie there and play dead."

"If you're fighting Abyr, that might be the better tactic."

"You enjoy the fight."

Umbra's lip curled, and they looked away. "I'd be disappointed if you gave up. I like that you don't. But people like Vermillion...they like to win."

"They won this morning, didn't they?"

"They are faster and stronger than me, for the moment. Practice."

Elliot spent too long slashing with the knife as though he were trying to gut Umbra. He got one cut across the leather. But eventually his arm became lead. He shook it out.

Umbra watched him. They took a sip of nectar before offering it to Elliot. He shook his head, needing water. He put the knife on the table and went to the bathroom to take large greedy gulps. The shirt clung to his skin.

Umbra followed and watched from the doorway as they carefully unlaced the padded waistcoat. "We'll do more with the knife tomorrow. I want to know how you fight."

Elliot turned and rested against the basin. "What do you mean?"

"You squirm and kick."

"That's all there is. No secret."

Umbra shook their head. "The first time I grabbed you, to save you, you broke my hold. You kneed me. I kneed Vermillion in the pods today...it was effective."

"In the pods?"

"Seed pods." They pointed at their groin.

Another reminder that Umbra was Kin, not human, and that enjoying being bitten was weird and probably wrong, and he definitely shouldn't be thinking about anything else. He glanced away. Fighting was a much safer topic.

"The way you fought me this morning...is that how the Kin fight?"

He walked toward Umbra, not sure if he was about to put himself deeper into trouble. There was an edge between them now. They were teaching each other how to wound better. While he wouldn't have called what they had trust, they'd never had that, they were using each other. Working out the rules as they went. That he wasn't chained like a dog prone to wandering was a relief. If Umbra tried that, he'd make plans to flee early, even though he needed Umbra to get his brother. He didn't like needing people.

Deliberately, he faced Umbra and put his forehead to theirs. "You do this, and push." He gave Umbra a shove, and Umbra resisted. "Pretend I'm strong enough to move you, to pick you up and shove you against a wall. That's what comes next?"

"It is. How do you know that?"

"Because that's what you do to me, every bloody time." He shoved again, and this time, Umbra took a few steps back. Elliot matched him and kept their foreheads close. It was odd, watching feet not face. "Vermillion had you against the door this morning. I heard the crash."

"This isn't a fight, it's a show of strength. Antlers can get tangled and broken if it goes too long."

"Grab them."

"No!"

"If you're fighting for your life, you have to." He gave Umbra a shove, and then used his foot to hook his leg so he stumbled. Umbra recovered quickly and pressed back with his forehead.

Elliot grabbed a handful of hair and tugged, but Umbra didn't drop to their knees like a human would have. They twisted away, leaving Elliot holding hair. He let the pink strands fall from his fingers. This wasn't working.

"Do it, push me against the wall."

Even though he was ready, it still took his breath to be lifted as though he weighed nothing and held there with his toes barely on the ground. Umbra did the forehead thing, and Elliot stuck his finger up Umbra's nose and yanked.

"Fuck." They stepped back, dropping Elliot, and clutching their nose.

"No rules against that?" They checked their hand for blood, but there was none. He'd been gentle. "If you do it hard enough, you can tear their nose open."

"Why haven't you done that before?"

"Because we have a deal, and I'm not being driven by some raging bloodlust I can't control. The person who gets angry and loses control loses the fight."

They wrinkled their nose. "Knee to the pods, fingers up the nostril. What else?" Umbra was gentler this time pressing him against the wall the way one might press a lover. For a moment, he thought Umbra might kiss him, and he didn't know how he'd react to that. Probably kiss him back. They were very pretty, even with their sunset pink eyes and pointed smile. It was almost better when they were rougher.

"A hit to the throat." He'd had to do that one night when a client had gotten too rough. "Or you could melt." Elliot relaxed and slithered down the wall. Umbra stopped him and hauled him up, so they were face to face.

The look in their eyes wasn't blood hunger or the wild feral look that had been there this morning. This much more serious.

"If you were stronger, you'd be dangerous."

Elliot took that as a compliment.

"Wounding Vermillion would be worse than killing them. Remember that. It has to be fatal."

"What about you? You can't let them beat you up whenever they want."

"For the moment, I will."

"Then don't bring it in here, or I will rip your nose and snap your antlers."

Umbra smiled. "I was furious with you, because you had snuck out and been caught. Do better."

Elliot crossed his arms. Was he in trouble not for leaving, but for being seen? "Don't get caught?"

"Vermillion's human guards will be expecting you tonight. If you're caught, this will be over. I will have to deny knowing you. I cannot reveal what I am doing. Not yet."

As much he wanted to slip out tonight, that wouldn't be the smart thing to do. "I'll wait a few days."

And he wouldn't go to the kitchen. Maybe that had been his undoing. Too much food and comfort was making him lazy and complacent.

He glanced at Umbra's bed. "I'll sleep on the chair tonight."

CHAPTER 18

ost other Kin returned to their rooms before Umbra
went to theirs. They liked that they could resist the
urge to sleep better than the others, though the human blood in their
body was making it more difficult.

Elliot was playing the solo version of ossic when Umbra returned.
He glanced up but didn't speak. He'd offered to sleep in the chair, and
while it would be nice to lie in their bed again, he didn't entirely trust
Elliot not to slink out the door the moment their eyes closed.

Umbra glanced at their bed, the one they had refused to sleep in
with Elliot in case they accidently bit him in their sleep. While the
bloodied sheet was no longer on it, there were marks on the blanket
beneath where the blood had soaked through. He hadn't noticed the
discomfort of the chair while he'd slept, only when waking with a stiff
back, but it was nothing that a sip of nectar didn't erase.

"Vermillion has worked everyone up to believe we are in danger
from a human invader intent on killing us all."

Elliot's hand hovered over a piece, but he didn't speak.

"I wouldn't move that one. The game will be over in three moves
and you'll lose." Umbra walked over and moved a piece that appeared
to have been forgotten on the side. "Don't be so direct."

"Are you talking about the game or Vermillion?"

"Both. You have played into their hands. They're itching to start a war with the humans. They want to wet their sword and prove their leadership." Umbra gave him a half smile. "Of course, a true leader doesn't need to prove how good they are."

"When do I get to leave your rooms?"

"Not yet. Let them be paranoid."

"People will die if they attack Fotyna."

"They won't attack. The humans will." Umbra shed their waistcoat and shirt. They really needed to let the cleaners come in, but what would they do with Elliot while the cleaners were tidying up and taking the laundry? It would have to wait a few more days.

"Why would we do that?"

"Why wouldn't you?"

Elliot scowled. Umbra left him to his contemplations while they went into the bathroom and washed. The sun across the lake was weighing heavily in their bones. There was no need for them to stay up past the others, but they liked having the hall almost to themselves.

Most Kin locked their doors at night, not trusting even the most well bribed servant not to kill them. Vermillion left their pet and guards in the outer room and locked the inner.

Umbra brushed their teeth with their finger and the grit. They paused and looked more closely at their reflection in the mirror. Were their fangs a little longer? They drew back and examined their face, then smiled. Yes, their fangs were longer. The tips more visible. The side of their hair that had been shaved to scalp now had a soft down of hair. A little longer, and they'd be able to cover their shame a little better with the braids they wore.

They spat and rinsed, then unraveled all the braids. They could've worn something much simpler, but as prime it was their right, and they didn't want to give Vermillion any chance to forget who they were dealing with.

They finished in the bathroom, and Elliot went in. Umbra used those moments alone to change into soft sleep pants. They weren't sleeping in their clothes tonight. Other changes were starting to happen—beyond hunger and liking the taste of blood. Their pods were definitely swelling, as was their stem. They ran their hand over the strange contours. They were going to have to get new leather pants made, but not yet. Vermillion would demand to know why, and Umbra wanted to make sure the change was well established.

Some said the changes caused by female blood were easier because aside from the growth of breasts for feeding the young, everything else was internal. They shuddered at the memory of Vermillion groping their chest.

Umbra drew the curtains and dimmed the lights until the room was almost dark, then they slid into bed to wait for Elliot. They needed a feed before they slept. In bed, it was harder to fight the pull of sleep, so they sat against the pillows instead of lying down.

Elliot came out of the bathroom. "You want some."

Umbra nodded.

Elliot didn't do that look or the walk, like he wanted more than being bitten. He sat on the edge of the bed, back to Umbra, and waited. Even though Elliot didn't look at them, the longing was still there. They wanted to pull him closer and feel him pressing against them. They wanted to brush his hair aside and bite his neck and hear him moan.

Instead, they lifted his hand, holding it carefully. They had to be gentle. This morning's savagery was a stain on their consciousness.

They licked the skin, feeling the pulse, then bit. Elliot drew in a breath, his body going tense for a moment, before he relaxed. Umbra slid their other hand around his waist to steady him. At least, that was the excuse they used. Elliot didn't brush them off. It would've been easier if he did.

With a final taste, Umbra drew back. In the red light, the fresh bite shimmered silver. Elliot pressed his fingers over the punctures, then got up and had a sip of nectar before licking his own wrist.

A little part of Umbra wanted to do more than bite him. They wanted to dip him in nectar and lick him all over.

He moved toward the chair.

"Bed," Umbra said.

Elliot glanced at them.

"I want to make sure you don't leave."

"I won't."

"You told me that once before."

He winced at the truth but got into the bed, lying on his back as close to the edge as he could manage.

It had been a while since they'd shared a bed with another. It was something they missed. While they should lie on their side of the bed, they needed to be able to feel if Elliot moved. It might rouse them enough to stop him. They hooked a foot over Elliot's ankle.

Elliot glanced at them, then moved closer, turning his back. "You sleep like a corpse anyway."

Umbra smiled and put their arm over him. Elliot tensed for a few breaths before he relaxed. Then Umbra let the need to sleep drag them under like a hungry leviathan.

～

They had to ride out to the human city tonight. After spending the last couple of nights mostly in their chambers, teaching Elliot to fight or at least be able to defend himself, Umbra didn't really want to leave the castle. Everything they needed was here. But nothing was as it had been, and that was their fault.

They were working together, but every so often, Umbra would glimpse the wariness in Elliot's gaze. They saw it when Elliot used the knife, even though the weapon was still awkward in his hand. That moment of fear when he wasn't quite sure, but he threw on a coat of braveness as he practiced. Umbra learned much more about the way humans fought. There were no rules and less honor. They twisted away like a worm escaping a hungry beak. Humans fought for survival, not to win or save face.

Umbra braided their hair and checked them in the mirror.

Even though they were living in such a small space they were giving each other more distance. Even when they bit Elliot, it was more formal. When they fought or slept, that was the only time they truly touched. So far, Elliot hadn't slipped out again.

They pulled on their pants and laced them up. They were bordering on uncomfortable, pinching in places where there shouldn't be any pinching. With their pants on, they could look in the mirror and recognize themselves. They readjusted their pants.

Elliot knocked on the door. "You've been in there forever. You'll be late, and then Vermillion will be angry."

Vermillion was always ready to erupt, but Lapis had backed off. Though Umbra was sure they were still being closely watched.

They opened the door. Elliot stood on the other side holding a shirt and waistcoat. He glanced at Umbra's brown pants then back at the clothes.

"I got these out for you." Dark stubble shaded his jaw.

Umbra wanted to run their fingers along his skin to feel the roughness, taste it on their tongue. They took their clothes. They wouldn't usually wear that shirt with these pants, but it would be passable. Light blue with dark brown. The waistcoat was brown and only lightly patterned with darkened vines scrolling across the chest. "And what coat do you suggest I wear?"

"The one with the suns...or I can get you something else. I wanted you to hurry up so I could bathe."

Umbra bit back a smile. "I wasn't stopping you from coming in."

The bath was made for more than one person.

Elliot's gaze lingered before he snapped it away. "I want to shave today."

"I think I should introduce you when I get back." The change was clear, though not complete. "After that, I can have someone come and shave you."

"I wouldn't trust another to have a knife at my throat."

"I won't be able to sort something out before I go. But I will." They pulled on their shirt and slipped on the waistcoat, then checked their reflection. The combination worked.

Elliot walked in and turned the knob so the bath started to fill. He'd wanted to know where the hot water came from, so Umbra had tried to explain and ended up finishing with a rather lame promise to show him. He couldn't resist watching as Elliot stripped off his shirt and draped it over the lip of the bath. No doubt he'd wash it.

"Take another shirt if you need."

Umbra ran their tongue over the tip of their fang. They had bitten him before getting out of bed but seeing him half-dressed made him hungry and his pants even tighter.

Elliot glanced over his shoulder. "I can see it in your eyes. I can feel it. It's like something rippling beneath my skin. I may not be tasting your blood, but I have still been tamed."

"You aren't tamed. You are a temporarily caged wild thing."

They didn't want a tamed pet. They couldn't think of anything more boring. Elliot could've stabbed them with the antler in his knife while they slept, but he hadn't. If he tried, they'd have a rather interesting fight.

Their pants became downright uncomfortable. This was ridiculous.

Elliot gave them a half smile. "At least you aren't trying to be polite and fight it."

Under the red-light, small parts of Elliot's veins gleamed silver, a glint on his neck and wrists that caught the light when he moved.

They didn't want to admit it, but it had been better since they'd stopped fighting the need to feed. They'd tried to restrict it to once a day, but now it was two or three times. They hoped it lessened soon. Many Abyr fed on blood less than once a sennight. But Umbra was only a sennight into the change.

They walked over, and Elliot watched. It wasn't fear or resignation or that look from his first night here. It was something else. He swept his hair off his neck and tilted his head. Sometimes he thrust out his wrist and Umbra accepted, but they liked the neck. They liked being able to hold him. It was more personal. Elliot hadn't offered his neck in a few nights.

Umbra ran his tongue over the skin, making it softer so the bite would hurt less. Elliot moved closer, and Umbra put their hand on his hip and the other on the back of his head, their fingers tangling in his dark curls. They bit, their teeth sinking deeper now that they were longer. Elliot gasped, but didn't pull away. His heart quickened, and he smelled even better, sweeter somehow.

Umbra moved closer, he was hard against their hip. They wanted to touch him. They wanted him to touch them. Heat flooded their veins, and they wanted to see the same in Elliot's eyes.

Someone hammered on their outer door.

They drew back too fast.

Elliot's eyes were half closed, his lips parted in desire. Blood trickled down his neck. "Go."

"One moment," they called out even though they couldn't be late. They still needed boots and a coat. They gave Elliot's neck a final, longing lick, wishing they had time to taste more and figure out what humans did with lust. "Abyr will still be roaming the castle."

"I'll wait here." He touched Umbra's lip, and his finger came away bloody.

They didn't want to go at all. Screw Vermillion and their trading party. They turned away before they could change their mind.

From the wardrobe, they grabbed the coat Elliot had suggested and threw it on. It was tight across the shoulders even though it had been made specifically for them. They grabbed their boots and their curved blade as well as their sword. Then they pulled the bedroom door closed. It clicked behind them as Elliot locked the door.

Elliot was smart.

He'd be fine.

CHAPTER 19

*E*lliot rubbed his neck, and his fingers came away red. He dipped a finger in the nectar as he walked past and rubbed it over the bite. By the time he walked back into the bathroom, the small punctures were healed. They'd stopped hurting before he'd even locked the door.

It wasn't real pain, a small sting and then…then he liked it far too much. The more it happened the more he liked it.

He wanted Umbra to bite him. He needed more than a bite, and when Umbra looked at him, he thought he saw the same hunger.

But in bed, nothing happened beyond biting and sleeping. After being bitten, Elliot lay awake, entangled with Umbra, his dick hard and needing more. Would Umbra sleep through him stroking himself to completion? Of course, then there was the mess.

He gave his dick a rub through his pants. If Umbra hadn't been called away, then maybe… Would that make this whole thing weirder? Would he be selling more than his blood? Did he really want sex or was that a side effect? It didn't matter while he was alone. The bath was half full, and he was going to steal a little enjoyment like he had the previous times Umbra had left him alone.

Steam coiled off the bath. He stripped off his pants and tossed them to the side. He'd get clean clothes out of Umbra's wardrobe. Already, he was used to the finer fabrics. The clothes he'd worn when he'd arrived were neatly folded in a faded, scruffy pile of mismatched colors.

He eased into the bath and the heat slid into his bones. For a moment he lay there, the water running, but he couldn't linger, so he twisted the knob shutting off the water not wanting to waste it—even though there were no servants pumping it and heating it. While most of the Kin were out of the castle, he had plans. He'd been making them for days, waiting for the opportunity, and he couldn't waste the chance to speak with Dayne in private. Once Umbra introduced him to the rest of the Kin, he may not get the opportunity.

Vermillion wouldn't be impressed with Umbra's deception. Elliot was expecting an all-out fight, and he hoped it didn't end in death. If Umbra was killed, he was screwed. Which was why he needed to make plans. He'd been very good and hadn't slipped out since that first day. It was one thing to creep about when no one knew he existed and another to know they were waiting for him, believing him to be an intruder.

He ran his hand along his dick. The heat had wilted it a little, but his touch brought it back to full hardness. He tried not to think about being bitten while he stroked, he tried to think about previous lovers. About being in Killian's bed and his kiss. About a few other nameless men he'd enjoyed. But his body kept remembering the feel of Umbra against him. The hardness that pressed into him. A hardness that had definitely increased in size since they'd been biting.

His breathing quickened as he imagined being naked and rubbing against Umbra as he was bitten. His body tensed as he came. The lust cut deep, and he gasped. The old bites throbbed as he spiraled down and released a shaky breath.

He hoped that when these twenty-eight days were over, and he was no longer being bitten, that this quirk would fade away. That he'd go back to his more usual imaginings like lips on his dick or an ass being offered up for fucking.

With a last shudder he got up, water streaming off him, and

grabbed the cloth to dry. He brushed his teeth with the grit—which tasted better than anything he'd ever used—and ran his fingers through his hair. Umbra had braided it once, pulling it into an elaborate style like many of the Kin wore. He wasn't sure who'd enjoyed the quiet moment more.

He had more physical contact with Umbra than with many of his lovers. Most of the time he never stayed the night. That he liked sleeping next to someone…even being held was dangerous.

He didn't want to need anyone.

If he needed someone, they would leave or die. It was much better to be independent.

Alone.

When he got Dayne back, he wouldn't be alone. They'd have each other. And that was all he needed, along with the occasional lover. He dressed in a shirt and loose pants, the same as always. Then he stopped…should he wear leather? He wasn't used to wearing it or fighting in it, and while he wasn't planning on fighting, he wanted to be prepared.

This was a visit, nothing more. A chance to see his brother. Hopefully. If Dayne wasn't there, at least he would've gotten out of the chambers and done something.

Umbra had taken their knife, so Elliot grabbed the one Fife had given him. He wasn't going out unarmed. He belted it on, then put on Umbra's socks and his own boots. The buckles were cheap and already spotted with rust. He'd been satisfied with his clothes and life before. Well, maybe not satisfied, but he'd been doing okay and certainly better than many. Now, when he looked at his things, he saw the poor workmanship. The battered, worn leather of his boots and the worn-out soles. His entire room would fit in Umbra's bathroom, and his bed didn't feel like sleeping on a cloud. His floor wasn't warm beneath his feet.

He wanted to go back, but at the same time he knew what he'd be going back to. Without a job, he was going to be scratching and whoring to get by. Maybe that's all he was good for. He fell into it so easily. Even here.

He flung open the balcony door and breathed in the sweet, warm air. The rolling ink dark hills stretched as far as he could see, and the orange sun burned in the deep blue sky. He'd even grown used to this endless never-night never-day.

While he couldn't see who was on the balcony next door, he could see the railing, and if he leaned all the way out, he could glimpse similar furniture. That was Vermillion's balcony. Their chambers were next door because they were supposed to be Umbra's mate. Elliot grinned. They could still be mates, there'd just be no babies.

He went back in and grabbed the bloodied bed sheet from the pile of laundry on the floor. Whoever came in to clean up when Umbra finally allowed it was going to have a lot of washing to do. That Umbra had so many clothes was a boon. Elliot would've already run out. Umbra's wardrobe could dress them both for another sennight at least.

Carefully, he tied the sheet to the railing. He tried not to look down or think about what would happen if he slipped or the knot unraveled. The fall would kill him. Umbra's plans would unravel, and Dayne would be trapped. Falling wasn't an option.

Sweat beaded on his back. All he had to do was climb over the railing, jump, and grab the other balcony. He ran back inside and tied a pair of trousers around his waist, then tied the diagonal corner of the bed sheet to the trousers, paying close attention to his knots. If he missed, he'd have to climb back up and try again...or dangle there like a worm on a hook until Umbra got back and gave him a bollocking for not staying put.

It was the getting back once he was over that was more concerning, but he'd figure it out when it became a problem.

He checked his knots again and tugged on his makeshift rope. Nothing slid. This was as safe as it was going to get.

Elliot shook out his hands, then carefully climbed over the railing. He turned so his back was to the railing and his heels balanced on the lip. It wasn't that far to jump. He drew in a breath, but his lungs were tight, and his pulse was beating loud in his ears. If he didn't do it soon, he'd lose his nerve.

He wanted to look down, to see how far he'd fall if his knots unraveled. He forced his gaze up, to the green roof reaching for the sky, then carefully lowered it to the opposite balcony.

Vermillion had ridden out.

He could see his brother for the first time in over a month.

All he had to do was jump.

The moment of being weightless was sickening. Then, he was falling. His fingers caught the edge of Vermillion's balcony, the stone smooth. He hung there for a several heartbeats then carefully shifted his grip, one hand at a time until he held the railing posts. His legs dangled, and he hoped no one was walking beneath and looking up.

He swung one leg up and hooked the toe of his boot into the railing, then pulled himself up to standing. A smile split his face. He'd done it. He almost fell over the railing in relief. Then he untied the pants that were around his waist and knotted them to the railing so he could swing home. He checked he still carried the knife. It was there, a cool comforting presence.

The curtains were mostly drawn so he crept over and peeked in.

The bedroom was grander than Umbra's. The bed was bigger, and there were art and weapons on the wall. He was about to give up, thinking the room was empty, when he saw movement near the bed. A chain snaked over the floor...toward Dayne.

Elliot couldn't breathe.

He wanted to knock on the glass to get Dayne's attention, but he wasn't sure his brother was alone. It killed him to wait. Those precious moments slipped by as he watched the room. Dayne sat on the floor, eyes closed as though he were already dead. He had no games or books within reach. Elliot's heart broke.

After what felt like forever without seeing anyone, Elliot risked making a small sound on the glass, the softest tap. He held his breath.

Dayne opened his eyes and lifted his head. He looked around, then his gaze settled on Elliot. Elliot pressed his palms to the door and grinned. Dayne stared, and eventually a smile formed. He crawled toward the door, but the chain yanked on his neck before he even got close.

No guards came running.

Elliot tried the door handle. Locked. If it was like Umbra's, it was a simple catch. He drew the knife and slid it between the frames of the glass panels. He'd break the bloody glass if he had to.

No. Today was a sneaky visit. No one needed to know.

He jiggled the blade until the latch lifted, and he got the door open. Metallic, hot air, like the workshop after soldering spilled out.

Dayne opened his mouth, but Elliot put his finger to his lips. He moved quietly over the floor to his brother and held him close. Until that moment, Elliot hadn't believed. Dayne returned the embrace after several heartbeats.

"You shouldn't be here." Dayne's voice was rough from lack of use.

"I came for you." He didn't want to leave him, now that he had him.

"I'm gone."

"You're here." Elliot drew back to take in his brother and the shadow he'd become. His eyes were hot, and tears slid down his cheeks. He hugged Dayne again. "I'm sorry." He should've taken better care of his brother, the way he'd promised. "Why are you chained?"

"I'm a pet."

So was he, but Umbra didn't make him sleep on the floor. "Are you okay?"

Silver gleamed along his brother's neck, his veins highlighted the same way Elliot's were starting to shine.

Dayne stared at him. "Why are you here?"

"To get you. I have a plan." He smiled. Why wasn't his brother more excited?

"No one escapes."

"I made a deal." This man didn't have the spark Dayne had once had. "We'll get you home, and it will be fine. I kept your job open and—"

"I'm devoured."

"I know. But we can work it out." An awful thought stabbed him through the heart. "Do you want to stay...like this? What do you do all day?"

Dayne looked away. "Not like this. I thought I'd die here. I don't want you to die, too. Leave while you can."

"I can't. When I leave, you're coming with me. We can do this." He gripped his brother's hand, but there was no fight left. Dayne had been kicked too many times to have hope.

Dayne touched the silver mark on Elliot's neck. "You should've left me for dead."

"I'm not devoured. Just selling my blood." He shrugged as though it were nothing. It wasn't really, and it was less hassle than anything else he'd sold.

Dayne shook his head. "They're dangerous."

"I know." He'd seen the furious side of Umbra and was risking it again. "I should've come sooner. I'm sorry it took me so long."

His brother looked like he might cry for a moment. "I like it when they bite, and I like their blood. I'm broken."

Elliot's throat swelled so all he could do was nod. "Do you sit by yourself all night?"

Dayne shook his head. "No, usually I am with them. I'm kept by the leader. Vermillion."

"I know. But I can get you out."

"Now?"

Elliot shook his head, and the silence settled. He couldn't leave when he'd only just arrived. But every moment he stayed was risking discovery.

"Can you play ossic?" Dayne asked.

One game wouldn't matter. "Yes."

"I've never played, only watched."

The chain was too short for Dayne to sit on the chairs, so they sat on the floor with the board between them. A spark flickered in Dayne's eye's as he moved his pieces, and he won with a grin.

"Can we play again?" Dayne asked, and for a few moments they were kids again, and Dayne was begging him to play some more instead of letting Elliot go off to play with his own friends. This time, he didn't mind.

"Sure. But last one for today." He didn't want Dayne to think he'd been forgotten.

Dayne smiled, a fragile thing as though he'd forgotten how. "Are you the spy Ver's been talking about?"

"I'm not a spy." But Dayne could be. He must hear a lot of what Vermillion said. "What else does he talk about? I know there are some Kin here he doesn't like. There are more humans here than I thought, too."

"They couldn't run the castle without us...but they fear us." Dayne moved his piece on the board. "One Kin told me to stop drinking Ver's blood. I tried. The hunger eats me from the inside."

Elliot bit the inside of his lip and stared at the board. "It'll be okay."

Dayne nodded. "When can we leave?"

"A fortnight." A little longer than that in truth. "I'll be coming to the main hall soon, so I'll be able to see you more. You aren't on your own." He reached over and touched his brother's hand.

"When they took me, I thought I'd never see you again."

"What were you doing when you were taken?"

"Just out." Dayne shrugged, but Elliot didn't believe him, Dayne was venerie, but had he been caught by the marshals and handed over, or had he been fighting the Kin when taken? "How did you end up here?"

"I met a Kin and made a deal. Same as always, really." Elliot smiled even though he didn't feel like it. His brother was half missing. Where was the laughter? "Do you need anything?"

Dayne glanced around. "No. I have food and such."

But he was still wearing his old clothes. Vermillion hadn't dressed him. "Why doesn't he let you look at the books or play the games?"

"I haven't asked."

Elliot studied Dayne's face. He had a patchy beard, but seemed clean and well fed. "Does he hurt you?"

Dayne blinked. "Only if I don't behave. I try to behave." His eyes widened. "You should go." He shoved the board away and pieces scattered, clattering over the floor.

Elliot gathered the pieces to put the game away, but they both froze when the door between the bedroom and outer chamber opened. A human man entered, and his gaze fixed on Elliot.

"You." He drew a knife. "What are you doing in here?"

Dayne hid behind the bed, cowering with his hands over his head.

"Visiting a friend." Elliot remained crouching, the wooden game board in one hand and some loose pieces in the other.

The man approached, knife held too comfortably in one hand while he beckoned with the other. "Come with me."

Not a chance. "I can get myself back to my chambers."

"You won't be going there. Vermillion has been waiting to talk to you." As he stepped closer, Elliot threw the pieces. The man slipped, and Elliot sprinted to the glass door.

Pain burst in his calf and he stumbled, his hands hitting the floor. The man was getting up. Elliot pulled the knife out of his leg.

Dayne watched wide eyed.

A second guard came at him. Elliot kept the knife in his hand as he got up. He let the other man attack first, then defended in hard slashes the way Umbra had taught him. It was hard to dance in and out of range when his leg throbbed, and blood made his sock squish.

He ducked and grabbed the wooden board, then swung it up at the man's face. It connected with a crunch, and he dropped like a stone. Elliot backed toward the glass door, his gaze on the other guard.

The guard moved toward the outer chamber.

"He'll get help," Dayne whispered.

Blood and bother. Elliot went after the guard. He had to stop him from reaching the door and calling for help. The guard turned before Elliot could smack him over the head with the board, so he used it as a shield, catching the blade, but the strike forced it from his hand.

Elliot put a chair between them, and the man kicked it over. He needed to stop this man, but the man anticipated every move he made. Inner thigh, throat…but that would kill him, and he didn't want to kill a human. Vermillion would kill him. His calf burned.

"Sit and we can talk," the guard said.

"You want to hand me over." Elliot slashed and caught the man's arm.

Was the door unlocked? There was a key hanging next to it, but he wouldn't have time to unlock doors. Even if he fled out the door, Umbra's chambers would be locked, and he didn't know any good hiding places in the castle. He needed to drop the man and get across the balcony.

The man wanted this over too. He slashed, then charged, knocking Elliot off his feet. He hit the ground hard, but was already twisting away, dodging the swipe of the knife. He stabbed his blade into the man's buttock. He screamed, and Elliot rolled away. The man followed, and his blade bit into Elliot's stomach. For a moment, Elliot couldn't do anything. He forgot how to breathe as hot pain filled him.

The man yanked his knife out. "Got you."

Elliot slashed the man's groin. His pants turned crimson, and his smile faded as he fell.

Breathing hard, Elliot stood. Blood spilled between his fingers, and he staggered back to the bedroom. "Where's the nectar?"

Dayne's eyes widened. "There's none."

He wasn't going to be able to make the jump while holding his guts in.

"Are you dying?"

"It's not all my blood." It was mostly. "I'll be fine. I'll go out the door."

He stepped back.

"Ver's going to be mad at me."

"Blame me. I'm sorry." He leaned against the doorframe. He needed nectar. Then he needed to fix this. He didn't know how to make this right. Umbra was going to chain him to the bloody bed after this. But he couldn't think that far ahead when his fingers were touching his slippery insides.

Elliot stumbled through the outer chamber and grabbed the key from by the door. When he tried the handle to Vermillion's chambers, it opened. No one was outside, so he limped to Umbra's door. Locked.

He cursed Umbra for being so cautious.

He tried the key, and it fit. Perhaps they all had the same lock on the outer door. The door clicked open.

"Elliot!" his brother screamed.

He turned to see the first guard coming out of Vermillion's door. "You little shit."

Elliot shoved open the door, then slammed it closed behind him. The key was still in the lock on the other side. He dragged a chair over as the man started trying to get in. *Shit.* The nectar was in the bedroom, and the bedroom door was locked. His shirt was stained red; blood dripped on the floor with every beat of his heart. He'd be dead before Umbra returned.

He was breathing too fast as panic and fear danced.

He needed to get the bedroom open, and it wouldn't be as easy as opening the glass door. He dragged another chair over. The man called for help. Kin would come.

He slid the knife into the gap but couldn't get the lock to shift. He tried putting the blade into the lock, but it was too big. In desperation, with his sticky bloody hands, he twisted off the hilt and tried the thin piece of antler.

The chairs moved as the guards shoved.

Panic made his heart beat faster, spilling more of his blood on the floor. He needed something smaller. He glanced wildly around until he saw the buckle on his boot. He cut the leather and pressed the tongue of the buckle into the lock. It caught something but didn't budge. "Come on."

He yanked on the tongue, so it came off in his hand, then he fed that slip of metal into the lock and jiggled it one way and then the other.

The chairs squealed as they slid over the floor.

The lock clicked, and Elliot stumbled through. He slammed the door and locked it, then shoved a chair against it for good measure. He grabbed the nectar and took two swallows before pouring the rest on his stomach and calf. Then he collapsed in the chair, well aware that he was bleeding everywhere when it should be stopping.

CHAPTER 20

*U*mbra stood with Lapis and Weld behind Vermillion, less of an honor guard and more of an actual guard in case the humans decided to attack rather than negotiate. Across the desk was the human in charge and three of his green coated marshals. The lord of the city always insisted they meet like this, as if the desk would somehow protect him. It wouldn't, but the ride through the city was perilous. Umbra could taste the anger on the air.

It wasn't only the ridiculous pomp that grated today. Today, they noticed the clothing, the human's boots and coats and the building they met in. These were the people who traded for nectar but didn't share it with those in need the way they should. If they weren't treating the ill, what were they doing with all the nectar?

Umbra wanted to interrupt and ask, but Vermillion was seething and giving the lord a lecture. Vermillion was like a child discovering that the world wasn't fair for the first time. It was clear Vermillion had planned how this meeting would go, and they wanted something very specific.

Was Vermillion hoping the humans would declare war?

It would be over before they left the room. Four humans, even with poisoned blood, would not be able to take on four Abyr. How many marshals waited beyond the door?

Umbra blinked, realizing Vermillion had stopped talking. The humans looked unimpressed. The man opposite fiddled with the cuffs of his shirt and coat—neither of which were frayed. "We will ensure that you have more offerings and that they are prepared so you do not need to wait for the poison to leave their blood."

Vermillion slapped their hand on the table. "We do not want to be fed. We have pets for that. We like to hunt, and the Dark City is poisoned."

The man nodded his head, and the small bald spot in the center gleamed in the red light. Who was he to trade away the lives of others? "We will try to ensure there are more—"

"You will do better than try. You will get half the nectar and orbs until such a time as the problem is fixed." Vermillion stood.

They didn't need to hunt. They didn't need that much blood. They weren't changing an entire army because there was a war on their doorstep. Were they? The battle tales that Vermillion liked to listen to were of the blood-soaked days when the humans invaded and took nectar and slaughtered the unchanged. Humans had never reached the forest of old ones…but what if they had and all that knowledge had been lost? Would they have burned them where they lay, helpless to fight because their antlers had become the size of trees?

In the old tales, the changed went from being outcasts to being saviors. They suppressed a shudder. Vermillion was no hero leading the first army of the changed.

The human man stood. "I'm sure we can reach an agreement."

Vermillion turned, a smile on his lips. They'd gotten what they wanted. It had never been about negotiating, only about telling them their supply was getting cut and making it appear it was their own fault.

Umbra followed Vermillion out to where the beasts were parked and the other Abyr waited with the load to be traded. "Give them half."

Without question, half was unloaded.

The lord lingered in the doorway as though hoping it would offer protection, but the Abyr had been invited in once and that was enough.

"You'll get more offerings next time. Double," the lord whined.

Umbra flexed their fingers, resisting the urge to stomp over and snap his neck. He was offering up people when he had no right. They were criminals, but if what Elliot said were true and their only crime was being poor?

Vermillion ran a hand down Umbra's back, mistaking their annoyance. "Patience. We will have our battle, but not tonight."

Umbra nodded and kept their revulsion, at the touch and the idea of battle, hidden. It was a relief when they rode away through the dark streets toward the shore and home. Not all the night had been wasted. They'd be able to spend some with Elliot.

Vermillion rode beside them. "You should collect your pet. You need more blood."

Umbra didn't glance over. "I already have."

They felt Vermillion's shock rather than saw. "You must introduce us. They must be seen in the hall."

"I didn't want to change in the first place, and I had no desire to do so in public with everyone watching. I feel that maybe it is time, though." They tilted their head as though conceding even though they had decided already.

Elliot wasn't a tamed pet, and Umbra doubted he could play the part. He had too much mischief in his eyes, too much fight in his heart. Thinking about him made Umbra's pants uncomfortable in a way that wouldn't have been a problem a sennight ago.

Vermillion's gaze was still on them, their beast staying true on the road that lead through the dark part of the city. No hunting tonight, for which they were glad.

And no stopping to speak with the hopeful that waited on the shore. Devoured, according to Elliot. They'd been bitten and tamed with Abyr blood, then discarded. Honestly, Umbra was surprised any were returned when Vermillion had such a thirst for death.

They rode over the causeway, the water still and dotted with stars.

No leviathan had drifted too close to the castle and waited too long before heading out to sea. The mist that clung to the castle became the walls as they drew closer. They glanced back, but the shore was wreathed in fog, and they couldn't see the bonfires of the humans that waited for one more taste of Abyr blood.

They shuddered.

This wasn't a peacetime castle, maintaining trade with the humans like Octadine. This was a castle preparing for war. Stoking the flames until there was a reason to strike the first blow. Umbra was almost on the side of the humans. War was brutal, and they didn't want the lake stained red; it would attract too many leviathans and that was never a pretty sight.

A human servant ran toward Vermillion before the beasts had even been stabled. Vermillion listened, and their gaze landed on Umbra.

Their stomach sank. What had Elliot done? Could he not be trusted for even one night? They liked the fight, but they wanted trust. They needed someone on their side, and if Elliot kept throwing them at Vermillion's feet, he was an enemy not an ally.

Vermillion got off the beast, leaving it for another to tend. Umbra's beast came to a stop, and the others went past, casting glances over their shoulders, wanting to know what the drama was but not wanting to be close enough to catch any spatter.

Vermillion put their hand on Umbra's thigh. "You have a *rat* in your chambers."

"I have a *pet* in my chambers." They got off the beast and stood toe to toe with Vermillion. Had Vermillion's guards broken in while they were out? "I do hope my rooms have not been invaded."

Vermillion glared at them, and their lip twitched. "Upstairs. Now."

Well, that was where Umbra wanted to be anyway. They had visions of Elliot captured and hurt. Vermillion thought him the rat—which he was in that he was the unknown human in the castle—but he'd done nothing wrong. Nothing that would warrant Vermillion killing him.

"My pet is allowed to wander."

They strode after Vermillion. Through the hall and up the stairs.

"Only after they are known. You have kept them hidden." Vermillion stopped on the stairs above Umbra. "Tell me the truth this time, *mate*. Is your pet male?"

Their heartbeat quickened. "He is."

Vermillion came closer. "I will starve you of blood and make you start over. Do you have any idea how babies are made among the changed?"

"You will not starve me. No one can be forced to change." Umbra put a hand on Vermillion's shoulder. "We're siblings now. We share blood."

It disgusted Umbra; Vermillion didn't deserve the honor of having the same blood as them.

Vermillion's eyes narrowed, then he slammed his forehead into Umbra's. Umbra stumbled down a couple of stairs, recovered, and then gave chase, needing to reach their chambers first. Vermillion moved quickly but they stopped short on the walkway.

Umbra reached the top step and stared. There was blood, dark human blood, on Vermillion's door, on the wall and the floor, and all over Umbra's door—which was hanging open. Several guards, human and Abyr, waited inside. While in theory anyone could enter the outer chamber, in practice, it was usually invitation only, and plenty of Abyr kept their chambers shut.

They'd locked this door when they'd left.

"Who opened my door?"

"The rat took the key from…" The guard glanced at Vermillion and stopped talking as Vermillion strode over.

"You had a key to my chamber?" Umbra would deal with that invasion of privacy later. They touched a sticky smear of blood on the door and brought it to their lips. Elliot's blood. It was all Elliot's blood.

Vermillion finished talking to the human guard and smiled. "My pet is unharmed, fortunately."

"Of course he is. They're brothers. This wasn't an attack," Umbra snapped. They tried to open the door to the bedroom, but it was locked. There was a puddle of blood by the door, bloodied footsteps.

Elliot had run from the outer chamber door to the inner, dragging the chairs and bleeding everywhere. So much blood. They didn't want to start imaging Elliot dead, but it was there in a hundred different variations, cutting at their heart. "Or at least it wasn't an attack on your pet."

"Your pet killed one of my guards," Vermillion snarled.

Your guards may have killed my pet. Umbra closed their eyes for a moment and listened. If Elliot was alive, they should be able to hear his heart. After several breaths, they heard it. Faint but there. The fear and tension eased enough for them to think. They pulled the tiny key for the bedroom from their pocket and unlocked the door. The door wouldn't open. Something was blocking it. Elliot's body? They shoved, and the door moved a little.

Vermillion put their hand on the door and whispered in Umbra's ear. "Your pet broke into my chambers, was in my bedroom. There are penalties."

Umbra lifted their gaze, their hands sticky with Elliot's blood, their heart desperate to get inside. "And your guards attacked a pet. There are penalties they will have to pay. If my pet is dead, I will demand satisfaction."

"If he is dead, you will fast."

"I will not. If you want a child so bad, you fast and carry it. That is what castle leaders do." Umbra gave the door a shove, widening the gap.

Vermillion stepped back. "Tend your pet, and if they live, present them in the hall, so we no longer mistake them for a rat." They took all but two of the human guards with them and spoke to others on the walkway. There would be Abyr posted at the door to their chambers. It wasn't Elliot who had to present to the hall, but them.

They shoved hard, widening the gap enough that they could slip through. The human guard went to follow them in.

Umbra put a hand on his chest. "You're not invited in."

"I have to view the rat...pet."

"You can wait there." They shut and locked the door.

For several heartbeats, they didn't move, just pressed their back to the door and breathed as they surveyed the room. There'd been no fight in here despite the blood on the floor and the shattered goblet. Elliot was alive, for the moment, passed out on the chair.

The glass door to the balcony was open. Umbra strode over and was about to shut it, but they saw the sheet tied to the railing, and the way it was tied to Vermillion's balcony. They leaned out but couldn't see anyone. That was part of the design, but the illusion of privacy had been ruptured.

They couldn't fault Elliot's bravery; the fall would've been fatal. The need to see his brother must have been all consuming.

Umbra sighed. Now there was all kinds of trouble simmering. Vermillion wouldn't let this pass. Too many had seen the evidence, and word travelled faster than flies to a corpse.

With a muttered curse, Umbra went back in and shut the door.

Elliot hadn't moved.

There was no nectar in the room. He'd used it all. If there'd been none to drink, he'd no doubt be dead. The night was still young, and death was still a possibility.

They clenched their fists as fury burned hot and bright. One more night...

"Fuck your impatience." Umbra leaned close, antlers bracketing Elliot's face, torn between shaking him awake and not wanting any freshly healed wounds to tear open. "You fucking lied to me again." They closed their eyes and clenched their teeth.

No other Abyr would tolerate such behavior from a pet, but Elliot wasn't truly a pet and wasn't bound by blood. Had they made a mistake? The cold fury in Vermillion's eyes had been clear. They wanted to starve Umbra and force feed them female blood.

Their status as mate or guest could be revoked. Worse, if it was determined Elliot had broken into Vermillion's private chambers, there could be compensation to be given.

"Fuck." They drew back and sat on the table.

Elliot lay there as though he were dead. He'd be less trouble if he were dead.

Someone knocked on the door.

"Fuck off."

"You are to bring your pet to the hall."

"What, now?"

There was more than one person in their outer chamber, and they were talking too softly for Umbra to make out the words.

"Umbra, *mate* of Vermillion." Lapis said. "A trial is being convened."

"A stay until tomorrow." They needed time to think and for Elliot to wake.

"It will be dealt with before sunrise. Do not waste our time." Clipped footsteps faded.

"Fuck." This time it was a whisper. They opened the door, startling the human guard. "Fetch me nectar, and I will be ready sooner."

"I can't leave."

"Then call for someone. I don't care how you get it." They shut the door harder than needed, and Elliot's eyelids flickered. The edge of danger pressed firmly to Umbra's throat. They needed time to plan.

There was no way Elliot was being presented in the hall looking like he'd been in a fight and should be dead. Umbra stalked into the bathroom and turned the knob. Hot water poured into the bath, they tossed in the soap, then went back to Elliot and scooped him up, boots and all. He was trying to wake. Umbra was tempted to drop him into the filling bath, but didn't want to make the damage worse, so they stepped in. In their boots and pants.

They put Elliot down and then shrugged out of their coat—not wanting to ruin everything they were wearing—and tossed it out the door. They stripped off Elliot's blood-soaked shirt and dropped it on the floor. His stomach was smeared with blood. What had happened. They grabbed the sponge and started cleaning off the blood, trying to determine the extent of the damage. Was he still ripped open on the inside?

How much nectar had been in the goblet? They couldn't remember.

Elliot batted at their hands, his eyes still not open. They'd seen more ferocious new-born kittens.

The water in the bath turned pink. Was there another wound?

They grabbed Elliot's face, the stubble rough on their fingertips and not at all unpleasant. "Wake up."

When that failed, Umbra splashed water in Elliot's face. That got more of a response. A grunt, and his eyes flickered open as though he were struggling to wake. He'd be struggling to breathe if Vermillion had their way.

Someone hammered on the bedroom door.

They tapped Elliot's face with a wet hand, then tapped him a little harder. His eyes opened that time. And his expression went from confusion to panic in less than a heartbeat.

Umbra grasped Elliot's jaw. "You are going to do exactly as I say, or we will both be in the lake come dawn. You don't want to see how a leviathan eats up close. They have tiny little mouths with beaks. I'm told it takes a hundred bites to die."

Vermillion might do it in ninety-nine.

CHAPTER 21

Umbra released him and got out of the bath. Elliot's head fell back against the stone base. Water lapped around his ears. Every breath felt like something was tearing inside of him, and Elliot really didn't want to explain what had happened. He'd hoped he'd have time to clean up before Umbra returned. Come up with a convincing reason.

He didn't have even have half a reason, and from the way Umbra's eyes glittered, pink and furious, he was about two words away from being thrown up against the nearest wall. He really didn't have the strength to fight.

Umbra stalked back into the bathroom. They hauled Elliot up, so he was sitting instead of in danger of drowning. "Drink."

Elliot didn't argue. The sweetness of the nectar was welcome and sated a bone deep thirst. He stopped after half, but Umbra tipped the glass so he had to finish.

"Clean yourself up. Vermillion has ordered a trial." Umbra put the goblet next to the sink, and Elliot struggled to get up out of the bath. Why was he in the bath in his clothes, and boots? Umbra put a hand on his shoulder, forcing him to sit. "I don't even want to look at you at the moment."

When they stepped away, their fingerprints remained on his skin.

"Why the fuck did you go into Vermillion's rooms?"

Elliot opened his mouth.

"Don't even bother. I don't want your excuses." They paced away, then turned. "Your words mean nothing when you say one thing and do another."

The air around Umbra seemed to crackle. Elliot couldn't take his eyes off them; it wasn't safe.

"Get cleaned up. We don't have time to waste, and I have to think. Your inability to follow even the simplest of instructions has put everything in danger."

"I was coming back. No one was meant to know."

Umbra glared at him. They dropped to their knees next to the bath. "That doesn't make it right. Your brother would have told of his visitor. Vermillion can control him, force the truth from him."

"I wanted to see him."

"And you were going to."

"I needed to be sure you were telling the truth."

Umbra looked away, disgust hardening their features. "Unlike you, I stand by my word." They reached over the bath and pulled off Elliot's boots. "We don't have time for this."

"Why?"

"The trial. We need to get to the hall, so it doesn't happen in our absence—no chance to defend ourselves then."

"What did you do wrong?"

"I didn't introduce my pet, I failed to control a pet...and that pet broke into Vermillion's chambers."

"You knew he wasn't going to approve of me." This trouble had been coming from the moment they'd made the deal.

"I did, but this is not on me. You made this mess. Vermillion not liking you and my choice of change is very different to invading the private chambers of a leader. Get your pants off." Umbra tugged at his clothing.

Elliot's skin tingled, like it wanted to peel off. The room was sharp at the edges, and the lights were too bright. He squinted and scratched at his arm. "I don't feel so good."

"Too much nectar." Umbra threaded their fingers into his hair.

"No." Elliot turned away, not wanting Umbra to bite while they were in a mood.

Umbra released him. "Fine, see what happens."

"What will happen?" He scratched harder until blood welled, but it wasn't enough. "You made me drink it all."

"Because I didn't know how wounded you were. I didn't want you to die before I had the chance to kill you. Vermillion would like a chance, too."

"What?" Elliot tried to scramble away but his coordination was gone.

"If you weren't so injured, I would've tossed you a knife. Practice can hurt when nectar can heal the wounds. I stained many a floor with my blood when training."

His nails were hurting, turning red. He thrust his arm toward Umbra. Umbra didn't need a second invitation.

Their teeth sank into Elliot's arm, and the relief was almost instantaneous. With every swallow, the tightness faded. They drank deeply, more than usual. Elliot groaned as pleasure tingled through every nerve. Umbra lifted their gaze, and for a few breaths, the anger was replaced with something much more terrifying: desire.

Elliot wanted to revel in it, see where it led. With their gazes locked, Umbra sucked and swallowed, and Elliot became dizzy with desire. His body ached even though his wounds were healed.

Umbra gave his wrist a final lick, then stood in one smooth motion. "Finish washing. I'll find you something to wear."

"What will happen?" He shut off the water and shucked off his sodden pants. His stomach wound was healed, as was his leg. It was hard to believe he'd been injured, but he remembered the pain and the blood. The bite mark on his wrist healed as he watched. His nail beds were still dark. His dick was still hard. He'd love to blame that on the nectar.

Umbra returned with clothes. Their gaze dropped before slowly lifting to Elliot's face. "I either hand you over, surrender you to Vermillion for them to deal with or keep, as they see fit, or I have to fight and prove that I can be trusted to keep a pet. One more incident, and this will be over."

Elliot took the cloth, but the soft fabric did nothing to hide the jut of his dick. "What will you do?"

"I don't know."

"Well, you've gotten what you wanted…" He dried not caring if Umbra watched with half hidden glances.

"Why should I keep my word when you break yours? I have tried to protect you. I have warned you. But you don't care about me. All you want is your brother, and you only think one step ahead, not three or five or more."

"I can't think that far ahead. I've always had to get through one day and then the next. I don't know how to plan two days or a sennight ahead." But he'd paid the rent before he left. That had been a kind of plan. Coming here was a kind of a plan.

"Then you have to learn, or you won't last the rest of the month. You have compromised my position and while I am still a guest, I have brought trouble to the castle. I'm no longer a potential mate. At best, I'm now Vermillion's blood sibling. Trust me, the Abyr sibling bond is not as strong as yours."

"I don't want to be Vermillion's. My brother…" Elliot didn't know how to describe it, and when he tried, the words caught in his throat and made it ache. "He isn't himself."

"I told you, he's been tamed with blood. He's still your brother, but he wants to please his Abyr." Umbra unfolded a cream shirt and held it out. "I doubt Vermillion treats their pets with kindness."

Elliot took the shirt and pulled it on, his dick softening far too slowly when Umbra was so close. "He was chained to the bed. I wanted to free him and leave." He didn't want to be chained up like that. He'd fight and break antlers before that happened. "He wasn't allowed to play ossic or look at books. I sat with him a bit. That's all."

"You're too kind. You let one guard live instead of killing them

174

both. We'll have to train until there's blood on the floor. Pants on; I've seen enough of your stem and pods."

Elliot snatched the pants. "I've got no shoes."

"I don't care. You won't need shoes because you won't be going anywhere, will you?" Umbra laughed. "I don't know why I bother asking. You'll lie to my face."

He walked out of the bathroom without waiting for an answer.

Somehow that was worse. Elliot wasn't even worth the fight or the argument.

His shoulders slumped. Umbra was giving up on him.

He pulled on the pants. He had to prove he was worth something, that his life had value. He ran after Umbra and dropped to his knees in front of them. He reached up to clasp Umbra's hand.

"Please. Don't give me up." If Umbra let him go, he'd have no chance of getting Dayne back or getting home. That was all he was here for. That's what he was doing wrong. He was only thinking of himself and his brother the way he had for so long. "I'll do as you say. What do you need me to do?"

"I don't know. I may not even get a choice. Maybe I should've done what was expected. Served out the year and day and then gone home." They grimaced as though they'd eaten rancid meat.

Elliot knew how to choke that down, but Umbra didn't. They were prime and used to being obeyed, having power. Here they had none.

Umbra ruffled their fingers through Elliot's hair. "How do you do what needs to be done when you know it could destroy you?"

"Because if I don't, everyone I have ever loved will die. My father vanished. My mother died of the Dark City cough. My brother…" He swallowed hard.

Nothing he did ever worked. Everyone left. All he did was keep flinging himself at the wall hoping that something would change. A door would open or something.

He rested his head against Umbra's leg, their fingers were still threaded through his hair. "It's nice not to work, to worry about my next meal or if there's enough wood for a fire. I'm not sad I came."

And if he died, then he'd tried, and like so many others born in the dark, his fate ended with the Kin. Maybe that was all he was good for, food. Did the cattle in the field know that they'd be eaten and make the most of everyday? He hadn't even done that. He'd been too busy surviving.

"But you're not ready to die?"

Elliot glanced up. "Are you?"

"No. But until we get down there, I don't know what plan to use."

"But you have plans?"

"I always have plans. That doesn't make them good or guarantee they'll get used. Behave like this down there, and we might have a chance."

Elliot frowned and sat back on his heels. "When you arrived, did you plan on being Vermillion's mate?"

"No." They pulled a clean shirt and waistcoat out of the wardrobe. "I thought about fleeing, but Vermillion wouldn't have been as forgiving as my sire, and there are things worse than death. It took me a few nights to understand who was in favor and who obeyed out of fear." They stripped off their old clothes and pulled on the clean ones. "Then I started resisting. I'd have been quite happy staying in Octadine, learning more of the old songs and practicing my fighting. My parents had other plans."

"What plans do you have now?"

Umbra smiled, all teeth and sly like a fox. "I cannot say in case I lose you tonight and Vermillion forces you to tell all our tales." They tossed a waistcoat to Elliot. "I want you dressed properly."

"Why?"

"Because no one else bothers here. At home, a well-dressed pet was expected."

Elliot put the waistcoat on, but it didn't do up. He didn't have Umbra's lithe lean body. He got to his feet. "Am I well-dressed even though I'm wearing your sleep pants?"

Umbra considered him for a moment. "None of my pants fit you?"

He shrugged, but he knew. He'd tried on everything.

"Yes or no, Elliot. I know you were in my wardrobe."

"No."

"I figured. They don't fit me so well either anymore. I'll have to summon the tailor from the town. Boots?

"The blue pair are wider and fit me best."

The boots and a pair of socks were handed over, and Elliot put his old pants on with the new boots. Well, new to him, and they looked almost new. The leather wasn't scuffed, and the creases were barely there. He knotted the laces, feeling rather like a fancy gentleman who lived up the hill, even though theirs had buttons. He took a moment to admire the boots on his feet. They were a little snug across the toes, but they'd give. A finger width too long if he were being fussy, but when it came to boots, as long as they kept the water out and didn't crush his toes, he'd always been pretty happy. These were something else. He grinned, not sure he'd be able to wipe it off his mouth.

Umbra knelt and undid the laces, tying them instead in neat bows. "Keep them." They stood and pulled out the leather coat with the orange suns. "This too. It no longer fits."

"What?"

"My shoulders."

Elliot stared at him. "I hadn't noticed."

Umbra inclined their head and smiled. "That's very polite of you."

No, he really hadn't noticed. "Do the Kin pretend there's no change or something?"

Umbra shook their head. "Most announce when they start and celebrate with new clothes. New clothes are never a bad thing, but I wish the reason were better."

Elliot slipped on the coat. While the waistcoat had been made for Umbra's body, the long coat wasn't as tight and did up, almost hiding his scruffy pants beneath.

Umbra put on a coat with green embossed butterflies that trailed up one arm before splitting and spinning down their chest and back, re-meeting on the opposite side. They checked their knife was at their hip and then shut the wardrobe door. "Ready?"

Elliot bit his lip. He felt silly wearing these clothes. "I'm over-dressed."

"I'm not having my pet look like I can't afford to dress him."

"Vermillion won't be happy."

"He's not happy anyway. What's one more cut? Besides, I have a reputation to maintain. They need to be reminded that I am not some low-level warrior fresh from the heartland."

As much as Umbra didn't want to be a warrior or change, they certainly liked the status it brought.

Elliot followed Umbra out of the chambers. Umbra stopped to order a guard to send up a cleaner before leading them down the sweeping stairs to the hall. Elliot didn't have time to admire the delicate arrangement of orbs hanging from the ceiling or the intricate carvings on the walls. Instead, his gaze was on the long table filled with Kin, their hair a rainbow of colors, their clothes a mix of leather and cloth. Some plain brown, others bright, but few seemed as well dressed as Umbra. Their clothing rivaled Vermillion's.

It wasn't just the clothing. Many wore their hair loose or had a single braid. Umbra had many. Elliot had watched them neatly braid and entwine them even though they couldn't see the back of their own head. Only Umbra had one side shaved, and today it was mostly hidden.

This was a display of some kind, and Elliot was part of it. All eyes turned to them, and Elliot carefully kept his eyes on the back of Umbra's heels. He had to behave like a pet. He still didn't know what that meant exactly.

He glanced to where Vermillion sat. Dayne was on the, floor chained to the chair. Alive.

Elliot breathed a little easier, but his heart rattled his ribs, and he could barely swallow.

Umbra sat in the empty seat to Vermillion's left and greeted the leader loudly enough for everyone to hear. "Blood sibling."

Vermillion forced a smile that looked like it hurt. Whispers ran along the table.

Elliot went to sit on the floor at Umbra's feet.

"Stand behind me, pet."

So he stood, where everyone could see him when all he wanted to do was hide. The coat was heavy and hot, and even though he wasn't looking at Vermillion, he could feel the weight of the Kin's stare and the prickle of hate like the tip of a knife running down his back.

Vermillion stood. "As I'm sure you've all noticed, Prime Umbra has taken a male pet. The brother to mine, doing me the *honor* of becoming their sibling in blood." The way they spoke, it was clear they didn't consider it an honor. "Your sire will no doubt be pleased with your choice."

Yeah...Elliot was pretty sure that wasn't going to be the case.

Umbra hadn't moved. They sat like they were made of stone, and Elliot had no idea what expression they were wearing. Boredom? Amusement? It wouldn't be fear. Elliot was struggling to keep it off his face, though. The pressure of his teeth on his lip was the reminder to be calm.

If he'd died this morning instead of drinking the nectar, none of this would be his problem. If he'd decided not to make the jump, this wouldn't be his problem either. He was here for Dayne, and if he didn't stop thinking of only that goal, he'd fail. He lost every game of ossic he played with Umbra because they were so many moves ahead.

What was Umbra planning? He didn't believe Umbra had taken him for no reason other than to annoy Vermillion—though that had worked.

"I have already written." Umbra inclined their head.

Had they? Did they need to? Was Umbra expecting their parents to ride in and do something? Elliot struggled to keep his gaze fixed on Umbra's shoulder blades, but if he was careful, he could watch Vermillion from the corner of his eye.

Vermillion's upper lip twitched. "As much as this is a celebration of my new sibling, it is also a trial. The rat has been found and must now answer for his crimes."

Elliot was grabbed by the arms and pulled away from Umbra. He struggled, but Umbra put up a hand up, and Elliot remembered to obey his Kin and stilled.

"Pets are allowed to wander. They do not have to be chained," Umbra said as though bored of the whole thing.

TJ NICHOLS

"Pets?" Vermillion slapped the table. "You have not introduced him. We still do not know his name."

"Elliot. Though I'm sure you had your pet reveal that." Umbra stood. "My pet did roam the castle."

Vermillion leaned forward. "He roamed while as we slept. While we were in the city, he broke into *my* chambers and killed one of *my* guards. Elliot cannot be trusted as a pet. You cannot deny that."

"No, I don't. He tied the bedsheet to the balcony and jumped across because he was desperate to see his brother." More whispers broke out along the table, and Umbra let them swell before softening. "I do like a pet with a reckless urge."

"He is untamed," Vermillion said. "And a danger to us all. He could break into our chambers while we sleep and kill us."

"He had my permission to go to the kitchens to get food."

Elliot blinked. Umbra knew where he'd been.

"And I confess I did promise him that he'd get to see his brother."

"Your pet's failings reflect poorly on you, Umbra. He wears your clothes and stands. Who has been tamed?" Vermillion laughed.

Some of the other Kin joined in, but some knew that something was going on.

"I confess, I do follow the ways of Octadine, my home. A pet should be well kept, and if one cannot trust a pet, then they should not be kept at all. Chains shouldn't be required. They should want to offer themselves. I couldn't sleep knowing that if my pet got free, they'd choke me with the chain that bound them."

Why did Umbra keep confessing?

None of the Kin laughed now. Those with pets chained at their side glanced at the human sitting on the floor.

"This isn't Octadine," Vermillion snapped.

"I am aware." Umbra appeared to be relaxed as they rested their hands on the back of their chair. "What would you have me do? Ban my pet from going to the kitchen? From seeing his brother?"

When said like that, it seemed ridiculous. Vermillion's lips thinned to a flat line as though they realized that control was sliding away, and they were the ones looking foolish.

"But he didn't just see his brother. He broke into my chambers."

"Yes, and played ossic with your pet until your guards attacked him." Umbra turned to face Vermillion. "Do you really want to continue this in public?"

Vermillion placed their hands on Umbra's chest, but didn't push. "Your pet needs be punished and brought into line. If you won't do it, I will."

"Punished how? What is it that you do here since the ways I am used to are not appropriate?"

"You will surrender him to me for a month." Vermillion smiled.

Umbra shook their head. "The error was mine, not his. I should have asked if they could sit together when we rode out. I will not have my pet pay the price." Umbra glanced at him. Elliot couldn't read his expression and didn't know what he was planning if anything. "You want him chained in public, very well."

Elliot gasped, but Umbra held his gaze as he was pushed to his knees. A collar was placed on his neck, so tight every swallow was constricted. The guard held the end.

"He is tamed." Umbra walked over to claim the end of the chain. "No more going to the kitchen for extra food."

"There's still the matter of my dead guard," Vermillion said.

"I'll give you blood price for him," Umbra said as though money meant nothing. What was a human life worth to the Kin?

"I want blood not coin."

Umbra froze. They didn't move for several heartbeats, then they turned. "We are siblings. We shouldn't fight."

"You should've thought of that before letting your pet run wild. My decision is final. If I win, I will take your pet for a month and teach him manners."

He'd be dead before the month was over. Vermillion would force him to drink their blood. He glanced up at Umbra, but no words formed. Their pink eyebrows were pinched, and worry filled their sunset eyes.

Finally, Umbra spoke. "And if I win?"

Vermillion almost laughed. "If you win, he's yours."

"If I win, I want your pet for a month."

"No."

"If we cannot agree to terms—"

"You don't get to agree, you are at fault. All heard your confession."

The watching Kin nodded.

"I will not give up my pet this early in the change."

"You don't have a choice. Lapis." Vermillion pointed to the two staffs crossed on the wall behind Vermillion's chair, and Lapis took them down. "You confessed to mismanaging your pet. I will remedy that."

The guards dragged Elliot back by the chain. He tried to stand but wasn't allowed so he had to crawl toward the wall, the fine coat dragging on the floor. Umbra was going to lose, and then he'd be Vermillion's. He be chained all the time like his brother with no hope of escape.

He'd rather be dead.

Umbra took off their coat and draped it over their chair, then they rolled up the sleeves of their shirt. They said something to Vermillion who was doing the same. Vermillion put a hand over Umbra's. White bloomed on Umbra's skin from the pressure, yet they didn't flinch. They held Vermillion's gaze, cool and steady.

Elliot had seen them angry, the fury glittering in their eyes. But this was somehow worse. Did they not care? They seemed resigned and reluctant.

He wanted to claw at the collar and take it off, but that would only prove he was untamed. He couldn't go to Vermillion. The guard next to him was wearing a knife. If Umbra lost, Elliot would arm himself and fight to the end.

No, he should be thinking further ahead than the next few minutes. But his heart was beating too fast and too loud and all he could do was watch as Umbra checked the glass tip on both ends of the staff. They spun the deadly stick, tips glinting blood red in the light. They were fluid as they turned, a faint smile on their lips.

As swiftly as they'd started, they stopped, staff horizontal before them.

Vermillion did the same and nodded.

While Elliot knew Umbra was fast—he'd fought with them enough times—he hadn't realized how fast. Umbra had been holding back. The staffs clashed as Vermillion attacked and Umbra retreated. Vermillion almost had them, but Umbra's feet left the ground and they spun over the staff and landed low, striking up and forcing Vermillion back. The smug smile Vermillion had been wearing vanished.

Was Umbra changed enough to match Vermillion?

Vermillion moved quickly, but Umbra was always just out of the way, half a move ahead. Umbra wasn't faster, they were better.

They used the staff to launch up and over, Vermillion striking where Umbra's feet had been and following them up. But Umbra was already on the ground, kneeling. A drop of blood hit the floor next to them.

Elliot held his breath. Whose blood was it?

Umbra held the staff horizontal. Their back lifted with each breath.

Vermillion stood on the table, blood dripping from a scratch on their forearm. Their lips twisted, and for a moment, Elliot thought they were going to retaliate, but they held the staff out.

Umbra had won. That was a win, wasn't it?

Vermillion jumped down from the table. "Well done, sibling. You keep your pet. Just remember where you are."

"I will not forget." Umbra stood and handed the staff to Lapis.

Vermillion turned the staff catching the back of Umbra's hand as they handed it back to Lapis. "Oh, how careless of me. No point in wasting it." They beckoned to Elliot.

No. The guard didn't care. He dragged Elliot over and he couldn't help but resist. Vermillion knew he hadn't been tamed by blood. This had all been a game. Win or lose this had always going to be his fate.

Umbra's face was set in a mask, their smile was there but it was still and didn't reach their eyes. The promise they'd made was just another broken between them. Umbra took the chain out of the guard's hand.

"Taste, pet." Their fingers were in his hair drawing him closer to the bright kin blood he didn't want.

He couldn't refuse, but he couldn't taste it either. Umbra watched him. Elliot lifted his hands to take the offered one. Bright blood dripped over Umbra's fingers. He didn't need to taste it, it only needed to look that way. Elliot smoothed over the cut with his thumb and licked the unmarked skin above, hoping he wouldn't get caught.

Umbra gave him a single nod and pulled their hand away. "Satisfied? Did you think we have unruly pets in Octadine. Our methods are different, but the result is the same."

"When you return to Octadine you may do whatever you like. While you are a guest here, *sibling*, you will obey my rules." Vermillion sat and indicated for Umbra to do the same.

Umbra looked like they'd rather stab Vermillion through the eye, but they arranged their face into something more pleasing. Elliot wanted to return to the safety of their chambers. For days, all he'd wanted to do was leave, but the castle was not the big empty place it had been when he'd explored.

While Umbra kept hold of the chain, they motioned for Elliot to stand behind them as he had before. From his place, he had a clear view of all the Kin. The closer to Vermillion, the more in favor? The Kin called Lapis sat on Vermillion's other side. Many didn't have pets, or at least none that Elliot could see. Human guards stood at the edges. What had they been offered to not kill Vermillion in their sleep?

Had they been ordered to kill Elliot if he was seen wandering?

Food was brought out. Great platters of fruits and cheeses, breads filled with other things, some so warm they steamed, roasted vegetables in piles of color and soaking in sauce. More food than Elliot had seen, even in stores. His stomach grumbled.

The Kin started feasting, and it became clear he wasn't going to be allowed to sample any of it. He almost licked his lips, but he couldn't be sure it wasn't marred by blood. Had he tasted it by accident? Was an accidental drop enough to make him devoured?

In the corner of the hall, more Kin were gathering and setting up drums and instruments he didn't recognize. It was a welcome distraction from the food he couldn't eat. They started to play. The main drum beat solemnly, but then a faster tempo joined, and one of them started to sing in a clear high voice. Before he could grasp the words, a deeper voice joined in, singing what appeared to be a completely different song.

No one else seemed bothered by the apparent disjointedness.

The song went on, and Elliot realized the deeper voice told the events while the higher one sung a chorus of sorts, repeating endlessly. It was hard to focus on the different words and melodies, but he gathered enough to know the humans had invaded and there was a bloody war.

When it ended there was a round of applause, and Vermillion seemed well pleased, pouring more mead for themselves and Umbra. Umbra sipped a little and ate less, tasting bits and pieces before giving up and eventually passing their plate of leftovers to Elliot.

Elliot wouldn't have cared if Umbra had licked everything before handing it to him. He held the plate with his bloodied hand and ate with the clean one. And he ate fast, not knowing when it was going to be taken off him. The vegetables were sweet and the bread soft and fluffy like eating a cloud. His favorite cheese was on the plate out of the six or so that were on the table to choose from. It was almost as if Umbra had made this plate for him. He slowed down. Had they?

The Kin bard sung another song of battle. When it ended, Umbra lifted a hand. "Sing of the old ones."

"Any tale you want to hear?"

Umbra shook their head. "Anything that doesn't end in bloodshed."

Vermillion leaned over. "You do not like songs of glory?"

"Do you want a song made for you?"

"Don't you?"

Umbra sipped their mead as though considering. "It does have an allure."

Vermillion smiled. "We aren't that different. Let us put aside this bitterness and make plans. The bards can sing our song."

Elliot edged a little closer. Umbra passed him the glass of mead, giving him reason to be even nearer. He sipped warily, remembering the incident in the bath as he scanned the table. The Kin had stopped looking at him and Umbra and were having their own conversations. Making their own plans.

This was a game of ossic and they were the pieces. The Kin knew that; Umbra had been trying to show him. Why did it take him so long to understand?

"What kind of plans?" Umbra tilted their head toward Vermillion as though they were friends.

"War is coming."

"Yes, it is." Umbra lifted their hand, and Elliot returned the goblet.

Vermillion watched the interaction. Elliot suppressed a shudder. "Perhaps you would join me in my chambers for a more private game."

"I'd be delighted." Umbra smiled.

Elliot wished he'd fallen to his death. That would've been less painful.

CHAPTER 22

The chain was light in their fingers. Silvery and delicate and Umbra hated it. One shouldn't have a pet if they needed to be restrained all the time. Where was the fun?

Vermillion unlocked their chambers but didn't stop in the outer room. They lead Umbra and Elliot through to their bedroom. Which was the last place Umbra wanted to be. There was no blood on the floor, no sign anything had happened in here. Vermillion hooked the chain to the foot of the bed. Dayne obediently sat, gaze on the floor.

Umbra took a chair at the table and let the chain drop to the floor. They put their boot on the end, a nod to Vermillion's need to be in control. Elliot sat at their feet, tense like he was ready to flee. It was too late for that. The game had shifted, and they had to play to the end. Where force had failed, Vermillion had moved onto coercion. That would fail too as Umbra had seen beneath Vermillion's smile and swagger. Vermillion wanted power, a bloody battle song to sing of their glory.

Vermillion had led a bloody coup, killing all the older Abyr to seize the castle. To be fair, there had also been trouble with the humans— though how much had been manufactured, Umbra couldn't say as it had happened soon after their birth and no song had been made to remember the details.

Umbra had every intention of having a song written for Vermillion, but they wouldn't be the hero. They would be the villain who destabilized a castle and a city for glory. It would be a cautionary tale for all. They could almost imagine the haunting refrain. They had been sent to be Vermillion's mate, but it would be much more glorious to unseat the bastard and take over. Their birther would be proud, even their sire would have to grudgingly admit that it was the right thing to do.

Elliot leaned against their leg. A reassuring presence, though one that couldn't save them. After tonight's public defeat, Vermillion needed a private win. Something that could be whispered around the castle.

"Dice?" Vermillion place the weighted set on the table.

"What is the wager?"

"A taste to cement our bond."

"We do not have to wager that which I would give freely." Umbra smiled as sweetly as they could manage. They ruffled Elliot's hair. "You like to be bitten don't you, pet?"

"Yes," Elliot said with forced joy.

"I underestimated you. I thought you'd been sent willingly to my bed."

"I have never said that wasn't possible, only that I wouldn't bear a child. Do not conflate the two."

Vermillion toyed with the dice. Dice were wonderful for those who liked cheating and chance, and while Umbra could take advantage of both, they preferred strategy. They wanted to spend what was left of the night with Elliot, not waste it here with someone they could barely tolerate and respected less.

"If I win, you'll stay until dawn. If I lose, I get a taste of your pet."

"That sounds like you win either way." Umbra tried to sound as though he liked the idea of playing with Vermillion and their weighted dice.

"I don't expect anything less." They pushed the dice over to Umbra.

There it was. Vermillion had expected Umbra to hand over Elliot for a month—which might as well be forever. While it appeared on the surface Vermillion was accepting of Umbra's choice, inside they seethed at being defied.

Umbra rolled, then took their second roll. The dice were familiar now; they could manipulate them. They wanted to. They wanted to win and get out of Vermillion's chambers. There would already be talk that they were together, that the rift wasn't as large as it seemed, that it was a culture clash and nothing more. If Vermillion hadn't gossiped about getting a mate, maybe they could've saved face and been honored they shared the same blood. But Vermillion didn't want an equal, even in a mate. They wanted someone they could control.

Vermillion rolled, and Umbra watched. Even cheating, Vermillion lost the first round.

Umbra lost the next two deliberately. Vermillion was smiling and relaxed as though they didn't realize or care they were being played. Umbra trailed their fingers through Elliot's hair and along his stubble roughened jaw.

They won the next one, unable to bear another loss. Perhaps Vermillion would play so badly they lost. Perhaps all they wanted was a taste of Elliot to be sure the pets were brothers.

Vermillion held the dice. "Your change is established?"

"Yes." No rules would be broken if they were to spend what was left of the night together, though it was more customary to wait the full month. "Though if you win, you can claim later if you'd feel more comfortable."

"Why delay?" Vermillion rolled a perfect hand. Fool. Did they think Umbra didn't know about the dice?

Umbra held the dice, their heartbeat like a bard's drum in their ears. Elliot's much faster rhythm blended in. Surrender Elliot or themselves?

They glanced at Vermillion. They needed to get them on side and less suspicious. They would have to do what needed to be done.

They rolled, their stomach aching as the dice fell badly.

"You are more skilled with a staff than with dice."

189

I was raised a warrior, not a conniving liar. But they smiled. "The old ones favored you tonight."

Elliot glanced up, his eyes wide and dark.

Umbra took their foot off the chain. "Return to my chambers."

He opened his mouth to argue, but Umbra put a finger on his lips.

"A guard will escort you so nothing untoward happens," Vermillion said. A guard appeared in the doorway and took the end of Elliot's chain. "We can share my pet tonight."

"How generous."

Dayne hadn't moved. He sat on the floor at the end of the bed, eyes downcast, not even looking at his brother. How much blood did Vermillion feed the young man? Too much for him to be of any use.

Vermillion got up and shut the bedroom door.

Elliot was on his own. As were they.

Vermillion placed their hands on Umbra's shoulders and leaned in. "I had hoped it would be different between us. That you would see my point of view and understand what I need." Their thumbs stroked Umbra's neck. "That you would surrender your trouble-making pet and change your mind, as well as your body, to something more suited to the task." The pressure increased. "You were sent for my bed."

They'd stalled and thought by taking a male pet, they could avoid that. They should've known Vermillion wouldn't accept defeat.

"I am here."

Vermillion gripped Umbra's throat and hauled them up. "Do not defy me in public again."

They flung Umbra toward the bed and stalked over, tearing off their shirt and waistcoat. "I am the leader, and your games will end."

"My parents had no right to set up this expectation."

"You should have upheld it regardless. You should've obeyed." They grabbed Umbra's shirt collar and dragged them up. Fabric tore. "You've been disobedient from the moment you arrived."

Umbra broke their hold and stripped off their coat before it could get damaged. "Why do you think my parents sent me away?"

Vermillion slapped them across the face. Their head snapped back, and they lost their balance falling back onto the bed. Vermillion pounced, but Umbra threw them off and rolled away. "We don't have to be at war."

"You'd prefer me to woo you with song and clothing?"

"That would be nice."

"I'm not an unchanged bard—yes, I know about your dalliances. I have heard plenty about you, and I look forward to grinding you into submission."

∾

*T*he sun was rising across the lake; Umbra could feel it dragging down their blood. With only the slightest limp, they made their way across the fortunately short distance to their chambers. They locked the outer door and turned. Elliot stood in the bedroom doorway wearing only sleeping pants. The collar and chain were gone.

"Tell me there is some nectar remaining." They made their way to the doorway and leaned against the frame, wishing they weren't so tired or hurt.

"Why did you stay? Why didn't you win?"

"Because sometimes you have to lose to get into a better position." They dropped their coat on a chair, glad to see the laundry had been taken and the floors cleaned.

Elliot pressed the goblet into their hand. "Vermillion wants to kill you."

"They can't. My parents sent me here to pull me into line, but they'll be extremely angry if something happens to me." Their hand shook as they took a deep swallow of nectar.

Elliot cupped their jaw and studied them far too closely. They should have pulled away, saved some dignity and kept some secrets.

"I saw."

"How?"

Elliot indicated to the balcony. "I wanted to go in and stop it, but I figured you'd be angry I was even there."

191

Umbra closed their eyes. Elliot couldn't follow an order, and it made them smile. A laugh bubbled up. "When are you going to learn?"

They pulled Elliot into their lap, wincing as he pressed against what was probably a broken rib.

"Maybe when you do." He moved aside his hair, offering his neck.

Umbra nuzzled against his skin. "Vermillion needed the win, or they'd have been impossible. We need to appear to be behaving. You need to be very careful, or you'll end up in their chambers." Their teeth raked his skin. They wanted to taste Elliot's blood and feel him pressed against them. "I want to wash first. The sun is rising, and I'm exhausted."

Elliot got up and offered his hand. "At least when I do what you did, I get paid, and I don't get hurt. You're doing it wrong."

"I'm not human, and you know nothing of the Abyr."

They stripped and washed, scrubbing blood and other fluids from their skin, not wanting to think too much about it. They'd done what needed to be done. Let Vermillion have their temporary win. Five moves later, they'd be pinned to the wall with antler in their throat.

CHAPTER 23

*E*lliot woke entwined with Umbra, but he didn't pull away. He'd gotten used to sharing a bed, and they no longer left a polite gap. After last night, Elliot was surprised Umbra wanted to be touched at all. Dark purple bruises bloomed across their skin, skin that had been split. A human wouldn't have survived Vermillion's roughness.

He'd stood on the balcony, venerie blade in hand, realizing what a fool he'd been. Umbra was barely fighting back. They weren't striking Vermillion, only defending. Then the clothes had come off, and Umbra had seemed almost willing. He'd recognized that look, that touch, because he'd done it a dozen or more times. It made his stomach turn to see Umbra perform like that for Vermillion.

He turned over, his back to Umbra, wishing he hadn't seen anything. He should've stayed in this room like a good pet.

Umbra reached out and drew him close. "It's only sunset. A little longer."

Elliot closed his eyes even though sleep was far away.

It had taken too long to arrive. Umbra had fed and fallen asleep, and Elliot had held them as though he could protect them when it was perfectly clear he stood no chance if he ever had to fight a Kin. All those fights, the training with knives…it was only now he realized Umbra hadn't been trying to hurt him. If Umbra had wanted to punish him, it would've been quite simple.

Umbra's hand moved against Elliot's belly, tracing the line of hair from his navel to the waist of the pants. They liked it, their fingers always finding it and tracing along it. Their lips pressed against the back of Elliot's neck, and then they moved as though to take their first feed of the night. Then Elliot would slide out of bed and take care of the wood that formed. It wasn't a bad way to wake up, and it had been a bloody long time since he'd woken up to something as intimate.

"Show me how to do it right," Umbra whispered, their fangs scraping Elliot's skin.

Elliot startled. They didn't talk when they woke. Umbra fed, and then they both pretended they didn't like it as much as they did and got on with the night. Usually, that involved something to do with knives or ossic.

What Umbra now wanted was for more dangerous than fighting.

"I think you know how to bite."

Another toothy kiss on his neck right over his pulse. A shiver raced through his blood to his groin. He tried to think of something dull, like his busted boots.

"That's not what I meant."

"I know." Elliot turned to face them. It was almost dark, yet if he tilted his head, their lips would meet. Would it hurt, being kissed with fangs? "We weren't doing this."

For good reasons, although he wasn't sure what they were now. If he died tomorrow, he'd regret not trying everything.

Umbra's hand fell away. "I know the deal was blood only." Then they turned away, putting space between them.

Elliot reached out and moved over them, sure he'd been thrown off in about three heartbeats. "After last night—"

"I want to wash the memory away." Their fingers tunneled into Elliot's hair and pulled him closer so their lips were almost touching.

"You could have anyone." But he was convenient.

"I don't want anyone."

"I'm not Kin, I..." *I can't find a good reason not to.* "Are there rules about this kind of thing?"

"The unchanged don't have anything to do with humans or the changed, but that is the only rule. Or at least it was at home."

"You'll regret it. It won't erase the memory."

"You think I've never woken up in a bed and wondered how I got there before?" They moved, and their lips brushed along his jaw.

He couldn't imagine Umbra creeping through the castle boots in hand after a chance get together with someone they probably shouldn't have been with.

"I always know how I got there." He wanted Umbra's hands and mouth on him.

"And you don't always like it."

He might like this, and then where would that leave him when their deal ended? "I know enough to know what I like."

"And I don't, not in this body. It irks me that I didn't get that chance first."

"Irks you?" Elliot sat back, deliberately sitting over Umbra's hips. "That's it?"

"I did what had to be done, as you say."

It took Elliot a few breaths to find the words. "I'm sorry. I shouldn't have...it was supposed to be safe."

"Nothing here is safe. That's how Vermillion likes it. It's how they keep power." Umbra's hand slid up his thigh. Elliot's heartbeat quickened in expectation. "It's usually an honor to be the one chosen to try out the changes."

Elliot smiled. "Well, when you put it like that..." But that still didn't make it a good idea, no matter how tempting.

Beneath him, Umbra was hard. They didn't feel that different to when he was with a human man. Umbra found the line of hair again and traced it from navel to the top of the pants. Then their finger dipped lower to where Elliot's hard dick pressed against the fabric. He didn't move, could barely breathe.

"I can hear the change in your heartbeat."

Elliot closed his eyes. "Is nothing a secret?"

"I don't know your thoughts."

"And I don't know yours," Elliot countered.

"I told you mine. I want you to erase the memory."

"I'm not that good." He was sure he couldn't erase the memory of Umbra getting thrown. Elliot didn't mind a little rough play, but that hadn't been play. It had been all about pain. This wouldn't be the same. He hoped.

"Try." Umbra tugged on the strings that held his pants up, and they came undone. "Or walk away. If you don't want me or you'd rather hold fast to the original deal say so." They stopped touching him.

Fuck it. Maybe one nice memory of the castle would be a good thing. He leaned over, his lips a whisper away.

"Remember, I'm human, not Kin."

"I won't hurt you. I swear by the old ones."

That didn't mean he wouldn't die, only that it wouldn't hurt. He pressed his lips to Umbra's in a soft kiss that didn't have to go further. Umbra's fingers tangled in his hair, and their tongue traced his lip. He opened his mouth and tested the point of Umbra's fang with his tongue. Umbra returned the kiss, pressing their fangs to Elliot's lip, but they didn't break the skin. He turned his head so Umbra could bite.

They kissed down Elliot's throat, and Elliot ground against them. If he didn't think, he could be in any dark room after a night at the Moss. Hands slid down his back and gripped his hips, pulling him down harder. A groan slithered out of his throat.

Then Umbra bit. It was quick, barely a bite, and he wanted more. His pants were sliding down. With one hand, he tugged them down further. Umbra got the hint and freed his dick. He tried to get Umbra's pants undone, needing to feel skin on skin.

Umbra flipped him onto his back and followed, but before Elliot could get their pants open, they were moving. Trapping Elliot's legs between theirs, then kissing and licking down his chest, then lower following the trail of hair until their lips brushed the head of his dick.

"You do use mouths?" they murmured.

"Yes." It had been a long time since someone had sucked on him. With lust coiling tight around him, that was all he wanted.

The wet heat of Umbra's mouth closed around him, and his fingers curled into the sheets. Then Umbra gripped his hips, rocking them while his tongue moved. His dick was caught between their tongue and the roof of their mouth and the scrape of fangs on the sides. He flung one arm over his head to grasp the headboard. His other hand strayed to Umbra's hair, tangling in the braids that hadn't been unraveled before bed, but he didn't tug or pull. He let Umbra continue, doing what they needed to put aside last night.

He closed his eyes and tried not to sink into the need, but it was impossible. It was far too easy to pretend they were lovers and that this little interlude was his perfect life.

He bit his lip and opened his eyes, barely able to make out the shape of Umbra's body and his antlers. That didn't help, so he shut his eyes again. "I need to—uh."

The tension uncoiled in a rush as he came.

Umbra drew back, but it was too late. He was done and without a final suck or stroke. His breath came in hard pants, and he needed a moment to catch his scattered thoughts. All his thoughts were about how good that felt, though.

Umbra gave him a lick that made Elliot shudder. He changed his mind; he didn't want Umbra to touch him. Everything felt too sensitive.

"You definitely can't carry a child?"

"What? No." He could barely speak. He shivered. What kind of question was that?

"Good." Then Umbra was over him. They rubbed their hard length —though it wasn't that long—in the mess on Elliot's stomach.

He reached down to stroke, but Umbra shifted a little so their... dick? Stem? Whatever thrust between his thighs. They kept Elliot's legs pinched closed with their knees. Their breath was on his neck. He looped an arm over Umbra's shoulders and turned his head.

His breath caught at the familiar kiss and the press of teeth. It was deeper this time. He could feel the heat and the suction, and for a moment, it felt as though he were coming again, everything twisted inside of him before releasing.

Umbra groaned, thrusting a couple more time, and wet heat spread between Elliot's thighs. For several breaths neither of them moved. He could feel Umbra's rapid pulse against his chest, and his breath on his neck. There was an antler dangerously close to his face, the tip against his cheek.

He couldn't move even if he wanted to—which he didn't. He wasn't getting kicked out of bed, and he wasn't kicking anyone out, which made a nice change. Umbra eased back and placed a soft kiss on his lips. He didn't taste blood even though he'd expected to. Then Umbra rocked back on their heels.

Don't say anything. Just let it be.

"That wasn't so different to what I knew as an unchanged."

Elliot sighed. They were talking. "You could've fucked me…or I you."

"I just did. And I don't have a channel anymore." They picked up Elliot's hand and brought it to their body, to the smooth skin of their thigh and then higher to the slight swelling at the base of their dick. "The pods seal it up, and the stem grows." They guided Elliot's hand over their dick. Soft now, it was even smaller.

"But if you were to drink female blood, it would come back?"

"The pods would go down, and my stem would go back to how it was. Seeing yours made me quite concerned. I didn't want something so ungainly."

He'd never thought of it that way, and he'd seen plenty of dick. "You don't need a channel; you have an ass."

Umbra tilted their head and didn't release Elliot's hand.

"I'm guessing the Kin don't offer up their ass." His face was heating, and he was so glad it was dark.

"No. No one sticks anything in anyone. The unchanged don't anyway."

"But you asked me."

"Because I didn't know if you had a channel hidden under that undergrowth. I didn't want to accidentally slide in."

Elliot bit back on the laugh. "I wouldn't have complained."

Their antlers tilted as though Umbra were considering him. "You can show me another time."

Another time... Had it been what Umbra needed? "Did you like it?"

"Yes. It soothed the memory better than any nectar." They leaned in and took another kiss. "I look forward to your lips on my stem."

"So do I." Would Umbra taste different?

Elliot lay there feeling boneless and warm.

Umbra stood and offered their hand. "Come I'll run a bath."

He accepted the offer and let himself be dragged to his feet. He would try not to break any rules today.

CHAPTER 24

A line of red opened beneath Elliot's collarbone. He was getting faster. Practicing everyday with the threat of injury was making him work harder. But they were running out of time. It was sliding through their fingers, and not just because a fortnight had passed.

Vermillion was making plans, and Umbra wasn't privy to them.

Elliot brought his fingertips to the cut and then glanced at his bloodied fingers. "That was close."

"It was nowhere near your artery." They took a sip of nectar; they always made sure there was a full goblet before practicing in case it all went horribly wrong.

They stepped in and licked the cut, enough nectar on their tongue for the wound to heal immediately. Elliot's blood in their mouth was sweeter than nectar. They then took Elliot's hand and licked his fingers clean of blood. Elliot's heartbeat quickened, and while it would be tempting to stop, they'd barely gotten started.

Umbra released his hand. "When you score on me, we'll stop."

"Then we'll be here all night."

That didn't bother Umbra; it was better here than in the hall. "You that keen to wear the chain?"

"I want to see Dayne. I haven't seen him since…"

Umbra didn't want to think about the fight with Vermillion anymore than they already did. As much as they'd like to skewer Vermillion on the end of their antlers—they didn't care if they snapped off at the skull—Lapis would simply take over, and Lapis already hated them.

Vermillion merely wanted to control them. Control they could deal with; hate was much harder. Hate was irrational, and Lapis was far smarter than Vermillion realized. For the moment, it was better that Vermillion was in charge, no matter what that entailed.

"I know. I have been told he's alive." That wasn't all they were told, but they didn't want to push Elliot into recklessness again. The last few days had been calm.

Elliot tossed the knife and caught it with his other hand, looking decidedly unconvinced. They'd gotten him his own curved blade and his new clothes were ready for collection. Despite Elliot's protests, Umbra had ordered him a complete outfit—pants, two shirts and underclothes, a waistcoat and coat. They would not send Elliot back to the city with nothing.

They didn't want to send him back at all. Not when the situation in the city was worsening. Vermillion had cut the amount of nectar being traded again and refused to supply any new orbs until the Kin could hunt freely.

Umbra stepped back. "Ready?"

Elliot inclined his head, a few dark curls clung to his forehead. He attacked swiftly, and Umbra danced back, almost colliding with the table. They swung around, putting it between them. They shadowed Elliot when he darted left or right. The goblet of nectar sat precariously in the center. Umbra put their foot on the chair and launched up.

Elliot smacked their inner thigh with the blade as he slid beneath. "You're dead."

Umbra landed and turned, hooking their blade across Elliot's neck, pulling his head back and exposing his throat. "You didn't make the cut."

He didn't move. "If you make that cut, not even nectar will save me."

Umbra removed the blade and kissed Elliot's pulse. "Again."

~

*J*t was much later when they went downstairs. There'd been blood to clean up and when they were together, bathing took three times as long and was at least three times as fun. They were getting used to the changes and liked the way Elliot felt against them. They were far too attached to a man who wasn't really their pet.

Foolish.

But they couldn't stop.

Many of the Abyr were absent from the hall. Probably in the human city. Or had they gone to the heartland town for supplies? Umbra needed to be more interested in the running of the castle, but that meant subjecting themselves to more of Vermillion's attention and Lapis's hatred.

Lapis had to be removed, and that would be difficult.

Vermillion lounged in his chair, reading something and making notes. Umbra sat and let the chain fall to the floor, barely keeping their pet restrained as Elliot sat.

"You're getting later and later. If you'd been here earlier, you could've gone into the heartland." Vermillion didn't look up.

Umbra shrugged. "I was otherwise occupied."

Vermillion glanced up from the papers. "Doing what?"

"Training my pet, of course." Umbra ruffled Elliot's hair. The soft, still damp curls were like silk on their fingers. "And where is yours? They've been noticeably absent, and people have been...well, you know how gossip is." Umbra smiled. They'd started the gossip.

What they needed was some small snippet on Lapis. Something to create an edge between Lapis and Vermillion. There were fracture lines all through the castle that they'd missed when they'd first arrived, simply because they'd been the outsider, unchanged and no threat.

Now...now they'd made it clear they weren't Vermillion's plaything and would not be treated as such, and that had made some a little less loyal.

Vermillion's lips thinned. They put down the papers. "My pet should've known better than to play with yours. They have been banned from leaving my chambers."

"A bored pet is one that will get into trouble. Better to keep them occupied, is it not?"

"Give them too much to do, and they think they can have the run of the castle." Vermillion glanced at Elliot.

Umbra kept their face fixed, but Elliot's night wanderings had been noted and reported. He'd been out twice, and both times, he'd sworn he was armed and careful even though he'd spoken to some of the humans. Most of the humans here had been born in the castle and knew nothing else. The old ones remembered a time before Vermillion. They remembered the takeover and the slaughter. There was a reason why no Abyr had bigger antlers than Vermillion.

Many of the Abyr were supporters of Vermillion's rebellion, but not all. Some had come from other castles either because they wanted a mate or they'd been sent when there was a flare up in the city ten years ago.

"If you have to chain them, are they really yours?" Their tone was light, but Umbra saw the moment it struck.

Vermillion's gaze hardened as they turned to study Elliot. "Your pet wants to see his brother."

Umbra rested their hand on Elliot's shoulder; tension thrummed in his body.

"Why should I entertain you? What can you give me?" Vermillion said to Elliot.

Umbra spoke before Elliot could. "Let's have a little game." They leaned forward. "You win, and you get me. I win, and the pets can play."

Vermillion smiled. "That is better." They reached their hand over the table to clasp Umbra's. "You know how to make things interesting."

You wait. When I figure out how to kill Lapis, things will get really interesting.

Their smile was genuine. But they knew if they killed Vermillion and Lapis, it would be all out civil war until a new leader was picked. They couldn't make the mess and walk away. They might have to run the castle, something they hadn't expected to do for at least a century. And it was Octadine they were supposed to inherit, a border castle that had already found stability.

Elliot glanced up at them, a frown knotting his eyebrows. Elliot would soon be in the city, and if Vermillion had their way, the Abyr would have free hunting in the dark while the humans up the hill continued to thrive. Elliot would be a target. They would have to do something before Elliot left, but didn't know what.

"Dice?" Vermillion pulled out their favorite weighted set.

"Why not? A quick resolution is good for all."

Vermillion won the first hand, but Umbra won the next two, using the dice just so. They had to win this; there was no way they were going to spend another night in Vermillion's chambers.

Vermillion grinned, confident in their hand. Umbra rolled and took their second roll, stealing the victory and earning the pleasure of seeing Vermillion's eyes narrowed in confusion. "Another time?"

Vermillion snatched up their dice and summoned a guard to fetch Dayne.

There was a reason Dayne hadn't been in the hall. Yellow-green shadows marred his jaw, and dark circles haunted his eyes. He sat on the floor next to Vermillion's chair and stared at the ground. Umbra's grip on Elliot's shoulder tightened. This was far worse than the rumor they'd started or the whispers they'd heard.

"Your pet could do with some nectar."

"My pet will learn his place, and you will not tell me how to treat him." Vermillion gathered their papers and stood. They beckoned Umbra to follow. They stepped away from the table, and Elliot moved closer to his brother, embracing him. Umbra could see his lips moving but could not hear him.

"You were sent here, and I opened my castle to you as a guest and my mate. You are not serving your purpose. Perhaps you feel the pressing need to return home."

Umbra nodded. "I do miss home, but I am having more fun here." They touched the collar of Vermillion's coat. "There's less rules for a start."

"There are rules." Vermillion removed their hand. "I no longer need you. Lapis is to be my mate."

The announcement was hardly news. They twisted their hand to grasp Vermillion's as though they were friends. "You need the legitimacy of my bloodline because all you have is an assortment of warriors with no history."

Vermillion shrugged. "I had no history, and yet I run a castle. Blood means nothing."

"So why make a deal to have me sent here? You need someone to ride at the front and lead the battle. I have six generations of blood. My family was one of the first. That is history that cannot be bought for any price." Umbra released Vermillion's hand. "The city is boiling. When they race across the lake to take what they can, the invasion will be one of songs. How do you want your name remembered?"

"And here was I thinking you'd slept through those meetings."

One never slept through trade meetings. It was the things that weren't said that were important, but Vermillion had never had that training. They thought force was the only weapon.

"Not at all. I could be useful here. I have been trained in strategy since I could walk." And if Umbra controlled the warriors, they would control the castle. Vermillion would rule in name only. They wouldn't even need a coup. All Vermillion needed to do was fail when the humans invaded.

Making peace would simply mean supplying the humans in the dark with what they needed to overthrow the bloated leeches on the hill. Umbra glanced at Elliot, still fussing over his brother.

If Umbra failed, they wouldn't be welcomed back at Octadine. They'd be shunned—assuming Vermillion didn't stake them out in the center square for dawn.

"I'm planning a raid tomorrow. I was going to let Weld take the lead, but perhaps it is a chance for you to prove yourself. Lead it successfully, and I'll consider your offer."

"What is the goal?"

"I want the lord's son. It might motivate the father." Vermillion pressed two pieces of paper to Umbra's chest. "Fail, and I will break you and then feed you to the leviathan." They stepped back. "Pet."

Dayne glanced up, and his smile faded. He wasn't going to last until the end of Elliot's month. They were going to have to break their agreement.

CHAPTER 25

"*L*et's leave the castle." Umbra tucked the papers Vermillion had given them into their coat.

Elliot tore his gaze off his brother and stared up at Umbra. He didn't want to go anywhere. His brother needed him. He needed nectar and to be away from Vermillion. He glanced at Dayne as he followed Vermillion up the stairs. He was already out of reach. Elliot closed his eyes. Would Vermillion hurt him again? His fingers curled.

Umbra tugged on the chain. "You can't help him right now. Let's collect the clothes."

"I don't care about the clothes," Elliot snapped.

"It's not about the clothes," Umbra hissed. Elliot had to get up or choke. He reached out to snatch the chain out of Umbra hands, but at the last moment, he remembered he was supposed to be tamed. He drew in a breath and let his hand drop.

Umbra walked and Elliot followed, gaze down, seething, his blood boiling.

They walked in silence to the stable, then Umbra stopped. "I forgot my coin. Get my beast ready." They handed over the end of the chain.

Elliot held the chain and stared at them. Umbra had told him what he needed to do to wake a beast, but he'd never done it. "And then what?"

"Then you wait. You won't be allowed to leave without me." They pointed at the gate that was closed most of the time. That was the gate that lead to the heartland and the town that supplied the castle.

When he left with Dayne, it would be through the other gate, to Fotyna.

Umbra left him standing there. He had to do this on his own, prove he could accomplish step one of his eventual escape.

It was dark in the stable except for the glowing red hearts of the beasts that all beat at the same time, making the air pulse. Their ribs cast long shadows on the walls. They weren't animals, though maybe they had been once. Now, they were skeletons that lived to serve.

One was Umbra's. He should be able to find which one. All the horns were different, and more than that, Umbra had let the beast taste his blood. It should know him. With no noses or tongues, though, Elliot had no idea how that was possible. He wasn't sure he wanted to know.

As he moved deeper into the stable the pulsing increased, and he could feel their attention on him, even though they had no brains or eyes. Sweat formed under his arms, and all he wanted to do was run out into the eternal twilight sun.

He had to do this. The horns on Umbra's beast weren't even; the right one tipped up while the left was straight. If he was carrying his knife, he'd have pricked his finger. Would that wake the beast and make it creep forward? They all seemed like they were about to wake and pounce.

He walked up to the one he thought was Umbra's and held his hand out as if the beast were a dog getting to know him, but the beast didn't respond. It wasn't alive in the way he was used to.

"What you doing?" a gruff voice demanded.

Elliot startled and spun, but it was only the old man who seemed to spend all his time sweeping. "Getting a beast ready."

"You have to touch it. And if you don't have permission, you'll lose a hand."

"I have permission."

"I bet you do. Your master isn't like the others. He needs to watch his back." He swept the doorway but didn't enter. "You'd be wise to watch yours, too. Someone has their eye on stealing you."

"How do you know that?"

"I'm nothing but a part of the castle. I'm invisible. But I've seen you about, and I know you aren't a pet, no matter how chained up you are."

Elliot stepped forward. "How."

"You don't look like a kicked dog for a start. And when your master looks at you, you almost smile. Humans here don't smile if they want to live."

The man ducked his head and moved out of the doorway. Elliot saw the shadow of antlers; his heart clenched and missed a beat.

Umbra appeared in the doorway. "Still not ready?"

"This one." He pointed at the one he was standing near.

Umbra gave a single nod. "You will have only heartbeats next time. You need to move faster."

Elliot placed his hand over the beast's smooth bone forehead. It woke with a grumble. He wanted to step away as the beast crept forward but didn't, even though his legs were shaky and he felt like the beast's dinner. He grabbed a horn and swung on the way he'd been told to, knowing he was infinitely less graceful than Umbra. Umbra stepped aside so Elliot could steer the beast out, not that he really needed to. The beast wanted out.

Elliot moved back so Umbra could take control. He even offered Umbra the end of the chain, aware that the sweeper was watching and noting everything. Who else was he whispering his findings to?

Elliot put his arm around his Kin's waist. The beast gave a purr and sped toward the gate. A few words with the guards and they were through, into the fringes of the Kin heartland. A place no human should be.

Once out of the castle, the beast raced, and Umbra made no effort to slow it. Umbra leaned forward as though encouraging the reckless-ness. The wind stung Elliot's eyes and made them water. It was all he could do to hold on so he didn't die. He wasn't sure if it was fear or excitement rushing through his blood. Eventually, Umbra eased back, and the beast slowed, then stopped.

"Can't do that in the city." Umbra got off. They weren't anywhere near the Kin town, but he could see it. Behind him was the castle, a tall blot on the skyline. "We're going to the town, but you'll get us there. I need to know you can do this part." They fingered the chain then tucked the tail into Elliot's pocket. "I can't take this off. A loose human in the heartland would cause a panic."

Elliot nodded. He knew the feeling a hunting Kin caused in the Dark City. "The old man said you need to watch your back."

"I need to watch more than my back. If he wasn't so old, I'd ask him to be my guard."

"Why don't you have any?"

"Because I don't trust any of Vermillion's staff. If you know anyone trustworthy who wants a well-paying job, you can send them my way."

"What about me?"

Umbra shook their head.

Elliot clenched his jaw. Why couldn't he stay in the castle? "That's right. I'm only good for one thing. Sorry, two things." Their first tentative deal had become something bigger and all-consuming, and he liked it. He didn't want to give it up and go back to the pathetic life he'd had. But Dayne needed to get out, and he'd need care. In that moment, he hated his brother for getting taken and damning them both.

"Yes, you are good at those two things." They reached out, but Elliot leaned back, not wanting to be wooed. They let their hand fall, and their smiled melted. "I have bigger plans and I need your help."

"And what if Vermillion tames me and makes me devoured?"

"He won't have a chance. You're leaving tomorrow."

"But there's nearly a whole fortnight remaining. Don't you need my blood?" He didn't want to leave when he was enjoying living and had learned how to fill his nights with something other than work.

"I'd like to keep you." Their tongue touched their fang. "But your

210

brother needs to leave. Vermillion isn't giving him nectar, and he is weakening from blood loss. He'll be too weak to escape if you wait."

Elliot hadn't even considered that was why Umbra encouraged him to drink a little every day. "That's why he has bruises."

"Did Dayne say anything?"

"He said he was fine." Even though he clearly wasn't.

"He was probably told to say that and couldn't get the words out to say more." Umbra rested against the beast. "I have to lead a raid tomorrow. Vermillion wants the lord's son. If I don't get him, it will be safer for you to be in the city."

"Why are you helping them?"

Umbra stared at their boots and was silent for several breaths. "I haven't forgotten or forgiven the other night. Or any of the other nights. That was not the first time, only the worst time, and it will not be the last while they live. But one cannot overthrow a leader on a whim. It has to be planned." Umbra looked up. "Do you understand?

"You're plotting ten steps ahead."

"Yes." They studied Elliot as though trying to figure out if he could keep up. Probably not. "I didn't come here for that. At first I wanted to fit in and survive, but I can't buckle under and let Vermillion continue."

"You're going to kill them?"

"Eventually. But Lapis is far more dangerous. They also love Vermillion, and I don't need an enemy. While Ver doesn't trust me, I have a bloodline that makes them hungry."

"And why do you need me?"

"I'll keep my end of the deal and help you get your brother out. I may also visit you in the city from time to time. I'll bring you nectar. Dayne will need it, and I don't want you getting hurt and not being able to heal. You will always be my pet." Umbra reached for him, and this time Elliot leaned into the touch.

Why couldn't he be a pet in the castle where he got a bed and a bath and didn't have to scrounge for every coin?

"I can't walk around the Dark City with nectar." People would be begging or stealing it from him. "You have no idea how much one single goblet is worth."

"I do, and the price is going up. Ver wants a clean hunting ground. Until they get it, they're rationing nectar and orbs."

"To clean the Dark City, the marshmallow processing plant will have to be shut down." With no leaf, there'd be no protection from the Kin. "And then what? Vermillion kills whomever he wants?"

"They want war, Elliot. They want the bards to sing their name the way they sing my birther's."

"There won't be a war, the rich will close the plant and let us be hunted."

"Ver will stop giving them nectar. If they want it, they'll have to come and get it. I'm going to help them have their war. And so are you."

"Why would I do that? I don't want to be hunted, and I don't want my friends to die either. We'll be the ones the rich conscript to fight." The rich would stay safe up the hill.

Umbra gave him a small smile then pulled out a map. "The hill." They pointed to a small area on the paper. "The dark, the shore, and the causeway. I want you to lead your people against the rich. They sit there in their luxury in their shiny boots. I've seen yours and the room you live in. That's not right. Your people know it's not right."

"Says the Kin who lives in a castle with servants sweeping and guarding."

"And they were all born there. They are given, or at least should be given, the chance to leave. In Octadine, few did. Would you if all you had to do was guard my door?"

"No. That'd be the easiest job I've ever done. And I'd get to live somewhere nice." That's why people happily worked in the castle. He could think of ten people who'd jump at the chance. "But you don't want me here."

"What I want doesn't matter. Hasn't since the day my sire cut this deal. But this can't continue. Constantly keeping the border on a simmer isn't the sign of a well-kept castle, but it is the sign of someone who likes to rule by fear. If I take over, I can end that."

Elliot had no doubt they could. "That won't change things in the city."

"Not on its own." Umbra grabbed his arms. "But I will make changes with your help." They were excited, their eyes were bright and their smile wide.

"I don't know how to do that. I didn't know how to use a knife until a fortnight ago."

"And now you can."

"I'm not a leader. I couldn't even keep my family together."

"That's not what I see. I see a man who'd do anything for those he loves."

And he still failed. He wanted to believe it was possible but didn't see how. All he saw was dead man's room waiting for him and Dayne.

"And that's still not enough. People won't listen to a no one."

"You came to the castle and rescued your brother. You tamed a Kin." Umbra leaned in and kissed him. "I can't do this on my own."

He hadn't rescued Dayne on his own either, but would anyone believe he'd made a deal with a Kin? He was going to have to sing his own legend into existence.

"What happens to me after, when you rule? Am I an inconvenience to be dealt with?"

"If you want to come back, you can. My door will always be open for you. That's assuming we both survive." They drew back, their fingers lingering on Elliot's jaw. "I can't promise that."

"So, save Dayne, derail the war, and make it a revolution?"

"Something like that." Umbra made it seem so easy.

Living here, he'd forgotten how tired he usually was. He'd forgotten what hunger was, the gnawing in his belly a memory from long ago. People in the dark didn't have time to rise up. They feared losing what little they had. He had no job waiting; Fife would've already taken an apprentice. "You don't hunt in Octadine."

"No, there are enough volunteers. It wasn't perfect, and I don't think it ever will be, but it was better. There was peace, and nectar and blood flowed across the border."

That was all this was about, nectar and blood. But in Fotyna, those that gave the blood never tasted the nectar. He wasn't sure he could live his life never tasting it again…never being bitten again.

"I'll do it. Or at least try."

"The bards will sing our names either way."

Elliot didn't want to be a line in Vermillion's victory song.

~

The town was as beautiful as the castle, all stone and wood and covered with engravings of vines and trees. Elliot was stared at, and he tried not to stare at all the unchanged Kin. They were different to those in the castle. Slighter, shorter, and with smaller mouths and fangs. And while their hair was still colorful, it wasn't as bright. Umbra would've stood out as they fled into the heartland, marked by the generations of human blood in their veins.

The Kin gave them a wide berth, as though expecting trouble. From him or Umbra? They rode slowly through the streets, past a few other beasts that had been left outside a building.

Umbra stopped at a small shop. They gathered up the end of the chain and expected Elliot to follow without a word. Elliot did his best pet performance while Umbra examined the work. The shop smelled of leather and something else he couldn't place. He wanted to be free to examine all the colors and patterns on display. He fidgeted, his gaze darting around until the tailor glared at him. He bit back a sigh and focused an Umbra's lower back.

Umbra paid for the clothing, and Elliot carried the heavy bundle back to the beast.

"I expected there to be more." The package was too small for all the clothes Umbra had ordered.

"My clothing isn't ready. I knew you'd need yours first."

He wasn't going to be able to run around the city wearing a Kin-made coat. As much as he loved the delicate leatherwork and fine cloth, it would probably get stolen right off his back. Even though he hadn't wanted the clothing, he couldn't refuse it either. When he saw his clothing in Umbra's wardrobe, he was embarrassed—and they'd been his good clothes. They weren't even fit to be cleaning rags. "Thank you."

Umbra smiled. "When we get out of the town, do you want to practice again?"

For an answer, Elliot placed his hand on what the beast's skull to wake it. It didn't look any different, but there was a change in the vibration around the bones.

When they were far enough from town for no one to care, they swapped so Elliot sat at the front, Umbra's arm around his waist. "Try and pick up some speed this time."

Elliot steered the beast for the castle, but it knew, and as Elliot leaned forward it got faster. He was going to die. There'd be nothing left of him but a smear on the rolling hills of the heartland. Given his options, that wouldn't be a bad way to die.

~

*I*t was late when Umbra returned to their chambers. They put some papers on the table, and the smile that had been there in town was gone, replaced with a grimness that Elliot was used to seeing about three days before payday when the coins and food were running out. Money wasn't Umbra's problem.

"Planning went well?"

"Planning went fine, it's the mission I disagree with."

Elliot didn't really care if the mayor's son got snatched up and devoured like a solstice goose. It was about time those up the hill got bitten. He shrugged. "Someone has to die...why not him?"

Umbra opened their mouth, then shut it. They started unbraiding their hair, and Elliot walked over to help. Their hair felt different, thicker and rougher than human hair. Umbra stopped, and let Elliot do it for them.

After a time, Umbra spoke. "No one has to die. And this death will only pour oil on what is already becoming a fire."

"If none of the Kin changed and we just traded for nectar, then... then you wouldn't need pets or anything." Elliot had finally figured out the engravings. He'd seen the trees wrapped in vines as they'd ridden to the town. The vines flowers dripped nectar, feeding the tree even as the vine fed on the tree. There were plants engraved everywhere. But at the border, it wasn't just plants being fed on. Humans were the tree constantly being fed on but at the same time being healed. Without the drips of nectar, the trees died.

"But humans get greedy, they want more nectar because they can sell it and get rich. You invade and take too much, and our whole world crumbles. Nectar is our food." Umbra turned and pulled Elliot into their lap. "Did you try on your clothes?"

"Yes. They all fit." And he was never going to have a finer set of clothes.

"Of course they do. But will you wear them?"

"I don't know. Can I leave them here and come and get them?"

"No, you must wear them tomorrow. I have arranged for you to spend the night with Dayne while I'm on the raid. You'll be under Vermillion's *care*." Their fingers traced down Elliot's spine.

Elliot's stomach knotted. "Your idea or his?"

"He offered, and I accepted." Their hand slid over his knee. "Tomorrow will be your best chance. We'll return late, and Vermillion will come down to view the spoils. I'll leave a bag in the stable with my beast, but it will be up to you to get down there and be on the causeway as the sun comes up. If you're caught, fight, because your life will depend on it, and I won't be able to help you."

"And what about you?"

Umbra held his gaze. "I knew there'd be a cost to helping you."

Elliot shook his head. He'd seen the price that would be extracted. "No."

"No what?" Umbra picked him up and set him on the floor. "No, you don't want to save your brother and you want to watch him die, because that's what will happen. This is not the first time, nor will it be the last, that Vermillion has killed a pet. I think they rather like it. Or no, you don't want me to be in their chambers? They want to think they control me and know me, fine. That's a weakness I can exploit."

"You'll get hurt."

216

Umbra cupped his face. "Elliot." They kissed him, deeply. "I've broken over thirty bones, shed enough blood to fill that bath several times over. We never train for taps or almost strikes, it's always for blood."

"What if you bleed out? Don't you die?"

"No. There are worse things than death for Abyr. That cut you didn't make," Umbra touched their inner thigh, "would've made a mess, and without nectar, I would've slipped into the waking sleep. Aware of everything, but unable to move."

"But nectar would've healed you."

"The only way to kill us is with our own antler. Not a cut."

"What about cutting off your head?"

"That kills everything, except for resurrection snakes." They pulled a face. "Have you ever butchered an animal?"

Elliot shook his head. "I've never killed anything bigger than a centipede."

"Beheading is hard, and a cut to the throat we can survive."

"You think I'm going to have to fight my way out?" He couldn't fight well, and Dayne couldn't fight at all. What if he failed and they were recaptured? "Maybe I should wait."

"You need to be ready to fight." Umbra placed their forehead to Elliot's and pushed.

Elliot twisted away, earning a grin from Umbra.

"With everyday that passes, your brother will weaken. Much longer, and you won't be able to flee." They took off their waistcoat and shirt, dropping them on the floor to be cleaned later.

Elliot let his gaze linger on his lover's body. He wasn't sure if it was different because he hadn't seen much of it before, but he liked the smooth, hairlessness of their chest, and the lithe, lean muscle. Next to them, Elliot didn't feel so scrawny even though he was just a dark born no one. He had no fine blood line and nothing to his name.

Umbra stifled a yawn. "Come. Let's not waste the little time I have left awake." They held out their hand, and Elliot accepted the offer.

Their lips met, then parted. Umbra tasted like nectar, and it was no longer too sweet on his tongue. He unlaced Umbra's pants and thrust his hand inside to run his fingers over their dick. Their flesh hardened and swelled with each touch. They pulled off Elliot's clothes as though desperate to feel him. The kisses quickly became hungrier and more demanding.

Umbra sat and dragged Elliot down onto their lap. Elliot moved closer to better grind against them, and as he did, Umbra kissed his neck. A shiver of lust traced through him a heartbeat before Umbra bit. He couldn't stop the moan of pleasure from sliding past his lips. Umbra wrapped their hand around both dicks, stroking and feeding.

Elliot closed his eyes; he kept a hand on Umbra's shoulder for balance as he gave into the pleasure coursing through him. It was only then Umbra withdrew their fangs. Elliot drew in a few shallow pants. The room spun, and he was strangely weightless. He'd never come while being bitten. It was a rush he wanted again.

Umbra flipped him onto the table so that his legs rested on one of Umbra's shoulders, their arm around his shins. For a moment he thought Umbra would sink into him, but they didn't. They thrust between Elliot's thighs, the table rocking and their face a picture of concentration until they spent. They lowered their head, chest heaving and a smile on their lips.

Elliot reached up, and Umbra clasped his hand. The room was still a moving thing, billowing around him. It was Umbra who moved first, reaching out to pick up the nectar. Somehow, the goblet hadn't gotten knocked or spilled.

They dipped their finger into the liquid and dripped it onto his lips. "You need to drink. I took a lot."

Elliot licked Umbra's fingers and propped himself up to accept the nectar. "One last feed?"

"There's still tomorrow." Umbra smiled, but there was something hidden about it.

Umbra held the goblet for him, which given the unsteadiness of the room was a good idea. The red orbs spun like stars across the ceiling. Umbra was still pressed between his thighs. Elliot eased back, nectar spilling on his skin.

"Enough. I don't want to be…" He didn't know how to describe the feeling of having too much nectar in his body. "I don't want to be like one of them and explode in a flash of light."

He smiled. Umbra didn't.

They lowered the goblet and then his legs before leaving to get a cloth. They wouldn't bathe together tonight; they'd fall into bed and sleep. Tomorrow they'd wallow. Umbra returned and wiped his stomach and between his thighs. "Are you okay now?"

Elliot nodded, and the room didn't even bounce. "How do they work?"

Umbra glanced up at the lights. "You know how to turn the dial."

They never went off in the castle, unlike in the city. "That doesn't explain how they work."

"I don't know how they work exactly." They sighed, their movements slow as the sun rose in the human city. Such a change from the way Umbra moved at night. "The oil glows, and when connected to the silver, it can be controlled." They sat heavily on the bed. "Why?"

"We're taught to handle them carefully in case they explode. I've seen the damage." The half-destroyed workshop, all charred and melted glass. "I dropped one once, thought I'd destroyed the city, but when I opened my eyes, it was at my feet, whole and undamaged." He eased off the table and padded over.

Umbra wasn't watching him; they were staring up at the lights. "Sun nut oil reacts to blood." They glanced at him. "Sun nuts grow on the tree that the nectar vine grows and feeds on."

"And the nectar feeds the tree. It all balances...it all should. It doesn't anymore."

They lay down, and Elliot let himself be drawn into Umbra's embrace. He was going to miss this. The healed bite on his neck still tingled, and his bones were still weak from being fucked and enjoying it far too much. He wasn't sure if he was selling blood and more for his brother or if he was giving it away freely.

It didn't matter what he thought or wanted. He was going home, and all of this would mean nothing.

CHAPTER 26

*U*mbra delivered Elliot to Vermillion's chambers. The collar chafed his neck, and Vermillion was all too happy to take the chain and tug too hard. He stumbled, his feet deliberately bare. His new boots were with his new coat in Umbra's room, but he had put on his new pants, shirt and the waistcoat. He was overdressed, but Umbra had enjoyed dressing him—and then temporarily undressing him so they could steal another kiss and taste and fall back onto the bed to delay the inevitable. Umbra didn't want anyone thinking they didn't care for their fake pet.

If they were hoping Vermillion would feel shame, they were wrong.

"Have a good raid," Vermillion said before shutting the door.

Umbra had already been walking off as if they had better things to do.

"If your master fails, you're mine."

Elliot suppressed a shiver and lifted his gaze, careful to keep his expression dead. "And if they succeed?"

Vermillion smiled. "I'll worry about that if it happens."

Umbra had been set up to fail, and Elliot could give them no warning. Vermillion watched him closely, so Elliot dropped his gaze again and shuffled as though not sure what to do next. He wanted to go to his brother.

After several heartbeats, Vermillion yanked on the chain and led Elliot into the bedroom. Dayne didn't even look up. He was a bruised shadow of the man he'd been—and he'd barely been a man. Elliot's heart clenched, and he had to remember to breathe.

What kind of life were they going to have when they left the castle? He closed his eyes as desperation and despair scrabbled like rats in a trap. The rats had no plan beyond escape; he was no smarter than a rat destined to die.

Vermillion gave him a little push, and Elliot dropped to his knees next to Dayne. There would be no games this time. No conversations about the future. The Kin hooked Elliot's chain to the foot of the bed with Dayne's. Dayne put his head in Elliot's lap like he had when he was younger, when he'd been smaller than Elliot, and Elliot ran his fingers through his hair, wanting to make more promises he couldn't possibly keep.

It was never going to be all right.

No matter what he did, it wouldn't be enough.

He'd promised Da that he'd look after Mama and Dayne. Promised Mama that he'd look after Dayne. And he hadn't. His eyes burned, but he refused to give Vermillion anything.

After a while, Vermillion got up and left. The bedroom door shut, and they were alone. A test? Probably. It wouldn't be dawn yet. He unfolded his legs and leaned against the foot of the bed. Dayne moved with him, still resting on him like a child in need of an adult to make things right.

"How are you?" Elliot kept his voice soft in case the guards were at the door.

"You shouldn't be here."

"Neither should you."

Dayne turned slightly to glance up at him. "It will be worse when you leave."

"They wanted me here today. You won't get into trouble this time."

"I thought they'd killed you. There was so much blood..."

Silence blanketed them. He wanted to tell his brother that they'd be escaping but couldn't. Umbra had made him swear not to reveal any plans, not even to Dayne. It was a promise he had to keep.

"Why don't I tell you a story?" He didn't wait for agreement.

Dayne had always liked the tale about the mice outsmarting the cat. He started the story as he always did, talking about how clever the mice were and how their homes got damaged when the cats fought, forcing the mice to spend time fixing their houses. Without houses they were vulnerable. The cats spent their time preening or pulling apart the twigs the mice had woven into shelter, and sometimes they ate one or three. One day, the mice decided they'd had enough, and instead of building small houses, they built something much bigger.

Elliot paused. He'd always thought this story had been about the Kin hunting them. But it wasn't. It was the mice revolting against the cats, the ones who ruled.

"A trap. They built a trap for the cat," Dayne whispered.

"Yes. They did. And when one cat got trapped, others came to help, and they got trapped too. Eventually, the rest fled. The mice dropped the trap into the lake, and after that, they had no trouble. Everyone left them alone."

"I want to be a mouse."

"We are the mice," Elliot said. They always had been.

"We can't build a trap."

Not yet they couldn't...or at least not on their own. "Maybe we need the help of the rats."

Dayne gave him a half smile.

The door clicked open, and Vermillion walked in with a plate of food and more papers. They sat and started to eat, offering none to Elliot or Dayne. He wasn't surprised. Was he going to have to beg for a sip of water and a bite of bread?

He'd gotten lazy, having meals brought for him.

Vermillion worked steadily through their papers and the plate of food. They sipped nectar and completely ignored the two humans. In much the same way Mama had ignored the mouse Elliot had pretended was his pet. Feeding it and making sure it had somewhere to sleep—right up until the mouse brought its family and they'd gotten into the barley.

He'd had to help Da set the traps.

"Pet."

Dayne got to his knees and went to Vermillion, or as close as the chain would allow.

Vermillion walked over, and Dayne lifted his wrist. There wasn't enough left of his brother to feed Vermillion. Elliot went to stand, but Vermillion's cold glare made him stay on one knee.

"Have me." He pushed his shirt up, exposing his wrists. The silvery lines were now webs that stretched up his arms from all the feeding. He had a few on his inner thigh, too.

Vermillion smiled and walked past Dayne. Dayne opened his mouth, his face a mix of horror and disappointment. Dayne wanted to be bitten even though Vermillion hurt him?

Elliot lifted his hand, and Vermillion grabbed it. They examined the silver marks. "I've been waiting. Perhaps you'll be my next pet. You'll find things different in my chambers. I'm not a trusting fool. I know humans, and you reek of dishonesty."

There was no softening of the skin, just the tearing of teeth into his flesh as Vermillion bit and then bit harder, as though they were chewing on his wrist. Elliot gasped but couldn't pull away as Vermillion sucked and worked their teeth deeper. They swallowed several times, drinking far more than Elliot was used to, then drew back and wiped their mouth. They released Elliot's arm; he was still bleeding, and bleeding too much.

"Too sweet from too much nectar." Vermillion sat back down and went back to his paperwork.

Elliot pressed his fingers to the wound. It wasn't neat or small. He'd need a bandage or nectar or something. Dayne tore a strip off his shirt and handed it over without a word. Elliot tied it around his wrist and watched as it turned red.

"Can I use the bathroom?" He might be able to stem the flow with a towel.

"You can wait until someone comes to clear my plate and feed you."

Elliot closed his eyes, keeping pressure on the wound and hoping the blood flow would slow from all the nectar in his body. Dayne leaned against him. Gradually, he released his wrist, happy he wasn't going to die before even attempting to escape.

But he was bored, too used to spending his time either fighting or bathing or looking at the pictures in Umbra's books. Sometimes, he played the solo version of ossic even though he still wasn't very good. This doing nothing, not even talking, was torture. The night was taking too long to pass.

Was the raid underway?

He needed to know but couldn't ask. Could they not even go to the hall and listen to the bard play? He bit his lip as he ran through the different escape options that he'd discussed with Umbra. There were too many Kin in the hall. He'd be caught before he reached the beast. From this room, they had the best chance. He looked at his wrist and the stained makeshift bandage. Would he be able to make the jump?

If he couldn't make the jump, he'd have to kill both human guards. Variations to the plan formed and spun out in his imagination. He almost gasped as he realized he was thinking beyond the next step.

Vermillion glanced over, their gaze as sharp as the curved blade at their hip. Elliot turned toward Dayne and closed his eyes. As much as he'd like to kill Vermillion for Umbra, that was impossible and would also mess up Umbra's plan which was far more complicated than his small part.

It was another lifetime before the door opened and a human came in with water and plain bread. She placed them on the floor almost out of reach, then cleared away Vermillion's plate. He'd left food and not even offered it to the pets.

The goblet of nectar was still on the table, half full. He'd only need a sip and a splash on his wrist. Dayne could have the rest, and he'd start to get better.

Vermillion glanced up and sipped their nectar. "Enjoy your meal. Then I'll release you to use the bathroom." They drained the goblet, never breaking eye contact.

Elliot's fingers curled as rage bubbled. He remembered too late to drop his gaze. He wanted to unclip the collar and use the chain to choke Vermillion until their face turned purple. It wouldn't kill them, but he could do that slowly and make them suffer the way Dayne suffered. Dying a little every day.

But in the castle, Elliot had never felt more alive. His life here was something he couldn't have imagined before. From his clothes to the bed, to the food to how he spent his time. He'd never been so...not tired. He hadn't even realized how tired he was until he wasn't. And he was going back to less than he'd had before making the deal.

He didn't think he could do it. How would he survive knowing what was over the causeway?

He used his foot to hook the plate closer and then the jug of water more carefully. There was barely enough for one person, so he tore the bread. It wasn't the soft and fluffy stuff Umbra had given him or the one full of seeds and fruits that was sweet and best with the soft cheese. There was no cheese on the plate, no fresh fruit or vegetables. Just the coarse bread. Just like home. He gave the biggest piece to Dayne, and they ate in silence.

When he'd swallowed the last piece, he drank deeply, then passed the jug to Dayne. He was still picking at the bread as if food no longer held any appeal. By the time Dayne was done, Elliot was itching to get up and go to the bathroom if only to have something to do.

Vermillion was true to their word. They unhooked Dayne first, but Dayne didn't go straight to the bathroom. He waited on his knees staring up at Vermillion. After several heartbeats, Vermillion bit their wrist and offered it to Dayne.

Elliot looked away too late. Even then, he could hear his brother drinking Kin blood as though that were all he needed in the world. Devoured. Dayne wasn't himself anymore. Elliot bit the inside of his lip. He'd known...but now he'd seen.

He glanced back over and Dayne was smiling, his eyes bright as they had once been, but it was a lie.

Elliot waited for his turn. Vermillion unhooked him but didn't offer his wrist, and Elliot didn't beg for it either. He stood, his legs cramped after sitting still for so long. They grabbed his jaw, so Elliot was forced to look into their brilliant green eyes. They could've been beautiful, but Elliot had seen too much cruelty enacted by them to see anything other than the ugliness of their heart.

Their grip tightened. "I don't know how they did it, but you aren't tame at all." They tilted Elliot's head toward the red orbs. "And yet, I quite like it. If you were tamed, you wouldn't care about your brother's pain. This way, I wound you and him, and it's much more interesting to see you wriggle like a worm beneath the claw of a crow." They released him with a shove. "Don't take too long. I have work to do."

Elliot stumbled toward the bathroom, his heart beating hard and his wrist weeping.

The truth now spoken.

Like Umbra's bathroom, there were no windows and no easy escape, but for a few moments, they weren't being watched. "Is it always like this?"

Dayne nodded. "Sometimes I have to ask for blood...usually they give me a taste." He talked too quickly, as if he'd been saving up all of his words. "You should try it; it makes you feel...bright. No don't try it. I shouldn't have...but I didn't have a choice." Dayne turned to him. "You know that? You don't blame me?"

"I don't blame you." Elliot stepped behind the screen. When done, he washed his hands and inspected his wrist. It was a mess, like a piece of half chewed meat. It hurt, but he splashed water on it, hoping the cold would stem the flow further, but it didn't.

Dayne peered over Elliot's shoulder. "You shouldn't have moved. They get hungry and tear the skin."

He hadn't even flinched. Vermillion had done it deliberately.

"Hurry up, pets. My riders are back," Vermillion called.

Elliot's heart leaped but he blanked his expression before going out. Vermillion reclipped the chain to the collar but didn't gather the chains. "Be good and wait here. I'll return you to Umbra, if they were successful." Vermillion reached down and grabbed Elliot's wrist. "I'm a little hungry today."

They bit hard, tearing at the already damaged skin. Elliot wanted to fight, to twist away and trip them, slam their head into the foot of the bed. He didn't. He let the Kin feed again, drawing blood, ripping up his wrist until it ached and dizziness threatened to send him to his knees. His fingers curled and a sob escaped. It was only then Vermillion let him drop to the floor.

They picked up their coat and swept out of the room.

Elliot rested his head on the cool floor, cradling his wrist, blood seeping between his fingers. They had to go now. They couldn't wait. They needed the nectar in Umbra's chambers.

Carefully, he straightened, ignoring the dizziness that made the room slide around the edges, then he undid the collar. Blood dripped on the floor as he walked to the table. A few drops of nectar remained in the glass.

"You shouldn't. They'll be angry. Please don't make Ver angry."

He didn't care if Vermillion was angry or sad or anything in between. Elliot held the glass until a few drops fell on his torn open arm. He sucked it a breath at the sting and watched, waiting for the nectar to work its magic. "I'm bleeding too much. There's more nectar in Umbra's room."

Dayne shook his head, but Elliot unclipped him anyway.

"What are you doing? We have to wait here."

Elliot yanked the sheet off the bed, then helped himself to a pair of sleep pants. "Going outside."

"You can't."

"I'm not their pet. I'm not anyone's pet. Neither are you. We have a life in the city." He hugged his brother. "Their blood has made you feel good but when it wears off, you'll feel bad again. Limp and half dead. Look at yourself in the mirror."

Dayne shook his head. "If he catches us, he'll hurt us."

"What do you call this? Umbra has never bitten me to wound." He'd known that they could, but Umbra had bitten for pleasure. It would've been easy to hate them and distrust them if they hadn't spent all their spare time helping Elliot prepare for this day.

Dayne appeared confused for a moment. "You don't want to live here?"

"No. We don't belong here. Please. We can go home; I know how." Elliot offered his good hand, hoping Dayne would take it and come with him.

And what if he didn't? He couldn't deal with the thought. It was too big and too painful. It made his heart tear like the bread they'd shared.

He couldn't leave his brother…but if he didn't leave, he wouldn't be able to help Umbra take over by twisting Vermillion's war into something else. If there was no Vermillion, at least Dayne would be safe. If he lived that long.

What were the odds Dayne would be allowed to live after Elliot escaped?

Not good.

Dayne reached out a hand. "It won't hurt anymore?"

"No. Our room is waiting for us. I swear it will all be fine. Better than it was." He'd make sure it was better, even if he had to sell his ass every night. He'd make sure Dayne wasn't one of those people down on the shore who forgot to eat and lived only for a taste of Kin blood.

Elliot opened the balcony door, tied the sheet to the rail, and secured the pants around his waist, nice and tight. He could do this, though it looked further today.

Could Dayne do this? He would've once. He'd always been the one climbing roofs and getting into trouble. Elliot had been the one following, trying to get him down before he broke something.

"I'll go first, yeah? Then I'll throw it back and you can jump across."

Dayne looked at the sheet and then at the balcony they could barely see the edge of. It wasn't a straight jump, but a leap out, hoping to catch the edge.

"Do you want to do it with me? Get another sheet and pants?"

"I don't think we should." The rush of Kin blood was fading from his eyes, and the haunted look was back. Would his bruised body start to hurt again? They had to do this before his strength faded.

"There's nectar and a plate full of cheese and fruit." He held up his still bleeding wrist, knowing he needed to fix it properly before he fainted. That he was dizzy wasn't a good sign. He needed to be able to haul himself up, and he wasn't sure he'd be able to.

Dayne went inside and returned with a sheet and pants. Elliot helped tie it up, though his wrist made his grip weak. Those few drops of nectar hadn't done much.

"Ready?"

Dayne shook his head.

"Come on, you used to do this kind of thing all the time while I was the one yelling at you to stop." Elliot climbed over the railing and held the edge. The ground fell away. He blinked and stared at Umbra's balcony.

Maybe Umbra would be there waiting.

Or maybe they were already dead.

He swallowed hard. One thing at a time. Get nectar. Then escape and then… He'd worry about living in the city when they got there.

Dayne awkwardly made his way over the railing, all his grace gone. It would come back. He needed to eat and sleep and be away from here. "And we jump?"

"Yeah and climb up." Elliot smiled and tried to believe it would all be fine. "We can do this. We can go home."

"I don't want to be caught." He glanced up.

A breeze tugged at Elliot's sheet. He wanted to ask if Dayne had been in there when Umbra had sacrificed themselves but couldn't. He didn't want to think about that or what would happen to them when it was discovered both pets were missing.

Umbra didn't have to do any of this, not for him anyway. If it was part of Umbra's plan, then it was so many moves ahead Elliot couldn't even work out what was going on. But he didn't want Umbra to be hurt. He wanted the chance to kiss them again and wake up in their bed.

He drew in a breath. That wasn't for him no matter how much he wanted it. Somethings were out of reach.

He focused on the railing opposite.

229

"We won't be caught. Ready? You must push off hard. If you don't make it, you'll have to climb up the sheet and try again." There weren't enough sheets to climb all the way down. If there were, Elliot would rather be doing that. The arm that was holding on was starting to ache, his other arm wasn't going to be much help. "On three."

Dayne nodded.

"One. two. Three." Elliot waited a heartbeat longer to be sure Dayne jumped. He did, and Elliot followed. The moment of weightlessness was something that couldn't last. He hit the edge hard and slid before grabbing at the railing. He needed both hands even though one was weaker. His brother was beside him, smiling like he once would've. Then they were climbing up and over. They untied the pants from around their waists and went in.

Umbra's chamber was empty, but as Elliot had promised there was food and nectar. Umbra had made sure there'd be enough for both of them before leaving. Elliot took a large swig and poured more on the wound before encouraging Dayne to drink the rest. While Dayne ate Elliot pulled out his old clothes. He put on the raggedy coat, even though he really wanted to wear the one Umbra had gotten for him. It was a thing of beauty, but something he couldn't wear in the Dark City. He probably couldn't wear it up the hill either. Finally, he picked up the venerie blade and shoved it in his pocket. The curved blade would be waiting for him in the stable with the beast.

But what if Umbra hadn't come back?

Would their beast be back, or would he have to coax another into action? Or would they have to run as fast as they could across the causeway, hoping to avoid the leviathan if there was one and the Kin who'd be chasing them, and that they reached the shore before the sun took away the causeway. There were too many maybes.

Elliot grabbed a piece of fruit and cheese and ate fast. Then he took another chunk to be sure. He didn't know when he'd get to eat this well again. He crept to the main door, unlocked it, and peeked out.

The main walkway was clear. All they had to do was make it around the corner and through the door to the walkway that the servants used—the same one Umbra had lead him through when he'd first come to the castle.

Dayne walked up beside him, his feet bare, but there was nothing that could be done about that now. His feet were too big to borrow Umbra's shoes. "Follow me and move fast."

"Where are we going?"

"Home."

Dayne frowned as though they hadn't discussed this at all.

"Are you feeling better? Did you finish the food and drink?"

"I don't like the drink."

"It's medicine. You need it." He shut the door. "Go."

Dayne walked back to the table. There was still food on the plate.

Elliot snatched up a few more pieces. He needed Dayne to hurry.

"Drink up. Look." He showed Dayne his wrist. The bleeding had stopped, and while it still looked awful, it wasn't as deep. It burned on the inside as it healed.

Dayne made a face, but he choked down the nectar and ate a little more of the food. From the main hall there was shouting. Celebrating or fighting? He grabbed Dayne's hand and pulled him toward the door. They were out of time. He cracked the door and checked the walkway again. Clear.

He pushed Dayne out the door toward the little corridor, then closed the door behind himself. His heartbeat almost drowned out the noise in the hall, and while he was tempted to look, he didn't. He thought he heard Umbra crowing his success but couldn't be sure, and he didn't want to hope too much.

Once the dark of the corridor consumed them, he breathed a little easier, and with his hand tight around his brother's, he ran. He didn't look out at the sea or check for leviathans. He couldn't think about Umbra and the fallout from the missing pets. He had to leave.

This had always been the plan. Umbra expected and needed him to follow it. What did Elliot need?

The easy answer was Umbra.

Caring about a Kin was something that shouldn't have happened, but it had, and he couldn't treat the ache with nectar. There was no wound to heal. Yet. But there would be. No one he loved survived. No matter how hard he tried.

At the base of the stairs, he paused. They'd have to run across the courtyard to the stable. He didn't know how close to dawn it was. If he waited too long, there'd be no causeway; he didn't want to end up in the ocean or the lake. If he went too soon, the Kin would follow. He listened for what felt like forever, chest tight, teeth digging into his lower lip, before edging out of the shadow. The sweeper was there, cleaning the cobbles as usual. He opened a smaller door and flicked his hand as though signaling Elliot.

Elliot frowned. Did the sweeper know he was there?

When he did it again, Elliot pulled Dayne along and ran for the door.

The sweeper nodded. "Won't be too long until dawn."

"How do you know? Why are you helping?"

The sweeper nodded at Dayne. "My boy was their pet before him, and I did nothing. Didn't know how. When I put my broom back, it'll be time to go." He shut the door, and darkness wrapped around them.

Elliot leaned against the wall of the small storage room. They weren't safe. The old man could be lying. He didn't want to wait. The need to leave was an itch in his blood. This halfway time was danger- ous. If they were caught, everyone would know they were trying to flee. Dayne slumped on the floor.

"You okay?"

"This is bad. It's going to hurt."

"It's not going to hurt. They won't hurt you again. I promise." His wrist was burning, and the lies were heavy in his heart. The air became hot. They couldn't stay in the cupboard.

Outside, people shouted.

Elliot squeezed his eyes shut. Vermillion had noticed they were missing.

The door was yanked open. "Go. It's almost dawn but be careful because they're looking."

Elliot squinted at the light, even though it was the same orange sun and inky sky as always. Always dusk, the edge of dark and light.

He pulled Dayne up. It wasn't far to the stables, just across the courtyard.

"Thank you."

They ran. The cobbles were uneven, as though trying to stop them. Elliot kept glancing around, searching for Kin. They were halfway across when Lapis appeared out the servants' door they'd used.

"Run." Elliot gave Dayne a shove toward the stable and drew his knife. He kept moving, no longer running, but watching Lapis.

They didn't run either, but they were gaining. They had that languid stroll that Elliot had seen too many times before Umbra came to bed. Lapis was older than Umbra and more vulnerable to the sun.

Lapis grinned, all fang. Their orange hair was coming loose from its braids. "You have stolen something that wasn't yours."

"He was my brother before their pet."

They pulled their knife. "Killing you will gut Umbra."

"I'm surprised you didn't kill them on the raid. Couldn't find time for treachery?"

Lapis lunged, a move Elliot had seen before. He defended the way he'd been taught. The straight knife was different to the curved one he was used to training with, and he failed to make the cut, but he was ready for the next strike. Lapis wasn't as fast as they should've been. They were evenly matched, but even then, he was forced backward. He made sure each step took him closer to the stable.

They snarled and intensified the attack, slashing and hooking, catching Elliot's old coat and tearing it. The leather waistcoat beneath saved his skin. They pressed forward, and Elliot saw an opening. He dropped and slid, smashing his knee on a cobble but slicing deep into Lapis's groin. Blood splashed over him, and the Kin dropped to their knees.

Not dead.

Just bleeding.

Elliot fumbled with the handle until it came off revealing the antler spike. He stood and thrust the antler into Lapis's neck.

They were already turning as though to cut Elliot's belly, then stopped. Where the antler had struck their neck, black bloomed, first like spider legs then thickening and spreading like spilled ink. They grabbed at their neck, but Elliot was already stepping back, the cobbles slick with bright Kin blood.

He'd killed a Kin. With a venerie blade.

Lapis dropped to the cobbles. Elliot hesitated, then stepped on one of their antlers, it snapped. Lapis clawed at his pants but couldn't find purchase with their weakening fingers. Elliot grabbed the broken antler and ran for the stable. Dayne crouched on the floor, clutching his head. He hadn't watched the fight at all. "Up. Come on."

Where was Umbra's beast?

Elliot scanned the dark room until he saw the one with uneven horns. He put his hand on the skull without hesitating, and it woke with a purr. Behind it on the floor was a bag. Elliot swung the bag over his shoulder and got on the beast, easing it forward until he reached Dayne by the door.

"You killed Lapis."

"I did. Now let's go." He held out his hand, willing his brother to get up. "Before they lock the gates." Before the causeway vanished in daylight. Before his luck ran out and they were eaten by a leviathan. He hoped Umbra knew what they were doing, or there would be nothing but blood and bother in their future.

Dayne didn't grab his hand, but he did get up. The beast headed for the gate. It was open and unguarded as though the Kin didn't expect anyone to come across or try to leave. Elliot leaned forward, and the beast got faster. They cleared the gate, and Elliot let out a whoop of joy.

The layer of water over the causeway splashed his legs. A grin broke his face. They were out. In front of him was the familiar dark area between red lit hills and the bonfires on the shore. The sun was cresting the hills and the houses of the rich. The shadows of the hill were stretching, but the sky was getting light. He leaned further forward, knowing that when the sunlight hit the water, the causeway would be gone. They had to reach the shore.

The sun was racing them. The beast was tiring having already been out that night.

No.

Sunlight caught the shore and spilled golden on the water, getting faster now. The beast faltered as the sunlight hit them. There was nothing under its wheels, and they sunk. Elliot gasped as the cold water closed around them. But his head didn't go under, he pushed off the bottom and kicked toward the shore. Where was Dayne? He turned as Dayne surfaced beside him.

They swam for the shore and stumbled out of the water, their clothing heavy and dripping. He tripped and sat. The castle was gone. Nothing more than mist gathered in the center of the lake. Elliot lay back on the shore and laughed.

Dayne was silent, staring at the lake. "Ver will hunt us."

Elliot gazed up at the golden dawn sky. Had sunrise always been so grand? "Not today they won't. Today, we are free."

PART II
BOTHER

CHAPTER 27

$\mathcal{U}$mbra watched as the sun addled older Abyr tried to respond to Vermillion's alarm. They leaned on the railing, yelling for the missing pets to be found. But those who could still rouse themselves were not exactly rushing to do their bidding.

It was dawn over the lake. They had to sleep, and they had no choice.

It had all gone very splendidly, and it was all they could do to keep the smile off their face.

"You can't rest here." Umbra put a hand on Vermillion's arm.

They snarled and threw Umbra off. "You did this."

"How could I? I was on the raid. *You* had care of them."

Vermillion stifled a yawn, their face contorting with rage and exhaustion. It would be so easy to kill them now. Kill all the ones loyal to Vermillion while they moved slowly and weren't locked behind closed doors for their slumber. But Umbra wasn't as underhanded as Vermillion.

Umbar knew all about the coup Vermillion had led from talking to the human survivors. There'd been an uprising in the human city, but only after, only when Vermillion brought in a new way of doing

239

things. Those in power across the lake had seen the changes and seized the opportunity to enrich themselves.

"You blame me?" Vermillion's eyes glittered with fury.

"You let my pet escape, and I haven't finished my change." They tried to sound upset, but in truth, any male blood would do. He liked Elliot...probably too much. It was for the best their arrangement was over early. But their lies rung hollow and off key.

"You should've tamed him." Vermillion stumbled, their body demanding rest.

Umbra supported them instead of letting them fall. For the moment, they were a solicitous friend. The one equally devastated by this loss. The one Vermillion should trust. Their own bones were heavy as the sun crept higher. If Elliot wasn't across the lake now, he'd be having to swim. Hopefully, he could swim and there were no leviathans trapped in what was no longer an ocean.

Together, they staggered toward Vermillion's chambers. The door hung open. The human guards kept their eyes down as Vermillion walked past, but that didn't save them.

"You let them go. How did they get past you?" Vermillion managed to stay upright, but if Umbra let go, they'd crumple to the floor. That Vermillion was even keeping their eyes open was a feat.

The rage was keeping them going. Something to remember.

"They left on a beast!"

"Lapis is dead!"

The shouts from the hall made Vermillion stiffen. They couldn't fight the urge to sleep much longer, but they were trying. They shoved at Umbra and lunged for the doorway, holding themselves upright on the frame. "Dead?"

"What do they mean dead?" Umbra didn't have to fake being shocked. Killing Lapis hadn't been part of the plan. But if they were truly dead, that was the best news they'd received today—beyond breaking the careful plans that had been made for the raid and turning it into something successful instead of a suicide raid with Umbra's death as the end result. Vermillion had been stunned to see them return with the lord's son who was now in a water level holding cell.

Umbra ran to the railing, every step like wading through nectar. Humans were darting about; did they actually care pets had escaped or were they just trying to look busy? Several Abyr were slumped at the table, unable to wake until dusk.

"Dead," one of the Abyr in hall repeated.

"But how?" It wasn't their place to ask. Vermillion should be asking. Umbra glanced over their shoulder. Vermillion was still against the doorframe, eyes barely open.

"How do you think?"

"Antler."

The word was barely a whisper. Elliot had reclaimed the venerie blade and used it.

Their initial joy that Lapis was dead faded fast.

The one person who had been able to control Vermillion was dead. While they didn't like Lapis and had planned on killing them at some point because they were far more dangerous than Vermillion, Vermillion was ruled by their ego and could be controlled, now Vermillion would want vengeance.

Elliot's blood and their own.

They stepped away from the railing, tiredness seeping through them like too many jugs of mead. Elliot had killed an Abyr, no easy task. All those questions about death, all that training about how to fight. They'd expected Elliot to use those skills at some point, possibly to kill humans, but not an Abyr.

Had they underestimated Elliot's ability to plan and fight or had he simply seen a chance and taken it, knowing that Umbra wanted Lapis dead?

"Your pet is wild."

"Yes. They should be willing to offer their blood." But a pet who turned an antler on any Abyr should be punished. That was a crime. Though was it still a crime if Lapis had attacked first, determined to drag Elliot and his brother back to the castle?

They should be grateful. One problem had been sorted.

But who had they been sharing their bed with? A man who only cared about his brother, or a man who wanted revenge on all Abyr?

"Your pet killed Lapis. You will lie with me while we rest, and we will discuss the venerie problem come dusk."

Umbra glanced at the leader, barely awake. The last thing they wanted was to share Vermillion's bed, even if it was only to sleep. They shook their head.

"That wasn't an offer. Our pets have absconded. Yours is venerie." Their words were slurred. A guard stood close in case Vermillion lost their battle to stay awake.

Venerie, yes. But Umbra had trusted him. They didn't want to see Elliot's eyes dulled with the need for Abyr blood until it consumed all his thoughts and left no room for anything else.

"Assist me," Vermillion ordered.

Umbra wanted to turn and retreat to their rooms, but that would only save them for one day. Better to act like they were on the same side.

They hooked their arm around Vermillion and helped them undress so that they may sleep comfortably. Vermillion lifted their hand to backhand Umbra across the face, but Umbra caught it. They were stronger at the cusps when the sun and moon battled for control. "There is no need."

"Do not tell me what is needed. I will extract payment from your flesh for this." They yanked their hand back, their movements slowed by the dawn.

"Do it then. Why wait?"

Vermillion turned and charged, backing Umbra against the wall, forehead to forehead.

"You want to fuck me?" Umbra cupped their face and kissed them the way they'd done to Elliot.

Vermillion bit Umbra's lip, drawing blood. "You'll keep until tonight. Then you'll give me everything I want. Like last time, all kicking and biting. I love the way you fight."

They laughed and walked naked to the bed. Asleep as soon as they lay down.

Umbra remained leaning against the wall, for several heartbeats before releasing a slow breath. They had gotten lucky the sun was so high and Vermillion had run out of fight. If not, it would be their blood on the floor until Vermillion took their pleasure.

They couldn't go through that again. They would not be a plaything for Vermillion to torment and break. They shuddered even though they had banished most of those memories and buried them beneath more pleasant things. But Elliot wasn't here to soothe the sting. Nor could they flee the castle as easily.

Umbra locked the door with shaking hands. There was no point in trying to leave. And even if they did, the guards would tell Vermillion. They flexed their fingers and paced as exhaustion swelled within them.

When Vermillion woke, they would make good on their threat unless Umbra had a plan in place. They draped their coat over a chair and took off their knife. For a moment, they toyed with the idea of slitting Vermillion's throat but discarded it just as fast. That wasn't a plan; that would only create chaos. And chaos was destructive.

There would be plans made tomorrow to retrieve Dayne and Elliot. Vermillion wouldn't let this act of rebellion by the pets go unpunished. However, without Lapis, there was an opening to be filled, and if Vermillion were smart, Umbra could fill it. All Umbra had to do was make sure Vermillion's ego was petted and fed until such time Umbra was ready to feed them to the leviathans.

Or stake them out in the city.

They hadn't decided yet.

They stripped off their clothes and slid into the bed. Vermillion didn't move.

Even though the rising sun was sucking them dry, it was a long time before Umbra could close their eyes and sleep. Worry formed a knot of their innards and drew tight. Fear of what to come, or more precisely, the pain and shamble back to their chambers to heal and the whispers that would follow.

They were a prime. They shouldn't be getting treated like a

common warrior. Vermillion should be honored Umbra was even sharing their bed.

They wouldn't be. With each passing night, Umbra was glad they had chosen a male pet. Bearing Vermillion's child would be no honor. But with Lapis dead, there were no other volunteers.

And with no pet, Umbra had no blood, and they still needed to drink regularly for the next sennight. It was entirely possible Vermillion would try to starve them and force them to change. That gave them a month. One month to tear apart the city and the castle and rebuild.

It was one thing to have a plan and an idea for revenge on the monster lying next to them, but another to actually have the first move in play. And while Elliot had started the game, Umbra wasn't sure how well they could trust their partner. Now that Elliot was free, he may want nothing to do with the Abyr...

Dayne on the other hand...well it wouldn't be long until he burned for another taste of blood.

～

Umbra's sleep wasn't restful. They were chased across an ossic board always being pursued. They couldn't win while running, but they couldn't stop running. When they woke, it was like being dragged from the depths of the lake and thrust into the harsh, hot light of the bonfires. They wanted to get out of this bed and retreat to safety.

They drew in a breath and let their heartbeat calm a little. It would do them no good to tuck tail and flee. Vermillion would only see that as a challenge. All this time they'd been pushing them away, trying to escape their interest, but they'd been playing the game wrong. They'd been playing it the way Vermillion wanted them to play.

New tactics were required. They turned onto their side to watch Vermillion sleep. They were attractive in rest, but their face took on a harshness that did them no favors when awake. Their hair was dark green in the dim glow of the lights. Green had never been one of Umbra's favorite colors.

Elliot's worn green coat came to mind, a muted shade that was closer to gray. Would he have taken that with him? Or had he left some small reminder for Umbra to cling to? They wanted to see what was left in their room and what was missing. Perhaps he'd taken everything of value, Umbra wouldn't blame him if he had.

They shouldn't blame him for killing Lapis. If he hadn't, he and his brother would've been dragged back, and Dayne wouldn't have lived for another sennight. Blood loss, lack of food, and a lack of will to go on. All unnecessary cruelty.

They reached out a hand and ran it over Vermillion's chest. They could let them sleep, but where would be the fun in that? Their hand slid lower, beneath the blanket, and skated over their hip.

How much longer did Vermillion need to sleep? Their antlers weren't so huge they couldn't wake until the sun had completely set. But then Umbra's weren't so big they needed to wait until the sun was sinking. They had watched the sun rise and set soon after arriving. Before drinking blood, that had been easy to do. They had loved watching the castle shift between worlds at home too. They would miss it when their antlers got so big, they couldn't resist sleep.

Vermillion's hand closed over theirs and dragged it to their soft stem. Umbra didn't pull their hand away. They closed their eyes and pretended it was someone else. That Elliot was first in their mind was not comforting. Elliot's stem felt different. It was bigger even when limp and terrifying when hard; he could not imagine that being stuck inside any part of them even though Elliot assured him that it was common practice among humans. Licking and sucking him didn't count.

It was going to take thoughts of Elliot to rouse their body to action, so while Vermillion lay there, struggling to wake, they remembered what Elliot's mouth had felt like, the way his body moved when his legs had been wrapped around their hips and they ground together. Or the way he'd rolled his hips as they'd sat in the chair, thrusting into Umbra's willing hand, the taste of his blood on their tongue.

Their heartbeat quickened, but Elliot wouldn't be waiting next door. Their bed would be cold. They would be safe from a man who was now venerie. They'd be obliged to hunt him and kill him. Obligation and desire warred. For the moment, that wasn't their concern.

They rolled to lay over Vermillion, the way Elliot had with them. They didn't try to kiss Vermillion the way they would've kissed Elliot, but they had learned how to put on a convincing performance. A look, a touch, those first few things they hadn't wanted Elliot to do...until they had wanted him to look at them like that and mean it.

Had he, or had it been an act?

Vermillion's eyes flickered open. They stared up, unfocussed and stiffening beneath Umbra. For a moment, Umbra was repulsed with themselves and Vermillion. How did Elliot do this for coin?

"Are you awake yet?" Umbra rolled their hips, wondering what kind of creature they'd become. But if it got them permanently kicked out of Vermillion's bed, it would be worth the debasement.

Vermillion groaned. "What are you doing?"

"You wanted me here, so I thought we could dally in bed a little longer?"

Vermillion gave them a shove, and Umbra rolled onto their back, expecting Vermillion to follow and continue, but they didn't move. "You thought wrong."

Umbra propped themselves up, biting back on the smile. Was their acquiescence that much of a letdown? Better than the rough treatment and deliberate causing of pain. Just because they could heal didn't make getting hurt fun. That wasn't their preference. They much preferred Elliot's more sensuous movements, his smile and kiss. His touch.

They blinked. They had to stop thinking of their now free pet. They were nothing to each other. A pleasant moment in time that couldn't be stretched any further.

Vermillion closed their eyes as though asleep. They weren't. What were they planning? Something unpleasant, no doubt.

Don't fight back.

This time, they had to give Vermillion nothing. They had failed every other time. Had lashed out which had made Vermillion enjoy it more. For every blow they landed, Vermillion had repaid thrice. But they were more evenly matched now, and while last time Umbra had let Vermillion rebuild their damaged pride, this wasn't the same. They shouldn't have fought back at all last time, but they hadn't been able to stop. Their own pride had refused to let them submit. They swallowed, knowing that had been a mistake.

They were too used to being prime and being obeyed.

Vermillion reached out and grabbed a fistful of hair, tugging Umbra down. They didn't resist. They shoved down the blankets and climbed between Vermillion's legs as though eager. A little dark green hair clung to their pods, a sign of the length of time they'd been drinking blood or amount they'd been drinking. Umbra didn't want to ever drink enough to get hair, but they liked to run their fingers through the dusting on Elliot's chest, feel the roughness of his leg hair as they moved together.

They licked and lapped as though there was nothing they wanted more.

Vermillion shoved them over again and followed. Umbra simply opened their mouth for the offered stem. No fighting, even though they wanted to bite it off and their fingers were curling into fists.

Vermillion drew back, barely hard. "No fight in the morning?"

"We need to be united in this disaster." Umbra forced their hand to trail up Vermillion's thigh.

They snatched Umbra's hand away and pinned it to the bed. It took everything Umbra had not to struggle.

Be compliant.

The change in strategy worked as Vermillion softened.

Vermillion leaned in close, gripping their jaw. "Were you fucking your pet?"

"Why not get maximum value? Weren't you?"

"You disgust me," Vermillion said.

"Did I break another rule? That kind of thing didn't matter in Octadine."

"I'm sick of hearing about Octadine. Your home is here. You will obey my rules. We don't fuck pets, and we don't leave them wild." They got up and stalked away to grab clothes out of the wardrobe. "I haven't forgotten, nor will I forget. You deceived me, made it look like he tasted your blood. When they are recaptured, I will feed him my blood to make sure it is done right."

CHAPTER 28

The sun had never felt so grand on his skin, but it did little to warm him. Elliot turned his face to the sky as he walked, keeping hold of Dayne's hand as they made their way from the shore toward town. The icy water had washed the blood from his clothes and hands, but everything he wore was wet, and the breeze was cold, chilling him immediately. It was tempting to stop at the bonfires and warm up, but he wanted to get home and get inside.

It had only been a fortnight, but the city wasn't the same.

Green coated marshals were everywhere. It wasn't uncommon to see them walking in pairs in daylight, but already Elliot had counted ten and they were only halfway home.

The markets were emptier too. At this time of the morning they should've been full of people haggling for their daily bread. There were less stalls too. They made their way deeper into the Dark City. In daylight, it wasn't dark just grimy and cloaked in shadows from the tall buildings and skinny streets.

Had it always been so run down? He noticed the broken windows, the charred buildings where some made do with meagre shelter. As they walked deeper into the dark part, the cobbles ended, and the roads became hard packed dirt. They narrowed so a cart would barely fit. The stink of night soil tossed into the gutter filled his lungs. Had it always smelled this bad?

He kept hold of Dayne's hand and forced a smile when all he wanted to do was cry with the reality of being back home. "Almost there."

He'd always thought their building one of the best. But as he stared up at it now, he realized it was as rickety and worn as the others. Nothing special. It wasn't a castle with running water in a private bathroom or fancy orb lights. The beds weren't huge and soft, and he wouldn't be sharing it with a lover.

There'd be no breakfast delivery. No new clothing on a whim. No lingering in bed and finding new ways to occupy themselves.

His life was as threadbare and frayed as everything else here. He was going to have to patch something together so they could get by.

He kept his smile in place and pulled his brother on, they passed another pair of marshals. They never usually came this deep into the dark unless there was trouble, and even then, murder wasn't enough. It had to be a riot or fire. Death was nothing special.

The landlord sipped tea on the front step as usual. He looked up, eyes widening.

"My room still there or did you think me dead?" Elliot said with far more bravado then he felt. If he didn't have a room, everything was going to be that much harder.

"Still there." His gaze slid to Dayne. "I didn't think you could do it. How did you?"

Elliot licked his lip and wondered how much to tell. "I made a deal."

"With a Kin?"

"Yeah." He'd made more than one...he'd agreed to help Umbra overthrow Vermillion. All he had to do was lead a rebellion against those up the hill. They were the ones telling everyone that the Kin were blood thirsty monsters, but they never lifted a finger to fight them because of the nectar and orbs.

The landlord offered his cigarette. "You might be needing this again. I'll get your key."

Elliot took a drag and coughed. The smoke burned his throat and tasted worse than he remembered. He offered it to Dayne who just shook his head. Would the Kin blood in Dayne not mix with the leaf? Elliot coughed again, not sure how he'd ever liked smoking leaf or if he even should. What if Umbra turned up at his window looking for a feed?

If they brought nectar with them, he'd bare his neck and more.

The landlord returned with the key and reclaimed his cigarette. "Good to have you back. Both of you."

"It's good to be back." The words fell off his tongue even though he didn't mean them. This was where he belonged. This was home. But as he climbed the stairs to the top, he wanted to be back in the castle, warm and wrapped in Umbra's arms.

~

*I*t didn't take long to get settled. The room was cold and stale, so Elliot flung open the window and set the oven so it was ready to light once the room had aired. He had no idea where his flint was. And while the rent was paid for another fortnight, he didn't have any coin for food. That could be solved tonight. He was running through what needed to be done, but he'd seen how others lived and had tasted what it was like to not worry about where the coin was coming from. He wanted more than surviving.

Dayne stood in the middle of the room, his head not much below the rafter. "What happened to our room?"

Elliot pulled off his sodden coat. He was as cold in it as he was out of it. "I couldn't afford it."

"Oh…" Dayne stared at the floor.

"I tried. I worked your job and mine, waiting for you to come back, then looking for you down by the lake. But I couldn't keep it together, and then the rent went up. And then I met Umbra."

Dayne's gaze landed on him again, and there was something calculated in it. If Vermillion got him, he'd be forced to spill all their secrets. His brother was back, but not as he had been.

251

"What's with you and them?"

"They said you were at the castle, and that if I was their pet while they changed, I'd be able to see you. I wanted you back."

Dayne shook his head. "No...you don't crave Kin blood."

"I never tasted it."

Dayne opened his mouth, and his eyes lost focus. "It's like being alive in a hundred different ways at once. How am I going to get it?"

"I don't know yet. Let's get out of the wet clothes and get the fire going."

"Ver will look for me."

"They can look all they want, but they can't take you. I won't let them. I won't fail you again."

Dayne undressed silently.

Elliot did the same. He dried off on the coarse cloth and pulled on dry pants, hoping the pants Umbra had given him wouldn't be ruined. Between the two of them, they strung a line and hung up their sodden clothing. Water dripped on the floor, staining it dark.

Elliot tipped out the bag that Umbra had left for him. The curved blade fell out, along with his flint, a leather pouch that clinked rather hopefully, and a small glass vial filled with liquid gold. The nectar was worth more than anything Elliot could sell. He kissed the vial and grinned at Dayne.

Dayne didn't smile. He picked up the curved knife and examined the blade in much the same way that Umbra had handled the knife. "Where is the one you used on Lapis?" Elliot reached in the pocked of his coat and pulled out the venerie blade. Dayne took it and pulled the hilt free, exposing the blood-stained antler. "You killed them."

"Yes." He watched his brother. Dayne knew what to do to reveal the antler.

"Where did you get this?" Dayne wiped the antler, then the hilt and blade before putting it back together.

He'd rescued his brother...but who was he?

"From a friend who thought I might need it." Dayne handed it back and Elliot added it to the pile on the bed. "How did you know what it was?"

Dayne was silent as he sat on the other narrow bed, head in his hands. Dripping water filled the silence.

"When did you become venerie?" Elliot pressed.

"Months ago. I had to do something. I saw them hunting round here all the time."

Dayne had courted trouble instead of being safe. Anger bubbled in Elliot's blood. All of this could have been avoided if Dayne hadn't gotten involved with the venerie.

"And how did you get caught?"

Dayne shrugged. "I don't know. It just happened. I never got the chance to kill one. Why didn't you kill Ver?"

He didn't really know. He could've. But Umbra had a plan, and Vermillion was better alive for the moment. He couldn't tell Dayne that, though. "I didn't carry the blade. Couldn't. They'd have smelled the antler or something."

"You didn't kill Umbra in their sleep either."

"I had no need to. They aren't cruel. Things are different where they're from." He hid the nectar and the venerie blade, then poured the coins onto the bed and grinned. He didn't know where Umbra had gotten the coins and didn't really care. "I think we should go to the Moss and celebrate your return."

Dayne stared at him. "Have I returned? I'm devoured. You can't hide from that. I can't. I can feel the craving gnawing in my belly."

"We'll fix it. Maybe if you sip nectar."

"That might work for a bit, but the craving will get too strong. It tears and hurts. I'll lose my mind, thinking only of a taste. I've seen them on the shore. I'd be better off dead."

"No." Elliot dropped to his knees and clasped his brother's hands. "We can do this."

"*I* will have to do this. You can't fight this battle for me." He pressed the back of Elliot's hand to his cheek. "I'm not a child anymore. You don't have to tell me pretty lies when I've lived the ugly truth."

Elliot embraced his brother. "We'll celebrate and be back inside by dark. We'll plan and find a way to get you Kin blood. Please let us enjoy this day." For one day, could they not pretend that everything was fine?

His brother's eyes were liquid and filled with pain. "One day. By the end of it, the craving will be taking over."

❧

*D*espite Dayne's protests, they ended up walking to the Moss and Mallow for the simple reason that there was no one Dayne wanted to see at his favorite tavern, and the Moss's ale was about ten times better which more than made up for the lack of women—or at least that's what he'd promised Dayne.

It was early so those coming off night work would be there to have a drink before bed. Excitement buzzed in Elliot's veins. He'd done what everyone thought was impossible. But when he glanced at Dayne, the way he hunched his shoulders and stared at the ground as he walked, Elliot knew it wasn't over.

They passed a couple of marshals whose gaze lingered on them a little too long as though expecting trouble.

"Was there a riot or something?" Elliot muttered. He'd only been gone a fortnight.

"Dunno, but something is off." Dayne sniffed as though he could smell rotten meat. "Maybe they're looking for my kind."

Elliot frowned, then realized what Dayne meant. "Where do they meet?"

"Not at the Hare and Wick." He almost smiled.

So definitely at the Hare and Wick. "I thought you went there for the company."

"I did at first. That's where Serene works." His brother blushed. "But things happened."

"And you don't want them to know your back."

"They'll know. They know everything, Elli."

"Then why not—"

"Because I don't want Serene to see me blood addled and wanting what no one should want." He lowered his voice. "I don't want her pity, and I don't want to see her turn cold."

"Love isn't that easy to kill."

"Tell me exactly how many men you have loved with your heart, not your body."

Elliot opened his mouth and shut it just as fast. Killian didn't count. Sure they had a thing but neither of them were thinking about living together. Before him, there'd been a list of others who'd been equally as trivial but important at the time as he reclaimed his body for his pleasure.

Dayne stopped and stared at him. "Have you ever loved anyone?"

"You." But it wasn't the answer Dayne was looking for.

"You have to. I'm your brother."

"I could've left you there. You'd have been dead within a fortnight."

Dayne nodded. "Now I get to suffer." He shoved open the door and went down the three steps.

There was a small crowd. Less than Elliot expected. He scanned the faces, smiling at the ones he knew. He wanted to tell tales of his adventure, but Dayne's sullenness sucked the joy. His brother would rather be dead.

Death was too final for Elliot. At least while he was alive, he could fight.

He ordered two ales and they sat at the bar. Everyone here was tired; he could see it in their eyes and the way they huddled over their drinks. How was he going to lead a rebellion when no one had the time or energy?

"Didn't expect to see you again." The bartender put the drinks down.

Elliot grinned. "Course I was coming back. No one waters ale like you."

"Shh. It's gonna get a whole lot more watered soon. Word is, not much coming into the city. Trouble with the Kin and trading."

"So it'll be liquor only?" Umbra had talked about trade, something to do with nectar and orbs, but Elliot hadn't paid much attention because he didn't care what the rich did with their ill-gotten spoils.

He didn't really like liquor, and his experience with mead had only solidified that opinion.

"Don't know yet."

Someone threw an arm around his shoulder and kissed his cheek. "I thought you were dead for sure." Killian dropped onto the stood next to him. "You did it then?"

"Yeah. That's my brother." Elliot grinned.

"Hey, brother."

"I'm not sitting here while you catch up with your boyfriend." Dayne got up.

"He's not my…" But it was too late, Dayne was making his way over to a quiet table in the corner. Elliot sighed. "He's got to get used to being back."

"Is he back or is he…you know?" Killian glanced at Dayne, but was still leaning in, close enough that Elliot could kiss him if he moved a little. Killian's hand was on his lower back, and if he closed his eyes, he could pretend that everything was fine.

Elliot's smile faded, and he sipped his ale. It was more watered than usual. "You know."

"I'm sorry. And you?"

"Me…I'm just me."

Killian was staring at him now. Could he see the silvery lines that marked his neck and wrists? But there were no red orbs here, only simple lanterns, and when Elliot glanced at his wrist nothing was visible.

"You're a mad fuck, going to the castle and stealing your brother." Killian kissed him, and Elliot turned his head to catch his lips.

"You should've seen it. More food and drink than you'd believe."

"What did you do while there?"

Elliot turned the glass. He couldn't tell Killian or anyone the truth, not all of it. "I traded my blood for Dayne."

"That's all?"

"That's all. They have people working in the castle. Beyond the castle is a whole other place filled with Kin. It's like another country or something. We disappear when the sun rises, and there's an ocean.

Water as far as the eye can see where the lake was. The monsters are leviathans that get trapped when the sun rises."

Killian stared as though Elliot was telling tall tales best suited to children.

"We don't vanish, they do."

"From their side, we vanish."

Killian frowned. "But we don't."

Elliot almost argued but stopped himself. "I'm glad to be back." If he kept saying it, it would become true. He had Dayne and they had their room and it would be fine. "I have to sort out some work. Hear anything?"

He knew where he'd end up if there was nothing else.

"I'll let you know. But I don't like your chances."

"What's with all the marshals?"

"They've been out prowling, looking for trouble for the last sennight. Picking up people for no good reason, and we all know where they'll end up. People will want to know how you did it." Killian nodded at Dayne. "'Cause most of them won't be coming back."

He'd gotten his brother...but what about all the others? The ones who weren't pets, but were killed for Vermillion's sport? He couldn't save them all.

"Marshals are taking on people, but you have to have the coin for a coat. I'm saving up. Pay's better. You should join me."

Be a marshal and round up the poor to feed to the Kin so the rich could feast on nectar? Never.

"I need a job first." Elliot jerked his head at his brother who was still sitting alone and slid off the stool. "I should go sit with him."

Killian put his hand over Elliot's. "Don't disappear again, okay? Maybe come around some time?" He smiled as though nothing had changed.

He could already see Killian in marshal green.

"I'd like that," he lied easily, knowing it wouldn't happen, then turned away.

The Moss was filling now. People slapped him on the shoulder as he walked by.

"Back from the dead."

"Poke the Kin in the eye."

"I hope you killed a few of the bastards."

Elliot smiled, and they bought him drinks. They wanted to know how he'd gotten over and how he'd escaped. How many were dead. He downed the ale and basked in their attention. He'd saved his brother.

This was the celebration he'd wanted, but it felt wrong somehow. They pressed close, wanting him to tell the part where he killed Lapis again and again. Their eyes lit with hate and desperation. They were hungry for blood. The wrong blood.

He jumped onto a chair, not sure if it wobbled or he did. "Listen, before the rumor outstrips the truth."

Some of the men laughed.

"I've been to the castle and returned with my brother. Here's what I see after being gone for a fortnight: marshals hunting us, locking us up to be handed over, and those up the hill want their cure-all and orbs, but they don't want to pay for it. We pay for it. With our blood, with our lives, and we accept it. Who here hasn't lost someone? Who here hasn't gotten a job because someone went missing? And if you know of any work, let me know because in a fortnight, I'll have no room either." He tried to make light of it, but it was the biting truth and they all knew it.

They looked up at him. "And what would you have us do?"

The door swung open, and four green coated marshals pushed in, batons out.

Elliot's eyes widened. *Blood and bother.*

Someone pulled him off the chair. They couldn't be here for him. Could they? Elliot shoved through the crowd and grabbed Dayne's sleeve.

"We've got to go." Elliot dragged Dayne clear of a fight, and they slid behind the bar. Marshals blocked the door. They couldn't get out.

Dayne crouched low, hands over his head. The sound of flesh being struck made Elliot wince. People were shouting and screaming.

The bartender gave him a kick. "Pretty words up on the chair, but no action when the trouble arrives."

Elliot glanced up. He needed to do more than talk. But what? He'd spoken on a whim, not a plan.

"Where's the one boasting about escaping the Kin?" one of the marshals shouted over the noise. "Hand him over."

"Shove that baton up your ass." Glass shattered.

"Is there another door?" Dayne asked.

"We can't go. We have to help," Elliot said.

"We can't help. If we stay, we'll be arrested. We'll be handed to Vermillion." Dayne glanced at him, eyes wide.

"It's my fault." He shouldn't have said anything, but he wanted people to know who the real enemy was.

Dayne shook his head. "Someone told."

"Why would they tell?"

"To earn extra coin."

Elliot gasped. No one spoke to the marshals unless they were forced to.

"Got you." A marshal stood at the end of the bar.

Elliot scrambled up and ran toward the other end of the bar. A chair crashed into the bottles, sending glass and alcohol over the floor, his clothes and skin.

Every other time, when he'd slipped out the back to make good use of the wall and the man he was with, no one had blocked his way. Now there were men everywhere, fighting and shoving. The green coats were outnumbered. They could take them. And what? Kill them?

That's what rebellion meant. They were fighting to live. Not all of them would survive.

Dayne grunted.

Elliot turned and lashed out to stop Dayne from being dragged away. Elliot kicked the marshal's knee, and he dropped to the floor with a howl.

"Move it." He grabbed Dayne's arm and pushed past. He took a blow to the shoulder, from a baton and elbowed a marshal in the jaw but didn't stop to make sure he was down. Elliot kept moving. Once they made it to the corridor it was better, past the piss room, past the storeroom.

The back door swung open. Another pair of marshals.

"Fuck," Dayne swore.

"Piss room," Elliot said, backing up. He opened the door, the smell thick on the air and dragged Dayne in before slamming the door. There was no way to lock it and the window wasn't made to be opened. "Get the window out."

The door vibrated against his back. His heart hammered. He hadn't gotten out of the castle to be thrown in prison and handed over. Vermillion would kill him. Vermillion couldn't have ordered a search already. The Kin would all be sleeping.

Dayne was right.

"One of us summoned the marshals." Elliot didn't want to believe it, but there was no other explanation.

"Yeah." Dayne used his knife to lever the small window out of the wall. "How do you think I was named and caught? Someone told the Kin where we'd be. Some were killed, but Ver wanted a pet. Someone he could break."

"Did he?"

The window came free. "I don't want to think about those first few days. But then I was lost in the blood haze and it was easy. Then you show up, and it all starts over, but with less blood. They want you, not me. You should go first."

"You go." Elliot drew the curved Kin blade. Dayne was in no state to fight. His hands shook and his skin was ashen.

"You kill a marshal, they'll be hanging up pictures with your face."

"They'll be doing that anyway." Elliot jerked as the door was hit. "Go up to the roofs."

"I'll see you at home." Dayne pulled himself up and out the small window. There was nothing but a brick wall on the other side. Just enough room for a man to walk between, or there would've been if it weren't filled with rubbish.

With his brother clear and the marshals shoving at the door, there wasn't much Elliot could do but let them in. He readied himself. It was only a few steps to the window, but he wouldn't get that far. Not without a fight.

The next time they struck the door, he sprung forward, and three marshals tumbled in and landed in a heap. A fourth tried to jump over them to get to Elliot but tripped. Elliot sheathed the blade and dragged himself up to the window. He was almost out before one got a hand on his boot. He wasn't about to lose the nicest pair he'd ever been given. He kicked, the laces held fast, and he wormed his way out. There was shouting at the end of the alley as he climbed upward to the roof.

Then he crept along the tops of several, making the small jumps without looking down. His heart was beating too fast and sweat dampened his underarms. He couldn't go home yet. Not while they were looking for him.

Elliot perched on what was left of the roof of a shaky building that had partially collapsed last summer. Two sides were still up; the rest had been cannibalized to build something new. With his back to the chimney, he waited for the fuss to die down and the marshals to disperse.

He was home. This was supposed to be easy. He was supposed to be able to enjoy his success and have his brother back. But he wasn't even sure who his brother was.

A pet. A venerie. Not the boy Elliot thought he'd been protecting.

CHAPTER 29

*E*lliot kept his snood up and his eyes down. He stayed among people as much as possible as he bought enough food to last them a few days. Everything had gone up. Not much but enough that he noticed. Even though it was noon, he was chilled to the bone after sitting on the roof waiting for the fuss to die down. How could the men at the Moss have sold him out to the marshals?

As casually as he could, he made sure he wasn't being followed by ducking down alleys, circling around, and trying not to check over his shoulder every other pace. When he was sure he was alone, he went into the boarding house, and then ran up the stairs. The room was unlocked. Dayne sat on his bed, knees drawn up like a child.

"Are you okay?" Elliot dumped the food on the table. He checked the fire and added wood before warming his hands.

"No," Dayne whispered. He stretched his legs, their father's boots on his feet.

"You hurt?" Elliot couldn't see any blood.

Dayne shook his head. "Nothing you can see." His lips twitched. "I used to wonder about the devoured. How they could live wild on the shore, scavenging when they remembered to eat. But my first thought was to run to the shore. To go back to the Kin like that was safer."

"They control you?"

"I don't hear orders...but there's something broken inside me. Why would I go back when I know what Ver will do? Yet that's what I want more than anything."

"Not all the Kin are like them."

"I'll end up on the shore when I can't resist."

"And I'll bring you back and make sure you eat." They could do this. Umbra would give Dayne blood, and they'd make it work.

"I saw the look in your boyfriend's eyes. He knew what I was. Don't you see? There's no devoured in the city, there never has been. Families let them go for a reason."

"Would you have let me go?"

Dayne was silent for too many heart beats.

Elliot spun away but there was nowhere to go to in the tiny room. "Fuck you. I risked everything to save you."

"And what have I got left? You didn't save me for me, you did it because you couldn't live knowing I was there."

"You're the only family I have."

"You have to stop thinking I'm family. If Ver offered me blood, I'd sell you out in a heartbeat." His lips twisted. "I don't want to, but I know I would. Because I can feel the hunger scratching at my veins. I know that food will lack taste, and water won't quench the thirst. When all I want is one little taste of hot Kin blood, what will you do?"

"I'll look after you."

"You can't watch me all the time. One of us should get to live. And it won't be me."

"Don't talk like that. We'll find a way."

When was he going to find time to create a rebellion to help Umbra?

"I knew the moment I was caught, I was done. I survived the first and then the second night...I wish I hadn't survived the third. Then I was given nectar and blood and questioned again about the venerie and my family. Da was venerie, Elli. He hunted the Kin."

"No. He wasn't. He worked in the field."

"And at night he hunted. He used to go to the Hare and Wick. Mama let him go."

Elliot shook his head. "I'm not letting you go to the shore to waste away."

"You can't fix everything. I watched you pull yourself apart for Mama. I know what you did when you went out."

"You weren't supposed to know."

"I didn't, not at first. But you got a look and snapped if anyone brushed against you when you sold yourself. And I heard Mama telling you not to."

Elliot blinked, his eyes hot. "So? If I don't find work, I'll do it again." He'd be keeping them both afloat when it would be so much easier to sink.

"You don't have to."

"I promised Mama I'd look after you."

Dayne glared at him, his forehead creased. "I'm not a kid. You don't have to look after me."

"Clearly, I do."

"I didn't ask you to rescue me."

"You were dying."

"Don't tell me it was a noble sacrifice. You didn't get that look when letting the Kin fuck you."

Elliot checked on the clothes strung across the room, so he didn't have to look at his brother. His cheeks heated, but he ignored the burn. The socks were almost dry. His coat wasn't. Dayne needed a new coat. The coins they had would soon be spent. "How did you know?"

"I heard a lot of gossip sitting at Vermillion's feet."

So the whole castle knew. "And what did they think about that?"

"That Umbra is weak."

"And what do you think about that?"

"That you'd fuck anything with a dick and a pretty face for free."

Elliot bit his lip and kept his back turned. "Was that an insult or a compliment?"

"Neither, just fact. You don't have to worry about getting anyone pregnant. Maybe it's easier for you to have fun." Dayne pushed the wet pants aside. "You deserve some fun."

"So do you." They deserved better than just getting by.

Dayne's expression shuttered. "I don't want to talk about it."

Because it still hurt. He'd seen the way Dayne had reacted to the fight in the Moss. Before, his brother would've been joining in and looking for trouble.

"Then we won't. And you don't get to press me about what I did in the castle either."

"I wasn't going to ask what deal you made because I'll tell. But I know you made one that went beyond blood and sex. Ver will want me back, and you have to promise not to come after me again."

"I can't do that."

"I'm a danger."

"You're my brother." Vermillion would want him too, just to spite Umbra.

Dayne hugged him. "You're an idiot."

"I know. When did you get so smart?"

"I wasn't sleeping while you were working."

No, his brother had been getting into trouble with the venerie.

Killing the Kin wouldn't change anything. They had to stop the rich leeches from sucking them dry.

"Will the venerie help us?"

"Probably not. Helping would put them all at risk."

"I have to look for work. You want to look for a coat at the market or will you walk to the shore?" How much supervision would Dayne need?

"We should stay in."

"I'll be back by dark." The Kin would hunt tonight. Vermillion would tear apart the city searching for his lost pet.

"I don't want you to leave. I might hate you tomorrow because you stopped me from getting blood."

He could look for work tomorrow. There'd be just as few jobs. If he didn't go out, he could stay nice and warm. "Okay. You want to play cards or something?"

Dayne nodded. "You wanted to pretend like everything was fine for today. So let's do that."

But every time the stairs creaked, they both looked up as though expecting someone to batter down the door. It was late afternoon, the sunlight golden honey as it spread across the floor, when someone did knock on the door.

Elliot got up, hand already on the curve blade at his hip as though he'd been a warrior for years not weeks. "Who is it?"

"Serene."

Dayne winced and shook his head. She'd heard the news. They lived in the same boarding house, so it had only been a matter of time. Elliot opened the door a crack and peered out, but it was only her. He moved his hand from the hilt.

"Is it true?" She tried to look past him.

"What?"

She smiled. "He *is* back. Is he in?"

Elliot stepped aside, and she slithered past, ducking under the laundry. Dayne did his best to act like nothing had changed and that he still wanted to marry her. Elliot couldn't be here for this. There was no privacy to be had; as kids they'd never worried about it, but how had their parents managed to talk without every word being overheard?

He left the room, so he didn't have to hear them kiss and whisper. He sat on the top step in the dark, the old house breathing around him. Was Dayne breaking it off or keeping the lie alive?

After a few more moments, he got up and walked down the stairs. Might as well go looking for work now.

~

*I*t was getting close to dusk when Elliot returned, cold to his bones and without a single prospect. He'd been told to queue at the leaf processing plant with every other hopeful even though he'd worked there before. He'd stopped in at the nightsoil dump, but there was nothing there, and Killian hadn't been there either. He'd tried a few other places but had gotten the same response. He wanted to go and see Fife but didn't want to be out past dusk. Not the first night, maybe not ever.

He jogged up the stairs, the only part of him that was warm was his toes because of Umbra's nice blue boots. A few people glanced at him as he passed. Did they know who he was? Would they report him to the marshals?

He opened the door, expecting Serene to still be there from the smell of cooking, but Dayne was alone.

"How did it go?"

Dayne didn't look at him, too focused on the pot he was stirring. "I told her it was over."

"Why would you do that? She loves you."

"No, she loved who I was. I'm not that person anymore."

"You are."

Dayne shot him a red eyed glare. "I'm devoured. I know that. You need to accept that. Things will never be how they were, no matter what you do. I need Kin blood. By morning, it will be all I can think about. By nightfall, I'll be unthinking."

"I'll get you blood."

Dayne shook his head and turned back to the oven. "Yeah. Your Kin going to knock on our door and offer himself?"

"Most likely the window, and they've already been invited in so…" His stomach knotted like boot laces. Inviting Umbra in probably hadn't been a smart move, but it was too late to uninvite them. Would Umbra turn up to feed or would they make do with a devoured on the shore?

"How could you do that?"

"I had to. I did what I had to," he said softly. That was his whole life.

He looked at dead man's room. The wind whistled outside, and the building creaked. He'd always been satisfied before, hadn't he? Known this was his lot and that he couldn't expect more. But now he'd tasted more, and he knew what it was like to wake up rested and fed and to not have to worry about where the next meal was coming from. He wanted that. He wanted Umbra even though he shouldn't. He hadn't tasted Kin blood, but he was still addicted.

"Did you talk to any of the people who worked in the castle?"

"No." Dayne dished the stew into the bowls. It was mostly beans with a little meat and some vegetables to spread it out further. "I didn't get to do anything."

"And you knew that?"

"When the high wore off, yes, until the craving began. But the most dangerous part was that in between. Ver liked me to be alert for the beatings."

Elliot accepted his bowl and stared out the window. The castle was forming out of mist on the lake, solidifying with every breath. "I spoke to some. They'd worked there for generations. Some were the children of pets. No new people have been accepted to work there since Vermillion took over. The Kin worried about being stabbed."

"You could have killed them all while they slept."

Elliot ate so he couldn't answer.

Dayne stared at him, then nodded. "It's like that, is it? A coup?"

"Blood and bother. They're riding tonight." Elliot pointed to the red glimmers crossing the lake. Dinner turned leaden in his stomach. He wasn't ready.

"Guess we'll find out if your Kin will betray their welcome." Dayne drew the curtains.

"If you go to the shore, you'll be taken." And getting his brother back would be that much harder a second time.

"Maybe I'll take a piece of that antler with me and stab them."

They both knew that wouldn't happen. In Vermillion's presence, Dayne would obey their every command.

They finished eating washed the dishes and turned out the light. The room was cast in the flickering shadows of the fire when the first thump on the roof echoed too close to their heads. They both glanced up, but neither spoke.

Someone knocked on the window. Dayne got up, but Elliot grabbed him and shoved him to the bed, pinning him down so he couldn't get up. Dayne struggled, fighting back, his eyes lit from within.

"Let me in," Vermillion purred.

Elliot clamped a hand over Dayne's mouth. His brother bucked and struggled, desperate to obey the Kin blood in his body. Sweat made his skin slick and he was strong.

Outside the window, Vermillion laughed. "You can't resist me all night."

Dayne bit Elliot's hand, and in the moment of shock, was able to toss Elliot off. Elliot scrambled up. Vermillion was right. They couldn't do this all night. Elliot hooked his arm around his brother's throat and held on until he went limp.

Elliot lowered him to the floor and kissed Dayne's temple. "I'm sorry."

He hadn't realized how strong the pull would be. Had Dayne?

For several heartbeats, there was total silence. Then, Vermillion thumped on the window. "You have something of mine, venerie."

"My claim on him is greater," Elliot called.

"You have no claim."

"The same blood is in our veins."

"Yes...yes, it is. And you will have mine too soon enough." There was a thump and then nothing.

Elliot slumped to the floor. He checked that Dayne was still breathing and that he hadn't accidentally killed his brother with one of Umbra's fancy moves. But Umbra had told the truth, and Dayne was alive, just unable to obey.

~

He hadn't slept well even after Dayne had woken and gone to bed without speaking. There wasn't anything to say.

When dawn came, Elliot was gritty eyed and frayed. He couldn't do this every night, and yet what other option was there?

He dressed, pausing only momentarily to admire his boots. If he

269

had to, he could sell them and get something cheaper. But the odds of him ever having such nice boots again were non-existent. He should've brought the coat, that he could've sold. But he didn't want to part with it, even if he couldn't wear it. He had expensive clothes that would last for the first time in his life.

He tied the laces; it was odd not having cheap buckles or the buttons those up the hill had on their boots. He pulled his coat on; it was finally dry, and possibly a little cleaner after being dunked in the lake.

Dayne watched from his bed. The man who'd been his brother was gone, replaced by a fevered shell, his eyes hot with visions only he could see.

"I'm going looking for work. Will you be okay?" He needed to get Dayne blood soon. The little sips of nectar were barely making a difference.

Dayne eventually nodded.

"You won't go to the shore?" *Or jump out the window?* It wasn't called dead man's room for no reason.

Dayne didn't reply. The listless pet he'd been in the castle had returned. It would pass; the devoured by the lake weren't this bad. They just forgot to eat and take care of themselves.

"If I don't get a job, I'll be back soon. If not, I'll be back before dusk." Would the Kin hunt again? Every night until they made a mistake and were captured?

He drew back the curtains to let a little light in. The castle was slowly becoming nothing more than mist on the lake. "I'll crack the window so you can have some fresh air."

Elliot didn't expect an answer, and he didn't get one.

He ran down the stairs and out onto the street, heading toward the leaf processing plant and hoping someone wouldn't show so he could take their place. Outside the air was sweet and smoky, something was burning, but no bell was sounding.

There were others on the street heading to work or hoping to find something, but they were all scanning the sky for smoke.

"Fields are on fire!" yelled a boy as he ran down the street.

Elliot looked at the woman next to him, both of them puzzled like everyone else.

"The marshmallow fields are burning!" another cry went up.

Elliot didn't wait for a third call. Like many of the others, he ran. If the fields burned, there'd be nothing to smoke. No leaf to process and no way to keep the Kin from eating them. His lungs ached by the time he reached the edges of the city where the houses were little more than huts. Beyond the stream that ran for the lake were the fields. Smoke drifted up and the ground was licked with flames as the marshmallow plants burned. Marshals stood by the stream, armed with baton instead of buckets.

Why weren't the marshals acting?

Why weren't the bells ringing?

Seeing the swelling crowd, the marshals straightened up. "Get to work or you won't have a job."

"Won't have a job if there's no leaf," someone shouted as they splashed across the stream, only to be shoved back by a marshal.

"Kin set fire to the fields. We can't put them out," another green coated marshal said.

"The Kin never come this far out," Elliot shouted.

The marshal fixed him with a glare.

The people on the city side of the stream shifted nervously. There were more of them than there were marshals. There was muttering about jobs. If he left now, he could pick up work for the day. But what would happen tomorrow? How many would lose their jobs if the processing plant closed? He dithered, unsure what to do as the flames spread.

"We need to save what we can," Elliot said, barely loud enough to be heard over the shouting.

"Why? Too much has burned," the man next to him said.

"We could grow our own."

"And risk jail time? We all know where that leads." The man jerked his head in the direction of the lake.

"Clear off the lot of you," one of the marshals shouted. "Get to work."

As tempting as a day's work was, this was bigger.

Elliot stepped forward, closer to the stream. He had the marshals' attention now. He licked his lips, wanting nothing more than to slink back and be unseen, the way he'd always lived. But they would've heard of him even if they didn't know who he was. The fame he'd wanted for escaping the castle and saving Dayne had circled around to catch him. The dice had been thrown. All he could do now was make the best hand he could with his second roll. He was much better at dice than ossic.

"The Kin don't care if we smoke leaf; it only takes a few days to clear our blood. Those up the hill never have to worry about leaf. They feed us to the Kin. Our blood buys their safety."

People were looking at him now. Elliot stepped into the stream, and the cold water bit his ankles. He took two steps into the middle. The marshal on the other side drew his baton. Elliot didn't have his knife. Didn't think he'd need it for a day looking for work.

Several other people joined him in the river.

"Save the marshmallow!" someone called.

Then they surged forward, a mass of bodies, desperate to do anything to stop the Kin from drinking them dry. The marshals swung their batons, and fists connected with flesh. Elliot kept his hands up protecting his head; he caught a blow across the ribs but pressed forward. The marshals were outnumbered and fell back, but the fire was behind them. The batons changed hands, and the marshals were forced into the river or into the fire.

People were there with buckets and pots now, and they made chains filling them with water and passing them along, wetting the marshmallow that were unburned. Others shoveled dirt onto the flames. It was hot, and the ash and smoke stung his eyes.

The marshals returned, more of them this time, but still they didn't help. They broke up the water chains and arrested people. Elliot put some dirt and small plants in his pockets. He encouraged others to do the same. They couldn't stay; they needed to use the smoke and confusion to leave. The marshals shouted, and people were yelling. The fire was still burning. Spreading and crackling. They were losing.

Like the others, he slipped away.

The ash was bitter on his tongue. All they'd done was fill the jail, not save the plants. Using the smoke as cover, Elliot disappeared into the fringes of the city. The sun was barely visible through the smoke, an angry red ball that reminded him of the one in Kin lands. With all chances of getting work today gone and unwilling to go home and see Dayne in the grip of blood hunger, he wandered around until his feet took him toward the Moss and Mallow.

The moment he stepped inside, the bartender shook his head. Other men looked over, their gazes hardening as they realized who he was. Elliot turned and fled. With his head down and his snood drawn up, he made his way through the streets. He ignored the marshals but could feel their gaze as they watched everyone too closely.

His feet took him to Killian's. The building was rotting away around its occupants. He went in and knocked on Killian's door. Maybe it was too early. Or maybe he'd gone drinking. Or he was sleeping. Elliot knocked again. A woman stuck her head out of the room next door, her eyes narrowed.

Elliot glared at her until she shut her door. He pulled one of the plants he'd rescued out of his pocket and left it in a pile of dirt by the door. Killian would need it now that the fields were gone. It was a pathetic little thing that probably wouldn't survive. With Killian wanting to be a marshal, it was much like their relationship.

He'd wanted to come back and reclaim his life...but the life he'd had before was gone as though it had never truly been his, just something he borrowed for a time. He walked out of the building and stood on the steps, trying to work out where to go next. There was nothing for him to do and no place to go. No one wanted to know him, all because he'd done the impossible.

With his eyes no longer on the ground, he saw the posters everywhere. He stalked over and pulled one off the wall. And while he couldn't read the words, he knew his own face. How much was the reward?

CHAPTER 30

*L*apis's wrapped body was placed on the cart. No one cried. The blood had been cleaned off the cobbles after Vermillion had inspected the body after dusk. It had been a good kill, a cut to the thigh and then the antler to the neck. Quick. Much better than being stabbed in the leg and having the time to watch death creep over your skin. But Umbra doubted that was Elliot's reasoning.

While Dayne was venerie, Elliot hadn't known how to fight until Umbra had showed him. And if they hadn't, Elliot and Dayne would be here now, and Lapis would be hailed a hero. It was better Lapis was dead.

Throughout this whole ordeal, they'd been as tense and concerned as the rest of them. Most of that wasn't an act.

The unchanged Abyr from town clicked their tongue and hauled the cart forward. The gates shut with a whine and were locked. The escape had made Vermillion tighten security. Vermillion was so worried about appearing weak, they were exposing that very flaw at every turn. All Umbra had to do was sit back and watch. Vermillion would bring themselves down.

"Condolences for losing your pet at such a critical time." Weld stood next to Umbra.

Umbra nodded as though it were a horrible shock.

"There's good money on you being picked to be their second."

Umbra didn't look at Weld. "They won't do that."

That wasn't what Umbra wanted. And even though Vermillion didn't know what to do with Umbra, honoring them would never happen. For one, Vermillion loathed them, especially now Umbra was so keen to share their bed. Vermillion wanted someone they could control, and Umbra no longer fit the requirements. Two, Vermillion didn't trust them. They were unpredictable. 'Impetuous child' had been the words Vermillion had used.

For the moment, there was an uneasy truce between them. Umbra would help get the pets back, and Vermillion would leave them alone. The incentive being that Umbra wasn't allowed to drink blood from another source, so if the pets weren't back within the month, they would change again.

What Vermillion didn't know wouldn't matter. Umbra would play the game, but the moment Vermillion wasn't looking, Umbra would feast on male blood, even if it wasn't Elliot's.

"Why? You have the bloodline." Weld glanced at them. Had they put money on that bet?

That was the third reason why. Umbra's bloodline stretched back to the earliest of border wars. Not something they were proud of, but it was useful because it stopped Vermillion from throwing them into the lake for leviathans to nibble on.

"Exactly." Umbra gave Weld a smile.

Weld's blue eye's widened for a moment, then they nodded. "I see."

Vermillion strode over. "We will ride tonight."

Umbra nodded. They'd expected that.

Vermillion reached out and fingered the end of one of Umbra's braids. They'd arrived with their hair out and no status, but now they braided their hair like they were prime of this castle and set to inherit. It was possibly a little too much, but as Weld had said, they had the bloodline. They might as well flaunt it.

Vermillion unraveled the end, a smile on their lips that revealed their fangs. They stepped closer. "Careful. Your hair shouldn't surpass mine."

Umbra flicked them a glance and lifted their eyebrow. "Shall I wait to see how you braid yours before doing mine?"

Their eyes were ice for a moment, then they leaned in, their lips almost brushing Umbra's ear. "Remember your place and dress accordingly. That shouldn't be too hard." Vermillion gave the unraveled braid a tug.

If Umbra had been sent to any other castle, they doubted anyone would've been so petty. But Umbra's point had been made, and everyone had been reminded who was born to rule and who had obtained the role through a coup, slaughtering those who were loyal. Brutal, and effective, but generally frowned upon unless the leader was incompetent. They hadn't been from all accounts. There had been peace.

Weakness, to Vermillion's mind.

"I'll do my best not to let my hair offend you in the future," Umbra murmured as though contrite. They'd do what they wanted with their hair, though they wouldn't be at all surprised if Vermillion started wearing their hair in a manner that was well above their position. No one here would call them out for stepping too high.

Umbra turned on their heel and walked toward the stable. They'd been given Lapis's beast since theirs had been stolen, and it was taking time to get to know it. The first time they'd ridden it, they'd been thrown off, much to the amusement of Vermillion and a few others.

They bit their thumb and smeared the blood between the horns. The beast gave an angry rumble that set Umbra's teeth on edge. The others were coming, and they needed to have the beast under control today.

"Play nice with me." They stroked the length of one horn, its tip arched forward in a threatening manner. "And I won't stop you if you want to play mean with others."

The rumble dropped to a purr. They could understand why this was Lapis's beast. They got on, and the beast didn't tip them off—

which was a better start than last night. Umbra let the beast ease out of the stable and into the courtyard.

They were watched, of course.

Seeing Umbra ready to go, the others claimed their beasts, not waiting for Vermillion who was still talking. Umbra didn't need to say anything, just put themselves in places where they could be viewed as the leader.

When Vermillion was finally ready, the gates were opened. Umbra waited, the beast straining to be free beneath them. They were last out, as planned. They leaned forward giving the beast free rein. It wove and roared between riders, swinging its horns and nearly throwing Umbra off, but they had the feel for the beast today. They were the first to reach the shore. They grinned with exhilaration, their heart beating fast.

From the inky lake a long black, tentacle reached toward the causeway, slapping the water too close to a rider. Another followed, and this time it was successful, snatching the rider up. They screamed, then were dragged under.

Umbra stared, their heart still as shock consumed them. They waited for the Abyr to resurface. But the lake was still. "Fuck."

The abandoned beast lay on the causeway, wheels spinning. That was why they didn't hunt every night, why someone was supposed to check to see if there were trapped leviathans. Since no one had assumed Lapis's job, no one had checked. Vermillion hadn't thought to check in their rush to hunt.

The rest of the riders reached the shore, horror etched on their faces. Umbra kept their fear tightly bottled. There was no other way home. They'd have to cross the causeway again before dawn. Would the leviathan still be enjoying its feed or be ready for more?

"Get better control of that beast," Vermillion snarled at Umbra before leading the way toward the city.

A few looked at Umbra before peeling off to follow Vermillion. The attack wasn't their fault, the oversight was Vermillion's. Just because the Abyr didn't get eaten often, didn't mean it didn't happen. They glanced over their shoulder at the now still lake.

The hopeful at their bonfires moved closer, calling for blood. Offering themselves. They couldn't take the time to stop and feed. Not tonight. They drew in a breath and followed the trail, catching up swiftly. The air was sweet on their tongue. A scent they should know from Elliot's hair and clothes when they'd first met...marshmallow. Poison to their blood. And they were breathing it in.

When they stopped in the square, they tore a strip off their shirt and wrapped it over their nose and mouth. "The air is full of marshmallow."

It wouldn't kill, but it would have unpleasant side effects. This whole ride was cursed. They should have stayed in the castle and drunk to Lapis, told tales of their exploits as was more customary instead of following Vermillion's quest for revenge.

Was Vermillion so petty that they didn't want anyone else to be spoken well of?

Others did the same as Umbra, covering their nose and mouth with strips of cloth. They'd all pay the price later with retching. If ingested in poisoned blood, there be retching and a fever, and then a sleep that never ended. Not even with nectar. Those who were poisoned were usually killed swiftly with antler to the heart.

"Let's get this done." Umbra got off their beast.

Vermillion scowled. "Hunt freely while we locate the missing pets."

No promise to collect them tonight. Returning empty handed once had been a big enough dent in Vermillion's pride.

There were still people in the streets. In this lit area, they scuttled indoors, gazes cast aside as though they weren't even seeing the Abyr. It was them Umbra wanted to snatch and feed on. But these people weren't the ones making the trade deals. They lived further up.

"How is your new pet?" Umbra asked.

"He never shuts up, begging and crying." While they couldn't see Vermillion's mouth, Umbra was sure they were smiling. "But I want the other one too. The venerie can't be allowed to get away with this insult."

The lights became more spread out, then stopped until only moonlight lit their way.

It wasn't just the smoke on the air that was different. People didn't look away as they passed. Someone spat on the ground. Vermillion was on the man instantly, slamming him into the wall until his skull broke with a wet crack.

"Know who owns you," Vermillion said to the watchers in the shadows.

"No one owns us." A man no older than Elliot stepped out with a double ended blade in his hand. One blade silver, one white antler.

Vermillion grinned and drew their blade. They glanced at Umbra, expecting them to do the same.

"We have other plans tonight," Umbra muttered. They didn't want to kill the venerie, and they didn't want to be seen helping Vermillion or enjoying the violence. They liked a good fight as much as the next changed Abyr, but Vermillion wanted to kill.

Umbra kept their blade sheathed.

Other humans moved around them. The humans had lost their fear. Or maybe they had nothing left to lose.

Vermillion snarled. "You're as pathetic as an unchanged bard."

Umbra smiled at the compliment. "I did always fancy myself as a tale teller." The scars on their back for pursuing that dream had almost faded to nothing.

The venerie attacked Vermillion with a speed and surety that Umbra had never seen in a human before. He moved as though trained, and his attack emboldened the others. The whisper of metal as blades were unsheathed. Clicks as the antler was revealed.

This wasn't how they were going to spend the night. They ran at a wall, the human there lifting their knife in defense, but Umbra launched over their head, feet on the wall and pressing higher for a hand hold before swinging on to the roof.

They crouched and watched the fight. There would be trouble for not joining in, but that was preferable to being hated by the humans. Umbra would need them when the time came. "Stop wasting time," they called to Vermillion.

Vermillion didn't look up. Soon they would be attacked on all sides. Their plan would not work if Vermillion died tonight.

Umbra drew their blade, wishing they had their staff instead. "Leave while you still live."

Several humans were bleeding, spilling their life onto the dirt street.

Umbra watched a moment longer, choosing a target, then dropped down to the street. Their leather coat flapped like wings and they landed like a feather, knife to the throat of the young woman with close cropped blond hair. She smelled of liquor and marshmallow and elbowed him in the gut. He grabbed her hand so he could keep the antler in sight.

"Hold still and listen," Umbra whispered. "I helped one of yours escape. I will call on that favor, and you can kill Vermillion another day."

"Liar." She stomped on their toe and wriggled like a worm on a hook, not caring about the blade to her throat and the way it bit her skin, leaving a line of red.

"Tell Dayne I send my regards."

She went still, and Umbra released her.

She spun, and for a few moments they traded blows, metal on metal. Then, she whistled and backed away, watching him like a cat promising the mouse they'd be back.

Two humans were dead, or at least so wounded that come dawn, the result would be the same. Vermillion's mask had slipped, and they grinned like a fool. They wiped their bloodied blade on the clothes of a fallen fighter but didn't ease their suffering.

Umbra carried a small vial of nectar, more for Elliot so he stayed well. But this man needed it now. They put their hand in the pocket, feeling for the slightly bigger vial and hid it in their palm before crouching to wipe their blade. They pressed the nectar into the man's hand. He stared up, blood on his lips, confusion in his eyes. Umbra closed the man's fingers around the vial, then stood.

"Now can we go to the pets?"

Vermillion pulled up their mask. "You need to spend more time fighting and less time fucking humans. You disgust me."

Umbra shrugged. "Everyone has preferences. I can't help it."

280

"Try." Vermillion launched upward, and Umbra followed.

They ran over the roofs to the now familiar building. Vermillion landed with a thump and made deliberately heavy steps before dropping to the window. Umbra followed more softly. The curtains were open this time.

Elliot sat on a chair staring out.

Behind him, Dayne was gagged and tied to the bed in the grip of hunger. The worst would pass in a few more nights. Four or five. Then he'd be like the hopeful, hungry but functioning. If one could call living only to be fed truly living. But tonight, Dayne's focus and desire had narrowed to a single point.

Umbra crouched on the windowsill with Vermillion.

Elliot got up. "You may not enter."

The reminder might work on Vermillion, but it wouldn't work on him. As Elliot opened the window, Umbra wanted to step in. They didn't. If Vermillion knew Umbra could enter, there'd be trouble.

They faced each other. Vermillion snarled but couldn't cross the threshold. They looked like a fool, carrying on. Even Elliot seemed bored by the performance.

How had Vermillion ended up in charge? Had they made promises of battle and glory, how had the other Abyr all fallen for the lie? How many had been freshly changed and eager to fight?

Elliot crossed his arms. "My brother needs Kin blood. I'm prepared to make a trade."

Dayne whimpered.

"My blood for yours," Elliot continued.

"There will be no trade. He belongs to me," Vermillion snarled.

"And he left. Is it not the way that pets are meant to volunteer?" Elliot asked.

Umbra didn't bother to fight the grin that formed; it was hidden by the mask of cloth.

Vermillion tugged down the cloth on their face. "Not here. We have hunting rights."

"Then perhaps you should hunt among those who have the power to grant those rights. The people here don't benefit from your deals."

"I don't care about your excuses. Return my pet." Vermillion glanced at Umbra. "What have you to say?"

Umbra pretended to weigh the situation. "I'll make that trade. I want your blood."

"You will not." Vermillion shoved them, and Umbra fell from the window ledge before catching themselves on the next one. Their curtains weren't closed, and a child screamed at the sight of them.

They jumped back up. Vermillion was making more tiresome threats.

On the street, there was shouting.

Humans hunting them, or humans fleeing from them?

"Come closer so that I may bite you." Umbra lowered their mask.

Elliot held their gaze, then calmly picked up a knife and pulled up their sleeve. "There will be no biting. You will go to the roof, and I will place the bowl on the windowsill. You will drink and then bleed into it."

This wasn't necessary, Umbra had a vial of blood for Dayne, but it was an interesting development.

"I will get him back. He will wind up by the lake, and I will feast on his blood, draining him until he wishes for death. I will hunt you and kill all of the venerie," Vermillion snarled.

Elliot considered Vermillion for a moment. "We all need goals. I need a job. Dayne needs blood. There are plenty of people who'd be happy to sell their blood for nectar or coin."

While Umbra had left some stolen coins for Elliot, they weren't going to be enough. They'd have to get more. Keeping a human pet alive in the Dark City was harder than they expected.

"We hunt, we do not shop for blood." Vermilion shot Umbra a glare. "Will you take blood from a bowl like a kitten?"

"Yes."

Vermillion let go and dropped all the way to the ground.

Elliot cut his arm. His nose wrinkled as his skin split, then blood was trickling into the bowl. "You will have to go up or they will know."

Umbra nodded and flung themselves up. From here, the castle

loomed in the center of the lake, tall and gray with green caps. Fog eddied around its base as if it were floating. Below, several Kin had surrounded the building and Vermillion was making themselves busy by testing each window to see if they could enter.

This ride wasn't getting any better.

The bowl appeared on the ledge, so Umbra dropped down. They sniffed then emptied the bowl on the street below. "It's poisoned."

They wanted to be able to drink from Elliot, but another would do. They were happy to trade, unlike Vermillion. They put the vial on the windowsill.

"The fields were burned. I helped fight the fire and breathed in the smoke. The Kin were blamed…but you didn't light the fire, did you?"

Umbra shook their head, then bit their wrist and let some fall into the bowl. "For later." Elliot took the bowl and the vial, and Umbra put their hand over his. "This is far from over."

"I know." He glanced down.

"We didn't burn the fields, but Vermillion demanded free hunting with no poisoned blood."

"So the rich burned the fields to make it easier for you to hunt us." Elliot pulled away.

Cries echoed through the building. "I should go, make sure Ver hasn't gotten in."

But they didn't want to go. They wanted to enter, to bite, to kiss and grind. They threw themselves off the ledge before they did something stupid.

They had no doubt another was watching from a roof. Should they have not touched Elliot's hand?

CHAPTER 31

*E*lliot shut the window with shaking hands. The building echoed with the cries of people tormented by Vermillion's threats. Even if Vermillion could trick one into letting them in, they still wouldn't be able to get into this room. They were safe—as long as Dayne didn't talk.

His arm bled, but not badly. A scab would form if he left it alone. It certainly wasn't worth wasting nectar on when Dayne would need every drop. Elliot forced himself to sit and wait until the Kin gave up and the building went quiet.

Dayne gave up his struggles as though he'd realized Vermillion wouldn't be back.

After checking the window, he carefully he untied the gag. "I'm sorry. I had to."

Dayne started to cry, which in turn made Elliot's eyes prickle with tears.

He turned away and grabbed the bowl. The blood was bright, almost human but wrong somehow. The wrong shade of red, or a little too luminescent, or something. He was almost tempted to taste it.

"Here. Don't take too much." He held out the bowl. There was maybe a glassful. How much blood did Dayne need? The vial Umbra had given him didn't hold that much nectar, a couple of swallows at most. "Maybe we can wean you off it until you no longer crave it."

He expected his brother to flick the bowl away like a petulant child, but he grabbed it with his free hand and drank like a starving man, draining the bowl before Elliot could take it off him. Red smeared his brother's lips.

Elliot gagged, his stomach flipping over, but he managed to keep his face bland. Dayne dropped the bowl in his lap and then used his finger to wipe around it, licking it clean. Next time, Elliot would have to ration the blood because Dayne couldn't, not even to help himself.

"Feel better?" Could he untie him, or would he throw open the window and call to Vermillion?

Dayne wiped his mouth on the back of his hand and looked up. He swallowed and took a breath. "Can I have some water?"

"Yeah. Do you want some dinner too?"

Dayne nodded as he worked the knot free on his wrist. When in the grip of craving, he hadn't even thought to do that. He got up and put the bowl in the sink. "I'd have invited them in."

"I know."

"No, you don't. I'd have done anything they asked. If they'd said kill you, I'd have done it just to get their blood." He ran his tongue over his teeth. "That tasted different."

"That was Umbra's. Does it matter whose?"

"Doesn't seem to." Dayne closed the curtain. "Even if you get me blood every other night, how long can we do this for, honestly?"

Elliot bit his lip, so he didn't have to answer, but it wasn't long. They needed a plan, and he'd never been able to make one that went past a day.

*I*t was gray pre-dawn when Elliot slunk out of the building. No one was up and no one was on the street as he made his way to the workshop. He'd travelled the route so many times he could do it half asleep. Often had.

Even though he didn't see anyone about, he kept his snood up. When he reached the road where the first of the lights appeared, he breathed a little easier. Getting home would be a problem once the marshals were patrolling, they'd be out soon. Even the green coats locked themselves up at night when the Kin hunted.

Red light spilled out of the workshop, and a man worked inside. The windows had been fixed while he was in the castle. He hesitated, his teeth worrying his lip. This wasn't where he worked anymore. There was a reason he'd been putting this off. He didn't want to hear that his job was gone and that he'd never get another chance at being a lightman. He'd had the best job going for people like him, and he'd let it slip through his fingers.

Elliot forced a breath out between his teeth, and it whistled through the gap in the front. The cold seeped through his pants, but his feet were warm. He'd be warmer if he were wearing the coat Umbra had bought for him. That had reached past his knees. But wearing Kin-made clothing would make him a target even if the marshals didn't know who he was.

He crossed the road and knocked on the open door.

Fife glanced up. "Was wondering when you'd show up."

"Had a few things to do." He ran his fingers over the familiar countertop. The hole in the ceiling had been fixed.

"I heard. There's posters up everywhere."

"I don't know why." He hadn't stolen or killed. He hadn't even started the fight in the Moss. He eased his snood down and ran his fingers through his hair, the dark curls knotted around his fingers. Umbra had brushed it smooth, braided it all fancy as though he were a prime who never cut their hair.

Fife fixed him with a look. "You stole from the Kin."

"They stole from me first."

"That's not the way it works. What you did gives people in the dark hope, and some folk don't like that." He put down the light he'd been fixing. "Do you have the stomach to finish what you've started?"

Elliot scuffed his boot on the floor, through the metal filing and glinting fragments of glass on the wood. The workshop was a mess. "You got a new apprentice?"

"Yeah. Had to after three days. He's shit, always late and can't sweep."

"You said the same about me once. You can't..." He couldn't say the rest.

Fife just shook his head. "You know that's not how it works. I would if I could. Maybe. You're a dangerous man to have around now." He walked over, grabbed one of Elliot's hands, and turned it over.

It the red light of the workshop, his skin was tracked with silvery lines.

His heart stopped, and he didn't draw breath. Those marks were everywhere Umbra had bitten.

Fife released him. "You had to pay for your brother."

Elliot breathed again. "Did you really think I'd die or fail?"

"You're as mad as your father, taking risks and stirring up trouble. If the Kin don't snatch you back, the marshals will grab you and hand you over."

"What did my father do?"

"You'd have to ask the venerie."

If he went to the venerie, he could get answers. He could sell them Lapis's antler, which would solve some of his coin issues.

"You should be off. Don't come back." Something must have shown in his face because Fife turned away. "I wish I had better news. But jobs..."

"I know. Once lost." No one wanted to know him. He was a no one who'd suddenly become a someone all because he'd gone after Dayne and succeeded. If he'd failed, no one would've cared.

"Stay lost," Fife finished.

In much the way the devoured were meant to stay lost.

287

He left Fife to his work. A boy ran down the road toward the workshop, slowing as he saw Elliot. The boy's eyes widened, and Elliot pulled up his snood and walked away.

There were people on the streets as he made his way back, heading to work and setting up their stalls. He bought a hot pastry filled with cheese and ate it as he walked home. Marshals were appearing like mushrooms after a good rain, lurking at crossroads and watching everyone.

Sweat made his shirt stick to him. If he got caught, he'd be handed over to Vermillion, and after last night, Vermilion was well angry. But nothing about him stood out. He was just another dark haired, poorly dressed man, making his way somewhere.

He slipped down a side road and looped through some of the alleys to be sure. He didn't know if that was safer than being part of a crowd, but it made him feel better to have fewer eyes around to remember seeing him.

The landlord was sitting out the front drinking his tea as usual, an unlit cigarette in his hand. The price of leaf was about to go up. If there'd be any at all.

"Got a moment, kid?"

He had all day. "Sure."

He offered the landlord his flint to light the cigarette.

The landlord took a couple of puffs then pinched the end to put it out. "So, the fields burned, and the processing plant is closed."

"I guess so." Elliot nodded.

"There's going to be a lot of people looking for work." He sipped his tea.

"I'll make sure you get your rent. I'm still paid up for another sennight."

"About that..." The landlord pulled some coins from his pocket and held them out to him.

A sennight's worth of rent.

Elliot didn't take the coin. The cheese pastry settled like a stone in his stomach. "I need to check on my brother."

"You need to pack, kid. You brought the Kin to our door."

"But they didn't get in."

"This time. The boundary that stops them is thin. If someone hadn't claimed the room as theirs, they could've gotten in, and once in, it's a whole lot easier to scare a few more into weakening."

"They may not come back. They didn't get Dayne."

"Or they'll come back every night until they get him." The landlord put his hand on Elliot's shoulder. "What you did was brave. A good thing, but a foolish thing. If I didn't know you like you were my own, I'd hand you to the marshals myself."

"What do you want?"

"I think it would be best if you and your devoured brother moved out." He put the coins on the step between them.

"But what about Mama and your promise?"

He sipped his tea and was silent. Elliot didn't move either. This was the only home he'd ever known. It was safe, and the Kin couldn't enter.

The landlord stared at his cup. "If it were just you, I wouldn't have a problem...but he's devoured. He's luring them here. Perhaps you should send him back."

Elliot stood. "He's my brother. A person. He's not a toy or a borrowed tool."

He sighed. "The devoured aren't like us. You've seen them by the lake."

"They are like us, they're just addicted." What did the Kin call it? "Tamed by Kin blood. We can't leave the room. Where else will we go? Who else will rent the room?" With so many out of work would they all end up on the streets?

"Dunno...but they won't bring the Kin with them." He stood. "Good luck, kid." Then he walked inside.

The coins glinted on the step. He didn't want to pick them up on principle but couldn't afford to leave them either. He'd been evicted. Or more correctly, Dayne had been evicted, and he was just tagging along. There was the temptation to walk away, to give up and run far from this liminal city that touched the Kin lands. But he didn't know anything else. He knew this city and how it worked. And Dayne was all he had.

He blinked a few times, then picked up the coins and shoved them in his pocket. They jingled as he walked up the stairs, each step harder than the last.

It was a year before he reached the top step, but it felt like he was fifteen again, Mama just in the ground, and he was coming home with no breakfast for either of them because they were out of coins for the fortnight. He'd seen the disappointment in Dayne's eyes. He'd tried so hard to be both Mama and Da for his brother. Always doing what had to be done, never taking what he wanted or needed.

What about his life and what he wanted? He hadn't even known what another life could even look like until he'd gone to the castle. He put his hand on the door and squeezed his eyes closed, not knowing how he was going to tell Dayne, but this wasn't something he could hide or lie about.

It took several deep breaths before he was ready to open the door.

The hinges squealed. Dayne was folding his clothes, and he had a bag on the bed as if he were packing to go somewhere. "What are you doing?"

"Landlord came up to tell me we were out because of the Kin." He rolled up his spare socks. "I know it's because of me. You can tell me to leave."

Elliot shook his head. "No...it's both of us they want." They would have to face this together, same as always. "We'd best pack fast and see what we can find for the night."

Dayne pressed his lips together. "I think we should go to the Hare and Wick. We should see the venerie."

Elliot didn't know if they'd help, but they could at least get a drink and have a think about where they could stay that might have enough of a boundary. Otherwise, they might as well wait for the Kin at the causeway.

CHAPTER 32

*T*he furniture in dead man's room wasn't theirs, but even so, there was a lot to carry. Elliot had been tempted to leave some of the pots but rebuying them later would be costly. There was a chance that they could leave some things with Dayne's venerie friends.

The Hare and Wick was a small bar, barely big enough for a handful of people. It was half full when Dayne strolled through the open door like it was a second home. The broken antler dug into Elliot's back, hidden in his bag. The nectar was inside his spare socks to protect the vial. Both antler and nectar were things he could sell if he had to. Fife's reaction to the silvery lines on his skin meant he couldn't go back to the brothel he was known at; they wouldn't want him now. He wouldn't do that work in the dark part of the city where there were no red orbs to give him away. The price was too low.

Was there any job he could do?

Serene was behind the bar, a scarf around her throat, her short hair unbrushed. She watched Dayne with a dead expression, and Elliot wanted to back out the door and leave them to their quarrel.

"You have some nerve," she put two glasses on the counter.

"It's not you I've come to see."

"'Course not. Drink, or are you just here to make a mess?"

"A drink would be nice." Dayne sat at a table pressed against a wall. He shoved his bag underneath.

Elliot did the same. He could feel the stares of the others boring into him. They would've seen the posters offering coin for him. They were everywhere.

Serene put a glass in front of Elliot. "I don't want the kind of trouble you made at your place."

"I'm not here for trouble." He'd had enough to last a lifetime already. And all of it traced back to Dayne and the venerie. Maybe being here would end it.

"I'll let him know you're here."

"Thank you." Dayne put his hand over Serene's. "It's for the best."

"Shut your mouth." She blinked and turned.

Dayne stared at her back like he wanted to follow. He shouldn't have broken up with her. His brother was an idiot.

"She really liked you."

"It's called love, dickhead." Dayne picked up his ale and drank.

How long did they have before someone slipped out and let the marshals know they were hiding there? But no one left. And no marshals burst through the door. A youthful looking man stuck his head through a side door and beckoned to them. Elliot drained his glass and stood, hauling his bag over his shoulder.

The bar was small but the room out the back was twice the size, and the door was all but invisible unless one knew where to look. The only furniture were wooden chests, and the floor was heavily scarred.

"Have a seat," the man said. In part, Elliot thought, because he was a little shorter than him, and Dayne was a good bit taller again.

But they both sat. They weren't in a position to argue.

The man crossed his arms and studied them for several heartbeats. "I'd like to throw you both out...but I can't. No one has ever come back, and I need to know how you did it." He fixed Elliot with a stare. "And I need to know why you aren't a half-crazed mess down by the lake. Serene said you were devoured, and yet here you are."

Elliot licked his lip and stared at his Kin-made boots. At first glance they didn't look that different, but the laces gave them away. He could see the tails hanging down.

"It would be best if you started talking," the man said.

Dayne nudged him, and Elliot winced.

"Dayne had been gone a month. I'd looked for him down by the lake, worked his job and mine hoping he'd come back. I was half asleep," And half dead, "when a Kin pressed me to a wall." He could still remember the fear when Umbra had covered his mouth and whispered in his ear. He'd thought he was gone that night. "He was hiding me from Vermillion. I learned from him that they had Dayne. They needed a favor from me and in return would help me get Dayne back."

"And what was that favor?"

"They wanted my blood to change."

"Yours…why?"

"They didn't want to be female."

The man gave a laugh. "And they can pick and choose like we change our clothes."

"It's not that easy." But looking up at the man, Elliot wondered if he was one of the Kin-touched. Different on the inside to the outside and trying to make them match.

"And you're the expert?"

"I was there for a fortnight. I'm not devoured, and I learned a few things about the Kin and their other border cities. I also know Vermillion wants a war."

"That's no secret."

Elliot swallowed. He had to tell someone, and the venerie were about all he could trust. "The Kin who took me was some kind of royalty. Right blood, right parents. Sent to be Vermillion's mate. They rebelled by becoming male. They want to put things right."

"What do you mean?"

"They want to oust Vermillion. When war comes, the Dark City needs to turn on those up the hill instead of fighting for them."

The man continued to stare at him for a beat, then they pivoted and stared at Dayne. "And you? what excuse have you got?"

"I made a mistake."

"You were the only one to live. They slaughtered the rest. They were hunting us specifically." The man paced away, got halfway across the room, and came back. "Vermillion wants you both back."

"I'd rather be dead," Dayne said, his voice flat. "It's bad enough when I feel the craving wrap around me, smothering every other want."

The man studied Dayne. "You have blood, though."

"Umbra, the Kin I made a deal with, gave him some," Elliot said.

"And what does this Umbra look like?"

"Bright pink hair, likes clothes."

"I know the one. I'll put the word out not to kill them. It's only fair since they didn't kill one of ours last night. I'd offer you a place, but with the marshals hunting you, I can't draw attention. You can leave things here, though. They'll be safe."

Elliot shook his head. "We'll be dead by dawn. Will no one take us in?"

"Too much of a risk."

As Umbra would say, *fuck*.

"What are we supposed to do?" Dayne leaned forward. "I'm one of you, have been for three years."

Elliot turned and stared at his brother.

"Your money might be good at Eastward Inn. Might be far enough from the lake that the Kin won't bother you."

Elliot scrunched his toes in his boots. It wouldn't matter, they'd be found. And renting a room by the night would burn through what little coin he did have. "I have some antler. What's it worth?"

"How big?"

"About the length of my forearm with three branches."

The man whistled. "How fresh? And is the Kin dead? Or is that why they want you?"

"I killed them a couple of nights ago. Didn't have time to get both antlers." He wished he had.

"Owning that could get you arrested."

"Just breathing could get us arrested, Benton." That was the first time Dayne had used the man's name.

Benton scowled. "You can't be selling that in the street."

"Give us a fair price," Dayne said.

"Fifteen halves," Benton offered.

Dayne shook his head. "Fifteen full, don't be cheap."

"You'll be dead before you can spend it all."

"Half now, half in a sennight. If we're alive."

Benton considered them for a moment. "Twelve full, half now, half in a sennight, but you don't darken my door between."

Dayne stood. "Deal."

They shook hands as though they were old friends. Elliot pulled the antler out of his bag. Benton took it almost reverently, running their fingers over the velvety surface. Already it was losing it, becoming hard and bone like.

"You both appropriately armed?"

Elliot drew aside his coat to reveal the Kin blade and the venerie blade. Two knives were better than one.

"I can fight. I can help you," Dayne said.

"I can't trust you. I'm sorry." Benton put the antler into a chest and locked it, secreting the key on their person. "I'll get your coins."

While Benton did that, Elliot and Dayne quickly created a pile of things they wanted to leave here. Elliot guessed if they didn't come back for the rest of their coins, their stuff would be sold on. He kept one small pan just in case they had a fire and a block of cooking fat. They had dried beans and a few other essentials, but everything else, they'd have to buy as they needed. Some things didn't change.

Their unneeded things were carefully put away in chest.

"Go and have a drink, Dayne. See if you can't fix Serene's mood." Benton grabbed Elliot's arm to stop him from leaving.

Dayne noticed, his gaze flicking between their faces before leaving. The door softly closed after him.

"So, you killed a Kin. Under other circumstances, I'd welcome you." He drew in a breath. "Your deal with Umbra. I want to know more."

"I don't know more. All they said was when the war came, we fight those up the hill. It seems like a better plan than being pinched between Kin and rich."

Benton rubbed his chin. "Where were they from?"

"Octadine." Elliot hoped he got it right.

"Hmm. That makes sense."

None of it made sense. "They said it was different there."

"It is, at the moment. But all the border cities have their troubles. It's our turn at the moment. Before we were born, there was peace here. But the way your Da told it, the trade weren't that much different. Rich took most."

"Now they take all. I'd offer to help, but you don't want it."

"I don't want Dayne's aid; he'll tell everything to Vermillion. You... I don't know if you can keep your mouth shut."

"I can...I only shared Umbra's plan with you because you have fighters to command. The marshals harass us at every turn. Can we not retaliate?"

Benton considered him for a few heartbeats. "When you see Umbra, tell them I want to meet."

"Where?"

"Top of your old building. Serene will keep an eye out. No other Kin, but you can be there."

Elliot didn't know what use he'd be, but he wasn't going to let Umbra step into what could be a trap. Dayne might trust Benton, but Elliot didn't.

"Don't bring your brother, and don't tell him either. He'll bring us all down."

*L*ooking for some place to stay wasn't easy when the whole of the dark side of the city was crawling with marshals. Elliot ripped a poster off the wall. In the picture, his hair curled around his face and brushed his shoulders.

A couple of marshals walked toward them.

"We need to move on." Dayne grabbed his elbow. "There's nowhere to stay anyway."

They'd asked at a couple of places, but they either had no rooms or they didn't want the man whose face was plastered all about staying. "Maybe you should be the one asking since I'm on the poster."

The marshals were definitely following them. "Hey, you two."

"Shit." Elliot moved faster, slouching down and trying to hide in the small knot of people. The first alley they come to, he ducked down, diving behind a pile of refuse that stunk of death and mold and brought bile to his throat.

Dayne gagged as he joined Elliot behind the rubbish.

They pressed against a wall that felt the trickle of nightsoil every morning. They were going to stink. There was no bath or even a bucket to wash in, to look forward to later. He closed his eyes and breathed through his mouth, sure he could feel the smell sticking to his teeth and seeping into his clothes. The luxury of Umbra's chambers was so far away. The heat of the water, the soap that was more like fancy butter...

Dayne snatched the crumpled poster out of his hands and studied the picture. "It could be half the men in the Dark City."

"Thanks." He knew he blended into a crowd and was nothing special. People didn't pay that much attention to him. But Umbra had. He'd been too visible in the castle.

"It's your hair, too long. Most keep it short."

He knew keeping it short was more practical, but he liked it longer. He'd liked the way the Umbra had played with it. That didn't matter now.

"That won't stop those who know you, and what you did, from putting it together. But it might stop the marshals. They're looking for a man with pretty curls."

Elliot drew the curved blade as it was sharper, and handed it to Dayne. "Try not to cut yourself."

Dayne took a moment to admire the blade. "This is very fine work. I can't believe you took it from your Kin."

"They aren't *my* Kin, and I didn't steal it. They gave it to me."

297

"Your Kin gave you a knife?"

"And taught me how to use it."

"How?"

"What do you mean how? We'd fight." To blood, as Elliot had gotten better. That had been terrifying, even though there was nectar to heal the wound. One wrong move here and it would be fatal. They didn't have enough nectar to heal anything more than a minor wound.

"You fought with your Kin?"

"Are you going to cut my hair?"

"I just can't believe you had time to do anything other than—"

He turned and glared at Dayne. "I have another knife and stabbing you would solve many of my problems." He never would, but if he hadn't rescued Dayne, his life wouldn't be in this mess. If he hadn't gone after Dayne, he'd have never lived in a castle or learned to fight or done anything. His life would still be in the same rut. "I didn't mean that."

Dayne tugged on Elliot's hair and hacked it off. "You were always so good at everything. Looking after Mama and me, making sure that we had a roof. All I had to do was go to work, and I hated even that. It was a stupid, boring job that paid a pittance, but I knew I was never going to get anything better. When you came home really late and in that weird mood, I knew where you'd been. I used to wonder why you bothered coming home." He hacked away at Elliot's hair, tugging at the locks, then letting them fall into the filth. "I knew even then that you could've taken off, become some rich man's plaything and lived a pretty life. But you always came back. You came to the fucking castle to get me.

"I know I should feel grateful, but by blood, I'm never going to be as good at anything as you. So, give me one thing to stir you on. It's all I have as your brother." Dayne held out the knife. "No one's going to think you're pretty now. Sorry. I know how much you liked your hair."

Elliot sheathed the knife. "I was barely keeping it together. I never thought about leaving." He'd had offers, though. A room in the lower lit part, a few discreet meetings a week. But he hadn't wanted to be somebody's.

Until Umbra.

Dayne plucked a curl off Elliot's pants and handed it to him. "It'll grow back."

"I know." He ran his fingers over the lock of hair then slipped it into his pocket. "I always thought I was failing. I know Mama wanted you to continue at school, but I couldn't make things stretch that far."

"Don't need to read to process leaf."

They were both silent. There was no more leaf to process. With less work about, neither of them were likely to get jobs in the near future. Elliot sighed. "Did you notice the humans working in the castle? Wouldn't that be something?"

Dayne shook his head. "I'll always be a pet."

"I was, too."

"Yeah, but it was different. So different." Dayne stood. "Come on, the smell isn't getting any better."

~

*A*s much as Elliot would like to stay in the Dark City, there was nowhere to hide, and there were far too many marshals. But Dayne's talk of him leaving to be some rich man's...pet for want of a better word...had given him an idea.

"Where are we going?"

"Somewhere nicer." They didn't walk up the streets because that would've attracted attention, but there were alleys where the nightsoil was collected, and they walked through them, twisting around corners and gradually making their way uphill to where the buildings had stone foundations. If they kept going, the houses would be made of stone, and only one family lived in each of them.

"I don't think any of the places up here will take us." Dayne slowed. "Do you know where you're going?"

"Yes." He'd forgotten Dayne had never come up this far. "This is my old light route, though obviously I'd be on the street not round the back."

"Let me guess. Killian worked the back and that was how you met?"

Elliot shook his head. No hair tickled his ears. His head was noticeably cold, even with the snood up. "No. We met at the Moss. A while ago, there was a fire. Bakery beneath took the levels above with it. Last I was here, it was untouched. I thought we might claim it." He grinned like it was the perfect solution to their problems.

It wasn't, and they both knew it, but it was all he had right now.

They turned another corner, and there it was. Three stories of burned out wood above a solid stone base. There were no ovens left in that bakery, that stuff had all been taken. But the whole place smelled of smoke and bread anyway.

"Home. What do you think?" Elliot waved his hand at the building.

Dayne pressed his lips together. "I don't know if the Kin will think it's home."

"But it was a home, and we're going to make it a home this afternoon."

"And when one of the neighbor's reports people in the building?"

Elliot glanced at the two buildings pressed up on each side. There were no windows; no one ever wanted to look at the nightsoil alley. According to Killian, everyone liked to pretend they didn't shit. "As long as we don't go out the front door, we'll be fine. Come on."

He pushed open the gate. Something scuttled in the yard. Rats or cats or both?

They entered the bakery, thick with a layer of soot and dust, and wandered through to what would've been the entrance. He'd never been in one of these shops before. Well, not past the door anyway. The shop had a separate entrance to the residence. The stairs that lead up from the entrance had been wood and were half missing. "Hold my bag, and I'll see if they'll take my weight."

He didn't give Dayne a chance to argue, thrusting the bag at him. He reached up and grabbed the step. It creaked and groaned as he pulled on it a few times before hauling himself up. It wasn't too bad. He moved up a step. "Okay, give me the bags."

Dayne tossed them up, one at a time, and Elliot threw them up to the next level. The step moved beneath his feet. He scampered up again.

"There's a reason no one is living in here."

"Yeah, can't keep the place warm." There was a chunk of roof missing, along with a good third of the building. "It'll be fine. Just for a few nights."

Dayne shook his head but pulled himself up. The step dropped, and Elliot sucked in a breath, but it held and Dayne clambered up.

"Come on, let's find a homely corner." He had no idea what it took to make something a home, but he doubted they were going to find it in what was left of daylight.

They disturbed the birds that had claimed the second floor, but up here, the front rooms were untouched. The glass was still intact, and they could close the door. There was no oven in the room. It might have been a bedroom, but all the furniture was gone.

Dayne glanced up at the ceiling. There were char marks, but it seemed sound. "It could be worse."

"Yeah." Elliot dropped his bag. It wasn't home, but it might do in a pinch.

"Do you reckon we can light a fire?"

"Only if we can cover the window." Otherwise, it would be visible from the street. He stood to the side and gazed out. For the first time in his life, he had money that he couldn't spend. He drew in a breath, not knowing what to do or quite how it had come to this. If Umbra were here, they'd be laying out a plan step by step. Plotting a way to get out of this mess and come out in a far better position.

How was he supposed to get the people of the Dark City to turn against the rich?

But so many no longer had jobs. Like him they would be out of their rooms and on the street. Then what?

"This is only temporary," Dayne said.

If they couldn't keep the Kin out, it would be very temporary. He couldn't think what to do. He should know. He should have some idea about how to lead a rebellion. How could he do that when he couldn't even find a place to stay?

He slid down the wall to the floor. When he ran his fingers through his hair there was nothing to feel, the strands too short to grab. "We need to make a plan."

"How about you get dinner since you know your way around this part of the city, and I'll try and turn this into a home?"

"Then what?"

"We wait for the Kin to find us."

Elliot nodded. What he wanted was to drag the lord and his friends to the Dark City at night so they could know what it was like to be afraid and cold and hungry. He wanted them to pay for their nectar with their own blood. "There's more of us than them up the hill."

"They have the green coats at their command."

"And most of us are untrained and unarmed." But plenty had time on their hands with no job. And he was already wanted. He could join the desperate in the job lines and make suggestions. "Where could we meet?"

"Get dinner. You'll think better on a full stomach." Dayne offered his hand. He drew Elliot up, then pulled him into a quick hug. "You'll figure it out."

◇

He didn't shop for dinner in the lit part of the city. Too expensive for a start, and his clothes were wrong. He passed Fife and his new apprentice as they started their shift, but he didn't stop and speak to them. He kept his head down and slipped into the back alley, clinging to the growing shadows, dinner cooling in his hands and a bottle of ale in his pocket, banging against him with every step.

He slipped into the back yard and then into the building. The other stairs had survived the fire better, and he stuck to the wall, knowing that there were holes in some of the centers. A flock of birds startled and launched upwards. For a moment, he was disorientated, but he went up again. The door to their little room was shut.

Tomorrow, he'd steal a few clothes off the lines of the fancy houses. A blanket or two as well. If they were careful, they could stay here for a bit. There was no one to kick them out when the Kin came. It might be fun to watch the Kin terrorize the Lit City for a change. They shouldn't be terrorizing anyone, but there was nothing he could do about that. Blood would have to be spilled for there to be change.

He pushed open the door. In the growing dark, he could just make out Dayne resting on the floor. "Dinner is ready."

A black shadow pooled around Dayne's body. The scent of blood crawled down Elliot's throat. "No." He dropped dinner and ran to his brother's side almost slipping in the spreading blood.

Dayne groaned as Elliot rolled him onto his back. "What happened?"

Where was he bleeding from? He felt Dayne's chest for wounds, but there was nothing there. It was only then he saw the knife held loosely in his brother's hand. "Dayne!"

What had he done?

Where was his bag?

Elliot pulled away. He found the bag in the shadows and rummaged through it, not caring about the tacky feel of blood on his fingers and the way it would smudge on everything. His chest was tight with fear Dayne would die. He finally found the vial of nectar.

With shaking hands, he spilled a little on his fingers and wiped them over the split skin of Dayne's wrists. Then he forced a little down Dayne's throat. He moaned and choked on the liquid. "You don't get to die on me."

He hadn't fought this hard to lose Dayne now. Dayne batted at Elliot's hands, and he dropped the nectar. Elliot scooped it up before too much spilled. He poured the nectar that remained down Dayne's throat, determined to save him. What if it wasn't enough? He was sure Umbra had made him drink more.

He dragged Dayne out of the blood puddle and pulled him close.

The wounds on his wrists were healing, but the puddle on the floor was so big. His heart cracked.

Rain hit the roof. A few drops at first, then it became a downpour.

He squeezed his eyes closed to stop the tears, but he failed again. The chill of the house wrapped around them, sucking away what little body heat Elliot had. Dayne was cold in his arms.

He didn't care about hiding from the Kin anymore. He needed their nectar and their help. As the darkness deepened and the cold seeped into his bones, his brother's breathing was the only sound he heard. The only thing that mattered.

CHAPTER 33

$\mathcal{U}$mbra basked in the heat of the fire in the hall. The remains of the feast covered the table, but many had drifted away. Two deaths so close together was viewed as bad luck. Of course, it had nothing to do with luck, and everything to do with poor leadership. But Umbra hadn't said that. They didn't need to say anything.

Vermillion knew everyone was watching them and counting the mistakes. They weren't riding tonight even though the lake was clear; Umbra had checked, a hunger for blood scouring their veins. Another night without. Their room and bed were empty and unwelcoming so they were in no rush to spend any extra time there.

After warming themselves by the fire, they cleared a place at the table and pulled out ossic.

The bard helped themselves to a goblet of mead. "Did you want to hear something?"

"You're done for the night, it is okay." Umbra continued to lay out the pieces.

"I think I have one more in me. I feel your tastes are a little different."

Umbra lifted an eyebrow and glanced up. "If I'd had my way, I'd have become a bard. I know a few of the older tales."

The bard smiled politely as if they knew that Umbra's blood would have never let them pursue that path. It would've helped if Umbra had obtained that wisdom earlier instead of on the end of a whip.

"You know the one about the seeker?"

"In the forest of old ones?" The bard nodded. "That's a very old tale, and an unusual request for a border castle."

"I'll never get to see the forest myself, but I can imagine. Give me your version so I can add to the image in my mind."

"Few go to the forest, even among the unchanged. I went once."

That got Umbra's full attention, the game pieces forgotten for a moment. "And?"

Was the ground truly the bodies of the old ones? How tall were their antlers? And the animals, were they somehow different too?

"And it is as beautiful as it is terrifying. There is hunger and magic enough to ruin a mind if you were to stay too long." They sighed. "I'll sing it for you."

"Thank you."

The bard collected the younger one, and they took up their instruments. The tune was familiar. One that Cerulean had liked to listen to. If they closed their eyes, they could be at home. But they kept their gaze on the board, moving pieces, trying to beat themselves. It was quite easy to lose.

The bard sang of the seeker, searching in the forest of old ones for so long they became an old one themselves. Their antlers became tangled, and they became part of the forest, taking their place instead of pursuing childish dreams. Weld slid into the chair next to Umbra and poured themselves a drink. They didn't speak; they just watched Umbra play.

A few others were still in the hall. Umbra felt their gazes and their judgment for requesting this song. If they wanted war, they wouldn't get it from them.

The last notes of the song faded away. Umbra closed their eyes for a breath. The forest would live in their mind. They'd never wanted to be part of the forest, only to see it and hear the whispers of the old ones, though according to the song, the whispers were prone to cause madness in the listener. A terrifying place that most songs skipped over. Maybe it was better that they'd never had their fantasy ruined with reality.

They turned and nodded at the bard, who bowed in return.

It was then Weld spoke. "You play an interesting game."

Umbra didn't glance up from the board. "Playing alone sharpens my skill."

It gave them a chance to experiment with how many moves they could plan ahead and how many branches those moves could take. It was much harder to do when someone was talking to them.

"When do you plan to stop playing alone?"

Umbra drew in a breath and made three quick moves. "What makes you think I have any of those plans?"

"I've watched you since you arrived. I was told to."

"And what did you observe and report?" Umbra claimed a few more pieces. They might win this game. Although there were many players who thought that only to find they'd defeated themselves by making one wrong move midway through the game. They couldn't afford to make that error.

"That you arrived scared, alone, and status-less. You left home in disgrace with your hair shorn."

"That's true." They smiled. A part of that had been deliberate. They didn't want to stroll in with braided hair, acting like the prime of the castle. Hair loose and no attendants had been planned, but the fear had been real. From the moment they'd arrived, Vermillion had made sure they'd known who was in charge even though they had presented no threat.

"Why?"

"Why should I tell you?" Anything said would be reported to Vermillion. That they were absent only added fuel to Umbra's suspicion this conversation was a set up.

"You don't have to. Unless you have eyes on this castle and want help to take it." Weld reached out and moved a piece.

Umbra stared at the board. That would've been their next move.

Did they put it back and do something else, or play on and ignore the interference?

"You never ask the bard to play songs of war. Octadine has known peace for decades. I don't think you want blood to run the streets of the human city," Weld pressed.

Were they that obvious? Perhaps the next song they'd get the bard to play would be their birther's takeover of the castle. There was enough violence in those verses to please even Vermillion.

"What I want doesn't matter. Ver rules."

Weld leaned back. "I haven't reported everything I've seen. I saw you visit your pet and gain entrance to his home before you brought him here. Yet, you were unable to enter the other night?"

Umbra's heart gave a hollow beat. They hadn't noticed they were being so closely followed.

"I realized something was going on, and I needed to pay attention to what you were doing. Not for Ver, but for me. Now I could tell all my tales, but I'm no bard, and I prefer the songs you choose."

Umbra left Weld's move and played on. "Then you should know that for the moment I play alone." Umbra looked up. "But when I'm ready, I'll invite you to join me." They glanced at the others.

Weld gave a nod.

"Why are you so keen to play?"

"I fought with Cerulean once. I do not want my name in the type of songs that others want written." Weld stood. "You are three moves from winning."

"I know." Umbra made the moves, the board empty except for the five pieces standing proud in the designated places. Taking the castle would not be as easy.

~

It was dawn over the lake. Umbra's heart was slowing, calling them to sleep, but they had two more things to do while the castle was almost at rest. They were the only Kin up, and they liked these moments the best.

They made their way down to where the lake washed the floor and seeped into the cells. There weren't many, and they were meant as a deterrent to Kin. Humans shouldn't be housed there, yet one young man was. Maybe man was too generous. They didn't look as old as Elliot, and Elliot wasn't very old at all.

"What do you want?" He jerked his chin up in defiance.

"Are you being fed?"

"Yes. My father will kill you all for this."

Umbra considered the lord's son for several breaths. Vermillion wanted to push the humans into making the first strike. "Maybe. Do you ever think about all the humans you let die?"

"What do you mean? I haven't killed anyone."

"The ones in the dark of the city die every day so you can have nectar and orbs."

He shrugged. "You're the ones doing the killing. They should work harder and move to the lit part where you aren't allowed to hunt."

"We can hunt anywhere we want. That we follow your pathetic rules is a courtesy. Perhaps it is time you started to pay for your nectar with your own blood."

The man edged away, the bravado melting away. "That's not how it works."

"Why? When did it start?"

"I don't know. It's just the way it is. The trade deal works for everyone."

"Except those in the dark."

"They're poor, and it doesn't really matter as there's plenty of them." He crossed his arms.

"I felt sorry for you. But now I'm looking forward to watching Vermillion kill you."

"He can't. The rules."

"What rules? We're renegotiating terms, and I think well fed humans will taste a whole lot better than the skinny offerings in the dark." They bared their fangs even though they had no intention of biting him. He wouldn't taste like Elliot, and he'd probably squeal and carry on as though he was dying. His pride was all bluster with no backing.

They didn't want a meek pet; they wanted an equal. Someone they could trust while they slept. Pets were supposed to guard. This man would stab them while they slept and then cry about being stuck in the castle.

Umbra stalked away. The guilt they'd carried for capturing him melted away. He felt no concern for the lives of the humans in the dark of his city, a city he'd been brought up to rule. Umbra glanced back at the man who should've been their human counterpart. Like Vermillion, they wanted the glory without the responsibility.

They dragged themselves up the stairs, running out of time as the sun crept higher. The causeway was gone, and the tang of salt was in the air. The old man was sweeping the courtyard same as always.

Umbra made their way to the stable to spend a few moments with Lapis's beast. More blood on bone, but they were gaining an understanding.

The old man stood in the doorway.

"Yes?" They didn't want to hear the latest gripe the humans had. They couldn't fix it right now.

"It's been several nights since your pet left. Do you need feeding?"

Yes, they did. "I can't feed on staff."

"I'm offering."

"The mark will be visible." And then there would be questions. "And I don't want to weaken on old one."

"I don't think you're that hungry."

The beast beneath their hand rumbled as though the talk of blood was pleasing.

The old man rolled up his trouser leg, revealing a plump, knotted vein tracing up his calf. "No one sees my legs."

Umbra swallowed. They should resist until they saw Elliot and could safely drink his blood, but they were too new to the change, and Vermillion wanted to starve them. "That doesn't mean you won't be forced to talk if something is suspected."

"No one sees me. I'm just the stable hand. A relic who served the previous ruler and who wouldn't mind seeing the castle change hands again."

"You shouldn't say such things aloud."

"We don't. We whisper while you lot sleep. Your pet did a lot of listening."

The blood pulsing in the old man's veins was too tempting, the hunger they'd been smothering surfaced.

The old man drew in a breath, and his eyes widened for a moment as if sensing the change. He put his foot on a stool. "Before I change my bloody mind."

CHAPTER 34

*T*he rain was a light drizzle. Enough to slip down the back of a collar and eventually soak him to the skin if Elliot went outside. The Kin hadn't found them. He wished they had. He was so cold. Dayne's body across his legs had numbed them, but he didn't want to disturb his brother, his breathing was shallow and his skin like ash. He was cold to touch as though he was already dead.

They couldn't stay there without a fire. And while he could light up what was left of the house the smoke would bring the marshals to put it out. No plan had formed overnight. In the gray almost dawn, he still had nothing.

He was so useless.

Dayne's wrists were fully healed. It wasn't the wound that was making him sleep; he'd lost too much blood and he needed more nectar.

There was nectar up the hill, but he didn't know where the rich kept it, and he couldn't wander through their houses unnoticed. The room lightened, and the blood on the floor went from the black to dark, sticky red.

He needed to piss. He wasn't dead or halfway there, and his body needed attention, but he still couldn't force himself up. He didn't want to keep fighting for every breath he took.

Carefully, he eased Dayne off his legs and laid him on the floor. He didn't wake. Elliot flexed his feet, his muscles cold and cramped. They pricked back to life, making him gasp before he even stood, and hobbled around the room. Dinner was on the floor cold and forgotten in its paper wrapping; it would be fine for breakfast. He opened up the door to the room and stepped out to use the more burned side of the building to relieve himself. By the time he walked back to the room, the pain in his legs had stopped, but he was shivering. It was warmer in the room, but not by much.

Dayne needed heat, and Elliot couldn't give him that here, hiding from the marshals. He also couldn't run if he was dragging Dayne with him. He leaned against the door frame and worried at his lower lip.

He'd thought they needed a boundary to protect themselves from the Kin...maybe they didn't. Umbra could hear his heartbeat and find him that way, which meant Vermillion could do the same. But Dayne wasn't himself right now. His heartbeat was different. If he hid his brother with the devoured and their fires, would he be safe?

He'd be warm, which was more than Elliot could offer him.

All he needed was a way to get his brother to the lake.

What he needed was a cart.

Nightsoil.

He checked on Dayne again, then scooped up the cold dinner and went downstairs to wait. He'd lied to Dayne; this had been Killian's route. They'd seen each other working before making the effort to meet after establishing they did in fact like the same kind of ale.

Hopefully, it was still Killian's route and he wasn't going to be a pain in the ass. Or worse, report him to the marshals to claim the money. He expected that from people he didn't know well and wouldn't begrudge them the coin. But Killian was a friend, and he wanted to join the marshals. He needed the coin too.

What other options did he have? Dragging Dayne through the city would draw attention. Leaving him in the cold would be fatal.

He waited by the gate, leaving it open a crack. The sun was staining the sky but hadn't peeked over the hill yet when the donkey and cart rolled down the lane. Killian had a mask pulled up over his face, for warmth or against the smell? Probably both.

Elliot waited until Killian had served the house opposite before stepping out. "Nice morning."

Killian startled and swore. "What're you doing here?"

"Testing out a new neighborhood."

Killian's gaze flicked to the burned-out house. "I heard you were moved on. Kin trouble."

Elliot nodded.

"You had trouble last night?" Killian pointed at Elliot's blood-stained clothing.

"Dayne, he…" *Tried to kill himself.* But the words wouldn't form.

"I'm sorry." And he looked genuinely sorry, sadness filled his eyes before he turned away. "I can't stop. You know how it is."

"Can you come back after?"

"We can't…I can't. I still have things to lose, and you're a dangerous man to know." He shrugged. "I don't want it to be like this between us…"

Then don't let it be. But Elliot knew fear when he saw it. He'd seen it all his life, but now he recognized it. The constant worry that it could all be taken away with one wrong word to the marshals or one sick day.

And Killian wanted to be on the other side. It felt wrong. Those in the dark stuck together. They didn't become the brute force of the enemy, mostly because they couldn't get the coin together for the coat.

"I want to borrow your cart. Take Dayne to the lake." It was probably for the best that Killian thought Dayne to be dead. "The devoured have their own rituals and such."

"I don't know."

Elliot didn't know either, but maybe they did. Maybe it didn't matter. Elliot held up a full coin. It glinted gold in the dawn. "I'll make it worth your while."

"Where'd you get that?"

"You don't want to know. You want to be safe." He was almost sure he was never going to have that luxury again, but he didn't care about the illusion of safety that a room and job provided. He wanted actual safety, so he didn't have to worry about where his next meal was coming from.

Killian eyed the coin. "That's half my recruitment for the marshals."

"You really want to do it?"

He shook his head. "But I don't want to do this either. Green coats get paid better and smell less."

"And when you have to arrest me?"

Killian glanced away. "Got to do what needs to be done. There's talk we'll invade when the moon turns dark. Kill some Kin."

A senninght until blood ran in the streets. There was no need to invade the castle. Those up the hill didn't need the orbs or nectar, they just wanted them. And once again, they were prepared to use others to get them.

"The Kin want the war and the lord is too stupid to realize he's playing exactly the way the Kin..." Elliot paused, mouth still open. All those games of ossic that he'd so badly lost, he'd been reacting to Umbra's moves instead of planning his own. He hadn't understood what Umbra had been telling him when he said plan three moves ahead because he didn't see how that was possible when he didn't know what move Umbra would play. He'd never been playing his own game.

He still wasn't. He was playing the way he was supposed to. Running and hiding until he was cornered and taken off the board. The chances were, he was going to get taken off the board anyway, so he might as well leave a mark.

"What? You have that look on your face."

"There aren't enough marshals to arrest us all. The prison isn't big enough."

"Yeah, and?

"There's so many out of work, what will they do?"

Killian frowned. "Most likely green band them, so they can fight the Kin. They're recruiting and training now. It's tempting, but not permanent."

Killian wouldn't throw a job away for a temporary part in a battle. He was smart and looking for ways to climb out. Elliot wanted to break down the walls, so no one had to climb. If everyone refused to fight the Kin, what would happen then? What if the dark turned on the light and devoured it whole?

He understood what Umbra had been teaching him.

He glanced up at Killian. "I don't think they'd green band me even if I applied."

"Probably not. Maybe when the fuss dies down, we'll both be marshals together, move up to the edges of the Lit City."

Once, that would've been an attractive offer. But if he'd wanted to be a marshal, he'd have sold his ass every night for a fortnight to pay his way in and been done with it. He wouldn't sell his life and body to the rich to damn the poor. Maybe that's why the thing with Killian had never blossomed. They were too different, and convenience wasn't love.

Love was what he'd felt those last few days in the castle with Umbra, but he hadn't recognized it at the time. Elliot smiled, but it wasn't for Killian.

The odds of him making it to the end of the war were small, but if he could lead the rebellion and help Umbra overthrow Vermillion, then everyone would be better off. "So you'll bring the cart back?"

Killian pressed his lips together.

A door opened. People were starting to wake.

"I'll come back. Just stay hidden."

Elliot nodded, plans forming. There were too many in the dark for the marshals or the Kin to kill. Instead of being picked off one by one, they needed to rise like a trapped leviathan and lash out as one beast.

*T*he cart rolled through the alley at the back of the Lit City, Dayne lay in the back, bundled up in a blanket that Elliot had taken from the yard of a house a few doors up. He'd also taken a coat and pants, both of which were a little too big, but they were still a better quality than what he had been wearing.

Killian had looked at the brighter clothes and said nothing.

He'd said nothing as they'd carried Dayne out, but his gaze had lingered on the blood.

The alley way ended, and they were on the street, turning away from the center of town, the sun creeping higher. Killian stifled a yawn. The cobbles gave way to muddy streets that wouldn't dry out now that the first of the spring rains had arrived. The dark part of the city would be a slick and stinking swamp before the summer heat arrived, bringing with it biting bugs and sickness. As much as he hated being cold, it was better than the muggy, swollen air of summer.

The city fell apart into small houses. Where the temporary lean-tos should've been there was only rubble, smashed up wood, and scraps of cloth.

"What happened here?"

"Marshals, probably looking for you." Killian gave him a glance that suggested he was having second thoughts.

Or the marshals had wanted to have a little fun, stealing from those who already had nothing.

"You didn't have to help me."

Killian stared straight ahead. "I couldn't turn down the coin."

No one ever turned down coin.

"Did you tell them where I was staying?"

"I thought about it."

Elliot winced. There was no affection left between them. He stared at the lake. The surface was clear, and he could see the farms on the other side.

"If not me, then someone else."

Was he asking permission? Elliot studied him and realized he didn't know Killian that well. Maybe if there'd been more between

317

them, he'd have been happy for Killian to try and claim the reward. They could've made a plan and split it in half. But Killian expected him to fail and fail fast.

"You won't help me overthrow the lord?"

"You don't have an army. You have an idea. I have a job, and I'm not going to throw it away." He sighed. "I like you, that was never a secret, but I thought we wanted the same things. Ever since you came back, I don't know who you are."

That made two of them.

"Going to the castle gave me a clearer view of the city."

"Or the Kin got inside your head and turned you against humans."

"I'm not against humans." The bonfires on the beach were burning. Less than there had been, but they still dotted the shore, clustered more tightly near the causeway. "Why are we so eager to forget the ones who paid with their blood?"

"Because we can't help them." Killian glanced over his shoulder at Dayne. "I know he's the only family you have, but I think you should've let him go. The Kin aren't our friends. And if you try to fight the marshals, you'll be caught."

"If they pay you enough, you'll tell them?" Elliot said with a smile.

Killian stared straight ahead. "Move on. I don't want to know where you're staying in case I'm tempted."

Elliot's smile remained frozen on his lips. If Killian was willing to turn him over for a price, how many others would?

Killian parked the cart near the first fire. "I'll help you get him out. Then I'm going to try not to cross paths with you again."

"Are you that scared of me?"

"Not of you, of the trouble you'll bring." He jumped down.

Elliot watched him for a few heartbeats. He'd once convinced himself that he'd been in love with Killian, but he hadn't been. He'd been in love with the idea. With the discovery that he could have something just for him, something he didn't have to share with anyone, and that he didn't have to buy or sell. Beyond drinking and fucking, they had nothing in common.

He wanted to shake Killian out of the fear that held him trapped, but Elliot had been the same. Bound up until Umbra had shown him the way the rest of the city worked. At some level, Elliot had known, but it was easier not to see. He didn't have time because he was so busy surviving.

Elliot climbed down. The donkey started nibbling at the shrubs, more concerned about eating than anything else. "And when everything changes?"

Killian glanced at him. "Then I'll be happy to say I was wrong and bow to the new lord of Fotyna." He gave a half bow. "Just remember you'll still need your shit shoveled."

"I don't want to be lord."

"Well if not you, then who? If you don't pick someone then those who want power will take it, and we'll be back to this." He jumped into the back of the cart and picked up Dayne under the arms. "Does he even realize how lucky he is to have you?"

Elliot's teeth clamped shut. He shrugged unable to answer. Dayne wanted to die because he didn't want to be devoured, and Elliot couldn't respect that wish. Had he done the wrong thing in trying to save him? Again?

He glanced at the bonfires and the people huddled around them. Their eyes were sunken, and their faces pinched. They'd sit and stare at the flames all day, only rousing when the sun set and the Kin rode.

He'd seen people down here offering them food. With less of that to go around, how long until they died, alone and forgotten? Next time, he'd bring food.

Killian and Elliot lifted Dayne off the cart and carried him to the first bonfire.

"I need to get home."

Elliot nodded. "I'm going to stay here for a bit."

"Are you sure?" Killian's eyebrows drew close.

"Yeah. They won't hurt me."

Killian glanced at the lake and then at the devoured. Then he shrugged. "You won't stay here until dark, will you?"

"I don't know. I haven't decided what I'm going to do." He didn't know how to start a rebellion. Or lead one.

Killian touched Elliot's shoulder. "When you figure it out, I'm sure it will cause trouble." He trudged back to his cart, head bowed. He was only a couple of years older than Elliot, but the weight of living was already crushing him. He climbed up and glanced back.

Elliot lifted his hand.

Killian did the same then got the donkey moving.

He watched until the cart was gone. Maybe he hadn't loved Killian, but he liked him, and they had fun together. Their time together had always been a bright star in an otherwise endless night. That might have been enough for him if he'd never been to the castle.

For a while, Elliot sat next to Dayne, thawing his bones, staring at the flames like he'd tasted Kin blood and lost his mind. Maybe he had. What kind of idiot thought they could change things? He tossed a twig on the fire and watched it burn. Then another. Aside from the crackle of the hungry fire, the shore was silent.

Down here, the marshals wouldn't bother him...but he was vulnerable to the Kin. He checked Dayne's pulse. Still too fast, but at least he lived. Would the change in heartbeat be enough to hide him?

He doubted this simple plan would work, but there was nothing else he could do for Dayne.

The heat soaked into Elliot, melting the ice at the core of his bones as he stared at the lake. He closed his eyes remembering the flutter of freedom as he'd fled the castle with Dayne and the feel of the beast beneath him. That morning, everything had been possible.

He opened his eyes. Umbra's beast was in the lake, not far from the shore.

Humans didn't ride beasts.

But he was changing the rules.

He touched Dayne's hand, but he was still cool despite the warmth of the fire. Elliot offered him a little water from the flask at his hip. Most of it spilled out of his mouth, but he swallowed a little. Elliot took a swig and closed the cap. Then he forced himself up.

He stripped off his coat and shirt and then his boots and pants. A few eyes watched, but no one moved. He hoped his stolen clothes were there when he got back.

In his undershorts, he ran down to the lake. The water was clear before darkening as the bottom dropped away. As a child, he'd thought the lake was bottomless. It had terrified him, even though he could swim a little. If he stayed in the shallows, he'd be safe.

He waded in, the water dragging the heat from the skin, then his muscle. The causeway was here at night. Where was the beast? If it had sunk to the bottom of the deep water, he wouldn't be able to get it. The water lapped at his knees and then his thighs. His teeth chattered.

Carefully, he walked farther into the lake. How many beasts had been lost over the years? Was there a pile of them at the bottom? Or were they in a leviathan's stomach, or at the bottom of the ocean in the Kin world?

He scanned the bottom of the lake as he searched for the red heart, the orb. He almost walked past the beast, a jumble of white bones that could've belonged to one of the cattle across the lake. It was lodged in the drop off as though it were slowly sliding into oblivion. Elliot reached down but couldn't grasp it. He was going to have to go under.

The dark water was still and deadly, like staring into the darkest night. If he slid off the edge he'd fall forever. No. He could swim; he wouldn't sink. His heart thumped against his ribs. They rattled with cold and fear. He edged closer, stirring the sediment at the bottom. His toes slid off the edge, and he gasped as the water swallowed him. He came up spluttering and scrambled for the firmness of the shallows. The beast hadn't moved, but he wasn't getting any warmer or braver.

This time, he dove for the beast and grabbed the horns. With a jerk it came free, the water clouded, and Elliot felt the weight of the beast drag him down. He was sinking. Bubbles escaped his mouth.

He kicked hard, the surface wasn't that far away, but with the weight of the beast to haul up, it was like trying to climb a rain slicked building.

His back bumped the vertical drop off. He kept kicking, almost on his back with the beast on top of him. His lungs burned. If he let go, the beast would be lost. His head broke the surface, and he drew in a breath, and didn't sink. His ass touched the lake bottom. The beast's bones jabbed him in all the wrong places, but he'd done it. A grin split his face.

Shaking with cold, he stumbled up and dragged the beast with him. The beast made no effort to help. No red heart glowed. The wheels creaked. It was just a collection of bones held together with sinew. He dragged it up the shore to the bonfire, then basked in the heat until he stopped shaking and could pull his clothes on. The beast remained silent.

Was the beast broken or dead?

~

*H*e spent the day by the fire with Dayne and the beast, its red heart like a broken light. His gaze narrowed, then he squatted down to study the orb lodged in its ribs. Bones and Kin magic held it all together, but he knew where to get the sun nut oil filled orbs from, and he could fix them. Fixing a beast couldn't be that much different to fixing a light.

But first he needed to get it back to the bakery he was calling home. While he didn't want to be out at night, he didn't want to be hauling a beast back in daylight either. So, he waited until the sun was setting. Then took the same backstreets and alley that Killian had this morning. The people in the alleys were invisible to those who lived in the houses.

He was sweating in his stolen coat by the time he reached the burned out building. He parked the beast in the yard and took a drink, but didn't dare take his coat off, because when the sweat cooled, he'd freeze. His stomach growled as he considered the beast, knowing that he was running out of time to get things done.

With his snood up, he made his way through the streets like he was hurrying to work. The workshop wasn't far away, but he didn't have long to collect his tools before Fife started. He didn't bother with the front door, instead going straight for the roof. The repair was easy to see. Dark, new tiles against old. He gave a new tile a tug and it slid out, so he lifted three others making enough of a hole for him to climb through.

He lowered himself through the roof and onto the workbench, then he jumped to the floor. He took a moment so his eyes could adjust to the dim interior. The smell of metal caused a familiar ache. Bits of lights lined the shelves. A box of dead orbs sat ready to be handed back. Elliot checked the contents of his old work bag that now belonged to the apprentice and added a few more bits including a run of solder and some flux. That would have to do.

He hopped up onto the workbench.

The lock in the front door clicked.

Elliot tossed the bag onto the roof and scrambled after.

Fife's cursing reached Elliot as he replaced the tiles. "I know it's you. You'll get yourself in trouble thieving."

Elliot stared down at Fife. "I'll return them." Maybe. "Besides, it's for the venerie." He put the last tile on before Fife could respond.

Since he was venerie—he'd killed a Kin after all—it was for the venerie and he wasn't lying, and while Fife wasn't a member, he did run messages. Fife had been the one to hand over the knife, without which he'd be dead. With the familiar weight of the bag over his shoulder, Elliot ran across to the next building, and then to another, clearing the small alley between. He grinned even as his feet slipped on the slick tiles. So much of his life had been spent staring at the cobbles instead of at the sky.

In an alley, he climbed down and made his way toward the house. It was getting dark, and the lightmen would be turning on the orbs soon. With the bag, Elliot looked the part even though he was alone. He doubted anyone would notice or care. He turned on a few orbs, their red glow spilling onto the street. The next orb, he released from its cradle and slipped into his bag. That was all he needed, but he took two more to be sure.

The orbs clinked gently in his bag he as slipped off the street and into the alley to wind the rest of the way to what he was thinking of as home. In the gathering dark, the husk of a house wasn't welcoming.

He doubted his decision to leave Dayne at the beach, but Dayne wouldn't survive another night in the cold. Elliot may not survive the night if the Kin came calling. It wasn't home enough for there to be a boundary. He had to be ready to fight and flee from both Kin and marshals.

The bones of the beast gleamed white in what had been the storeroom of the bakery. He ran his fingers over the cool bone, but there was no response. Not a growl or a purr. He put the bag down and sat on the floor so he could reach up under the ribs and grab the heart. It was locked in differently to what he was used to, but he'd be able to figure it out.

Before he did anything though, he needed more light. For that he needed to get the spare stolen orbs working. There'd be spare connections in the bag. He rummaged around until his hand closed around the box of silver studs. No bigger than his thumbprint, they fitted into the dimple of the orb. The silver made them glow. Blood made them explode.

He pulled out a stolen orb and pressed the connection in. The orb lit, filling the storeroom with its bloodied light. The bones cast long shadows as he inspected the cage of ribs. On his back, he wiggled under the beast, dragging his bag close.

In the red light, a web of silver lines gleamed on his wrists. The marks of bites long healed. The memory hadn't faded as fast. He needed to see Umbra, get more blood for Dayne. And more nectar. Dayne would recover. Better to be warm on the beach than freezing indoors. He only wanted to see Umbra for Dayne, not himself. He didn't want to be bitten. He repeated the litany in his head in the hope of making it true as he attempted to pry the dead heart out of the beast.

After much fiddling to figure out how to release the heart, it dropped out and rolled across the floor. Elliot held his breath, all those warnings about handling them carefully echoing in his skull. But the glass didn't crack, and the orb didn't explode.

He stared up at the underside of the beast. The silver cage that had held its heart was empty. It would be nice if he could swap out his heart as easily. A new heart with no troubles or cares that wasn't weighed down by other people's demands. He shoved the selfish thought aside. Looking after Dayne wasn't a burden.

He wanted to believe that Dayne would've done the same for him. Except they'd had that conversation, and Dayne would have followed the rules and gone on as though Elliot had never existed because that's what they were taught to do.

Ignore the Kin. Ignore the devoured.

Go to work. Go home. Eyes down. Don't draw attention.

He picked up a new orb. It pulsed in his hand. Fuck them all and their rules. The only people the rules kept safe were the ones up the hill. He wanted to make the lord and his kind feel the same kind of worry those in the dark lived with. He needed to lash out.

And he knew how. He held a weapon in his hand.

The Lit City would burn.

His lips curved as he carefully positioned the new heart and closed the cage that held it in place. While the heart glowed, the beast still didn't wake.

Blood and bother. Elliot slithered out and leaned against the wall, knowing he should retreat upstairs to the illusion of safety the room provided. "What do you need? Or did the water kill you?"

He wasn't sure the beast was truly alive enough to drown.

It was a collection of bones with hide wrapped wheels. But when he'd ridden it, he'd felt its will. The beast had wanted to push faster, it knew where to go even without Elliot steering. It may not be alive, but it wasn't dead either.

Blood. It needed blood.

He made a cut on the back of his hand and pressed it to the beast's forehead between those deadly horns. Nothing happened for several heartbeats, then it seemed to shudder and cough before grumbling rather too loudly.

"Shh. You're in the human city and they'll pull you apart." He didn't want to be ripping the heart out to keep it quiet. The mouth he could smother was full of pointed teeth and had no lips to muffle the sound.

Elliot rubbed the skull. "You know me. I fixed you up."

The beasts grumble became a softer purr.

The beast barely moved, but Elliot felt the push. The need to do something. He could hide in the room on the off chance the Kin rode or...

He had a couple of orbs, some blood, and a beast. He could make some trouble.

The marshals wouldn't be able to catch him, but he needed a way to hide the glowing heart that would give the beast away.

"I'll be back."

He scrambled upstairs and grabbed his old blood-caked coat and slung it over the beast's back, then tied the arms around its bony neck. The light was better hidden. It wasn't perfect, but it would do for the moment.

With the bag over his shoulder, Elliot eased the beast out of the yard, then out onto the main street. He glanced downhill toward the lake, then turned his gaze away.

"Where do the Kin take you when they travel all the way to the top?"

CHAPTER 35

*U*mbra watched the lake. Tonight, its inky surface was still. Stars glimmered in the surface, diamonds of light. They let their gaze drift to the beach, to the bonfires and the hopeful. Dayne would be hungry.

They were hungry.

The old man's blood did what it needed, but it wasn't what they wanted. They wanted to feel Elliot's skin against their lips, taste his blood and more. It was a problem they weren't willing to share with anyone.

They lifted their gaze to the city. The band of dark between the fires and the red lights on the hill. Someone came up the stairs to join them. They sighed, not ready to have their peace broken.

"You should come in. Ver is having a feed; maybe you can talk them into riding." Weld leaned on the railing. "It is safe to ride?"

"Yes." Umbra had taken on the job of watching the lake. It gave them a chance to stare at the city in peace and without question. They wanted to ride, but Vermillion had lost their nerve after the leviathan attack.

"You want your pet back." It wasn't a question. Could Weld sense the longing?

"I'm newly changed. Of course I want my pet." They couldn't get the right snap into their voice.

Red light flared on the top of the hill.

Umbra blinked. Had they imagined it?

"What was…" Weld stared at the city.

Umbra squinted, trying to see further. "It looked like an orb exploding." Whatever it had exploded near was now on fire.

Another flash.

"What are they doing?" Weld scowled.

Umbra smiled. "Let's find out."

Together, they raced down the stairs to the hall. Had Elliot stirred up trouble? Umbra didn't care; it was an excuse to ride.

Umbra stopped as soon as they entered the hall. The bard sung a song of blood and battle, of the slaughter of humans and the first of the changed Abyr—one of Vermillion's favorites. The lord's son was on the table, barely alive. Several Abyr looked up. Blood stained their lips.

While the young man had shown nothing but disdain for his fellow humans, this wasn't right. It wasn't how the Abyr behaved.

Weld muttered a curse.

"The hill in the city is on fire, and the lake is clear. We should ride," Umbra said.

Vermillion wiped their face. "That is my decision to make. Not yours. You are nothing here, no matter the braids in your hair."

That again. They were entitled to wear their braids; Vermillion hadn't the lineage or accomplishments to wear theirs. Truly though, Umbra hadn't done anything except been born to the right parents. That would change soon.

"My error. I shall take a seat while the lord's house burns and our trade deals go up in flames." Umbra sat at the other end of the table, leaned back, and waited for the others to finish feasting on the dying man.

A few stepped back, their gazes dancing between Umbra and Vermillion.

Vermillion deliberately bit the man's wrist again, never breaking eye contact with Umbra. Only two others joined in. Umbra noted them carefully. Lines were forming, and Umbra needed to be sure of who they could trust. Their own name was the only one on the list. Weld was on the maybe list. Loyalties were fickle, and if it looked like Vermillion could turn things around, Weld might switch back. Just because one didn't like a leader's methods didn't mean one didn't like the results. Trouble was, at the moment Vermillion had neither. Nor did Umbra.

All they had was hope. Umbra was a chance for change. That was all.

Umbra held Vermillion's stare.

Vermillion glanced away first. "Get him ready. We'll return him to his father. Maybe the lord will be more inclined to negotiate."

A dead child would only make the lord furious and more prone to violence. The war would start. Maybe it already had.

"The lord will most likely be dousing his house." Umbra stood. "Are you sure you don't want him as a new pet?"

Annoyance flared in Vermillion's eyes.

Umbra bit back the smile that wanted to form. It was becoming easier to play Vermillion.

"I do not give up pets. Get him ready to travel." Vermillion brushed past Umbra. "We will ride. Perhaps the lord needs our help to get his city under control."

Only weapons were taken, no orbs or nectar for trade, though Umbra tucked a vial of nectar and blood into their coat. Despite the clear lake, and their own desire to cross the causeway, something sat wrong in their gut.

There were too many hopefuls on the beach. As the Abyr drew closer to the shore, the humans drew closer to the causeway. Metal glinted in the moonlight.

Umbra eased back, slowing their beast. "They aren't hopeful. They're an army."

The army formed up, blocking the Abyr from leaving the causeway.

Vermillion drew their blade. "Clear a path."

The humans drew swords. A sharp wall of pointed metal. "You will not enter our city."

"Nonsense. I am entitled to hunt," Vermillion shouted for all to hear.

"You've failed to uphold your end of the treaty." The front row blocked the causeway.

There was so many of them. The Abyr could only fight two at a time on the causeway, and even that would be a tight squeeze. They had limited numbers. Speed and training only went so far against a tide. Even if the Abyr killed half the human soldiers, they'd still be overrun. They had to protect the border and stop the humans from accessing the heartland. If they stayed and fought and died, they'd be leaving the castle open to all who wanted to invade.

"You failed to uphold your end. I demand to speak with the lord." Vermillion stood on the footrests of their beast. The beast was perfectly balanced. Had it ever wanted to toss its rider into the lake?

"And I demand you return my son," a man spoke from the back. He was lifted up, protected by a dozen rows of soldiers.

The lord had aged since Umbra had last seen him. His face had sagged, and his eyes had sunk. But it was more than just the stress of losing a loved one taking a heavy toll; he'd run out of nectar, and his body's age was showing.

Desperation could make a man do many silly things. Umbra glanced up at the fire on the hill. Then the lake. The humans didn't need to use the causeway to cross it. All they needed was a boat and a certainty that there was no trapped leviathan.

Umbra was sure the lake was empty. They'd thrown meat in to be certain. But that didn't mean the leviathan wasn't lurking at the bottom, waiting for something far tastier than a chunk of dead flesh. Living flesh was what leviathans preferred.

And the Abyr could live without dying for a long time. They didn't want to dwell on whether the taken one was still silently screaming, no air in their lungs, as the leviathan nibbled on their flesh.

"Consider it done." Vermillion beckoned Weld forward with the body. Weld lay the young man down and stepped back. "He is alive. I trust you have enough nectar to heal him."

The lord's mouth flapped for several heartbeats before words came out. "What have you done?"

"Hunted. Your stock was contaminated."

"They will be clean within days; the fields have been burned. Take what you want, but give us nectar." He reached a hand forward, begging.

Begging for himself or for his son?

Umbra was betting on the former.

The army shuffled and parted as two men in green coats pushed through to pick up the lord's son.

It would be possible to push the beasts hard and get through several layers of humans, but then they'd be on their own, surrounded, and the lord would get away.

"I don't have any with me." Vermillion shrugged. "You refused to trade."

"You took my son." The mayor raised his voice. "Attack. I want the nectar in the castle."

Fuck.

Umbra drew their knife, the hooked blade like a sliver of moon. They were all going to die on the causeway, and the castle would fall. Even if they didn't die, they'd never live that defeat down. Cerulean would disown them at best, more likely come up with a creative punishment that would occur while they retook and secured the heartland.

The humans ran forward. It soon became clear most of them were unskilled swordsmen, barely knowing which end to hold, but that didn't stop them from trying. The lord stayed at the back, yelling orders. Vermillion and Tiba fought at the front, slashing at the humans until they fell screaming.

There wasn't much for Umbra to do in the actual battle. They turned to Weld. "Take three others you trust and secure the castle. Do not let any of the humans enter."

"You should come."

"No. I must be here." Maybe there was something they could do, maybe there wasn't. But keeping the humans from invading was what they'd trained for.

"This mess should never have happened."

"Too late for that. We are up to our elbows in blood and must wade through. Go!"

Vermillion wouldn't appreciate Umbra giving orders from the back, but this wasn't a glorious battle to be sung about. This was a disaster.

The humans pressed forward, but that hindered them as much as the Abyr.

Behind the humans, the hill burned. The first few explosions had become something more, spreading. What was Elliot doing? What he should be doing was attacking the army from the back. But Elliot wasn't a warrior. This attack hadn't been coordinated and planned.

"What about your burning city? Do you not care for that?" Umbra shouted over the noise of metal on metal and the groans of the dying. "Retreat and we can parley. Make a new agreement."

Vermillion spun, another taking their place. "You do not have that right."

Umbra inclined their head and lowered their voice. "But if I did…I would be seeking new terms before we slip in our own blood."

"Weakling." Vermillion turned back to the battle.

But the lord was watching now. "You are few. I have a whole city that will fight."

"Do you? You think the people in the Dark City will obey you when you offer their lives for yours?" Some of the soldiers to the sides appeared uncertain. "They know nothing will change for them. They'll still be fighting each other for jobs that barely keep them fed while you and a select few keep all the spoils for yourselves." Umbra drew in a breath, their voice already hoarse from shouting over the din. They risked a glance back at the castle gates. They were closed. "As long as a few of us live, the castle will not fall. You will not take what isn't yours."

Vermillion spun and leaped toward Umbra. They grabbed their

braids and pulled them down from their beast. "You will keep your mouth closed. This isn't a negotiation." They glanced at the castle. "Who ordered the retreat? You? Are you trying to make us appear as cowards?"

"I'm defending the castle. Something you should prioritize before your own glory." Umbra brought the blade up, cutting their braid and leaving Vermillion with a handful of pink hair at the back of the battle. Umbra made their way to the front, to defend. To fight. And talk. Though that was hard while dodging the poorly manned swords of the humans. They didn't all have the bright green coat of the marshals; the ones fighting at the front had green armbands. The ones in green coats were a few layers back, yelling orders.

"Go for the ones wearing green," Umbra shouted. They defended more than attacked, pushing back or sweeping humans off the side where they floundered in the shallow water. Their blood pumped hard through their veins. The urge to fight filled Umbra with a power they'd only heard in songs or tasted when training Elliot. It was different to when they'd fought as an unchanged. Hotter, brighter. They were stronger and faster, and this was fun. As Umbra pressed forward, they weren't sure if they would go back even if they could. They were starting to like the changes instead of hating them.

The scent of blood and fear was in the air, but they didn't stop to feed. They tried not to wound. These weren't equals seeking a battle. The humans were being forced to fight. Reason floated through Umbra's mind, thin and faint.

Behind the soldiers were the hopeful. They called out for blood, acting like children afraid of a fight and not knowing whose side to pick. It would be unfair to call them forward. The soldiers would surely turn on them.

The green-coated soldiers tried to back away from the fight, now aware they were being targeted.

"This fight isn't yours," Umbra said as they shoved another green-armbanded fighter into the lake. Bodies lay in the shallow water on the causeway, impeding progress but too wounded to move to avoid being stepped on.

The clashing of blades behind them made Umbra glance back. Humans had swum around and climbed onto the causeway. They were surrounded. *Curse Vermillion.*

"Fight the ones in green," Umbra yelled again.

That earned them the attention of several green-coated fighters. Umbra was faster and had no qualms about killing them. A cut to the throat, a slice to the belly. Steal a sword and fight with a blade in each hand.

They stepped back. They needed to end this disaster. Where was Vermillion?

With luck Vermillion would be almost dead. Struck and bleeding or underwater. Umbra wasn't fussed which.

Of course Vermillion was alive, though. They'd merely been bending down to feed off a soldier. Umbra wanted to shake them, then run them through with his own antlers—and they didn't care if they snapped off in Vermillion's chest. The sacrifice would be worth it. "We must retreat before we cannot fight our way back."

To be caught on the causeway come dawn would be fatal.

"We will not. We will kill them all." Vermillion didn't bother to wipe the blood from their lips.

"They will keep us here until dawn. And what then?" The causeway would vanish, and they'd burn in their forced sleep, or be killed by the humans. Or sink to the bottom of the lake until night fell. They were all unattractive options.

"You'd better fight faster, weakling."

Umbra thrust the sword through the throat of a soldier. "Knowing strategy is no weakness."

Vermillion shouldn't have been allowed to rule a castle. Someone should've stepped in to take it off them. A thought snagged, but they couldn't catch it, not now. The humans were pressing closer, feeling success within their grasp.

The castle would be safe. Weld would ensure that.

Umbra stepped closer to Vermillion. "Call a truce. Make a deal. We cannot fight like this," they hissed. The night was filled with the sounds of dying. While the Abyr were faster, they still tired. No one could keep this up all night.

Above the din, the lord was yelling orders. The soldiers were shouting. There was no way back to the castle because it was blocked by dozens of enterprising, but wet, humans. All in green coats.

"Make for the lord." Kill him and this would be over until the humans found someone else to lead them.

The Abyr around Umbra obeyed.

Vermillion was left fighting the humans on the causeway. "Don't listen to Umbra."

No one wanted this to be a routing, going for the human leader made sense, so the Abyr ignored Vermillion.

Umbra pressed through the humans, slashing and stabbing with both blades, Abyr at their back as they arrowed toward the shore and the lord, still held high on his litter. The lord realized what was happening and called his soldiers to him. The humans retreated to the shore, but they didn't sheath their swords and go home.

Their arm stung, and there was blood on their sleeve. Theirs from the color, though it was hard to tell. There was human blood on their clothing, too. Their boots were dark with it.

"Call off your men," Umbra yelled to the lord.

"You aren't the leader." His lips curved in a sneer.

Umbra reached into their pocket and held up the vial of nectar they'd planned on giving to Elliot. That wouldn't happen tonight.

The lord's mouth opened, and his tongue slid over his lips.

"Call off your men, and you get the nectar for your son and your soldiers." It wouldn't be enough to save the grievously wounded, but many would live.

A blade pressed against Umbra's back. "What do you think you are doing?" Vermillion's breath was hot on their ear.

"Ending this before you lead us to disaster."

"You had that on you. Why?"

"For my pet, so I can feed."

The blade breached the leather of their coat and sunk into their flesh. Umbra staggered forward as the cold metal was yanked free, leaving the wound feeling too hot and the pain too big for their body.

They sucked in a breath. "You're a vain fool."

"And you are done," Vermillion whispered. "Captured by the humans. Do not return unless it is with my pet."

"No." Umbra fought the reaching hands, but the vial was in one and their short-curved knife in the other wasn't enough.

"Protect the castle," Vermillion called.

"Get the nectar!" the lord screeched.

Umbra stepped back. They were not getting trapped on this side of the lake.

Vermillion thrust their blade into Umbra's back again. "Protect our retreat." The order was loud enough for most to hear.

Had anyone seen the blade dig deep? There was blood on their tongue. Their own. They couldn't step back because Vermillion's blade was waiting. Blood soaked their shirt, their pants, and spilled from the deep wounds.

Umbra turned to look at Vermillion. "You will pay for this."

"I will send my condolences to your family." Vermillion smiled. "You could've ruled with me."

Humans clutched at Umbra's coat, trying to get the nectar from their hand.

There was only one way out. The water was dark like ink that had been spilled before it could tell its tale. Umbra sheathed their knife, shrugged out of the coat, and dove off the causeway.

CHAPTER 36

*A*fter parking and hiding the beast at the house, Elliot watched the fire from the roof of a nearby building. The bell was ringing, and the marshals were trying to put out the blaze. It was chaos. And it felt good to be the thorn in the sole of the shoe that was holding him down. If enough thorns pressed deep, maybe the foot would ease back.

The lord's house was untouched by the fire. He hadn't been able to get close to that one, but there were others around it to target. The lord's friends and family, the business owners. Those that were happy to sell the poor to the Kin.

He turned away from the fire, to see if the Kin were riding, hoping they'd add to the confusion. He squinted into the night trying to work out what was going on at the causeway. There seemed to be far too many people and not enough beast hearts lighting the night.

Was Umbra there?

His gaze flicked to the fire where he'd left Dayne, but it was a good distance from the causeway. He was about to climb down and investigate, when he saw someone watching him from another roof top. Her hair gleamed white in the moonlight. Elliot lifted his hand in greeting, but his stomach tightened. Would the venerie be displeased?

Did he care? They weren't helping him. They hadn't wanted anything to do with him or Dayne.

He dropped down to street level, merging with the confused crowd that was whispering questions and searching for answers. Had the Kin set the fire? Had any Kin crossed? What was happening by the lake? He added to the murmurings, reminding people that the rich had burned the fields. Asking if they should really be fighting the kin when they could seize this chance to bite the hand that was holding them down. Fear and anger eddied through the streets. Elliot could almost taste the change on the air.

Someone tugged at his sleeve, and he turned. Serene pulled him into the doorway of a closed shop. "You seem pleased with yourself."

"Maybe." He struggled to hide the grin.

"Where's Dayne?"

The joy that had been spreading evaporated like spilled water in summer. "He…" Elliot glanced down at his Kin-made boots. "He tried to kill himself."

Serene covered her mouth with her hand. "Why?"

"Because he's addicted, and he can't deal with it. He just needs a little Kin blood every day, and he's fine." But Dayne didn't see it that way. "He's safe. He needs time to heal or nectar."

"Can I see him?"

"Why should I let you? You kicked us out."

"That wasn't me. Benton takes our safety seriously, and you're too well known. The marshals will work out it was you that caused the fires."

Elliot shrugged. "Maybe."

"They aren't stupid. The price on your head is enough that I was thinking about it."

"Really?"

"No, Dayne would kill me." She bit her lip and glanced down the street. "Where is he?"

"Why? You aren't anything to him now."

"He broke up with me." She scowled. "I didn't break it off with him. I should know better. He's devoured."

"If he gets blood, he's himself."

"If."

"Umbra will make sure he gets it."

"Yeah, the one who gave me this?" She pulled aside her snood revealing a healing cut on her throat.

"If you were attacking them, be glad that's all you got."

"You trust that one?"

Elliot nodded. "I was hoping they'd visit tonight."

Serene shook her head. "The lord ordered the marshals to block the causeway. No Kin crossed, hopefully plenty died. Were you helping the Kin tonight?"

"No." But he was glad that he'd diverted the marshals' attention all the same. His gut knotted with worry. Was Umbra alive? Had they been on the causeway? "And the devoured? Are they safe or did the marshals clear them out?"

"They were ignored as usual...why?"

"Because I left Dayne there. He needed the heat of the bonfires."

"You left him alone? What if the Kin had gotten through and taken him?" She slapped him on the arm.

"They don't pay attention to the devoured. That and his heartbeat was too different for him to be tracked."

Serene stared at him. "What do you mean?"

"They can hear the heartbeats of those they've kept as pets." He was never going to be able to escape that. All he could do was hope that when Dayne recovered, Umbra would've dealt with Vermillion. "We should check on him."

"No. Your new hair cut won't fool many. I'll go." She drew away.

Elliot grabbed her hand and pressed the vial of Umbra's blood into her palm. "Give him a little of this. Guard it well. It's all I have until I see them again."

"Where on the shore?"

"Third bonfire to the left off the path. He wasn't awake when I left him."

She nodded, then turned and disappeared into the cluster of

people. No wonder they were all so brave about being out tonight. The Kin hadn't been able to cross.

But no crossing meant no nectar and no more blood for Dayne.

He drew up his snood, her warning about being too well-known ringing in his ears like the bells calling for water and help to put out the fires. He shoved his hands into the pockets of his stolen coat; it was a nice blue and much warmer than he was used to.

As he wove his way back to the house, always looking over his shoulder, he was sure he was being followed. But he couldn't stop now that he'd started unravelling the city. The marshals had been weakened. The lord wasn't getting his nectar and orbs. Lights were going out, and the city was on edge. Now was the time for the Dark City to rise up and push back and demand an end to the sale of their lives.

A hand pressed over his mouth. He fought off his attacker, throwing them to the ground. He was three steps away before he realized his attacker had pink hair.

"Umbra?"

They groaned. "I trained you too well."

Elliot crouched down next to them. They were in the alley, but if they made too much noise, someone might stick their head out. He ripped off his snood and put it on Umbra, covering their hair as much as possible. "What's wrong?"

Why were they not getting up?

"Umbra?"

They took a great breath that seemed to take a part of their soul. "I am gravely wounded. I ask you to shelter me and guard my body. I will give you whatever you ask in return." The words were spoken with a formality Elliot had never heard before. Umbra grasped his hand. "Will you do this for me?"

"Yes." Elliot helped them up and realized they were soaking wet. "What happened?"

"There was a fight on the causeway. I saw the fire on the hill. You?"

Elliot nodded. They needed to get into the house and out of sight. Rats moved in the alley way, rummaging in the rubbish that wasn't cleared as often as it should be but still more frequently than it was in the Dark City. "If I'd known the lord was planning an attack, I'd have done more than set a few houses alight."

"There was nothing you could've done, unless you have an army at your disposal."

He didn't tonight, but tomorrow? Maybe.

People were disgruntled about the loss of the marshmallow fields and the closing of the processing plant. That the marshals had watched everything burn. He was sure Serene would make sure the venerie claimed responsibility for the fires up the hill, and that suited him fine.

They made it around the corner and into the yard. Elliot closed the gate and shoved a length of wood against it. It wouldn't stop a determined invader, but it would deter the casual interloper. Umbra lifted their head. "You have a beast."

"I pulled it out of the lake and replaced its heart."

Umbra stared at him. "You replaced a heart?"

"Should I not have?"

"I don't know. Others do that. People in the towns."

Elliot glanced up. "Can you climb? There is a room on the second floor."

"I need a room without sunlight. I need nectar and blood." They stumbled, and Elliot caught them. His hand came away sticky with blood. Now that he had time to look, he could see the cuts and blood on the back of Umbra's shirt. His heart gave a panicked flutter at the idea of losing Umbra. They were Kin, they couldn't die…not unless stabbed with antler. But that didn't mean they couldn't be weakened.

"I don't have any nectar." He led Umbra inside and helped them up the stairs that were becoming more dangerous with use. The charred wood giving way beneath their combined weight. He dragged Umbra up them.

"What did you do with it all? Sell it?"

"No. Dayne needed it."

"He needs blood more than nectar."

Elliot threw open the door to the room. Dayne's blood was now a dark stain on the floor. A shadow that never moved. "That enough blood for you?"

Umbra lurched to a stop at the door as though they'd hit a solid barrier. "I can't enter."

"What do you mean?"

"I can't cross. You have to invite me in."

"I've only slept here one night." That wasn't enough to make a barrier, was it?

"But you've bled and cried and lived in that one night. It became home. Is he alive?"

"Barely. His…Serene took him what was left of your blood. I have to be careful. There's a price on my head."

Umbra leaned against the door frame. Their face ashen, lips pale and drawn, a ghost of themselves. "May I enter, Elliot? Or would you rather me stay in a different room in your house?"

Elliot swallowed, then nodded. "You may enter."

Come dawn, Umbra would be vulnerable and would need protection. They'd be safer with someone else; he couldn't look after anyone.

He pulled open another door that led to a smaller room. There were racks on the wall. It was probably where clothes had been stored, though it was bigger than the closet Umbra had. Elliot struggled to imagine having so many clothes. When would they all get worn? "This is probably the safest place. There's no fire, no blankets."

Nothing.

"It is enough." Umbra slid to the floor, wincing as they did and leaving a smear of bright Kin blood on the wall.

"Do you want me to look at your back?"

"It's healing. I drank the nectar I had planned on bringing to you tonight." They rested their head against the wall, their antlers poking out of the snood. "Vermillion stabbed me during the battle."

"Should I pretend to be shocked?" He wasn't shocked, but he was worried that Vermillion would strike again while Umbra was weak.

"I was. I didn't think he'd go that far." Umbra grimaced, the tips of their fangs visible against their lip. "He expects me to die come daylight."

"And what will you do?" What would he do? Umbra couldn't stay with him. All those whispered plans were nothing but hopeful dreams. They wouldn't be overthrowing anyone. They were barely surviving. He bit his lip, realizing that he wanted to believe Umbra could change things for the better.

"Not die. Go back." Even though they'd drunk nectar, they were still clearly in pain. Every movement caused a wince, and their words were carefully measured.

He didn't want Umbra to go back and risk death. "So he can stab you again?"

"I'd hoped to stab them first. I may have left that a little late. My plan needs work."

If the marshals blocked the causeway, Umbra wouldn't be able to get across tomorrow night either. Even if they got across, they still needed to get into the castle. "You need to heal before you can go back." Elliot sunk to his knees at Umbra's side. "And if anyone finds you here, you'll be staked out in the center square."

"I know. But this was my only chance. It wasn't easy getting this far into town in my state." Umbra reached for him. "I'll be fine come dusk. I'll take the beast."

"Oh will you?" He'd rescued and fixed the beast; it was his.

"Elliot, if you're found with it, you'll be in trouble."

"More trouble." The Kin had brought him nothing but trouble. But he liked it. He just wanted it to stop at some point, so he could live again without watching over his shoulder. "The venerie want to meet with you."

Umbra snorted. "I'm sure they do."

"To plan. Not to kill you."

"You trust them?"

"As much as I trust anyone."

"Including me."

Elliot tilted his head in agreement. He'd never seen Umbra so fragile, so wounded. Even after spending time in Vermillion's rooms, they hadn't looked this broken. "I think you need the venerie as much as they need you."

"Maybe. For the moment, I only need you." They pulled Elliot into their lap and held him close.

Elliot expected a bite, but it didn't come. It was just a simple embrace. Elliot relaxed a little and rested his cheek against Umbra's much cooler one. He closed his eyes and pretended that they were back in the castle, warm and safe. That they'd wake up in Umbra's bed tangled together.

Umbra's fingers threaded through what was left of Elliot's hair. There was nothing to grab, no curls to wind around their fingers. "You cut it off."

"I had to. There's posters with my face up everywhere." The hair cut wouldn't fool everyone. Not when the reward was so high. He should've left it long because he liked the way Umbra toyed with the strands.

"Vermillion wants you both back." Umbra's grip on the back of Elliot's head tightened. "They would've made sure the lord did everything in his power to return you."

"They are as bad as each other." And he didn't want to be thinking about Vermillion or the lord.

Umbra shook his head. "The lord is worse. How long has he ruled?"

"I don't know, all my life at least."

"And how old does he look?"

Elliot drew back to stare at Umbra. In the darkness, their face was unreadable. Not much light from the window reached the closet. "Not that old, but he lives up the hill and never has to work."

Umbra cupped his face. "You really do not know? Nectar heals humans, but if one takes a little everyday, it does more. Aging is the body unable to keep up the repairs."

Elliot frowned. "What do you mean? Them up the hill drink it every day? They don't...they don't get old because they drink it?"

"Your lord has been ruling this city since the sweeper in my castle was a boy. He turns seventy this year."

Elliot had only seen him a handful of times at the opening of a new factory or the like. He'd never really paid much attention. But he was certain the lord barely looked middle aged.

"The humans in your castle don't drink every day?"

"No. It's for healing. It sustains the unchanged as well, but it's not meant to be drunk so frequently by humans."

"But I drank plenty while I was there." What had it done to him?

"And it would've done you no harm. But your lord has been drinking nectar for a very long time. He doesn't want to get old, and he doesn't want to give up power. He'd do anything to get nectar. He will do whatever Vermillion asks."

"The lord is immortal like you?"

"I'm not immortal. I can assure you I'm close to death." Their word were sharp with pain even though their tone was light.

"But only antler can kill you."

"There is something between life and death. And tonight, I have drunk my fill of it." They lifted Elliot's hand to their lips and kissed his knuckles. "May I?"

Heat traced through Elliot's veins in anticipation. "How much will you take? There's no nectar to heal me."

"Not much. Enough to get me through the day." They turned Elliot's wrist over and kissed the skin, their mouth hot against his flesh. Their tongue swept over his pulse before their teeth pressed in.

Elliot hissed but the pain was gone just as fast, replaced with sucking and the drawing of life out of him. But his body reacted as though it were something most delightful. Lust tumbled through him, and he fought the urge to roll his hips and enjoy it that little bit further. Umbra groaned with something more than hunger, then pulled him closer. Despite their injuries, they were hard. Elliot pressed a little closer.

Umbra gripped his hip, so they ground together. The sucking became more of a lick, then they drew Elliot down for a kiss. Their lips were hot with the taste of metal on their tongue. His blood, he realized, but didn't pull away.

"I've missed you in my bed."

The words made Elliot's heart tighten with hope he didn't want to feel. Elliot had missed Umbra's bed and everything about living in the castle, but they couldn't go back to that. "You should rest."

"I should. But I don't want to." Their fingers traced Elliot's jaw before they kissed him again. They moved and grunted in pain.

"You're still healing." But need hummed in Elliot's blood.

"I'm healed enough to not bleed everywhere, but not enough to do anything more than rest."

"Your kind doesn't know what it's like to be mortal and sick where only time will tell if you'll recover or be buried." Elliot sighed and stood. "Get your rest."

Umbra's hand wrapped around his calves. They looked up and there was a moment when Elliot was sure that his heart stopped beating. "Unbutton your trousers."

He could have stepped away. He could have told Umbra to sleep while he stood guard, but dawn was a long way off, and Umbra wanted more than just blood. His good sense deserted him as he undid the buttons and freed his dick. He didn't need to do anything but close his eyes and surrender to Umbra's tongue.

His fingers traced the ridges of Umbra's braids—the patterns intricate beneath his fingers—as Umbra drew him deeper, the edges of their fangs pressing close but not cutting. Heat travelled down his spine and sank into his balls. Umbra's tongue feathered over the slit and around the crown, and Elliot's breath hitched. He shuddered as he spilled.

It was several breaths before he could step back and button his trousers.

If that was payment for his blood, Elliot didn't mind the price at all.

~

*E*lliot woke long before dawn. A lifetime of waking early to turn off the lights was far harder to shake than it should've been. His head was in Umbra's lap. Umbra leaned against the wall, their hand on a drawn blade. Guarding Elliot while he slept, as though he needed protection. Though it was the first night he'd slept soundly since returning to the city.

"Go back to sleep." Umbra smoothed their hand over Elliot's head.

Elliot turned onto his back. Umbra's eyes were closed, and their free hand moved to loop over Elliot. He yawned. If they'd been in a bed, he might've gone back to sleep. But the floor was cold, he was stiff from sleeping awkwardly, and there were things he needed to do. "I need to speak with the venerie. You need to speak with them."

"No. They'll know where I sleep come dawn."

"We will meet them elsewhere." Elliot pushed himself up and turned to face Umbra. "We may not get another chance to plan. Are you well enough?"

Umbra sighed. "Yes, though I'm not at my best."

Elliot's lips curved. Umbra was still more finely dressed than any of the venerie. He stood and offered Umbra his hand. Umbra hesitated.

"We'll be back here before the sun crests the hill," Elliot reassured them.

Umbra still didn't move.

"What's wrong?"

"I've never been on this side of the lake when the sun rose. I don't know what it will be like. I've heard tales and I know, or rather, I've been told my skin will burn. My birther staked someone out. I watched them do it and helped collect the remains the next day. But I don't know what the sleep will be like. What if I can't rouse myself?"

"I'll stand guard. I swear."

"You are one person in a city of thousands. There are more people here than I have seen in my entire life. The Abyr aren't plentiful like you."

Elliot squatted down and cupped Umbra's jaw. "You'll be safe. I swear." Umbra leaned their head into the touch. Was this the first time they'd ever been truly afraid? Elliot didn't know what else to say. "But if you'd rather return to the castle you have time to take a boat and cross the lake."

Umbra glanced down as though weighing their options. "If I stay, you're in danger."

"I'm in danger anyway." He wasn't ready for Umbra to leave. "Are you healed enough to face Vermillion?"

They grimaced and shook their head. "I'm not healed enough to stay, either."

Umbra accepted Elliot's hand and stood. For a moment, they were unstable on their feet, and Elliot doubted if they would get across the lake to the castle in a rowboat. "Are you sure you don't want to rest here the day?"

Stay with me a little longer?

"I should. If you had nectar I would. But the city is aflame, and it will be safer for everyone if I return to the castle after meeting the venerie."

Elliot swallowed and nodded. This wasn't about him and what he wanted or needed. "And Vermillion?"

"Will not be safe from me." Umbra's fangs flashed.

～

The shore was cold and dark, no glimmer of dawn yet, though the sky was no longer inky. Elliot had woken Serene, he knew which room she slept in in his old building, and she had roused Benton who lived above the tavern. Together, they had made their way through the sleeping city. Soldiers slept near the causeway, and a few stood guard as though expecting trouble.

They crept south to where the boats were kept, upturned for winter. In summer, they'd be used most days during daylight before being dragged up on the shore when the insects came out to feast on blood. The bugs were a warning that the Kin would be waking. As a child, the Kin had been the danger he had to watch for. Now he was helping them.

"Where is Umbra?" Benton whispered. He'd wanted to meet on the roof of Elliot's old building, but Elliot had insisted on the change. This was Umbra's plan now.

Had they not made it? Elliot scanned the boats and the path, panic gripping him. Then he saw a boat by the water, as if ready to be taken out. A shadow moved, then Umbra stood and came over. From here, they couldn't see the soldiers; the sweep of the shore hid them. As soon as the boat went out though, it would be visible. Would the soldiers go after Umbra?

Umbra's hand rested on the hilt of their blade. "You wished to see me?"

There was a haughtiness that Elliot hadn't heard before, that he didn't like. Umbra wouldn't meet his gaze either.

"We need to plan and act together," Benton said. "What actions are you taking?"

"I will be removing Vermillion. That is no secret. You need to clear the beach of soldiers."

"There isn't enough of us," Benton hissed.

"There is enough of us in the Dark City. They're already angry and seeking an outlet," Elliot said.

Benton shook his head. "They fear the Kin more than the lord."

"I will not negotiate with your lord or his kind," Umbra said leaving no doubt that point was unnegotiable. "He's been driven mad by nectar and seeks only to live longer at the expense of others."

"Then who do you expect to rule the city? To trade with?" Benton asked.

"I will trade with the venerie only. You will ensure that any nectar is given to those in need, not those who hunger for power."

"A fine idea until those up the hill kill us and take over," Serene said.

Benton rubbed his chin. "Suppose the venerie ruled the city. A council if you will."

"That could work. Though if something happens to Elliot, we will have no deal. You'd best make sure that he doesn't get caught." Umbra grinned, all cold menace.

"Just take him as a pet if he means that much," Serene snapped.

"I'd rather have someone I trust here." Umbra glanced at Elliot. "You will always be welcome at the castle, though."

Welcome, but not able to enjoy the luxury. He scuffed his boot in the dirt. He was only good for blood and bedding. He knew that, but he'd expected more.

Umbra grabbed his chin and forced him to look up. "I mean that. I need you here. Whatever happens. No matter what I do. You have to trust me." They released Elliot and fixed Benton with a glare. "This will be a mess before it's over."

"And what about the mess you Kin have already left?" Serene flung her hand out in the direction of the bonfires of the devoured. "Will you take them back? What will you do with Dayne?"

Elliot had assumed his brother would be taken care of, but Serene wanted to be sure.

Umbra pressed their lips together. "If they get blood, they'll be fine, but they require it regularly." They hesitated. "We have human staff for the running of the castle. They could assume positions there, though I suspect some will be too damaged from waiting too long."

"We aren't disposable," Benton said.

"Look to your own treatment of them. You turn your backs on them and offer no help." Umbra shook their head. "The practice of taming a pet and addicting them to blood is not one that is needed if there is trust." Their gaze flicked to Elliot. "I can't vow that will never happen, but I do promise they will be taken care of." Umbra sighed, their gaze on the hill. "I will act tonight. You must do the same. And I must go."

The sky was lightening. Dawn was coming.

"We need more time," Benton said.

"You don't have it. Remove your lord and his kind. They will be aging fast now, their bodies betraying the truth. It shouldn't be hard to draw them out with a promise of nectar." Umbra smiled. "I'll even bring some come night, if I can get through."

They turned, giving Elliot one final glance. The back of their shirt was ripped and blood stained, but they moved more easily, pushing the boat they had prepared into the water before climbing aboard and rowing out.

"That was bloody useless. I thought they'd be more helpful in getting rid of the poxy lord." Benton shoved his hands into his pockets.

"They have their own problems." And he had his. "I need to check on Dayne."

Like Benton, he'd been hoping Umbra would help them overthrow the lord. Instead, it was up to them. Would the people in the Dark City really care who was in charge?

Serene walked next to him as they made their way back to the bonfires. Elliot's gaze kept sliding to the lake where the little boat was getting further from the shore, closer to the castle and curving toward the causeway.

"They'll all get help if Umbra succeeds." Serene sounded hopeful. "The Kin should never have cast them off."

Elliot nodded. "And we should never have allowed the Kin to hunt us. Why were deals never made that meant the one wanting nectar had to pay?"

Maybe they had been like that once, before greed had taken over.

"We can change it. Make it better."

"Will it be better? How long until the council doesn't want to give up power? What do we do if Umbra fails?" If they failed, they'd be dead, and Dayne would be nothing more than a shell of himself. Always hungry for Kin blood, waiting on the shore for succor that would never come.

"Even if they fail, we can still take down the lord," Benton said from behind them. "The Kin won't fight our battles. Even Vermillion will want to trade eventually. They'll want blood. Check on your brother, then return to the Hare." Benton peeled away and disappeared up the path.

Elliot stood for a moment. The sky was gray, streaked with pink. The boat was close to the causeway now. The marshals who'd been on watch were pointing and talking.

He checked the sky again, not wanting to be on the streets come daylight. The marshals would be looking for him, and the price on his head tempted even him.

They made their way to the fire where he'd left Dayne. "How was he?"

"He wasn't awake. I poured the blood down his throat. Most of it anyway. I had to give some to the man who'd been watching him," Serene said. "Will he wake?"

Elliot's teeth worried his lower lip. He wanted to say yes, but he didn't know. "He needs nectar. He lost a lot of blood."

The lord's long life had been bought with the lives of others. It was sick. All of them up the hill were the same. It wasn't just one lord they had to remove; it was all of them. But if that were easy, someone would've done it before now.

Elliot looked at the people huddled round the fire, thin and hungry, but no food would ever fill the gap. If no one fed them; they died of starvation where they sat. To the people in the Dark City, where every coin mattered, they were a mouth to feed that couldn't work. "We should get them fed, look after them."

"People do come. It's hard to turn your back on family."

He peered at the faces, looking for Dayne. "I don't see him."

"Neither do I. Maybe he got up." But Serene sounded just as worried.

Elliot squatted near one of the devoured. "Where's my brother?"

Serene was doing the same, asking the devoured where Dayne was.

A woman stared up at him with sunken eyes and spoke with cracked lips. "He's lucky. Gone now."

"Gone where?"

The man who'd been looking after Dayne spoke up, "The Kin took him. Gave him blood. Gave us all blood."

"Which Kin?" But he knew. Umbra had already had the boat in the water.

"Pink hair, the kind one."

Elliot stood, fury pulsing through his veins. "I'm going to fucking kill them."

Umbra had taken Dayne, knowing Vermillion would hurt him.

Elliot stormed toward the lake where the soldiers camped

blocking the causeway. Serene grabbed his arm. He threw her off. She took him to the ground, face in the dirt, arm twisted behind his back.

"What do you think you're doing?" she hissed in his ear.

"Getting him back." He struggled, but her weight was on his back, and her hand was clawed against his cheek.

"The marshals will arrest you. They are already looking over. Be smart." Her voice softened. "We can't help him anyway."

She didn't know how bad it had been for Dayne over there. He'd never survive.

"He'll get better eventually. We just have to look after him." He needed to believe that Dayne would've healed, that he'd have returned to being his little brother. If he hadn't been kicked out of his room, Dayne would've been fine. He may not have tried to take his life. "I only brought him here to stay warm since I know you lot wouldn't help him."

"Shit." She got off him. "Marshals."

Elliot sprung up, and with a final glance at the marshals and the causeway, he ran after Serene. A few marshals gave chase, but it was easy to lose them in the fringes of the city. They leaned against a wall panting but trying to breathe quietly.

"Vermillion will kill him," Elliot whispered.

"I want him back, but there's only two of us against all those marshals," Serene said. "We don't have a plan, and we'll never reach the castle before it vanishes."

The sky was pink now. Was Umbra inside the castle? Or waiting to be let in, bartering with Dayne's sleeping body. What would happen to Umbra if he wasn't let in? Would they huddle by the gate all day, hoping a leviathan didn't snatch them into the sea?

He hated that he cared. The lump in his throat swelled until he could barely breathe.

"We need to raise an army." He'd take the bloody castle himself.

CHAPTER 37

*U*mbra walked into the hall and gently placed Dayne's body on the table. Their hands were raw from rowing. They'd expected a leviathan to grab them the whole way across, and then the human soldiers to grab them before the gates opened.

The guard hadn't wanted to let Umbra in; they had orders. But when Umbra had showed then the missing pet, the gate opened. Tension drew their gut tight and made their heartbeat too fast. Now Dayne was in the castle, and they couldn't let him be killed. Elliot would never forgive them. Dayne needed to be here, not only to buy Umbra's return, but also to wake.

The sun crested the hill as Umbra entered the castle. The need to sleep dragged at their wounded body, but they forced a smile for the benefit of those still in the hall.

Vermillion wasn't there. They would've already gotten ready for bed, but someone had been sent running, and they appeared above, leaning on the railing. "I didn't expect you back so soon."

"Your pet is almost dead. If I'd delayed, I'd have been bringing you a corpse."

"Give him nectar and bring him to me."

"No." Umbra stood by Dayne. Their heartbeat was weak and fast. It had been unrecognizable, but they'd found him by the smell and the look of him. They'd expected Elliot to realize or to try and stop them. Would they have left Dayne behind or told the truth about why they needed him if questioned?

Dayne needed nectar. Umbra needed Dayne. It was a fair trade even though Dayne hadn't made it himself. And Elliot would've never made it for his brother.

"No? Did you not learn your lesson?"

"What lesson would that be? That you got so swept up in the battle you forget to guard the castle? That you happily stabbed me in the back." They turned so all could see the rips in their shirt and the blood stains. "You wanted me to die, but I have friends in the city."

"Your pet." Vermillion spat the word. Their knuckles were white as they gripped the railing. The sun was climbing, and the need to sleep was becoming harder to resist.

Umbra wanted nectar before they rested. Where was the jug?

"Leave my pet. I'll deal with him come dark. No one is to help my pet or Umbra. If the sun weren't so high, I'd have you sent to the cells. You could take yourself," Vermillion grinned, "but I no longer trust you to follow orders. You are a traitor." They stepped back. "Sleep well, Umbra."

Umbra wouldn't be sleeping well at all. They wouldn't sleep well until Vermillion was either dead or worse than dead.

"Where's the nectar?" Umbra looked at each of the Abyr in turn.

"We are not allowed to have it out anymore. Vermillion rations it. I must sleep." The red-haired Abyr left the hall.

Where were Weld and the others Umbra had sent to protect the castle?

"Does anyone want to help, or are you scared of them?" Umbra indicated up, to where Vermillion had been standing. They couldn't do this on their own. They needed the nectar.

"We thought you gone."

"And did they tell you they'd stabbed me? What kind of Abyr stabs someone in the back? There's no honor in that, but they lack the grit to face me in a fair fight." Anger bubbled through them. They tried to tamp it down, but the rage was a swift, sharp current.

"It will be sorted come dusk. Your accusations will be dealt with."

Then Umbra was the only Abyr in the hall. The others abandoning them to sleep safe in their chambers. Humans moved around the edges, waiting for them to go to bed so they might clean or dance or whatever they did while the Abyr were forced to sleep.

"Where is the nectar? He will die without it." And they would remain in this weakened state. Should they have stayed in the city for the day? While there would've been no nectar, they would've had extra time to heal, to feed. More time with Elliot.

They never had enough time with him. Was it a dependence or something else?

They placed their hand over Dayne's, feeling his pulse beneath their fingertips. Elliot wouldn't understand why they'd done this... would Dayne?

None of the humans approached. Vermillion had instilled fear in every part of the castle. Undoing the damage would take time. They needed people they could trust. Could they trust any of the human staff? Where was the old man?

They rested their head on Dayne's hand, knowing they should return to their chambers and lock the door, but unable to lift their head and take those steps. Sleep dragged them down like a hungry leviathan. They didn't resist. Elliot had shown them that a locked door meant nothing.

They'd sleep here and pretend they had no fear of anyone or anything. Their heartbeat told the truth. Their pulse in their ears whispered the ways they could fail, could die, could be worse than dead.

A hand on their back was enough for Umbra to force their way to the surface. Their body didn't want to obey, their eyelids weighted.

"Drink." The word was whispered too close to their ear.

The glass was pressed to their lips. They were sure they smelled nectar, and they drank because it was the best way to be left alone to go back to sleep. It was only after they were sinking again that they dreamed they'd swallowed poison.

Their dream was every fear. They watched from a worse than death state, kept in the main hall while Vermillion debased everything a border castle should be. Humans came and died. Blood stained the floor. Elliot appeared, blaming Umbra until his last pained breath.

Even the Abyr blamed them. The song the bard sung was about a failed rebellion led by an upstart youth who had fallen in love with a human.

All they could do was watch, helpless even as their birther visited. Cerulean didn't claim their body and take them home to heal. They looked straight at them.

Finish the job.

Umbra startled. Their skin was sticky with sweat. People were moving around them. They cracked open an eye after several attempts. The sweeper was there. They closed their eyes again but didn't want to sink back into the nightmare that had stalked them. The hand beneath theirs was warm. The pulse was stronger.

And they didn't fall back asleep.

It must be dusk. With every breath they roused a little more, though they didn't feel well rested. The horror of failure and watching the castle become a place of death lingered. Cerulean's words echoed.

They had been sent as mate to Vermillion. To learn how to run a castle.

They lifted their head.

That's what everyone had been told.

Perhaps they'd been sent to run the castle. Cerulean would never have approved of the way things were being run. Had their sire? They had ties to Vermillion, which perhaps made them the perfect pawn. No one would've stopped them from entering, not even Vermillion. An unchanged one, who didn't even want to fight. Hardly dangerous. But everyone knew they had teeth now.

They had to finish the job.

CHAPTER 38

*E*lliot paced the Hare, fury burning his veins. He raked his fingers through what was left of his hair and scrubbed a hand over his face. He should've left Umbra to die. Should've, but hadn't been able to because he'd thought there was something between them. Something more than blood. Something more than an unsteady alliance.

They had no alliance.

Whatever happens. No matter what I do. You have to trust me. They'd already had Dayne in the boat and were reminding Elliot they were on the same side.

He picked up the glass of liquor that had been poured for him and drank. The sharpness burned his tongue and throat. It wasn't the weakened ale he was used to. Perhaps it was the spirit those on the hill preferred. Warmth spread through him, fueling his anger.

Every time he closed his eyes, he saw the boat ready to go.

His lips twisted, and a tiny part of him knew Umbra would give Dayne the blood and nectar he needed to get well. Elliot couldn't even give Dayne a bed to sleep in. But how could Umbra protect Dayne from Vermillion when they couldn't protect themselves? They were fighting a useless battle. Dayne had realized and tried to end his part, and Elliot hadn't had the grace to let him go. Twice.

If Dayne didn't want to be saved, maybe it was time he listened.

Elliot put his glass down too hard and liquor splashed over the rim and onto his hand.

"Elliot, were you listening?" Benton topped up Elliot's glass.

He lifted his gaze from the liquor and loosened his grip, so his knuckles no longer looked like bone. "Yeah. We need to rally the jobless and homeless and anyone else."

Lead people into a fight that some of them would die in. He didn't want to do that.

"You need to get out there. People know you escaped the Kin. They see the posters."

"And they'll turn me in for the reward."

"We'll protect you."

"Only because Umbra said you had to. You didn't want me anywhere near you a few nights ago." No one wanted him.

"You bring trouble."

"I don't bring it, I find it." Elliot downed the rest of his glass and luxuriated in the burn and heat that filled him.

Other venerie drifted in, Serene doing her job of waking them. They all gave Elliot a hard glance before taking a seat.

Dayne should be leading this fight. He was venerie in his spare time. Dayne had time to fight the Kin while Elliot did everything he could to keep food on the table and a roof over head. Even his brother had used him and cast him aside.

The liquor became bitter in his mouth and threatened to upend his stomach.

Those few weeks in the castle, he'd lived only for himself. While he hadn't been free, no one had forced him to do anything, not even Umbra. He was trying so hard to hate them. And he did, a little, for taking Dayne and putting them back to where it had all started. But he loved them more for showing him what life could be like. For teaching him how to fight and plan and for making him feel like he could be more.

The dozen venerie muttered about this and that. Lack of work. Lack of food. Lack of leaf. A thin cigarette was passed around. They seemed happy to sit and gossip like the chance of a lifetime wasn't within reach.

Elliot tapped his glass on the bar until they all turned to him. He forced a smile, like he knew what he was doing. He'd been to the castle and returned, and that counted for something. "Is this what you do when you meet? Bitch about the Kin and your neighbors?"

"We fight the Kin!"

A few of them lifted their fists. Most glared at Elliot like he'd just pissed on their last piece of bread.

"What has that ever changed? The whole trade is broken. The rich selling us to pay for their pleasure. Their extended life."

"We kill all the Kin, and we'll be free," a man smoking marshmallow said.

"You can't kill them all. When we can't see the castle, it exists somewhere else. There are more of them. The castle is there to stop us invading their lands and taking nectar. We need to take the power off the lord." But someone would still have power, and living forever must be a strong temptation if life was easy. No one in the dark wanted to live for longer than they needed to. "We need to stop the marshals. March up the streets to the lord's house. Refuse to work."

"Then others will take our jobs."

"We fight the Kin, not the rich."

They weren't listening. The Dark City would be crushed between the rich and Kin.

Benton poured another glass of liquor. "Elliot has been to the castle and talked with the Kin. He should be listened to."

"He's not one of us. If we put him under an orb, will he glow silver?"

The cigarette was offered to Elliot. "Or perhaps he's selling his blood for favors."

Elliot took the cigarette and drew the smoke into his lungs. The burn at the back of his throat and the taste were familiar, but he stopped missing it by the time he breathed out a cloud. He handed the cigarette back. No one would be sipping on his blood for a day or so. A small measure of relief flowed through him even though it would mean nothing in the end. The Kin would wait for his blood to be clean before draining him.

"I sold my blood to get Dayne back." He shrugged. "It's my blood to sell. Our blood. Our choice. That's all I'm saying. If you want to buy nectar and live forever, go for it. But don't ask others to pay the price. We need to fight those up the hill who see us as little more than chickens waiting for the ax. Drag the lord to the lake so he can pay for what he has taken." The lord's death wouldn't bring back all the lives lost. "The devoured that we have been taught to abandon and treat with fear only need a little Kin blood to be returned. How many of us have left family by the lake to die?"

"I have." Serene was leaning against the wall. "My aunt was taken when I was six. I went looking for her, found her, and brought her home. Ma nearly died, and I got a whipping for going to the lake alone. If we were to take our family back and listen to what they say, we might have learned the truth a while back."

A few others stared at the tables. They all knew someone who'd been taken.

"We need to rally today. Make trouble, clear the marshals from the shore before tonight."

"So the Kin can join the fight. You work for them," the smoker said.

"The Kin will have a new leader come dusk." Hopefully. "If Vermillion is still in charge, then you can hunt the Kin all you want. Today, I ask you to help me topple the lord."

"You set fire to the hill?"

"I did." Elliot sipped his drink, his confidence in the plan growing.

"We could turn you in and claim the reward."

"No one will be doing that today. Elliot is our link to the Kin," Benton said. "Though if Vermillion is still in charge by the end of tonight, I'll be handing him to the lord myself and putting the reward on the bar."

~

*T*he city was split up so they could cover more ground. Some were heading toward the barracks to hassle the marshals there. Others were spreading through the Dark City to rile up the cold and hungry into taking what the rich kept for themselves. They were all to meet at the center square at midday and march up the hill.

The sun was bright, but not warm. Winter still gripped the city, even though spring gave teasing promises. A good day to start a riot.

Elliot led Serena through the alleyways until they reached the house he was staying in. The stain was still on the floor, and the beast was hidden under a stolen blanket. He grabbed his bag of tools.

Serene stared at the blood but said nothing. She'd been silent the whole way—thinking about turning him in or worrying about Dayne? At least he'd be safe in the castle while the Kin slept.

He slung the bag over his shoulder but left the beast. Even the venerie didn't know he had it. His job was to get more orbs and teach Serena how to use them.

"The lightmen don't work during the day. People'll ask questions or send the marshals our way." He glanced at her, wanting some kind of input. She was venerie; she should be better at this than him.

She frowned. "I'll stand watch. You'll be quicker."

Elliot peered out the alley at the closest light. People walked along the sidewalk in brightly colored clothes, not a patch or frayed hem to be seen.

He would be faster, but that didn't mean it was going to be easy. They couldn't walk up the street. They'd have to be smarter. "I'll do this one, then we'll run through the back streets and take another. Working toward the square."

Serene nodded. "Do you think Umbra will win?"

Elliot pulled the tools he'd need out of his bag. He was trying not to think about Umbra because every time he did, he saw the boat by the lake. *No matter what I do. You have to trust me.* "I think we can't wait to find out. If we bring down the lord, then maybe whoever is in charge will negotiate with us."

If they failed, the marshals would turn them all over to the Kin without even blinking.

"All these folk won't be happy with the changes."

Elliot watched a family walk by. The kids didn't have hollow cheeks and tired eyes. "Maybe not, but they benefitted from selling us. If their ma is dying, they just hand over a few coins, someone grows richer, and the Kin eat us. They'll still get nectar if they need it. They'll just have to pay the Kin with their own blood."

Serene stepped closer. "Do you think they're all really old like the lord?"

He studied the passersby. None of them ever glanced down the alley. "I hadn't." And it was a disturbing thought. The men passing by looked his age, but they could be fifty or a hundred if they'd been sipping nectar daily. He shivered.

Serene leaned closer. "If you had enough money each sennight that you had coins left over, what would you spend it on?"

"Clothes." He'd get knee high boots that buttoned up the sides and beautiful coats like Umbra had. Like he'd left in the castle.

"You're rich; you already have lots of fancy clothes."

"I'd buy some for others. Get a tutor and learn to read."

"And then what?"

"Buy a house."

"And then?" She nodded at the sidewalk. "They have all of that stuff."

"You think they drink it for fun? Buy an extra year?"

"Or decade? In the dark, we're all worn out by the time we hit thirty. We drag ourselves around for another decade, maybe two before dying of the cough or injury. These people don't get sick, and the parents look as bright as the kids."

"How long would you really want to live for?" If he owned businesses and didn't work, he'd have to fill his days. Living forever would get dull after a while, but he wouldn't mind giving it a chance.

"I don't know." Serene shrugged. "A tipple of nectar once a month to stay healthy. I'd sell my blood for that."

"And you'd still be washing vomit off the floor and fending off drunks at the Hare."

She elbowed him in the ribs. "If Dayne is safe in the castle, maybe I'll join him. I can clean floors anywhere. You'll be going there if Umbra wins?"

Elliot pressed his lips together. He liked it there, but it wasn't real. It wasn't where he belonged, not when there was so much to fix here. "I'd like to visit, but I don't think I could live there knowing what it's like over here. We can't all pack up and leave to clean the castle. We have to make the city better."

"You're right. And he doesn't want me anyway." She blew out a breath. "Go get an orb so I can start stabbing marshals."

Elliot waited a moment then stepped onto the street, eyes down, striding toward the light. He could feel the hot glances of the rich on him. They saw him. A speck of mold on their bread that didn't belong.

He climbed the post and opened the box with the key. He freed the orb and dropped it into his bag, no longer concerned about holding them gently. Then he shut the light and started climbing down. Halfway down, his gaze accidentally locked with one of the finely dressed folk. His bright red coat was striped with darker red and the trim was white. Proper cloud white, not too-often-washed-gray.

For a moment, neither of them did a thing.

"You." The man pointed. "Thief!"

Elliot jumped. His feet hit the ground, and he was running. He skidded into the alley, but the rich saw them now. They knew there were alleys and that people used them, but they preferred not to see those kinds of people. Now, there was no unseeing.

They ran through the alley, the cobbles slick with moss and the excrement that fell out of Killian's cart. Serene threw herself around one corner and then another. They panted for a few moments and listened for sounds of pursuit.

She grinned at him. "Ready to go again?"

"Sure. Maybe this time you could actually help instead of hiding."

*B*y the time he had five orbs in his bag, the marshals were searching for him. They were scouring the area and guarding the lights. From the roof of a building, Elliot watched them scurry. It was almost noon, and they had other places to be.

Serene climbed up to sit next to him, lunch in her coat pockets. On the street, the pie maker was yelling about a thieving girl. People were declaring they didn't know what was going on. What was wrong with people? Didn't they know their place?

She pulled two pies out of her pocket and handed one to him. Elliot bit into the flakey pastry. There was actual meat inside not just gravy and a few odds and ends that were best not to think about. He closed his eyes and enjoyed the burn of each bite as he ate too fast. If he had coin, he'd never buy cheap food again. He wanted the nice stuff. Real meat and unwatered ale.

"Do you hear that?" Serene whispered.

With his eyes closed, he listened. The pie warm in his hand, the sun on his face. The noise on the street below faded. Beyond it was something else. A rhythm. Shouting.

The center square was only over the block. He opened his eyes. If he could hear the people marching up the hill, could those on the ground?

He glanced down. The marshals that had been placating the pie seller and guarding the lights turned as another green coat ran toward them.

This was it. They knew the Dark City was rising.

He shoved the last piece of pie in his mouth and licked his fingers. "You might actually get your blade wet this time."

"Have you ever killed?"

He was about to say no, but that would be a lie. "Only a Kin when I escaped."

This time, he'd be fighting other humans. He wasn't sure he was ready to draw his blade and spill dark human blood, but the marshals wouldn't hesitate to spill his. They'd never hesitated before. Those that lived in the dark were nothing, cattle at best, rats to be removed at worst.

He climbed down the building into the alley behind with Serene close by, then handed her the bag of orbs. "You know what to do?"

"Yeah." She clutched the strap. "I hope your Kin keeps their end of the deal."

Elliot nodded, unable to speak. He had to believe they could make a change and life would be better for everyone, otherwise why was he fighting? This had been Umbra's plan. Take the city and the castle in one neat move. But it wouldn't be neat. There were too many people who'd suppressed their anger for too long. Their shouting filled the air like the coming of a summer storm.

Elliot and Serene made their way quickly through to where the alleys and lights ended and joined the crowd. People were yelling their grievances as they marched up the hill. They brandished their tools, rakes, shovels, or hammers. Some only carried sticks or pans. A few carried knives that were no doubt blunted by age and wear as much as poor craftsmanship. Cheaply made for those that couldn't afford better.

His Kin-made knife cut through clothing and flesh like they were little more than cooking fat.

The marshals formed a line at the start of the Lit City. The one in the center cracked a whip over the heads of the crowd, and while the first few rows, faltered the tide behind them didn't. It seemed like every person who lived in the dark had downed tools for the day and was marching.

Elliot wasn't at the front, but he could see the whip move and snap over heads. When that failed, the whip no longer danced overhead. He felt the change in the crowd before the first cry of pain as the whip found a target. The howl only fueled their anger. The marshals were armed with batons and swords and whips; they tried hard to hold the line but were forced back by those who'd never been trained to fight.

While some who lived in the dark had saved up and become marshals, there hadn't been many. With the Kin trouble, the lord had handed out green armbands to swell the ranks of soldiers. How many holding the line were raising their weapons against friends and family to support a man who cared nothing for them? Or was it just a job, one that paid well and gave them a step up toward the Lit City.

"Charge them!" a cry went up, and the crowd ran at the line.

The marshals' line broke, and the tide ran uphill. A marshal's whip snapped across Elliot's shoulder. He turned, but the marshal was already fighting for his life. He didn't get his sword out fast enough. The club being wielded didn't need finesse to do its job. Elliot looked away before wood met head with a solid crunch.

A chant formed. "Our blood. Our choice. Pay for your own nectar." He recognized his words on the tongues of so many.

In the crowd, the venerie stoked the fire until it lived on its own, consuming all it touched. The people who lived in the Lit City, who'd strolled the sidewalk in their pretty clothes not that long ago, had vanished. Marshals lined the streets and harried the edges of the crowd. Glass shattered as shops were raided.

He lost sight of Serene, but when something flashed and a building caught fire, he figured she'd gotten ahead of the crowd. He jostled along with everyone else. When the people near him fell back to tangle with marshals, he kept going. When attacked, Elliot fought back, his knife in his hand—though he couldn't remember drawing it.

A green-coat came at him sword drawn, and Elliot defended himself, not wanting to kill. They were doing their job, but they could strip off their coat and join in if they wanted. They didn't.

Elliot got in close so the sword was useless and slammed the hilt of his knife into the man's temple. Someone crashed into him, and he stumbled, dropping his knife. An elbow caught him in the face, and his cheekbone became fire. A hand reached out to help him up and he took it.

Killian.

He smiled, thinking Killian had changed his mind about becoming a marshal.

"Knew I'd find you thick in the trouble." Killian's club caught him across the stomach, stealing his breath. It was then Elliot saw the green ribbon tied around Killian's sleeve.

"Traitor," Elliot spat the word and pulled his hand free of Killian's

"You're the traitor." Killian struck again with the club.

Elliot put his hand up to protect his face and tried to step back into the crowd, to vanish into the sea. But it threw him back into Killian's painful embrace.

Where was his knife? He thought he saw a glimpse, but it was behind Killian.

"Just because you didn't get your way, you ruin it for everyone." Killian struck again, and heat radiated through Elliot's forearm. "The reward is mine."

Elliot ducked low beneath the next strike and barreled into Killian. Killian side stepped, and Elliot saw his knife. He dove for it, clasped the hilt and rolled.

Killian was on top of him. The end of the baton struck his ribs and stopped his heart. Elliot bucked, trying to throw him off, but every breath burned. Killian slammed the hand holding the knife against the cobbles. Elliot's knuckles exploded on the stone, and the knife was lost again. Killian pressed the baton to his throat.

"Even if you stop me, you can't stop them. Things are changing." Elliot clawed at Killian's wrists. The edges of his vision turned red then black.

"Things never change. They just appear to."

CHAPTER 39

$\mathcal{W}$ ith great effort, as it was still too light and the sunlight was making their blood thick in their veins, Umbra sat up. A pile of clean clothes had been placed on the table.

Dayne had been washed and changed, and his heartbeat had slowed into a steady rhythm. Umbra ran their tongue over their teeth. They had drunk nectar during the night, they were sure of it. Their shirt clung to them, damp with sweat and reeking of old blood. They should bathe and change, but they didn't want to leave Dayne alone. If they were rousing, other Abyr would be, and they couldn't take that risk.

There would be time for luxurious baths afterward. Or there'd be bigger things to worry about if this all went bad.

There was water on the table, fruits and other simple breakfast foods. That wasn't what they needed, though. They needed more nectar, blood, and a day in their own bed.

They wanted Elliot. It was a sensation they weren't sure what to do with and couldn't dwell on.

They stood and forced themselves to move. Their knife was still at their hip. Their back no longer ached, the wounds now only deep scars that would continue to heal until they vanished to little more than a memory.

They stripped off their old shirt and poured water on the cleanest sleeve to wash as best they could. Though it couldn't really be called washing when it was more a case of spreading the sweat and blood around and hoping to remove some of it. They pulled on the clean shirt. It was one of theirs. One that smelled of Elliot. They tied the cuffs, then took off their boots and socks and stripped off their old trousers and undershorts, hoping the pants could be salvaged, and finished washing. They dressed in the clean pants and fresh socks and sat to put on their boots, their strength not fully back.

Their gaze landed on Dayne, the beat of his heart too tempting. He needed to get up. He had to be awake. Umbra tugged Dayne up to sitting. His head lolled for a moment before his eyes fluttered open.

"So nice of you to wake and join me."

Dayne blinked a few times. "No." He batted at Umbra's hands and succeeded in falling back onto the table, smacking his elbow in the process. Dayne winced and lay still. "I'm not dead."

Umbra lifted their eyebrows. "I realize that was your plan, but Elliot thought it was a rather stupid one. I agreed."

"You don't understand."

Umbra grabbed Dayne's shirt and hauled him up so they were nose to nose. "I understand fine. Your brother has done everything he could to save you, and you threw it away like an ungrateful brat."

"I don't want to live like this."

"Like what? Here in the castle where you don't have to worry about a thing? Where you'll get the blood you need to stay yourself?" Umbra let go. "It's more than he'll get."

More than he could offer Elliot. There would too many humans dependent on the Abyr already. No one would thank them for taking another, especially not one who could be their eyes and ears in the city.

Dayne regarded them with the same dark eyes Elliot had. But where Elliot's gaze was filled with wonder and more, Dayne's was harder. "I never asked him to do a bloody thing for me."

"Do you care so little about your own blood? There isn't a part of him left that hasn't been sold or traded." It should be Elliot here, enjoying the castle. He could learn to read. He could learn to make the fine glass windows he'd been so entranced with. He could do whatever he wanted with his life. It was his to spend, and he should spend it the way he wanted.

"I know." Dayne looked away. His gaze tracked around the hall, his eyes widening with each breath. "You brought me back."

"Yes. It was the only way to save you." If not for Elliot, they wouldn't have bothered.

"I need to leave. I don't want to be..." His gaze jerked up. "Ver will kill me."

"You wanted to die, so why the sudden panic?" They knew; there were quick deaths where one didn't feel much after the first cut or the slow death that Vermillion would give an errant pet.

"You can't let them kill me. Elliot won't like it."

"Elliot isn't here. So here is the deal, Dayne." Umbra put their hands on the table, bracketing Dayne's legs. "I am going to seize power today if all goes well. You want that to happen because I am the only person who can stop Ver from killing you in a very painful and degrading manner. You will pretend to be much sicker than you currently are. You will go to his side until I make them an offer. You will play this game with me and be a willing and grateful pawn. If you fail to play your part, you will be pulled apart piece by piece. Elliot will hear only that I couldn't stop Ver. He will be devastated, but his life will be much simpler if he isn't constantly supporting you."

Keeping Dayne here would have the advantage of lifting that weight from Elliot's shoulders. He'd done a noble thing in raising his brother, but it was time for Elliot to find his own life. Hopefully there would be a place for them in some small way.

"Do you understand the knife edge you and I walk along? Or should I end you myself? One bite in the wrong place..." Their fingers curled against the wood. This man was supposed to be venerie, a fighter, and yet they had seen nothing of that. They saw a man who had been happy to let Elliot wear away, so he didn't have to make hard decisions. A man who broke at the first test and again at the second.

Dayne would not become their pet. He wasn't worthy.

Dayne nodded.

"Seal it with blood." Umbra bit their thumb and offered it to Dayne. He hesitated for a moment before licking and sucking on the offered blood. Umbra jerked their hand away and snatched up Dayne's hand. He bit Dayne's thumb, taking only the smallest drop even though they wanted more. "Keep your word, for I will have no trouble keeping mine. Lay down and be weakened."

Dayne slumped back onto the table. His heartbeat was running footsteps.

Umbra didn't trust him, but there wasn't much else he could do.

They sat and worked the tangled braids out of their hair, running their fingers through strands that smelled of lake water, sweat, and death. Then, they started the process of rebraiding, concealing the area that had been shaved and weaving in the short strands where they'd cut their own braid to spite Vermillion. Their fingers knew the patterns and the meaning behind each one. Tonight, their loops and lines were the same as their birther wore before battle, their history shown for all to see.

Their own heavy heartbeat drowned out Dayne's. There were a dozen different ways this could play out. Some they won, some they lost. Some could scatter into a hundred different plays. They wouldn't know until Vermillion appeared which possibility was going to start the game they played.

They finished the last braid. The sun was fully set, and Vermillion should be up. The wait was part of the ploy. The moment Umbra walked away from Dayne, there would be no chance. Despite what they'd said, they didn't want Dayne to get hurt any more than he already was. Their anger at the suffering Dayne had put Elliot through wasn't theirs to exploit. That was between the brothers.

Umbra dragged a platter of food over and ate, waiting for the others to rise and for the drama to begin. They didn't taste the bread or cheese, but they knew it was Elliot's favorite.

They wanted this over.

Two Abyr came down the stairs. Umbra glanced at them and weighed the odds of success before deciding it was worth the test. "Fetch me a coat."

Anil glanced at Umbra and then Dayne on the table. "You have returned."

"The green one I think will look best." Umbra didn't bother to answer the most obvious question. Some Abyr were good warriors, but not good leaders.

"We were told you were wounded in battle and fell into the water. How much of that is true?" Falu asked.

"All of it, though parts were omitted. The blade that wounded me was held by a *friend*." They picked up a piece of dried fruit and chewed. "My coat?"

They could refuse; Umbra wasn't Vermillion's mate and had no special status anymore. However, lines had to be drawn, and Umbra needed to know who was going to be on their side and who was going to play for Vermillion. They didn't want another bloody coup.

Anil turned back and went up the stairs. Umbra watched as the door to their chambers opened. Falu didn't join them at the table but lingered at the side.

Vermillion's door opened, and they strode out dressed in finery. They stopped when they saw Umbra still at the table. Had they been waiting for Umbra to leave Dayne unattended? Umbra bit back a smile. *Fool.*

"You have returned with my pet and accusations."

Dayne flinched, his heartbeat a mess of tangled rhythms.

Umbra ate another piece of bread as though they had nothing to be concerned about.

Vermillion strolled down the stairs. "You gave orders when you had no right to. You could have lost us the battle."

"A battle you have been hungry for." Umbra stood. Behind Vermillion, Anil came down the stairs holding their coat. They wanted its protection even though Vermillion had cut through the last one. "The castle must be protected at all cost. That is why we are here. Everything else is a byproduct or a bonus. Though I am sure the bards would sing of a breach should there be one."

Vermillion's lips drew back revealing their fangs. "I have already sent word of your demise. How did you survive?"

There was a chance Vermillion was lying. If they weren't, Umbra could send a rider to intercept the news before it reached their parent's ears. Perhaps they should've faked their death instead of changing, but the heartland was not for them. This was their life now.

"I fed and rested and found him amongst the hopeful on the shore. There was quite the feast there, and I found myself revived come pre-dawn." Umbra walked over and took the coat from Anil.

Vermillion noticed, and their scowl deepened. No one rushed to Vermillion's side. The Abyr clung to the edges of the room, slowly filling the hall, knowing the tension that had been building would be cut today. Settled.

Some would want more blood and battle and would side with Vermillion; others wanted change. They had seen what was happening and had been waiting for someone to take the risk and stand against Vermillion.

The same could be said of the city. Most knew those up the hill were corrupt, but few realized how deeply, and fewer had the energy to make the change. One step at a time. First the castle, then they could help with the city.

"How lucky." Vermillion ran their fingers up Dayne's arm. "He should be awake."

"He is weakened from blood loss."

Vermillion glanced sharply at Umbra. "You fed off my pet because your own will not feed you?"

"Your pet was so reluctant to come back, they tried to take their own life." Umbra tilted their head. "To treat a pet so poorly—" Vermillion's hand snapped out to strike Umbra, but they caught it. "To treat a pet so poorly reflects ill on the owner." Umbra lowered their linked hands. "So, I propose a game. Let us play for this pet. If you win, you keep him and do as you will. If I win, he is mine."

Vermillion snatched their hand back. "He is mine, and I do not need to play your games." They shoved Dayne. "Get up and serve me."

Dayne did his best to act as though he were just waking, but his heart betrayed him. There was nothing that could be done about that.

"Someone helped you both last night. I have traitors in my castle." Vermillion's voice rose with each word.

There were traitors in the castle, but Vermillion would need a mirror to see them.

Dayne sat on the table, his gaze on the floor.

"We do not need more bloodshed," Umbra said.

Vermillion faced them. "You have caused nothing but upset since you arrived, a poisoned gift from your birther. I was at Octadine when you were born. A nasty little bundle of noise that ensured I would never get the castle despite my loyalty. I left and made my way here, bided my time until I could take over. Your sire praised me and offered you to me as a way to heal the wound. But it was never about healing was it? Tell me!"

If it had been about anything else, Umbra hadn't been told. They shrugged. "I was sent to be your mate because my parents were tired of my antics. Surely, my reputation preceded me. I'd rather have been a bard than a warrior. I do not lust for battle with every breath. I grew up in a castle knowing peaceful trade with the humans. You have humans on that hill who have prolonged their life with nectar while keeping it from those who need it."

"Better to have consistent rule than to dance in the breeze." Vermillion's hand rested on the hilt of their knife.

"Did you want me to turn my back again so you may strike me more easily?" Umbra drew in a breath, then spun, giving Vermillion a chance to prove their dishonor. No blade bit their back.

Vermillion pulled the weighed dice out of their pocket. "Winner takes all."

"And the loser?"

"Leaves," Vermillion snapped.

If Umbra lost, they wouldn't be leaving alive. They'd be tossed in the lake, worse than dead. "You expect me to go home? My parents already think I am dead."

"Try not to disappoint them again." Vermillion sat.

Umbra sat opposite Vermillion. Vermillion grabbed Dayne's wrist and bit. Dayne gasped and tried to pull away, but Vermillion laughed and forced him to the floor next to their chair.

No one else stepped closer to take a seat.

The platters of food that had been put out for them at sunset remained untouched.

"I should kill you for your insolence." Vermillion rolled the dice in their hand.

"You tried once and failed. Perhaps your luck will be better today?"

"You have brought this on yourself." They rolled the seven dice, then picked up two and rerolled.

A standard hand with a reasonable score, but not so high it could be called into question. "Someone to score?"

Anil collected the peg board that kept track of such things when the stakes were high and placed it on the table. Vermillion moved their peg.

Umbra held the dice for a moment. They didn't want to reveal they could play the weights too soon nor leave it too late that they lost. They rolled and made the best of what they had, ending a point behind.

Vermillion wasn't so conservative the second time. The hand they produced was well above average, even for a good player.

Umbra did the same, using the weighted dice to their advantage.

Vermillion's smug expression slid off their face.

"Perhaps you have brought this on yourself, by encouraging violence and ruling by fear. No human would help you if you were trapped in the city. No pet would come to your side and offer their blood."

"I take what I need." Vermillion snatched up the dice and didn't hide their cheating. "A pet is nothing but walking food. You are weak from growing up in a place where battle was shunned. Your birther became soft as their antlers grew. Their tales of war are dusted with age."

Umbra smiled. "I would rather rule in peace than awash in blood." They rolled, cheating better than Vermillion with a perfect hand. Each of the seven dice displayed their highest symbol.

"That's impossible."

Whispers raced around the hall.

"Your dice. My castle. My pet." Umbra stood. "I am the new leader."

Vermillion drew their knife, the curve gleaming red in the light. They sprung forward, going for Umbra's throat. Umbra leaned back and lifted their arm, deflecting the blow. Vermillion fell back and hit the floor with a sickening thud.

Umbra leaped over the table, ignoring the burning of their forearm and the hot blood running down their skin. Dayne knelt on the floor, his hands and shirt bloody. A cheese knife stuck out the side of Vermillion's neck. A puddle of bright blood spread, tracing the gaps in the stone, pooling in the uneven surface.

Vermillion scrabbled for the knife, their fingers like a hungry spider reaching for more. They were bleeding out, and no one stepped forward to help.

"You all stand witness to the gamble that Vermillion lost. They then attacked and were attacked in kind by the pet they mistreated. Let that be a warning to you all. I will not punish a pet who takes vengeance." They turned slowly, taking in the faces of the watching Abyr. "If you wish to leave, do so now. If you wish to stay and make good the damage done, then you are welcome."

Umbra knelt next to Vermillion. Their lips worked but no sound came out.

"You stabbed me in the back and cheated, but still you couldn't win." Umbra leaned closer. "No bard will sing your name. You will be forgotten forever."

CHAPTER 40

*E*very breath stabbed. One arm ached with a pain that radiated up to his teeth, and his other hand pulsed with each heartbeat. Elliot wanted to go back to the dark place where he didn't hurt.

He tried to move but couldn't. Panic fluttered close by, but he didn't have the energy to join the dance. He moved his fingers and sucked in a pained breath. Rope bit into his wrist. He tried his other hand, but the pain was worse. He drew in several quick shallow breaths that stopped his chest from burning.

"I know you are awake, so how about you stop keeping me waiting?" The voice was cracked and dry.

Elliot swallowed, his throat swollen. He didn't open his eyes. He needed a few more moments to let Killian's betrayal stop smarting. The man Elliot had thought he knew was gone replaced by a sneer and a snarl as he'd fought and pressed the baton to his throat. He'd climbed out of the dark and didn't want his victory to be snatched away. Why wouldn't Killian want things to be better for everyone, not just himself?

Bony fingers gripped his cheeks and forced his head up. Elliot opened his eyes. The lord stared at him, his blue eyes sharp and bright even though his face had sagged and was spotted with age. All that remained of his hair were a few wisps of white. He'd aged a lifetime in a few days. Was this his true age?

People in the dark wore out before they got old. Those that did get old relied on family when they could no longer work, often looking after the children of the boarding house in exchange for a meal. The old woman in his building had died when he was five. After that, the next oldest child was in charge. They'd been eight.

"I had to pay out your reward. Only half, of course, because you lot don't know what to do with coin." The fingers dug in. "You don't know when you have it good."

"Good? You live in the Dark City at night and see how good it is." His words were twisted by the ache in his throat and the fingers digging into his cheeks.

"I give the city stability. Without me, you'd be overrun with Kin. You'd all be dead." The lord released him and stepped back, wiping his fingers on a cloth offered by a servant dressed in black.

"That's a lie."

The lord slapped him in the face. Elliot's head snapped back, and the shock jolted every injury. He wanted to crawl into bed and hide under the sheets—except it wasn't his bed he was picturing, but Umbra's.

If he didn't get his hand fixed, it would be busted for life. If he didn't get his arm set, it would mend crooked. He wouldn't be able to work at all. Did he have the coin to pay for that? Or did the venerie know a bonesetter who'd do it cheap?

That was assuming he lived.

The lord wiped his hand as though Elliot was something dirty and contagious. "I know about your little stunt at the castle. Word travels uphill swiftly when I throw a few quarters in the gutter. You think you know all about the Kin?" The lord shook his head and the loose skin around his neck wobbled. "You only know what they want you to know."

"Why would you tell me the truth?"

"Because we need the same thing. Nectar."

His breaks would mend without it. The lord was getting old fast, his age catching up with him. How many nights until he died?

"Nectar has kept this city stable. My leadership has brought great things."

"Like what?"

"Trade, wealth—"

Elliot forced a laugh. "We don't see a lot of that down the hill."

A marshal tipped the chair. Elliot yelled as his arms were pinched between the floor and the wooden slats of the chair back. There was nothing he could do but pant through the burning agony that wanted to rip him apart.

The lord walked around so Elliot could see him. Beyond the halo of white hair, the ceiling was painted with a forest. There were deer and rabbits and other animals, most Elliot couldn't name.

His vision went white at the edges. He wanted to throw up.

"Not everyone can benefit. Some people have to be the workers. We let you have marshmallow. Even pay you to grow it and harvest it. Still not enough. What do you people want?"

"Not to be hunted. To have access to nectar."

"You can get nectar. It's available. Or at least it was until you started agitating." The lord motioned to the marshals and the chair was dragged up right.

Elliot groaned, and the pain scraped through his body like it was trying to find a way out. "We can't afford it."

"That's not my problem."

"I'd have given my blood to save my mother. Traded directly with the Kin."

The lord stared at him. "From the silver on your skin, you have already given your blood. We can't have everyone doing that. It would be chaos. Who would manage it?"

"The venerie."

The lord chuckled. "A band of troublemakers who hate the Kin. No, nectar needs to be controlled." The servant carried a seat over, and the lord sat carefully as though he'd exhausted himself. "What is it you want? Your brother is with the Kin again; he's devoured, I believe. Beyond hel—"

"All he needs is blood."

The smack came from behind and jerked Elliot's head forward, so his arms tugged on the rope. The pain blinded him for several heartbeats.

"Don't interrupt me when I'm speaking. Do you not learn manners?"

"No schools." Those that did claim to be there to teach the poor were too expensive. Who had coin for books and uniforms?

Another slap that made stars explode and his teeth rattle.

"Don't lie. I went to great effort to make sure there are schools."

"Can't afford the uniform." There was blood in his mouth. He swallowed it instead of spitting it at the lord. He couldn't keep getting hit. It was hard to think past the pain.

"So I'm supposed to do everything?" The lord leaned forward. "You spend your coin on leaf, don't go to school, and so don't aspire to anything. You're little better than cattle. Dumb and easily led. But you know that. You led them up the hill. Took advantage of them." He drew his thin lips into a smile that created deep creases in his face.

He hadn't taken advantage. There were less jobs, less food. People were done with barely existing while seeing those up the hill prance around like they were somehow better.

"You could go far. I'm sure if you were bathed and dressed better, you could be passed off as nobility. Your manners could be worked on. You could even make those in the Dark City your cause. Everyone likes a cause, somewhere to throw their extra coin."

Elliot frowned. What was he suggesting?

"Have you forgotten how to speak?"

Elliot winced but the strike didn't come. "What is it you want?"

"I want you to negotiate for the nectar. You have need of it as much as I do. In return, you will be given a place on the hill, a share of the trade, and you can dabble in the cesspit until you realize it can never be cleaned up. Some people don't want to better themselves. You aren't one of them."

"What about my brother and the other devoured?"

The lord drew in a breath. "The devoured by the shore have been dealt with."

"No!" Elliot rocked forward trying to stand. The chair was yanked back. He tucked his head in as he fell back. The scream that left his lips wasn't a voice he recognized. One of the marshals put his boot on Elliot's chest and pressed down. He couldn't breathe as shards of hot pain radiated through his chest and down his fingers. The marshal smiled. Then he was picked up and the chair set to rights.

He stared at the ceiling, wishing to be anywhere but here. Trying to find a way to breathe that didn't hurt and failing.

"If you need more motivation…" The lord indicated to the marshals. Elliot twisted in the chair trying to see what was going to happen.

One of them grabbed his busted hand and straightened his fingers against the wood of the chair. A baton connected with the palm of his hand. Elliot cried out.

The lord nodded. Another strike. Warm blood dripped down his fingers. His knuckles were on fire, and his hand throbbed.

"I know that nectar can do all kinds of wonderful things, but I don't know how good it is at setting bones straight. It would be interesting to find though, wouldn't it? It wouldn't take much to break all your fingers and twist that break in your arm. Lock you in a room for a few days with only water and see how you feel about helping. It's an option. I was hoping that you'd be smart. You are smarter than the average dark dweller. You got into the castle and back." The lord leaned forward.

"You don't have a few days," Elliot said through gritted teeth.

The lord got up and gripped Elliot's face again. "I will not have everything I have built torn down by an upstart pup who doesn't know his place." His nails bit into Elliot's skin. This close, Elliot could see the cloudy edges in the lord's eyes. He was dying, and he was afraid. "Break his fingers. One at a time."

It took three before Elliot agreed.

CHAPTER 41

The city was burning again. The bonfires on the shore had swollen in size and were spewing out thick, black, oily smoke. There were marshals guarding the causeway but only a dozen, and none of them wearing green coats. But the lake was a mirror. Stars glittered in its surface, promising a beautiful night if they stood still to admire it.

There would be other nights. It was time.

This wasn't the first act Umbra wanted to do as leader, but it had to be done. Maybe it was their second act, their first being freeing Weld and the others from the towers where Vermillion had jailed them for following Umbra's orders to secure the castle during the battle.

With a sigh, Umbra turned and went down to the main hall.

"The lake is empty. We will ride to the city," Umbra announced. "We will make a new trade deal and put this bitterness behind us. We are not at war with the humans. That is not our way...unless they invade. And they are less likely to invade if we treat them fairly." They made eye contact with each of the Abyr who had enjoyed Vermillion's hunting trips. "We will not hunt, but there will be enough blood flowing our way for hunting to be unneeded." They turned and nodded at Weld who returned the gesture. Vermillion's body was ready. "Does anyone beg for leniency on behalf of Vermillion? Is there a kindness about them that is worth saving?" The list of charges had been read out before Weld had removed Vermillion from the hall and prepared them. The bard had listened to every word.

Vermillion had seized the castle through underhand methods. They disrupted trade and put the border at risk. They had killed and brutalized numerous pets. No one had spoken when the charges were read, and no one spoke now.

Some lowered their gazes to the floor, as though hoping to be forgotten.

Umbra had promised a second chance, but not a third. Two had left, ridden away so they never had to face their shame at not standing up to Vermillion. The rest had stayed and vowed to do better. For the moment, Umbra believed their word until given a reason to doubt.

"Very well. Vermillion is to be consigned to the depths as befitting one who betrayed the Abyr for their own hunger." The punishment for the changed was far worse than for the unchanged, but the job the changed did was far more dangerous. It was easy to become thoroughly corrupted.

A few winced, and Umbra didn't blame them. The lake was clear tonight, but the next leviathan would find the body and feast for days. Nibbling at the flesh with their beak, squeezing and tugging with their tentacles. The only mercy Vermillion could hope for was that the leviathan would rip their head off before they started eating.

Umbra strode out of the hall and down to the cells were water lapped the floor. They didn't glance at the one where the mayor's son had been held but instead walked to the end where the body was being guarded.

They were aware Vermillion would be listening to everything. Watching. Panicking. Umbra closed Vermillion's eyes. "Is this what you did to the previous ruler or did you give them the grace of a quick death?"

Vermillion didn't answer. Couldn't. They were paralyzed.

Weld opened the door. The lake stretched out before them, a

swathe of black and broken glass. For a moment, Umbra couldn't breathe, and they were the ones sinking beneath the water to exist in the dark and await the death that came in a million bites.

They lifted their chin. "Send them down."

The guards picked up the body and dropped it feet first into the water. Vermillion sunk fast. Umbra stepped forward, fingers curling as though to grab them at the last moment. They wouldn't. Couldn't. Then they were gone. Swallowed whole, worse than dead.

CHAPTER 42

The coat was too tight and made from the shiny fabric those up the hill favored. The lace cuffs itched Elliot's swollen hand. Getting changed had been painful and made worse by the way the two marshals had watched and prodded him to move faster with their batons.

If they hadn't broken his fingers, he'd have been quicker.

But he'd been smart enough not to speak. He didn't need another broken bone.

The pain ebbed and flowed through him, always there. Sometimes hot, sometimes a gut gripping twist that took several breaths to fade.

The pants were no better than the coat. More shiny fabric, and they only went to his knee. They'd taken his Kin-made boots and given him button up boots that met the pants. He couldn't button them. Even if his fingers weren't broken, the buttons were too awkward to reach. A servant had to do it for him.

Why he couldn't stay in his own clothes, he didn't know. He'd only agreed because he hadn't had another choice. Or at least not one that he liked. The marshals would've broken every bone in his body.

With the sun now set, everyone was watching the lake instead of the crowd that shouted outside the lord's house, refusing to offer their blood for the lord anymore. The lord's lips were pressed into a thin line. He blamed it all on Elliot, while at the same time puzzling how Elliot had so much power.

All Elliot had done was tell the truth and given the anger an outlet. He'd hoped the crowd would rush the lord's house and break in, but it was too well walled and guarded. So they waited outside. They hadn't left even though it was dark and the Kin would be coming.

The fog gathered in the center of the lake, thickening as dark settled and the stars appeared. Then the castle appeared out of the fog, but it brought no fear or dread the way it once had, only a longing to go back. Hopefully, Vermillion was dead, and Dayne was alive.

If Umbra hadn't taken Dayne, he'd have been killed along with the other devoured on the shore. While he couldn't quite feel gratitude, there was a measure of relief. Of course, if Dayne was dead, he was going to snap Umbra's antler and stab them with it. That was assuming he lived through the night and the lord didn't order his legs be broken so he couldn't escape.

If the Kin rode, the lord planned to meet them.

If the Kin rode and Umbra was at the head, Elliot had a chance.

A small one, but he'd slipped through that gap before. His whole life could be measured in slim chances and opportunities that begged to be stolen.

The lord thought Elliot was the sacrificial piece. If he failed to get nectar, he'd be killed, no loss. But Elliot had played enough ossic to know that move didn't always work.

For it to work, Umbra had to care about Elliot enough that they'd give up nectar for his life. Even if Umbra did want to do that—and Elliot was pretty sure Umbra wasn't that reckless—Elliot didn't want them to. He wanted the lord to wither and die.

Since their conversation this morning, the lord's eyes had taken on a milky tone, and his words came slower. His skin looked like the color of laundry water. Elliot couldn't be sure he looked much better. His cheek was tender and split, one broken arm, the other hand looked more like raw sausages than fingers. While he wasn't dying, he wasn't able to fight either. If his bones didn't mend straight, there

TJ NICHOLS

wouldn't be much work for him. He looked down, staring at the shiny toes of the black boots.

Once he'd fancied button up boots that gleamed like a mirror. But their soles were soft and the boots more of an annoyance than use. His old buckle up boots had been sturdier. His Kin-made boots had been the best he'd ever had. He'd never doubted his step, knowing the soles wouldn't slip and slide. Once he'd gotten used to the laces, they'd been a fine pair that he was already missing.

What had happened to his clothing? When this charade was over, he'd be needing them back. This outfit wasn't good for anything besides standing around and admiring oneself.

"They're riding," someone said.

Elliot's heart sank. He'd be stepping out to face the crowd a liar. Better to get it over with.

"Good. Perhaps now they'll scurry away like roaches." The lord indicated for one of the marshals to open the door to the balcony.

When it was open, the lord was carefully carried out. A chair had been placed on a platform so all could see him. He'd happily sell the lives of everyone gathered so he could live another day. Elliot was offered no such courtesy; he was shoved out onto the balcony.

The crowd booed and threw rotten food. The food hit the wall, not the balcony. Elliot scanned the rooftops, searching for the venerie.

Had anyone noticed he was missing?

Flames licked several of the wooden buildings, but the lord's house was built of stone. He didn't seem to care his city was on fire and his people were angry with the way they'd been treated.

The lord lifted his hands for quiet, but all that did was fuel the chanting of the crowd. Their fury washed over Elliot. Even though it wasn't directed at him, it soon would be. They'd see him as a traitor, believing he'd sold them all for a life of comfort up the hill.

This had never been the life he'd wanted. All he'd wanted was for everything to be a little easier. He should be able to work and live without finding his pockets empty three days before payday. He didn't need fancy clothes and such.

He wanted the chance to get a better job. To be able to buy medicine if he needed.

Simple things.

"Be silent. Your lord will speak," a marshal yelled.

A bell was rung. Elliot turned and glanced up at it. He'd never gathered outside of the lord's house before. No one in the Dark City really did. What was the point of listening to the lord's decrees when he didn't listen to the pleas of his people? They didn't care about new trade deals or the weddings between those up the hill.

A hush gradually fell.

The lord drew in a breath. He was dying even if he didn't realize yet. His skin had taken on that look. His body giving out after too many decades of use. Nectar could heal, but Elliot was reasonably sure that it couldn't undo the aging that was taking place as he watched.

The lord lifted his hands again as though he'd hushed the crowd. "I have watched you march, heard your anger, and spoken with the man who lied to you and led you here. I am not your enemy. I have ruled you for over a hundred years. Given this city stability that other border cities don't have."

"Our blood, our choice," the chant started to rise again.

"The Kin demand blood. They are the ones you should be rising against. Cross the causeway. Seize the castle. They are riding for you. To hunt you."

A ripple went through the crowd. For a moment, Elliot thought they might scatter. But they didn't.

The lord's hand shook as he reached for Elliot. "Speak as you were told, or I will see to it that your bones never mend."

Elliot doubted the lord would see sunrise, but if not the lord, someone else would step up and rule. Unless they were all in a similar desperate state.

Were they at home in front of their mirrors watching as lines formed and their bones became fragile? The thought was a glimmer of hope in an otherwise dark night.

"Here is one of you. Elliot Brand. He riled you up with promises, but I have spoken to him, and he understands the way things are supposed to be."

It was a marshal who pressed him forward to the railing. Three stories up. Enough of a fall to kill him or kill the people who tried to catch him? Directly beneath the wall were more marshals, their swords sticking out like silvery whiskers. They'd probably point their swords skywards and impale him if he jumped. Beyond them was a hastily erected wooden barricade and another row of marshals. The barricade was being pulled apart by the people at the front. When it was taken down, there would be a battle in the streets.

A baton nudged him in the back.

His throat was dry and his heartbeat too loud.

People stared up at him. If they knew him, it was only by reputation, and he wasn't sure how much of that was true and how much was embellishment. Perhaps they only knew the price on his head.

He hoped Killian choked on the coin, that it bought him a case of pox that swelled his balls and shrunk his dick and that only burning pus flowed out the tip.

"I'm Elliot Brand." His voice was too quiet.

The slap of the baton across the back of his legs confirmed it. "Speak up, and do not stray from the words."

He'd had to memorize the speech. The lord had handed him a written copy. And while he saw the letters on the paper, he didn't know the sound each one made. He couldn't put them together into words no matter how hard he tried, and he wasn't going to be able to learn in an afternoon. To be fair, memorizing the speech had taken his mind off the pain.

"I'm Elliot Brand. Some of you will have heard how my brother was taken by the Kin. How I went to the castle and took him back even though I knew the rules. What the Kin take the Kin keep." He swallowed. People looked at him, their eyes full of hope. He wanted to tug at the collar of the too tight coat. Rip it off. He didn't belong up here, trussed up like those ducks in the shops up the hill. "In taking back my brother I broke the law and angered the Kin. They will no longer trade with us."

That was wrong, and he'd tried to tell the lord that, but he hadn't cared. The lord needed someone to blame.

"I am sorry." He wasn't. He'd do it again. He moved his arm and winced as he put his busted hand on the railing. "But I'm now working with the lord to undo the damage and return the city to proper rule." His words faltered. The rumble of beasts filled the air.

"Keep talking," the lord said.

Elliot licked his lip and forced the words out. "We need consistent leadership by the lord to make the city prosper." The words were ash. The prosperity never rolled down the hill to the Dark City. "I see that now. We need to be united against the..."

The baton hit the back of his legs and he stumbled into the railing. "The Kin."

"You heard him. He is one of you. We must remain united against the Kin. They are dangerous, but I accept the risk of trading with them for the sake of the city. I have sacrificed everything for you." Spittle flew off the lord's lips.

Some parts of the crowd were still chanting. Others were edging toward the shadowed alleys. There were calls of traitor directed at him.

Elliot hung his head.

"I hear your demands and agree." Their voice barely reached Elliot, but he knew it. *Umbra.*

Elliot lifted his gaze. The Kin edged their beasts closer and the crowd parted. They'd be surrounded and ripped off their beasts, pulled apart by a crowd that wanted blood and an end to being hunted.

"What are they doing?" The lord squinted.

"Negotiating with the crowd."

"What? No. Attack the Kin. Kill them all, and we will invade the castle and take all the nectar we need," the lord screeched.

No one attacked. They parted, letting the Kin move deeper into the crowd. There were only ten of them and more people than Elliot could imagine counting.

"The castle is locked and will only be unlocked when I return. If I don't return, there will be no more nectar. Ever. We do not need blood to survive. My predecessor was a hungry fool. He wanted war, and your desperation gave him an excuse."

"Then your pet will die." At the lord's order, a marshal put a knife to Elliot's throat.

He'd been waiting to feel the bite of metal since he'd been arrested.

Umbra looked up at him his face unreadable. "I have his brother. Why would I need him?"

Elliot smiled. Dayne was safe. That was all he'd wanted.

Everything else...that hadn't been him. That had been him trying on different lives to see if any fit. He wasn't venerie. He wasn't a tamed pet.

He was Elliot Brand, and he'd saved his brother. That was all the mattered. He closed his eyes, waiting for the metal to sink in and end the pain scouring his veins.

CHAPTER 43

*U*mbra tried not to let their gaze fix on Elliot. Elliot was too far away for them to do anything. And while they hadn't meant what they said—they wanted Elliot back—they'd had to tell that lie. Elliot's life wasn't a coin to be gambled with, but this wasn't a rescue either. They'd come to negotiate new terms and help the venerie take down the lord.

If Umbra reached out, they could touch a handful of humans. They pressed close, jostled by the crowd. The human's fear and anger bubbled around them, making them unpredictable. A herd rather than an individual. The beast snarled and growled beneath them, unhappy with being hemmed in, and Umbra had to agree. Behind them, the Abyr were silent. They had muttered their objections when Umbra had started riding up the hill—though they hadn't objected to riding through the few marshals that had been left to guard the causeway.

If the crowd turned on them, they'd be ripped apart.

Umbra wouldn't bet on this roll, not even with Vermillion's weighted dice in their hand.

They glanced at Elliot. His eyes were closed, the blade was still at his throat, but the marshal hadn't cut. There was still time. They scanned the rooftops, seeking out the venerie. They were up there, waiting. All of the training Umbra had received on strategy and fighting melted away. Confronting the lord while he was beset by unrest had seemed like a good idea. Now that they were in the midst of the swarm, Umbra wasn't so sure.

"I'm here to negotiate a new trade deal. I'm happy to give you nectar, but you pay for it with your own blood. Those are my terms." Umbra lowered their gaze and looked at the faces of the humans that watched them with hostile eyes and clenched fists. They edged the beasts forward, and no one stepped in front. They lowered their voice. "If you have an ill loved one, you may bleed for them. Nectar is for all not the few."

Their words created a ripple of confusion.

"They pay for me. That has always been the way," the lord shouted, his voice thin and mewling.

"When did they agree to that?" The beast crept forward, the crowd parting for them. "I didn't, and I am the Abyr you must deal with now."

"I am lord of this city." The words were spoken like he'd never had anyone question his authority before. Maybe no one had. Those that lived up the hill benefited from the lord's doings, so they kept their mouths shut and their eyes averted from the truth.

Umbra stood on the footrests of the beast and spread their arms. The beast remained perfectly balanced beneath them. "And? I have removed one corrupt leader tonight, and I am happy to dethrone another." The humans watched them. "Are you happy with your lord's rule?"

The crowd's attention shifted from Umbra to the lord.

"Kill the Kin. What are you waiting for they are the enemy! They're dangerous." The lord pointed at Umbra still standing on the beast.

The beast crept forward. It would take a year to reach the barricade. And when they got there, Umbra still wasn't sure what they were going to do. "Yet you are the one with the knife to the throat of an innocent man. You are the one who surrendered the people in the

Dark City to the Abyr. You ignored their plight and never once pled for mercy on their behalf. Who is the enemy of the people?"

The lord who'd only days ago appeared to be a man in his prime was now hunched and withered and behaving as though he'd been wronged. "He stole from you." He pointed at Elliot. "He arranged this gathering he is hardly innocent." The lord swept his arm out. "Venerie, is it not your job to kill the Kin? Defend me."

Umbra could almost smell the panic rolling off the lord.

"I want to hear what the Kin have to say. Hear the terms of their trade," Serene shouted from the roof. "No rush to kill them; it's not like they're going anywhere fast."

They were in the center of the crowd now. All they could do was move forward. Their heart quickened, but it was too late for doubts. Their birther may still get to arrive to grieve their death, though there would be no body, only a collection of pieces. Maybe not even that.

"Perhaps it's time for another to rule. A hundred years is a long time. How many of those who live up here are your blood relations? How many have lived long past their human years?"

"Why should we have short lifespans when you live forever?"

The crowd was thinning now, and they were almost at the barricade. Umbra pulled an orb from their coat. "The Abyr do not live forever—or at least not what you would call living. Our antlers weigh us down as we get old, and we lie down to be part of the forest." They nicked their wrist with their fang. "I don't think you'd like to be part of the forest."

They dripped the blood into the dimple in the orb. It warmed their hand for the few heartbeats they held it before throwing it at the barricade. The barricade burned. The people around Umbra watched. They understood. They'd been given the weapons to fight back but hadn't known how to use them. The power had been in their hands all along.

All this time they'd let the lord lead them, fuel their fear and promise a prosperity that never came because it was horded for the few.

"You must have really liked working with Vermillion." Umbra stared up at the lord. They were close now. Fear was etched deep in the lord's face. Elliot's eyes were still closed. If his throat was cut, Umbra wasn't carrying enough nectar to save him. But they had to think of the city, not one man. And now they knew how Vermillion had taken the castle. They hadn't done it on their own. The lord had helped; they had made a deal. Who had been played? Or had they used each other? Vermillion hunting freely and the lord making the Kin the enemy so the people didn't look up the hill and see who was really causing their pain.

"They knew their place," the lord hissed. "Give me the nectar."

"Nectar cannot reverse aging. It will heal you enough every day that your body will keep going. Is that what you want?"

"I am the lord of this city."

"You have children who could take over…or perhaps it is time for no lords. Perhaps the people would rule themselves. A council of representatives to ensure nectar and trade benefits all."

They could hear the ripples spreading through the crowd, but their gaze was locked on Elliot. He knew how to fight, but he wasn't doing anything. He was waiting for death as though he no longer cared.

Umbra stopped the beast in the barricade. The fire burned on either side of them. The marshals stood close, their swords drawn but not raised.

"I ask again. Who will pay for your nectar? If you want this man to be your lord for another hundred years, step forward."

Silence. No one raised their hand or called out.

Umbra edged their beast through the barricade. This close, they could see that Elliot's face was pinched and pale. His hand on the railing was swollen and dark. That was why he wasn't fighting; he was injured.

"Kill the Kin. Kill them all," the lord shouted. "I will take your castle. I will claim your lands."

The marshals raised their weapons and moved forward. Umbra reached behind and pulled free their staff. The glass tipped ends glittered. To his side, more of the barricade exploded and burned. The crowd was arming themselves with orbs and fighting. People were shouting, giving orders, but they weren't attacking the Abyr. They were attacking the marshals.

A few marshals stripped off their coats and left them on the ground before fleeing. Umbra didn't blame them. They vowed to uphold the law, not fight their neighbors. Those that remained attacked. The rest of the Abyr were behind them, the opening in the barricade too small to allow more than one to pass through.

Umbra slashed at their opponents, the staff keeping them back. While they didn't want to kill, there was little choice. They wanted to get to Elliot before the lord made good on his threat. Umbra had thought the lord desperate enough to make a new deal; they had underestimated his selfishness. A man who didn't want the best for his people wasn't a leader. He was a coward who believed his own bard tales.

The marshals surrounded them, as they swept at the ones on their left, the ones on their right pressed close. These marshals had nowhere to run to. Their backs were to the wall of the lord's manor. In front of them was an angry crowd. The marshals fought because they had nothing else. The crowd did the same.

Blood filled the gaps in the cobblestone and streamed downhill.

CHAPTER 44

*E*lliot opened his eyes. Umbra was surrounded by marshals. The Kin were pushing through the burning barricade, fighting. The crowd had turned on the marshals and were dying for their efforts. This wasn't how it was meant to be. There was supposed to be a new deal. "You said you'd negotiate."

"I say a lot of things. Why make a deal when I can take it all?" The lord turned to the marshal. "Kill him."

He didn't want to die; he wanted to live. He didn't know what that meant or what it would be like, but he deserved the chance to do more than survive.

The sleeves were tight, keeping his broken arm secure. As the blade pressed to his skin, Elliot leaned away and brought his arm up. The strike made stars bloom in his eyes. He wouldn't be able to take the knife with his preferred hand, and he couldn't make a fist, but he still had two working legs.

He stamped on the marshal's foot then kneed him in the balls. As he folded, Elliot slammed his forehead into the man's temple, taking the blade from his hand. The marshal stumbled and a knife appeared in the green coat, blood staining it red. Elliot looked up to see Serene on the railing. She grinned, then pulled her knife free, ready to face the marshals who saw her as the threat, not Elliot.

The lord was shuffling as fast as he could to the door, scurrying like a roach in daylight. Elliot hooked his good arm around the lord's throat and held the blade to his belly. "I'll give my blood."

He said it again louder as he dragged the lord to the edge.

"I'll give my blood. Put down your weapons. We'll negotiate. Kin, lord, venerie. Anyone else?"

The lord struggled. "You can't do that. You have no authority."

Umbra held his staff out level. "The man with the knife to your soft parts usually has quite a bit of authority."

"I will not negotiate," the lord said.

"Then you will never taste nectar again." Elliot cut the front of the lord's fine coat. The slippery fabric tore open. "I care more about the people in the city than you do. You were happy to see their blood run the streets." He cut the shirt, revealing pale wrinkled stomach skin. "Let the Kin in and sit at your fancy table to talk. Get your nectar. You are no better than the devoured, craving what has been denied to you."

"Help me," the lord begged.

But where there had been marshals, there were now only venerie, and they watched with hate in their eyes.

"We'll help you the same way you have always helped us," Serene said as she opened the door. "Be glad you're getting nectar. If it were me holding the knife, you'd be dead."

Elliot wanted to slit his belly. It wouldn't take much, but then who would they be left dealing with? Without negotiations, they'd be back to where they were.

He looked out at the crowd, who'd spilled through the burning barricade, Kin and humans standing together. "What do you want?" he asked them.

"Kill the lord," the chant went up.

"You have to do it now," Serene said softly.

"He won't," the lord spat. "He knows they'll hate him if he does it.

You are a bunch of illiterate children who need someone to tell you how to thi—"

Elliot pressed the knife into the papery skin of the lord's belly then dragged the blade across before pulling it out. Blood gushed over his hand. The foul stink of ruptured guts made him gag. He stumbled back, bile burning the back of his throat.

Serene caught Elliot and lifted his hand, still clutching the bloodied knife. "Your hero. The lord is dead." Elliot glanced at her. What was she doing? "Elliot has stolen from the Kin, he has fought for his brother, for you and will lead us." She cheered, still holding up his arm.

"I don't want to rule." His words were a whisper beneath the shouting of the crowd.

"Too bad." She was still grinning; her lips had barely moved. "They supported you. They want you to make it all okay."

How was he supposed to do that?

But the battle had stopped, and everyone was staring up at him, expecting him to know what to do. He had to say something.

"Let the Kin in so we can talk."

~

*E*lliot eased into a chair in a room that was far more ornate than anything he'd ever seen. He wasn't even sure the furniture was made for sitting on. It was too delicate, the fabric on the seats too soft. He sat behind the desk with Benton and Serene at his side. There was paper and ink and documents covered in writing that could've been important or a shopping list. Umbra sat opposite. Their sleeve was cut but otherwise, they seemed unharmed.

His hand throbbed and the bones in his arm ground together in a way that made his skull hurt. He really wanted to find where the liquor was kept and drown in a glass or three so someone could fix up the breaks and he could forget.

But instead he was playing lord.

He was even dressed the part.

Behind Umbra stood Weld and another Kin with bright yellow hair and equally yellow eyes.

"Congratulations, Elliot." Umbra inclined their head.

He couldn't tell if Umbra was mocking him or being serious. "How is Dayne?"

"Well. Everything went well."

Elliot nodded and winced. "Um..." He glanced around the room. "You'll honor what you said? That you'll only trade the blood of the willing for nectar?"

"We will. In return, you will not attack us."

"Unless you step out of line," Benton said. "That was always the venerie's role."

"There should be penalties for humans who seek nectar for their own enrichment. No one stopped the lord."

"Perhaps they tried. It was too long ago for anyone to remember."

"Question the others, drag them from their fine houses and make them answer to all who've lost loved ones." Elliot was out of patience. "We'll set up a care house. A place where the ill can be brought. You will visit and the trade will be made?"

"Yes. A building closer to the lake would suit us better."

"We will find one. Is that all? Can I resign now?"

Everyone, human and Kin, shook their head.

"You must make these changes and make them stick," Benton said.

"But we'll make sure it happens. You're the figurehead we need to fix our city," Serene added.

He closed his eyes and immediately felt unsteady, so he opened them just as fast. He put his good hand on the table. Blood smeared the papers. "This isn't what I wanted."

Umbra gave him a small smile. "Maybe not, but this is what you have ended up with." Umbra pulled a vial from their pocket and placed it on the desk. "As a show of good faith, you get this one for free. Next time, you pay."

Would there be a next time? Would he get to go to the castle? Would he ever feel Umbra's lips on his again or was this it?

"Dayne will remain with you?"

"For the moment." Umbra stood. "Come and see him in a few nights."

"Won't I be too busy here to leave?" He'd be a prisoner in this fancy house, enslaved to the will of the city.

"I can't be expected to always be the one crossing the causeway. Besides, I'm sure that in three nights, there will be more to discuss. The gate will be opened for you." Umbra frowned. "If that is what you want?" Elliot gave a small single nod. Umbra almost smiled. "Otherwise it will remain shut." Umbra nodded at Benton and Serene, then left with the other two Kin.

The vial of nectar gleamed in the soft red light. As much as he wanted to drink it all now, if his bones weren't lined up straight, they'd heal wrong. He stared at the vial for a few more heartbeats, knowing that there was more pain to come before he'd feel better. "Benton, know a bonesetter?"

CHAPTER 45

*U*mbra rode across the causeway, water spraying in their wake. The gates to the castle were locked; they hoped they'd be opened for them and there hadn't been a coup while they were in the city.

Every time they blinked, they saw Elliot's tired pinched face. They'd wanted to bring him here, but that was impossible. At least for the moment. Maybe when things settled down and the city became stable...

Maybe by then Elliot wouldn't want to come. He'd have carved a place for himself and decided that he didn't want Umbra or anything to do with the Abyr. They didn't quite believe that, but the doubt was there like a stone in their boot.

The gates eased open, and Umbra rode through. There were beasts in the courtyard. Six of them. They stopped, not bothering to put the beast in the stables and strode toward the hall. Who had been let in while they were in the city?

They'd left orders for no one to enter. Annoyance flicked through them and settled on their tongues ready to spill in harsh words. They pushed open the doors and stopped.

In their seat at the head of the table was Cerulean, their soft lilac hair intricately braided on top of their head. They stood. "I was told you were dead. I came for your body or for revenge." They walked around the table, toward Umbra.

Umbra knew they should move, but they couldn't. Their parents had thought them dead and cared enough to claim their body. "Vermillion is worse than dead."

"So I have heard." Cerulean studied Umbra. "And you are now the ruler of this castle. No longer prime of Octadine."

Umbra nodded.

"I had expected it to take you longer."

"Vermillion was heartless and cruel. They tried to force my change. They killed pets and hunted in the city. I couldn't live like that." Annoyance became anger. They didn't need their birther's approval. "You sent me here as Vermillion's mate."

"I thought you would be for a time. But I knew you wouldn't let things fester."

Anger bubbled up. "You should've warned me. Told me what you wanted me to do."

The corner of Cerulean's lip turned up. "A ruler doesn't take orders. You had to set your own plan. You did that and were successful." They stepped closer. "You have done well."

Had they? Vermillion was at the bottom of the lake, and Elliot was now the reluctant ruler of the city, not here with them.

"Then why doesn't it feel like success?" Umbra said softly.

"Because there will always be a problem to solve. Enjoy the small wins when you have them, but always be ready for the next battle." Cerulean took their hands and kissed their knuckles. "I am glad that I have found your body and do not need to take it home."

CHAPTER 46

W hen his fingers had healed, Elliot went to the burned-out house and collected the beast and the rest of the things he'd left there. It wasn't much, and he didn't know why he bothered. There was everything he could ever imagine needing in the lord's house.

The beast he parked in the grand entrance. The shiny clothing, he'd donated.

With Serene and Benton and some of the other venerie, they had quickly made a few changes and turned them into law. No more school uniforms for the schools in the Dark City and no more book buying requirements. It would be supplied. Benton went through the city ledgers and discovered that a lot of nectar was sent out of the city at huge profit that had all fed into the lord's coffers.

Some of the other nobles who lived up the hill had come begging for nectar with bony chicken feet-like hands. They had gotten none and had been told to gather at the care house to trade with the Kin like everyone else.

Young nobles were now old, like their dying parents. They had cursed and yelled and cried about the unfairness. Elliot sat and listened, his heart as cold as mid-winter and as dark as the new moon.

Today, he'd had enough. He'd taken them in their finery to the Dark City, showed them what it was like, and then left them there to find their own way back.

How dare they ask for compassion when they had none for the lives they'd destroyed.

The farmer who'd lost his crop of marshmallow leaf had sown the fields with food crop. If people wanted marshmallow, they could plant it in their yards, if they had yards, or in pots. He didn't have a clue how marshmallow grew.

He didn't have any idea how the city ran. None of them did, but they were starting to find out. The lord's secretary had been most helpful, perhaps realizing that she wasn't going to lose her place if she could assist.

He flexed his fingers. They still ached but not as badly as his arm. He'd had enough nectar to get the healing process started, but not enough to complete it. Would Umbra think he was crossing to the castle for more?

"You going to the castle?" Serene leaned against the doorframe.

He nodded. He'd been riding the beast around the city, not for long though as it jarred his arm.

"Can you give Dayne a message?"

Elliot nodded. Hopefully his brother had come to his senses.

"Tell him…" Her teeth worried at her lower lip. "Tell him I'm going to be running the care house, and I could do with some help."

"We're all helping."

Serene had taken on the responsibility of the care house once they'd found a building. People who'd kept their devoured hidden and cared for came forward, still afraid that they'd be punished for doing the wrong thing.

She rolled her eyes. "I'm giving him a reason to come home. I want him to come home. I don't care that he's devoured."

"Oh. I'll tell him that, too." Though perhaps Dayne wouldn't want to leave. The castle had everything. He wouldn't leave if he didn't have to.

"You'll be back?"

It was his city, and he could help fix it. Instead, all he wanted to do was walk away and do something that he wanted. Not that he knew what that was either.

"Yeah. I have to come back."

She stared at him but didn't say anything.

He placed his hand on the beast's forehead and it rumbled to life. It purred as they left the grand house and rode down the hill to the lake. The moon glittered on the surface. He waited, watching the surface, and then to be sure he skipped a rock over the water. Nothing.

Last night, there'd been two of them in there, their tentacles reaching out and sweeping the beach and crashing onto the causeway as they'd fought or mated—maybe both.

He swallowed and waited a few more breaths. Cold sweat trickled down his spine. But the lake was as still as glass.

"As fast as you can go." He leaned forward, and the beast leaped, racing over the causeway as if it were desperate to get home. Water arced to the sides of him, the beast going so fast that Elliot was sure if he fell off, it wouldn't stop or care. He squeezed his eyes closed and gripped the horns tighter.

Then they were slowing. The gates loomed in front of him, and for a moment, he didn't think he'd be let in. Then they opened.

What kind of person willingly visited a Kin castle? Not once, but twice?

As he entered the courtyard and stabled the beast, he stopped caring. The air here was sweeter, and he breathed deeply. But there were more beasts than he remembered. Maybe he shouldn't be visiting. He was human after all, nothing more than a short-term pet.

With more caution, he made his way to the hall doors that stood ajar. He risked a peek before entering. There were definitely more Kin here, but Umbra sat at the head of the table. Umbra lifted their gaze and looked at Elliot. They smiled and tilted their head as if inviting him in. He wasn't walking in as prey.

He straightened his brown wool coat, now damp at the edges from the lake spray, and strode into the hall like he had every right to be there. Some of the Kin scowled, but most ignored him.

407

Umbra said something to the lilac haired Kin next to them. They turned and nodded, and the scowls were rearranged into something closer to puzzlement.

Umbra stood and beckoned him over. "The new lord of the city."

Elliot bit back the wince as he closed the distance. He wasn't a lord. "I've yet to take a title but that won't be it." He scanned the hall searching for Dayne but didn't see him.

"Do you still claim the title of my pet?" Umbra said more softly.

Did that mean Dayne wasn't taking that place? "If it is still available."

"Of course it is. I had hoped to see you last night, though I'm glad you didn't risk it."

"I rode to the shore and watched for a while before turning back."

"It is leviathan breeding season," the lilac haired Kin said. "They come into the shallows to mate."

Come summer, the lake would be teeming with eels, or baby leviathans he now realized. Some would escape to the sea when the castle vanished each day. More would be eaten by the people of Fotyna

"Elliot, my birther, Cerulean. They are visiting for a few nights."

"Leaving later tonight. Castles do not run themselves."

"Neither do cities." Elliot smiled and hoped he sounded like he knew what he was doing.

"And you have things to discuss." Cerulean studied him. "Fresh blood on both sides can only be a good thing, though it will take time for the wounds to heal."

Longer for the memories to fade.

He curled his fingers by his side. They ached after the ride, but he loved riding the beast more than he should. He loved being here more than was safe. When he looked at Umbra, he wasn't sure what he felt, only that he shouldn't be feeling it.

"Yes. Trust takes time." There were still some in the city who were opposed to bleeding for the Kin while still asking when the nectar would be arriving. Benton was far more diplomatic than Elliot was. "I think the care house will help."

"Your brother is upstairs, if you'd like to see him first?" Umbra inclined his head toward the stairs. "Then perhaps we can sit down and go through what has happened."

Elliot nodded at Cerulean. "It was nice to meet you."

That was the polite thing to say to Umbra's parent, right? He'd heard tales of their battles when he'd been here before, but it was probably best not to ask them about that.

They smiled, their eyes as calculating as Umbra's could be. The tilt of their lips was ever so similar. "I have no doubt you'll enjoy your visit."

Heat crept up Elliot's neck. He turned away before it could reach his cheeks and started up the stairs. He glanced back to see Umbra hugging Cerulean, their antlers not touching. They said something, and Umbra nodded. Were they talking about him or was he nothing but a pet while he was here? Umbra hadn't greeted him as a pet.

But in a hall full of Kin, he was an easy meal.

He knocked on the door to Umbra's chambers. "It's Elliot."

Was Umbra making Dayne lock himself in?

The door clicked and then opened. Dayne was wearing human clothes that had seen better days. While the blood had been cleaned off, they were frayed and patched. But Dayne looked healthy. His skin was no longer gray, and the gauntness was gone.

He launched himself at Dayne and hugged him tight. He didn't know what to say to him, he was just glad that he had that chance. Dayne put his arms around Elliot as though he was a stranger and he wasn't sure if he should be hugging him.

Elliot drew back. "What's wrong?"

"You saved me."

"Did you think I was going to let you die?"

Dayne pressed his lips together. "I wanted to at the time. Now, I don't know. I keep hearing whispers about what happened and here you are in a nice new coat. Is it true? Did you kill the lord?"

"Only after he'd broken a few of my bones."

"And you're the new lord?"

"Not lord. The venerie are a council, and we want to make the city better for everyone. Serene is in charge of the care house. There are other devoured, too. You'll all get the blood you need to be whole. Serene wants to see you again."

Dayne glanced away. "Come in so I can close the door."

Elliot stepped in and shut the door. "What's wrong?"

"I know you helped me, and Umbra too, and I know I should be thanking them. I know I need their blood, but I can't be here. I want to go home, but I don't want to fade away on the beach. I don't know what to do." He raked his fingers through his hair.

"Is someone here hurting you?"

Dayne shook his head.

"Threatening you?"

Dayne shook his head again. "I killed Vermillion, stabbed him in the neck. Since then, I've been in here, only opening the door when Umbra brings up food."

"You don't have to stay in here."

"I do." He clenched his hands and kept his gaze on the ground. "I don't trust them. I don't like them like you do."

"Then go home and help Serene with the care house."

"Umbra said something about how I should be grateful because you wouldn't get to be here. They're going to want blood soon. I've had some of theirs every day." He closed his eyes. "I want to hate it, but I can't because it tastes so good and it stops my body from jittering like a roach on a hot pan."

"You'll still get it at the care house. No one is keeping you here." He hugged Dayne again, and for a moment, it was like when they were kids and Elliot was trying to make him feel better about not having any dinner. Dayne clung to him as though trying to believe. "I'll take you with me when I leave later tonight."

"You'll give Umbra blood?"

"Probably." *Hopefully.*

"And Serene doesn't hate me?"

"No, she's been worried about you."

"I wish you'd let me die. It would've been easier."

Elliot already knew Dayne wouldn't have come after him if he'd been taken to the castle. "Next time I will, okay?" He forced a smile. "So, if Umbra hasn't been sleeping here, where has he been sleeping?"

"Next door." Dayne grabbed his arm near the break, and Elliot sucked in a breath. "You don't have to feed them for me."

Elliot smiled. "I'm not. I'm doing it for me."

EPILOGUE

*M*ayor Elliot Brand waited on the shore. His leather coat flapped in the warm breeze.

He'd been elected again. Third year running.

The sun dipped below the lake, swallowed up in a single bite. The fog gathered once it was dark. The lines of the castle formed in the shifting shapes.

The lake was still. The fishermen had been out all-day, hauling eel to salt and sell. Some would go to other cities. Elliot preferred it fresh and in pie now that he could afford such things.

Benton had made visits to several cities that had no link with the Kin. Some had visited them, asking for nectar. They had set up a care house for visitors seeking the healing power of the Kin. They paid in gold—and Umbra had agreed because nectar was not endless. It had to be grown. So far, they hadn't been able to grow it in the fields around the city.

Tucked inside his coat was an invitation for Umbra to attend the naming day for Serene and Dayne's first child. Umbra wouldn't attend, of course. They hadn't attended the wedding because they knew that Dayne still held a fear of the Kin that had never diminished.

The castle solidified as the night deepened, the causeway was there, just below the water. The beast purred, content with their regular visits though Elliot was sure it liked tearing around the city and out to the farms—that was his job since he had the beast, and he quite liked the travel.

"Ready to go home?" He straddled the beast and it gave a rumble. They tore across the causeway, coat flapping like wings, his dark curls streaming behind him.

Umbra would be waiting.

Maybe next year he'd lose the election and they could renegotiate terms. For the moment, a few nights a fortnight was the best they could do.

THE FINAL VERSE

Beyond the curtain, people whispered. They'd slept late; the sun was well set.

"Did you want to get up today?" Elliot propped himself up on one elbow.

Umbra couldn't move their head, just their eyes, to look at him. "I should."

They needed to make the effort, but it was getting harder every moon. Even though Elliot helped hold the weight of the antlers and their neck and shoulders had thickened, it wasn't enough. Their antlers were too big for their head. They'd been too big to get through a doorway for the last five years; a part of the main hall had been turned into their bedroom so they didn't have to navigate the stairs.

Elliot's dark eyes were only filled with concern these days. They were both far too old.

"Sire, you need to get up. There are people here to see you," a servant said from the other side of the curtain.

Umbra closed their eyes. They couldn't go on like this. Shouldn't. But no border Kin had ever lived this long. Azure would make a good leader; the venerie were used to dealing with them, and Umbra hadn't gone to the city in over a decade. Elliot hadn't either. His family knew of his legend but not him.

Elliot got up and dressed before helping them to sit. He braided Umbra's hair, while Umbra braided their beard. Two hundred years of blood drinking had rather cemented the changes. Just sitting gave them an ache in their neck and skull. Elliot stood in front and offered his hands. Umbra pulled him close until he sat in their lap, needing to make the most of these moments.

Elliot kissed him and looked away.

They both knew, but neither of them was ready to say it. Elliot slid off their lap. He still looked twenty-nine, the age he'd been when he'd stopped being the mayor and had come to the castle permanently.

His hair was long, almost to his waist, and before the antlers had weighed them down they'd braided it for him. They'd been able to live. As tempting as it was to ask for their antlers to be sawn off, they couldn't.

With Elliot's help, they stood and made their way through the curtain and into the hall, Elliot behind them, holding the antlers.

Three white clothed unchanged stood there, eyes wide before they bowed. "We didn't realize."

"Realize what?"

"The situation...your antlers."

Umbra sat in a chair designed and built by Elliot, which took some of the weight. Elliot sat by their side, the same place he'd been for the last two hundred years or there abouts.

Azure sat on the other side, prime of the castle.

The three unchanged produced a document and handed it over with a flourish. Umbra read it, then closed their eyes.

It was the invitation that no border Kin had ever received. They had come to take them to the forest. To take their place so their wisdom lived on forever.

For the longest time, Umbra had been obsessed with it. Now, they'd rather die by antler than become part of the forest. Alive but not living. A part of something that could never be tasted or experienced again, feasting on memories that lost their flavor with each tasting.

They pushed the invitation toward Elliot.

"We have the cart and everything ready. We would've come sooner but we didn't realize. We're sorry to have left you this way," the unchanged said. Their voices like the whispers of leaves. Their job was to tend to the old ones.

"And Elliot?" What would happen to their pet, their lover, their everything? Would he come only to die in Umbra's arms leaving them alone for eternity?

"No human may enter."

Umbra would've nodded but couldn't. Instead, they lifted their hand in acknowledgment.

"This is an honor. The first...you wanted this." Elliot said, his lips by Umbra's ear.

Once, when they'd been young and foolish.

Now, they couldn't imagine living without Elliot. They'd rather die with him.

"I think I'd rather cross the causeway and watch the sun rise."

There were gasps from the unchanged.

Azure grabbed their hand. "You don't mean that. You'd die in heartbeats."

Yes. That sounded perfect.

They tilted their head to see Elliot, who'd been silent.

Elliot considered them for several heartbeats, then nodded. "I will need to stop drinking nectar to prepare."

"But you have had lasting peace for two hundred and thirteen years," one of the unchanged said. We need you in the forest."

"That long?" No wonder their head was heavy. They were old. They'd lived and loved and raised their prime.

"We need you in the forest."

"No. The bard will tell my tale better than I ever could. Three nights, and then we cross the lake?"

"That sounds like a plan." Elliot smiled, his eyes far older than his face.

The unchanged stayed, and on the third night, a grand procession filed out of the castle. Umbra rode in the cart, Elliot tucked by their side. His age had caught up with him fast.

They were met on the shore by an honor guard of marshals, the venerie council, and the human mayor. No one had heard of such a thing—an Abyr choosing to die by sunlight. The unchanged still whispered how wrong it was.

But now Umbra had crossed the lake, it felt right.

The cart was turned to face the hill. The sky lightened. It was too late to turn back.

They glanced at their lover. "The sun rises, Elliot."

Elliot opened his eyes, his skin a fragile silvery thing now that the nectar no longer healed all his ills. He placed his hand over Umbra's chest as the first rays appeared.

They fought to keep their eyes open, so sleep wouldn't steal these last moments.

Their blood heated with every breath.

Elliot's heart faltered.

Their blood became molten.

Umbra gasped as the sun consumed them, turning them to ash and smoke.

To keep up with my news join my newsletter.

Newsletter: http://www.tjnichols-author.com/lp

If you want more dark fantasy check out the completed Studies in Demonology trilogy.

"Engaging characters, interesting and compelling world, and outstanding story telling." - Joyfully Jay

Angus Donohue doesn't want to be a warlock.

But he's caught up in war he's not ready to fight. As his understanding of magic grows so does the danger...and the forbidden love for his demon. With the fate of two worlds hanging in the balance Angus will have to pick a side. Human or demon?

Studies in Demonology is a complete mm fantasy romance series, full of magic, danger and forbidden love, with a reluctant human hero and a demon mage who should know better than to fall for a human warlock.

OTHER BOOKS BY TJ NICHOLS

Studies in Demonology trilogy

Warlock in Training

Rogue in the Making

Blood for the Spilling

Mytho series

Lust and other Drugs

Greed and other Dangers

Envy and other Cravings

Vanity and other Monsters

Sloth and other Delights

Wrath and other Troubles

Gluttony and other Hungers

Familiar Mates

The Witch's Familiar

The Vampire's Familiar

The Rock Star's Familiar

The Vet's Christmas Familiar

The Detective's Familiar

The Siren's Familiar

The Soldier's Familiar

The Billionaire's Familiar

The Firefighter's Familiar

The Bodyguard's Familiar

Outcast Pack (Familiar Mates world)

Wolf Heart

Wolf Blood

Wolf Soul

Wolf Mate

Wolf Lust

Wolf Hunt

A Summer of Smoke and Sin (historical urban fantasy)

Liminality (fantasy)

Captured Earth trilogy

Resist

Regroup

Revolt

Holiday novellas

Elf on the Beach

The Vampire's Dinner

Poison Marked

The Legend of Gentleman John

Silver and Solstice

Solstice Wishes and Christmas Kisses (novella collection)

A Wolf's Resistance

Hood and the Highwaymen

ABOUT THE AUTHOR

TJ Nichols is the author of the Studies in Demonology and Familiar Mates series. They write mostly gay fantasy and paranormal romance, but sometimes gay action/horror as Toby J. Nichols.

After traveling all over the world and Australia, TJ now lives in Perth, Western Australia.

You can connect with TJ at:

Newsletter: http://www.tjnichols-author.com/lp

Ingram Content Group UK Ltd.
Milton Keynes UK
UKHW020652240723
425668UK00013B/558

Telephone and Reception Skills

Thelma J Foster

Fellow of the Royal Society of Arts

Chief Examiner to the Royal Society of Arts for
General Reception

Formerly Senior Lecturer, Business Studies Department,
Worcester Technical College

Second Edition

Stanley Thornes (Publishers) Ltd

First published in 1980 by Stanley Thornes (Publishers) Ltd
Old Station Drive, Leckhampton
CHELTENHAM GL53 0DN

Reprinted with minor corrections 1982

2nd Edition 1985

British Library Cataloguing in Publication Data

Foster, Thelma J.
    Telephone and reception skills. — 2nd ed.
    1. Receptionists
    I. Title
    651.3'743   HF5547.5

    ISBN 0–85950–223–6

Also by Thelma Foster and published by ST(P)

OFFICE SKILLS
TYPING SKILLS — Book I
TYPING SKILLS — Book II
TYPING SKILLS — Book III (in preparation)
OFFICE SKILLS ANSWER BOOK
OFFICE SKILLS ADDITIONAL EXERCISES (in preparation)

Typeset by Tech-Set, Gateshead, Tyne & Wear.
Printed and bound in Great Britain at The Bath Press, Avon.

Contents

PREFACE TO SECOND EDITION   vii

INTRODUCTION   viii
Telecommunications in the modern office

LIST OF EXERCISES   ix

PART 1   **TELEPHONE SKILLS**   **1**
Telecommunications in the modern office

Chapter 1   TELEPHONE TECHNIQUES IN A FIRM   3
Quiz on the use of the telephone — making telephones mobile — correct dialling — telephones available to rent or purchase — answering the telephone and dealing with messages — inside and outside calls — telephone etiquette — telephone style — a telephonist's personal alphabet — telephone dos and don'ts — internal staff directories — remembering names and status of staff — coping with indistinct callers — telephonist's reference books

Chapter 2   TELEPHONE CHARGES   22
How telephone calls are charged for — the telephone bill — how to keep charges to a minimum

Chapter 3   THE SWITCHBOARD OPERATOR   28
What the different telephone tones mean — payphones — telephone systems in a firm — how a switchboard operator should deal with calls — fashion tips — latest developments in switchboards

Chapter 4   EXAMPLES OF TELEPHONE CONVERSATIONS   38
(1) Between an efficient operator and a secretary
(2) How not to deal with an external call
(3) The nervous junior

Chapter 5   TELEPHONE EQUIPMENT   43
Telephone answering machine — callmakers: punched card, tape, developments in — special telephones: loudspeaker, intercom, carphone — tannoy or public address system — flashing lights — paging — help for the handicapped

Chapter 6   TELEPHONE SERVICES   54
             Special telephone services: alarm call, person-to-person call,
             fixed time call, message call, ADC call, information services,
             transferred charge calls, Freefone, telephone credit cards,
             emergency calls — international telephone services — picture
             and computer services: Confravision, Prestel, Datel, facsimile
             transmission

Chapter 7   TELEPRINTERS AND TELEX   68
             Telex and its advantages — teleprinter keyboard and dialling
             unit — making a Telex call — Telex abbreviations — reference
             books for the Telex operator — sending messages automatically
             — international Telex calls — latest developments in teleprinters
             — Teletelex and Telex Plus

Chapter 8   TELEMESSAGES   83
             Telemessages and their cost — sending a telemessage — inter-
             national telegrams — coded telegrams

PART 2   RECEPTION SKILLS   89

Chapter 9   RECEPTION DUTIES IN A SMALL FIRM   91
             Reception duties — guidelines for receiving visitors — escorting
             visitors

Chapter 10   THE RECEPTIONIST IN A LARGE FIRM   94
             Duties of a receptionist — appearance — voice — the ideal
             receptionist — types of caller — greeting callers and dealing with
             visiting cards — using names — the receptionist's desk — job
             vacancies for receptionists

Chapter 11   THE RECEPTIONIST'S RECORDS   107
             Callers' register — appointments book — staff 'in and out' book
             — dealing with lost property — messages — notices in reception
             area — producing notices — displaying notices

Chapter 12   THE RECEPTION AREA   123
             Giving a good impression — keeping tidy — a comfortable
             design for the visitor — arranging samples of products to
             advantage — flower arranging — looking after flower arrange-
             ments — using artificial flowers or grasses — care of plants —
             choosing plants

Chapter 13   EQUIPMENT AND REFERENCE BOOKS   135
             The things you need — looking up information — information
             about your firm

Chapter 14   FORM LETTERS   140
               Saving time — sample letters

Chapter 15   SAFETY AND SECURITY IN THE RECEPTION AREA   146
               What to look out for — identifying personnel — bomb warnings
               — letterbombs

Chapter 16   FIRST AID FOR THE RECEPTIONIST   153
               What is First Aid? — minor injuries and ailments — more serious
               conditions — very serious conditions — if the patient stops
               breathing — other emergency situations — general guidelines —
               procedures for recording accidents

Chapter 17   BUSINESS ENTERTAINING   164
               Serving tea and coffee — preparing for parties and lunches —
               serving wines — making introductions

Chapter 18   BASIC OFFICE ARITHMETIC   175
               Exercises: addition and subtraction of money, working out per-
               centages, travel, time, converting imperial to metric measure

GENERAL EXERCISES   179

ADDITIONAL EXERCISES   185

INDEX   198

Preface to Second Edition

A second edition of *Telephone and Reception Skills* has become necessary for several reasons. One of these is the disappearance of the telegram, which made a whole chapter obsolete, another is the rapidly changing technology which is affecting telecommunications, and must be mentioned in a textbook on the subject, even though many thousands of offices will be operating efficiently with equipment which they have used for many years, without any of the advantages of the new automation. Students must be made aware of some of the developments in the telecommunications world, so that if they are confronted with new equipment when they start work, it will not be wholly unfamiliar to them.

Additionally, the second edition has been enlarged to meet the requirements of the Royal Society of Arts syllabus for General Reception, and I hope that this will make the subject more interesting to students, whatever examination they are hoping to sit, as it should give teachers ideas for practical assignments – so essential in the presentation of this subject.

My grateful thanks are due to my husband, Mr RAD Foster, for his section on calculator practice, also to Mr Peter Longville, Manager, Offices Services, BOC Cryoplants Limited, Angel Road, London N18 3BW, who was kind enough to give up some of his time to show me the very latest teleprinter equipment in his firm, and to check the section of my manuscript which dealt with it.

THELMA J FOSTER
Studley, 1985

Introduction

Telecommunications in the Modern Office

The telephone has joined forces with the computer, micro-electronics and television technologies creating entirely new areas for handling, processing and transmitting information – telex, word processing, facsimile transmission, viewdata, telephone, data transfer and confravision.

The complete electronic office system has among its main features spelling and typing corrections, electronic noticeboards, diaries and multiple addressing. The telephone is connected to a visual display unit (VDU), microprocessor or word processor by means of this service and it is then possible to receive and send information, ranging from a memo to a telex message, to and from people in various parts of the world. In addition, a record-keeping system could be set up, if required.

Access to this system is available from overseas countries.

List of exercises

	Quiz on the use of the telephone	3–4
1	Telephone messages	9–10
2	Internal telephone directory	15
3	Telephone alphabet	18
4	The Classified Trade Directory (Yellow Pages)	19
5	Answering the telephone	20–1
6	How telephone calls are charged for	23–4
7	Telephone charges – dialled direct calls	24–5
8	Questions on a telephone bill	26
9	Telephone tones	29
10	Answering a telephone extension	34–5
11	The switchboard operator	36–7
12	Examples of telephone conversation (1)	38–9
13	Examples of telephone conversation (2)	39–41
14	Examples of telephone conversation (3)	41–2
15	Communications in firms other than by telephone	51–2
16	Telephone equipment	52–3
17	Telephone services	57–8
18	Telephone services	58
19	International telephone services	60–1
20	International telephone calls	61–2
21	International direct dialling	65–6
22	Switchboards, etc.	66–7
23	A Telex message	73
24	A pre-coded punched tape teleprinter message	74
25	Telex	75–6
26	The telephonist's or Telex operator's reference books	77–8
27	A morning in the switchboard and teleprinter office	80–2
28	Telemessages	85
29	Telemessages	85–6
30	Coded telegrams	87–8
31	Reception of visitors in a small firm	92–3
32	The receptionist's duties	95
33	The receptionist's appearance	98–9
34	The receptionist's responsibilities	104
35	Job vacancies for receptionists	106
36	Callers' register	107–9
37	Callers' register	110–11
38	Questions on callers' register	111
39	Staff 'in and out' book	112–13
40	Lost property	115
41	Lost property	115

42	Writing notices	117
43	Writing notices	118
44	Colouring notices	120
45	Notices in reception area	120–1
46	The receptionist	121–2
47	Designing a reception area	125–6
48	Flower arranging	130–1
49	Receptionist's reference books	136–7
50	Receptionist's reference books	137–8
51	A receptionist's form letters	140–4
52	Revision	144–5
53	Safety and security in the reception area	151–2
54	First Aid and safety in reception	160–2
	Emergency situations for the receptionist	162–3
55	Setting trays	166
56	Suitable food for business entertaining	166–7
57	Laying tables	169–70
58	Serving wines correctly	171–2
59	Making introductions	173
60	Making introductions	173–4
61	Addition and subtraction of money	175
62	Working out percentages	176
63	Travel	176–7
64	Time	177
65	Converting imperial to metric measure	178

General exercises:
66	Revision	179–80
67	Practical work on reception	180
68	A complete revision	181–4

Additional exercises:
	Telephone equipment	187
	Telephone services	187–8
	Miscellaneous	188
	Telex	188–9
	Telemessages	189
	Special exercises	189

	The receptionist	189–91
	The reception of visitors	191
	Tricky situations	192
	Designing outfits	193

| | Some final questions and exercises | 193–4 |
| | Crossword | 196–7 |

PART 1 **TELEPHONE SKILLS**

CHAPTER 1

Telephone Technique in a Firm

Quiz on the Use of the Telephone

Before we begin, let's see how much you know already! You may like to copy out the questions and answer them in your office practice folder, if you have one.

Is it true that:

1) Answering the telephone in an office is one of the most important jobs that most office workers do?

2) Every business firm, however small, has a telephone?

3) Answering the telephone in a firm is the same as answering the telephone at home?

4) Answering the telephone in a firm is easy – no special training is needed?

5) A pleasant, polite and friendly voice is the most important part of answering the telephone?

6) Office workers who do not often answer the telephone answer it badly because they are nervous?

7) Appearance — make-up, hairstyle and clothes – is a very important part of answering the telephone?

8) Switchboard operators are employed by firms to deal with all incoming and outgoing telephone calls and British Telecom will train switchboard operators for firms, free of charge?

9) Some switchboard operators also look after a firm's visitors, and act as receptionists?

10) Two people can talk to each other on the telephone at a speed of 150 words a minute or more, over thousands of miles of oceans and land?

ANSWERS TO TELEPHONE QUIZ

Score: 2 for a right answer
1 for an answer which is half-right
0 for a completely wrong answer

1) *Yes, it is true* that answering the telephone in a firm is one of the most important jobs office workers do.

2) *Yes*, every business firm, however small, has a telephone. Much day-to-day business is done over the phone, and no firm could afford to be without one. They would lose a great many customers if they had no telephone, because all business people want to be able to obtain information from other business people, as quickly as possible. Letters take too long.

3) *No – this is not true.* When you answer a telephone in your home it is correct to give your number, followed by your name, if your caller is a stranger. In a firm, you must give the name of the firm first (so that the caller knows at once that he has the right number) followed by a pleasant 'good morning' or 'good afternoon'.

4) *Yes, it is true* that answering the telephone is easy in a firm – when you know how! Score one if you have answered 'true' to this question, but score two if you have added 'but you must know the right way to do it'.

5) *Yes, true.* It is important for everyone working in an office to use a pleasant voice every time they answer the telephone. An offhand, curt voice may give a caller the impression that whoever is answering is in a bad temper. Every telephone call is another, unknown individual.

6) *Yes, true.* It is important for all office workers to know how to answer the telephone efficiently.

7) *No, not true.* No one can see you when you answer the telephone (at least, no callers on the telephone can see you). The most important asset you have is your voice.

8) *Yes, quite true.* All BT-trained switchboard operators are very efficient. The first person a caller on an outside line speaks to in a large firm is the switchboard operator and it is essential she gives a good impression of her firm.

9) *Yes, true.* In many firms, the receptionist also looks after a switchboard. Obviously, *her* appearance is as important as her voice.

10) *Yes, quite true.* It is possible to talk to someone on the telephone at a speed of 150 words a minute or more; – this is the speed at which many people speak, in normal conversation. Telephoning to Australia from the UK is also possible, and to many other distant countries.

How did you get on? If you scored over 15, you have a good knowledge of the importance and use of the telephone already. Well done!

If you scored between 10 and 15, you have a useful working knowledge.

If you scored less than 10, you have a lot more to learn about the telephone.

Making Telephones Mobile

Extra telephone sockets can now be installed quickly by telephone engineers, in homes or offices, for around £30 per socket.

This will be especially useful in offices, because frequently the arrangement of the files, desks and other equipment has been governed by the telephone sockets. Now the office layout can be changed and the telephone sockets moved without too much fuss or expense.

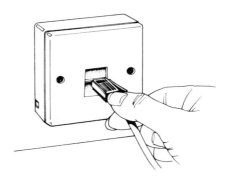

Bring mobility to the telephone

Correct Dialling

According to British Telecom 1000 million calls fail each year, mostly because of misdialling. How often have you had to feel embarrassed and say, 'Sorry I must have the wrong number'? If you follow the following suggestions made by British Telecom you should make fewer mistakes!

Check the number first from your own records or the telephone directory for that area.

Write the number down if it is given to you orally.

Wait for the dialling tone before dialling.

Telephones Available for Rent or Purchase

Mickey Mouse telephone

Snoopy telephone

Telephone with dial

A model of one of the first telephones

A twenties model

Modern telephone

Press-button telephone

New shape telephones

No hands telephone!

Dial and handset combined

Wall-mounted press-button telephone

A trimphone with press-buttons

Dial from a written record.

Dial with care. Pull the dial right round to the finger stop and let it return freely.

Don't pause too long between each figure.

Don't be a dozy dialler! But if you do make a mistake, replace the receiver and start again.

Wait up to 15 seconds for the equipment to connect you and, above all, *concentrate*.

Dial right round to the finger stop   Dial the number very carefully

The latest types of telephones have press-buttons instead of dials. There is less likelihood of misdialling (the correct expression for using a press-button telephone is 'keying') and it is quicker, as there is no waiting for the dial to return to position before dialling the next number.

Eventually, press-buttons will replace dials on telephones.

When pressing buttons, make sure each button is fully depressed and be careful to press only one button at a time. Press at a steady rate.

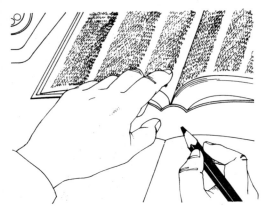

Record the numbers you often use

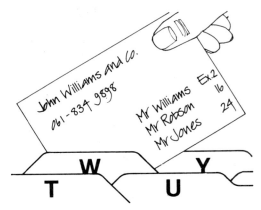

A card index for recording numbers

Answering the Telephone and Dealing with Messages

Always pick up the telephone receiver with the hand you do not normally write with. This will make it easier for you to write down a message if you have to!

Preparations for dealing with messages can be made before the telephone even rings.

By the side of every telephone should be:
- something to write *on*
- something to write *with*.

Better than a writing pad is a pad of telephone message forms, similar to the one on page 10, so that the headings remind whoever is answering the phone of any questions they should ask the caller before he or she rings off.

It is always better to write messages down, at once, then read them back to the caller so that they can be checked, rather than to try and remember what was said.

After a message has been checked, it must then be taken to the person it is intended for without delay.

A caller may not be willing to leave a message. As an alternative, he could be asked:

- if he would like to phone back later;
- if he would like to be phoned back – he may suggest a suitable time.

In any case, he must be asked for his name, address (or his firm's name and address), telephone number and extension number, if he has one. The extension number is the number of his internal phone, and if it is known, the caller can ask for it and save the switchboard operator looking it up.

Never let a caller go without finding out who he is and his address.

If his name is a fairly common one, such as Smith or Jones, his address will be essential to identify him. There are a lot of Smiths in any telephone directory!

Exercise 1

TELEPHONE MESSAGES

Rule up four copies of the telephone message form, putting in the headings. Then complete them correctly, with the details in the following telephone messages. Sign the forms yourself.

1) The Manager of the Swan Hotel, Oxbridge, telephone number 344567, rang up to say that arrangements for the staff dinner on 4 March at 1930 hours are now complete. A room has been booked for 30 people. Menus and prices are in the post. The message is for Mr C Bailey of Personnel Department.

2) Mr Vernon of ABC Group Services Ltd, Milchester, telephone 733552 extension 8, telephoned to say he will be in the neighbourhood on 1 February and would like to see Mr Kendall, Sales Manager, at 1000 hours on that day, if it is convenient. Could Mr Kendall's secretary please confirm, or otherwise.

3) Would Mrs J Grant, Typing Pool Supervisor, please telephone Mrs G Hughes of J V White & Co Ltd, Blandwich, telephone 811356 extension 11, to let her know whether a demonstration of the offset-litho duplicator will be convenient on Monday 31 January at 1200 hours?

TELEPHONE MESSAGE

FOR *Mr. P. Jenkins* . . . . .
DATE *Jan. 25th 198-* . . . .
TIME *10.30 hrs* . . . .

URGENT / ~~NON-URGENT~~

FROM *Mrs. P. Barker* . . . .
TEL NO *436551* . . . . EXTN *23* . . .
COMPANY NAME *Barker and Lane* . .
ADDRESS *Highfield Trading Estate* . .
. . . . *Kidderminster* . . . .
. . . .

TAKEN BY . . . . . *P. Hill* . . . . .

Mrs Barker regrets that she cannot call as arranged (at 11.30 hrs today) as she has been called away unexpectedly.

She would be able to come on Friday 27 January at the same time. Would you please telephone her office to confirm?

P Hill

4) Miss H Edmonds, 21 Grace St, Warley, telephone 333812, rang to let Mr K Daniels of the Purchasing Department know that she has flu and will not be at work for a few days. She will ring again when she knows definitely when she will be returning to work.

Inside and Outside Calls

Small firms may only have one telephone for receiving *outside* (or *external*) calls. Calls on an outside telephone in a firm should be answered by announcing the name of the firm, first, followed by 'good morning' or 'good afternoon'.

Larger firms will have two telephone systems – one for receiving and sending outside (external) calls and the other for offices to phone each other (internal calls).

Another type of telephone system will deal with both internal and outside calls. The type of call can be distinguished by the tone of the ring.

An *inside* or *internal* telephone should be answered by announcing the name of the office, followed by your own name: 'Sales department, Jane Jackson speaking'; or 'Mr Thompson's secretary speaking'.

In large firms where all outside calls are received by the switchboard operator, she will have given the name of the firm, so an incoming call would be taken by announcing the name of the department, office or manager. There is one important thing to remember with an outside call. It is that no caller must be left hanging on indefinitely while the person he wants to speak to is being found. He must be told frequently that he has not been forgotten, and can also be asked if he would like to be phoned back. This saves him wasting time and money.

Telephone Etiquette

WHAT TO DO IF YOU ARE CUT OFF

If you are cut off in the middle of a telephone conversation, replace the receiver, and wait for your caller to dial again, if it was an incoming call. If *you* made the call, you dial again, after replacing the receiver.

ENDING THE CALL

It is considered polite not to conclude a call if you are the person who was *called*. In other words, the person paying for the call should be the one to end it.

A Telephone Style

There are certain *slang expressions* which should never be used on the telephone:

'Hang on'
'Hello' – always name of firm, name of department, or name of boss.
'OK'
'Okey-doke'
'So long!'
'Cheerio!'
'See you!'
'Ta-ta!'
'Hang about a bit.'

Everyone uses some of these during normal conversation, but on the telephone they sound familiar and not very polite.

Neither should callers be addressed as 'dear', 'my dear', 'duck' or 'love' for the same reasons.

Some people may be inclined to chat unnecessarily, especially if they ring up frequently. This should not be encouraged – 'chatty' callers can be dealt with quite politely by being told that someone else is waiting to use the telephone.

11

Any telephone conversations which are overheard should never be repeated. They may not be confidential – but in any case should always be treated as if they are.

At the end of a telephone call, thank the caller for ringing and replace the receiver quietly. If you bang it down, it may reverberate in his ear – not pleasant.

When talking on the telephone, speak almost normally, but rather more slowly than usual, holding the receiver so that the mouthpiece is close to your mouth. Remember, it is a small microphone so you must speak directly into it. *Shouting* is no good at all – it merely distorts the sound.

A Telephonist's Personal Alphabet

A *Acknowledging* caller promptly.
B *Being brief* – calls are charged for by time as well as distance.
C *Courteously* dealing with all callers.
D *Dialling Code Booklet* – must be up-to-date.
E *Engaged tone* – learn to recognise it and ring off.
F *Finishing* a call with 'Thank you for calling'.
G *Greeting* caller by name, if known – if not, using it as soon as it is known.
H *Helping* callers as much as possible.
I *Index* of frequently used numbers – saves time.
J *Jotting* down messages as they are given, not afterwards.
K *Keeping caller informed* that you are trying to connect him.
L *Looking up numbers,* not trying to remember them.
M *Making* caller feel that he is being dealt with efficiently.
N *Number unobtainable tone* – check number with British Telecom.
O *Offering* all possible help to callers.
P *Paytone* – caller is in a callbox and may run out of coins, deal with quickly.
Q *Quickly* connect callers.
R *Reading* messages back to callers as a check.
S *Speaking slowly and clearly* – not shouting.
T *Telephone message pad* – always to hand.
U *Up-to-date International Telephone Guide* for telephone information.
V *Very pleasant voice.*
W *Wrong number* – if you dialled it, apologise.
X *(E)xpress service to callers.*
Y *Yellow Pages* (Classified Trade Directory) – another essential telephonist's reference book.
Z *Zealously* carrying out correct procedures on the switchboard.

Telephone Dos and Don'ts

Do Give name of firm followed by 'Good morning' or 'Good afternoon', to a caller on an *outside* line.

Don't Say 'Hello'. It tells caller nothing.

Do Give name of office, or extension number, to a caller on an *inside* line.

Don't Say 'Hello', for the reason given above!

Do Answer the telephone as soon as it rings.

Don't Ignore a ringing telephone. Caller may be in a call-box.

Do Remain calm, polite and helpful.

Don't Lose your temper even if caller loses his.

Do Be brief – calls are charged by distance and length of call.

Don't Encourage callers to chat.

Do Speak normally, but a little more slowly.

Don't *Shout!*

Do Tell the caller frequently that you are trying to connect him.

Don't Let the caller wait in complete silence – he may think he has been cut off.

Do Thank the caller for telephoning and replace receiver quietly.

Don't *Bang* receiver down!

Do Remember to ring a caller back, if you promised to do so.

Don't Forget to write a note on a Telephone Message Pad to remind you to ring the caller back.

Do Have a pad of special Telephone Message Forms by the telephone with a pencil *always*.

Don't Take a message and let the caller go without asking name, address, and telephone number.

Do Write down incoming messages.

Don't Try to remember messages.

Do Read messages back to callers as a check, before they ring off, especially messages which contain numbers.

Don't Let the caller go without making sure the message you have written down is correct.

Do Write out beforehand a message that you are going to telephone.

Don't Rely on your memory.

13

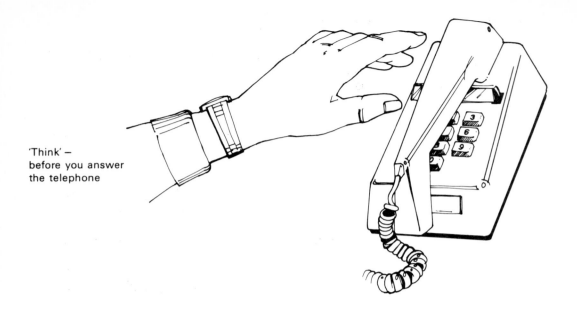

'Think' —
before you answer
the telephone

Internal Staff Directories

Each member of staff who uses an internal telephone (a telephone extension), announces the extension number (followed by name of office) when answering the telephone. A list of extension numbers should be arranged alphabetically under the names of the offices, with an alphabetical list of names beneath, as below:

ACCOUNTS DEPARTMENT		
		Extension
Alan Atkinson	Wages	35
Mary Burns	Wages	36
John Dunn	Cashier	34
Tina Eames	Cashier's Assistant	30
Arthur Grant	Chief Accountant	27
Hugh Harris	Wages	33
Jill Jackson	Secretary to Chief Acct.	28
Simon Lowndes	Assistant to Chief Acct.	26
Beverley Pratt	Wages	31
Lynn Turner	Cashier's Secretary	29
Peter Wells	VAT	40

Exercise 2

INTERNAL TELEPHONE DIRECTORY

Re-arrange the list of names, and departments below, in an order suitable for an internal staff directory.

SALES DEPARTMENT		Extension
Norman Knight	Advertising Manager	101
Elaine Scott	Secretary to Sales Man.	158
Michael Pickard	Sales Manager	157
James Abrahams	Sales Manager's Assist.	159
Beverley Zimmer	Secretary to Advertising Man.	102
Margaret Meacham	Advertising Manager's Assistant	103
Katherine Lynwood	Artwork Section	106
William Benn	Artwork Section	105
Mary Straker	Area Manager (Northern Division)	133
Elizabeth Pym	Area Manager (Southern Division)	132

Remembering Names and Status of Staff

In a large firm it is quite a difficult job to remember people's names and status, and it is important to make an effort to do so as quickly as possible, especially for receptionists. They will be in contact with many members of staff regularly, and should be able to address them by name as a matter of courtesy.

The internal directory (see above) can be used to learn people's names and titles, and an additional help is a brief description by the side of each name (e.g. wears glasses; has red hair; has a beard; very tall). Photographs, sometimes issued to everyone working in a firm for a company pass, could be used, too, with the name and status written underneath. Using people's names whenever possible is appreciated, even when you are not quite sure you are right – if done politely, most people will put you right with a smile, *but* will expect you to learn quickly — they will not be as patient in six months time!

Coping with Indistinct Callers

Sometimes your caller cannot hear you, even though you are speaking slowly and clearly. The line may be 'crackling' or your caller's English may not be very good. There is an internationally recognised way to spell out words, which all telephone operators use, called Standard Letter Analogy or Telephone Alphabet.

TELEPHONE ALPHABET

A	Alfred	J	Jack	S	Samuel
B	Benjamin	K	King	T	Tommy
C	Charlie	L	London	U	Uncle
D	David	M	Mary	V	Victor
E	Edward	N	Nellie	W	William
F	Frederick	O	Oliver	X	X-ray
G	George	P	Peter	Y	Yellow
H	Harry	Q	Queen	Z	Zebra
I	Isaac	R	Robert		

To use the telephone alphabet, you would spell out the word your caller couldn't hear like this:

The word she cannot hear is *parcel*

P – Peter, A – Alfred, R – Robert, C – Charlie, E – Edward, L – London and then repeat the word *parcel*.

FIGURES

There is a special way to pronounce figures so that they are not mis-heard on the telephone.

0	OH	Long *O*
1	WUN	Emphasise *N*
2	TOO	Emphasise *T* with long *OO*
3	THR'R'EE	Slightly rolled *R* and long *E*
4	FOER	One syllable long *O*
5	FIFE	Emphasise first *F*
6	SIX	Long *X*
7	SEV-EN	Two syllables
8	ATE	Long *A* emphasise *T*
9	NINE	One syllable: long *I*; emphasise first *N*

Say each figure separately.

12 is 'one, two'.

But for 100 to 900 say 'one hundred', 'two hundred' etc., and for 1,000, 2,000 to 9,000 say 'one thousand', 'two thousand' etc..

Pauses. Break numbers down into pairs from the right and pause between pairs. For example:

251 is 2, 51, two – five, one

1234 is 12, 34, one, two – three, four

38125 is 3, 81, 25, three – eight, one – two, five

Doubling. If a pair of numbers are identical say 'double one' etc, but do not double if the figures are separated by a pause.

3322 is 33 – 22 (double three – double two)

but:

2332 is 23 – 32 (two, three – three, two).

Now all you need is a little practice. Try the following as a well-trained telephone operator would say them:

675	665571
52183	5885
1000	667711
50000	499942

Speak more slowly and
clearly than normally

Don't shout!

Thank you
for calling.

Replace the receiver quietly
after thanking the caller

Don't bang the receiver
down!

Exercise 3

TELEPHONE ALPHABET

1) Make a copy of the telephone alphabet for your office practice folder, and then practise using it in class by spelling out your own name, and then perhaps each other's names.

2) If there is a cassette or tape recorder available, tape short conversations spelling out some of the words, and including numbers.

The Telephonist's Reference Sources

The following books would be needed by a competent telephonist and Telex operator:

- Local *Alphabetical Telephone Directory*. This lists all the subscribers in the area, in alphabetical order of surnames.

- *Classified Trade Directory* (also called *Yellow Pages*). This lists people and organisations etc. in alphabetical order of their professions, occupations or trades, so that it is possible to find most florists, plumbers, hairdressers or poodle parlours in an area, when their individual names are not known.

- *Telephone Dialling Codes* booklets. These list all dialling codes – both overseas and inland.

- *British Telecom International Guide*. This gives information about overseas telephone services.

- *World Atlas*. This helps to locate foreign places.

- *Telex Directory*. Telex Directories for other parts of the world.

ALPHABETICAL INDEX

The most frequently used numbers, both internal and external, should be listed for quick reference under the name of the subscriber. An extension number in addition to the external number is useful, too, wherever possible.

Exercise 4

THE CLASSIFIED TRADE DIRECTORY (YELLOW PAGES)

1) Give the name, address and telephone number of a car hire firm.

2) Give the name, address and telephone number of a watch repairer.

3) Give the name, address and telephone number of a kennels.

4) Give the name, address and telephone number of an estate agent.

5) What is the telephone number and address of your nearest motel?

6) Give the name, address and Telex number of a florist with a teleprinter.

7) Give the telephone number and address of a riding stables.

8) List the hairdressers in your area.

9) List the plumbers in your area.

10) List the car hire firms in your area.

MICROFICHE TELEPHONE DIRECTORY

The latest British Telecom telephone directory is available on microfiche and the complete UK set of alphabetical telephone directories, including Telex, fits in one small drawer file – saving shelf space of 15 feet. It is automatically up-dated.

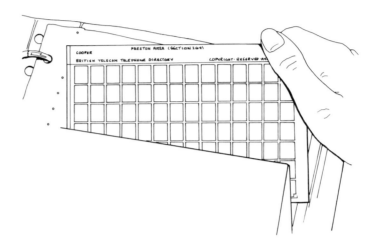

Exercise 5

ANSWERING THE TELEPHONE

Write these notes in your folder, filling in the missing words and phrases.

1) For recording the most frequently used telephone numbers a _Alphabetical index_ is useful.

2) When answering the telephone, pick up the receiver with the hand you do _less_ with.

3) By the side of every telephone should be: something to write with, something to write _on_ .

4) After writing messages down _Repeat_ them back to the caller so that they can be _Understood_.

5) After receiving a telephone message and writing it down, it must be taken to the _Member of Staff_ without delay.

6) If a caller is not willing to leave a message, he should be asked to: phone back later or _to write in_
to call in

7) Before he rings off, he must be asked for his name, address (or his firm's address) _telephone_ and extension.
number

8) Never let a caller go without finding out who _he/she is_ and his _company_ .
number.

20

9) Answering an outside (external) call on a telephone should be done by saying _Good Morn._ *Good afternoon* after the name of the firm.

10) When answering an inside (internal) call in a firm, the name of the office should be given followed by _name of person_

11) With an outside call, a caller must never be left _waiting_ indefinitely.

12) He must be told frequently that he has not been _forgotten_ and can also be asked if he would like to be _called back later_

13) If you are cut off in the middle of a telephone conversation _replace_ the receiver and _wait._ if it was an incoming call.

14) If it was an outgoing call (you made the call) dial again, after _replacing the receiver._

15) It is considered polite not to _call back_ if you are the person who was called. The person paying for the _call_ should be the one to _telephone. back._

CHAPTER 2

Telephone Charges

How Telephone Calls are Charged for

It is possible to dial most calls. Charges for these are recorded automatically on a meter at the telephone exchange. Charges are based on:

- Distance between caller and the person to whom he is speaking
- Time of day
- Day of the week
- Length of time the call takes (duration)

A Local Call is one made within the area around a town or city extending to about 900 square miles.

A Trunk Call is a call made outside this area. A trunk call can be dialled or made via the operator.

Cities and large towns now have all-figure telephone numbers. This means that there is a number code which has to be dialled first, before the telephone number of the person or company who is wanted is dialled. All the codes now available are in the Dialling Code Booklet. Before you dial it is very important to check that you have the right code.

On STD calls (Subscriber Trunk Dialling) there are no 'pips' to show how long the call has lasted. 'Pips' are only given on trunk calls (long-distance calls) connected by the operator. These 'pips' can be heard every three minutes. Below are charts for the rates of charges for different types of telephone calls.

All inland calls

Charge rate period	Mon	Tue	Wed	Thur	Fri	Sat	Sun
6.00 pm-8.00 am	Cheap rate						
8.00 am-9.00 am	Standard rate						
9.00 am-1.00 pm	Peak rate						
1.00 pm-6.00 pm	Standard rate						

International dialled calls

Charge rate period	Mon	Tue	Wed	Thur	Fri	Sat	Sun
8.00 pm-8.00 am Does not apply to Charge Band 5B	Cheap rate						
8.00 am-8.00 pm	Standard rate						

Value Added Tax
Telephone **charges** are VAT exclusive and a sum for VAT is added to the bill at the appropriate rate.
To help you, call **costs** (to the customer) of all the examples of telephone calls shown include VAT at 15%.

Dialled direct

Local calls

| | | Approximate **cost** to the customer including VAT | | | | | Time for one unit |
		1 min	2 mins	3 mins	4 mins	5 mins	
Local *L*	Cheap	5p	5p	5p	5p	5p	8 mins
	Standard	5p	5p	11p	11p	16p	2 mins
	Peak	5p	11p	11p	16p	22p	1 min 30 secs

National and Irish Republic calls See note 6

		1 min	2 mins	3 mins	4 mins	5 mins	Time for one unit
Calls up to 56 km (35 miles) *a*	Cheap	5p	5p	11p	11p	16p	2 mins
	Standard	11p	16p	22p	32p	38p	45 secs
	Peak	11p	22p	32p	43p	54p	30 secs
Calls over 56 km (35 miles) connected over *b1* low cost routes See note 3	Cheap	5p	11p	16p	22p	27p	1 min
	Standard	16p	27p	43p	54p	70p	24 secs
	Peak	22p	38p	54p	76p	92p	18 secs
Calls over 56 km (35 miles) *b*	Cheap	11p	16p	22p	27p	38p	48 secs
	Standard	16p	32p	49p	65p	81p	20 secs
	Peak	22p	43p	65p	86p	£1.08	15 secs
Calls to the Channel Islands *b*	Cheap	11p	16p	22p	27p	38p	48 secs
	Standard	16p	32p	49p	65p	81p	20 secs
	Peak	22p	43p	65p	86p	£1.08	15 secs
Calls to the Irish Republic from Great Britain and the Isle of Man	Cheap	22p	43p	65p	86p	£1.08	15 secs
	Standard	43p	81p	£1.24	£1.62	£2.05	8 secs
	Peak	43p	81p	£1.24	£1.62	£2.05	8 secs

Exercise 6

HOW TELEPHONE CALLS ARE CHARGED FOR

Write these notes in your folder, filling in the missing words and phrases.

1) Charges for telephone calls are recorded automatically on a _____ at the telephone exchange.

2) STD means Subscriber _____ .

3) On trunk calls connected by the operator _____ are heard every three minutes.

4) A _____ call is one made within the area around a town or city within about 900 square miles.

5) A trunk call can be _____ or made via the operator.

6) On STD calls there are no _____ to show how long the call is taking.

7) Telephone calls are cheapest on Saturdays and Sundays. On weekdays, after working hours, they are cheapest between _____ and _____ .

8) On weekdays, during working hours, a telephone call is cheaper after _____ and before _____ .

9) Most cities and large towns are now on all-figure telephone numbers. This means that there is a number code which has to be dialled first. All the codes available are in the _____ .

10) VAT is _____ to all telephone bills.

Exercise 7

TELEPHONE CHARGES – DIALLED DIRECT CALLS

From the charge bands on page 23 work out the following:

1) Ten minutes at the cheap rate for a local call.

2) Ten minutes at the peak rate for a local call.

3) How much time you get for 5p at standard rate for a local call.

4) How much time you get for 5p at cheap rate for a local call.

5) Five minutes at standard rate for a call over 56 km (35 miles).

6) Five minutes at peak rate for a call over 56 km (35 miles).

7) Five minutes at cheap rate for a call over 56 km (35 miles).

8) Four minutes at peak rate for a call to the Isle of Man at peak rate.

9) Two minutes to the Isle of Man at cheap rate.

10) Ten minutes to the Irish Republic at standard rate.

11) Six minutes to the Channel Islands at cheap rate.

12) Three minutes local (peak rate).

13) Three minutes local (cheap rate).

14) Five minutes up to 56 km (35 miles) standard rate.

15) Ten minutes over 56 km (35 miles) connected over low cost routes.

16) Four minutes to the Irish Republic from Great Britain and the Isle of Man.

24

The cost of these calls includes VAT at 15 per cent.

17) What is the cost of them *without* VAT?

18) How much time is allowed for a local call during the cheap rate period for 5p?

19) How much time is allowed for a call over 56 km at peak period for 5p?

20) How much time is allowed for a call to the Irish Republic at standard period for 5p?

21) Make a list of the different types of *inland* call.

The Telephone Bill

Telephone calls are paid for every three months, when an account is sent to each subscriber (a subscriber is a person who rents a telephone from British Telecom). This account lists calls via the operator, reversed charge calls separately but adds together all dialled calls (STD and local). VAT at the current rate is added to telephone bills. There is also an additional quarterly rental for the telephone.

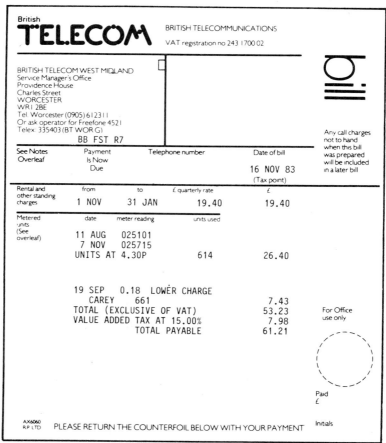

Any subscriber who forgets to pay his or her bill is disconnected, after a warning has been given, and has to pay an extra charge, on top of the bill for the preceding quarter, before the telephone is reconnected.

Any faults in a telephone system will be repaired by British Telecom engineers usually without charge. They should be reported clearly and as accurately as possible from another telephone, giving the number of the faulty one, to the number given in the Dialling Code Booklet and the local telephone directory.

Exercise 8

Questions on the telephone bill on page 25.

1) What is the period for which rental will be paid?

2) What is the date up to which the calls are being charged?

3) How many units have been used?

4) What is the price per unit?

5) What is the total cost for the units?

6) What is the total cost without VAT?

7) What is the amount of VAT?

8) What is the total payable?

9) The date of the bill is 16 November. When is payment due?

How to keep Telephone Charges to a Minimum

It's not the number of calls that makes the bill high – it's the number of *units* recorded on the meter at the telephone exchange. A unit is measured by the length of the call, the distance between callers, the time of day and the day of the week.

Calls should be kept as short as possible.

Using the operator to make calls increases the cost – dial whenever possible.

Dial carefully – dialling a wrong number can cost a lot of money, when the wrong person answers, from a long distance.

Avoid 'person-to-person' calls and transferred charge calls unless absolutely necessary – the extra charge for these is now quite high.

The hour between 0800 and 0900 should be used as much as possible for telephoning (the 24-hour clock is explained on page 177). Now that many firms use flexitime, offices are open earlier and calls are cheaper at this time.

The afternoon is the next best time to make calls, especially long-distance ones. This is cheaper than making them in the morning.

The cheapest time for telephoning calls at home is on Saturdays or Sundays, or after 1800 hours Monday to Friday.

Note that British Telecom *do not charge* if a caller is cut off by faulty equipment, or has to re-dial for a wrong number, where the person called answers, *provided* that the operator is called and told. If not, the meter ticks up as usual and the charges go on the bill of the person making the call.

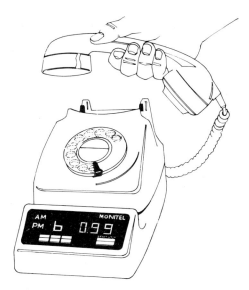

A telephone which tells you how much your call is costing while you talk

CHAPTER 3

The Switchboard Operator

What the Different Telephone Tones Mean

When you pick up a telephone receiver you should hear a low-pitched 'burr-burr'. This tells you that the telephone is working, and that you can go ahead and dial the number you want. This is known as the *dialling tone*.

After you have finished dialling, you should hear a repeated double ring (the *ringing tone*) which tells you that the number you have dialled is ringing.

If you hear a single, high-pitched note, repeated at intervals, you know that the person whose number you dialled is already talking to someone else on his telephone. What you can hear is the *engaged tone* – an engagement ring in fact, but not the sort you can wear on the third finger of your left hand!

If the number you dialled is out of order, you will hear a continuous, high-pitched note. This is the *number unobtainable tone*.

Answer the telephone with a 'smile in your voice'!

THE PAY TONE

If you hear a series of rapid, high-pitched pips when you pick up your receiver to *answer* the telephone, don't hang up – hang on. This is the *pay tone* and it means that someone is calling you from a public telephone box. You must announce your number as soon as the *pay tone* stops and then give caller time to put his money in. Until he does this, you cannot hear him, but he will be able to hear you.

Exercise 9

TELEPHONE TONES

Write these notes in your folder, filling in the missing words.

1) A continuous, high-pitched note means that the number dialled is _____ .

2) This is called the _____ tone.

3) The engaged tone is a _____ note, repeated at intervals.

4) The engaged tone means that the person whose number has been dialled is _____ .

5) The dialling tone is what you hear when you pick up the receiver of a telephone before you start to dial. The dialling tone is a low-pitched _____ .

6) After you have finished dialling, you should hear a repeated double ring, the _____ .

7) A series of rapid, high-pitched pips is the _____ .

8) This means that someone is calling from a _____ .

9) As soon as the _____ stops, you must announce your _____ .

Payphones

Telephone boxes are a familiar sight all over the country. In many large stores, pubs and other buildings used by the general public, payphones have been installed for our convenience.

The latest type of payphone can be used for inland and international calls (see page 30) and when they are out of order the local repair centre is informed automatically.

The coins inserted are held and the amount shown on an illuminated display. As the call proceeds, the amount of credit goes down and a 'bleep' is given as a warning ten seconds before the credit finally runs

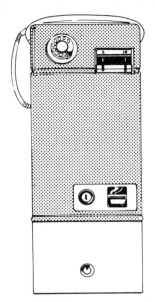

The most familiar type of payphone

out. There is a request displayed to insert more money and a final 'bleep'. The caller is then disconnected unless more money is inserted.

Any money not used at the end of the call is returned to caller.

Illustrated below is a press-button payphone in use.

A modern payphone

It is possible to buy (at some post offices, tobacconists and newsagents) slot-in cards, usable only on specially adapted payphones, installed, at the moment, in some larger towns (usually in railway stations or airports). You simply slot in your card (40 units can be bought for £2 or 200 for £10), 'key' your number and watch the window which tells you how fast your units are being used.

TWO-IN-ONE TELEPHONE

There is now available a telephone which is small enough to be placed on a desk and can be switched from ordinary use to a payphone at the turn of a key. This is ideal for small businesses such as hairdressers, pubs, wine bars and shops which want to provide payphone facilities for their customers or visitors.

It could also be used in a home where frequent outgoing calls are made by younger members of the family!

Two-in-one payphone

Telephone Systems in a Firm

The switchboard operator deals with all incoming (external) telephone calls, re-routing (connecting) them to the person who has been asked for. The switchboard operator also connects the employees in the firm to the number they have asked her for. The exchange which this type of operator uses is called a PMBX (Private Manual Branch Exchange). A cordless PMBX is shown in the picture overleaf. This one has three exchange lines (one for each row) and twelve extensions (the number of switches in each row) but there are models of other sizes. The operator can either use a headset or a telephone.

31

An operator using a PMBX switchboard

How a Switchboard Operator should deal with Calls

Answering an external (outside) call. Give the name of the firm, followed by 'good morning' or 'good afternoon'.

The caller then states who he wants (giving the extension number if known). If he does not know the extension number, the operator will look it up from the alphabetical list she has near at hand, and dial it. If it is answered, the caller is connected. If no one answers, she tells the caller, and asks him whether he would like her to try again or prefer to phone back later. If the caller decides to wait while she tries again, and there is a delay of some minutes, the operator frequently comes back to the caller saying 'still trying to connect you' so that he does not think he has been forgotten, or cut off.

Answering an internal (inside) call. This will be someone working in the firm who wants an outside call. The operator will reply 'switchboard' and wait for the caller to tell her the number wanted. It is not fair to expect a busy switchboard operator to look up a telephone number, except on the rare occasions when it is impossible to find one – i.e. in a part of the country for which there is no directory available. Also, asking for the extension number saves a delay after the call has been answered at the other end. The firm's telephone operator there will be able to put the call straight through.

An automatic exchange is the type which allows employees to dial direct without the operator's help. This is known as a PABX (Private Automatic Branch Exchange). Incoming calls are still routed by the firm's operator. A disadvantage of PABX is that an extension number may be engaged on an internal call but the operator can break in and interrupt. The picture opposite shows an operator using a PABX system.

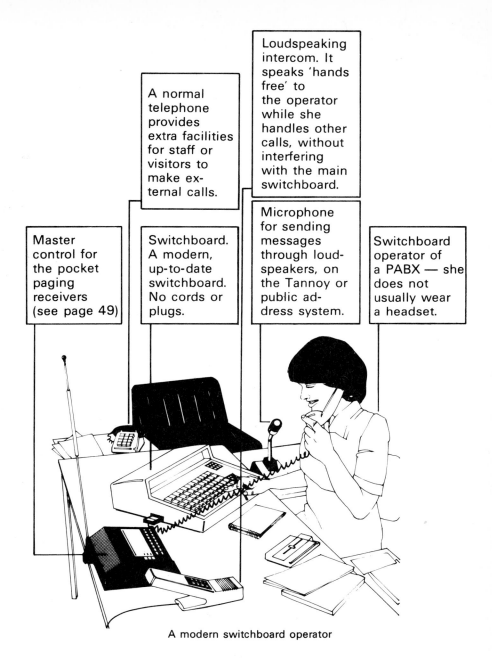

Loudspeaking intercom. It speaks 'hands free' to the operator while she handles other calls, without interfering with the main switchboard.

A normal telephone provides extra facilities for staff or visitors to make external calls.

Microphone for sending messages through loud-speakers, on the Tannoy or public address system.

Master control for the pocket paging receivers (see page 49)

Switchboard. A modern, up-to-date switchboard. No cords or plugs.

Switchboard operator of a PABX — she does not usually wear a headset.

A modern switchboard operator

Internal telephones in firms are automatic – that is, employees are able to dial, and get, the number they want, which connects them to another office in the same firm.

Most offices are supplied with an internal telephone and an external telephone, usually in different colours; a different ringing 'tone' is also a help in identifying which telephone is ringing, or similarly a flashing light.

Exercise 10

ANSWERING A TELEPHONE EXTENSION

The following messages are telephoned through to an extension. The student answering the extension telephone when it rings has to:

(a) *answer with the extension number, followed by her name;*
(b) *listen, while the person telephoning explains what he/she wants;*
(c) *answer sensibly and offer to take a message;*
(d) *take down a message from dictation;*
(e) *read back the message to the caller, checking especially dates, telephone numbers, any other numbers, and perhaps the correct spelling of names.*

To conclude the Assignment, the messages will be checked against the originals, for accuracy, neatness, correct layout (e.g. is the date and time of the message included, and has the message form been signed by the student taking the message).

1) Message for Mrs Foster: Please tell her that 40 copies of the latest Classified Trade Directory are now in the cupboard by the window at the back of M 234. Out-of-date copies of the Classified Trade Directory may now be destroyed.

2) Message for Mrs Passmore: Please tell her that her dentist's appointment is for Friday, 9 April at 1145, instead of Monday, 5 April at 1030. Ask her to let the dentist know if it is not convenient. He has a new telephone number – it is Blacking 7099.

3) Message for Mrs Ellis Jones: Please ask her to ring me at Sandhoe 36271 – James & Galway (Mr Southam). She has an appointment for tomorrow and we shall have to cancel it. Suggest Thursday at 1000 as an alternative.

4) Message for Mrs Craig, Business Studies Dept – Secretarial Section. Can she collect the books from A O Jones as soon as possible? Any problems, please ring me, John Moore, Horton 32176, Ext 21.

5) Message for Mrs Foster: Can you ask her to ring me as soon as possible? Malcolm Davies, Gateley, Waring and Co on Oldport 38911. If I'm not there, then I shall be on Elton 82164.

6) Message for Mrs Passmore: Will she telephone Mr John Hancox, Robbins Hayward & Co 021 775 3261, Ext 374 – it's about her new car. It will be ready for collection from them tomorrow at 1700.

7) Message for Mrs Davies: The time of her meeting on Wednesday is changed to 1830 from 1900. The meeting is in the Tutorial Room of the College Library. If she cannot go, please telephone Mrs H Jones, the Tutor Librarian before 1200 today.

8) Message for Mr P Sherriff: Please telephone Hugh Markham and Simpson (Blacking 798551, Ext 4). Mr Simpson would like to speak to him about the appointment he made to call and see him on Friday this week.

9) Message for Mrs P Moore: Tell her that the speaker she had arranged to come next Monday at 0930 is unable to do so. Please telephone back between 1400 and 1600, 021 3436 9784, Ext 9, tomorrow (Tuesday).

10) Messages for Mrs Foster: Mary Jenkinson of 8 Laurel Street, Handley wishes to re-sit shorthand-typing duties section of SSC examination. She wants to know the date of the examination and the last date she can enter. Could you please let her know? Not on the telephone at home, but can be contacted between 1400 and 1700 on Shiphampton 543218, Ext 5.

11) Message for Mrs Ellis Jones: Miss Frances Knight is unable to come to College today because she is ill. She is a student on a Day Release Course (2nd year shorthand-typing) and hopes to be able to attend next week. She works for Gadgets Unlimited, Personnel Dept.

12) Message for Mrs Davies: Miss Kathleen Carson, 43 Snowdon St, Blacking, has applied for a position as a junior clerk at Palmer and Loe, in the Accounts Dept. The Personnel Dept of Palmer and Loe would like you to let them have a reference for Miss Carson.

Two Small Fashion Tips

If you have long fingernails get a special *telephonist's ball-end* pen.

If you have to operate an old-fashioned switchboard with head-phones, try to choose a suitable hairstyle which will not be spoilt.

Latest Developments in Switchboards

British Telecom's latest range of switchboards offer even the smallest office a choice of facilities previously found only on large switchboards. These latest small switchboards are often called 'call connect' systems, and take up very little space (less than 2 square feet for some systems).

One switchboard automatically routes incoming calls to another extension (if one line is engaged) and repeats the last number dialled, so that if it was engaged, it can be tried again without re-dialling the number.

Each of these small switchboards can be expanded after installation, as the business grows, if required.

LARGER SWITCHBOARDS

The new, up-to-date large switchboards provide the facilities available on the smaller 'call-connect' systems, but in addition, offer faster methods of handling calls so that staff are not waiting around for engaged numbers to be free, and many other automatic services such as 'logging' (keeping a record) of all calls.

British Telecom provides training on these switchboards after they have been installed to make sure that the operators (and the office staff) get maximum benefit from the new technology incorporated into the switchboards.

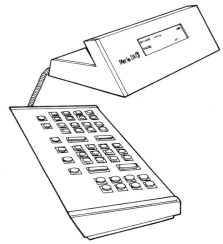

A recent switchboard model

Exercise 11

THE SWITCHBOARD OPERATOR

Write these notes in your folder, filling in the missing words and phrases.

1) The switchboard operator answers an external call by saying _____ .

2) She answers an internal call by saying _____ .

3) PMBX means _____ .

4) Internal telephones in firms are _____ ; that is, employees are able to _____ .

5) The most up-to-date types of telephone exchanges are _____ .

6) When the operator is not able to connect a caller to the person he wants immediately, she will ask him if he would _____ or if he would _____ .

36

7) It is a help to a busy switchboard operator to give her the number you want as well as the _____ number whenever possible.

8) On the more up-to-date type of switchboards, the operator does not always have to wear a _____ .

Examples of Telephone Conversations

(1) Between an Efficient Switchboard Operator and a Secretary

Scene: The switchboard in the Majestic Engineering Company. An incoming call is indicated on the switchboard.

Operator	Majestic Engineering Company. Good morning.
Caller	Good morning. May I speak to Mr Gibb, please?
Operator	Mr H Gibb, Personnel, or Mr J Gibb, Buyer?
Caller	Mr J Gibb, please.
Operator	Who is calling, please?
Caller	Lennox – David Lennox, of the Office Supplies Co.
Operator	Just hold the line, please – I'll put you through. (*Short pause.*)
Operator	I'm sorry, Mr Lennox but Mr Gibb is away today and tomorrow. Would you like to speak to his secretary?
Caller	Yes, please. (*Another short pause.*)
Operator	I'm trying to connect you, Mr Lennox. (*Further short pause.*)
Operator	You're through to Miss Dawes, Mr Gibb's secretary.
Caller	Thank you.
Secretary	Good morning, Mr Lennox, Mr J Gibb's secretary speaking.
Caller	Good morning, Miss Dawes. I'm sorry to have missed Mr Gibb. He asked me to telephone when I was in the area as he had one or two matters to discuss with me. Could I make an appointment to see him on his return?
Secretary	I'll look in his diary. Would you hold on a moment, Mr Lennox? (*Pause.*)
Secretary	Sorry to keep you waiting, but I was trying to find half-an-hour when he would be free to see you and it was rather difficult. He is very busy for the next few days. The only time I can suggest is 9 am on Thursday – and he has an appointment at 9.45 am so he won't have much time to spare, I'm afraid.
Caller	I'll make a note of that date and time and call then. Thank you for your help, Miss Dawes.
Secretary	Glad to have been of assistance. Goodbye Mr Lennox!

Exercise 12

TELEPHONE CONVERSATION (1)

1) Why did the switchboard operator ask which Mr Gibb the caller wanted?

2) Why did she say 'I'm trying to connect you' when she was putting the caller through to Mr Gibb's secretary?

3) The operator told caller the name of Mr Gibb's secretary before she put him through. Why did she do this?

4) As well as asking caller if he would like to speak to Mr Gibb's secretary, what other course of action could she have suggested?

5) The secretary also called Mr Lennox by his name. How would she know what his name was?

6) Why is it important for switchboard operators and receptionists to use people's names as soon as possible?

7) Rewrite the script, adding what the switchboard operator said to the secretary and the secretary's reply, before she was connected to Mr Lennox.

(2) How not to Deal with an External Call

Scene: A small office in a firm of builders. It is empty except for a typist, who has only been working in the firm for a short time. The secretary whom she helps and who normally answers the telephone is out of the office temporarily. The telephone rings.

Typist	Hello?
Caller	Is that the Burroughs Building Company, please?
Typist	Yes.
Caller	May I speak to Mr Burroughs, please?
Typist	He's out.
Caller	Oh, dear. It's rather important. When will he be back?
Typist	I've no idea.
Caller	(*after a short pause*) Is his secretary there?
Typist	No, she's out too.
Caller	Will she be back soon?
Typist	I shouldn't think so – she's gone for coffee.
Caller	Could you put me on to someone who could help – some of your workmen are here and I'd like them to stay and do one or two more jobs for me instead of leaving and perhaps not be able to come back for some weeks . . .
Typist	(*interrupting*) You'll have to speak to Mr Burroughs.
Caller	Perhaps you could ask him to telephone me?
Typist	OK but I don't know when.

39

Caller	My name is Nixon – Mrs Nixon, and my address is . . .
Typist	Yes, ta – got that. Cheerio!
	(*Puts the receiver down.*)
	(*Caller has been disconnected. Enter secretary.*)
Secretary	Did I hear the telephone?
Typist	(*airily*) Oh, yes, but I coped OK.
Secretary	Who was it?
Typist	A Mrs Nixon. She wanted to speak to Mr Burroughs. I told her I would ask him to ring her back.
Secretary	Didn't you offer to take a message?
Typist	I never thought . . .
Secretary	Well, never mind. Only I might have been able to help if I'd known what it was about. Which Mrs Nixon was it – we are doing work for three at the moment.
Typist	(*rather subdued*) I didn't ask for her address.
Secretary	You didn't handle that very well at all, did you? One of the three Mrs Nixons we do work for is a *very* good customer and has been for years. I hope it wasn't her.
Typist	So do I. What shall I do?
Secretary	Find the three files for Nixon and then I'll ring each Mrs Nixon and try to find out tactfully which one has been telephoning this morning.
Typist	(*now very subdued*) I'm terribly sorry . . .
Secretary	You'll learn. But it is very important to deal with the telephone in an efficient manner, as so many of our customers ring up about work and it can make all the difference how they are spoken to – we don't want to lose any of our customers.
Typist	I'll get the files for Nixon.

Exercise 13

TELEPHONE CONVERSATION (2)

1) The typist should not, of course, have replied 'Hello' when answering the telephone. What should she have said?

2) Her manner was rather abrupt. How could she have re-phrased 'He's out' and 'I've no idea'?

3) When answering the enquiry about Mr Burroughs' secretary, what should she have said instead of 'She's gone for coffee'?

4) What should the typist have said instead of 'OK'?

5) The typist should have offered to take a message, of course, but as well as saying she would ask Mr Burroughs to telephone Mrs Nixon, what else might she have suggested could be done?

6) What would have been more polite than 'Yes, ta – got that. Cheerio!'?

7) Rewrite this script as it should have been written had the typist handled the telephone call efficiently. Fill in any missing details.

8) Fill in a telephone message form as if Mrs Nixon had left a message and sign it with your own name.

✗ (3) The Nervous Junior

Scene: Office in a firm. It is empty except for office desks, typewriters, the telephone and the office junior.

One of the telephones rings. It is on a desk near the junior, and she jumps, nervously, but does nothing. The telephone goes on ringing. Finally, the junior picks up the receiver and the following conversation takes place:

Junior H-h-h-hello?

Caller Is that Mr Graham's office?

Junior I-I-I'm not sure. I'm just delivering mail.

Caller Isn't there anyone else there – his secretary?

Junior No, only me.

Caller Look at the telephone – is it extension 37?

Junior Yes, it is.

Caller Then it *is* Mr Graham's office. Write this down and leave it on his desk, please.

Junior Hang on – I haven't got anything to write on.
(*Pause while she searches desperately for some paper.*)

Caller Ready?

Junior Yes – OK.

Caller I want Mr Graham to know that I have to go to London unexpectedly and I'm catching a train at 11 o'clock this morning. I shall be away until Friday, 12th, and I'll have to postpone the meeting with him that I had arranged for Thursday, at 2 pm in my office. Got that?

Junior Sorry, my pencil's broken. Half a mo while I find another.
(*Rather long pause while she looks frantically.*)

Caller (*Now very cross and impatient*) Oh do be quick – I've a train to catch!

Junior Oh dear (*getting very flustered*) I'm doing my best – I'll try and remember the message – could you repeat it?

Caller Tell Mr Graham that I have to go to London today, at eleven o'clock and I shall be away until Friday, 12th, so the meeting I had arranged for Thursday at 2 pm in my office will have to be postponed. Have you got that?

Junior Y-y-yes. I think so.

Caller I think you'd better repeat it – it is rather important, but be quick, I haven't much time.

41

Junior　Er – um – I have to tell Mr Graham that you are going to London on Thursday at 2 pm and the meeting arranged for today is to be postponed. Is that right?

　　Caller　No, it *isn't* right. I'll send someone down from here with a message – at least, that will make sure that it *is right*. (*Rings off.*)

Exercise 14

TELEPHONE CONVERSATION (3)

1) What should the junior have said first on picking up the telephone receiver?

2) What should every telephone (whether internal or external) have by the side of it?

3) What should the junior have said instead of 'OK'?

4) What should she have said instead of 'Hang on'?

5) What should she have said instead of 'Half a mo'?

6) It is always better to write telephone messages down as the caller dictates them, asking for anything to be repeated that is not quite clear. What should the person answering the telephone do *after* having written a message down?

7) Even if the junior had managed to remember the message correctly and pass it on correctly, she had forgotten to ask one very important question. What was it?

8) Write out the message on a telephone message form, as it should have been taken down by a really efficient junior.

9) Rewrite the script, changing it so that the junior handles the caller and his message efficiently.

10) What is the difference between answering an outside call on the telephone, and answering an internal call?

CHAPTER 5

Telephone Equipment

Telephone Answering Machine

A telephone answering machine can be connected to a telephone to answer calls when the office is closed, and there is no one to answer the telephone.

It makes use of a tape recorder. An incoming call starts the tape, which then plays a pre-recorded message. When the message ends, the set switches automatically to 'record' and the caller has a short time in which to give his name, address, and telephone number, followed by his message. The telephone answering machine then switches itself off until the next incoming call.

This equipment is particularly useful for doctors, veterinary surgeons, and dentists or any one-man businesses. People who wish to make appointments can telephone at any time.

Busy secretaries find a telephone answering machine useful, as it enables them to concentrate on urgent work without constantly being interrupted by the ringing of the telephone. The calls on the tape can be dealt with at a later, more convenient time.

Firms, such as travel agents, often give a telephone number in their advertisements (perhaps a Freefone number) to enable the public to telephone during the evening when their offices are closed, and give names and addresses for brochures advertising holidays to be sent to them.

A telephone answering machine

Callmakers

PUNCHED CARD CALLMAKER

With a punched card callmaker, the card can do the dialling for you. This can be done quickly and it eliminates the possibility of a wrong number. Each card can record up to 16 digits, and numbers are changed by punching a fresh card. An unlimited number of cards can be stored, each with one telephone number.

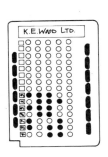

A punched card

Punching a card

The way to operate the callmaker is quite simple. You lift the handset and when you hear the dialling tone drop the appropriate card into the slot at the front of the callmaker unit. The number will be dialled automatically and the card drops through on to a tray. The picture below shows what a callmaker looks like.

Using a callmaker

44

TAPE CALLMAKER

A tape callmaker is an alternative to the card callmaker. A magnetic tape stores 400 telephone numbers and each one can have up to 18 figures. Numbers can be altered, added, or removed when necessary. The magnetic tape has a writing surface with an index down the left-hand side. To make a call, the tape is moved until the required entry appears between the two guidelines on the window at the front.

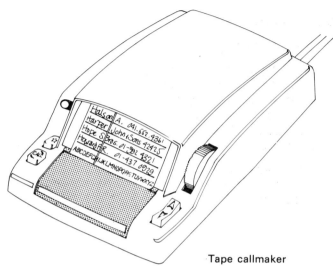

Tape callmaker

DEVELOPMENTS IN CALLMAKERS

The latest callmakers provide a telephone which incorporates a memory that can store up to ten frequently used numbers of up to 16 digits each. These can be called at the touch of a button. The last number called can also be redialled automatically.

A callmaker

45

In some models a display shows the number being called or stored in the memory and gives a stopwatch timing of calls. When the telephone is not in use, the display may become a digital clock.

Special Telephones

LOUDSPEAKING TELEPHONE

A loudspeaking telephone has a louspeaker incorporated into the normal telephone dialling arrangement, which can be switched on when a call is being made, so that both speakers in the telephone conversation can be heard by other people in the room. When the loudspeaker is switched off, the telephone conversation is carried on normally, i.e. only the two people speaking to each other can hear.

This telephone is quite different from an intercom, because it is part of an *external* telephone system. An intercom is part of an *internal* telephone system.

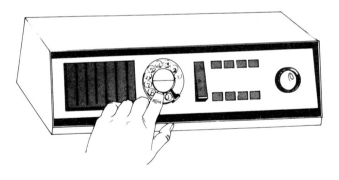

Loudspeaking telephone

INTERCOM

Communication from office to office (between the boss and his secretary for instance) is often done by an intercom. The message is relayed through a small loudspeaker so that all the secretary has to do is press a button and then she can hear.

The latest type of intercom is shown below. It can be left on a desk or picked up and used as a telephone receiver.

Free standing one hand telephone

CARPHONE

The driver of a car may contact anyone on a telephone by means of a carphone. He presses buttons on the carphone and the call is automatically switched through to its destination.

The car driver can also receive calls direct from any telephone in the UK, contact ships at sea and oil platforms in coastal waters.

He can also receive telephone information services (see page 55).

Pocket paging can be used with a carphone (see page 48).

Tannoy or Public Address System

Loudspeakers are necessary in noisy areas, such as factories, to call people to the telephone, which is situated in a quieter part of the building.

The picture shows some of the equipment for a public address system (left to right: a microphone for making a call; a telephone for answering a tannoy call; and two types of wall-mountable loud-speakers).

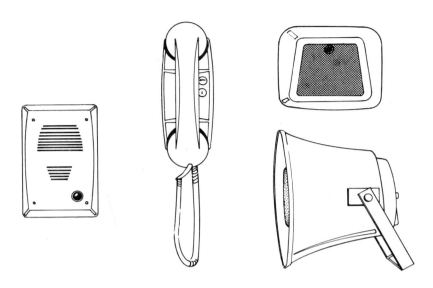

Flashing Lights

Where the ringing of a telephone disturbs people's concentration (where office workers may be spending most of their time on calculating figures, for example) different coloured lights which flash to indicate that someone is wanted on the telephone, are a noiseless alternative. Each member of staff will know which colour refers to him.

Other users of flashing lights are hospitals, where doctors are called from the wards for emergencies by this system, and in doctor's waiting rooms, where a different coloured light refers to a different doctor.

Paging

People do move around – to meetings, to other parts of a large building, outside to other buildings, and it becomes very difficult for the telephonist to locate them either to give them a message which may be urgent, or to get them to speak to a telephone caller. One way to make sure that managers and other staff who are frequently away from their own telephones can be contacted is by using 'pocket paging'.

Pocket paging consists of a lightweight receiver, small enough to be carried in a pocket, or hooked over a belt, which 'bleeps' or vibrates when the telephone operator presses the button on the master control which she has close to her switchboard. When the pocket receiver 'bleeps', the person carrying it knows he or she has to go to the nearest telephone as quickly as possible.

The radius (distance) at which pocket paging can be operated from a switchboard is approximately one mile.

RADIO PAGING

This is the system operated by British Telecom. Transmitters are based in most of the large cities such as London, Manchester, Birmingham, Liverpool, forming a national grid which covers most of the UK. The distance over which this system can be operated is about 20 miles.

The British Telecom pager has a display panel which shows numbers up to a maximum of 10, which could show telephone numbers, or be used as a code (agreed with the user) to carry out various instructions – e.g. about prices or which customer to visit next.

British Telecom Radiopaging

SOME EXAMPLES OF WHERE PAGING WOULD BE USEFUL

Lost executives cause inefficiency

Phoning back is expensive

Plant breakdowns cost money

Emergency

Mountain rescuers using radio pocket paging

A doctor in contact by radio pocket paging

WHY 'PAGING'?

This is because years ago the only way of sending messages to people who were somewhere around a building was by sending a page-boy – usually a young boy in his first job after leaving school. He would go round shouting 'Paging Mr Jones, Paging Mr Jones' until Mr Jones eventually heard him and came forward to collect his message. Now it is done by 'bleeps'.

Small pocket paging sets usually operate over a distance of about half-a-mile, which is sufficient for most business firms.

In very noisy areas, where the 'bleep' would not be heard, the receivers vibrate until the wearer switches them off.

Help for the Handicapped

FOR THE DEAF

An earpiece can be supplied by British Telecom with an adjustable volume control. There are special bells available in varying tones, so that people who are deaf can choose the bell which they hear best.

Flashing lights instead of bells indicate an incoming call and may attract a deaf person's attention more quickly.

FOR THE BLIND

Specially marked dials can be obtained from British Telecom. The Royal National Institute for the Blind (RNIB) supplies instructions typed in Braille.

For partially-sighted people (those with a little sight) there are Dialling Code Booklets in large print.

PEOPLE WITH THROAT AFFLICTIONS

Special equipment can be supplied by British Telecom which increases the volume of outgoing speech, so that it sounds normal to the person called.

Exercise 15

COMMUNICATIONS IN FIRMS OTHER THAN BY TELEPHONE

Choosing the correct answer from the three given under each question.

1) Flashing lights are used:
   a on police cars
   b in areas in firms where quiet is essential
   c on advertising signs.

2) In areas which are very noisy, a wall-mounted loudspeaker will relay messages. This is called:
   a an annoying system
   b a public nuisance system
   c a Tannoy system or public address system.

3) Pocket paging is:
   a keeping a diary
   b a small portable receiver
   c keeping a pocket book.

Exercise 16

TELEPHONE EQUIPMENT

Write these notes in your folder, filling in the missing words and phrases.

1) The switchboard on which the operator deals with *incoming* and *outgoing* calls is a _____ .

2) The switchboard on which the operator deals only with *incoming* calls is a _____ .

3) Pushbuttons on a telephone in place of a dial provide a quicker method of dialling and are also _____ .

4) A telephone answering machine is particularly useful for _____ .

5) A punched card callmaker dials automatically when the punched card is dropped into a slot at the front of the callmaker. This is a quicker method than ordinary dialling and is also _____ .

6) A magnetic tape callmaker stores up to _____ numbers.

7) A loudspeaking telephone can be switched on when a call is made so that _____ .

8) Communication from office to office (e.g. between a boss and his secretary) is often carried out by means of an _____ .

9) In noisy areas a _____ is useful for calling people to the telephone.

10) Where the ringing of the telephone would disturb people's concentration, _____ are often used.

11) When someone moves around a factory a great deal and it is difficult to contact him by telephone _____ is useful.

12) The machine connected to a telephone which records an incoming telephone message is a _____ .

13) When the pre-recorded message has finished, the set switches automatically to record and the caller _____ .

52

14) Paging equipment is especially useful for doctors, veterinary surgeons and _____ .

15) People who wish to make _____ can telephone at any time.

16) Firms such as travel agents often give a _____ telephone number to encourage the public to telephone in for travel brochures.

17) _____ uses punched cards which dial telephone numbers automatically.

18) _____ uses magnetic tape which stores up to 400 telephone numbers and dials them automatically.

19) When several people want to hear a telephone conversation at the same time, a _____ is useful, as the caller's voice is amplified.

Suggest a suitable item of telephone equipment which could be useful under the following circumstances:

20) For a manager who is frequently travelling by car around the UK and receiving (and sending) information about his latest orders.

21) A Production Manager who spends a great deal of his time in the factory away from his office (the factory is noisy).

22) An office where the workers are engaged on jobs which require great concentration and interruptions are a nuisance.

23) A manager who has to speak often to his secretary in the next office.

24) A supervisor who has to convey instructions to three of his staff from the manager in an office three floors above.

25) A firm which is frequently telephoned after the office is closed.

CHAPTER 6

Telephone Services

Special Telephone Services

ALARM CALL

For a small charge, the telephone operator will ring at any time of the day or night, and go on ringing until the telephone is answered.

This is a useful arrangement when an early train or plane has to be caught, or for an urgent, early appointment.

PERSON-TO-PERSON CALL

A *person-to-person* call does not mean a friendly, chatty telephone call. It is one where there is no charge until the person asked for actually speaks on the telephone (apart from a small, additional charge by British Telecom). A person-to-person call avoids paying for the time wasted trying to find someone who may be out of his office frequently.

FIXED TIME CALL

A fixed time call is a way of making sure that the person called is by the telephone when caller rings. A fixed time call is especially useful for overseas calls, to countries where the time is different from the time in the British Isles.

MESSAGE CALL

A message is recorded and is delivered automatically to a given number at a specified time.

ADC CALL

The caller may need to know how much a telephone call has cost, if for instance, she is telephoning from someone else's telephone. The call must be made through the operator (it cannot be dialled) the operator then asked to ring back at the end of the call and let the caller know the cost. This is known as Advice of Duration and Charge.

INFORMATION SERVICES

Information about gardening, weather, motoring, skiing, cricket scores, Stock Exchange prices, tourist facilities, the latest road, rail, sea and air information is available in nine areas of the UK 24 hours a day, seven days a week – this service is called Traveline. The correct time, bed-time stories and even recipes and a hit record can all be obtained over the telephone by dialling the number given in your telephone directory.

The services are not free – the charges are the same as for ordinary calls, and the length of the call may be restricted.

TRANSFERRED CHARGE CALLS

Another name for a transferred charge call is a *reverse charge call*. This enables the caller to make a telephone call without payment, but first she must ask the operator to ring the number of the person she wishes to speak to and ask if they are willing to pay for the call. Only when permission has been given will the operator connect the caller. This service is used in some firms by their representatives when they wish to telephone in whilst they are travelling around on firm's business. The switchboard operator would have a list of representatives and also keep a note of the transferred charge calls made.

FREEFONE

Firms use this method to encourage customers to telephone them and ask for advertising material to be sent to them. A special Freefone number is published in their advertisements in newspapers and magazines, and all that the caller has to do is to ask the operator for the Freefone number. The cost of the call is added to the account of the firm.

TELEPHONE CREDIT CARDS

These are used by businessmen travelling around, who may need to telephone their offices frequently from public call boxes.

Credit cards have a number on them, and it is this number which has to be given to the operator by the caller before he tells her what number he wants. The cost of the call goes on to the account corresponding to the credit card number. It is not necessary to use coins, but as all credit card calls have to go through the operator, they are more expensive.

EMERGENCY CALLS

There are three main emergency services:

- Fire
- Police
- Ambulance

and three other emergency services:

- Coastguard
- Cave or Mountain Rescue Services
- Lifeboat

To call any of the above services, dial 999. The operator will answer and ask which service you want. Then wait until the emergency service you have asked for speaks to you. They will want to know:

- The address of the person requiring help (not necessarily yourself)
- Directions to where they can be found (i.e. if they live in a very long road, it may be helpful to give a landmark such as a pub or church).

If you can keep cool and give helpful directions, this will save the emergency service wasting precious time looking for the house or area.

It is worthwhile practising making a 999 call in the dark – try it with your eyes closed. The figure 9 on the telephone dial is the last figure but one at the bottom of the dial. The last figure is 0. It is also important to remember to turn the dial carefully as far as it will go before dialling again, to make sure you do not dial the wrong number. Get a friend to watch you while you practise, *but leave the receiver on the hook during practice!*

If you have a pressbutton telephone, try working out a way to dial 999 in the dark for yourself!

It may one day be necessary to dial 999 in a darkened room and your practice will have been most useful.

One emergency which you do not dial 999 for is if there is a smell of gas. In this case, the Gas Board operate a 24-hour service and their number is in the telephone directory under Gas.

Make a note of it by the telephone, together with numbers for:
- Water Board (in case of leaking pipes)
- Plumber
- Electricity Board
- Nearest doctor
- Nearest hospital with casualty department
- Taxi Rank
- British Rail enquiries

Exercise 17

TELEPHONE SERVICES

Write these notes in your folder, filling in the missing words and phrases.

1) If it is essential to be woken at any time of the night the British Telecom telephone operator will ring and continue to ring until the telephone is answered. This is known as an _____ call.

2) To avoid unnecessary expense when telephoning someone who may not always be near to his telephone, a _____ call cuts down the cost, as no charge is made (except a small surcharge) until the caller actually speaks to the person he wants.

3) It is possible to make a telephone call without payment, from a call-box, by asking the operator to ring the number required and obtaining the permission of the person called to paying for the call. This is known as a _____ call.

4) People who travel around and have to make frequent telephone calls to their head office will find a _____ very useful, as this enables them to telephone from a call-box without using coins – all they do is to give the British Telecom operator their _____ number.

5) Firms when advertising encourage the public to telephone them and ask for samples, catalogues etc. by using a special number which they can use free of charge. This is called _____ .

6) Booking a telephone call for a certain time of day is known as a _____ call.

7) It may be necessary to know how much a telephone call has cost if it has been made from someone else's telephone. The British Telecom operator will ring back and tell caller if an _____ _____ call is asked for beforehand.

8) There are many telephone information services and they cost the same as _____ telephone call. The length of an information call may be _____ .

Exercise 18

TELEPHONE SERVICES

Suggest the correct telephone service for the following:

1) Caller is using a payphone and discovers he has no money – the call he has to make is an urgent one.

2) A secretary has to telephone New Zealand for her boss and she wants to be sure the person being called will be at his telephone when she puts her call through.

3) A telephone call has to be made to a manager in a firm where he is frequently out supervising the building of new offices.

4) A manager has to catch a plane at 0300.

5) A salesman has to drive to Edinburgh in January and wants to check on the state of the roads in Scotland.

6) A visitor to an office asks if she may use the telephone to make a call to France, and wishes to pay the cost of it before she leaves the firm.

7) A firm wishes to encourage the general public to telephone them free of charge in answer to advertisements.

8) Salesmen travelling around and making frequent telephone calls to their offices.

International Telephone Services

It is possible to dial direct by International Direct Dialling (IDD) to most overseas countries. A full list is given in British Telecom's *International Telephone Guide,* which will be supplied free by dialling 100 and asking for Freefone 2013.

Countries on IDD are also listed in the Dialling Code booklet.

If IDD is not available, an international call should be made by dialling 100 and asking for 'International Operator' or 'Continental Service' (depending on where the country is).

It is possible to dial direct from public call-boxes or payphones to many overseas countries, but not all. Countries beyond a certain distance cannot be telephoned from payphones because the cost would involve putting in too many coins.

International dialling codes are in the Dialling Code booklet. To obtain up-to-date lists of international dialling codes dial 100 and ask for Freefone 2013. They are supplied free of charge.

For a free demonstration of dialling tones dial 100 and ask for Freefone 2070.

British Telecom's *International Telephone Guide* also gives details of charges for telephone calls abroad, as well as the time differences between the British Isles and other parts of the world. It is known as 'ITG'.

Ships at sea can be contacted by telephone.

DIALLING INTERNATIONAL CALLS ON IDD

- Write down the *full* number before starting to dial.
- Dial steadily, without long pauses between numbers.
- Be prepared to wait up to a minute before being connected.
- Tones used in other countries are often different from those in the UK.

SPECIAL SERVICES

Transferred charge calls
Person-to-person calls
Credit card calls
} Ask the international operator to which countries these services are available.

International calls

		Approximate **cost** to the customer including VAT					**Time for one unit**
		1 min	2 mins	3 mins	4 mins	5 mins	See note 1
Charge Band A	Cheap	38p	70p	£1.08	£1.41	£1.78	9.30 secs
	Standard	43p	86p	£1.30	£1.73	£2.16	7.50 secs
Charge Band B	Cheap	49p	97p	£1.41	£1.89	£2.32	7.05 secs
	Standard	59p	£1.14	£1.68	£2.27	£2.81	5.85 secs
Charge Band C	Cheap	59p	£1.19	£1.73	£2.32	£2.92	5.65 secs
	Standard	70p	£1.35	£2.05	£2.70	£3.35	4.85 secs
	Peak	76p	£1.46	£2.16	£2.92	£3.62	4.50 secs
Charge Band D	Cheap	81p	£1.62	£2.38	£3.19	£4.00	4.10 secs
	Standard	97p	£1.95	£2.92	£3.89	£4.86	3.35 secs
Charge Band E	Economy	81p	£1.62	£2.38	£3.19	£4.00	4.10 secs
	Standard	97p	£1.95	£2.92	£3.89	£4.86	3.35 secs
Charge Band F	Cheap	81p	£1.62	£2.38	£3.19	£4.00	4.10 secs
	Standard	£1.08	£2.11	£3.19	£4.22	£5.24	3.10 secs
Charge Band G	At all times	£1.08	£2.11	£3.19	£4.22	£5.24	3.10 secs

Note

1   Dialled calls are timed and charged in whole units of 4.7p excluding VAT (5.405p including VAT at 15%). The time allowed for each unit depends upon the destination dialled and time of day. You pay only for the number of units registered during your call. The tables above show examples of the approximate cost to the customer (including VAT at 15%) of calls of various durations. All these approximate costs are rounded to the nearest penny.

2   Your Dialling Code Booklet, Telephone Directory or International Telephone Guide (ITG) shows which charge letter or International Charge Band applies to the call you wish to make.

3   If calls to distant exchanges are connected over low cost routes from your area, charge letter **b1** will be shown against those exchanges in your Dialling Code Booklet.

4   Telephone exchanges are arranged in groups for the purpose of calculating charges for calls between places within the United Kingdom and the Isle of Man, and for calls from Northern Ireland to the Irish Republic. A call made to an exchange within the same charge group or to an exchange in an adjacent group is usually a local call.

Other calls are generally charged on the basis of the distance between the charging point in the group in which the call originates and that in the group containing the called exchange. Special rates apply to calls from Great Britain and the Isle of Man to the Irish Republic.

5   Cheap and Economy rate periods are normally extended throughout Christmas Day, Boxing Day, New Year's Day and other Bank Holidays as they apply in England, Wales, Northern Ireland and Scotland and, for Economy rate, throughout weekends adjoining those days. Details will be announced before each holiday but if you are not sure ask the Inland or International operator.

6   **National** calls were formerly known as **Trunk** calls.

> **Additional information**
> For more copies of this leaflet or information about other charges for telecommunication services dial 100, during normal office hours, and ask for **Freefone 2500**. Separate leaflets containing charges for service from rented payphones are available on request. **Freefone BTI** can provide a free copy of the International Telephone Guide which gives a selection of principal area codes for each IDD country and international time difference information. Freefone numbers for other services are given in your Telephone Dialling Code Booklet.

Exercise 19

INTERNATIONAL TELEPHONE SERVICES

Write these words in your folder, filling in the missing words and phrases, and answer the questions.

1) IDD is the abbreviation for _____ .

2) Countries on IDD are listed in _____ and the Telephone Dialling Code booklet.

3) Calls can be dialled direct from payphones to certain overseas countries, but not to those beyond a certain distance because _____ .

4) The _____ gives the time differences between the British Isles and other parts of the world.

5) A free demonstration of dialling tones will be given if 100 is dialled and Freefone _____ asked for.

6) When dialling calls on IDD, you must write down the _____ number first.

7) Be prepared to wait up to a _____ before being connected.

8) Tones used in other countries are _____ from those in the UK.

9) Where are the overseas countries listed to which it is possible to dial direct?

10) If it is not possible to dial direct, how would an overseas call be made?

11) What does 'ITG' stand for?

12) Three special services are available to some overseas countries. What are these services and how would you find out if they were available to the country which you were telephoning?

Exercise 20

INTERNATIONAL TELEPHONE CALLS

Use the Dialling Code Booklet to answer these questions.

1) How many cities can you dial direct in Russia?

2) Is it possible to dial a call from a public callbox to New Zealand?

3) What numbers do you dial to ask for supplies of leaflets giving dialling codes for separate countries?

4) There is information in the Dialling Code Booklet about ringing and engaged tones in Europe and North America. What numbers would you dial to ask for free demonstrations of dialling tones for (a) North America and (b) Europe?

5) If a call had to be made through the operator for any reason, to a country overseas, what number would you dial?

6) The charges for international calls are divided into 'bands' with differing amounts of time allowed for 3p. The 'bands' are numbered from 1 to 5B. Which is the cheaper of these two bands?

7) How much would it cost for a dialled call to Paris lasting for 6 minutes sent at 1500 hours on a Monday?

8) Which would be the more expensive – a call to Greece or a call to Italy?

9) Charges for international calls made from a callbox or payphone are slightly different from those made by an ordinary line. What is the difference (i.e. are they cheaper or dearer from a callbox)?

10) How much would it cost for a dialled call to Hanover lasting 9 minutes?

11) Which would be the dearer call – 6 minutes to Australia or 6 minutes to Austria?

12) Is it possible to dial direct to Canada from a callbox or payphone?

13) A traveller abroad may wish to telephone to his firm in this country. What is the code for the United Kingdom which has to be dialled first when making a call to this country from overseas?

14) After dialling this special number, what numbers would the traveller dial next, when making a call to the UK?

15) The countries marked as 'not available from coinbox telephones' are on chargebands 4, 5A and 5B. Why do you think this is?

Picture and Computer Services

CONFRAVISION

Confravision is a British Telecom service which links people or groups of people in different cities by television. There are Confravision studios in seven large cities in the UK which can be booked for meetings, discussions or negotiations at distant locations and save the expense and time of travelling over long distances.

PRESTEL

Prestel is the world's only Viewdata system. It links television by telephone to 200 000 pages of information from an enormous library to which a subscriber can refer at any time. It also supplies up-to-date news.

An electronic 'mailbox' service allows Prestel users to send messages to each other by means of a simple 'keypad', on which a message is tapped out to another Prestel user. The message appears on their screen the next time the television set is switched on.

Gateway allows banks and airlines to plug their computer databases into Prestel.

Television sets have to be modified to allow Prestel to be used, and there are extra charges for this service.

DATEL

DATEL enables a computer installed in a firm to communicate with distant sites. Most Datel services can be used to much of Europe, the USA and a number of other countries. Datel (otherwise known as data transmission service) operates over the telephone network.

FACSIMILE TRANSMISSION

 Facsimile transmission (Fax for short) is the transmission of a document, picture or letter using the telephone system and is a system which reproduces an accurate copy of the original at the receiving end.

 Fax works by scanning the original document on the transmitter and electronically encoding its image. The coded information is then sent down a standard telephone line. At the receiving end, another Fax machine decodes the message and prints out an exact 'facsimile' copy of the original document.

Fax is faster than Telex (see pages 68–77), transmits both words and pictures and is as easy to use as an office photocopier.

 The latest machines are capable of transmitting at speeds of under a minute per document.

A page of urgent information can be sent from London to Aberdeen for about 8½p.

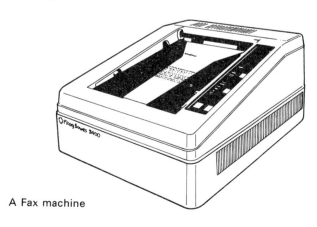

A Fax machine

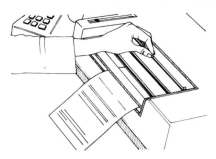

1) Place the document to be sent in the machine

2) Set the carriage levers to either side of the document

3) Switch to 'send'

4) Telephone to the recipient

Sending (above) and receiving (below) a document by facsimile transceiver

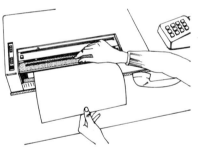

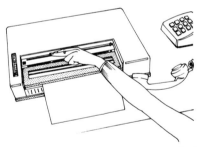

1) Place special paper in the machine

2) Switch the machine to 'receive'

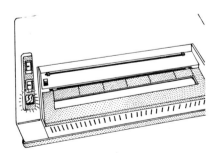

3) Switch machine to telephone line

4) After the machine has stopped the sender and recipient switch back to the telephone to confirm receipt of the document

64

There are several different makes of facsimile transmission machines available for installation in offices.

British Telecom operate a Fax service for use by firms without their own facsimile transmitters (Bureaufax).

The Post Office offers Intelpost, which gives a similar service, but the documents copied are delivered by post or collected.

It is possible to send documents by facsimile transmission to many parts of the world.

Senders (and recipients) of Fax have to have a special 'Fax' telephone number. A directory of 'Fax' numbers is at present being compiled. Firms print their 'Fax' numbers on their letterheading.

Exercise 21

INTERNATIONAL DIRECT DIALLING

1) What country is Sydney in?

2) What is the code number to dial for Sydney?

3) Is there a service to Papua New Guinea?

4) What is the Freefone numbr to dial to ask for extra International Direct Dialling leaflets?

5) What is the code to dial for New Zealand?

6) Which country is Vienna in?

7) What is the code for Vienna?

8) Which country is Brussels in?

9) What is the code for Brussels?

10) Which country is Quebec in?

11) What is the code for Quebec?

12) Which country is Copenhagen in?

13) What is the code for Copenhagen?

14) Which country is Helsinki in?

15) What is the code for Helsinki?

16) Which country is Athens in?

17) What is the code for Athens?

18) Which country is Milan in?

19) What is the code for Milan?

20) Which country is Tokyo in?

21) What is the code for Tokyo?

22) Which country is Oslo in?

23) What is the code for Oslo?

24) Which country is Lucerne in?

25) What is the code for Lucerne?

26) What is the code for Moscow?

27) Why is the charge for a call to a country in Europe different from the charge for a similar call made from a non-coinbox telephone?

28) What is the French for 'Who is speaking?'

29) What is the French for 'What is your number?'

30) What is the French for 'I am speaking from London'?

Exercise 22

SWITCHBOARDS, ETC.

Write these notes in your folder, filling in the missing words.

1) When answering an outside call on the switchboard the operator should say _____ .

2) Another name for an internal telephone is a _____ .

3) A trunk call is _____ .

4) A fixed time call is _____ .

5) An ADC call is _____ .

6) PBX means _____ .

7) PMBX means _____ .

8) PABX means _____ .

9) A 'person-to-person' call is _____

Apart from 999 calls (these are free), which *three* telephone services allow a caller to telephone from a call-box without putting in any coins?

10) _____ .

11) _____ .

12) _____ .

What *five* reference books would a switchboard operator need?

13) _____ .

14) _____ .

15) _____ .

16) _____ .

17) _____ .

18) STD means _____ .

19) What helps a telephone operator to spell out awkward words to a caller who cannot hear? _____ .

20) Telephone calls are charged for by _____ and _____ .

21) Telephone messages should always be _____ to the caller as a check before he rings off .

22) When answering an internal telephone call, the person answering should say _____ .

23) What is the name of the equipment which plays a pre-recorded taped message to the caller, and then records his answer on tape, after the office is closed? _____ .

24) An alarm call is one which _____ .

25) Telephone calls are cheapest between 1800 hours and 0600 hours, when offices are closed. The cheapest time to telephone during office hours is between _____ and _____ .

CHAPTER 7

Teleprinters and Telex

Telex and its Advantages

Telex enables someone to type a message to someone else without posting it. It is like sending a letter by telephone! The typist taps the keys in London, for instance, and the message can be printed out in Birmingham, or a message from Manchester can be received in Milan.

Telex messages are quick – an expert operator is able to transmit at about 50 words a minute. Telex messages are less likely than telephone messages to be misunderstood if in foreign languages, as translations can be made carefully from a written message. Technical information is also received without errors.

Letters may take days, especially those from foreign countries.

Telex messages give a record both for the sender and for the person receiving the message. As the operator types out the message she is sending, it is automatically printed by the teleprinter receiving it. Up to six copies can be produced at once, if required. Black print indicates outgoing messages. Incoming messages (automatically received) are printed in red.

Incoming Telex messages can still be received even after the office is closed, at any time of the day or night, provided the power supply is left switched on and the teleprinter has a supply of paper left in it. This is especially useful for receiving messages from other parts of the world, where the time may be very different from the time in Britain.

Charges for Telex calls are based on distance between Telex subscribers and the length of the message (i.e. time taken to transmit a message). This is the way charges are calculated for telephone calls too.

The units which send and receive Telex messages are called *teleprinters*. They are available for rental from British Telecom. Rental charges include the maintenance of the teleprinter and there is an extra charge for the connection of each new Telex exchange line. Enquiries about the Telex service will be answered by British Telecom (see your telephone directory). Large cities have Telex bureaux where messages may be sent by firms who do not have a teleprinter.

Telemessages (see pages 83, 84) may be sent by Telex.

FIFTEEN STAGES IN SENDING A LETTER AND GETTING A REPLY . . .

Taking dictation

Typing from notes

Checking letter

Signing letter

Taking it to Mail Room

Sticking stamp on

Posting

Transporting

Opening

Reading and dictating reply

Typing a reply

Letter handed back for re-typing because of errors

Signing reply

Posting it

Recipient reading reply

. . . BUT ONLY FOUR STAGES USING TELEX

Taking dictation

Transmitting

Receiving message

Sending a reply

Teleprinter Keyboard and Dialling Unit

The teleprinter keyboard is similar to that on a typewriter. What is printed by the operator on her machine is printed at the same time on another teleprinter at the end of the line. Only capital letters are printed and there are certain keys:

FIGURES or **FIGS.** After this key has been pressed the machine prints figures or symbols shown on the keys and allows WHO ARE YOU and BELL to be used.

WHO ARE YOU. When this key is depressed, the 'answer back' code which identifies the other teleprinter operator is printed on both machines.

BELL. When this key is pressed an alarm bell rings on both machines.

LINE FEED. This key moves the paper upwards for the next line of type.

LETTERS or **LTRS.** When this key has been pressed the machine prints the letters shown on the keys as they are operated.

The dialling unit is similar to that of a telephone but there are four additional buttons:

DIAL   CLEAR   LOCAL   RESET

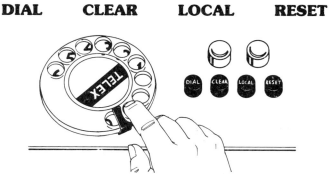

Making a Telex Call

British Telecom will provide free training for office staff. Here are the basic stages for making a Telex call:

1) The operator presses the 'dial' button by the dial.

2) She dials the Telex number she wants (she has found this in the *Telex Directory*).

3) A green light on the teleprinter shines while it is sending or receiving a message.

4) After the operator has dialled the Telex number, she expects to receive the 'answerback code' of the number she has dialled, which tells her that she is connected to the right number. If a teleprinter is left switched on, it will automatically transmit its 'answerback code'.

5) The operator sends her own 'answerback code' to identify herself.

6) The operator types her message.

7) Identical messages appear on both teleprinters as the call progresses.

8) At the end of the call, the caller sends her 'answerback code' and presses the WHO ARE YOU key to obtain the code of the other machine.

A teleprinter (Telex) operator

71

9) The called teleprinter sends its 'answerback code'.

10) During the call, either teleprinter operator can press the BELL key, which lights a red lamp on both teleprinters, and also rings an alarm bell. This would be done to call the operator's attention to something in the message which was not clear. The bell would stop and the red light go out when the SPACE bar is pressed.

11) A call can be ended by either operator (either the one sending the message or the one on the machine receiving the message) pressing a button on the dialling unit.

While an operator is being trained, the teleprinter would be switched to local use, which would not prevent incoming calls from being received. The alarm bell and red light would warn that the teleprinter should be restored to normal use if a local call were received during training.

Telex Abbreviations

CRV	Do you receive well or: I receive well.
DER	Out of order.
DF	You are in communication with the called subscriber.
EEE	Error.
NOM	Waiting.
NCH	Subscriber's number has been changed.
NR	My call number is _____ or: indicate your call number.
OCC	Engaged.
OK	Agreed or: do you agree?
R	Received.
RAP	I shall call you back.
RPT	Repeat.
SVP	Please.
TAX	What is the charge? or: the charge is _____ .
W	Words.
WRU	Who is there?
+	End of message.
++	End of last message (i.e. there will be no further messages).

Reference Books

When you are operating a Telex you will need the following books:

Telex Directory (UK)
International Telex Directory
Dictionary (Telex messages are *written,* not spoken, so check up on your spelling!)

Exercise 23

A TELEX MESSAGE

JAKVIN LPOOL

JOHNVAL LDN

ATTENTION MRS K N NORMAN

MAY WE REMIND YOU AGAIN THAT WE HAVE NOT RECEIVED OUR ODRER EEE ORDER 8/543. SVP DELIVER IMMEDIATELY. CFM

14.00

17.1.85

COL 8/543 14.00 17.1.85 ++

JOHNVAL LDN

JAKVIN LPOOL

---

1) What does EEE mean in the message?

2) What does CFM mean?

3) JAKVIN LPOOL is the 'answerback code' of the person to whom the Telex message is being sent. Who is JOHNVAL LDN?

4) What does LPOOL stand for?

5) What is LDN?

6) What does COL mean?

7) What do 14.00 and 17.1.85 mean?

8) What does SVP mean?

9) Why are 14.00 and 17.1.85 included?

10) What does ++ mean?

Sending Messages Automatically

Special equipment may be used on a teleprinter to speed up the sending of messages. This special equipment punches the messages on tape, in code, as the operator types them. This tape can then be fed through another machine called an automatic transmitter, which sends the message again at a speed of about 70 words a minute. There are some automatic transmitters capable of sending messages on punched tape at 120 words a minute.

While the teleprinter operator is not busy (during the first part of the morning, for instance) she would have an opportunity to pre-code messages on tape, which would be ready for sending. Sending pre-coded messages is a way of saving time, as they are transmitted more quickly than an operator is able to send them, so that pre-coded messages are cheaper to send.

Below is part of a message on punched tape. Messages can be understood from the punched tape, provided the code is known or is at hand.

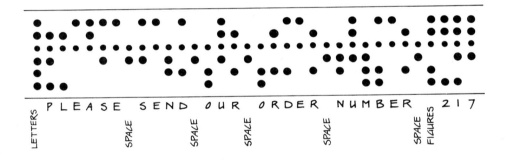

Exercise 24

A PRE-CODED PUNCHED TAPE TELEPRINTER MESSAGE

1) Instead of the word 'please' what could the operator have used to shorten the message?

2) If the operator had not pressed the key for figures on the teleprinter what would have appeared on the message instead of '217'?

3) What would be punched at the beginning of this message, and at the end of it?

4) As the message contains figures, what does the operator do before ending the message?

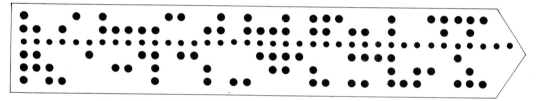

Punched tape code

DECODING

1) Below is part of another pre-coded message. Using the master code, write down what it says.

2) Try working out a coded message, perhaps in reply to the message above.

Punched tape

Exercise 25

TELEX

Write these notes in your folder, filling in the missing words.

1) The machine used for the Telex service is called a _____ .

2) The Telex service is an exchange service similar to the telephone service, and the word TELEX is shortened from the two words _____ _____ .

3) Teleprinters have a keyboard similar to that of a _____ .

4) A teleprinter has a _____ like a telephone _____ at the side of the machine.

5) A teleprinter prints only in capital letters and has no _____ .

6) A message printed on a teleprinter appears on the paper in the machine sending the message and on the paper in the machine receiving the message _____ .

7) A teleprinter is for _____ messages not _____ messages. In this way it is different from the telephone.

8) If a teleprinter is left switched on, messages can be received _____ .

9) In order to receive messages when the office is closed, a supply of _____ must be left in the teleprinter.

10) _____ copies can be printed at the same time on a teleprinter.

11) Answerback codes, Telex numbers and details of charges are all to be found in _____ .

12) Telex messages can be pre-coded by _____ .

13) It saves time to pre-code messages when the teleprinter is having a _____ .

14) On the normal teleprinters a message by punched tape can be sent at approximately _____ words a minute.

15) There are higher speed machines which can send messages at approximately _____ words a minute.

16) It is possible to dial a Telex number direct to most countries in Europe by dialling the code of the country first, and then the number of the subscriber. Numbers of foreign subscribers are not found in the Telex Directory, but the _____ _____ of the countries are included.

17) Some countries outside Europe can be dialled direct by using the codes in the Telex Directory. Calls to these countries are charged for in steps of one minute, and the minimum charge is _____ minute.

18) The main advantage of a Telex message is that it reaches the person for whom it is intended _____ whereas a letter will take at least 24 hours, probably more if not sent first-class.

19) The advantage of a Telex message over a telephone message is that it is a _____ message.

International Telex Calls

The Telex service is available to many countries throughout the world. It is possible to dial direct to New Zealand and to the United States of America, Canada and Europe.

Telex calls to other countries can be made through the London Telex switchboard operator.

International Telex Directories can be bought from the local Telephone Manager's office.

Exercise 26

THE TELEPHONIST'S OR TELEX OPERATOR'S REFERENCE BOOKS

In which book would you look to find the following:

1) The telephone number of an electrician.

2) The dialling code for Helsinki.

3) The telex number for Capetown.

4) The cost of a telephone call (standard rate) to Rome.

5) The telephone number and address of Mr J K Fowler.

6) Details about a trimphone.

7) In which country is the town of Macon.

8) Dialling code for Halifax, England.

Using the Telex Directory

9) What are the 2 digits that indicate the Birmingham Telex centre? _____ .

10) How are Telex calls charged for? _____ .

11) Can calls be dialled direct to the Irish Republic? _____ .

12) What is the signal for line engaged? _____ .

13) What is the number to dial to obtain Telex directory enquiries? _____ .

14) What is the Telex number and answerback code for Land's End Radio Station? _____ .

What are the names, Telex numbers and addresses of the following codes:

15) STV EDINBURGH? _____ .

16) ASSOC NEW LDN? _____ .

17) CG CROMER? _____ .

18) ZOOAN WEYBRIDGE? _____ .

Using the Telephone Directory (The West Midland Telephone Directory has been used here and elsewhere. It is suggested that tutors amend the questions to suit their own local requirements.)

19) What is the address and telephone number of Daniel Robert Food Group Limited? _____ .

20) What is the correct postal address for Croome? _____ .

21) What is the tone for number unobtainable and what does it mean? _____ .

22) What is the name and address of the Secretary of the Worcester Post Office Advisory Committee? _____ .

23) What is the function of the Advisory Committees? _____ .

24) What is the address and telephone number of the MEB Southern Area Office? _____ .

25) What is the number to ring to find out the weather report for Hereford? _____ .

26) What are the telephone numbers of the following hospitals: Ronkswood _____ , Evesham General _____ .

27) How much does the West Midland (Southern Area) Telephone Directory Cost? _____ .

28) Do subscribers have to pay this fee? _____ .

Classified Trade Directory (Yellow Pages)

29) Who do you ring if you wish to place an advertisement in the directory? _____ .

30) How much is an entry in Yellow Pages? _____ .

31) How can you make an emergency call in the dark? _____ .

32) How many squash courts are listed in the directory and where are they? _____ .

What are the names, addresses and telephone numbers of the following:

33) A toy shop in Pershore? _____ .

34) A house builder at Clows Top? _____ .

35) A recreation centre at Reddich? _____ .

36) A Youth Employment Centre in Droitwich? _____ .

The Latest Developments in Teleprinters

The latest teleprinters are equipped with:

- Automatic calling, message editing and storage of messages.
- Memory of about 4 pages of single line spacing (2,500 words).
- Automatic repeating of the same message to several different destinations.
- Facility to hold incoming messages in a memory and re-transmit them.
- Storage in the memory for the most commonly used Telex numbers – forming an internal directory.

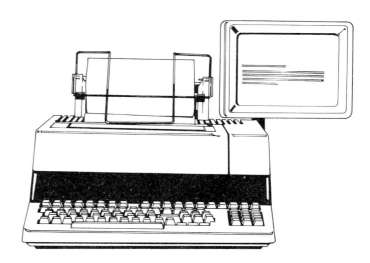

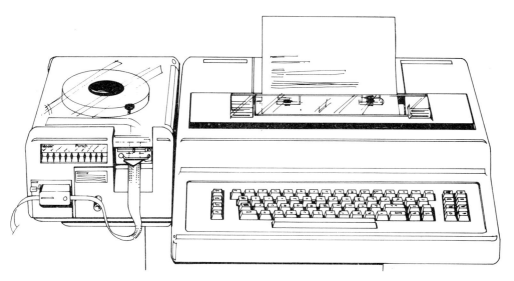

Two modern teleprinters
from British Telecom

79

The appearance of teleprinters has changed. There is no dial and calls are selected from the keyboard; the most comprehensive model now has a keyboard, printer and visual display unit (VDU) with a word processing facility for preparing and editing texts.

It is possible to link computers throughout a firm to the teleprinters, and messages can be transmitted direct from the computers. This is having the effect of dispensing with the need for an operator to sit all day by a teleprinter – most office staff are able to send their own messages.

Teletelex

This reproduces the messages with typewriter-quality texts. Offices will be able to send letters (and receive them) between offices instantly 24 hours a day, automatically.

Teletelex will send an A4 page of text in less than 10 seconds – 30 times faster than Telex. The text can then be stored until required and displayed on a VDU or printed. Many countries will be linked with Teletelex, as well as Europe and the UK.

Telex Plus

This service is available to all Telex users and saves the operator's time by sending the same message to up to 100 correspondents. It costs 10p extra for each UK message and 20p for an overseas message.

The messages are automatically repeated to each Telex number up to 64 times in 24 hours. Normal delivery time is 2 hours in the UK and countries on direct dialling.

Exercise 27

A MORNING IN THE SWITCHBOARD AND TELEPRINTER OFFICE

Copy the following in your folder, filling in the missing words using the list of words that follows.

List of words

Answerback	Punched tape
Telephone credit card	Transfer charge call
Person-to-person	Telephone alphabet
Chronological	Freefone
Alarm	Dictionary
Index	ADC (advise duration and charge)
Telex	

Jayne's job is to look after a small PMBX. In the same office with Jayne is Carole, who is the teleprinter operator. Both girls are able to exchange jobs and look after each other's equipment, when necessary. Jayne prefers operating the switchboard, however, as she enjoys the personal contact with callers. Carole is a very accurate, rapid typist, and likes operating the teleprinter.

At the side of Jayne's PMBX is a shelf on which she keeps her telephone directories, classified trade directories, Dialling Code Booklets, an atlas, and a _____ . In front of her, on the wall, is a large copy of the _____ which helps her to spell out awkward words, and near at hand is her alphabetical _____ of frequently used numbers, both external and internal.

Carole has a directory of _____ numbers and _____ codes on her bookshelf. Carole shares the atlas with Jayne. In addition, Carole needs a dictionary occasionally, as the messages she sends are printed, not spoken ones.

Jayne's first query on this particular morning was from the Typing Pool. One of the typists wanted to telephone to Edinburgh to ask about her father who was in hospital there. She was willing to pay for the call. The firm's rule was 'no personal calls', but exceptions were made for emergencies. Jayne asked the British Telecom telephone operator for the Edinburgh number, and also asked her to ring back at the end of the call and tell her what it would cost. The name for the call Jayne asked for was an _____ call.

The Sales Manager was worried about the state of the roads in Northumberland and also wanted to know what the weather was going to be like there in the next 24 hours. Jayne dialled the number for the telephone services, which give this information, and also arranged for the British Telecom operator to ring the Sales Manager at his home the following morning at 6 am. She asked the British Telecom operator, in fact, for an _____ call.

Meanwhile, Carole's teleprinter had been busy receiving messages, and these had to be distributed to the various departments as quickly as possible. At about 10 am a message came through from Paris in French, and Carole took this one to the Export Department, where one of the secretaries spoke and wrote fluent French, and was able to translate the message. While Carole was away from her machine, Jayne kept an eye on it. There was no problem about incoming messages as these were printed automatically, as long as the teleprinter was left switched on, but messages marked 'urgent' had to be taken to their destinations without delay. Fortunately, there were no urgent messages during Carole's absence, and Jayne was able to concentrate on her switchboard, which was busy, because the firm had been operating an advertising campaign for some weeks, during which members of the public were encouraged to telephone the firm and ask for free samples to be sent to them. There was no charge for these calls which were made to a special _____ number. Several of these calls had been made already this morning, and Jayne had to be very careful about making a note of the caller's name and address on the telephone message pad she always had to hand.

One of the minor queries Jayne had to deal with during the morning was whether to accept a call from one of the firm's sales representatives, who had some important information for the Sales Manager, but had no change for the call-box. It was against the firm's rules to accept _____ calls because any employee who was likely to telephone the firm frequently had his own _____ , and all he had to do was to give the number of this card to the British Telecom telephone operator, who then connected him to the number he wanted. However, Jayne used her initiative by accepting the call and put the sales representative through – he sounded rather desperate!

A _____ call came through for the Safety Officer during the morning. This was not at all unusual, as he was often out in various parts of the factory, and difficult to locate. Jayne asked the caller if he would like the Safety Officer to ring him back later, but the caller said he would prefer to wait. A _____ call is not charged for until the caller actually speaks to the person he has asked for.

Carole was having a quiet morning, so she used the time to put some messages on _____ for transmission later. This meant that they would be sent more quickly than Carole could type and thus cost less. Telex calls are paid for by units of time and distance, in the same way as telephone calls.

Jayne had a typewriter by her switchboard, and typed out the messages for people who were out. She kept a carbon copy of each message, in case of queries later, and filed the copies in _____ order.

Both Carole and Jayne had very important jobs to do, because the first person callers spoke to was Jayne, and both she and Carole had to make sure any messages received were passed on as quickly as possible. In addition, Carole had to type her Telex messages very accurately and be careful to dial the right Telex number. Mistakes cost money on the teleprinter as well as on the telephone.

Answer the following questions on this passage.

1) What does PMBX mean?

2) Why does Carole have no personal contact with callers?

3) Why would an atlas be useful to *both* Carole and Jayne?

4) A teleprinter will continue to receive messages automatically, even though it has been left unattended, provided it is switched on. What else must be done before leaving a teleprinter to make sure that messages are received?

5) Why did Jayne file copies of telephone messages, and why didn't she file them in alphabetical order?

CHAPTER 8

Telemessages

Telemessages and their Cost

Telemessages are a British Telecom service. They can be sent only by telephone or Telex, but not handed in at a post office.

To send by telephone – dial 100 (190 in London) and ask for 'Telemessage'.

To send by Telex – consult your Telex directory for the correct number to dial. Type TELEMESSAGE two lines down from your answerback number (see page 71) followed by the address and your message.

The Telemessage service operates to the United States of America and will be extended to other countries over the next few years. The American version of the Telemessage is known as a Mailgram.

The cost for a Telemessage is £3.50 for 50 words (but only £3 before noon). There is no charge for the name and address. The maximum number of words which can be sent is 350. After the first 50 words, £1.50 per 50 words is charged.

There is a specially reduced rate for Telemessages which are sent to a number of different addresses with identical messages. Freefone 2741 gives the details (call to be made during normal working hours). The service to ask for is 'Multiple Telemessage'.

There are Telemessage greetings cards available for special occasions such as weddings, christenings, anniversaries. These cost an extra 50p, but are supplied free with every Telemessage sent before noon on Mondays to Fridays.

Telemessages are delivered by the postman the day after sending, by first post. There is no delivery on a Sunday.

Telemessages are delivered in a bright yellow envelope with three blue stripes across.

A copy of the Telemessage you have dictated will be sent to you, if you ask for 'sender's copy'. A charge of 75p is made.

Special occasion cards

Baby for births

Telemessage envelope

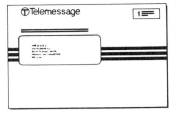

Bright yellow envelope with blue stripes

Sending a Telemessage

It is obviously necessary to write out a Telemessage first, before dictating it to the operator, when it is to be sent by telephone.

After drafting, count the number of words in the message, and if the total is more than 50, check to see if unnecessary words could be eliminated to avoid paying an extra £1.50.

Finally, dial 100 (190 in London) and ask for 'Telemessage'. When the operator answers, dictate the name, address and message. You will be asked for your own telephone number. The cost of the Telemessage will be added (plus VAT) to your telephone bill.

ⓉTelemessage

British
TELECOM

BMA1107 LLY6822 PJJ0008 P99 0505PERS

24 OCT 1983/1140

43 Cooper Street
Studley
Warwicks   B80 7BR

TELEMESSAGE   GREETINGS-A
MRS T GREEN
30 LONE ROAD
PERSHORE
WORCS

24 October 1983

Dear Sandy

This is a practice TELEMESSAGE, as a demonstration

Please keep it for me until Friday

Love to all

Gran

TO REPLY BY TELEMESSAGE SEE REVERSE SIDE

Exercise 28

TELEMESSAGES

Write these notes in your folder, filling in the missing words and phrases.

1) Telemessages can be sent only by _____ or telephone.

2) Telemessages can be sent to any place in the British Isles and also to _____ .

3) The cost of a Telemessage is _____ for 50 words.

4) The maximum number of words which can be sent in a Telemessage is _____ .

5) The cost for the first 50 words is _____ .

6) After the first 50 words _____ per 50 words is charged.

7) 'Multiple Telemessage' is the service for Telemessages to be sent to a number of different addresses with _____ messages.

8) A special greetings Telemessage can be sent for no extra charge _____ _____ on Mondays to Fridays. At other times it is _____ .

9) Telemessages are delivered on the _____ by _____ post. There is _____ on a Sunday.

10) Telemessage envelopes are _____ yellow with three _____ stripes across.

11) A copy of a Telemessage will be sent to the sender, if 'Sender's copy' is asked for. A charge of _____ is made.

12) Before a Telemessage is sent by telephone it is necessary to _____ _____ .

13) In London dial _____ for Telemessage service; outside London dial _____ .

14) The cost of a Telemessage sent by telephone is added to your _____ bill.

Exercise 29

Below are some messages which are to be sent by Telemessage. Re-write them in a suitable form, and work out the cost of each one:

1) Miss Elaine Harrison, 321 Strawberry Fields, Newtonville NC5 8KB.

Your interview arranged for 14 January is cancelled. Please attend same time 21 January and confirm.

Personnel Manager Spanmech Engineering Co Lambrove Trading Estate Cardiff.

2) (This is a greetings Telemessage which will be sent during the cheaper period for Telemessages.)

John Lane 2 High Street Freshley Warwickshire F80 7RB.

Congratulations on passing your exam. Love from grandad and gran.

3) David Gartside 88 Park Crescent Abberley Greatstone West Midlands G61 WM1.

Strike has been settled. Report for work Monday 9 January 0800.

Jones Works Manager Spanmech Engineering Co Lambrove Trading Estate Cardiff.

4) Miss Elizabeth Styles 437 Bristol Road Bridgetown Liverpool LP1 3HB.

The party planned for Thursday 7 January has been postponed because Tim has 'flu. Another party is planned for a later date but nothing certain has been arranged yet. Tim will be writing as soon as he is well enough. The message is from Tim's mother Mrs Warley of 88 Hamilton Drive Anychester 4AN 8GO.

5) Messrs Garner & Richards Norfolk House Bothampton 3BT 4RT.

The message is from the switchboard operator at Messrs Garner & Richards who is unable to go to work because she has laryngitis and has lost her voice. She hopes to be able to return in about three days' time. Her name is Mrs Lynne Brooks and her address is 5 Upper Cranbrook Road Bothampton.

International Telegrams

Telegrams may be sent overseas by dialling 100 and asking for 'International Telegrams'. It is no longer possible to send them from a Post Office.

Coded Telegrams

British Telecom allows telegrams to be sent in code, or cipher. Some countries (e.g. USSR) will not allow coded telegrams to be received. This is not only a way of sending messages which only the person receiving them can understand, but it is a way of cutting down on the cost of telegrams. Journalists sending reports from abroad use a special code. Hotels also have a code (though it may not be known in small hotels in out-of-the-way places). Here it is:

Accommodation required	Code word
1 room with one bed	ALBA
1 room with two beds	ARAB
1 room with three beds	ABEC
Two rooms with one bed in each	BELAB

Two rooms with two beds in each				BONAD
Three rooms with one bed in each				CIROC
Three rooms with two beds in each				CADUF
Child's bed in room				KIND
Sitting room				SAL
Private bathroom				BAT
Room with a good view				BELVU
Very quiet room				TRANQ
Very good quality of rooms				BEST
Good quality of rooms				BON
Simple quality of rooms				PLAIN
Air-conditioned room				ACOND
Length of stay: one night				PASS
Length of stay: several days				STOP
Lock-up garage for one car				BOX
Ordinary garage for one car				GARAG
Meet at station				TRAIN
Meet at port				QUAI
Meet at airport				AERO
Meet at motorbus terminus from airport				AEROZ
Cancel rooms previously booked				ANUL

Arriving	Morning	Afternoon	Evening	Night
Sunday	POBAB	POLYP	RABAL	RANUV
Monday	POCUN	POMEL	RACEX	RAPIN
Tuesday	PODYL	PONOW	RADOK	RAQAF
Wednesday	POGOK	POPUF	RAFYG	RATYZ
Thursday	POHIX	PORIK	RAGUB	RAVUP
Friday	POJAW	POSEV	RAHIV	RAWOW
Saturday	POKUZ	POVAH	RAJOD	RAXAB
This morning	POWYS			
This afternoon		POZUM		
This evening			RAMYK	
Tonight				RAZAM

Exercise 30

CODED TELEGRAMS

Change the following telegrams into the International Telegraph Code:

1) Hotel Splendid Paris France.
One single room; arriving Sunday morning; meet at station 10.30; staying one night. James Saunders.

2) Embassy Hotel Florence Italy.
Arriving Monday evening thirtieth; staying several days; one room with two beds and bathroom; meet at airport twenty-two hundred hours. Carole Dawson

3) Hotel Victoria Monaco.
One double room with child's bed and lock-up garage for car; arriving Friday night fifth June; staying several nights. Ian Mann.

4) Grand Hotel Oslo Norway.
Arriving Tuesday afternoon third July; very quiet room with bathroom and one single bed; staying one night. Peter Haigh.

5) Europa Hotel Salzburg Austria.
Arriving Wednesday morning eleventh; staying several days; ordinary parking for car; two rooms with one bed in each room; simple quality of rooms. Lynne Harrison

6) Baltic Hotel Copenhagen Denmark.
Arriving Saturday morning 0900 first September; meet at motorbus terminus from airport; two rooms with two beds in each; private bathroom; staying one night. John Moore.

7) Cancel rooms previously booked; arriving Friday afternoon twenty-first May; three rooms with one bed in each and one sitting-room; quiet and with good view; staying several days. Telegram to: Paradise Bay Hotel, Malta. From: Sunspeed Travel.

8) Arriving Friday night 2300; one room with one bed and one child's bed; airconditioned room; meet at port; staying one night. Telegram to: Rock Hotel, Gibraltar. From Mrs Jayne Ross.

9) Hotel Ricco Cascais Portugal.
Arriving this afternoon; staying several nights; one room with two beds; very good quality of room; lock-up garage for one car; private bathroom. Hinchcliffe.

10) Hotel Paso Majorca Spain.
Arriving Tuesday evening 1900; staying for one night; meet at port; three rooms with two beds in each room; simple quality of rooms. Worldwide Travel Agency.

11) Work out the cost of the telegrams in Questions 1–10: (a) when in code, (b) in full; assuming that the charge is 11p per word plus 70p surcharge.

Decipher the following telegrams:

12) RAMYK TWENTIETH STOP AERO NINETEEN HUNDRED HOURS ANUL TRANQ

13) BELAB TRANQ PASS BOX RAWOW

14) ANUL RACEX THIRTIETH AUGUST ALBA BAT STOP GARAG

15) RAFYG STOP BOX BAT KIND ABEC

16) ARAB POBAB QUAI PASS ACOND SAL ALBA

PART 2   RECEPTION SKILLS

CHAPTER 9

Reception Duties in a Small Firm

Reception Duties

Where a firm is too small to justify employing a receptionist in a separate reception area, many office workers will include among their duties the reception of occasional visitors to the firm. It is important to attend to callers promptly, pleasantly and politely. A notice over a bell stating curtly 'Ring and wait' in a draughty lobby without even a chair, is a bleak way to greet a stranger; worse still, is leaving him to stand in the lobby (after asking his name and who he wants to see) for a further wait. Anyone treated in this way could be forgiven for departing forthwith!

Receiving an occasional visitor to a firm should be the job of one or two of the office staff and they should be trained to do the job efficiently – reception should not be left vaguely to anyone who happens to be passing the main entrance.

Guidelines for Receiving Visitors

A visitor's bell just inside the main entrance is a good idea, as it allows a caller to draw attention to his presence at once. Nearby should be several chairs so that visitors may sit while they wait. A notice near the bell should be worded 'Please Ring for Attention and Take a Seat While You Wait'.

A telephone extension in the lobby is very useful, as a short call to the secretary of the person the caller wishes to see will avoid any further waiting.

The person responsible for attending to callers should respond *at once* to the bell (even though she may be in the middle of a job requiring all her attention, or it is the fourth time the bell has rung in the last hour).

Callers should be greeted as follows:
'Good morning/afternoon. May I help you?'

followed by:
'What is your name, please'.
'Who would you like to see?' and 'Have you an appointment?'

If the answer to the last question is 'Yes' then a telephone call can be made to check that the person the caller wishes to see is free and the caller escorted to the appropriate office.

91

If the answer is 'No' then a polite suggestion can be made that the caller could perhaps make an appointment, and call again; some firms have a policy of never seeing callers without appointments, in order to save wasting time listening to the sales talk of representatives trying to obtain orders for their products or services. A check with the secretary of the person the caller has asked for should be made, for her to deal with the matter.

Escorting Visitors

Walk in front of the visitor, when showing him to the office he requires, as he will, in all probability, be a stranger to the building, and will not know which way to go. Knock on the door of the office, when you reach it, and after hearing 'Come in' or 'Enter', open the door, stand on one side and announce the visitor:

'Mr Black, this is Mr Green, from Millard & Perkins Ltd. He has an appointment to see you at 10.30 (or whatever the time is).'

It is necessary to announce the visitor's name and to introduce him, because if you do not, the manager will look up and possibly see a total stranger standing there, who could be anyone. Then close the door quietly, and depart.

If a caller cannot be seen at once, for any reason, apologise, ask him to sit down (if he has not already done so) and go back to him at intervals to reassure him he has not been forgotten.

The above reception procedure is simple, helpful and makes a caller feel welcome. It must be accompanied by a pleasant manner and an attitude of polite interest.

Exercise 31

RECEPTION OF VISITORS IN A SMALL FIRM

Write these notes in your folder, filling in the missing words and phrases.

1) It is important to attend to callers promptly, pleasantly and _____ .

2) Receiving an occasional visitor to a firm should be the job of one or two office staff and they should be trained to _____ .

3) There should be several _____ near the visitor's bell.

4) A notice near a visitor's bell should be worded: _____ .

5) The person responsible for attending to visitors should respond _____ to the bell.

6) Callers should be greeted by saying: _____ , followed by: _____ and _____ ; finally by: _____ .

7) If caller has no appointment, a polite suggestion could be made that _____ .

8) A check with the secretary of the person the caller without an appointment wishes to see could be made for her _____ .

9) When escorting visitors _____ in front.

10) It is necessary to announce _____ and to _____ him because if you do not, the manager will look up and see a _____ standing there who could be anyone.

11) Finally, close the _____ quietly and depart.

12) If caller cannot be seen at once, for any reason, _____ , ask him to sit down (if he has not already done so) and go back to him at _____ to reassure him he has not been _____ .

CHAPTER 10

The Receptionist in a Large Firm

The Receptionist

All large firms (and organisations such as universities, hospitals, colleges, local authorities) have receptionists. In addition, many small firms find their services useful – estate agents, accountants, and solicitors, for example. Receptionists for doctors, dentists, hairdressers and hotels have to be specially trained, because they need some basic knowledge of the kind of attention their patients or customers require, and this book does not attempt to cover their duties; it deals with general reception, which applies to the majority of commercial offices.

Duties

The receptionist's main job is to look after the visitors to a firm. She will, however, have time during the day when there are no callers, to do other work. She may:

- Type
- Operate a switchboard
- File
- Give out brochures and handbooks issued by her firm
- Open and arrange for distribution of mail; receive parcels, and registered or recorded delivery mail
- Help with making tea or coffee for visitors – as it is essential that the reception desk is never left unattended, many firms have vending machines so that callers are able to help themselves to refreshments
- Be able to give simple first aid, when necessary.

Alternatively, there may be two receptionists – the head receptionist and her deputy – so that the reception desk is never left unmanned.

Visitors to a firm must never be kept waiting unnecessarily. They may go elsewhere if they are, and not return. Valuable business could be lost to the firm.

Exercise 32

THE RECEPTIONIST'S DUTIES

Write these notes in your folder, filling in the missing words and phrases.

1) The receptionist may have time during slack periods to do other work. This could include:

   typing
   operating a switchboard
   filing
   giving out brochures
   _____
   giving simple first aid when necessary
   making tea or coffee for visitors.

2) It is essential that the reception desk is never _____ and many firms have vending machines so that callers are able to help themselves to _____ .

3) Some firms have two receptionists – the head receptionist and her _____ so that the reception desk is _____ .

4) Visitors to a firm must never be kept _____ unnecessarily. They may _____ and not return. Valuable _____ could be _____ to the firm.

Appearance

As the receptionist is often the first person a visitor to a firm sees, her appearance is very important, as he forms his first impressions of the firm from her. She should be neat, smart, well-groomed (hair, nails and make-up) and look attractively competent.

GOOD GROOMING

This includes hair, complexion, hands, nails and teeth, as well as attention to clothes.

Hair should be shining clean and styled so that it does not quickly become untidy during even the busiest times. Long hair should be piled on top of the head, or tied back, not left hanging loose so that it sweeps the reception desk or obscures the view. Punk hair-styles are not suitable for anyone in a firm who may be seen by the public – illogical though it may be, people are judged, in the first instance, by their appearance, and an outrageous hair-style in all colours of the rainbow gives an impression of irresponsibility.

Unsuitable hairstyle for a receptionist

A simple daily routine which can be followed each morning is a great help and preferable to applying elaborate make-up one day and having to skip it the next because of lack of time. Making up at work is not a good idea – far better to arrive relaxed in the knowledge that you can face the most critical eye immediately.

DAILY ROUTINE

Leave as little as is reasonably possible for the morning. Bathe or shower the night before, so that an application of cleansing cream or lotion and a quick wash is all that is necessary before breakfast. Check deodorant and re-apply if necessary. Brush and tidy hair. After breakfast, brush teeth and apply simple make-up. Use a light toilet water rather than perfume – it is less obtrusive.

Shoes (polished the evening before) should not be allowed to look 'down-at-heel'. Have them repaired promptly.

It is a sensible idea to decide on an outfit the night before and put clothes ready, including matching tights and shoes, so that there is no last minute scramble to find the right article.

Keep a needle, cotton and scissors at work with make-up kit, for the occasional repair.

Nails and hands. These are very much in evidence in reception work. Nail varnish should be chip-free to look attractive. Touch it up the night before if it is beginning to peel, or remove it altogether. Three coats of varnish and a final coat of clear protective varnish should last almost a week. Nails should be reasonable in length – very long nails are a hazard on a typewriter – far better to settle for shorter nails with a reasonable chance of them remaining all the same length.

Once a week, thoroughly manicure nails, after removing varnish. Push back cuticles gently with cream cuticle remover and massage hand cream around base of nails. Give your nails a 'rest' occasionally from nail varnish, as it tends to make them split. If you bite your nails when under stress and cannot stop the habit, set yourself small targets of a day, three days, then a week, without biting. Their growth will give you encouragement to continue.

96

Use a good hand cream regularly (after washing your hands), and always last thing at night. Try to keep your hands out of detergents – use protective gloves.

Feet need almost as much attention as hands, although they are not 'on show' to the same extent. Rub a hand cream over them after a bath, especially around heels. Dry carefully between toes and keep nails short – cut them straight across. The occasional corn (which can be very painful) should be treated by a chiropodist. Clean, ladder-free tights should be worn daily.

Teeth should be brushed after every meal, and (most important) last thing at night. Keep a toothbrush and toothpaste at work and brush after lunch. This helps to freshen your mouth. Bad breath (halitosis) is a condition most people would hesitate to mention to even their closest friend, and thus the offender is often unaware of it. Regular six-monthly visits to a dentist, combined with brushing (as above) should ensure a healthy mouth. Avoid eating onions, curry, or garlic at lunch-time, as these are unpleasant 'second-hand' to other people. Heavy smokers can cause offence, too, with nicotine-laden breath.

OUTFIT

The right clothes give you confidence. An outfit should be comfortable when it is going to be worn all day, and skirts and trousers which feel tight in the morning will be even more so by mid-afternoon.

In a centrally heated building outfits can be lightweight, even in winter. A fine wool skirt and matching or toning jacket with a blouse in

polyester/cotton is ideal. Changes can be made with varying blouses and jackets. White collars and cuffs on a dark dress are smart, but the collar and cuffs must be detachable for frequent washing, so that they always look fresh.

In summer, cotton or a cotton and polyester mixture is comfortable to wear in hot weather but don't forget that a chilly summer's day can be very stark when the central heating has been turned off, and all you have with you is what you are wearing – a sleeveless cotton dress. Keep a spare jacket at work for emergency use. A spare pair of shoes to wear in hot weather is useful too – sandals or mules are cool and comfortable.

Receptionists are not always female – an outfit for a man would be jacket, trousers (linen in summer) with collar and tie, or polo necked sweater if weather is wintry.

Jewellery should be kept to a minimum – small stud earrings, a brooch, one or two rings at most, and a wristwatch. Leave anything really precious at home. Long necklaces and dangling bracelets can be dangerous when using a typewriter or other office machinery (e.g. duplicators) and are better worn after work.

Exercise 33

THE RECEPTIONIST'S APPEARANCE

Write these notes in your folder, filling in the missing words and phrases.

1) The receptionist's appearance is very important, as she is the _____ a visitor to a firm will see.

2) She should be neat, smart, well-groomed and look _____ .

3) A suitable hair-style for long hair would be _____ or _____ .

4) Elaborate make-up one day and _____ the next because of lack of time is not a good idea – a simple daily routine which can be followed each morning is a _____ .

5) A receptionist's hands are very much in _____ .

6) Nails should be thoroughly manicured once a _____ .

7) Feet need almost as much _____ as hands, although they are not 'on show' to the same extent.

8) The correct word for 'bad breath' is _____ .

9) This can be prevented by _____ combined with _____ .

98

10) An outfit should be _____ when it is going to be worn all day.

11) All large firms have centrally heated offices and it is not necessary to wear _____ clothes indoors, in winter.

12) Trousers, well-pressed and part of a _____ outfit look smart in winter.

13) A cool dress in summer with a _____ is useful.

14) An outfit for a male receptionist could be a jacket, trousers (linen in summer) with _____ and _____ or polo necked sweater if weather is _____ .

15) Jewellery worn to work should be simple and _____ .

16) Jewellery which might cause accidents includes _____ or necklaces.

The Receptionist's Voice

The receptionist's voice is particularly important; it should be pleasant and clear. Some visitors may be foreigners and have difficulty understanding English.

The Ideal Receptionist

Reception work is not suitable for shy people. A receptionist must be able to get on easily with strangers.

Generally speaking, an ideal receptionist should be aged 20 or over. She will have sufficient experience by then to be both confident and efficient at her job.

Types of Caller

CALLERS WHO HAVE MADE APPOINTMENTS might include:

- Applicants to be interviewed for vacant jobs
- Sales representatives
- Businessmen from other firms attending meetings
- Visitors from other firms, both in the UK and from overseas.

CALLERS WITHOUT APPOINTMENTS could be:

- People enquiring about vacancies for jobs
- Customers who have come to complain about the firm's goods
- Sales representatives hoping to see the chief buyer or a member of his staff.

REGULAR CALLERS NORMALLY WITHOUT APPOINTMENTS

- Postmen
- Security van drivers delivering cash for wages
- Delivery men from other firms
- Roadline delivery men
- British Rail (BR) delivery men
- Window cleaners, telephone disinfectant service staff, suppliers of pot plants
- People delivering letters and parcels from other firms by hand.

UNEXPECTED CALLERS WITHOUT APPOINTMENTS

These should be asked politely if they would like to write in for one. If they refuse to leave without making an appointment, the receptionist should telephone the secretary of the person the caller is hoping to see, and ask her when an appointment can be made.

Occasionally, callers insist on seeing the person they want without having made an appointment, and refuse to leave. This is where all the tact and patience of the receptionist is required. She should emphasise to the caller that the person he insists on seeing is at an important meeting and will not be available for several hours, or, alternatively, that he has gone to a meeting at another firm. Finally, if the caller still refuses to go, the receptionist should telephone the firm's security police, who will come and escort the caller out, but this is only as a last resort and, if the receptionist knows her job, should not be necessary.

Callers who have to wait because of an unavoidable delay should be looked after in the reception area, offered tea or coffee, and reassured from time to time that they have not been forgotten.

Copy.

What to do if all else fails!

Greeting Callers and Dealing with Visiting Cards

Using a person's name is friendly and makes a caller feel welcome. The receptionist's name should be either on a brooch pinned to her dress or on a stand in front of her, so that callers can see her name at a glance and use it at once. The receptionist's first question to a caller should be to ask his or her name and then use it. Many businessmen have business visiting cards and will give one to the receptionist. Business visiting cards have the caller's name, the caller's firm, firm's address and telephone number, and occasionally his home address and telephone number printed on them. Sometimes a card also gives information about the firm's products. The information on the business visiting card saves the receptionist asking the caller a great many questions. It also helps her to introduce the caller to anyone in the firm who may not know him.

Usually, business visiting cards (callers' cards) are left with the receptionist and she files them away in alphabetical order of the firms' names. Then, next time a caller comes whom the receptionist recognises, she is able to look up his business visiting card and refer to it for information.

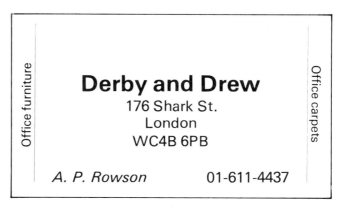

A business card

A card index box is useful for filing business visiting cards. They should be glued or taped to an index card, which makes them easier to handle and find. Business visiting cards form a useful record of callers and can be referred to for names and addresses for sending out advertising material.

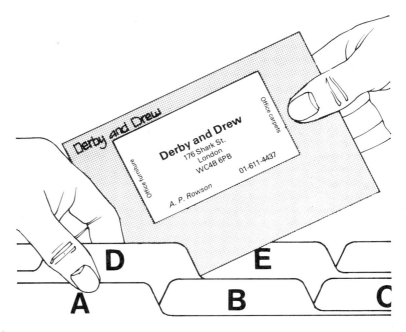

Filing a business card

Note that the card above is being filed under the name of the firm and not the name of the caller. This is because firms rarely change their names, whereas their employees frequently change their jobs, so it is easier for a receptionist to refer to a firm rather than to someone employed by a firm.

Using Names

It always sounds friendlier to use people's names. Callers are able to see at a glance what the receptionist's name is if she has it on a brooch pinned to her dress, or on a stand in front of her, on her desk.

A receptionist can quickly find out the name of a caller and his firm by asking for his visiting card.

The Receptionist's Desk

In some firms the receptionist may have a switchboard to look after. In all firms she will have two telephones: one for internal calls and the other for external calls. The latest telephones, however, incorporate external and internal lines in one instrument. She may also have a typewriter and a filing cabinet. She will also have her own records, consisting of:

- An index of callers' cards
- Records of callers (callers' register and appointments book)
- A staff 'in and out' book
- Lost Property Book.

Her name may be on her desk in front of her (or on a brooch which she pins to her dress).

She will have a plan of the firm on the wall behind her.

She will also have an organisation chart on the wall. This gives the names of the directors and managers of her firm.

The receptionist's desk should be near to the main entrance of a firm, so that callers are able to find it easily. The picture below shows how an efficient, well-organised receptionist has planned her desk and office equipment.

An efficient receptionist who is well-organised. The VDU may be used instead of an appointments book

103

Exercise 34

THE RECEPTIONIST'S RESPONSIBILITIES

Fill in the missing words and answer the questions.

1) The receptionist's *main* job is to _____ after callers at a firm.

2) Why is a receptionist important to a firm?

3) What effect might a 'couldn't-care-less' attitude have on callers?

4) Why is it important that a receptionist is well-informed about her firm's layout, products and staff?

5) What are the three different types of callers?

6) What sort of callers who call at a firm regularly would not normally have appointments?

7) Where should a receptionist have her name displayed?

8) Why is it important to use a person's name as soon as possible?

9) What is the correct procedure for dealing with a caller who arrives without an appointment?

10) The receptionist may be given a caller's card from which she can learn the _____ .

11) Other information on a caller's card may be _____ .

12) The receptionist will file callers' cards (business visiting cards) in alphabetical order of _____ names.

13) What are the two important uses of business visiting cards?

14) What information does an organisation chart give?

15) Receptionists are employed by doctors, dentists, hotels, colleges, opticians and veterinaries. What is the ideal age for a receptionist and what type of person should she be?

16) Where should the receptionist's desk be situated?

17) What is the correct way to look after a caller who may have to wait in the Reception Area for a rather long time?

18) Look at the advertisements opposite and answer the questions about them.

Job Vacancies for Receptionists

Young Responsible School/College Leaver

required as general administrative assistant.

Duties include: filing, photo copying, some typing and general office duties. Some relief reception work.

Minimum of R.S.A. Stage 1 Typing or equivalent required.

Preferably aged between 16 and 20.

Contact:

We are a successful group of Timber and Builders Merchants situated in various locations throughout South Wales and the Midlands.

TELEPHONIST/ RECEPTIONIST

We have an immediate vacancy for Telephonist/Receptionist, with a cheerful disposition, to work at our Group's Head Office in Studley.

The successful applicant will be working with the latest B.T. switchboard equipment and preferably be able to type.

An attractive salary is offered together with the usual large company benefits.

Applications should be made, in writing, together with details of previous experience to:

The Company Secretary

JUNIOR TELEPHONIST RECEPTIONIST REQUIRED. Training Given. Tel.

SWITCHBOARD OPERATOR/RECEPTIONIST
18-50 years

To work for a Rubber and Plastics engineers near to Stratford upon Avon. Operating a P.A.B.X. 7x30 switchboard, copytyping, receiving and directing clients. A knowledge of Telex useful. Ideal candidates should have relevant experience, good appearance and personality, with the ability to work under pressure. Excellent working conditions. Pay dependent on age, qualifications and experience. Write with full C.V. by 7th November to:

Telephonist/Receptionist

A vacancy exists in an export office for a telephonist/receptionist.

Small PMBX 5 x 25 Switchboard. Varied work with some other general office duties. A less than fully qualified applicant with the right attitude would be considered.

Hours 9 a.m. to 5.15 p.m. Monday to Friday with one hour for lunch. Salary negotiable, depending on age and experience.

In the first instance, telephone:

FULL TIME
RECEPTIONIST
REQUIRED

Smart, with typing and general office duty experience. Used to working as a team effort — sometimes pressure. Able to drive. Good with people, unflappable. This position offers variety and interest. Please state age and previous experience. Salary negotiable, Holidays flexible.

Apply in writing, including telephone number before 21st December.

R700

SECRETARY/RECEPTIONIST/ ASSISTANT

This interesting and varied appointment has, unexpectedly, become vacant. I am looking for someone with at least RSA grade II typing, preferably some knowledge of general insurance (particularly personal lines) and office routine.

Once trained you will be working much of the time on your own initiative. An attractive salary will be offered depending on age, ability and experience.

This is a career, rather than a job opportunity. Interviews will be held soon. Please apply in writing to:-

B700

RECEPTIONIST

A Bromsgrove Engineering Company has a vacancy for a receptionist, preferably a school leaver. Duties would involve switchboard, Telex and reception. Ability to type essential. Apply giving details of age, qualifications, experience and salary expected, to:

Exercise 35

JOB VACANCIES FOR RECEPTIONISTS

Look at the advertisements on page 105 and answer the following questions.

1) Which of the eight vacancies do you think would be suitable for a school/college leaver without any experience?

2) Which of these vacancies would appeal particularly to you?

3) Do any of the advertisements mention a definite salary?

4) How many ask for typing?

5) What does the expression 'working under pressure' mean?

6) What does the expression 'use your own initiative' mean?

7) What does the expression 'holidays flexible' mean?

8) Explain the abbreviation 'CV'.

9) What is a 'PABX'?

10) What does 'unflappable' mean?

CHAPTER 11

The Receptionist's Records

Callers' Register

One of the record books which the receptionist looks after is the *callers' register*. All callers to a firm sign this, with the exception of such people as postmen and delivery men.

A callers' register shows the name of the caller, his firm, or his home address, the time he arrived, who he saw in the firm, and whether he made a further appointment. Overleaf is a page from a callers' register, showing the callers at a firm on the morning of 21 November 198–.

Under the heading 'Action Taken' are details about callers who arrived without appointments. This column shows that the usual way to deal with such callers is to ask them to write in for an appointment.

Occasionally, a caller refuses to leave without either seeing the person he wants, or having made an appointment. In either of these cases, the receptionist should telephone through to the secretary concerned and ask to make an appointment.

Exercise 36

CALLERS' REGISTER

Now rule up a copy of the callers' register page, leaving it blank except for headings, and fill in with the following information. Use today's date.

1) Mr T G Robertson came at 1000 to see Mr H Roberts, Production Manger. Mr Robertson had an appointment for that time. His firm is: Messrs Barnet and Baker, Grosvenor Rd, Whitlock.

2) Mr James Brookes of S & J Electronics came at 1030 to see Mr J Ellis, Managing Director. He made another appointment on his way out for the same time and day next week.

3) Miss D Steele, 56 Forest Row, Bromyard, enquired about a vacancy in the Typing Pool and was asked to write to the Personnel Manager, Mr M Steele. She arrived at 1100.

4) Mrs G Forbes came at 1110 to see Miss B Burton, Typing Pool Supervisor. She had an appointment for 1115. Mrs Forbes' address is: Croft Cottage, Alemouth.

CALLERS' REGISTER

DATE 19_	NAME OF CALLER	CALLER'S FIRM OR HOME ADDRESS	TIME OF ARRIVAL	SEEN BY	ACTION TAKEN
Nov. 21	L. M. Parkins	J. Mann + Co. Ltd.	09 00	K. Jones - Buyer	
	Mrs H. Simms	18 Hilary Ave. Worcester	09 45	No appointment	Writing to Personnel Officer with details.
	B. N. Vines	Carson Engineering	09 50	Personnel Manager	
	Miss A. B. Tomkins	44 Scott Cresc. Evesham	10 00	No appointment	Personnel Man's assistant seeing her on 28/11 at 10.00
	Miss K. Lyons	219 Lake Ave. Worcester	10 30	Personnel Manager	
	F. Parkins	Pearson's Export Co.	10 35	Accounts Dept.	Made further appointment to see Chief Cashier 23/11
	Mrs. A. Drew	Wilchester Technical College	11 00	Personnel Manager	
	P. Lestor	Rejecta Paper Co.	11 05	No appointment	Appointment made to see K. Jones's assistant
	J. R. Smart	39 Market Place	11 20	No appointment	Writing to Production Manager with details
	Mrs. W. Moxon	Ofice Equipment Suppliers	11 30	Miss B. Burton Typing Pool Supervisor	
	Miss T. Baker	89 The Grove, Droitwich	12 00	No appointment	Writing to miss Burton with details
	B. M. Townsend	Bellevue Car Hire Co.	12 30	Transport officer	

108

5) Mr S Holmes, Mr A Simpson and Miss V Keene arrived at 1130. They all had appointments to see Mr H Long, the Sales Manager. All three callers were from Twist, Swindle & Dunnem, Chartered Accountants, Wordsworth Avenue, Champton.

6) Mr J Long called to see the Sales Manager and was asked to write for an appointment. Mr Long arrived at 1135. His address is: 12 Wood Lane, Martash.

7) Mrs Y Doughty, 18 Arden St, Earlsdon, Churchley, called to ask for an appointment with the Personnel Manager on an urgent personal matter and an appointment was made for her at 1500 tomorrow. Mrs Doughty arrived at 1155.

8) Miss T Taplow, Office Equipment Supplies Ltd, Blacking, arrived to see Mr Jones the Buyer at 1200, by appointment.

9) Mr C Vernon, Cast Iron Casting Co Ltd called at 1215 in the hope of seeing Mr G Kerr, Production Manager. He is writing in for an appointment.

10) Miss P Downs, 37 Bidborough Ridge, Plowsville, arrived at 1230. She had an appointment with the Managing Director for 1245.

To make sure you understand how the register works, try answering the following questions.

1) Which callers arrived without an appointment?

2) Mr F Perkins came to the Accounts Department. What arrangement was made for him?

3) Mr B M Townsend came to see the Transport Officer. What do you think the Transport Officer would be responsible for?

4) This was a busy morning for the receptionist – she would want a break for coffee some time during the morning. How could she arrange this?

5) Miss G P Tomkins had no appointment. The usual procedure is for the receptionist to ask a caller without an appointment to write in for one, but on this occasion she did not do so. What special arrangements were made for Miss Tomkins?

6) Some regular callers at a firm would not be expected to sign the callers' register. Give three examples of this type of caller.

7) What should the receptionist do if a caller refuses to leave until an appointment has been made for him?

8) Who is Miss Burton?

9) What does 'Personnel' mean?

10) Why would many callers to the Personnel Department have appointments to go there?

Exercise 37

CALLERS' REGISTER

The firm's receptionist has been away for the afternoon, leaving her relief in charge. The following are the notes left by the relief receptionist. Rearrange them into the correct chronological (time) order, and enter them on to a blank callers' register form ruled up by you.

Have typed these notes out for you, while I had a quiet half-an-hour in the middle of the afternoon. The early part, immediately after lunch, was quite busy, as you can see.

Miss Anne Mason called at 1415 to make an appointment to take photographs of the new Typing Pool for the firm's magazine – the House Journal, I mean. Miss Mason works for the Glossy Pics Photographic Co of Knightsbridge, London. She made an appointment to see the Typing Pool Supervisor at 1500 on Monday next.

Three salesmen arrived at the same time – 1430. Mr P James, Cavendish Carbon Co, Mr L Knowles, Orwell's Office Products, and Mr M Thomas, Neverwear Carpet Co. They all wanted to see the Chief Buyer (Mr S Downs) and were all asked to write in for an appointment (Mr Knowles was a bit persistent!).

Mrs G Lansdale called to see the General Manager at 1450, by appointment. Her address is: 8 Lilac Square, Barbourne. She made a further appointment as she left, for a fortnight today to see the GM again at 1630.

The Manager of the Star Hotel, Hightown, called to see Mr G Evans, the Canteen Manager, at 1500. His appointment was actually for 1630 but he wanted to know if the Canteen Manager could see him earlier than this as he had to go to London unexpectedly. Mr Evans was able to see Mr H Price (the Manager of the Star Hotel) at 1530. He had about half-an-hour's wait in the reception area.

Mr W Bury called to see Mr O Brown, Transport Manager. He had an appointment for 1530. Mr Bury came from the Majestic Motor Co, Park Ave, Gloucester.

At 1600 there was quite a crowd at the reception desk. Mr F Dale, a lecturer from Worcester Technical College arrived with a party of 20 students, to see the Mail Room. Mr Dale had made an appointment with Mrs K Coombes, the Mail Room Supervisor. I didn't make a list of all the students' names. Was this necessary?

Mr S Pearson and Miss K Burbage, from Dawson & Miles, Chartered Accountants, Gladstone St, Bristol 1, arrived at 1545 – forgot to mention them before. They had an appointment to see the Chief Accountant, but he was still engaged and they had to wait about 20 minutes. I offered them tea or coffee, but they didn't want it. Mr Pearson was nice!

While I was dealing with this party, there were several telephone calls, both internal and external and one or two callers had to wait while I sorted everything out. I remembered to ask the waiting callers to take a seat and they didn't seem to mind waiting. I found that a smile works wonders!

The last caller was a right one – a Mrs F McPherson arrived at 1650 and demanded to see someone about a faulty machine which had given her an electric shock. She refused to go away until she had seen someone, and finally I was able to get the secretary of the Sales Manager to come down and talk to her and make arrangements for her to see the SM next week. That was a tricky one! I found out later that Mrs McPherson is a relation of one of the Directors – just as well I remained patient! Appointment with the SM is for 1000 on Tuesday, 10 October. Mrs McP's address is 31 The Crescent, Hightown.

Some flagsellers arrived during the afternoon – I bought one for you and one for me and telephoned to Personnel Dept to ask if arrangements had been made for them to go round the offices, as they did last year. Flagsellers' names don't go in the callers' register, do they?

Exercise 38

Now answer the following questions.

1) Should the relief receptionist have made a list of all the students' names, do you think?

2) What is the difference between an internal and an external telephone?

3) Can you think of a reason why the relief receptionist would not be allowed to enter the names of callers in the callers' register?

4) Was she right not to ask the flagsellers their names for inclusion in the callers' register?

Appointments Book

This is used to record all future appointments and is used by the receptionist to see who is expected each day, and also to give future appointments to callers who arrive without one, or who have to make an additional appointment on leaving a firm.

A page from the appointments book for 21 November 198– is shown overleaf.

Rule up a copy of the page for an appointments book, leaving out the names and other details, and fill it in with the page from the callers' register which you have just completed.

Monday   21 November 198–

NAME OF CALLER	FIRM	TIME OF ARRIVAL	TO SEE
Mr. L. M. Parkins	J. Mann + Co.	09 00	Mr K Jones
Mr. B. N. Vines	Carson Engineering	09 50	Personnel Manager
Miss K. Lyons	219 Lake Avenue	10 30	"
Mr. F. Perkins	Peterson's Export Co.	10 35	Accounts
Mrs. A. Drew	Wilchester Technical College	11 00	Personnel Manager
Mrs. W. Moxon	Office Equipment Supplies	11 30	Miss B. Saxon Typing Pool
Mr B. M. Townsend	Bellevue Car Hire	12 30	Transport Officer

Appointments book

Staff 'In and Out' Book

Another important record book which would be the receptionist's responsibility is a staff 'in and out' book. In this, all staff working in the firm write the reasons for going out of the firm during working hours, with their names, time of leaving and date. They also sign again when they return, writing down the time they returned. This book provides a record of staff absences, so that the receptionist can tell at a glance who has gone out of the firm. It is a much more efficient system than leaving notes or messages, which are easily lost. Where a firm operates flexible working hours, it may not be necessary although it is still useful to know *where* staff have gone, as well as *when*.

Exercise 39

Below is a page from a staff 'in and out' book for 1 March 198–.

DATE	NAME	DEPT	TIME OUT	TIME IN	REASON

112

Rule up a similar page and complete it correctly from the following information:

1) Miss R Rhodes, Wages, went out to the bank at 0930 and returned at 1000.

2) Mrs W Thompson, Typing Pool, went to the dentist at 1030 and returned at 1130.

3) Miss V Marr, Mail Room, went to the Post Office at 1100 and returned at 1120.

4) Mr C Mann, Sales Dept., left at 1400 on a business visit to Cornwall.

5) Mr L Moore, Buying, left at 1430 to fly to Germany.

6) Miss C Cooper, Personnel Dept., left at 1530 to go to a funeral.

7) Mrs W Thompson, Accounts Dept., went home ill at 1600.

8) Mr R Spence, Cashier, went to the hospital at 1630 to see his wife and new baby daughter.

9) Miss B Crowle, Transport Dept., left at 1635 for a doctor's appointment.

10) Mrs J Timms, Typing Pool, left at 1700 to sit an examination.

Dealing with Lost Property

Articles which visitors leave behind are many and varied – ranging from umbrellas, briefcases, books, calculators, cameras and handbags to ballpoint pens, wallets and spectacles. The list is almost endless.

Briefcases, handbags and wallets may have the owner's name on a letter or credit card inside. This makes it relatively easy to trace the owner and telephone a message regarding the whereabouts of the lost property. Money is sometimes inside wallets and handbags, in which case they should be handed over to the Security Officer (or similar responsible person) for him to lock in a safe. When an article containing money is being claimed, it should never be handed over without first making sure of the identity of the claimant and checking on the amount of money – i.e. ask person claiming how much was in the wallet or handbag first.

Many articles do not have any identification – umbrellas, scarves, gloves, for example, in which case not much can be done except to store them away carefully until such time as they are claimed.

A lost property book is a help in identifying and returning lost property, as it keeps records of the dates on which articles were left behind (page 114).

LOST PROPERTY BOOK

DATE	DESCRIPTION OF ITEM FOUND	OWNER	ADDRESS	DATE CLAIMED	SIGNATURE
198—					
8 May	Calculator	Unknown			
	Wristwatch	Unknown			
10 May	Briefcase	Mr J. Bettes	Hill Top Long Lane Ponteland Newcastle NE31 7RN		
18 May	Eternity ring (diamond)	Unknown			
19 May	Umbrella	Mrs J. Carr	Instantprint Station Road Redley Warwickshire B80 7RB		
25 May	Wallet	Mr F. Dent	York Engineering Bradstone Work Wall Street York YE3 8MB		
31 May	Fountain pen	Unknown			

Anyone collecting lost property should sign in the Lost Property Book when claiming their property, as evidence that the article has been handed over, and to whom.

A notice should be displayed prominently in the Reception Area, reminding callers not to leave their belongings behind, and disclaiming responsibility for them (see page 119).

Often, items left behind are unclaimed, even when the owner has been notified. Many firms have a policy of keeping them for a certain period, say 6 months, and then either handing them over to the police (if valuable) or donating them to a jumble sale, for a charity, if not. There is a limit to the amount of space which can be allocated to lost property.

Exercise 40

LOST PROPERTY

Make a blank copy of the form on page 114 and complete with the following details:

On 4 February 198– Mrs Alice Samson forgot her shopping bag. Her address is: 99 Springfield Crescent, Studditch, West Midlands.

On 9 February, the receptionist discovered, when the firm had closed for the day, a camera and an overcoat. She had no idea who had left them.

On 18 February, Mr John Gilmour left his walking stick behind. He is an employee of Messrs Haldane & Fields Ltd, Anchor Works, Portsmouth, Hants.

On 28 February, the receptionist discovered a handbag, a pair of spectacles and a ballpoint pen – all owners unknown.

Exercise 41

LOST PROPERTY

Write these notes in your folder, filling in the missing words and phrases.

1) All lost property should be entered in a _____ Book.

2) When owners are known, they should be _____ .

3) When an article containing money is being claimed, it should never be handed over without first _____ and checking on the _____ .

4) When the owner of an article left in the Reception Area is unknown, the item should be _____ until such time as they are claimed.

5) Anyone collecting lost property should sign the _____ as evidence that the article has been handed over and to whom.

6) A _____ should be displayed prominently in the Reception Area reminding callers not to leave their property behind and disclaiming responsibility for them.

Messages

The receptionist's duties include taking messages, and passing them on, verbally as well as in writing. It is very important that these messages are passed on immediately. A special message form is a help, as it reminds her not to forget to ask for any vital item of information before caller has gone.

115

MESSAGE FORM

Date . . . . Time . . . . For . . . .

From . . . .

Address . . . .

Telephone No . . . . Extension No . . . .

Message (telephone / personal—cross out whichever does not apply)

. . . .

. . . .

. . . .

. . . .

. . . .

. . . .

Taken by . . . .

Use the form above to pass on the following details. Mrs D Knowles called to see Miss Burton, Typing Pool Supervisor, on an important matter. Mrs Knowles would not make an appointment, but said she would like Miss Burton to telephone her at home after 7 pm today. Mrs Knowles' address is: 226 Ashtree Avenue, Boyston, and her telephone number is Boyston 886555. Sign the message form yourself, and date it for today, adding the time at which you are writing the message.

PASSING ON MESSAGES

Messages must be delivered as soon as possible. As the receptionist cannot leave her desk, she must ask her relief or her assistant to deliver the messages for her. Alternatively, she may be able to ask one of the firm's messengers to take her messages. Sometimes firms' messengers are young school-leavers, or they can be older, retired men or ex-service men. Their job is to take messages, letters, parcels etc around a firm.

If there are no firms' messengers, the receptionist would have to telephone through to the secretary of the manager concerned, and ask her to send someone to collect the message.

A copy of each message should be filed in date order, each day's messages then being arranged in alphabetical order of the *surname* of the person *to whom the message is addressed*. This is in case of a query later on. Carbon copies could be made (on a typewriter or by hand) or photocopies taken of any very important messages.

116

Notices in Reception Area

COMPOSING NOTICES

Notices should be as short as possible and displayed in clear, large letters (the best effect is obtained by dark letters on a pale background). Notices should be easy to read at a distance – instant impact should be aimed at, with the information reduced to as few words as possible without losing the sense of the message or sounding discourteous.

The following notice is an example of one which is too detailed and could be misunderstood:

RING THE BELL IF YOU REQUIRE ATTENTION WHEN RECEPTIONIST IS NOT AT HER DESK. SHE WILL BE PLEASED TO HELP YOU ON HER RETURN.

A better wording of the above would be:

PLEASE RING IF RECEPTIONIST IS ABSENT.

The above is shorter, tells the caller all he or she needs to know and is polite.

A layout for the above notice could be:

> **PLEASE RING**
> **IF RECEPTIONIST IS ABSENT**

on matt white or pale background (shiny backgrounds are difficult to read in an artificial light).

Exercise 42

Re-word the following notices so that they are polite:

1) Shut the door.

2) Don't smoke in this part of the Reception Area.

3) Check whether you have left anything in the Reception Area before you leave.

4) Mind the step!

5) Use the litter bins.

6) Use ashtrays for cigarette ends not litter bins.

7) This vending machine is out of order.

8) Knock and wait.

9) All employees must show works passes on entering the building.

10) All employees must sign Staff IN and OUT book when leaving during working hours.

PLEASE CLOSE THE DOOR

When using stencils for lettering, close the gaps left in the letters by the stencil – this gives a more professional finish

Exercise 43

Write notices for the following instructions in a shorter form (don't forget to be polite!).

1) All briefcases, handbags and shopping bags will be opened and searched before callers enter the building. This is a necessary precaution in view of the possibility of bomb explosions. Your co-operation is requested. Any delay is regretted.

2) Callers without appointments will not normally be seen by the person they hope to speak to. The receptionist will help by asking if anyone can deputise, but it may mean a long wait.

3) If you feel ill, or have had an accident, let the receptionist know and she will give you some assistance.

4) Wear your visitor's badge at all times while you are in the building, otherwise you may be stopped and asked to leave.

5) Don't wander round the building without a member of staff to go with you.

Producing Notices

Printing notices is a job for professional printers or signwriters, but neat, clear notices can be prepared by anyone ready to take a little care.

118

USING STENCILS

These can be obtained from most large stationers, and are made with varying sizes of letters and numbers. Before starting to use a stencil, rule lines across the paper lightly in pencil to keep the letters level. These pencil lines can be erased gently when the lettering has been finished. Felt tipped pens are useful for closing the gaps left in the letters by the stencil when you have finished (see page 118).

Card will last longer than paper and can be obtained in various colours. A notice which is to be displayed for several months should be covered with a clear plastic adhesive film, to keep it dust free.

APPLIED LETTERING

This is a method for transferring letters or numbers from specially prepared sheets by rubbing with something smooth and rounded, such as the non-writing end of a ballpoint pen. These sheets can be obtained in many different typefaces, type sizes and colours, and used carefully give a professional appearance to your notices. As with stencils, lightly ruled pencil guidelines are necessary before using applied lettering.

Effective notices with stencilled lettering on A5 landscape

METAL BOARDS AND MAGNETIC LETTERS

A very useful arrangement for displaying notices is a metal board, to which letters bonded to small magnets can be attached quickly and easily. These too are obtainable in various sizes and colours.

119

Displaying Notices

Space out the lines – don't cramp them together at the top, making them difficult to read. Give prominence to the most important words by using a different colour and/or larger-sized letters. Draft out the notice beforehand on a sheet of A4 or A5 paper, so that you have some idea of the effect and colours you plan to use. Check the spelling carefully before you start the lettering properly.

Exercise 44

Below is a notice as a typist might have displayed it on A5 paper.

With felt pens, and a sheet of A5, write the notice as attractively as you can, using at least three different colours and sizes of letters:

1)

```
┌─────────────────────────────────────────────────────┐
│                                                       │
│            SECRETARIAL SERVICES                       │
│                                                       │
│        are available FREE on request                  │
│                                                       │
│    The receptionist will give you details             │
│                                                       │
└─────────────────────────────────────────────────────┘
```

Display the notices below, using colour if possible, on A4 paper, so that they can be read at a distance of about 10 metres.

2) French, German and Italian are spoken by members of staff. Please ask at the Reception Desk if you require their services.

3) Meals may be obtained in the Works Canteen between 1200 and 1330, if required. Please ask a commissionaire to escort you.

4) Writing paper and envelopes are provided for the use of visitors. Stamps may be purchased from a vending machine. There is a coin changing machine adjacent for the convenience of visitors.

5) Fire drills are held from time to time, without prior notice. Please follow the receptionist's instructions promptly and accurately. After all, you don't know whether it's a real fire or not!

Exercise 45

NOTICES IN RECEPTION AREA

Write these notes in your folder, filling in the missing words and phrases.

1) Notices should be as short as possible and displayed in clear _____ letters.

2) The best effect is obtained by _____ letters on a _____ background.

3) Notices should be easy to read at a _____ .

4) For writing notices, stencils, applied letter or metal boards and _____ are useful.

5) Notices should be _____ out beforehand on a sheet of paper.

6) It is important to check _____ .

7) Notices to be displayed for some time should be covered with _____ .

8) Card is useful for notices and can be obtained in several different _____ .

Exercise 46

THE RECEPTIONIST

Answer the following questions, as if for an examination. Remember that marks can be deducted for untidiness and spelling mistakes.

1) A receptionist's job is very important to the firm she works for because
   first impression

2) An ideal receptionist should be polite, friendly, *helpful* and *efficient*.

3) Besides dealing with callers, a receptionist may also:
   a _____ .
   b _____ .
   c _____ .

4) Her appearance should be smart, neat, and she should be
   well - groomed

5) A receptionist should be well-informed about three things:
   a _____ .
   b _____ .
   c _____ .

6) Some regular callers to firms do not normally have appointments. Give *three* of these.

7) Callers' business visiting cards have callers' names printed on them. What else might be printed on them?

8) What should an efficient receptionist do with the callers' visiting cards which are left with her?

9) What information does an organisation chart give?

10) As well as an organisation chart, what else should a receptionist have on the wall behind her desk?

11) In addition to the alphabetical card index of callers' cards, a receptionist is responsible for four record books. What are they?

12) Which of these record books is filled in *before* callers arrive?

13) Which record book is never used for *visitors* to a firm?

14) A message form is very useful for writing down telephone or verbal messages because ＿＿＿＿＿＿＿＿ .

15) Copies of message forms are filed by receptionists. Why?

16) Which name would be used to file copies of messages – the name of the *sender* or the name of the *recipient* of the message?

17) Give one way in which copies of messages could be made.

18) Explain another way in which copies of a message could be made.

19) A receptionist cannot leave her desk to deliver messages. What can she do to make sure they are delivered quickly and correctly?

20) Rule up a message form with suitable headings, which a receptionist could use. Then complete with the following message:
John Watts called today (1000 hrs) to speak to Martin Lewis, Chief Accountant. Can they meet on Thursday, 21 October, at Weeks & Co., Ragmouth, at 1000? Will Mr Lewis please ring back and confirm on Bagborough 327061 Extension 32.
Mr Watts is from Watts, Wainwright and Co, an engineering firm in Powick Lane, Trumpton.

CHAPTER 12

The Reception Area

Giving a Good Impression

This is where visitors to a firm wait, either because they have arrived too early for an appointment, or the person they have called to see may be unexpectedly delayed.

It is important that the reception area gives visitors a good impression because it is quite often the first part of a firm they see, and if it is not welcoming and comfortable, they may decide to transfer their business to another firm.

Keeping Tidy

The first things visitors notice on arrival may well be your own desk and equipment. The receptionist below is *not* likely to create a good impression. Can you see why?

How many things can you find wrong with this reception area?

A Comfortable Design for the Visitor

As well as being warm in winter, cool in summer, well lit and attractively decorated, the reception area should have comfortable chairs for the visitors, and it may also offer amenities such as vending machines for refreshments and cigarettes, toilets, payphone, coin changing machine, stamp machine and many other conveniences. Below is an assignment on designing a reception area, but first of all here is a picture of what the area near your desk should *not* look like. It is too small, visitors have nowhere to sit, and the receptionist has allowed a telephone conversation to go on for so long that a queue has formed.

A badly organised reception area. How many things are wrong?

Arranging samples of products to advantage

Showcases with glass doors are one of the best ways of displaying samples of a firm's products, when they are small enough. Good lighting in showcases is important, to show off the products to advantage. Larger articles can be displayed by photographs or posters mounted on partitions in the reception area.

Much obviously depends on the type of product. Lengths of material look effective draped on artificial models. Samples of carpets (about 50 cm) are often made into books containing different shades of each type of carpet available. A firm manufacturing large engineering equipment might have small scale models made to display in the reception area.

Exercise 47

DESIGNING A RECEPTION AREA

Trace the drawing of the reception area on page 126, which is carpeted, heated, lighted, but is otherwise bare.

Then trace the items below which would help to make a reception area more comfortable and attractive to visitors who have to wait for a short time.

Cut out your tracings neatly and glue them into appropriate places on your drawing. When the glue has dried, colour your reception area suitably.

Then on a separate sheet of paper make a list of everything in your reception area, under the heading 'An Ideal Reception Area'.

The assignment will be graded according to the neatness of your design and how well you make your list. After you have finished this assignment compare your design with that on page 195.

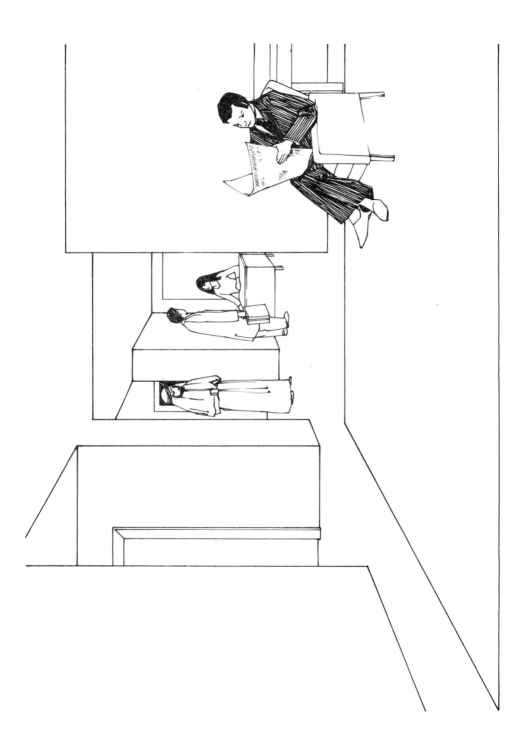

Flower Arranging

Flower arrangements in a reception area, and on the receptionist's desk, should be kept low, so that they do not obstruct the receptionist's or caller's view.

MATERIALS REQUIRED

Holders. Wire netting with 2″ (5 cm) mesh, cut into pieces to fill vases when crumpled. (A pinch of borax in the water stops the wire netting from rusting. Borax is obtainable at any chemist's shop.)

Pin holders – the best type are either held by suction at the bottom of the vase, or are weighted, to prevent them toppling over.

Water absorbent plastic foam – a green, spongy substance which can be cut, shaped and placed in the bottom of containers. After watering, this foam holds flowers securely and keeps them moist.

Scissors. A sharp pair is essential for neat trimming of stems.

Sprayer. Used to give a refreshing overhead spray of lukewarm water to flower arrangements, to counteract the drying effect of central heating. This helps to prolong the life of fresh flowers.

Containers. Shallow bowls or dishes,
rectangular or boat-shaped baskets with container inside,
square and rectangular troughs,
posy rings.

MAKING FLOWER ARRANGEMENTS

It is not difficult to make an attractive flower arrangement, but practice is needed to become reasonably expert. The following guide-lines will help:

- Keep arrangements simple.
- Cut flower stems to different lengths.
- Arrange flowers so that no one bloom hides another, thus using them to maximum advantage.
- Buy flowers when they are in bud – the warmth of most reception areas will quickly cause them to open.
- Keep to one of four basic shapes.

Crescent

Line basket or shallow rectangular dish with plastic foam.
Place three flowers (each with different length stems) at either end.
Place three short-stemmed flowers at centre point.
Fill in centre with flowers, stems cut to varying short lengths.
Mask gaps with foliage.

Crescent

L-shaped

Line a low rectangular container with plastic foam.
Place vertical bloom at left of 'L'.
Place horizontal blooms at either end of basket.
Fill in with blooms and foliage.

L-shaped

All-the-way-round

This is one of the easiest to do and one of the most attractive. It can be placed centrally on a low table and looks pretty from all angles.

Fill a bowl with crumpled 2″ wire netting.
Outline edges of bowl with flowers (small ones such as polyanthus are best).
Build up from centre until bowl is full.
Add leaves at random, and round edges to lighten final appearance.

128

All-the-way-round

Triangular

Fill a container with crumpled wire mesh or plastic foam.
Place longest stem in central position to mark top point of triangle (see below).
Choose two more long stems and place at right angles to form base (see below). This gives triangular shape.
Finally fill in body with flowers cutting stems shorter where necessary.

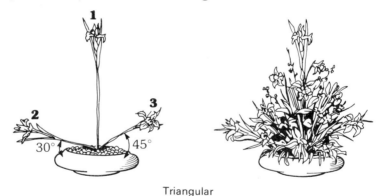

Triangular

Looking after Flower Arrangements

Keep flowers in a bucket of water in a cool place until needed. Remove leaves from stem (they deprive flowers of water if left on the same stem). Add two tablespoons of sugar (or a tablespoon of charcoal) to a quart of water (1 litre) to keep it pure. Carnations keep well in fizzy lemonade! Use tepid water only in containers, ensuring that pin-holders when used, are covered, topping up each container daily. It is not necessary to empty water out and refill daily. Each day spray each arrangement with clean tepid water and remove any dead flowers.

129

Using Artificial and Dried Flowers or Grasses

ARTIFICIAL FLOWERS

Today's artificial flowers (either plastic or silk) are very realistic and look particularly attractive when mixed with fresh foliage or small branches.

Artificial flower arrangements are particularly useful for centrally heated rooms, as they will remain fresh-looking indefinitely, but they will collect dust, and should be gently washed in warm soapy water occasionally.

DRIED FLOWERS AND GRASSES

These may be purchased from florists and large department stores and are attractive for winter floral arrangements. Dried grasses and flowers are available either in their natural colours, or dyed.

All artificial arrangements should be changed round from time to time to give variety to the reception desk and reception area.

Exercise 48

FLOWER ARRANGING

Write these notes in your folder, filling in the missing words and phrases.

1) Flower arrangements for a reception area, and on the receptionist's desk should be kept _____ so that they do not _____ .

2) Holders are of three main types, crumped wire mesh, pin holders and
   _____ .

3) To keep the wire netting from rusting, use a _____ .

4) Suitable containers for flower arrangements in the reception area and the receptionist's desk are: shallow bowls or dishes, rectangular or boat-shaped baskets with container inside, square and rectangular troughs and _____ .

5) There are five guidelines for beginners attempting flower arrangements:
   a keep arrangements simple.
   b cut flower stems to different _____ .
   c arrange flowers so that no one bloom hides another, thus using them to best _____ .
   d buy flowers when they are in _____ .
   e keep to one of four basic _____ .

6) The four basic shapes are:
   a triangular
   b crescent
   c L-shaped
   d _____ .

7) Looking after flower arrangements includes:
   a covering pinholders with _____
   b using _____ water in containers
   c placing flowers in a _____ in a cool place until needed
   d removing _____ from stems
   e topping up containers daily with _____
   f removing _____ flowers daily
   g spraying with _____ daily.

8) Artificial flower arrangements are very useful as they do not wilt but they should be _____ and _____ from time to time to give variety to the _____ .

Looking After Indoor Plants

Plants in offices can be as much a part of the furnishings as the carpets and looking after them is comparatively simple.

Many firms use plants in troughs and tubs as a screen to divide sections of offices, or to make an area visited by the public such as Reception (see page 197) welcoming and attractive.

It is possible to arrange for a specialist firm to supply the plants, look after them regularly, and replace them when necessary. This relieves the office staff of all responsibility regarding the care of the plants, but is an expensive service which can very well be managed by members of staff. It is a sensible arrangement for one or two people only to be involved in looking after plants in each office, so that their care is not forgotten – few things look worse than drooping, neglected plants.

GUIDELINES FOR THE CARE OF INDOOR PLANTS

1) *Position.* All plants need light, but most dislike strong sunshine, so a position near a north or east facing window is ideal. This will get no sunshine (north) or morning sunshine only (east).

2) *Temperature.* No indoor plants will tolerate frost, so do not leave plants touching a window in an unheated room on a frosty night. Move plants away from the windows on to the floor at the end of the day in the winter. Conversely, plants also dislike direct heat from radiators, so do not stand them on top of radiators, or too near them.

3) *Watering.* When the soil surface feels dry to the touch, water from the top until the water seeps out into the container. Drain away any surplus water after a few minutes *so that the plant is not left standing in water.*

4) *Feeding.* Indoor plants require regular feeding which is generally done at the time of watering. Once a fortnight in summer is usually adequate and about once a month in winter. A useful plant food is one which is long-lasting and can be applied once every six months.

5) *Humidity.* Centrally heated offices have a dry atmosphere which most plants dislike. Regular spraying of the foliage with tepid water will be beneficial; also, standing the plant pot on gravel or pebbles which are kept moist keeps the atmosphere moist around the plant.

6) *Pests.* The three most common pests on indoor plants are greenfly, whitefly and red spider. These can be controlled easily by one of the many proprietary chemicals available at plant centres. Spraying will have to be repeated several times to eliminate the pest completely.

Plants in troughs can
be used as screens

7) *Diseases.* The most common diseases on indoor plants are mildew and botrytis and these also can be controlled by using a proprietary brand of chemical. When using indoor sprays, extreme care should be used and the manufacturers' instructions followed closely.

Choosing Plants

Buy young plants – they will be cheaper than the larger, more mature plants and will adapt more successfully to the different growing conditions in offices. Choose plants which are short and bushy and have glossy, healthy-looking leaves. Flowering plants should have plenty of buds still to open.

FOLIAGE PLANTS SUITABLE FOR GROWING INDOORS

Shade-loving (can be away from the light)
- Aspidistra eliator (cast-iron plant)
- Asplenium
- Fittonia
- Hedera (ivy)
- Parlour palm
- Pteris
- Senecia mikanioides (parlour ivy)

Light-loving plants (but do not place in direct sunlight)
- Asparagus ferns
- Begonia Rex
- Chlorophytum (spider plant)
- Cissus antarctica (kangaroo vine)
- Dieffenbachia
- Dracaena
- Euonymus fortunei
- Ficus elastica (India-rubber plant)
- Maranta
- Monstera deliciosa (Swiss cheese plant)
- Peporomia caperata
- Philodendron sandens
- Sansevieria (mother-in-law's tongue)
- Tradescantia
- Zebrina pendula (wandering Jew)

Plants which will tolerate some sunlight
- Aloe aristata
- Buxus sempervirens
- Coleus blumei
- Echeveria derenberghii
- Fatshedra lizeii
- Grevillia robusta (silk oak)
- Kalanchoe
- Pittosporum tobira

Flowering plants suitable for growing indoors
The following will be attractive only during their flowering period and will then have to be exchanged for foliage plants:

Spring	Summer/autumn	Winter
Azalea	Begonia semperflorens	Cineraria
Clivia miniata	Begonia tuberhybrida	Hippeastrum
Cyclamen persicum	Chrysanthemum	Saintpaulia
Freesia	Exacum affine	Zygocactus truncatus
Primula	Fuchsia	
Schizanthus	Impatiens	
	Pelargonium	

Post-a-Plant

Plants (chosen from four varieties – parlour palm, grape ivy, sanseveria or devil's ivy) will be delivered by Royal Mail, packed into a box specially designed to protect the plant as it goes through the sorting office, anywhere in the United Kingdom.

A form has to be completed, giving name, address, postcode and telephone number.

State the type of plant ordered and size of pot required. A message card to be sent with the plant has to be completed.

The completed order form and Transcash form should be taken together with cash or cheque to any post office. The counter clerk will date stamp the order and the Transcash form.

Detached order then has to be sent to the address given on the reverse side of the order form.

CHAPTER 13

Equipment and Reference Books

The Things You Need

Your basic equipment will consist of the following:
Desk and chair
Telephones – both external and internal
Filing cabinet – for storing callers' letters and copies of replies to them
Paper and envelopes.

In some firms (but not all) you will also need:
Switchboard
Typewriter.

Looking up Information

Many callers at a firm will be strangers to the area and may ask questions about where to stay, where to find other firms, where to get a good meal and what sort of films etc. are being currently shown. The following are useful for looking up information:

AA or RAC Book – this contains information about hotels, as well as garages, market days, and early closing days all over Great Britain.

Post Office Guide – there may be foreign visitors to a firm, and they may ask the receptionist about postage rates to overseas countries and other post office services.

Telephone directories, trade directories, Dialling Code Booklet and *British Telecom International Telephone Guide.*

Maps and guide books of the area around the firm.

Entertainments guide for the area, and local newspapers showing 'What's on'.

Pub food guide and restaurant guides.

Your Firm's Own Information

Your firm may give you its own diary, reference book or house journal to help you provide information on its personnel or products. It may also even produce its own booklet on notes for staff, giving you details about the firm and its facilities. Gone are the days when you would simply have a notice on the wall like the one appearing on page 139.

Exercise 49

RECEPTIONIST'S REFERENCE BOOKS

Look up the answers to the first five questions in the Post Office Guide, or International Telephone Guide.

1) Is it possible to send a toy pistol to Cyprus?

2) What is the cost of a 10-minute telephone call to Japan?

3) How many seconds are you allowed for 5.405p (IDD rates) when telephoning Belgium at cheap rate?

4) Is it possible to send plants by post to France?

5) What is the cost per minute of a telephone call to Poland at standard rate?

Now look up the next five questions in your local Classified Trade Directory.
Find the name and address and telephone number of the following:

6) An adding machine manufacturer.

7) A duplicating and copying service in Malvern*.

8) A dress shop in Worcester.

9) A wholesale stationer in Bromsgrove.

10) A toyshop in Pershore.

*It is suggested that the tutor should replace some of the place names (here and in other exercises) with other place names in your locality.

The answers to the next five questions will be found in the Dialling Code Booklet.

11) What is the number for 'Dial a Disc'?

12) What is the code for Cardiff?

13) When is the most expensive time to make a phone call in the UK?

14) What is the code number for Glasgow?

15) What is the code for Knutsford?

Look up the answers to the next five questions in the AA Handbook.

16) What is the distance between Bristol and London?

17) What are the best hotels in Southampton?

18) What are the best garages for car repair in Cheltenham?

19) What is early closing day in Gloucester?

20) What is the distance between Wolverhampton and London?

Look up the answers to the five questions below in the West Midland Telephone Directory. (Tutors may substitute their own local examples.)

21) What is the telephone number of G W Richards, Greystones, Rowney Green?

22) What number would you dial to be able to listen to a bedtime story?

23) What number do you dial in Worcester to get the right time?

24) What is the telephone number of Mr J W Smith, Station Road, Pershore?

25) What is the telephone number of Mr J E Smitten, 4 Arosa Drive, Malvern?

Exercise 50

RECEPTIONIST'S REFERENCE BOOKS

Answer the following questions and state the name of the Reference Books in which you found each answer.

1) What is the distance between Bodmin and London?

2) Give the name, address and telephone number of a kennels in Pershore.

3) Find the telephone number of A Gardener, 8 Great Field Road, Kidderminster, Worcs.

4) What is the code number to dial when telephoning London from Edinburgh?

5) Which county is Liverpool in?

6) Give the telephone number of a fish and chip restaurant in Kidderminster.

7) Find the telephone number of A Gardner, 6 Gilmour Crescent, Worcester.

8) What is the population of Milnthorpe?

9) Find the code number to dial when telephoning Derby (from outside the Derby area).

10) What is the best hotel in Minehead?

11) Find the name, address and telephone number of a local wedding photographer.

137

12) What is the number to dial to obtain a recipe in your area?

13) What is the code number to dial for Torquay from outside the Torquay area?

14) Is it possible to send a football pools coupon to Canada?

15) What is the telephone number of your local gas showroom?

16) Find the name of a hotel in Torquay which refuses to take dogs.

17) What is the dialling code for Bearwood from your area?

18) What day is there early closing in Cullompton?

19) Find the name of a brewer in your locality.

20) Find the telephone number of your college, or school.

21) Find the name, address and telephone number of a local dentist.

22) What is the dialling code number for Radcliffe from your area?

23) How many miles between Warwick and Worcester?

24) When is early closing day in Wantage?

25) Find the name, address and telephone number of a boutique in London.

26) Find the cost of a three-minute telephone call to Greece from your area.

Question number	Answer	Book used

The following presentation may be useful

1. Godliness, Cleanliness and Punctuality are the necessities of a good business.

2. This firm has now reduced the hours of work, and the clerical staff will now only have to be present between the hours of 7.00 a.m. and 6.0 p.m. on week days. The Sabbath is for worship, but should any man-of-war or other vessel require victualling, the clerical staff will work on the Sabbath.

3. Daily Prayers will be held each morning in the main office. The clerical staff will be present.

4. Clothing must be of a sober nature. The clerical staff will not disport themselves in raiment of bright colours, nor will they wear hose unless of good repair.

5. Overshoes and top-coats may not be worn in the office, but neck-scarves and headwear may be worn in inclement weather.

6. A stove is provided for the clerical staff. Coal and wood must be kept in the locker. It is recommended that each member of the clerical staff bring four pounds of coal, each day, during the cold weather.

7. No member of the clerical staff may leave the room without permission from Mr. Ryder. The calls of nature are permitted, and the clerical staff may use the garden below the second gate. This area must be kept in good order.

8. No talking is allowed during business hours.

9. The craving for tobacco, wines or spirits is a human weakness and, as such, is forbidden to all members of the clerical staff.

10. Now that the hours of business have been drastically reduced the partaking of food is allowed between 11.30 a.m. and noon, but work will not, on any account, cease.

11. Members of the clerical staff will provide their own pens. A new sharpener is available, on application to Mr. Ryder.

12. Mr. Ryder will nominate a senior clerk to be responsible for the cleanliness of the main office and the private office, and all boys and juniors will report to him forty minutes before prayers, and will remain after closing hours for similar work. Brushes, brooms, scrubbers and soap are provided by the owners.

13. The new increased weekly wages are as hereunder detailed:

	s.	d.
Junior boys (to 11 years)	1	4
Boys (to 14 years)	2	1
Juniors	4	8
Junior Clerks	8	7
Clerks	10	9
Senior Clerks (after 15 years with the owner)	21	–

The owners hereby recognise the generosity of the new labour laws, but will expect a great rise in output of work to compensate for these near Utopian conditions.

OFFICE STAFF PRACTICES, 1853

CHAPTER 14

Form Letters

Saving Time

A *form letter* is one which has been printed beforehand, in readiness for use, with spaces for the date, the inside address and any other details which will change according to the person to whom it is sent.

Form letters save a great deal of time, as the receptionist only has to complete them with the missing details, and this could be done by hand, although they look much more business-like if they are carefully lined up on a typewriter, and the missing information typed on.

Sample Letters

There are three blank specimens of form letter on pages 141–3.

No 1 is to let the recipient know the day and time of an appointment.
No 2 is cancelling an appointment.
No 3 is a polite way of avoiding making an appointment.

Exercise 51

A RECEPTIONIST'S FORM LETTERS

Copy (or preferably type) the letters on pages 141–143 and fill them in as requested in the ten examples that follow. The letters should be very neat, without alterations (which are not acceptable unless very carefully done). Make sure that dates and times are accurate to avoid someone coming in the wrong day! You should make a carbon copy of each letter. (Where do you think it would be filed – under the name of the person with whom the appointment is being made?) When you have finished the letters type out an envelope for each one, putting the post town in capital letters and inventing a suitable post code. If you want to avoid wasting envelopes use pieces of paper of about 16½ by 9 cm.

HALL & GRIFFITH LIMITED

32 Lime Avenue
ELMSTOCK
Oakshire
Telephone Elmstock 36277

Ref MS/

Date as postmark

Dear Sir/Madam

Thank you for your letter dated

Mr/Mrs/Miss of   Department
will be pleased to see you on
at

Please come to the reception desk a few minutes before
your appointment to enable our receptionist to check
that   is free to see you.

Yours faithfully
HALL & GRIFFITH LIMITED

M Steele
Personnel Manager

HALL & GRIFFITH LIMITED

32 Lime Avenue
ELMSTOCK
Oakshire
Telephone Elmstock 36277

Our ref MS/

Date as postmark

Dear Sir/Madam

Thank you for your letter dated
asking for an appointment to see Mr/Mrs/Miss
                   of   Department.

Unfortunately Mr/Mrs/Miss
is away at present and is making no appointments for
several weeks.

Please write again next month if you wish to make
an appointment later.

Yours faithfully
HALL & GRIFFITH LIMITED

M Steele
Personnel Manager

HALL & GRIFFITH LIMITED

32 Lime Avenue
ELMSTOCK
Oakshire
Telephone Elmstock 36277

Our ref MS/

Date as postmark

Dear Sir/Madam

I regret to have to ask you to cancel your appointment
for   at
to see   as he/she has been called away
unexpectedly. When it is possible to make a further
appointment I will write to you again.

Please accept apologies from Mr/Mrs/Miss
for any inconvenience you may be caused by this cancellation.

Yours faithfully
HALL & GRIFFITH LIMITED

M Steele
Personnel Manager

1) Miss K Penrose, 9 Harbour View, Snowley, Sussex, wrote asking for an appointment to see Miss F Brown, Catering Dept., on Monday, 13 November at 9 am. Send a letter confirming this. Miss Penrose's letter was dated 2 November.

2) Write to Mr A Brown, Production Engineer, Metal Products Limited, Silverside Trading Estate, Grimley, Co Durham, regretting that no appointment can be made to see Miss J Hoyle (Buying Dept.).

3) Write to Mrs W Coombes of 20 Ivy Lane, Lower Sleepington, Worcestershire, cancelling her appointment for 22 November at 1600 to see Miss P Lynes (Sales Dept.).

4) Write to Miss Sally Ford, The Laurels, Park Lane, Seedworth, Essex, asking her to come to see Mrs K Price (Personnel Dept.) on Friday, 24 November at 1130.

5) Cancel appointment made for Mr J R Smart, 39 Market Place, Greendown, Leicestershire to see Mr W Wilson (Buying Dept.) at 1630 on Wednesday, 29 November.

6) Send a letter to Miss L Hyles, Lilac Cottage, South Holding, Hants, regretting that an appointment cannot be made for her to see Miss B Burton, Advertising Dept..

7) Send a letter to Mr J Smith, 321 Barrage Road, Bagworth, asking him to call and see Mrs C Mann (Sales Dept.) on 1 December at 1530.

8) Cancel an appointment for Mr R Simmons, Works Manager, Leyton Engineering Company, Aircraft Road, Noiseville, to see Mr H Roberts, Production Dept., on 21 November at 1100.

9) Write to Mrs O Hankins, Wonderboss Typing Agency, High Street, Lowton, regretting that an appointment cannot be made for her to see Mr K Thompson, Wages Dept..

10) Write to Miss P Perkins, Quire and Ream Paper Manufacturers, 32 Albrighton Street, Clockton. Cancel an appointment to see Mr M Lewis, Accounts Dept., on 24 November at 1200.

Exercise 52

REVISION

Please answer all the following questions. In an examination they would carry equal marks.

1) **a** Why is the reception area so important to a firm?
   b How can the receptionist help to make her area attractive to callers?
   c Why is the appearance and manner of the receptionist so important?

2) The main duty of the receptionist is to look after the firm's callers. Explain how an efficient receptionist carries out this duty, and what other duties she may have, in addition to looking after callers.

3) **a** Business visiting cards are very useful, both at the time they are handed to the receptionist, and afterwards, when they are filed away. Give two reasons why business visiting cards are so useful.
   b Explain an efficient system for filing business visiting cards.

4) **a** Rule up a page from a callers' register, write in the correct headings, and enter five callers – four with appointments and one without an appointment. Date for today, and use suitable times between 0930 and 1200. Invent any other details which would normally be entered in a callers' register.
   b Rule up a page from an appointments book, with correct headings, and complete with the details of the four callers with appointments from your callers' register.

5) Describe what a well-organised receptionist would have on her desk, and in her office near her. Explain the use of each item.

6) **a** Rule up a message form which would be equally suitable for telephone messages and personal messages.
   b Explain clearly how copies of these messages should be filed.

7) Rule up a page from a Lost Property Book, with correct headings, and complete with details of lost property on five days in December, 198– (just before Christmas!).

8) Explain how samples of a firm's products can be displayed to good advantage if they manufacture
   a jewellery
   b fur coats
   c lorries.

CHAPTER 15

Safety and Security in the Reception Area

What to Look Out For

As well as making sure that visitors to her firm are looked after, a receptionist is responsible for seeing that accidents do not happen to them in the reception area.

She should check that:

1) Carpet or other floor covering is not frayed or loose, and report it if it needs repair, to the person in the firm whose job it is to put it right.

2) There are no loose wires trailing from electric sockets to appliances such as table lamps.

3) Doors are kept clear of bags, brief cases and boxes.

4) Fire exits are not blocked.

5) Ash trays are adequate. Many fires are caused by cigarette ends smouldering or carelessly discarded matches.

6) A first aid box is available, stocked with a supply of sticking-plasters, bandages, aspirins, antiseptic and cotton wool, and that she has an elementary knowledge of first aid, in case of emergencies (see Chapter 16).

7) Lighting is adequate, especially in dark corners, or where there is an unexpected awkwardly placed step.

8) All electric appliances are not only switched off before she goes home at the end of the day, but that they are *unplugged.*

9) There is at least one fire extinguisher in the reception area (preferably two, if it is a large area) and that she knows how to use it.

10) She knows the firm's fire drill.

In addition the receptionist should take care over the following safety precautions in her own office:

1) Make sure that filing cabinet drawers are kept closed – they can easily be tripped over. If the two top drawers are opened at once, the whole cabinet may fall over.

2) Do not stack boxes, or files on top of the filing cabinet, in case they topple over accidentally.

3) Make sure that there is a fire extinguisher near her desk.

4) Do not overload adaptors by plugging too many appliances into one socket – this is a frequent cause of fires.

An unsafe
filing cabinet

Many firms instal fireproof filing cabinets, so that in the event of a fire at least some of the documents will be saved.

Theft is another hazard facing firms, and the receptionist can co-operate by closing doors and windows before leaving and locking away anything valuable. At least this makes it more difficult for burglars to break in.

An Act passed in 1974 – the Health and Safety at Work Act – lays very definite responsibilities on all employees for health and safety in offices, as well as on employers, and there are quite heavy fines for firms who do not try to make their premises as accident-free as possible. Employees are expected, under the Act (known as HASAWA for short) to do their part, too.

Identifying Personnel

Many large firms do not allow strangers to walk around the premises unaccompanied. They are escorted either by a messenger, a commissionaire, or a secretary.

In some firms, badges are issued to all visitors with the word 'Visitor' printed on. These will have to be handed back to the receptionist before leaving the firm.

A visitor receives his pass

So that the receptionist is able to check quickly whether someone she does not recognise is an employee or a visitor, *works passes* are issued to employees; these passes have the employee's photograph on, for identification, and are signed by him (or her) and dated. Employees can be asked for these passes on entering or leaving the works, by works police or commissionaires. They are usually renewed every year.

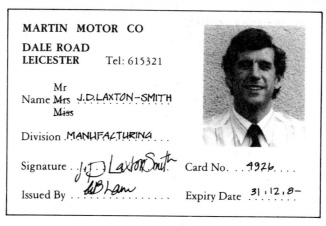

An employee's Works Pass

Bomb Warnings

In cities such as London, Birmingham and Belfast, where there have been many bomb explosions, all bags, including ladies' handbags, may be opened and searched in reception as a security precaution, especially if there have been recent terrorist activities.

The receptionist should know what the firm's procedure is if there is a warning by telephone that a bomb has been left in the building. Usually, the building is cleared of people at once (even if it is suspected that the warning is a hoax – no chances can be taken) and the receptionist informs the security officer at once.

149

Letterbombs have become more frequent of recent years and if a package or letter is at all suspicious, the firm will have a routine which the receptionist must follow.

The Metropolitan Police of London have issued the following guidelines, which they suggest should be printed on a card and hung up over the desk of anyone receiving or sorting incoming mail:

Look for:

Shape	Wrapping	Greasemarks
Size	Writing	Signs of wire or batteries
Thickness	Spelling	Postmark
Sealing	Wrong name or address	Unsolicited mail

If the package gives cause for suspicion send for the Security Officer AT ONCE. He will dial 999:

DON'T	*DO*
Open it	*keep calm*
Press, squeeze or prod it	*look for sender's name on back*
Put it in sand or water	*check with sender*
Put it into any sort of container.	*check with addressee.*

Then, if it is still under suspicion:
Leave it
Leave the room
Lock the door and keep the key.

Some firms do not allow cameras or large bags to be taken into the works and they must be left with the receptionist. Large bags could be used to smuggle out stolen goods and cameras could be used to take photographs of confidential work which might help rival manufacturers. Large bags should be safely stored away, not too near to the receptionist, in case they contain explosives!

Responsibility for any property left in reception rests with the owner, *not* the receptionist or the firm and large notices to this effect are usually displayed in the reception area (known as 'disclaimers' – see page 119). Of course, this does not mean that reasonable care will not be taken by the receptionist of visitors' property and anything left behind by accident in the reception area would be safely locked away until reclaimed by the owner.

Umbrellas, coats and hats in the reception area should be kept under observation by the receptionist, and visitors leaving the firm could be tactfully asked if they have anything to collect before they go.

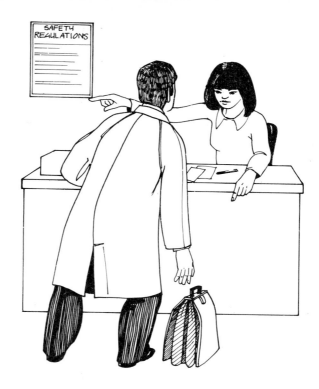

Exercise 53

SAFETY AND SECURITY IN THE RECEPTION AREA

1) How are many fires caused?

2) What can a receptionist do to try to avoid fires starting?

3) Fires can be started by electric appliances being left switched on. As well as *switching off* any electrical equipment at the end of the day, what else should you do?

4) There are three other precautions the receptionist should take with regard to fires:
   a know the firm's fire drill
   b know how to use the fire extinguisher.
   What is the third?

5) Many accidents are caused because people fall. What are the *three* points which a receptionist can check, and report if necessary?

6) Many minor emergencies may arise during the course of a day – cut fingers, splinters, headaches. What does a well-prepared receptionist have handy to enable her to cope?

7) Why can filing cabinets be a source of danger?

8) Boxes or files should not be stacked on top of a filing cabinet. Why?

9) How can filing cabinets be protected so that, in the event of fire, some of the papers inside them can be saved?

10) What should a receptionist do before leaving the reception area and reception desk to discourage burglars?

11) What is HASAWA short for?

12) When was HASAWA introduced?

13) What does HASAWA make regulations about?

14) Who has to carry out these regulations?

15) What do some firms issue to visitors so that the receptionist and other members of the staff can recognise that they *are* visitors?

16) What are issued to employees by many firms?

17) Why are brief cases, handbags and other large bags, searched in some cities?

18) What is the normal procedure after a bomb warning?

19) Why do some firms forbid cameras being taken in by visitors?

20) Property left with the receptionist, or in the reception area, is not the responsibility of the firm. This means that if it is stolen, the firm is not liable for replacing it. What do most firms do about visitors' property which is left with the receptionist, or in the reception area?

CHAPTER 16

First Aid for the Receptionist

What is First Aid?

First Aid means giving immediate help and comfort to anyone who has been taken ill suddenly, or who has had an accident, until skilled medical attention arrives. *Skilled medical attention* means a doctor, a trained nurse or other trained medical workers such as ambulance men. Instant action by a person who has had some first aid training may often save a life, and it will always make a casualty feel less anxious and more comfortable.

Minor Injuries and Ailments

A receptionist may have to deal with visitors' minor injuries, such as cuts or scratches, blisters, splinters; and minor ailments – sore throats or headaches. A well-equipped first aid box will enable her to cope with all of these and should contain the following:

Aspirins	Safety pins
Throat pastilles	Scissors
Adhesive plasters in assorted sizes	Tweezers
	Liquid antiseptic such as Dettol
Bandages – assorted widths	Thermometer
White lint	Indigestion tablets
Cotton wool	Two or three triangular
Antiseptic cream	bandages.

More Serious Conditions

NOSEBLEED

This is frightening, both to the patient and to people around. It should be dealt with by putting a bowl under the patient's head, and then by squeezing the nose. The patient should be instructed *not* to swallow, and to breathe through the mouth. This procedure usually stops the bleeding within a few minutes. If it does not, medical help should be summoned. Nosebleeds are not dangerous provided they do not go on for more than five minutes.

FAINTING

There are various reasons why people faint – hunger (caused, for example, by starting out without breakfast), standing too long in one position, feeling unwell, shock from bad news, anxiety about something unusual, or exceptionally hot weather. Generally, a faint lasts for only a few seconds and the patient recovers consciousness quite quickly. While still unconscious he should be gently turned on to his side with one leg forward and arms clear. This is known as the *Recovery Position* (see illustration below). Any tight clothing – belt, collar, etc. – should be loosened. If a patient does not recover consciousness, he should be covered with a blanket and medical help sent for without any further delay.

It may happen that the patient has fallen while fainting, and knocked his head. He may be concussed. He should be placed in the 'recovery' position, and covered with a blanket, but in addition, his pulse should be taken at regular intervals, and reported to the doctor or ambulance men when they arrive. The normal pulse rate is about 80 a minute.

Some people carry treatment cards with them (diabetics and epileptics) showing which drugs they take regularly. These cards help a doctor to decide what treatment to give to an unconscious patient, and save time if they can be produced quickly on arrival.

SHOCK

This is a state where, although the patient is conscious, he or she feels cold and looks very pale. Shock can be caused by bad news, an accident, or an emotional upset. The important steps are to comfort the patient, perhaps by saying 'I am trained in first aid, and know what I am doing'. Then cover the patient with a blanket, after loosening tight clothing round neck and waist. The patient feels better if she lies on her back with head low and turned to one side and legs raised. Recovery from simple shock is usually quite rapid. A cup of tea or coffee, sweetened (*not alcohol*) can be given if cause of shock is not an injury.

Hot water bottles should never be used, as they can cause serious blisters, especially to an unconscious patient, even through several layers of clothing.

154

Very Serious Conditions

SEVERE BLEEDING FROM CUTS OR OTHER INJURIES

The urgent need is to stop the bleeding as soon as possible. The total amount of blood in the body of an average adult is about 6 litres (about 10½ pints). If an artery or a vein is cut, bleeding may be so rapid that life is endangered very quickly. Blood from an artery is bright red and spurts. Blood from a vein is darker and flows continuously.

Raise the limb which is bleeding, after laying the patient flat. This slows down the heartbeat and reduces the flow of blood around the body.

Control the bleeding by squeezing the sides of the wound together.

Apply a clean dressing – ideally it should be sterile, but a clean handkerchief, a clean tissue or even some folded toilet paper will make a temporary dressing. Bandage very firmly. If bleeding does not stop, add further dressings – do not touch the original ones.

When bleeding seems to have stopped, lower the limb, but tell the patient not to move it.

Cover the patient with blankets and reassure. Bleeding is very frightening and the patient may also be suffering from shock.

An ambulance or doctor should be sent for as quickly as possible, but bleeding must be dealt with first. Someone near at hand can be instructed to telephone for a doctor while the patient is attended to.

BLEEDING FROM AN INTERNAL INJURY

The indications that there may be internal bleeding are:
The patient is very pale, cold and complains of being very thirsty.
There is a very rapid (much more than 80 per minute) and weak pulse.
The insides of lips and lower eyelids are very pale.

The patient should be made comfortable, by loosening tight clothing and covering with a blanket. *Nothing* should be given by mouth. A written note of the pulse rate should be kept.

The ambulance or a doctor should be sent for as quickly as possible.

BROKEN LEG (OR SUSPECTED BROKEN LEG)

Do not move the patient – it may only cause more injuries. Cover the patient to keep him or her warm, while someone sends for an ambulance or doctor. Treat the patient for shock.

BROKEN ARM (OR SUSPECTED BROKEN ARM)

Support the arm with a sling and keep the patient sitting in a comfortable position. Cover to keep warm. Treat for shock. Send for medical help.

155

RECOVERY POSITION

The 'recovery' position means simply turning a casualty on his side, with one knee forward, head to one side and arms clear, so that if he is sick he will not drown in his vomit. Merely doing this may save a life.

If the Patient Stops Breathing

An unconscious patient may stop breathing because the lungs are not receiving a sufficient supply of air. If the brain does not receive oxygen, the patient will die after five minutes, so something has to be done quickly. The sign of lack of oxygen is 'snoring' (stertorous breathing). Artificial respiration must be started at once, and continued either until breathing starts or a doctor arrives. There are two ways of carrying out artificial respiration, as follows.

THE HOLGER NIELSEN METHOD

This method of artificial respiration is not suitable when there are injuries to the arms, shoulders or ribs.

Place the casualty face downwards on a flat surface. His hands, one over the other, should be level with his forehead, and his head turned to one side so that his cheek rests on the uppermost hand.

A first-aider should kneel at the casualty's head (one knee on floor and foot of other leg near casualty's elbow).

Place his hands on his back just below his shoulder blade.

Count 'One'.

Keeping the elbows straight, rock forwards until the arms are almost vertical, exerting steady pressure on the casualty's chest.

Count 'Two, three, four'.

Grasp the casualty's arms just above his elbows and rock backwards, raising his arms until resistance and tension are felt at the casualty's shoulders.

Count 'Five, six, seven'.

156

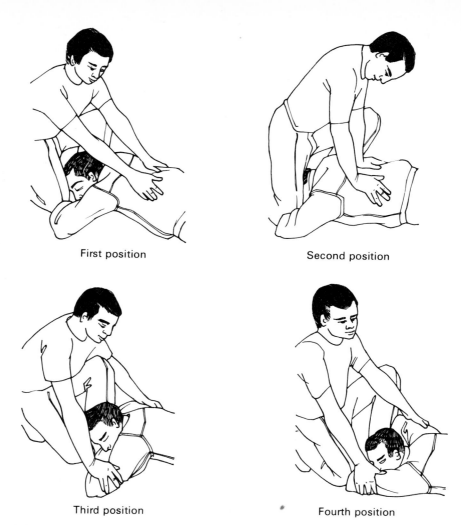

First position

Second position

Third position

Fourth position

Then drop his arms. The phases of expansion should each last 2½ seconds, the complete cycle repeated 12 times per minute. A count of 'one' to 'eight', rhythmically with each movement, is helpful.

Count 'Eight'.

MOUTH-TO-MOUTH RESUSCITATION

The other, more modern method of treating asphyxia (lack of oxygen to the lungs) is mouth-to-mouth resuscitation. The hand should be placed under the patient's neck. The patient should be lying on his back. Force the tongue forward by tilting the head back, after removing any false teeth, and nip the nose. Then spread your own mouth over the patient's mouth and blow gently. No force is required. Remove your mouth, then repeat until the patient starts breathing or a doctor arrives. A soon as breathing starts, place the casualty in a 'recovery position' to prevent inhalation of fluid or vomit.

157

It is very important to send someone immediately for medical help while one of the above methods of artificial respiration is being carried out.

Other Emergency Situations

OUTBREAK OF FIRE

It is important to prevent panic – even a small fire can cause a great deal of smoke. If fire *is* small and localised, deal with it by means of a fire extinguisher. Clear everyone out of the area, and prevent anyone from entering.

In the case of a larger fire, where smoke fumes may have caused casualties, drag unconscious people out by their shoulders. Do not try to go into a smoke-filled room to treat a casualty, or you will be another. Follow the firm's procedure for sounding the Fire Alarm (to clear the building), and also take steps to prevent anyone (except the Fire Brigade) from entering the building. Switch off and unplug electrical appliances. Close all windows, fire doors and other communicating doors. Leave the reception area and go to a previously agreed place of safety.

Follow procedure swiftly

TREATING BURNS

1) Place the part affected under cold running water or place it in a bowl of cold water.

2) Do not remove burnt clothing (it has been sterilised by the heat).

3) Do not break blisters – keep them in cold water if still painful.

4) Remove anything tight – rings, bracelets, belts, boots – before part starts to swell.

158

5) Cover the burn with a sterile dressing, or clean lint or handkerchief or clean tissue.

6) Bandage gently, to hold dressing in place.

ELECTRIC SHOCK

Switch off the appliance which is causing the shock at the socket and *unplug,* if possible. Do not touch the appliance. Remove the body without touching it, using, for example, a walking stick, if it is not possible to switch off electricity. Treat the casualty for shock, or, if unconscious, use the recovery position. The casualty may also have severe burns, which must receive attention.

General Guidelines

1) Check the first aid box weekly to replace supplies.

2) Know the firm's fire drill thoroughly, and how to use the fire extinguishers.

3) Remember at all times the importance of common sense and keeping calm when dealing with casualties, as well as knowing how to give first aid.

4) Keep very clearly in mind what to do first – always arrange for someone else to call for medical help, while you attend to the casualty – this may save a life.

5) Never leave an unconscious person – always stay with him until a doctor arrives.

6) Carry on with artificial respiration until breathing has started, or the doctor comes. If you become tired, perhaps someone else can take over.

7) Always try to reassure a casualty. Remember he or she will be frightened as well as shocked.

8) Ensure privacy – get rid of other people as quickly as possible – except those able to help.

9) Keep the casualty warmly covered, but make sure of fresh air by opening a nearby window or outside door.

10) Remember that anything you can tell the doctor, when he arrives, of the casualty's condition (e.g. pulse rate) will help to save time and may save a life.

Procedures for Recording Accidents

An accident book should be kept in the Reception Area, in which is entered details of any accident and any treatment that is given to visitors to the firm. A page from an accident book could be as below:

DATE 198–	NAME	ADDRESS	ACCIDENT OR ILLNESS
28 February	Graham Timms	34 Lynwood Close Roker Sunderland	Nosebleed – sent to surgery.
2 March	Maureen Evans	5 Willow Way Washington Co. Durham	Foreign body in eye – removed in Reception.
6 March	Janet March	78 Cathedral Way Durham	Burn on left hand – dressed in Reception.
	Paul Stokes	The Elms Cliffe Avenue Whitburn Co. Durham	Fainted – treated in Reception.
11 March	Debra Watts	106 High Lane Ponteland Newcastle upon Tyne	Fell & cut knee – taken to surgery.
	John Vine	299 Lilac Avenue Kingston-upon-Thames	Splinter in finger – removed in Reception.

It is important to keep a record of accidents, and treatment, however minor, in case of claims being made against the firm at a later date, should there be any serious developments from the accident, for compensation.

Exercise 54

FIRST AID AND SAFETY IN RECEPTION

Choose in each case which is the correct answer: **a, b** *or* **c**

1) The correct treatment for a nosebleed is:
   a lie the patient flat on his or her back
   b squeeze the nose, telling the patient not to swallow and breathe through the mouth
   c lie the patient flat on his or her stomach.

2) The total amount of blood in the average adult is:
   a 6 litres
   b 4 litres
   c 8 litres.

3) Arterial blood is:
    a dark red
    b very pale
    c bright red.

4) Venous blood (blood flowing in the veins) is:
    a dark red
    b bright red
    c very pale.

5) Blood which *spurts* out of a wound is:
    a venous
    b arterial
    c capillary.

6) The correct treatment for severe bleeding from an injured limb is initially:
    a do nothing, but send for an ambulance or a doctor
    b keep the patient standing while the limb is raised
    c raise the limb and lay the patient flat.

7) After the correct procedure for severe bleeding has been carried out, the next step is to:
    a bathe with warm water and antiseptic
    b apply pressure to both edges of wound
    c apply antiseptic ointment.

8) Finally, when bleeding has slowed down you should:
    a apply dressing, (preferably sterile, but certainly clean) and bandage firmly
    b bandage loosely over the clean dressing
    c leave unbandaged, after applying the dressing.

9) Hot water bottles should be used, for unconscious patients or those suffering from shock:
    a occasionally
    b only in winter
    c never.

10) Shock should be treated by:
    a raising the patient's legs, after turning him to one side, and lying him flat
    b keeping the patient in a sitting position
    c making the patient walk around the room.

11) Fainting should be treated by:
    a sitting the patient in a chair
    b gently lying the patient flat and turning him on his side with one leg forward and arms clear
    c fanning the patient with a newspaper.

12) Asphyxia (this means that the patient has stopped breathing) should be treated by:
   a artificial respiration
   b artificial inspiration
   c artificial instruction.

13) The other, more modern, method of treating asphyxia is:
   a mouth-to-mouth ventilation
   b mouth-to-mouth resuscitation
   c mouth-to-mouth inflation.

14) The best treatment to be given *immediately* for a suspected broken leg is:
   a to get the patient on to a comfortable chair
   b to cover the patient warmly where he is lying without moving him
   c to get patient to stand.

15) If the casualty has received a severe electric shock and is unconscious, the first step is:
   a to switch off the electric lights
   b to turn off the electricity at the mains
   c to switch off the electricity and unplug.

Answer the following questions:

16) What is the correct procedure when making an emergency call for an ambulance?

17) What is the name of the Act passed in 1974 which lays down laws about people's safety at work?

18) What three things can the receptionist do to make sure visitors to her firm do not have an accident?

EMERGENCY SITUATIONS FOR THE RECEPTIONIST

Read through the following, think about the circumstances, and then describe what you would do in each case:

19) It is a warm summer's day and there are several people waiting in the reception area. Suddenly Miss Parker, aged about 70, faints.

20) A pedestrian slips on an icy pavement outside your firm, and falls heavily. She is brought into the reception area, badly shocked.

21) An electrician, Tony Sparkes, is installing electric storage heaters in the reception area. Whilst connecting one of the heaters to the mains he receives an electric shock and becomes unconscious.

22) You are the first to arrive at your firm one morning, and can smell smoke from somewhere in the building.

23) An applicant for the post of the Sales Manager's secretary, waiting for her interview, suddenly has a violent nosebleed.

24) Mr Jenkins, from the Accounts Department, is coming downstairs and looking through some papers at the same time. He trips and falls down the remaining steps. You suspect that he has broken a leg – he is in severe pain.

25) Sue Jones, from the Filing Department, comes running into your office and trips over the bottom drawer of the filing cabinet which you have left open. She cuts her leg very badly, and there is heavy bleeding.

26) The telephone rings (it is an outside call) and a voice says 'There is a bomb in your building. It will explode in five minutes!'

27) A message arrives by telephone for one of the typists in the Typing Pool. It is to tell her that her boyfriend has been involved in a car accident and is in hospital. You telephone to the Typing Pool and ask her to come to reception so that you are able to pass the message on personally. She is badly shocked.

28) A visitor waiting in the reception area suddenly starts to cough violently and becomes unconscious. His breathing becomes stertorous and eventually stops.

CHAPTER 17

Business Entertaining

Serving Tea and Coffee

The most common form of business entertainment that a telephonist or receptionist will be called upon to arrange, is the provision of a tea or coffee tray for visitors. On the tray you will need the following.

A TRAY FOR TEA

A clean tray cloth
Stands for teapot and hot water jug
Tea pot
Hot water jug
Cold milk in jug
Sugar in basin with spoon (or tongs for lump sugar)
Slop basin
Tea strainer
Tea cups and saucers
Teaspoons.

A TRAY FOR COFFEE

A clean tray cloth
Coffee pot
Jug of hot milk or jug of cream
Stands for coffeepot and hot milk jug
Sugar basin and spoon (or tongs for lump sugar) (NB Many people prefer brown sugar in coffee)
Coffee cups and saucers
Coffeespoons (or teaspoons).

Preparing tray. Make sure that the items on the tray are evenly balanced for carrying. Place tea- or coffeepot on the right-hand side with handle facing guests for ease of pouring. Tea or coffee should be placed on the tray at the very last moment, so that it is served hot.

When serving coffee, guests must be asked if they would prefer black coffee, or coffee with milk or cream, *not* 'black coffee' or 'white coffee' – there is no such thing as 'white coffee'.

Preparing for Parties and Lunches

SHERRY PARTY

Arrange for the sherry to be poured into sherry glasses in a separate room from the party if possible (if impossible use a side table) and serve to guests from a suitable tray. Serve dry, medium and sweet sherry with small cheese biscuits, crisps and nuts, allowing one bottle of sherry for every 12 guests.

Also have available soft drinks and mineral water.

COCKTAIL PARTIES

Cocktail parties are more elaborate than sherry parties, requiring a variety of alcoholic drinks, means of mixing cocktails (possibly a professional barman to do this) and food. Suitable food at these parties could include:
Vol-au-vents with various savoury fillings
Savoury dips for biscuits
Cubed cheese
Paté
Spiced cocktail sausages
Mixed nuts
Crisps
Party pies (warmed)
Stuffed celery
Various sandwiches.

BUSINESS LUNCHES

To arrange a successful business lunch, you need the assistance of a specialist outside caterer, or your company executive canteen if you have one, and their staff. Suitable menus could be:

165

Summer	Winter
Grapefruit	Vegetable soup
Melon	Casserole of beef
or	Vegetables
Consommé	Jacket potatoes
Assorted salad	Side salad
Cold roast ham or chicken	Fruit pie and cream
Ice cream	Cheese and biscuits
Fresh fruit salad	Coffee
Raspberries or strawberries in season	
Cheese and biscuits	
Coffee	

Exercise 55

SETTING TRAYS

Write these notes in your folder, filling in the missing words and phrases.

1) When preparing a tray for tea or coffee, make sure that items on the tray are _____ balanced.

2) Place coffeepot or teapot on _____ with handle facing _____ for ease of pouring.

3) Place tea or coffee on tray at the very last moment, so that it is served very _____ .

4) When serving coffee, guests must be asked if they prefer _____ coffee, or coffee with milk or _____ .

Exercise 56

SUITABLE FOOD FOR BUSINESS ENTERTAINING

1) The allowance of sherry for 12 people is _____ .

2) Suitable for serving with sherry are _____ , crisps and _____ .

3) For people who do not drink alcohol, it is necessary to have available soft drinks and _____ .

4) For a cocktail party, suitable food could include sandwiches, savoury dips _____ , cheese, stuffed _____ and party pies (_____).

5) Cold food is suitable for business lunches in summer and might include melon (to start with), salad and _____ ,fresh fruit _____ , followed by cheese and biscuits and _____ .

6) Winter business lunches should consist of hot food and _____
   soup would be suitable to start with, followed by _____
   beef, vegetables, _____ potatoes and a side _____ .
   A _____ pie and cream or cheese and biscuits followed by
   coffee would be a suitable finish to the meal.

LAYING TABLES

The tablecloth must be clean and crisply starched. Make sure that the centre fold of the cloth is on the middle of the table – this ensures an even overlap all the way round the table.

In addition to cutlery, the following is also placed on the table:
Cruet: salt, pepper, mustard and mustard spoon
Vase of flowers
Ashtray(s)
Table number (if necessary).

There may also be:
Peppermill
*Rolls in a roll basket
*Butter pats (or portions in foil)
Bread sticks.

*The correct procedure is to offer rolls to guests after they have been seated, with the butter. (In a warm room butter will quickly go soft.)

CUTLERY

Cutlery laid on a table ready for guests depends on the food to be served, but a normal place setting consists of:
Soup spoon
Joint knife and fork
Dessert spoon and fork
Side knife.

The side knife should be placed on the side plate, at the left. The order for the remainder of the cutlery (from the right-hand side in) is:
Soup spoon
Joint knife and fork (either side of place setting).

Dessert spoon and fork are placed at right angles to knife and fork, at the top of the place setting.

CHINA

The side plate is placed at left of place setting. Other plates are brought in (warmed) as food is served and removed when finished.

GLASSES

A wine glass is placed at top right of place setting and is removed (if not required) and replaced by water glass or glass for soft drink, if requested.

Cutlery, china and glasses must be sparkling clean and shining.

Glasses and cutlery should be free of smears and fingermarks, and polished with a clean, dry lint-free cloth. Make sure both glass and china is free from chips and cracks before using.

SERVIETTES

These must match the tablecloth in cleanliness and crispness and should be placed between the cutlery of the place setting.

There are many ways of folding serviettes, some of them very complicated and suitable only for grand banquets. A simple one which is easily and quickly done is the best choice, as the serviettes then have the minimum amount of handling. Two such forms are described as follows:

1) Fold the serviette edge to edge twice, first into a square and then into a triangle.

2) Fold serviette into three (as shown), pleat, open out and place in wineglass where it will form a fan-shape.

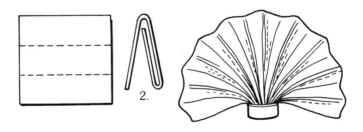

1. Fold the serviette into three in the manner shown in diagram 2

3. Pleat, open out, and place in a serviette ring or glass

The fan

3) Fold serviette into three, then fold corners down to centre line as shown; next fold flaps underneath, then fold triangular parts at centre line, finally curl triangular flat round, forming a cone shape (see illustration).

168

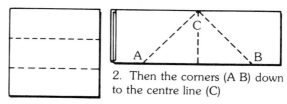

2. Then the corners (A B) down to the centre line (C)

1. Fold the serviette into three

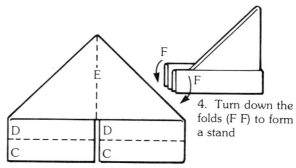

4. Turn down the folds (F F) to form a stand

3. Fold the flaps (C D C D) underneath then fold triangular parts at centre line (E)

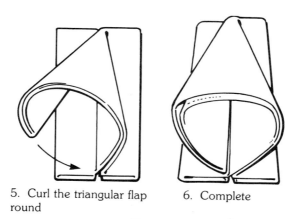

5. Curl the triangular flap round

6. Complete

The cone

Exercise 57

LAYING TABLES

Write these notes in your folder, filling in the missing words and phrases.

1) Make sure that the centre fold of the tablecloth is on the _____ of the table.

169

2) In addition to cutlery, the following is placed on the table:
cruet

_____

ashtray
table number (if necessary).

3) There may also be on the table:
peppermill
rolls in a roll basket
bread sticks

_____ .

4) A normal place setting of cutlery consists of:
soup spoon
joint knife and fork

_____

side knife.

5) The side knife should be placed on the _____ at the left.

6) The order for the remainder of the cutlery is (from the outside in):
soup spoon (_____ hand)
joint knife and _____ (either side of place setting).

7) Dessert spoon and _____ are placed at right angles to knife
and _____ at the _____ of the place setting.

8) Side plate is placed at _____ of place setting.

9) Other plates are brought in (warmed) as food is served and
_____ when finished.

10) The wine glass is placed at top _____ of the place setting.

11) If water or a soft drink is being served, a suitable glass should be
brought, if _____ .

12) Serviettes must match the tablecloth in cleanliness and _____ .

Serving Wines

There are a great variety of glasses available for serving wine, in all
shapes and sizes. Never use the champagne 'saucer' as the bouquet of
the wine and its bubbles are quickly lost in it. Avoid all coloured glasses
because they will make many wines served in them look terrible. A
wine glass known as the 6 oz Paris goblet is a good all-rounder. It can
be used to serve any wines – including sherry – and also for liqueurs
afterwards. Wine glasses should never be more than half full; this
leaves plenty of room for the 'bouquet' (the aroma) of the wine to fill
the glass.

170

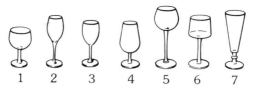

Shapes of wine glasses

1. Paris goblet 2. Tulip glass 3. Tulip glass 4. Sherry copita
5. Glass for German and Alsation wines 6. Anjou glass
7. Champagne flûte

There is no 'law' which lays down which wine should be drunk with a particular type of food, but traditionally, white wine is served with fish and fowl and red wine with meat and cheese. A sweeter white wine is served with desserts. White wine should be chilled – preferably in a refrigerator, or at least placed in as cool a position as possible – for several hours before serving. Red wine should be opened and left in a room for an hour or so before serving to reach normal room temperature.

Allow half a bottle of wine per person whatever the type of party, and the longer the event is likely to last, the more wine should be allowed. Never under-estimate – nothing is worse than having the drink run out. A party likely to last several hours may need nearer one bottle per person. Many wine shops allow wine to be sold on a sale or return basis, which means that unopened bottles will not be charged for. Many of these shops also lend glasses, or it should be possible to hire them cheaply.

Arrange sparkling clean glasses on trays (with tray cloths) which should be half-filled (two-thirds if sherry) as guests start to arrive; circulate constantly ensuring that no one is left with an empty glass, or without a glass. Before handing wine (or sherry) to a guest, ask if he or she will take it – some people prefer a non-alcoholic soft drink, which should always be available. Glasses should be refilled when empty, after checking what the guest is drinking.

Sherry is often served chilled, or even (in the summer) on ice; more usually, however, it is kept at room temperature. Guests should be asked if they would prefer dry, medium or sweet sherry.

Exercise 58

SERVING WINES CORRECTLY

Write these notes in your folder, filling in the missing words and phrases.

1) A useful 'all-round' glass is the 6 oz _____ .

2) A wine glass should never be more than _____ full.

171

3) Traditionally, _____ wine is served with fish and chicken and _____ wine with meat and cheese.

4) A _____ white wine is served with desserts.

5) _____ should be chilled (preferably in a refrigerator) for several hours before serving.

6) _____ wine should be opened and left in a room for an hour or so before serving to reach normal room temperature.

7) Allow at least _____ bottle of wine per person.

8) Always make sure glasses are sparkling clean by _____ them before use with a lint-free cloth.

9) Refill wine glasses after the first serving without _____ question.

10) Sherry is usually kept at room temperature and glasses filled _____ from the rim.

11) Guests should be asked if they would prefer dry, medium or _____ sherry.

12) Refill sherry glasses when _____ .

Making Introductions

Always introduce the man to the woman by saying:

"Mrs Jones, may I introduce Mr Smith, manager of Diddlem and Dunnem, Insurance Brokers?"

When introducing two women to each other introduce the younger woman to the older woman. Find out (if you do not already know) whether a woman is married or not, and whether she prefers 'Mrs' or 'Ms'.

If *you* are introduced to someone, shake hands and say, "How do you do".

The person to whom you are being introduced will reply: "How do you do" also, but does not require an answer. *Do not say* "Pleased to meet you".

HOW NOT TO MAKE AN INTRODUCTION

The scene is a midday sherry party in a firm. About 20 people have been invited. The receptionist has the job of receiving the guests and introducing them to each other.

Rec. (To new arrival) Good morning. May I have your name, please?

New arr. Good morning. I'm Margaret Johns (she is an attractive 25-year-old).

172

Rec.	Come this way, please (both go into party area).
MJ	I don't know a soul.
Rec.	Don't worry, I'll introduce you to the lady standing by the window on her own.
MJ	Oh, thanks.
Rec.	(Going up to the lady by the window, who has white hair and is obviously over 50) Margaret Johns – Mrs Marshall.
Mrs M	How do you do?
MJ	How do you do?

The errors in the above are:

1) The receptionist should have asked Margaret Johns whether she is married or single, and whether she wishes to be introduced as Mrs, Miss or Ms.

2) The receptionist should have said "Mrs Marshall, this is Mrs/Miss/Ms Johns".

Exercise 59

MAKING INTRODUCTIONS

Re-write the following, making the necessary alterations:

The scene is an evening cocktail party in the reception area of a large firm. The receptionist is helping to make people feel welcome.

New arr.	Good evening. I'm Stephen Grainger, from International Products Ltd, New York.
Rec.	Good evening, Mr Grainger. Please follow me and I'll introduce you to one or two of the guests.
SG	Thank you very much.
	They go into the party.
Rec.	(Approaching a middle-aged lady) Mr Grainger this is Miss Lester, of the Marshalsea Corporation. Mr Grainger is the Chief Buyer for International Products Ltd, New York.
SG	How do you do?
ML	How do you do?
Rec.	I see some more guests have arrived, I'll leave you to chat.

Exercise 60

MAKING INTRODUCTIONS

Copy the following notes, filling in the missing words and phrases.

1) Introduce the man to the _____ .

2) Introduce the younger woman to the _____ woman.

3) Find out if a woman is married or ＿＿＿＿＿＿ and whether she prefers 'Mrs' or 'Ms'.

4) When you are introduced to someone, say: ＿＿＿＿＿＿ .

5) Do not say: ＿＿＿＿＿＿ .

Take care when making an introduction

CHAPTER 18

Basic Office Arithmetic

Telephonists and receptionists may often find it necessary to work out some calculations. This is not a textbook on the subject, but offers a few exercises for you to practise some basic arithmetical calculations. You may use a calculator if you wish.

Exercise 61

ADDITION AND SUBTRACTION OF MONEY

1) A man pays £12.62 per week in National Insurance contributions. How much will he pay in a year?

2) You work in a small office and are responsible for making up the wages. The net pay of three people is: £38.45, £65.80 and £54.18. What is the total net pay of the three people?

3) You have to buy stamps for the office and require: 30 @ 16p, 40 @ 12½p, 8 @ £1.00, 12 @ 50p, 16 @ 30p and 12 @ 5p. How much money is required to pay for these stamps?

4) If you have £25.00 petty cash imprest in the petty cash box and spend the following sums: £1.48, £6.84, £2.30, 25p, £4.99, how much should be left in the box?

Exercise 62

WORKING OUT PERCENTAGES

1) With Value Added Tax (VAT) at 15%, how much tax would you pay on articles whose price less tax is as follows:
£3.00, £24.00, £38.50, £8.54, 84p, £125.60, £16.00, £9.30 (round up figures to whole pence).

2) You buy an article priced at £40.00 less 5% discount. How much will you pay for it?

3) How much VAT will you pay on the discounted price?

4) You are left some money in a relative's will and decide to buy a new car. The *list* price is £4320, but due to competition one dealer offers you 16% off the list price. How much would you pay for the car?

5) Refer to Question 4. Additional costs to get the car on to the road are:

Delivery   £25
Number plates   £5
Insurance   £230
Road fund licence   £45   (for six months)

How much will it cost you altogether before driving the car from the dealer's premises?

Exercise 63

TRAVEL

1) One of your managers has asked you to make arrangements for him to go to Paris by car. You do this, and tell him that from Le Havre to Paris by road is 224 kilometres. He wants to know how long it will take him to get from Le Havre to Paris if he averages 50 miles per hour.

Method:
One kilometre equals ⅝ mile, therefore there are fewer miles than kilometres. Convert kilometres to miles by dividing kilometres by 8 and multiplying result by 5, i.e. $224 \times ⅝ =$
Since he wants to know how long it will take, driving at an average speed of 50 miles per hour, you now divide the distance in miles by the average speed, which gives the driving time in hours.

2) Your boss asks you to hire a car for him to go to Manchester from Hereford, a distance of 120 miles. If the hire company charges £10 per day plus 8p per mile, what will be the total cost if the car is kept for two days and 30 miles are added for driving in Manchester before returning to Hereford?

3) The distance from London to Southampton is 180 miles. Your boss has an appointment in Southampton at 1430 hours. Assuming an average speed of 45 miles per hour, how much time can he have for lunch if he leaves London at 0900 hours?

4) You have an appointment in London at 1400 hours. Travelling by train from Birmingham to Euston (London) takes one hour and thirty minutes. From your office to Birmingham (New Street Station) takes 40 minutes, with a further 35 minutes' journey by Underground train in London plus 10 minutes to get from the Underground station to the place of the appointment. Trains leave Birmingham on the hour and at half past the hour. What is the departure time of the last train in Birmingham you must catch if your appointment is to be kept on time?

Exercise 64

TIME

Many people use what is known as the 24-hour clock system, where after 12 noon each hour continues the sequence of numbers on from 13 to 24 as a four-figure number. For example, 1 pm becomes 1300 hours and 4.20 am becomes 0420. To revert to 'normal' time you take 12 off the hour figure when this is 13 or more. To find '24-hour' time from 'normal' time, you add 12 to the hour figure from 1 pm until 11.59 pm. Times from midnight until 12.59 pm are the same in both systems.

1) You have calculated that a job will take 2.4 hours. How many hours and *minutes* does this mean?

2) You have to make a telephone call 50 minutes from now (which is a quarter past three). At what time will you make the call?

3) Convert the following from normal time to 24-hour time:
0.18 pm, 6.40 pm, quarter to eight in the evening, 4.30 pm, 2.45 pm, 5.25 pm, 12.30 pm, 11.55 pm, 3.00 pm.

4) The time in the Bahamas is 5 hours behind London time. Your boss has arranged to telephone the Bahamas office at 1015 hours their time. At what time in England should the call be made?

5) Business hours in Hong Kong are from 0900 to 1700. Their time is 8 hours in front of UK time. Your office hours are 0800 until 1700. Between what times should a telephone call be made to Hong Kong from your office, to be sure of talking to them before their office closes?

Exercise 65

CONVERTING IMPERIAL TO METRIC MEASURE

In answering Questions 1–4 assume that 2.5 cm equals one inch. To convert centimetres to inches, divide the centimetre sizes by 2.5; the answer is in inches.

1) It is proposed to instal a new word processor on your desk, which measures 48″ × 30″. The word processor measures 43 cm × 59 cm and the display unit base measures 32 cm × 40 cm. What is the size of:
   a the word processor ⎱ in inches?
   b the display unit ⎰

2) Find the length and width of the desk in Question 1 in centimetres.

3) The office plan gives the size of your office door as being 6′ 6″ high and 2′ 6″ wide. A new cupboard is being delivered, whose size in the manufacturer's catalogue is given as 25 cm high, 80 cm wide and 80 cm deep.
   Check by converting the cupboard size from centimetres to feet and inches whether the cupboard will pass through the door.

4) The internal dimensions of an index file card box you use are 5¼″ × 3″. File cards are now sold in metric sizes. Will a card 12.5 cm × 7.5 cm be suitable for the box?

5) One gallon of petrol can be assumed to be equal to 4.5 litres. If you are in France and want the equivalent of 8 gallons in your petrol tank, how many litres would you ask for?

General Exercises

Exercise 66

REVISION

Copy the following sentences, and fill in the spaces with a word (or phrase) chosen from the list below. Each word (or phrase) is used only once.

AA or RAC Book	message form	stand
appointments register	passes	switchboard
callers' business visiting cards	pinned	tactful
callers' register	pleasant	type
impression	polite	visitors' badges
main entrance	staff 'in and out' book	

1) The reception area in a firm should be pleasant and comfortable, as it gives callers their first _____ of the firm.

2) So that callers are able to find a reception area easily, it is usually situated near to the _____ to a firm.

3) As the receptionist may be the first person a caller speaks to in a firm, it is important that she has a _____ voice and a friendly, _____ manner.

4) However difficult a caller may be, the receptionist must remain calm, patient and _____ .

5) As well as looking after visitors to a firm, the receptionist may be in charge of a _____ and be able to _____ .

6) The receptionist should have near her desk an _____ for looking up names of hotels.

7) A record of callers is kept by the receptionist in a _____ .

8) Details of callers who have made appointments is kept by the receptionist in an _____ .

9) Two card indexes are very useful to the receptionist. One is an index of frequently used telephone numbers, and the other one is an index of _____ .

10) So that callers are able to use the receptionist's name when speaking to her, she should have her name on a small _____ on the desk in front of her, or _____ to her dress in the form of a brooch.

11) A _____ is useful for recording the absences of employees from a firm during working hours.

12) _____ are issued in some firms by the receptionist for security reasons.

13) All employees in some firms are given _____ once a year with their photographs on, which they have to sign.

14) A _____ is useful, because it acts as a reminder to the receptionist of what to write down when taking a message.

Exercise 67

PRACTICAL WORK ON RECEPTION

Choose a receptionist and make a name card for her to stand on her desk in front of her.

Arrange for five visitors with appointments.

Choose five callers without appointments. Perhaps one could be a little awkward, one could speak very little English, and one could be slightly deaf.

Arrange for three of your class to be employees of the firm who go out for various reasons. Two of them return.

You will need:
One page from a callers' register
One page from an appointments book
One page from a staff 'in and out' book.

Date them all for today.

At the end of this practical work, the callers' register should show the names of *all* the callers – both with and without appointments. It should also show what action was taken about those without appointments (including the awkward caller!).

The appointments book will contain only the names of the visitors who had made appointments beforehand.

The staff 'in and out' book should show the times employees went out and came back (if they did) and the reasons for their absences.

If there is a cassette recorder available, tape the conversations between the receptionist and the visitors, and then play the conversations back, for general criticism and discussion.

Exercise 68

A COMPLETE REVISION

This assignment attempts to cover all the learning objectives as far as it is possible in a written paper.

Answer all the following questions by ticking (in pencil) the correct answer at the side.

1) An organisation chart shows:
   a the layout of the firm
   b the names of all the executives
   c the names of all the secretaries
   d the names of all the organisers of fund-raising activities.

2) If you wished to arrange with a painter and decorator to redecorate your office, you would find a decorator's number by using:
   a the Telephone Directory
   b a Classified Trade Directory
   c a Pears Cyclopaedia
   d a Telex Directory.

3) Assuming you wish to send a telemessage, how would you find the number to dial in order to dictate it over the telephone?
   a consult your local Dialling Code Booklet or Telephone Directory
   b look among the 'Ts' for Telemessages
   c ask a friend and hope she can do it for you
   d look in the classified trades directory.

4) If you had to take down a telephone message, what would be the essential features?
   a the message and the name of the caller
   b the date and time of the message, the message itself, the name of the person for whom the message is intended, and the signature of the person receiving the message
   c the date and time of the message
   d the name of the person actually taking down the message.

5) In which order will business visiting cards be filed?
   a alphabetical order of the callers' names
   b numerical order of the firms' telephone numbers
   c alphabetical order of the firms' names
   d numerical order of the firms' Telex numbers.

6) If a casualty has received a severe electric shock and is unconscious, the *first* step is:
   a switch of electric lights
   b turn off electricity at the mains
   c switch off electricity and unplug appliance
   d call for an ambulance.

7) You are working on the switchboard of a firm. Would you answer a call with:
   a Hello. Can I help you?
   b This is Peggy Brown speaking.
   c The name of your firm.
   d Good morning, Peggy Brown speaking.

8) Certain subjects discussed during telephone calls may be confidential. To ensure that no confidential information she may hear is passed on, a switchboard operator should:
   a write everything down in a special code
   b never repeat *anything* she hears
   c only tell her *very* best friends
   d only tell people she can trust.

9) As a switchboard operator, you are trying to connect a customer to a certain department but the line is engaged. Would you:
   a tell the customer immediately that the line is engaged and ask him/her to telephone later
   b tell the customer the line is engaged and ask him/her if he/she wishes to hold the line, but keep him/her informed from time to time
   c tell the customer the line is engaged and ask him/her if he/she wishes to hold the line and, when the line is free (even ten minutes later) connect him/her
   d tell the customer the line is engaged.

10) Many firms make arrangements to protect themselves against claims for compensation for lost property by:
    a displaying large notices to this effect in reception
    b announcing it at frequent intervals over the loudspeaker system
    c displaying it on a noticeboard outside the firm
    d giving each visitor a copy of the notice to read.

11) There are six emergency telephone services. Five of them are:
    Fire   Lifeboat
    Police   Cave and Mountain Rescue
    Ambulance
    The *sixth* one is:
    Water Board   Electricity Board
    Gas Board   Coastguard.

12) The receptionist cannot leave her desk to distribute messages around a firm, so she arranges for them to be taken by:
    a a commissioner
    b a commissionaire
    c a commisariat
    d a commissar.

13) After dialling a number on the telephone, you should hear a repeated, single note. This is the:
    a dialling tone

b ringing tone
c paytone
d engaged tone.

14) If your office has a rule that employees pay for all calls, and you are making a call for yourself, how would you arrange to find out how much to pay to the office account?
a make a fixed-time call
b make an advise duration and charge call
c make a person-to-person call
d make a transferred charge call.

15) When some members of the office staff have telephone credit cards, so that they are able to make calls from a callbox without payment at the time, how does British Telecom eventually get paid?
a The firm pays a flat rate for the card so that the operator does not have to record the call.
b The operator is given the number on the card.
c The operator asks the telephone number from which you are calling and charges that number.
d The firm is told how many calls have been made, and they send a list to British Telecom for adding to the firm's account.

16) Where would you send a telemessage from?
a the Post Office (hand it over the counter)
b by telephone
c by ordinary post
d by airmail.

17) A receptionist should be able to cope with a threatened outbreak of fire by:
a giving up smoking
b joining the Fire Brigade
c knowing the fire drill and fire exits
d attending a first aid course.

18) You have been asked to spread some information quickly amongst all employees (works and offices). Which method would be the most effective?
a telephone
b pocket paging
c bells and buzzers
d loudspeaker system.

19) When you send a telemessage, you pay by:
a calling in at the post office
b asking for the bill to be sent to you
c sending a postal order to British Telecom
d giving the telephone operator your telephone number so that the cost of the telemessage can be added to your telephone account.

Complete the following questions.

20) Describe how you would care for the flower arrangements in your reception area.

21) Set out briefly what you consider to be the main qualities of a receptionist/telephonist. Include in your answer her manner, appearance and attitude to the public. Mention her importance to the firm she works for and the part she plays in the firm's communications.

22) Certain points should be borne in mind when dealing with callers. Mention:
   a three such points in relation to personal callers at the reception desk
   b two in respect of telephone calls.

23) What are the reference books and record books a receptionist will keep at her desk? Describe the functions of each.

24) What use would the receptionist/telephonist make of the following?
   a a House Journal
   b card index of callers' cards
   c form letters
   d plan of firm.

25) What do you understand by the following?
   a the telephonist's alphabet
   b a paging system
   c a telephone answering machine
   d a PMBX switchboard.

26) What is the name of the Act passed in 1974 which lays down the law about people's safety at work? Mention how this Act will affect the receptionist and what she should do to lessen the possibility of accidents to the staff and visitors.

27) **a** How would the British Telecom Telex service be of use in an office?
   b What are the advantages of using punched tape on a teleprinter?
   c How are Telex calls charged for?

28) **a** What is the importance of an internal telephone directory?
   b How should it be used?
   c How should it be arranged?

29) Describe how to set a tray for serving:
   a tea
   b coffee.

30) What cutlery and china is placed on a table before guests are seated?

Additional Exercises

Telephone Equipment

1) Under what circumstances would several people be likely to want to listen to a caller at the same time? What is the equipment they would need to enable them to do this?

2) What advantages has a telephone answering machine over a teleprinter? Compare these two types of equipment, and give:
   a their similarities and
   b the ways in which they are quite different.

3) Tape callmakers and punched card callmakers have one main advantage over the ordinary dialling systems. Explain what it is, and also give the other advantages of these two ways of dialling telephone calls.

Telephone Services

Copy the following sentences, and fill in the missing words.

1) If it is essential to be woken during the night, the British Telecom telephone operator will ring and continue to ring until the telephone is answered. This is known as an _____ call.

2) To avoid unnecessary expense when telephoning someone who may often be a long way from his telephone, a _____ cuts down the cost, as only a small surcharge is made up to the time the caller actually speaks to the person he wants.

3) It is possible to make a telephone call without paying anything at the time of the call, from a public call-box, by asking the operator to ring the number required and asking permission of the person called to accept the charge for the call. This is known as a _____ call.

4) People who travel around the country and have to make frequent telephone calls to their head office will find a _____ very useful, as this enables them to telephone from a public call-box without putting in coins – all they have to do is to give the British Telecom operator their _____ number.

5) Many advertisements encourage the public to telephone the firm advertising to ask for samples, catalogues, etc. by using a special number which they can use free of charge. This is called _____ .

6) Booking a telephone call for a certain time of the day is called a _____ call.

7) If a telephone call has been made from someone else's telephone, it may be necessary to know how much the call has cost, so that payment may be made. The British Telecom operator will ring back and tell caller the cost of his call if an _____ call is asked for beforehand.

187

8) There are many telephone information services but they all cost the same as _____ telephone call. The length of an information call may be _____ .

9) The cost of an emergency 999 call is _____ .

10) The important information to give to the emergency service is where the emergency is, what it is and _____ .

Miscellaneous

Answer the following questions.

1) What is the correct thing to do if there is a smell of gas?

2) Which emergency service would you ask for if you wanted a young kitten rescued from the top of a tall tree?

3) Which emergency service would you ask for if someone had fallen downstairs and was unconscious?

4) Which emergency service would you ask for if your house was badly flooded and the water was still rising?

5) Which emergency service would you ask for to rescue someone who had fallen down a cliff on the coast?

6) Compare the following three services and explain the differences between them:
Freefone
Transferred charge call
Telephone credit card.

7) A personal call is one made to a friend for a chat. Explain what a 'person-to-person' call is.

8) How could a businessman with customers abroad make use of fixed-time calls?

9) An employee of a firm travelling abroad frequently, with planes to catch, might find the alarm call service of use. Explain how.

10) There are many information services available through British Telecom. Which three might be especially useful to a businessman?

Telex

Answer the following questions.

1) Compare the Telex service with the telephone service.

2) Explain the use of punched tape in a teleprinter.

188

3) One of the advantages of a teleprinter is that it can be left to receive messages even after the office is closed. How would this be useful to a firm who transacted a great deal of business with countries in Europe? Or in other parts of the world?

4) What is Telex Plus?

5) Compare Telex messages with letters and explain the advantages and disadvantages (if any) of each.

Telemessages

1) How is a telemessage sent?

2) When is it delivered?

3) What is its minimum cost?

4) Is it possible to send a greetings telemessage?

Special Exercises

1) Whilst on holiday you are taken ill and cannot return to work when you should do so. Compose a telemessage to inform your boss.

2) On the first day of your holidays you discover in your handbag the key to your desk drawer, which you remember locking just before you left. In the drawer are several files which you know will be needed during your absence. Compose a telemessage to your boss explaining the circumstances and what you will do with the key.

3) Your boss is away on holiday in America when you have news that his son (at school in England) has had an accident. How would you word a telegram to break the news?

4) You are living in Bristol and have arranged to go home on Friday of this week for the weekend. Suddenly an interesting invitation reaches you. Compose a telemessage to your parents cancelling your visit to them.

5) Compose a greetings telemessage to send to your boss who has just been made an OBE while on a business trip in Scotland.

6) Explain your absence from the office one morning, after you have had three weeks holiday. You are stranded in the north of Scotland, your office telephone appears to be out of order and you are anxious to let your boss know what has happened to you. Your firm's name is: Freeman, Knightley and Grimes. Your boss is Mr Alec Freeman. Compose a suitable telemessage.

The Receptionist

1) Where should the receptionist's desk be situated?

2) The receptionist may carry out three other duties, as well as looking after visitors to her firm. What are they?

3) When a caller arrives without an appointment, what should the receptionist do first of all?

4) How does the receptionist file callers' business visiting cards?

5) There are two important reasons for filing business visiting cards. What are they?

6) What type of *appearance* should a receptionist have?

7) What type of *person* should she be?

8) Why is she important to a firm?

9) What must she be well-informed about?

10) What information does an organisation chart contain?

11) Select the appropriate word or group of words from the word list at the end to insert into each space.
   a Generally speaking the post of receptionist is offered to _____ staff only.
   b The receptionist is the first person in the firm that the visitor meets, and should always try to create a good _____ .
   c A receptionist should keep her work position tidy and in appearance she should be neat and _____ .
   d The reception office must be near the _____ to the building or suite of offices.
   e The best greeting is 'Good morning/afternoon. Can _____ ?'
   f Wherever possible callers should have previously arranged an _____ .
   g It is good practice wherever possible to ask to see a visitor's _____ .
   h A _____ should be kept to assist in recalling later who came, at what time, etc..
   i It is important not to disclose _____ information of use to callers.
   j When using the internal telephone it is best to speak _____ if there is any chance that a visitor may not be welcome.
   Word list: impression, impersonally, entrance, female, appointment, business card, register of callers, I help you, well groomed, confidential.

12) Suggest five pleasant remarks you might make to a caller while you were waiting for his contact to come down and collect him from the reception area.

13) List the chief qualities you would expect from a female receptionist. Select two of these qualities and explain why you consider them to be important.

14) A receptionist is often required to perform routine work during intervals of inactivity. What sort of activities might be carried out in this way? Explain why each is an appropriate activity for a receptionist.

190

15) A receptionist is faced by the following situations during a busy morning. Explain what action she should take in each case.

   a An important client from overseas is cut off by the receptionist. He was not ringing from his usual office, and the Sales Manager is annoyed.

   b The office boy is hit by a swing door and his nose bleeds furiously.

   c The local police call in to check security arrangements in connection with their campaign 'Look out – there's a thief about'.

   d The Post Department ask her to obtain postage stamps to the value of £10.00.

   e A parcel delivered by special messenger appears damp from internal damage. It also smells strongly rather like petrol or lighter fuel.

16) Outline how you would deal with a caller whose name and business you do not know.

17) Each list below contains one 'odd man out' – which are they?

   a *Pleasant Accessories for the Reception Area*
   Ashtray
   Plants and flowers
   Switchboard
   Low chairs
   Reading lamp.

   b *Receptionist's Reference Books*
   AA or RAC Books
   Telephone Directories
   Financial Times
   Post Office Guide
   Classified Trade Directory.

   c *Personal Qualities a Receptionist should have*
   Politeness
   Friendliness
   Tactlessness
   Patience
   Calmness
   Pleasant manner.

   d *Receptionist's Records*
   Callers' register
   Appointments book
   Card index of callers' business cards
   Post Office Guide
   Card index of frequently used telephone numbers
   Staff 'in and out' book.

   e *Receptionist's Equipment*
   Internal telephone
   External telephone
   Typewriter
   Vending machine
   Filing cabinet
   Switchboard.

The Reception of Visitors

1) Write a description about two-thirds of a page in length of a receptionist's duties, the equipment, records and reference books she uses, and the reception area in which she works and in which visitors wait.

   Use the words and phrases in the list overleaf at least once.

Caller's name
House journal
Company literature
Non-smoking area
Appointments book
Newspapers
Message form
Callers' register
AA or RAC Book
Lost Property Book

Post Office Guide
Trade journals
Business visiting card
Switchboard
Receptionist's name
Telephone directories
Classified trade directories
Callers without appointments
Messengers
Staff 'in and out' book

2) Discuss the following situations and then decide on the best way to deal with each one:

a A visitor calls without an appointment and asks the receptionist to telephone to the secretary of the person he wishes to see to enquire if he can be seen within the next hour. The receptionist telephones, and is told that on no account can an appointment be made the same day and that the caller must be asked to write for one. Write down the exact words the receptionist might use to the caller.

b Two callers arrive together at 1000. One had an appointment for 0930 and has been unavoidably delayed. The other is on time for an appointment at 1000. Which visitor would the receptionist send in first, and how would she handle the other one?

c A caller comes several times to see the same manager in a firm. Each time he has no appointment, refuses to make one, and the manager is too busy to see him. The caller seems annoyed – how would the receptionist deal tactfully with him?

d Several callers arrive within minutes of each other. As the receptionist deals with the first one, the telephone rings, and she has to leave the visitors while she attends to it. Write down what she should say when she returns to the waiting callers.

e A caller has been asked to wait in the reception area as the person with whom he has an appointment has been held up on his way to the office. How should the receptionist make the waiting caller feel that he has not been forgotten?

Tricky Situations

1) Mr Hill calls to see the Chief Accountant, who has forgotten that he has an appointment to see Mr Hill at 1245. The Chief Accountant is now at lunch at his club with an important overseas customer. How would a well-trained receptionist deal with the situation?

2) From your own experience of being 'received' in an organisation, devise a situation which will include some of the members of your group and act it out with them.

3) The young daughter of the Sales Manager comes into reception. She has run away from her boarding school and will not go back – she is very upset. The Sales Manager and his wife are on holiday in Italy for two weeks. You know the girl's uncle lives about 19 miles away. What action would you take?

4) Imagine you are a receptionist in an exhibition showground. What type of problems do you think you would have to cope with? Think of one and prepare to 'act it out'. Allocate different types of customers to the other members of your group.

5) Several people arrive at the same time at your reception desk, none of them with an appointment. One of them is determined not to go away without seeing the Chief Cashier and equally determined not to sit down and wait while you attend to the other, more reasonable callers. How would you deal with this situation?

Designing Outfits

Draw or trace two outfits which you think would be suitable for a receptionist to wear, one in the winter and one in the summer. Remember, she is often the first person whom callers see when they visit a firm.

Some Final Questions and Exercises

1) When would the telephone alphabet be used?

2) A new junior has been appointed in your office, one of her main duties being to answer the telephone. List four practical hints to help her.

3) **a** Draft out a specimen callers' card.
   b How would these cards be filed?

4) **a** At the front of a telephone directory is a page for emergency services and useful numbers including: doctor, hospital, taxi, British Rail enquiries. Make your own list.
   b Why would a receptionist keep a list of numbers such as those listed?

5) **a** What is a form letter?
   b Draft a form letter stating that an appointment which has been requested has been arranged.

6) True or false?
   a Tact is required when answering the telephone.
   b It is not necessary to ask a caller his name, because your employer will recognise his voice when you put him through.
   c When you answer an internal telephone in your office you should state the name of your company.

7) Why keep a reception register?

8) Would this register be kept on forms or in a book?

9) Who would be responsible for keeping the register?

10) On 20 May 1979 the following people called at the Reception Desk of Grosvenor Engineering Limited:

Mr Roger Brook of B & C Electronics saw the Managing Director, Mr Braithwaite at 10.15 am.

At 11.05 am Miss V Davids requested an appointment with the Personnel Department on private business. She was told to come back at 3.15 pm.

Miss Jane Brown, Pearson and Pepperton, made an appointment to see Mr J Hanson, Sales Department, next Monday 26, at 11.15 am.

The Marine Department received Mr C Kavil of A Peters Ltd at 4.00 pm.

Mr G T Robinson came at 9.30 am for an appointment in the Diesel Department to see Pete Davids. (He is a representative of Tabsco Ltd.)

Mr K Jamieson rang and is coming tomorrow at 10.30 am to see Mr Paul Cummings, Personnel. He works at Johnsons Ltd, Droitwich.

Mr D Samuels of Fitzroy Ltd arrived at 2.00 pm for an appointment in the Wages Department to see Mr M Jones.

   a Enter the particulars of these callers, in the order in which they arrived, in a callers' register. Use the 24 hour system. Invent any missing details.

   b Make an appointments book sheet for 20 May.

11) Give a list of the different types of caller you could expect to deal with if you were working as a receptionist.

12) What would the duties be of a messenger in the firm and how would they be of benefit to the receptionist?

13) The receptionist is at lunch from 1300 to 1400. There are four other employees who share the duty of relief receptionist at this time, and also when necessary during the day. They are Miss Brown, Miss Drew, Miss Fanshaw and Miss Glossop. Miss Brown is always absent on Monday, and Miss Drew on Thursday. Miss Glossop is not to be left in sole charge at lunch time as she is inexperienced, but it is desired to give her some opportunity of reception work at other times of the day. Miss Fanshaw, by special arrangement, always lunches from 1300 to 1400 so that she may care for her invalid mother.

Draw up a rota of duties to ensure that the reception desk is always manned.

14) Explain why a Lost Property Book should be kept by a Receptionist.

15) Draw up a notice for display to visitors in the reception area, informing them that as from the first Monday in the next month, the firm's hours of business will be changed to 8.30 am to 5 pm instead of 9 am to 5.30 pm.

Example of a well planned reception area

195

Crossword

Across

1 A receptionist should be polite and _____ (8)

3 She must not keep callers _____ unnecessarily (7)

7 Callers who have to wait must be _____ after by the receptionist (6)

12 The receptionist must _____ all messages to their destinations at once (4)

14 Callers' cameras, bags etc. should be kept _____ observation by the receptionist (5)

16 Callers should be escorted _____ and from the offices they are visiting (2)

17 As well as looking after callers, a receptionist may _____ as part of her duties (4)

22 _____ is a telephone service which firms use to encourage the public to telephone them (8)

24 First impression _____ a firm is given by a receptionist (2)

26 This should be removed from the ashtrays several times during the day (3)

28 _____ of the regular callers, such as postmen or delivery men, signs the callers' register (4)

29 A receptionist's _____ and nails, as well as make-up, should be immaculate (4)

31 Health and _____ at Work Act was passed in 1974 (6)

33 (and 21 down) A _____ _____ Call enables a telephone call to be made from a public call box without using coins (7, 6)

36 An _____ call will wake you early! (5)

37 A receptionist must never express _____ to a caller (5)

38 Speak more clearly (do not shout) to telephone callers who cannot _____ (4)

Down

1 Callers' cards must be _____ (5)

2 The staff 'in and out' book should be signed by staff *only* (yes or no?) (3)

4 The first _____ box in reception *must* be checked weekly (3)

5 As well as personal callers, a receptionist will have many callers on the _____ (9)

6 British Telecom International Telephone _____ gives information about telephone services to countries all over the world (5)

8 Look _____ for callers who may need extra help (3)

9 A receptionist should _____ the answers to almost any questions about the firm she works in (4)

10 The abbreviation for 'editor' (2)

11 French for 'of' (2)

13 It is impolite to callers for a receptionist to _____ while on duty (3)

15 The colour of an outgoing Telex message is _____ (3)

18 Any _____ should be written on a specially printed form (7)

19 No one can _____ the importance of a good receptionist to a firm (4)

20 Answer the telephone as soon as it rings – do or don't? (2)

21 See 33 across

22 _____ drill should be practised regularly (4)

23 The Gas Board should be telephoned if there is a smell of gas – _____ 999 (3)

25 A _____ letter is useful for sending confirmation of appointments, or cancelling them (4)

27 Is a receptionist usually a 'he' or 'she'? (3)

30 Appearance _____ less important than a pleasant voice to a telephonist (2)

32 A person who has had an accident may be _____ ful, and should be reassured (4)

34 _____ drivers do not sign the callers' register (3)

35 Girl's name (3)

Index

Answering a telephone extension   34–5
Basic office arithmetic   175–8
Business entertaining
     Making introductions   172–4
     Parties and lunches   165–9
     Serving tea and coffee   164–5
     Serving wines   170–1
Complete revision   181–4
Flower arranging   127–31
Form letters   140–4
General exercises   179–80
Internal staff directories   14–15
International telegrams   86
     Coded telegrams   86–8
Job vacancies for receptionists   105–6
Looking after indoor plants   131–4
Office staff practices 1853   139
Practical work on reception   180
Reception duties in a small firm   91–3
Receptionist in a large firm
     Appearance   95–8
     Callers' business visiting cards   101–2
     Duties   94–5
     Messages   115–16
     Notices   117–21
     Reception area   123–6
     Receptionist's desk   102–3
Receptionist's records   107–15
Receptionist's voice   99
Reference books for a receptionist   135–8
Types of caller   99–100
Remembering names and status of staff   15
Safety and security in the reception area
     Bomb warnings   149–50
     Dealing with an outbreak of fire   158
     First Aid   153–9
     Identifying personnel   148–9
     Preventing accidents   146–8
     Procedures for recording accidents   159–60
     Treating burns   158–9
Switchboard
     Fashion tips for operators   35
     Latest developments in switchboards   35–6
Switchboard operator
     Dealing with calls   32–3
     Telephone systems in a firm   31
     Telephone tones   28–9
Telemessages   83–6
Telephone
     Charges   22–7
     Coping with indistinct callers   16

Dialling   5, 7–8
Different types available   6
Do's and don'ts   13
Etiquette   11
Examples of telephone conversations   38–42
Messages   8–10
Mobile telephones   5
Pronouncing figures on the telephone   16–17
Style   11–12
Technique   3–5
Telephone alphabet   16, 18
Telephonist's personal alphabet   12
Telephonist's reference sources   18–20
Telephone equipment
     Carphone   47
     Developments in callmakers   45–6
     Flashing lights   48
     Help for the handicapped   51
     Intercom   46–7
     Loudspeaking telephone   46
     Paging   48–51
     Punched card callmaker   44
     Tannoy or public address system   47–8
     Tape callmaker   45
     Telephone answering machine   43
Telephone services
     ADC call   55
     Alarm call   54
     Confravision   62
     Datel   63
     Emergency calls   56–7
     Facsimile transmission   63–5
     Fixed time call   54
     Freefone   56
     Information services   55
     International telephone calls   59–62
     Message call   55
     Person-to-person call   54
     Prestel   62–3
     Telephone credit cards   56
     Transferred charge call   55
Teleprinters
     Advantages   68–9
     International Telex calls   76–7
     Keyboard and dialling unit   70–2
     Latest developments   79–80
     Making a telex call   71–3
     Teletelex   80
     Telex Plus   80
     Telex messages   74–5
     Telex reference books   72

Upgrading Your Home PC

Upgrading Your Home PC

Glenn Weadock
Photography by Emily Sherrill Weadock

SYBEX®

San Francisco   Paris   Düsseldorf   Soest   London

Associate Publisher: Richard J. Staron
Acquisitions and Developmental Editor: Ellen L. Dendy
Editors: Linda Orlando, Kari Brooks
Production Editor: Kylie Johnston
Technical Editor: James Kelly
Book Designer: Maureen Forys, Happenstance Type-O-Rama
Electronic Publishing Specialist: Maureen Forys, Happenstance Type-O-Rama
Proofreaders: Emily Hsuan, Dave Nash, Nancy Riddiough
Indexer: Lynnzee Elze
Cover Designer: Dan Ziegler Design
Cover Photographer: PhotoDisc

Library of Congress Card Number: 2001093081

ISBN: 0-7821-2960-9

Manufactured in the United States of America

10 9 8 7 6 5 4 3 2 1

To Emily, Carina, and Cecily,
who like gadgets as much as I do.

Acknowledgments

I'd like to thank the people at Sybex, who I found to be professional, friendly, patient, and dedicated: (in alphabetical order) Ellen Dendy, Kylie Johnston, Dick Staron, Rodnay Zaks, and everybody else who worked on this book but whose name I didn't get to know. Thanks go to my cheerful and excellent editors, Kari Brooks, Jim Kelly, and Linda Orlando. Special thanks go to my literary agent, Mike Snell, who put me in touch with Sybex in the first place. I also thank the many managers and public relations people who helped me with the book's research, including Duane Brozek of Viewsonic; Chris Bull of Logitech; Pedro Cabezuelo of Benchmark Porter Novelli; Katy Doherty of Hewlett-Packard; Bruce Friedrichs of Logitech; Katriina Laine of Weber Shandwick Worldwide; Shannon Lyman of Lexmark; Courtney Maloney of Kodak; Andy Marken of Marken Communications; Bradley Morse of D-Link; John Paulsen of Seagate; Ed Rebello of Adaptec; Will Reeb of Wacom; Emily Strickland of Lexmark; John Swinimer of ATI; David Szabados of Seagate; Richard Townhill of Adobe; and David Welsh of Everglide. Finally, I thank my wife Emily for all her help during this book's creation.

Contents at a Glance

Introduction . . . . *xiii*

Chapter 1 • Read Me First 1

Chapter 2 • Memory 15

Chapter 3 • Storage 37

Chapter 4 • Communications 63

Chapter 5 • Printers 85

Chapter 6 • Displays 115

Chapter 7 • Networking 143

Chapter 8 • Power 167

Chapter 9 • Of Mice and Multimedia 191

Chapter 10 • BIOS and CPU 223

Chapter 11 • Buses 249

Chapter 12 • References and Resources 275

Index *285*

Contents

Introduction . . . . *xiii*

Chapter 1 • Read Me First 1
Tools for Upgraders 2
Working with Electronic Devices 6
Opening a PC's Cover 7
Gross Internal Anatomy 12

Chapter 2 • Memory **15**
Intro to Memory 16
Determining Memory Capacity 19
    How Much Do You Have? 19
    How Much Can You Add? 19
    How Much Do You Need? 20
Determining Memory Type and Speed 21
    FPM (Fast Page Mode) 21
    EDO (Extended Data Out) 21
    BEDO (Burst Extended Data Out) 22
    SDRAM (Synchronous Dynamic RAM) 22
    RDRAM (Rambus Dynamic RAM) 22
    DDR (Dual Data Rate) RAM 23
    SRAM (Static RAM) 23
Memory Module Package Types 24
    SIMM (Single Inline Memory Module) 24
    DIMM (Dual Inline Memory Module) 25
    RIMM (Rambus Inline Memory Module) 26
Adding a Memory Module 27
Removing a Memory Module 31

Chapter 3 • Storage **37**
Intro to Storage 38
    Hard Drives 38
    Cartridge Drives 41
    Optical Drives 41
    Tape Drives 42
Adding an IDE Drive 43

Upgrading from IDE to SCSI 51
Adding a Zip or Jaz Drive 53
   Internal Drives 53
   External Drives 53
Adding a CD-R+RW Drive 54
   An Upgrade Example 55
   External vs. Internal Drives 58
   Disc Media 59
Adding a Tape Drive 60
Maintaining Your Storage Devices 61

Chapter 4 • Communications **63**
Intro to Communications 64
   Dial-Up Modems 65
   ISDN 67
   DSL 68
   Cable Modems 68
Dial-Up Modem Setup 69
   Installing an External Modem 69
   Installing an Internal Modem 74
Installing a DSL Router 75
Considering the Wireless Web 82
   Satellite 83
   Wireless Local Loop 84

Chapter 5 • Printers **85**
Intro to Printers 86
Printer Ports 91
   Parallel 92
   USB (Universal Serial Bus) 94
   Serial 94
   Infrared 96
   Network 97
Setting up an Inkjet Printer 99
   Printer Hardware 99
   Printer Configuration 103
   Head Alignment 104
Installing a Laser Printer 105
   Printer Hardware 105
   Configuring a Printer 108

Maintaining Your Printer 109
    Cleaning 110
    Lubrication 112
    Paper 114
    Ozone Filters 114

Chapter 6 • Displays **115**
Intro to Displays 116
    Viewable Area 117
    Desk Area 118
    Image Quality 119
    Adjustability 120
    Speed 121
    Options 121
    Warranty 122
Upgrading a Video Adapter 122
    Disabling Motherboard Video 123
    Adding a Video Card 123
Adding Memory to a Video Card 127
    VRAM 129
    WRAM 129
    SGRAM 130
    DDR 130
Setting Up Your Monitor 130
    Resolution 130
    Color Depth 131
    Refresh Rate 132
    Third-Party Calibration Utilities 133
Installing Multiple Monitors 135
Installing a Flat-Panel Monitor 136
Maintaining Your Monitor 141

Chapter 7 • Networking **143**
Intro to Networking 144
    Physical Connection 144
    Signaling Method 147
    Network Protocol 147
    Network Architecture 148
    Network Software 149
Installing a Wired Network 149
Installing a Wireless Network 159

Chapter 8 • Power **167**

Intro to Power 168

Upgrading or Replacing a Power Supply 169

    Adding a Connector 170

    Replacing the Entire Power Supply 170

    Replacing the Fan Only 180

Adding a Battery Backup Unit 183

    What Kind? 184

    How Big? 184

    Installing the Battery Backup Unit 185

Notebook Power Issues 188

    Care and Feeding of Extra Batteries 188

    On-the-Go Chargers 189

    Voltage Conversion Kits 189

Chapter 9 • Of Mice and Multimedia **191**

Intro to Input Devices 192

    Mice, Trackballs, and Joysticks 192

    Keyboards 195

Upgrade Input Devices 197

    Installing a Cordless Mouse 197

    Installing a Pressure-Sensitive Tablet 202

Intro to Multimedia 204

    Pictures 204

    Motion 205

    Music 206

Sound Investments 206

    Add Speakers 206

    Connect a MIDI Keyboard 210

Stills and Movies 214

    Using a Digital Camera 214

    Using an External Capture Device 216

    Buying a Webcam 220

Chapter 10 • BIOS and CPU **223**

BIOS Overview 224

Updating the BIOS 225

    How to Tell What BIOS You Have 225

    How to Get the Latest Version of Your BIOS 226

    Power Backup is Essential! 226

    Performing the Update 228

CPU Overview. 229
Replacing a CPU 232
    Replacing a CPU with a ZIF Socket 234
    The Other Kind ("Fork Required") 240
    Replacing Slot Cartridge CPUs 242
Adding a CPU. 246
    Adding a CPU to a Bare-Bones Motherboard 246
    Filling Out a Dual-CPU System (Windows NT/2000/XP) 247

Chapter 11 • Buses **249**

Intro to Buses 250
    Reasons to Upgrade 250
    Reasons to Add. 251
USB 252
    Installing a USB Host Adapter 256
    Installing a USB Hub 259
    USB Configuration Rules 260
    Measuring USB Power Draw 260
FireWire 262
    Installing FireWire 262
    FireWire Configuration Rules 263
SCSI 264
    Single- and Dual-Channel Controllers. 266
    Setting the Controller's SCSI ID 267
    Device IDs. 268
    Setting Termination. 270
    Other SCSI Settings 272
Notebook Bus Upgrades 272
Other Buses 273

Chapter 12 • References and Resources **275**

Internet References and Resources 276
    Web Sites 276
    Newsgroups 279
Print References and Resources. 282
    Magazines 282
    Books 283

Index 285

Introduction

f I were writing a doctoral thesis about why people love to improve their cars, houses, and computers, I'd probably explore the hypothesis that by making the things around us better, we are projecting a desire to make ourselves better. I'd also ponder the notion that improving something is an act of creation only slightly subordinate to building that something in the first place—and therefore simultaneously a rejection of our mortality and an affirmation of our power to control our environment.

Lucky for you, I'm *not* writing such a thesis, so I can simply state that upgrading PCs is fun, and you're going to have a good time with this book.

You're going to make your PC better, faster, stronger, more convenient, more capable, and more interesting. And you're going to save money in the process, because (at least up to a point) upgrading a PC is a lot less expensive than replacing it.

For all the talk about planned obsolescence in this industry, it's remarkable how long you can extend the lives of old computers with targeted upgrades. Come over to my office in Golden, Colorado, and I'll show you a PC that's eight years old but that's running Windows 2000 Server on my company network. I'll also show you the PC I used to write this book, a tiny home computer I bought three years ago for $500 or so and that I have hot-rodded to the point that it bears almost no resemblance to its original self.

Of course, you can upgrade new machines as well as old ones. In fact, given the current lamentable trend of manufacturers offering home and small-office PCs with marginal modem, display, and disk subsystems, you may well enjoy big performance jumps when bringing those subsystems up to a higher standard. And, of course, you may want to upgrade a PC to run the latest version of Windows, which is always more piggish of resources like memory, CPU power, disk space, and disk speed than the previous versions of Windows. (I should note here that 95% of this book's content is useful even if you don't run Windows; this is essentially a hardware book, and you'll find it handy even if you run Linux, Solaris, OS/2, DOS, or some other operating system.)

Now, admittedly, I spend a lot of time upgrading computers because it helps me learn about new products that I have to write about or advise my consulting clients about. I also have fun taking an old, slow machine and making it into an old, fast machine. You, on the other hand, may be interested in upgrading your PC for purely practical and prosaic reasons. You may need your computer to do something it doesn't do right now, or you may just need it to work faster, and you don't want to spend a lot of time or get a Ph.D. in computer science to get it done.

Happily, whether you're a gadget freak like me or somebody who couldn't care less about computer hardware, you should find this book useful. It doesn't spend a lot of time discussing the history of computing. It doesn't tell you in any great detail about how the underlying technology works in theory. The focus of this book is to give you a friendly, helpful guide to accomplishing the most common types of upgrades that people tend to perform with their PCs, in as few pages as possible.

The title of this book contains the words "home PC," but don't let that put you off if you're working in a small office. Most of this book is as helpful for small business users as it is for home users.

As you flip through these pages, you'll notice that the book has a lot of photographs but no line drawings. The goal is to show you the way this stuff looks in real life. The photographer and I shot every one of the photos you see in this book while going through every one of the upgrades that the book discusses. So this book is a little like those automobile manuals that advertise that they're "based on a complete tear-down and rebuild." (You always wonder if the car they tore down and rebuilt actually ran after the authors reconstructed it. Well, I can report that all our computers are working fine.)

You'll also notice that some of the upgrades this book discusses are inside the PC and some are outside. Connecting a digital camera to a computer and installing the supporting software necessary to communicate with that device qualifies as an upgrade just as much as adding memory inside the box. The book doesn't cover every possible device you might connect to your PC, but it does cover some of the more popular peripheral add-ons.

As to the book's organization, most chapters start out with an introduction to the particular technology, followed by some specific step-by-step procedures using typical hardware. The introductions serve a dual purpose: They explain the basics and simultaneously provide a miniature buyer's guide, with lots of purchasing tips. So, if you haven't already bought the hardware you're considering for a given upgrade, read the chapter about that hardware before you start shopping. If you've already made your purchase, that's fine too, because the chapters are full of tips for getting the most out of your hardware and avoiding problems during the upgrade.

Now for a few quick caveats. Although the step-by-step procedures are representative of how you'd usually perform a certain upgrade, you should always go by the detailed documentation you get with your new hardware, if such documentation is available. If you find a conflict between my recommended procedure and what your manual says, go by the manual. It's obviously impossible for any author to anticipate every possible wrinkle in an upgrade procedure. My goal is to show you how you'd typically execute the upgrade, but it's up to you to verify that the steps will work for your specific hardware.

The second caveat is to take sensible safety precautions. Turn devices off before opening them up. Don't work on a PC with the power cord still attached to the wall outlet. Read Chapter 1, "Read Me First," to get familiar with the tools you'll use. Heed warnings in the text about the risks of certain procedures. Also, use anti-static wrist straps where suggested. You want to protect yourself, but you want to protect the hardware you're installing, too.

Third, while upgrades are fun, educational, and potentially economical, if you're thinking about replacing a PC's video card, modem, processor, disk controller, *and* disk drive, you should

ask yourself if you wouldn't be better off buying a new system. Heck, the bundled software alone in a new system can save you considerable dollars. Also, if your PC is really old, you have to wonder if what you'll end up with is a turbocharged Yugo. If you have a 486 PC or a Pentium "one," you should think hard about simply replacing it rather than upgrading it.

Some of the procedures in this book will void your warranty with extreme prejudice. So, if your computer is still under warranty, you may want to make an anonymous phone call to your hardware vendor and ask if installing a memory module (or whatever) yourself would disqualify your machine for warranty repair. I've never seen a case where a vendor has refused warranty service for an upgraded PC unless the defective part was actually installed by the user or damaged by something else the user did, but you should consider that it could happen and some vendors are more understanding about these things than others.

Finally: This book contains opinions (gasp!). I don't pretend to be neutral about different technologies, companies, procedures, or products; some stuff I like, some I don't. The opinions in this book are informed ones, and I try to identify when I'm editorializing so you can accept or reject those opinions based on your own experience and judgment.

Chapter **1**

Read Me First

f you've ever installed a computer program, you've probably seen one or more little paper slips saying "Read me first" or "No, read *me* first," which contain details you should know before installing the program, such as "If you do not have a Ph.D. in computer science, please acquire one before proceeding." Many programs also place text files onto your hard drive with names like README.1ST and NOREADME.1ST to provide similarly vital information that you are likely to read for the first time two years later.

Well, this is your "Read Me First" chapter, and we even went to the expense of binding it with the rest of the book. This chapter contains information you're likely to need in several of the following chapters. Before you launch into this book's detailed procedures, take a look here for a few tips on tools, PC cover removal, and PC anatomy. Even those of you who've already performed one or more PC surgeries may enjoy a quick review, and for those of you who wouldn't know a motherboard from a cheese board, this chapter is *de rigueur*.

As I describe specific procedures in the chapters that follow, I'll describe (and include pictures of) any specific hardware relevant to the procedure. This chapter will simply serve to suggest some appropriate tools, lay down some basic ground rules for handling electronic devices, and help you get your bearings when you dive under your computer's cover for the first time.

Tools for Upgraders

Whether you're working on cars, fission reactors, or PCs, having the right tools makes all the difference. Don't attempt any of the procedures in this book if you don't have the tools I mention at the start of each procedure. You'll end up stripping screws, scratching circuit boards, and generally upgrading your PC right into the trash can.

Thankfully, the tools you'll need for the jobs I describe in this book are mostly common household ones: screwdrivers, flashlights, sledge hammers, etc. However, most of you won't have a dental mirror or Torx screwdriver in your collection, so picking up a few specialized items like these can make the difference between fun and frustration.

> **TIP** *I have yet to see a "PC toolkit" that has all the items on my list or that doesn't include at least a couple of tools that you'll never need. Also, tools that come in kits marketed for computer use tend to bend, break, or corrode after about five minutes of use. My advice is to get the individual tools from your local hardware store and make your own kit.*

The following descriptive list should help you fill out your PC upgrade toolkit. I'll start with the common items and work my way toward the more obscure ones.

- **Screwdrivers** are the most common tools you'll use (see Figure 1.1). However, you may need some smaller ones than those you use around the house:

  - I recommend you get two or three different sizes of both **slot** and **Phillips** screwdrivers for your PC toolkit. (For the Phillips-head screwdrivers, get sizes 0, 1, and 2.)

  - If you have a Compaq PC, you'll also need a set of **Torx** screwdrivers, which you can buy either at a PC store or at an auto parts dealer (Torx screwdrivers are used for adjusting American car headlights.) Sizes T-10 and T-15 are the ones you're likely to need.

  - Finally, you may want to have a set of **jeweler's** screwdrivers on hand, especially if you plan on working on your notebook computer. Like everything else on portable PCs, the screws are smaller than usual.

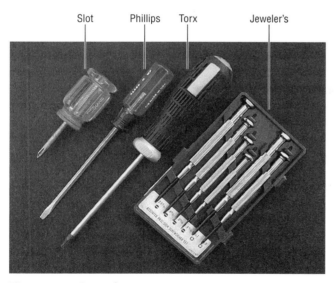

Figure 1.1 *Screwdrivers*

WARNING *Many screwdrivers nowadays come magnetized for ease of retrieving lost screws. Make sure you never work on a PC with a magnetic screwdriver. When in doubt, test the tool on a small screw.*

- **A nut driver**—the quarter-inch variety—is the only one you need. This tool is nothing more than a socket wrench without the wrench. You can sometimes use a nut driver to remove a screw that you can't get a good grip on with a screwdriver, for example because the slot has been stripped.

- **Flashlights** (see Figure 1.2) are a big help, especially with today's cram-everything-into-the-smallest-possible-space home PCs. I like to have two kinds on hand: the big square kind with a handle that use the US$10 lantern batteries are great for placing over the work area, and the little flexible-arm pinpoint kind are great for shedding light into tight corners. (You can also hold the small kind in your teeth if you have to.)

- **Needle-nose pliers** (see Figure 1.3) come in handy for fishing loose screws out of tight spots and for straightening bent connector pins.

- **Wire cutters** (also in Figure 1.3) aren't often necessary for cutting wires, but they are useful for cutting the annoying ties that sometimes come with a new device's packaging.

- **Electrical tape** isn't really a tool, but it should be in your PC toolkit because it's great for patching friction-worn areas on gray ribbon cables and for covering up connectors you want to make sure you don't use.

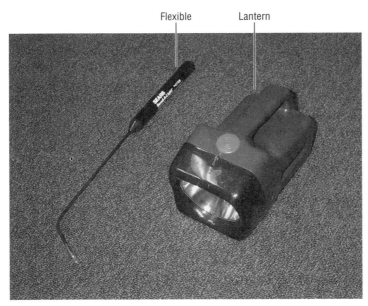

Figure 1.2 *Flashlights*

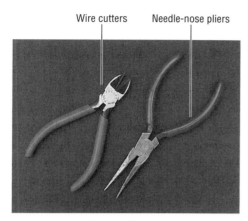

Figure 1.3 *Pliers and cutters*

- **Wire ties** also aren't really tools, but they are wonderfully useful both inside and outside the PC's enclosure. These plastic ribbons have one pointy, ribbed end that fits into a hole in the other end; when you snug up the loop, it stays tight.

- A **jar lid** or small **paper cup** is great for holding screws.

- A **dental mirror** is handy for situations when you need a circuit board model number or chip label or other printed information, and the component is situated exactly wrong for you to see that information.

- A **retrieval tool**, or *spider* (see Figure 1.4), is great for fishing out those tiny screws that we all drop from time to time, especially because I advised you a few paragraphs ago to avoid magnetic screwdrivers.

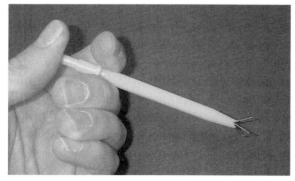

Figure 1.4 *A retrieval spider*

Working with Electronic Devices

With a few exceptions, such as monitors, most external electronic devices, such as keyboards, mice, and cartridge disk drives, don't need special handling. A commitment from you not to drop them onto a hard floor and not to spill beverages into them is usually all that's needed. Even devices that we traditionally think of as fragile, such as cameras, are really very rugged. (I dropped my digital camera more than once during the course of taking this book's photographs, and it didn't miss a pixel.)

When you start working with *internal* electronic devices, however, the rules change. Circuit boards, memory modules, processors, and the like require different handling precautions. Here they are in brief:

- **Don't touch the shiny parts**, especially the metallic connectors on the edge of a circuit card. The oil on your fingers leaves a corrosive residue that can interfere with good clean connections.

- **Handle devices by their edges**, preferably the edges that don't have metallic connectors.

- **Don't stack circuit boards**. They can scratch each other.

- **Watch out for static**. Even the pros have a tough time with static electricity. (I still remember the motherboard roundup in a popular PC magazine, in which the reviewers fried nearly half of the units they were supposed to test by inadvertently touching them when their bodies had built up a static charge.) Try not to work on carpeted floors (if you have to, then work barefoot); don't work in a wool sweater; wear an antistatic wrist strap; frequently ground yourself by touching the PC's metallic chassis or power supply box; humidify the work area; keep components in their antistatic bags until you're ready to install them; and try to get the job done in one sitting, so you don't have to get up and walk someplace and then sit back down, having built up a big static charge.

- **Doff your jewelry**. Remove your rings, wristwatches, bracelets, necklaces, and so forth; they can scratch circuit boards and also get caught in tight places. (You can leave toe, nose, and navel rings in place, unless you plan on doing things with your PC that I don't want to hear about.)

- **Don't force a fit**. Whether you're inserting a circuit board or connecting a plug into a socket, line the devices up first, and then make your connection. Pay attention to any *keys* (raised plastic areas) that ensure you can only connect something one way. Ribbon cables often have one end wire painted red or black; that end should match up with the "pin 1" designation on the circuit board connector.

- **Remove with care**. When disconnecting a device, if reasonable force won't release it, look for a plug, latch, or lock that you may need to press/twist/release. When removing a circuit board from a slot, rock it from side to side along its length while pulling up, and don't grab the chips to get leverage.

- **Keep things clean**. Dust is the enemy of electronics. It interferes with connections and traps heat. Wipe or blow dust away from the components you plan to work on before you start work. (You don't need a can of compressed air; just inhale deeply, shut your eyes, and blow.) Wash your hands. Wipe the table clean.

- **Always power down**. Don't ever connect the PC to AC power when the cover is off.

Opening a PC's Cover

When I started working with computers a couple of decades ago, opening the cover was very simple. You looked at the back of the PC, located the five screws that held the cover on, removed them, and slid the cover forward and off. Today, we have PC covers held in place by screws, knobs, snaps, and tabs; some designs are more complex than Victorian-era undergarments. However, the general technique for getting inside a PC hasn't changed greatly. Here are the usual steps for removing a PC's cover.

TIP *If you have your computer's user manual, it will contain a description that is both more detailed and more model-specific than what follows.*

1. Turn the computer off.

2. Disconnect everything from the PC's back panel: keyboard and mouse connectors, video connector, power cord, modem cable, network cable, and so forth (see Figures 1.5 and 1.6).

3. Locate the cover screws. These are usually Phillips-head screws at the back of the PC. Be careful, though: the screws that hold the cover on look a lot like the screws that hold the power supply in place. The power supply screws are typically a bit more "interior" than the cover screws, which live on the perimeter (see Figure 1.7).

TIP *Some PCs don't have cover screws; instead, they have tabs or latches holding the cover in place. Still other designs use knurled knobs instead of screws or latches.*

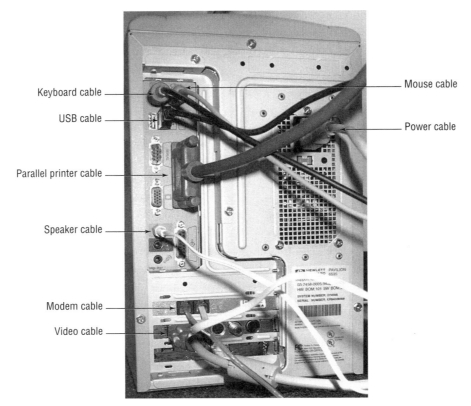

Figure 1.5 *A PC's back panel, dressed*

4. Remove the cover screws. Place them somewhere convenient where they won't roll away, such as an inverted jar lid.

5. Undo any latches that may secure the cover in place even with the screws off. Figure 1.8 shows two different types of latches that you may see. You may also have to unlock a cover lock, especially if your computer is a "business" model.

6. Slide the cover most of the way off (see Figure 1.9). The way most PCs work, you slide the cover about 80 or 90 percent of the way off, and the cover stops sliding. (If you have a PC where the cover just slides all the way off, you can skip step 7.)

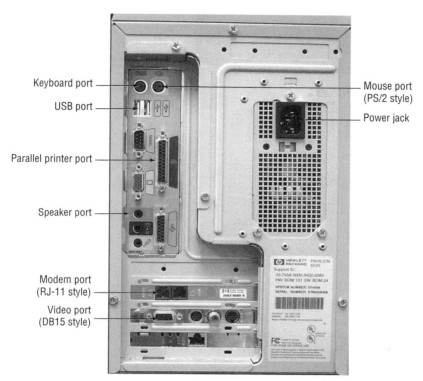

Figure 1.6 *A PC's back panel, undressed*

7. Lift the cover straight up and completely off (see Figure 1.10). You may need to pull the sheet metal apart just a little at the bottom in order to clear the chassis. Do this operation slowly so you don't bang any internal circuit boards or cables with the edge of the cover.

Reassembly is the reverse of disassembly, but here are two tips. First, be very careful when sliding that cover back into place, so that you don't catch and tear any floating ribbon cables. Figure 1.11 shows a PC (admittedly, not the greatest design) in which the cover has damaged an exposed disk drive controller cable. A bit of electrical tape can mend a small abrasion, but if you notice severed wires, a new cable is in order.

Second, take care that you've placed the bottom edges of the cover right where they need to be before you slide it into place. Many covers use a sort of tongue-and-groove construction, and the tongue of the PC's sheet metal needs to fit into the groove of the cover's edge in order to get a good tight fit. Clues that the cover is misaligned: one edge looks tighter than the other, or the cover screws don't seem to fit right. Take the cover off and try it again.

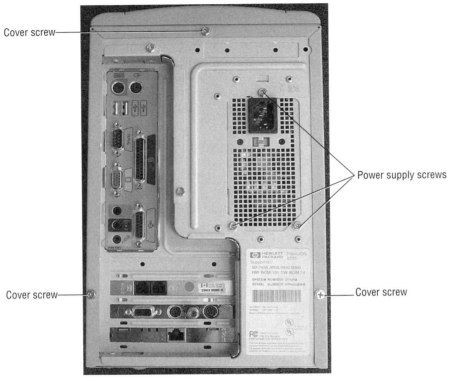

Figure 1.7 *Cover screws versus power supply screws.*

Figure 1.8 *Cover latches.*

Figure 1.9 *Sliding a cover most of the way off*

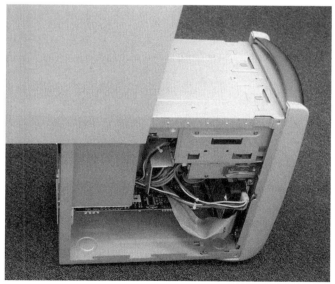

Figure 1.10 *Lifting a cover all the way off*

Figure 1.11 *Cable damage from cover removal*

Gross Internal Anatomy

The interior of a PC can vary quite a bit from one unit to the next, but all PCs contain the following major components:

- **Motherboard** (a.k.a. system board), hosting the CPU, memory, and various other integrated circuits

- **Expansion slots** (usually all you see are *PCI* slots nowadays—they're short and beige—but your PC may also have one or more *ISA* slots, which are longer and black, for older hardware)

- **Adapters** (add-on boards that fit into the expansion slots)

- **Power supply** (usually a silver-colored metal box with a yellow label)

- **Internal disk drives** (including usually one diskette drive, one or more hard drives, a CD-ROM drive, and sometimes a Zip drive)

- **Power cables** (groups of brightly colored wires ending in white connectors that plug into internal disk drives)

- **Signal cables** (typically, flat gray ribbon cables that carry data between the motherboard or adapters and internal disk drives)

Rather than describe these components in detail, Figures 1.12 and 1.13 show two fairly typical PC designs, the mini-tower and the tower, with labels for most of the major internal organs. Again, the documentation for your particular computer is likely to have a more relevant and detailed photo or drawing, so you should use that if you have it. (If you have a notebook computer, you're *really* going to have to depend on the manufacturer's documentation, because the interior layouts of these portable units vary even more than those of non-portable PCs.)

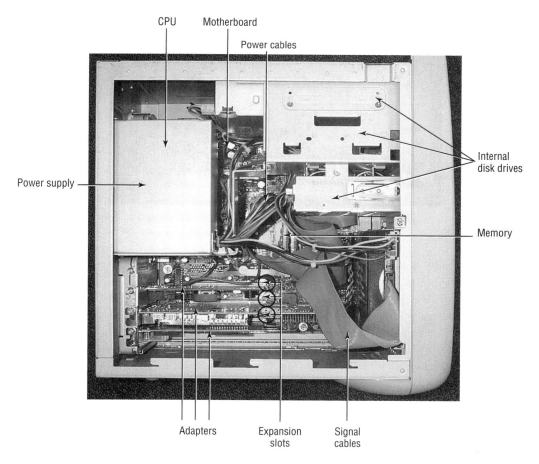

Figure 1.12 *Inside a typical mini-tower PC*

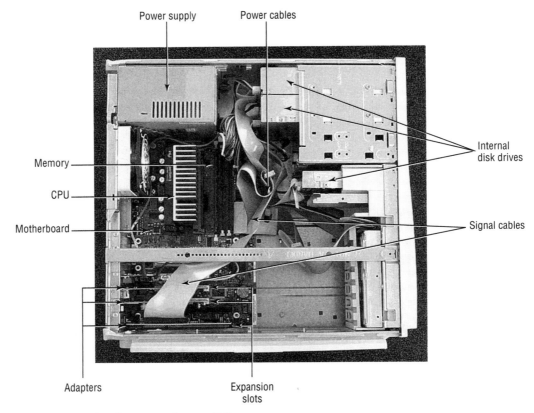

Figure 1.13 *Inside a typical tower PC*

Chapter 2

Memory

This chapter covers just about all you need to know about PC memory. I'll discuss how to determine how much you have and how much you need (the latter always being more than the former). I'll also explain the different types of memory, how their packaging differs, and how to install and remove memory modules.

Intro to Memory

The number-one PC upgrade is adding memory, and for several good reasons. First, it seems that the cheaper memory gets, the more memory new software requires. That's not really a surprise, considering that writing efficient software takes more time than writing wasteful code. "Bloatware" makes economic sense for software developers, if not for consumers!

Second, PC manufacturers wrestling with today's tough competition and minuscule margins often sell machines with too little memory in order to keep the total system price attractive. As I write this, several big-name PC vendors are selling Windows 2000 PCs with only 64 megabytes of RAM, which is just barely enough to meet the needs of the operating system before you add any programs. (That's a bit like selling a big, new sport-utility vehicle with a four-cylinder engine.)

Third, even if you buy a PC with a complement of memory appropriate for your needs, you're very likely to upgrade your applications (and maybe your operating system) to newer versions before retiring the hardware. Those software updates always need more memory than their predecessor versions. And finally, as time goes by, you're likely to discover the benefits of keeping multiple programs loaded in memory at all times, intensifying the need for more memory even more.

> **NOTE** *Your PC will still function with limited memory, because its operating system will typically use disk space as a slow substitute for RAM when no RAM is available; but this paging or swapping activity, as it's called, slows down your system very noticeably, even if you have a really fast hard drive.*

So the bad news is that you probably need more memory, either now or sometime fairly soon. The good news is that most memory is a terrific bargain in terms of the proverbial bang-per-buck ratio.

The other bad news is that you need to know several little-known facts in order to buy and install memory properly. The other good news is that you have this book to help you make the right decisions every step of the way.

The characteristics you should know before you buy memory are *capacity, type, chip speed, bus speed, packaging, error-checking, registration, buffering, pins, voltage,* and *contact material.* Here's a quick look at each attribute.

Capacity is simply memory size, expressed in megabytes (MB). Every PC will specify both a maximum total memory capacity and a maximum capacity per memory slot. (The maximum total capacity may be less than the maximum capacity per slot times the number of slots.)

Type can be FPM, EDO, BEDO, SDRAM, RDRAM, DDR, and SRAM. I decipher all this alphabet soup in the main part of this chapter. The only reason you need to know it is so that you can match new memory to your PC; a PC designed for SDRAM won't work with RDRAM, for example.

Speed can be rated a couple of ways. *Chip speed,* also known as *access time,* is expressed in nanoseconds and refers to the length of time between when the Central Processing Unit (CPU) asks for a memory datum and when the CPU actually gets it. Lower access time numbers mean faster memory. *Bus speed* is expressed in megahertz (MHz) and refers to the speed of the bus, or the *data communication channel,* between the CPU and memory; higher bus speed numbers mean faster memory.

Packaging is simply the physical layout of the memory module. The types you may see are SIMM, DIMM, and RIMM, as discussed later in the chapter. DIMM packages are by far the most common these days, but if Intel has its way, you'll be seeing lots of RIMM modules, too.

Error-checking is a yes-or-no proposition—it enables the PC to detect and even correct single-bit memory errors. When shopping for memory modules, you may see the acronym *ECC,* which stands for *Error Correction Code.* You can install non-ECC memory into a PC that can use ECC memory, but you lose the error-correction feature. *Parity* memory is related to ECC memory; it can detect, but not correct, a memory error. Unfortunately, most PC manufacturers have moved away from using ECC or parity memory, but if you have a computer that uses either technology, I recommend you add only RAM that also supports that technology. When you're filing your tax return online, you don't want even a single-bit memory error to mislocate a decimal point and raise the eyebrows of the Tax Man.

Registered memory allows more, and higher-capacity, memory modules to live on a single motherboard. However, you can't generally mix registered and unregistered modules on the same system. You typically see registered memory more often on servers and high-end graphics workstations than on regular workstation PCs; registered memory is also more common on high-capacity modules, like 256MB and higher.

Buffered memory is generally a tad slower than unbuffered memory. If your PC specifies buffered or unbuffered, you should match that criterion with any memory you add to the system.

Pins refers to the number of contacts on the edge of the memory module that plugs into the motherboard. These contacts don't really look like pins, but that's what they're called. The number of pins on the module needs to match up to the number of holes in your PC's memory slots. Get this wrong, and you won't be able to insert the module into your PC's memory slots.

Voltage is typically either 3.3 volts or 5 volts, and you have to match this to your PC or else the memory won't work (and you may ruin it, to boot). SDRAM typically operates at 3.3 volts, and RDRAM operates at 2.5 volts.

Contact material is simply what metal the contact pins are made of. This factor is often overlooked, but it can make a difference as to whether your memory module works well with others in the same PC. The options here are gold, which is gold in color, and tin-lead, which is silvery-gray. I don't like to mix gold contact modules with tin-lead modules in the same PC, but if the computer is a fairly slow one, you may be able to get away with it.

"Now wait a minute, Glenn," I hear you thinking. "Why do I need to know all of this stuff? Can't I just tell the computer component supplier what make and model PC I have, and let them specify the right memory module?"

In short, no. I've bought many gigabytes of memory over the years, and I've found that, most of the time, providing the make and model of the PC is enough to get the right memory. But if I want to be sure—and avoid the hassles of getting a Return Materials Authorization (RMA) number, paying additional shipping, and waiting additional days—then the only way is to get educated on exactly what kind of memory a PC needs, and make sure that the memory recommended by the mail-order house meets those specs in every respect.

Having said that, I do think it's a great idea to double check memory module specs with one or two online memory configurators, such as you might see at www.microwarehouse.com or www.pcconnection.com. These online forms let you specify make and model and then zero in on model numbers from one or more memory manufacturers.

> **TIP** *The bottom line: Don't trust any one source of information on which module you need without crosschecking the details. Memory incompatibilities can lead to intermittent and maddening errors, lockups, and crashes.*

Determining Memory Capacity

This section advises you on three issues: how much memory your PC already has, how much memory you can add to your system, and how much memory you should have for optimum performance.

How Much Do You Have?

First things first: Before you can determine whether you need more memory than you have, you must discover how much memory you have. Fortunately, doing so is a fairly easy task. Here are several methods you can use, depending on your specific hardware and operating system.

Check the startup screen. When you power on your PC and watch the white-on-black messages that the BIOS (Basic Input/Output System) provides, you're almost certain to see an indication of how much memory you have. That indication may be in megabytes (MB), but it may also be in kilobytes (KB), in which case you can just divide by 1024 to get the number of megabytes.

Run the BIOS setup program. The procedure for doing so varies from one PC to another, but you must usually press a function key such as F2 or F11, or a combination of function keys such as Ctrl+Alt+Enter, during the early stage of the PC's startup sequence. (The specific method for running the BIOS setup program will either appear on screen, for example in a message saying "Press F2 for Setup," or in your PC's user manual.)

Run a diagnostics program. If your PC came with a diskette or CD-ROM from which you can boot in order to run a test utility, that utility normally reports on the amount of installed RAM (and can test it for you, as well).

(Windows only) Check "My Computer." Right-click the My Computer icon and choose Properties. On the General tab of the property sheet that appears, you'll see how much memory you have in the system. This trick works on all current versions of Windows.

How Much Can You Add?

The next question is how much RAM can you add to your system. The answer depends partly on your motherboard design and partly on your willingness to throw away perfectly good hardware! As far as the motherboard design goes, the key considerations are

- how many memory slots exist,
- how many of those slots are filled vs. open, and
- what the motherboard's maximum capacity is.

You can determine the first and third items by consulting the PC hardware manual, but to be really sure of the second item, you'll need to open your PC's case and take a look.

EQUIPMENT YOU'LL NEED:

➡ *An appropriate screwdriver to remove your PC's cover*

INFORMATION YOU'LL NEED:

➡ *Your PC's user manual, spec sheet, or hardware reference*

If you don't want to throw any memory away, then take the number of available slots, multiply by the maximum size per slot (as detailed in your user manual), and add that number to your present capacity. That's your ceiling. On the other hand, if you don't mind discarding what's already there, you may be able to get even more capacity by upgrading from, say, a 32MB module to a 64MB or 128MB module.

WARNING *Don't assume that your PC's total memory capacity is necessarily equal to the maximum capacity per slot times the number of slots. Certain motherboard chipsets can only handle a certain amount of RAM even though it may appear possible to install more than that. Let your PC user manual be your guide.*

Generally it's OK to mix module capacities in the same PC. However, if you're adding memory to a machine that uses SIMM memory packaging, you'll need to add memory in pairs, and the two modules within a pair must be the same capacity. See the SIMM (Single Inline Memory Module) section later in this chapter for details.

How Much Do You Need?

INFORMATION YOU'LL NEED:

➡ *A diagnostic program to report actual memory use (optional)*

The last question to answer is the least obvious, but I'm opinionated enough to give you my thoughts, which you can take as open to argument but well informed.

As a baseline for a typical system running word processing, spreadsheet, Web browsing, and e-mail programs, I usually suggest 64MB of RAM for Windows 95, 98, ME, or NT 4.0, and 128MB for Windows XP/2000. Double those figures if you run demanding applications (such as image-editing software), or if you like to keep a lot of programs loaded in memory at one time.

If you're running Linux, you can generally get away with less memory than if you're running Windows.

If you want to be more scientific about things, run a diagnostic tool to see how much of your RAM is really in use. For example, Windows XP/2000 Professional comes with a utility called Task Manager that can show you total RAM usage and even break it down by programs. If you often exceed the amount of physical RAM, forcing the PC to use disk-based memory (the page-file), then adding memory is almost certain to make your system faster.

> **TIP** *Don't take half measures when it comes to upgrading RAM. Estimate how much memory you think you need to add, then add twice that much. You don't want to perform PC surgery any more often than absolutely necessary, and your time is almost certainly worth more than the cost of the RAM you're installing.*

Determining Memory Type and Speed

One of the keys to installing memory successfully is matching what's already in your system. Although you need to consider all the characteristics that I mention in this chapter's introduction—namely, error-checking, registered vs. unregistered, buffered vs. unbuffered, voltage, and contact material—the most important characteristics to match are type and speed. The following sections present details on different types of memory, discussing speed issues within each section as appropriate for that type.

FPM (Fast Page Mode)

FPM (*Fast Page Mode*) memory was common in older PCs; it is all but extinct today, because it can't keep up with modern processor speeds. Early FPM memory had a chip speed of 120 nanoseconds, while later FPM memory improved to 60 nanoseconds.

EDO (Extended Data Out)

Really a variation on the FPM theme, *EDO* (*Extended Data Out*) memory improves access times by 10 to 20 percent over regular FPM, but becomes a bottleneck when the system bus runs faster than 66MHz.

EDO RAM typically uses the SIMM packaging method (see the SIMM section later in this chapter).

BEDO (Burst Extended Data Out)

BEDO (*Burst Extended Data Out*) memory improves on EDO by processing up to four memory addresses at once, instead of just one. The system accesses the first address at the usual speed, but accesses the remaining addresses at a much faster speed—hence the "burst" in the name. BEDO had a fairly brief time in the sun because SDRAM followed quickly on its heels, as discussed in the next section.

SDRAM (Synchronous Dynamic RAM)

The most common type of memory in PCs today, *Synchronous Dynamic RAM*, or *SDRAM*, can work at much higher system bus speeds than FPM, EDO, or BEDO RAM. This type of memory synchronizes with the system bus and lets the PC access two memory addresses simultaneously. It also uses burst technology to perform subsequent data transfers at a much higher speed than the initial data transfer.

Because SDRAM synchronizes with the bus, its speed ratings match the PC's bus speed. The typical values are 100MHz and 133MHz, although older SDRAM modules run at 66MHz. You may see terms such as PC100 and PC133; these refer to the bus speed. (If you see the term PC SDRAM, it usually refers to the older, 66MHz modules.) If your PC uses a 100MHz bus, you must use PC100 SDRAM if you want reliable operation.

Most SDRAM uses the DIMM (Dual Inline Memory Module) packaging method (see the section on DIMM later in this chapter). Also, all SDRAM is 3.3 volts, so that's one less factor to worry about!

RDRAM (Rambus Dynamic RAM)

Rambus DRAM (or, more properly, *direct RDRAM*) is a newer and potentially much faster type of main memory than SDRAM. It uses a 16-bit wide data pathway as opposed to SDRAM's 64-bit channel, but data moves between the CPU and memory at much higher speeds (600, 700, and 800MHz!). RDRAM also works at a lower voltage (2.5V) to lower power consumption and heat generation.

However, RDRAM has had more than its share of controversy. RDRAM is more expensive, more complex for motherboard manufacturers, and (at this writing at least) not dramatically faster for routine tasks than PC133 SDRAM. Many motherboard manufacturers have revolted against Intel's promotion of RDRAM, but Intel has contractual obligations to Rambus Inc. for the time being and will therefore continue to promote and enhance the technology. You'll also see RDRAM in Sony and Nintendo game machines.

DDR (Dual Data Rate) RAM

DDR (Dual Data Rate) memory is a less dramatic and more evolutionary solution to the memory speed problem than RDRAM, but it's also simpler and less expensive as I write this, and it performs comparably. DDR works by taking SDRAM and doubling the number of data transfers that can take place in a single transfer cycle.

Although Intel has said that DDR is too slow for the Pentium 4, it remains to be seen whether that's absolutely true. The marketplace will probably be divided for a while between DDR and RDRAM for high-speed memory technology.

SRAM (Static RAM)

Static RAM, or *SRAM* (see Figure 2.1), is a special type of memory that PCs typically use for processor cache. This type of memory can retain data without being refreshed by the computer, as long as the power's on.

As you might guess, SRAM is very fast and very expensive, so what computer designers typically do is use a small amount of SRAM to store most-recently-used data from main memory. The amount of SRAM in any given system is usually 256KB or 512KB. For older PCs, you may be able to add to the SRAM on the motherboard, but for most PCs sold since 1997 or so, you can't change the amount of SRAM—it comes packaged with the CPU.

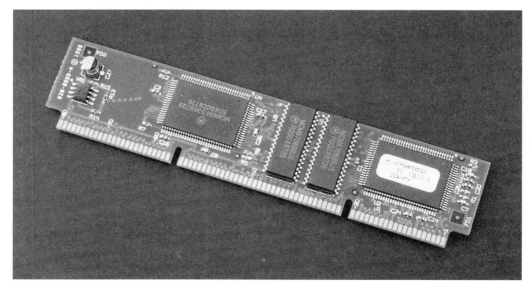

Figure 2.1 *An SRAM module*

Memory Module Package Types

Before you embark on installing memory in the section after this one, get familiar with the common package types. Thankfully, you're likely to bump into only three: SIMM, DIMM, and RIMM.

SIMM (Single Inline Memory Module)

SIMM is now a fairly old technology (common with Pentium and Pentium Pro PCs) but is still around in many working computers. The data path of a 72-pin SIMM module (see Figure 2.2) is 32 bits wide, although 30-pin SIMMs (see Figure 2.3) have an 8-bit-wide path. If you do run into a 30-pin SIMM, it may have memory chips on one side or on both sides, but it won't have a notch in the middle of the contact row as the 72-pin SIMMs have.

You have to install SIMM modules in pairs for Pentium family motherboards. (If you have an 80486 machine, you can install them singly.)

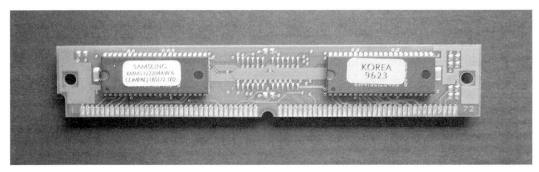

Figure 2.2 *A 72-pin SIMM module*

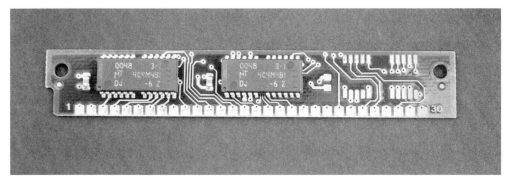

Figure 2.3 *A 30-pin SIMM module*

SIMM packaging appears most often with EDO and SDRAM memory. You can't necessarily tell whether a given SIMM is EDO or SDRAM just by looking at it.

WARNING *Some people buy SIMM stackers to convert their 72-pin SIMM slots to accept 30-pin SIMM modules. I haven't had very good luck with these devices in the past and can't recommend them. Your mileage may vary.*

DIMM (Dual Inline Memory Module)

DIMM improves on the SIMM by providing a 64-bit-wide data path. This is the most common memory packaging for Pentium II and Pentium III systems.

You can tell a DIMM right away because the contacts on the front and back sides aren't connected to each other (see Figures 2.4 and 2.5 for some typical DIMM modules). Unlike SIMMs, you can install DIMMs one at a time on Pentium family motherboards.

DIMMs come with 30, 72, 144 (for notebook PCs), or 168 pins (the most common configuration). DDR DIMMs have 184 pins.

DIMM capacities include 8-, 16-, 32-, 64-, 128-, and 256-MB modules. The chip speeds are typically 6, 8, 10, or 12 nanoseconds.

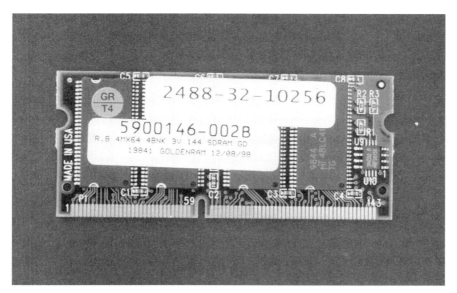

Figure 2.4 *A 144-pin DIMM module*

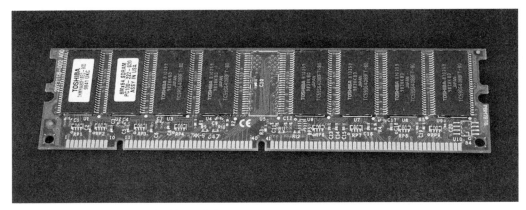

Figure 2.5 *A 168-pin DIMM module*

WARNING *Some motherboards include both DIMM and SIMM memory sockets. Generally, you can't use both at the same time, so don't think you can fill out every slot and get more total memory! The SIMM sockets are just there for convenience if you happen to have memory modules in that format.*

RIMM (Rambus Inline Memory Module)

RIMM is a unique package using 184 pins. Although its overall size is about the same as a DIMM package, the RIMM is laid out very differently (see Figure 2.6). The pin arrangement groups contacts into two rows separated by not one but two notches in the printed circuit board. RIMM boards also sport notches at both sides. Each RIMM package has its own cover plate which helps dissipate heat, at the same time reducing the effective density with which RIMMs can be placed by motherboard designers.

Unlike SDRAM, RIMM slots must all be filled, either with actual memory or with blank modules called *CRIMM*s (short for *Continuity Rambus Inline Memory Module)* or, sometimes, *terminator* modules. Also, some motherboards require RIMMs to be installed in pairs, just like the old SIMMs. You'll see RIMM technology in Pentium III and 4 computers.

A variation on RIMM is *SO-RIMM* (the "SO" stands for "small outline"), which is a smaller implementation for mobile computers.

WARNING *You can't retrofit RIMM modules onto a motherboard designed for PC100 or PC133 DIMMs.*

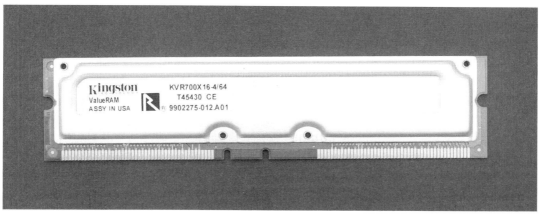

Figure 2.6 *A RIMM module*

Adding a Memory Module

Most of the time, you'll be adding memory to a PC rather than removing it, so this section deals with techniques for installing a new module of RAM to your system.

EQUIPMENT YOU'LL NEED:

➡ *Antistatic wrist strap (optional, but highly recommended)*

➡ *An appropriate screwdriver to remove your PC's cover*

➡ *Flashlight (optional)*

➡ *Stabilant-22 contact enhancement fluid (optional, but recommended; at available electronics supply houses, or Mercedes or Audi dealers)*

INFORMATION YOU'LL NEED:

➡ *Type of module (SIMM, DIMM, or RIMM)*

The installation method is almost the same whether you're using a SIMM, DIMM, or RIMM module; the only main difference is that when installing a SIMM, you must first insert the new module at a 45-degree angle and then bring it perpendicular to the motherboard. I'll point that out at the relevant step in the following instructions:

1. Disconnect the keyboard, mouse, display, power, and any other connectors.

2. Open the PC cover. (See Chapter 1's section titled "Opening a PC's Cover" for details if you need them.)

3. Remove any components (power supply, plastic airflow guides, etc.) that may be obscuring access to the memory sockets.

TIP *The precise location of memory sockets will vary from system to system. If you have your PC's manual, refer to it. If not, with the help of your flashlight, look on the motherboard for an even number of slots that are about half the length of the slots you'd use for an internal modem or video card. Typically, one or two of the slots will contain memory modules, and one or more empty slots will sit adjacent to them. The memory modules stand perpendicular to the plane of the motherboard.*

4. Disconnect any cables that may be in the way. Put a bit of masking tape on them and their respective connectors and then label them all with a felt pen so that reconnecting the cables is easy later.

5. Attach the antistatic wrist strap. One end goes on your wrist, and the other end attaches to the computer's chassis or silver power supply housing. (See Figure 2.7, which shows the cheap, semi-disposable paper kind; if you plan to do a lot of PC surgery, you may want to invest in a fancier cord-with-alligator-clip style strap that you can pick up at any Radio Shack.)

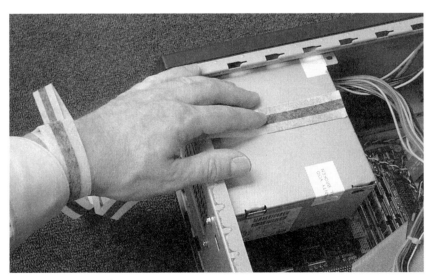

Figure 2.7 *Attaching an antistatic wrist strap*

6. Take the memory module out of its antistatic bag. (If it didn't come in an antistatic bag, or at the very least a plastic box of some kind, consider returning it. Who knows what damage it may have sustained during handling?)

7. The module has two sides: a short one and a long one. Along one of the long edges will be a row of silver or gold contacts. If you have Stabilant-22, apply a thin film of the fluid to the contacts, on both sides of the little printed circuit board (see Figure 2.8). This fluid improves connectivity between the module's contacts and the recessed contacts in the motherboard memory slot.

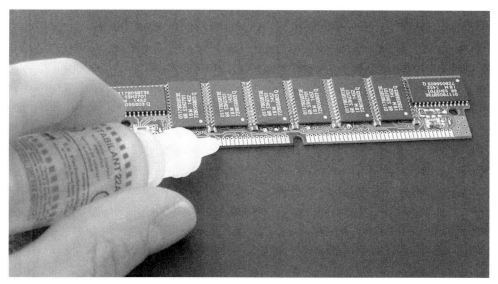

Figure 2.8 *Applying contact enhancer*

8. Take a look at the retaining clips at either end of the memory slot on the motherboard. If they're the kind that you can press down-and-out away from the socket, do so (see Figure 2.9).

9. Install the module, contacts down, matching the orientation of the new module to the ones that are already installed (for example, by paying attention to which side has the memory chips on it, if the memory chips only exist on one side of the printed circuit board).

   If you're installing a SIMM, you'll need to slide it into the slot at a 45-degree angle (see Figure 2.10), make sure it's positioned evenly in the slot, then while pressing into the slot, bring the module up so that it's perpendicular to the motherboard plane. Once you get to the perpendicular position, you should hear clicks as the retaining clips snap into place.

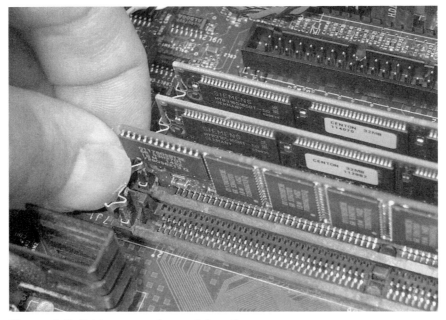

Figure 2.9 *Prizing apart the retaining clips*

Figure 2.10 *Inserting a SIMM at an angle*

If you're installing a DIMM or RIMM, drop the module straight down into the slot in a perpendicular orientation and press down; again, you should hear two clicks (they may occur simultaneously) as the retaining clips snap into place.

TIP *When pressing a memory module into place, go easy. You may need to exert significant pressure, but keep that pressure controlled. Be aware that in some cases it is possible to insert a memory module the wrong way around! So if you're pushing fairly hard and the rascal still isn't seating properly, pull it out and make sure you haven't got it in backwards.*

10. Gently wiggle the memory module to make sure it's properly seated and doesn't pop out of the slot in your hand.

11. Remove the antistatic wrist strap and reconnect any cables that you disconnected in step 4. You can remove the bits of masking tape that you used to help you remember what goes where, although it won't hurt anything to leave them in place.

12. Reinstall any components that you removed in step 3.

13. Put the cover back on the PC. Some people like to save this step for last, just so that it's easier to dive back in to the system if there are any problems, and that's fine. If you do so, however, make sure you don't run the system more than a few minutes. Some PCs need the cover in place to force fan air to the right places (mainly the CPU) in the right amounts. Granted, it seems odd that some PC components can get hotter with the cover off than with it on, but I've seen it happen!

14. Reconnect the keyboard, mouse, display, and any other peripheral cables.

15. Restart the PC and watch the BIOS to see if it reports the new memory size (the old size plus the new module). If it still shows the old memory size, then your new module is either defective (unlikely) or not completely seated (likely). In that case, follow the steps in the following section to remove the memory module, and then install it again. If that doesn't work, you may want to experiment with installing the module in a different motherboard slot.

Removing a Memory Module

You may never need to remove a memory module, but if you decide to max out your PC's RAM allocation, you'll probably need to yank out one or more lower-capacity modules and replace them with higher-capacity modules.

When I say "yank out," I really mean quite the opposite, because you need to go slowly and carefully to avoid ruining your motherboard! The annoying little clips that hold memory modules in place are notoriously fragile, and if you break one off, well, you can't use *that* memory slot anymore! Unlike other types of add-in circuit boards, like video boards or internal modems, memory modules need the clips to keep the modules securely in place so they'll work properly.

EQUIPMENT YOU'LL NEED:

➡ *Antistatic wrist strap (optional, but highly recommended)*

➡ *Appropriate screwdriver to remove your PC's cover*

➡ *Flashlight (optional)*

INFORMATION YOU'LL NEED:

➡ *Type of module (SIMM, DIMM, or RIMM; you may be able to deduce this information after looking at the memory, based on the details already provided in this chapter)*

The following steps apply to SIMM, DIMM, and RIMM modules. Where a particular instruction applies only to one or two of these packaging types, I indicate that clearly in the text.

1. Disconnect the keyboard, mouse, display, power, and any other connectors.

2. Open the PC cover. (See Chapter 1's section titled "Opening a PC's Cover" for details if you need them.)

3. Remove any components (power supply, plastic airflow guides, etc.) that may be obscuring access to the memory sockets.

TIP *The precise location of memory sockets will vary from system to system. If you have your PC's manual, refer to it. If not, look for an even number of slots that are between four and five inches long, usually black, with little plastic or metal clips at each end. Typically, one or two of the slots will contain memory modules (which are less than an inch tall), and empty slots will sit adjacent to them. The memory modules stand perpendicular to the plane of the motherboard.*

4. Disconnect any cables that may be in the way. Put a bit of masking tape on them and their respective connectors and then label all of them with a felt pen so that reconnecting the cables is easy later.

5. Attach the antistatic wrist strap. One end goes on your wrist, the other end attaches to the computer's chassis or silver power supply housing (shown in Figure 2.7).

6. Two plastic or metal clips hold the memory module in place. You must release these clips before you can remove the module. Use your flashlight to see exactly how the clips work. Generally, you'll press down and away on an angled surface of the clip (see Figure 2.11) to make the clip pivot around its retaining pin at the base of the memory socket and away from the memory module.

TIP *When pulling or pressing retaining clips away from the memory module, go easy. You may need to exert significant pressure, but keep that pressure controlled, even if your temperature is rising because the clips are scratching your fingers and bending your nails. If you snap off a clip—and some of them, especially the plastic ones, are mighty flimsy—you've done permanent damage to the motherboard. Also, I don't generally suggest using a screwdriver to prize away the retaining clips; if that screwdriver slips, it's just too darned easy to scratch a circuit trace on the motherboard and turn your PC into a boat anchor.*

Figure 2.11 *Releasing a memory module retaining clip*

7. Once both retaining clips are released, you can pull out the memory module. Here's where SIMM and DIMM modules vary a little: You have to angle the SIMM module forward in its slot before you can pull it out (see Figure 2.12). With DIMM and RIMM modules, you can pull 'em straight out.

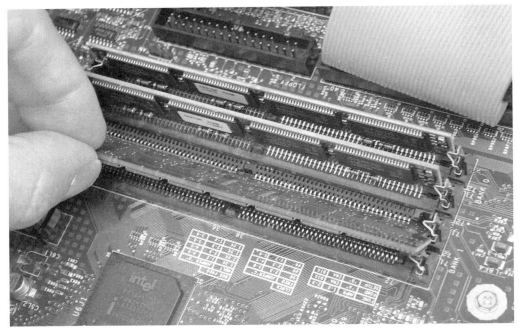

Figure 2.12 *Rotating a SIMM forward before removing*

8. Immediately put the memory module into an antistatic bag (see Figure 2.13) so static electricity won't zap it later, after you remove the antistatic wrist strap.

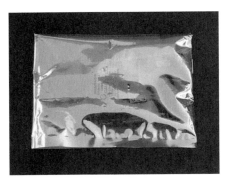

Figure 2.13 *An antistatic bag*

9. Shed the antistatic wrist strap and reconnect any cables that you disconnected in step 4. You can remove the bits of masking tape that you used to help you remember what goes where, although it won't hurt anything to leave them in place.

10. Reinstall any components that you removed in step 3.

11. Put the cover back on the PC. You can save this step for last, but see my comment in step 13 of the "Adding a Memory Module" section.

12. Reconnect the keyboard, mouse, display, and any other peripheral cables.

13. Restart the PC and watch for any BIOS errors that may indicate the system doesn't like the way the remaining memory modules occupy slots on the motherboard. If you don't see any such errors, the system should start normally. If you do, you may need to go back in and rearrange the remaining modules, for example, to make sure they're all adjacent with no intervening empty slots.

Chapter 3

Storage

As computer hardware components have become smaller and more efficient, software has moved stubbornly and consistently in the opposite direction. Operating systems have become so bloated that you now need a 2GB hard drive just to install Windows 2000 or XP—an amazing fact when you consider that you used to be able to fit a PC's operating system on a diskette. Sure, today's operating systems have more features, and they come with lots of non-operating-system stuff that some use and others don't. But are they *six thousand times* better? Surely not, but that's how much larger they've grown. (This is one reason why more and more folks are experimenting with Linux, which is considerably less voracious for resources like disk space.) Application programs have also grown enormous. Macromedia Dreamweaver takes 60MB; Adobe Photoshop, 100MB; Microsoft Office, around 200MB; and so on.

I won't go into the economics of "bloatware" here, except to note summarily that most software makers have little incentive to create compact code when the cost-per-megabyte of hard drives has dropped as steeply as it has in recent years. The result is that much of what we've gained in terms of storage cost-per-megabyte we've had to give back to feed the bloatware monster.

On the data side, the fact that today's PCs can handle digital music and video moderately well means that home users, especially, are likely to download and store these inherently large files more and more. Those MP3 music files can fill a multi-gigabyte disk in a matter of months, and those 30MB music videos can do so even faster.

So, you're probably going to need more storage before you know it. Even if you don't need more gigabytes, you may want faster ones. You may also come to realize that although your computer didn't come with a convenient way to back up all those megabytes in case of disk failure, you'd like such a backup system, and maybe you even need one. Or you may need a convenient way to exchange large files with friends, colleagues, relatives, or clients. So, it's time for a chapter about storage upgrades, and this is it.

Intro to Storage

Random access memory is technically storage, but when the term "storage" crops up in the context of PCs, it normally means "storage that doesn't go away when you turn off the power" or what computer nerds call *non-volatile storage*. That's a broad category that includes hard drives, cartridge drives, optical drives, and tape drives. Let's look at each of these in turn.

Hard Drives

Hard drives are the most common form of persistent storage, even more common nowadays than diskette drives. (The diskette drive is becoming almost vestigial, like the human appendix; I rarely use mine anymore and I bet you rarely use yours. I could compute pretty happily with a floppy-less PC, and we'll start seeing those more and more in coming years.)

Hard drives have a big impact on your PC's performance, and not just when you save data files, either. Those bloated operating systems I mentioned in the chapter intro (the ones that start with "W") spend a lot of time reading from and writing to the hard drive, especially on PCs with 64 and (gasp) 32MB of RAM, just for housekeeping chores. If you're into graphics, video, audio, or multimedia, then disk performance becomes a huge concern. So, how does one categorize hard drives?

The Interface

First, there's the *interface* that defines how the hard drive and PC communicate. Something like 95% of modern PCs use a variant of the *IDE* interface, which stands for *Integrated Drive Electronics*; the other 5% or so use a flavor of *SCSI*, or *Small Computer Systems Interface*. Normally, IDE drives connect directly to the motherboard, although you can upgrade your IDE capabilities by buying an add-in controller card. You usually have to buy an add-in controller if you want to put a SCSI drive into a small office or home PC, but so-called "workstation" PCs sometimes ship with an integrated SCSI controller. SCSI drives are generally faster, more durable, and more expensive than IDE drives, so one good PC upgrade to consider is bumping up to SCSI for your hard drive(s). However, you may be able to stick with IDE and make a significant hardware upgrade, as I'll discuss in the next section.

IDE drives have several variations. The fastest popular variant as I write this is Ultra ATA/100, also known as Ultra ATA DMA mode 5, which became widely available in the year 2000. The "100" part of the name means that this interface can handle a data transfer rate of 100MBps in short bursts. Ultra ATA/100 requires a 40-pin, 80-conductor cable (the extra wires are grounds to reduce electrical noise). A somewhat slower variation on the theme is Ultra ATA/66 (Ultra ATA DMA mode 4), which can move data around at 66MBps in short bursts, and which also requires a 40-pin, 80-conductor cable. Ultra ATA/66 drives were generally available as of mid-1999.

Ultra ATA/33 (Ultra ATA DMA mode 2) is an older and slower standard that supports a 33MBps data transfer rate, and works with a cheaper 40-pin, 40-conductor cable. Ultra ATA/25 (Ultra ATA DMA mode 1) supports 25MBps, and Ultra ATA/16 (Ultra ATA DMA mode 0) runs in 16.6MBps bursts, and both use the el cheapo 40/40 cable.

Just because you have an Ultra ATA/100 drive system doesn't mean you're running faster than someone with Ultra ATA/66, however! The reason is that although the interface may be able to handle the higher speed, most drives built nowadays aren't capable of providing the data that fast. Which brings me to the second way to categorize hard drives: rotational speed.

Rotational Speed

For a single-user PC (that is, not a network server), the most important single hard drive criterion from a speed standpoint is *rotational speed*—how fast the silly thing spins. Here's why: If your drive spins at a relatively slow speed, it's not going to be able to tax the capacity of either an Ultra ATA/100 or a SCSI Ultra160 interface. The drive simply isn't spinning fast enough to feed data into the communications channel at anything approaching its design's maximum speed.

Modern IDE drives usually come in one of two speeds: 5400rpm and 7200rpm. The slower drives are less expensive, often quieter, and more common in so-called "home" PCs. If your drive runs at 5400rpm, you should consider replacing it with a 7200rpm unit if you want to stick with IDE. You'll notice the difference, even though it may not sound like that big a jump. You'll definitely want 7200rpm if you're upgrading to an Ultra ATA/100 controller from a 66 or 33 controller; otherwise the controller upgrade is pointless because the drive won't be able to use the speed. Higher rpm drives tend to be noticeably louder than lower rpm unites. Having said that, Seagate's Barracuda ATA IV is a high-speed 7200rpm IDE drive that's so quiet you don't even know it's on. Some newer IBM Deskstar drives are very quiet too.

If you're willing to consider shelling out a few extra bucks and going for SCSI, then you enter a new world of speed possibilities. You can buy SCSI drives that run at 10,000rpm and even 15,000rpm. If you can find a 15,000rpm drive that doesn't sound like a dentist's drill and doesn't push your credit card over the limit, you'll never want to go back.

Other Features

Although the interface and rotational speed categories are the most important, you can also categorize hard drives according to *durability*, *seek time*, and *cache*.

Durability Most drives today are very reliable, and will run for four years or more without a problem, but SCSI drives usually have better durability than IDE drives. The industry measures durability with a number called *MTBF*, for *mean time between failures*; larger numbers are better.

Seek time The *seek time* is how long it takes the drive to seek a particular *track*, a concentric ring of data, on a disk. The seek operation is like placing a phonograph needle at the correct song on a vinyl LP (remember those?). You first have to move the read/write head to the right track (seek time) and then wait for the right sector on that track to spin around under the read/write head (*rotational latency*, which is lower for higher rpm drives). The *average access time* (how long the drive takes to find a particular bit of data) is the seek time plus the rotational latency. In most modern drives, the rotational latency is a bigger factor than the seek time, but the seek time can vary between drives having the same rotational speed, so you may want to be aware of it.

Cache All hard drives have some onboard memory (called *cache*) that they use to store recently read data. When the drive can transfer data from its cache memory instead of from the physical disk, the transfer speed can be much higher. As memory has become cheaper, today's drives use more cache than older drives. You'll see values ranging from 128KB to 2MB, and I've found that drives with more cache tend to perform faster in day-to-day use.

Cartridge Drives

Cartridge drives run at speeds equivalent to those of really slow hard drives, but their big advantage is that the media is replaceable: you can pop a disk out and store it, ship it, or archive it. Cartridge drives can be internal or external, and the interface can be IDE, SCSI, *Universal Serial Bus* (*USB*), or parallel; see Chapter 11, "Buses," for more detail on these interfaces. (By the way, when you hear "cartridge," think "magnetic" and not optical; these are magnetic media.)

Although other vendors such as SyQuest had been making removable cartridge disks before Iomega came along, the media didn't really take off until Iomega introduced its relatively inexpensive Zip drives. These 100MB devices have become very popular for backup and data exchange, although I think their popularity has crested now that optical devices are comparably priced and optical media are cheaper. If a 100MB Zip disk costs US$10 and a 650MB CD-R (Compact Disc Recordable) disc costs US$2, the cost difference between a US$100 Zip drive and a US$150 CD burner becomes just about insignificant.

Iomega introduced a 250MB version of the Zip drive that can read and write, but not format, the earlier 100MB disks. You should also know about the Jaz drive, a more expensive unit (around US$300 as I write this) that supports 2GB per disk. Data transfer rates for cartridge drives range from 1MBps to 8MBps, so they're a lot slower than typical hard drives.

Optical Drives

Optical storage on CD media has many attractive features: long-lasting media, good speed, imperviousness to magnetic fields, and readability on just about every PC in use today. Now that writeable optical, especially CD-R and CD-RW (Compact Disc Rewriteable), has become affordable, and you can buy 650MB CD-R and CD-RW discs for US$2 apiece, it's a great choice for backup and data exchange.

Your basic CD-ROM drive can read regular CD-ROMs and CD-Rs, and, if it's "multiread" compatible, CD-RWs. If you're thinking of upgrading your CD-ROM drive, don't just get a faster CD-ROM drive, get a "burner"—a device that can create CD-R and CD-RW discs as well as read all three kinds of CDs. These devices turn up the laser power in write mode and use low power in read mode. You won't spend much more money, and you'll get great technology for making backup copies of your data and even programs. If you exchange data with others, burning a CD beats making a Zip disk, in that you don't have to ask if the recipient has a CD-ROM drive (because CD-ROM drives are standard equipment on today's PCs).

WARNING *Just be aware that many CD-ROM drives can't read the rewriteable CD-RW discs, so you may want to mail out CD-R discs instead if you're not sure whether your recipient has a multiread drive.*

What about *Digital Versatile Disc* (*DVD*)? With capacities ranging from 4.2GB to a theoretical maximum of 17GB, this is a promising technology. However, as a storage medium, DVD is well standardized for reading (DVD-ROM), but not well standardized at all for writing. As of this writing, there are not one, not two, not even three, but four writeable-DVD standards in play: *DVD-R*, which is a write-once technology, and *DVD-RAM*, *DVD+RW*, and *DVD-RW*, which are rewriteable technologies.

It's a chaotic mess, and I'd suggest you stay away from writeable DVD until one or maybe two clear winners emerge from the standards wars. None of the writeable formats offer full compatibility with each other, or with current drives, so guessing wrong can be costly—especially when you consider that writeable DVD drives are in the US$1000-and-up neighborhood, lots more expensive than CD-RW drives.

TIP *You can buy compatibility with the read-only DVD-ROM standard for a smaller investment; I like the combo drives that read DVD-ROM and CD-ROM, and write CD-R and CD-RW.*

Writeable DVD media is close to CD-R and CD-RW on a per-megabyte basis. For example, DVD-RAM discs go for around US$20 a pop as I write this, for 5.2GB of storage. However, if you don't expect to fill a DVD-RAM disc, you'll save on media with the CD-based standards.

Tape Drives

Tape drives, still commonplace in server rooms the world over, are almost nonexistent in the home and small-office PC market. However, despite the existence of low-cost CD burners, tape is still a perfectly valid way to back up data. In fact, tape has three big advantages over cartridge disks and writeable optical: it's faster, it's more reliable, and you can back up an entire hard drive onto a single tape (meaning you don't have to hang around to change media, hurray!). Tape media is cheaper than cartridge disk media on a per-megabyte basis, too, although whether the media is cheaper than writeable optical depends on the type of tape drive.

Here are the main tape technologies:

Quarter inch cartridge (**QIC**) is a standard for drives that store data in parallel tracks along a 0.25" wide tape. Many variants exist; the most popular for PCs is *Travan*, which uses 0.315" tapes (so-called "QIC wide") with longer lengths and higher densities than regular

QIC tapes. Travan capacities range from 800MB to 20GB, and can move data at rates from 1MBps to 5MBps. These drives are generally slower than 4mm or 8mm tape drives.

TIP *Many Travan drives don't perform* Read-After-Write (RAW) *verification, an important data integrity check. Newer drives, particularly those that hew to the NS20 ("Travan 20") specification, do perform RAW, and these are the ones to get.*

4mm* or *Digital Audio Tape (**DAT**) is a popular Sony-licensed technology offering high capacity and good price/performance using small cartridges (2.9″ × 2.1″ × 0.4″). Cartridge capacity ranges from 4GB to 24GB, and the speed of data transfer can go up to 20MBps.

8mm tape drives from Exabyte, Seagate, and Sony offer higher tape capacity than 4mm drives on slightly larger cartridges (3.75″ × 2.5″ × 0.5″). Cartridge capacity ranges from 7GB to 60GB, and the speed of the data transfer is comparable to 4mm drives.

Digital Linear Tape (**DLT**) is a half-inch format using cartridges about twice the size of 4mm and 8mm tape with supporting capacities from 10GB to 35GB and transfer rates that can be up to twice as fast as 4mm and 8mm.

Tape drives can mount inside your PC using the IDE or SCSI interface, or they can be self-contained external units that connect to your computer via a SCSI, USB, or parallel cable. (If you have a network, you can even get tape drives that hook directly into a network hub.) Use a SCSI connection for optimum speed, or use a USB or parallel connection if you want to use the drive with different computers.

Travan drives are fine for workstation backups and notebooks, but I prefer units with RAW verification built into the hardware so you know without a doubt that your backup tapes are good. Expect to pay between US$200 and US$300 for a good 20GB Travan drive. If you use 4mm, 8mm, or DLT drives, you'll enjoy faster backups and more reliable hardware. Although you pay about twice as much for such drives, you often save on the media. For example, as I write this, a 10GB tape cartridge for an Exabyte 10GB drive costs US$4, significantly less on a per-GB basis than a typical Travan cartridge. So, the life-cycle cost difference between Travan and its fancier brethren isn't as much as you'd think at first.

The top tape drive vendors include Exabyte, Seagate Technology, Hewlett-Packard, Iomega, and Sony.

Adding an IDE Drive

The most common hard drive upgrade by far is adding a second IDE drive to a PC that already has one IDE drive. You may perform this upgrade to gain capacity, improve speed, or both.

EQUIPMENT YOU'LL NEED:

➡ *A Phillips-head screwdriver, medium point*

➡ *Other screwdriver(s) as necessary to remove the PC cover*

TIP *Normally you don't gain much of a performance boost by upgrading the IDE controller, but if you have an older controller (Ultra-ATA/33 or earlier) and you're adding a 7200rpm hard drive, you may want to buy a newer, faster controller if you can get a good deal on one. (Promise Technology is a popular vendor; see Figure 3.1.) You can generally figure out what speed controller you have by looking at the hardware specs in your user manual, or by looking at the IDE controller model number in Windows' Device Manager and then looking that number up on the Web. Note, however, that some newer IDE controllers require a specific version of the PCI bus, so check your PC's specs before you buy.*

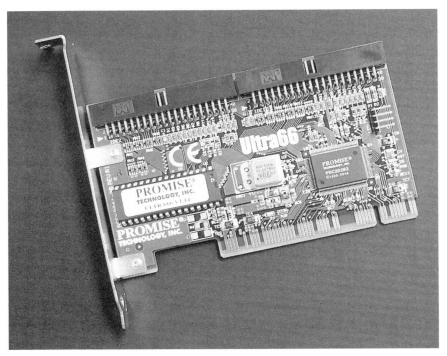

Figure 3.1 *An Ultra-ATA/66 IDE controller card*

The most important tip I can offer if you go through this upgrade is to move your more frequently used programs and data folders to the new drive when you're done, if the new drive is faster than the original one (which is highly likely). That way, you're using the original drive to boot your operating system, and the new, faster drive for day-in, day-out tasks.

This dividing of the workload between two drives goes by the name *load balancing* among IT professionals, and it's a big part of making your PC as fast as it can be. Yes, it's a chore to uninstall and reinstall your programs (you can't just move them with a file cut-and-paste operation), but you do it only once, and you'll enjoy the speed gains from that point forward.

Without further ado, here's the typical procedure for adding a second IDE drive to a PC that already has one IDE drive in it:

1. Turn off the PC and unplug it.

2. Remove all cables from the PC's back panel.

3. Remove the PC's cover. (See Chapter 1, "Read Me First," for details if you're unfamiliar with this step.)

4. Locate the present hard drive (see Figure 3.2). In a small-cabinet PC, you may have to remove the power supply, or one or two other components, to get to the drive. It'll have two connectors, one for power and one gray ribbon cable for data. Locations vary from model to model, but you're looking for a rectangular device measuring (most likely) 5.75" × 4" × 1".

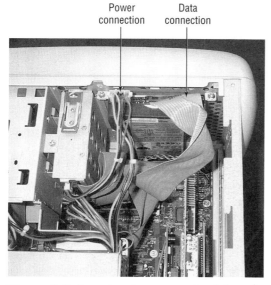

Figure 3.2 *Locating the present hard drive*

5. Look for an extra connector on the gray data cable (see Figure 3.3). It may be toward the end, or it may be between the present drive and the motherboard connector.

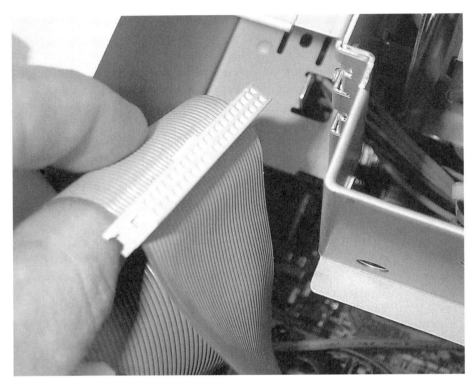

Figure 3.3 *Locating the unused IDE connector*

6. Place the *jumper* on your new drive so that the new drive is the "slave." (The existing drive is already set as the "master.") A jumper is a little plastic block with metal connectors inside, and it fits over two pins sticking out on the drive's back connector panel. Usually, you'll find a label right on the drive (see Figure 3.4) indicating how to set the jumper (or jumpers—some drives have more than one). Otherwise, check out www.ontrack.com or www.thetechpage.com for jumper information. Most hard drives ship with the jumper set to "master," so you'll almost always need to change it when adding a drive to an already-occupied channel.

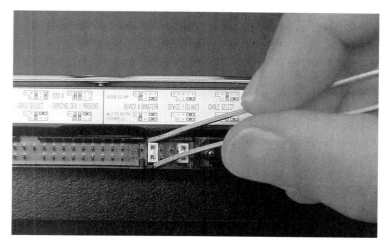

Figure 3.4 *Setting the master/slave jumper*

7. Attach *side rails* to the new drive, if necessary. Side rails (see Figure 3.5) are plastic or metal pieces, usually tapered on the front end, that secure to the drive's sides with screws. You then slide the drive into the bay by aligning the side rails with corresponding indentations, or channels, in the open drive bay's sheet metal. Your PC owner's manual should state whether you need rails or not. Rails don't come with new drives, but you can generally buy them cheaply from your PC's manufacturer or from your friendly local computer parts house.

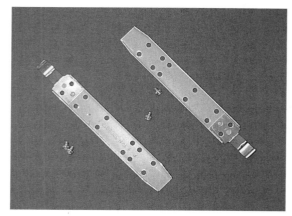

Figure 3.5 *Side rails*

WARNING *Some PCs have weird mounting requirements, so you may want to check with the manufacturer to see if you need nonstandard drive rails or other mounting hardware.*

8. Slide the new drive into place in any convenient, open storage device bay. It's usually easier to reattach the cables if you don't slide it all the way in; see Figure 3.6. (Also note that this particular drive enclosure doesn't require side rails.)

Figure 3.6 *Sliding the new drive into place*

9. Connect the data cable's extra connector to the new drive (see Figure 3.7). Most likely, it'll fit only one way, but if that's not the case, make sure the red wire lines up with the #1 pin. (Usually you'd have to really twist the cable around violently to connect it the wrong way.) It's okay if you need to switch connectors to make the cable work; it doesn't matter which connector goes to which drive. You should put your new drive on the same cable (or channel) as your first drive. The second IDE channel is for CD-ROMs and other slower devices, and if you mix a hard drive and a CD-ROM drive on the same channel, the channel runs slower and you'll stifle the hard drive.

Figure 3.7 *Connecting the data cable to the new drive*

10. Connect a spare power connector to the new drive (see Figure 3.8). The power connector is a white four-socket plug that fits into a mating socket on the drive.

11. Secure the new drive in its bay (see Figure 3.9). Different computers use different methods; some let you simply slide the drive into the bay until a spring-like metal tab clicks into place. Others require that you install four screws, two on each side, to mount the drive to the surrounding sheet metal. Still others have a removable caddy to which you mount the drive.

WARNING *Be careful about the screws you use! Ideally, get mounting screws from your PC manufacturer or from a computer parts supplier. If you go to the hardware store, it's very easy to get screws that are too long and that will effectively disembowel the inner circuitry of your new drive.*

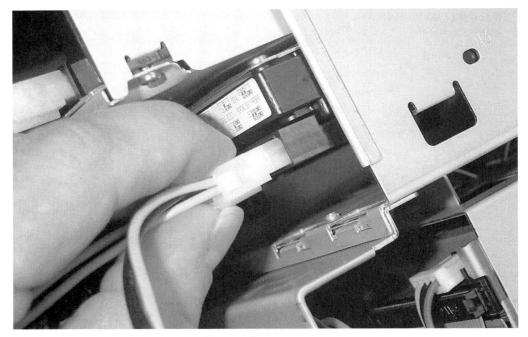

Figure 3.8 *Connecting power to the new drive*

Figure 3.9 *Securing the new drive in its bay*

12. Reconnect the cables you disconnected in step 2.

13. Turn the PC on, boot normally, and see if your new drive appears (for example, by looking in the "My Computer" folder).

14. If everything looks good, turn the PC off, disconnect the back panel cables, replace the cover, and reconnect the cables.

15. Restart the computer and perform a thorough disk test on the new drive to make sure it's completely healthy. For example, in Windows 9*x*, ME, and 2000, you'd right-click the drive in My Computer, choose Properties, click Tools, and click the Check (or Check Now) button. If you have an option to select a thorough test versus a standard test, choose thorough. The test may run for an hour or so, but at the end of it you can be quite confident that your drive is safe for programs and data.

16. (Optional) Partition the new drive. *Partitioning* is the process of dividing the space that a new drive provides into multiple drive letters. For example, if you install a new 20GB drive, you could partition it so that, to the computer's operating system, it looks like two 10GB drives (D: and E:). Partitioning used to be necessary to gain space efficiency and to avoid limitations in the operating system's ability to use large drives; with Windows 98, ME, 2000, and XP, however, as long as you use the FAT32 or NTFS file systems, the value of partitioning drives is minimal.

TIP *You can use a program called FDISK, which comes with DOS and Windows, to partition a drive, although I'm much more enthusiastic about a program from PowerQuest called Partition Magic (about US$60). In either case, read the documentation carefully before partitioning a drive. If you use FDISK, you wipe out all data on the drive when you partition it; if you use Partition Magic (carefully!), you can keep your data, under most circumstances.*

17. Run a utility to set the drive's data transfer mode. Some drives that are capable of using Ultra-ATA/66 or Ultra-ATA/100 use Ultra-ATA/33 by default for compatibility. Therefore, you have to run a small utility program to tell the drive to use the faster mode. Visit your drive manufacturer's Web site for details and to download the utility program.

Upgrading from IDE to SCSI

Although upgrading from one IDE drive to another is reasonably easy and can get you better performance, to get the most impressive speed gains—especially under an operating system like Windows 2000 or Windows XP—you should upgrade from IDE to SCSI. The downside is that the upgrade is more complex, you'll almost certainly spend more money on the hardware, and you may or may not be able to use your existing IDE hard drive anymore. If none of that bothers you very much, read on!

Upgrading from IDE to SCSI is different from adding a second IDE drive in two major respects:

- You're replacing an existing drive, rather than adding a second drive.

- You're most likely adding a new controller to your PC, rather than using an existing connection and cable.

Because you probably want to replace your existing IDE drive rather than keep it, you'll need to look at software to migrate everything from your present drive to the new drive. If you're already using a backup program that lets you make full backups, for example to a Jaz drive or a CD-R burner, then that's fine, but you'll have to reinstall your operating system on the new SCSI drive before you can restore your backup. A faster way is to use a utility like Drive Copy or Ghost to create a "mirror image" of your original drive on your new drive.

- If you use the utility method, you'll install your new SCSI controller and disk drive before removing the existing IDE drive. Your operating system will detect the new hardware and walk you through the process of loading *drivers* (small special-purpose programs) so that it can communicate with the new controller and drive. Then, delete any unnecessary files (such as the contents of your browser cache) and run your drive copying program to copy everything from the old drive to the new one. After that's done, you can remove the old drive and the system will be able to boot from the new one.

- If you use the backup program method, you'll make a backup of your entire disk. Then, you can remove the existing IDE drive and install the SCSI drive and controller. At that point, you'll reinstall the operating system onto the new disk, according to the operating system manufacturer's instructions. Finally, you can use the backup program to restore your programs and data files from the Zip disk or optical disk you backed 'em up to before you removed the IDE drive. This method is free, but slow.

The physical part of the installation is very similar to that for installing a new IDE drive, given earlier in this chapter (see "Adding an IDE Drive"), but you'll need to install a SCSI controller card if you don't already have one. You'll then run the data cable from that add-in card to your drive, instead of from the motherboard to the drive, as you would do with an IDE drive. You must make sure the drive has a different SCSI ID than the controller (boot drives are usually 0, controllers are usually 7). You must also make sure that the controller and drive are properly terminated. For more details on SCSI controllers, please see Chapter 11.

Adding a Zip or Jaz Drive

Although you should consider writeable optical if you're looking for a removable backup or data exchange storage solution, Zip and Jaz drives are attractive solutions for many users. This section offers a few tips for adding such drives to your PC.

Internal Drives

Adding an internal Zip or Jaz drive (see Figure 3.10) is almost identical to adding an internal hard drive (see the previous section, "Adding an IDE Drive"); the main difference is that you must use a drive bay that offers front-panel accessibility. You can choose to install the supporting software from the manufacturer, but I recommend that you try running your system without it first. Most versions of Windows reliably autodetect these cartridge drives and install the necessary software drivers automatically.

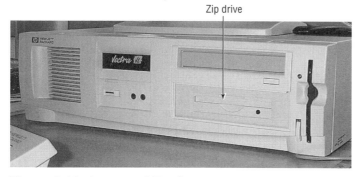

Figure 3.10 An internal Zip drive

TIP *If you install an IDE-type cartridge drive, you'll normally place it on your second IDE channel, along with your IDE CD-ROM drive. You wouldn't want to put a relatively slow device like a Zip drive on the same channel as a fast device like your primary hard drive. For one thing, the Zip drive will probably use PIO (Programmed Input/Output) rather than DMA (Direct Memory Access); CD drives also use PIO, but hard drives often use DMA for better speed.*

External Drives

The external flavors of Zip and Jaz drives offer three attachment methods: parallel-port, SCSI, and USB.

The parallel-port drive (see Figure 3.11) is the oldest and slowest option, but it's also the most flexible: you can connect a parallel-port Zip or Jaz drive to just about any PC. If you have more than one PC, you may want to consider a parallel-port Zip drive, because you can connect the unit to each machine you own, for backup purposes.

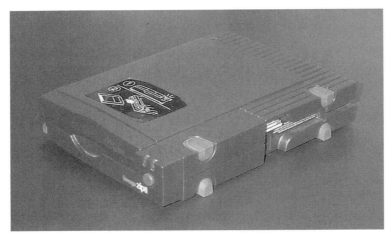

Figure 3.11 *A parallel-port Zip drive*

The SCSI interface is typically the fastest, especially if you have relatively recent SCSI hardware in your computer. That's the rub, though: Most PCs don't come with a SCSI controller, so you're looking at adding one unless you buy a "bundle" that includes both drive and controller.

The USB interface is middle of the road: It's faster than parallel and slower than SCSI. The appeal of USB versus SCSI is twofold. You probably already have a USB port on your PC, and you don't have to worry about stuff like "bus termination" and "device IDs" with USB.

Adding a CD-R+RW Drive

When writeable CDs came out, users exhibited some confusion about the different standards, but happily they settled out into two main categories: CD-R and CD-RW. The names even make sense: the "R" in CD-R means recordable, and the "RW" in CD-RW means rewriteable. So, you can write to a CD-R disc, but only once; you can write to a CD-RW disk many times. (CD-R is a subset of a larger class of write-once, read-many devices that fall under the acronym WORM.)

One of the best PC upgrades I know of is to either replace or augment your existing CD-ROM drive with a CD-R, CD-RW, or (best of all) combo drive. You may even consider getting a drive that can also read DVD-ROM discs, for maximum flexibility.

If you're installing an internal drive, you can replace the old CD-ROM or leave it in the system, depending on the available drive bays in your PC. Sometimes having two CD drives is pretty handy; you can keep a reference CD (such as a dictionary or encyclopedia) in the older unit and use the newer, faster, writeable drive for installing new programs or burning data discs.

An Upgrade Example

In this example, I upgrade an el cheapo home PC from a regular, internal CD-ROM drive (which I replace) to a combo CD-R/CD-RW drive. The interface is IDE.

EQUIPMENT YOU'LL NEED:

➡ *A Phillips-head screwdriver, medium point (for device mounting screws)*

➡ *Other screwdriver(s) as necessary to remove the PC cover*

1. See how your current CD-ROM drive is set up. Normally, it'll be the sole device on the second IDE channel, and will be set up as an IDE master. (In Windows, you could glean this information from the Device Manager screen, accessible from the Control Panel.)

2. Turn off the PC and unplug it.

3. Remove all cables from the PC's back panel.

4. Remove the PC's cover. (See Chapter 1 for details if you're unfamiliar with this step.)

5. Locate the old CD-ROM drive (see Figure 3.12). It shouldn't be too hard to find, since you know where it's located on the front panel. It'll have at least two connectors (power and data), and maybe a third (audio to the sound card).

6. Disconnect the cables from the old CD-ROM drive. You may want to mark the data cable (for example, with a piece of masking tape), because you'll be reconnecting it to the new drive later.

7. Remove the old drive's mounting screws (if any). Usually, you'll see two screws on one side and two on the other. Some drives, however, secure to the PC by one or more spring-mounted clips, in which case there won't be any screws to remove; you'll just release the clip (for example, by pressing it down) and slide the drive out the back.

8. Remove the old drive and set it aside. If it has mounting rails on the side (plastic or metal pieces that secure to the drive's sides with screws), you may need them to put onto the new drive so that it'll fit into your PC.

Figure 3.12 *Locating the old CD-ROM drive*

9. Set the jumper on your new drive. If the drive is the only device on the channel—the only device on the IDE cable coming from the motherboard—then set the jumper to the master setting. This is the most common setting. However, if another IDE device on the same channel is already set to master, you must set the new CD drive to slave.

10. Attach side rails to the new drive, if necessary. If your old drive had side rails, then remove the side rails from the old drive and attach them to the new drive in exactly the same way.

11. Slide the drive into place, but not all the way in.

12. Reconnect the data cable. Most likely, it'll fit only one way, but if that's not the case, make sure the red wire lines up with the #1 pin. The label on the back of the drive usually indicates where the #1 pin lies (see Figure 3.13).

13. Reconnect the power cable.

14. If you disconnected an audio cable in step 6, reconnect it now. If not, and you want to be able to hear CD audio through your PC's sound circuit, connect the CD burner's audio out connector to the audio input connector on your motherboard (or, on an older PC, the sound card) with the audio cable that was supplied with the new drive (see Figure 3.14).

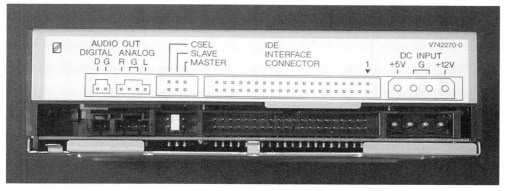

Figure 3.13 *A CD burner label shows the #1 pin location.*

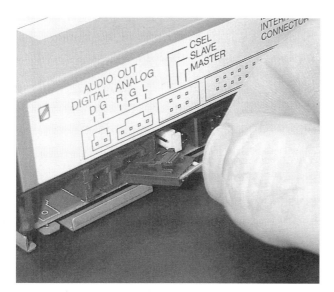

Figure 3.14 *Connecting a CD audio cable*

15. Secure the new drive in its bay. You may have to attach two screws on each side, or you may simply be able to slide the drive all the way in until a retaining spring clicks shut.

16. Reconnect the cables you disconnected in step 3.

17. Turn the PC on, boot normally, and check to see if your new drive appears (for example, by looking in the "My Computer" folder). You should also press the eject button to make sure the CD carrier is active and works properly.

18. If everything looks good, turn the PC off, disconnect the back panel cables, replace the cover, and reconnect the cables.

19. Install the manufacturer's software bundle and follow the directions to burn your own CDs.

TIP *You can use the discarded CD-ROM drive on another computer, sell it at a garage sale, use it to build a new PC from parts, or donate it to a computer smash event for a local charity.*

External vs. Internal Drives

The example I gave a couple of sections ago in "An Upgrade Example" looked at an internal drive, but if you have more than one PC, or if you travel a lot with a laptop computer, you may prefer an external unit. External CD burners (see Figure 3.15) connect via a SCSI or USB port on the back of your PC; they typically have their own power adapter. For laptop use, you can either use a built-in USB port or buy a CD-burner "kit" that includes a credit-card drive controller you insert into an available PC card slot.

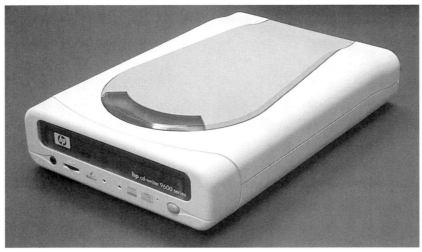

Figure 3.15 *An external CD-R/RW drive*

How do you decide between USB and SCSI? USB burners are easier to set up, but SCSI burners can go faster. I've found that in real life, unless you have a really speedy burner, you aren't likely to notice the speed difference, so my usual preference is for USB. (Some drives offer both, and let you choose.) Also, if you want to use SCSI, you'll probably have to add a SCSI controller to your PC, adding to the expense.

SCSI external drives need to have a unique SCSI ID, just as internal drives require; the difference is that on an external unit, you typically set the ID by a thumbwheel, dial, or similar device on the unit's back panel (see Figure 3.16). You'll also have to make sure the last device on the SCSI bus is electrically terminated, for example, by a resistor pack that you connect to the drive's extra SCSI connector.

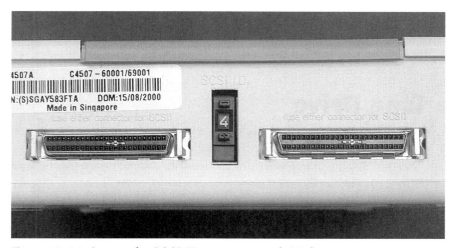

Figure 3.16 *Setting the SCSI ID on an external CD burner*

If you use only one PC, and it's a desktop with an available front-accessible drive bay, I recommend an internal drive. They're cheaper, they're faster than external USB drives, they don't take up desk space, and they avoid cable clutter.

Disc Media

The one thing you must know about disc media is that CD-R discs are compatible with just about every CD drive out there, while CD-RW discs work only with so-called *multiread* drives. (You may see labels or blazes on PC boxes touting the multiread feature: "Can read CD-RW discs!")

Many of today's better CD-ROM drives are multiread, and work fine with CD-ROM, CD-R, and CD-RW media. But lots of CD-ROM drives aren't multiread drives, and they'll have a tough time dealing with the different reflectivity characteristics of CD-RW discs. You may also find that one manufacturer's CD-RW drive doesn't read CD-RW discs made on another manufacturer's drive. So if you need maximum compatibility, use CD-R. (For example, when I make a capabilities demo for a prospective client, I always use CD-R.)

Now, about those rewriteability specs for CD-RW. You may have heard a figure of 1000 rewrites for this medium. You may see that if you wear latex gloves every time you handle your discs, but my experience is that 1000 rewrites is an optimistic figure. After about a hundred rewrites, I recommend you throw that CD-RW disc away.

Finally, longevity. True, optical discs aren't affected by magnetic fields, but they do oxidize over time. Handle discs by their edges, keep them in the mythical cool, dry place inside their little jewel boxes, and you may get 100 years out of them. Touch the surface just once with your greasy little fingers, and according to some experts, you cut that lifetime roughly in half. Here's my suggestion: Anything you need to keep forever, check it every 5 years for readability, and back it up (for example, onto another CD-R or CD-RW disc) after 10 years.

Adding a Tape Drive

Installing a tape drive is very similar to installing a hard drive (see "Adding an IDE Drive," earlier in this chapter). The tape drive slides into an empty bay inside the system unit, and you typically secure it with screws. You may also need to ground the device with a separate wire if the computer has plastic mounting rails instead of metal ones.

The better (read: faster) tape drives are SCSI, and if you install one of these, you'll need to set the SCSI ID number, connect the drive to your SCSI controller daisy chain, and plug a terminating resistor into it if the tape drive is the last device in the chain. (Don't forget to remove the terminating resistor from the device that used to be last in the SCSI chain.)

Figure 3.17 shows an internal tape drive's front view, and Figure 3.18 shows its hindquarters.

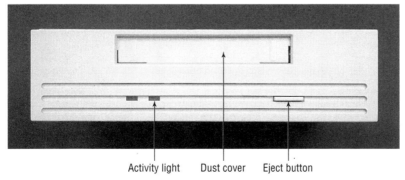

Activity light   Dust cover   Eject button

Figure 3.17 *An internal SCSI tape drive from the front*

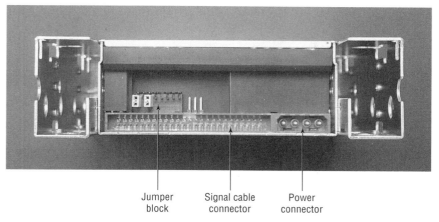

Jumper   Signal cable   Power
block   connector   connector

Figure 3.18 *An internal SCSI tape drive from the rear*

Maintaining Your Storage Devices

Excuse me? How can you maintain disk drives? Sure, the external drives need dusting every now and then, and the occasional going-over with a moist cloth, but how do you maintain an internal drive?

There is one thing you can do to improve the life of your hard drives, and that's to *defragment* them periodically. Defragmenting is the process of taking the little bits and pieces of files that get scattered across the disk over time, and consolidating them so that the file is one continuous piece. This process not only makes your PC run faster, because the disk's read/write heads don't have to bounce all over the place to read or write a file, but it extends the life of your hard drive, for the same reason.

How do you defragment a drive? You may have special-purpose software for this task, such as Norton Speed Disk from Symantec or Diskeeper from Executive Software, but most versions of Windows come with their own defragmenter. The usual method to get to this tool is to open My Computer, right-click the hard drive, choose Properties, click the Tools tab, and click the Defragment button.

The first time you do this on a PC that's seen a few months of use, defragmenting may take a long time, so do it overnight. Subsequent defrag runs go much faster, especially if you get into a routine of defragmenting once a month. (I defrag my disks at the office every week, but I use my PCs more than most folks do.)

If you install a tape drive, you'll need to clean the magnetic head from time to time. Follow the manufacturer's suggestions; typically, you buy a cleaning cartridge (make sure you get the right one for your model drive, as they are different!). In the rare event that no cleaning cartridge is available for your drive, the manufacturer may advise you to take a longish stick with a cotton swab at the end, douse the swab in isopropyl alcohol, and rub the swab back and forth over the read/write head a few times. A flashlight helps, because it can be a little tough to see the read/write head inside the tape drive.

Tape cartridges last a lot longer if you retension them periodically. Normally your tape drive will have a special retensioning program built into it that you can activate with a front-panel button. Or the drive may come with a utility program that you can run to retension a tape. Failing that, just put the tape in the drive, manually fast-forward to the end of the tape, and then rewind to the beginning. The conventional wisdom is to do this once a year, but follow the advice your tape drive manufacturer provides.

Chapter 4

Communications

PCs have become such good communicators that we're all beginning to realize the rather serious limitations of our decades-old communications infrastructure. The phone company seemed to be doing a fine job in the days when we used the phone to make voice calls only. Now, however, when I connect to my Internet Service Provider (ISP) at a paltry 26Kbps from my home office, I start wondering about the foresight of the telcos. Did they think modems were a passing fad? Or that they'd stay slow forever?

Qwest, the local phone company where I live, spends vast sums of money marketing voice mail, call waiting, caller ID, three-way calling, and other software-only features that cost Qwest comparatively little to implement. But when it comes to doing something about the substandard copper wires running to my house, sorry, you'll just have to live with that, Mr. Weadock, in fact, you're pretty lucky to be connecting at 26Kbps. To which my response is, you're pretty lucky to be a monopoly. When I then ask when I'll be able to get DSL, the amused rep explains that 45 minutes outside downtown Denver may as well be Siberia as far as they are concerned, to which I say I bet Siberia has better phone lines than I do, and maybe Qwest should consider upgrading to Russian telecommunications technology, after which the conversation generally goes downhill pretty fast.

The savvy PC user is not utterly helpless here. If you're like me, living in the exburbs (that's between suburbs and boondocks), you can take a few steps to improve PC communications somewhat. If you happen to live close enough to the cerebral cortex of a major metropolis that you regularly hear sirens, you can probably improve things more than somewhat. So, this chapter discusses how to perform some of the more popular communications upgrades. You may upgrade to gain speed, to reduce costs, or to do things you couldn't easily do before, such as share a fast Internet link with one or more other computers. Whatever the reason, given our increasing reliance on the Web, a communications upgrade can have an immediate and tangible effect on your PC's usability—even if the speed limit is still lower than we'd like it to be.

Intro to Communications

When you think PC communications, you think modems. Today, several different kinds of modems exist: dial-up, ISDN, DSL, and cable modems. (Some of these devices aren't technically modems, but rather "terminal adapters." A modem is a digital-to-analog-to-digital device; terminal adapters, like DSL and ISDN devices, are digital all the way.) This section takes a look at all four kinds.

Dial-Up Modems

Dial-up (*analog*) modems are the kind you're most likely to know already: the devices that your PC dials to connect via your phone line to the Internet or another public or private network.

Internal vs. External

Dial-up modems can be *internal* (fitting into an ISA or PCI slot inside your PC) or *external* (connecting to a serial or USB port on the back of your PC). The internal ones reduce clutter, but the external variety has its charms. You can see activity with the LED indicator lights, you don't have to sacrifice a precious PCI slot, and you can easily move an external modem from one computer to another, which can be convenient at times.

External modems have another plus. Sometimes, when you're communicating away, your modem will see a combination of data bits that causes it to freeze up tight. The only way to clear its poor little silicon head is to turn the power off and then back on. With an internal modem, the only way to power it down is to power the whole computer down, and the PC may take five minutes or more to reboot. With an external modem, unplug it or flip its power switch and you're back in action within 20 seconds.

Speed Kickers

If you have no other choice for faster "broadband" connectivity, or if the fees associated with the other choices don't work for you, then you may be surprised at what you can do with today's modem technology. First, let's talk speed. You may think that because you have a 56K modem, you're running as fast as possible. Chances are, that's not the case. If you're using an internal modem that came with your PC, it's probably a bargain-basement type called a *software modem*, *controller-less modem*, or *Winmodem*. All these terms are synonymous and signify a device that relies on your PC's CPU for all the heavy lifting. A *hardware modem*, by contrast, has its own processor and (according to my own informal testing) can perform as much as 15% faster when downloading a file in the background while you're doing something else with the PC in the foreground.

You probably wouldn't perform a modem upgrade solely to get a 15% performance boost, but wait—there's more. The International Telecommunications Union, or ITU, improved the 56K standard toward the end of 2000 with two new standards called V.92 and V.44 (modems that support one generally also support the other). The first of these standards is an improvement over the V.90 specification most modern modems use, in three areas:

- Modems that conform to V.92 make a connection as much as 50% faster than V.90 modems, partly by remembering the details of connections you make often.

- You can boost the upload speed of V.92 modems to 48Kbps instead of the 31.2Kbps limit of V.90 modems.

- If you have call waiting, *Internet Call Notification* or *ICN* (also called "modem-on-hold") is a part of V.92 that lets you take a voice call, hang up, and return to your Internet session.

The V.44 part is the modem's compression technology, which is up to 25% better than the V.42bis compression in today's common V.90 modem. That means that even if you connect at the same speed as with your V.90 modem, a modem that supports V.44 can still download Web pages faster, because it's packing more value into the same data stream.

The problem is that, as with most modem advances, it takes two to tango—that is, the remote computer's modem must be V.92 and V.44-compatible for you to realize all these benefits, not just your modem. And as I write this, Internet Service Providers like Earthlink, MSN, and America Online are dragging their feet on upgrading to these newer standards. So, let your ISP know you want a V.92/V.44 connection in your area, and tell your friends to do likewise. Meanwhile, if you're thinking of buying a new modem, get one that supports the newer standards; it'll cost you US$5 to US$10 more, and you'll be ready when the ISPs get their acts together. Manufacturers Diamond, Hayes, US Robotics, and Zoom are among the companies that make V.92/V.44 modems.

Voice Modems

You may see the term "voice modem," which usually means a modem that can also act as an answering machine. These devices work well, but as with any integrated device, you should ask yourself what happens if the modem breaks. Can you also afford to be without your answering machine? In addition, do you really want to leave your PC on all the time?

> **TIP** *Some external voice modems can perform their answering machine and fax-receive functions without the PC being turned on, which is a big plus.*

Multilink Modems

With Windows 98, ME, 2000, and XP, you can combine two communications channels to create a single "virtual" channel with greater speed than either individual channel. You can use the multilink feature with two analog modems if you have two phone lines. You can also mix digital (such as ISDN) and analog (traditional modem) devices, and you can use two devices that connect at different speeds (although the PC uses only the highest speed common to both devices).

So why haven't you ever heard of this capability? Because most ISPs don't offer it on their end of the connection. Still, you may want to ask your ISP, and if the answer is no, let them know you're disappointed.

ISDN

If you can't get DSL or cable modem service (both discussed later in this chapter), then you may be able to get *ISDN*, which does not really stand for It Still Does Nothing, but rather for *integrated services digital network*. ISDN works better over longer distances than DSL does. ISDN permits transmission of data, voice, audio, and video information over the same line, but you're most interested in the first two.

Competition from DSL has brought ISDN prices down a little in some markets, but the phone companies know that if you're asking for ISDN you probably can't get DSL, so ISDN still costs more than DSL even though it's slower, older, and more complicated. The only reason to use ISDN is if you need something better than the *POTS* (*plain old telephone system*) and you can't get DSL or cable modem.

Here are the salient facts about ISDN:

- ISDN "terminal adapters" aren't modems, strictly speaking, because modems do analog/digital conversion, and ISDN lines use digital signaling.

- Not all ISPs support ISDN connections. (For example, the leading ISP, AT&T World-Net, does not, which I find fairly appalling.) Make sure yours does before going this route. Also, find out if your ISP charges more for ISDN access (most do).

- You'll probably have to call your local phone company to get a quote on an ISDN line. Some telcos let you choose your own terminal adapter; others insist on supplying theirs (at a hefty markup).

- ISDN uses two types of channels: a B channel, which carries data at 64Kbps, and a D channel, for control.

- The *Basic Rate Interface* (*BRI*) flavor of ISDN uses two B channels and one D channel.

- Today's ISDN terminal adapters let you combine the two B channels for 128Kbps of throughput; when a voice call comes in, the terminal adapter throttles back to 64Kbps for the Internet connection and lets you talk on the phone via the other B channel. When you hang up, the terminal adapter automatically reconfigures to use both channels for data.

- ISDN has operating system support from Windows 98 forward (Microsoft published a Windows 95 add-in, which still ships with some ISDN adapters).

- If you want to share an ISDN connection, you'll probably want an ISDN router, which works much like a DSL router (see "Installing a DSL Router" later in this chapter).

- An ISDN line isn't shared with anybody else, so you get constant throughput (unlike cable modems, discussed later in this chapter).

DSL

Newer, faster, and cheaper than ISDN, *digital subscriber line* (DSL) is the weapon of choice among PC users wishing for high-speed Internet access. Not everyone can get DSL, however; you must be within a certain distance from the telephone company's central office (CO) to qualify. If you're further than 18,000 feet, you probably can't get it.

> **TIP** *You can do a bit of preliminary self-qualifying by visiting* www.dslreports.com, *which contains a page where you can enter your postal code and phone number to find out what services are available where you live. Don't take the results as gospel, but I've found them to be reasonably accurate.*

Many folks don't realize that DSL comes in several flavors. The most desirable is ADSL, which gives you the best speed by far (up to 2Mbps downstream and 640Kbps upstream); but if you're too far away to qualify for that variety, you may still be able to get IDSL, which is a lot slower than ADSL (144Kbps downstream) but still about three times faster than today's best analog modems. Other DSL variations exist between these two endpoints. All of them require that you have an Ethernet card in your computer for connecting up to the DSL terminal adapter.

You can expect to pay around $50 per month in the US for residential DSL to a single PC; the setup costs vary all over the map (anywhere from free to US$500 as I write this), so shop around. Usually, if you qualify for DSL, you can get the service from more than one provider.

> **TIP** *DSL service in the United States has become a bit of a gamble because the companies that provide it are going bankrupt left and right, caught in the telecom industry downturn. So, I recommend avoiding prepayments and long-term contract commitments; you won't get your money back if the provider fails.*

Cable Modems

Cable "modems" are devices that connect to the same cable you'd use for cable TV service. This broadband technology is comparable to DSL in both cost and speed, and it's probably your best choice for high-speed Internet access if you don't have access to DSL. (Even if you do have access to DSL, you may find that cable modem access is cheaper on a monthly basis.) As with DSL, you'll need an Ethernet card to connect to a cable modem.

The drawbacks to this communication technology are as follows:

- Unlike DSL, you're using a shared medium for your Internet connection—meaning that as more people in your neighborhood sign up, access times go down. If there was ever a technology tailor-made for the early adopter, cable modem access is it!

- Like DSL, not everybody has access to the service. Major metropolitan areas are more likely to offer cable modem service, but if you're in a location where you can't get DSL, the odds are that you can't get cable modem, either. The cable companies have to upgrade their infrastructure to support two-way communications (cable TV was initially designed as a one-way street).

- You may not be able to use your favorite ISP when connecting via cable modem.

WARNING *One other limitation is of special interest to telecommuters. Many cable modem companies require you to set up your PC as a member of a specific workgroup (you change this network setting from the PC's operating system—for example, the Windows 95/98/ME Network Control Panel). If you're a member of such a workgroup, you can't simultaneously log on to a corporate network domain, meaning that people working at home can't gain access to the company network. Some companies get around this thorny problem by setting up their network servers to "trust" the workgroup, but that can be a pain to set up and it does reduce network security. DSL users don't have this problem.*

Dial-Up Modem Setup

If you decide to add a modem to a machine that doesn't have one already, or if you simply want a newer, faster, and/or more convenient modem, this section looks at the typical steps for installing both an external modem and an internal one.

Installing an External Modem

The procedure for installing an external dial-up modem is really easy, although there's one step that almost nobody performs! (I'll withhold the details until later in the section in order to build suspense.)

EQUIPMENT YOU'LL NEED:

➡ *A modem*

➡ *A straight-through modem cable (normally, but not always, provided with serial modems; some modem models come with an integrated cable)*

➡ *A small slotted screwdriver (to secure cable at the back of the PC)*

➡ *Three telephone signal cables (with an RJ-45 connector at each end, and as short as will work in your installation)*

➡ *Stabilant-22a contact enhancement fluid (optional but highly recommended; buy over the Net or from a Mercedes or Audi dealer)*

INFORMATION YOU'LL NEED:

➡ *The number of the serial port (COM1, COM2, etc.; get from your PC owner's manual, the label on the back panel, or the Windows Device Manager)*

➡ *Connectivity details for your ISP connection (local access number, user ID, password, names of two DNS servers, incoming mail server, outgoing mail server, news server)*

In this example, I look at installing a serial port modem. Installing a USB external modem is even easier, the main difference being the connection at the back of the PC.

1. Locate an unused serial port on the back of your PC (see Figure 4.1). Today, because PS/2 style modems have eclipsed serial port modems, the sole serial port is probably free. Earlier PCs came with two serial ports, increasing your odds even more.

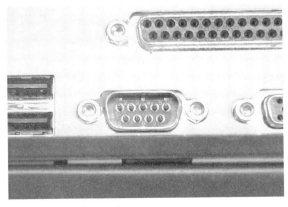

Figure 4.1 *A serial port*

2. Connect the straight-through modem cable (or the integrated cable, if your modem comes with one of those) to the unused serial port (see Figure 4.2). Most serial ports accept a 9-pin connector, and most modem cables have a 9-pin connector; however, if your cable has a 25-pin connector, you'll need a converter (see Figure 4.3). These are cheap, US$5 or so at the local electronics supply house.

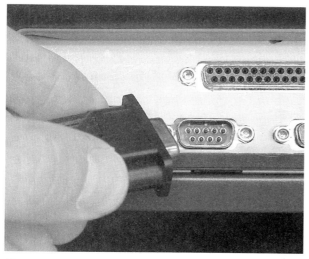

Figure 4.2 *Connecting the modem cable at the PC*

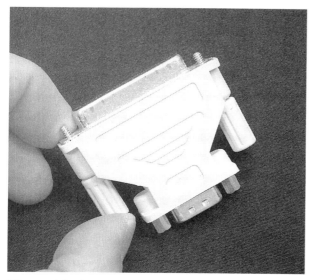

Figure 4.3 *A 9-to-25-pin converter*

3. Connect the other end of the modem cable to the modem. Again, if your modem comes with an integrated cable, the manufacturer has already made this connection for you.

4. Connect one end of the first phone cable to the wall jack. If you want to lubricate it with a drop or two of Stabilant-22a, that's a good idea.

5. Connect the other end of the first phone cable to—here it comes, the step most people don't take—*a surge protector* (see Figure 4.4). (You thought I was going to say "to the modem," didn't you?) Lightning can hit phone wires, so why risk frying your PC when your power strip probably already has connectors for the phone link? If yours doesn't, consider buying one that does (they're around US$20 at the local office supply store) or adding a standalone phone line surge protector (around US$10). Again, use the contact enhancer fluid if you have it.

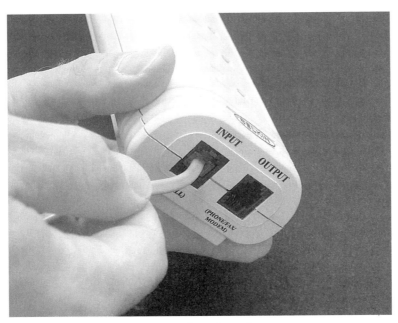

Figure 4.4 *Running the phone line through a surge protector*

6. Connect the second phone cable from the surge protector's second jack to the LINE IN connection at the modem, using the Stabilant-22a if you have it. Some modems, like the one in Figure 4.5, don't distinguish between the LINE IN and PHONE connections, in which case it doesn't matter which one you choose.

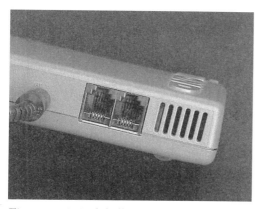

Figure 4.5 *Unlabelled phone jacks at the modem*

7. (Optional) Connect the third phone cable from the modem's remaining jack (if it's labeled, it'll say PHONE or show a picture of one) to your telephone, answering machine, or fax. If you don't have or need such equipment on this line, skip this step. You should also not waste your contact enhancer fluid on this connection.

8. Connect the external modem's power cord. It should run through a short self-test (the LED lights should blink) and then some of the LED lights should remain lit (as shown in Figure 4.6). Check your modem owner's manual to verify that they're the right ones.

Figure 4.6 *A modem that's passed its self-test*

9. Follow the manufacturer's suggested procedure for installing the modem's supporting software. (Here's where you'll probably need the number of that serial port; usually if you have only one serial port, it's COM1, and if you have two, the PC's back panel labels them for you.) If your modem didn't come with an installation CD, you may have to install its driver manually. In most versions of Windows, for example, you'd use the Add/Remove Hardware wizard in the Control Panel.

WARNING *What about Plug-and-Play? Don't rely on it. It works poorly for serial modems; the operating system probably won't even detect the modem after a reboot. (Note that if you install a USB modem, Plug-and-Play should work fine and the PC should autodetect the new hardware.)*

10. Set up your communications software to connect to your ISP or corporate network. Normally, this involves supplying an access number, user ID, password, DNS server address, backup DNS server address, outgoing mail server (name or address), incoming mail server (ditto), and news server, if you want to use Internet newsgroups. Your ISP, or your corporate network administrator, should supply you with all of this good stuff along with details on where in your operating system to add it.

11. Test your modem by connecting to the Internet or to a corporate network. (If the modem's speaker is on, and if you find that shrill screeching as appealing as I do, use your operating system's Modem Control Panel to turn the speaker off.) If you have problems, the chances that they're hardware-related are slim, so you should get on the phone with your ISP or corporate network's help desk and walk through all the settings. It takes only one wrong one to prevent you from connecting successfully.

12. (Here's another step most folks skip.) Once you're online, point your browser to the modem manufacturer's Web site, and see if any *firmware* updates are available for your modem. Firmware is the software-on-a-chip inside your new modem's box, and modem manufacturers update it from time to time, mainly to fix bugs but also to enhance performance. Those manufacturers also provide users with a downloadable utility to update the firmware from your PC.

TIP *If you update your modem's firmware, do it when the modem is not connected to a remote system.*

Installing an Internal Modem

Installing an internal modem (see Figure 4.7) is very similar to installing an external modem, with the following differences:

- You must remove the PC's cover (see Chapter 1, "Read Me First") and insert the modem card into an available PCI slot. (Don't buy an ISA bus modem unless you're all out of PCI slots, because the ISA devices are slower.)

- You don't have to mess with a modem cable; the phone line connections are built into the side of the card.

- You must typically install the serial port driver first, then reboot, then install the modem driver. I know, they're on the same silly circuit board, but the operating system considers the port and the modem to be two different objects that just happen to be cohabitating.

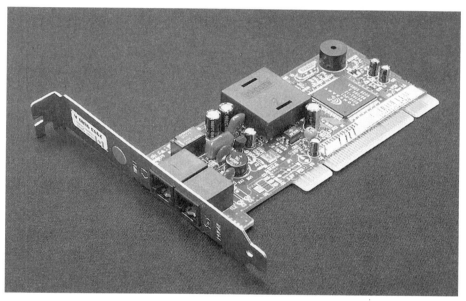

Figure 4.7 *An internal PCI modem*

WARNING *Windows users, don't be surprised if the operating system assigns your new internal modem an odd-sounding number, like COM4 or COM5. Windows is notoriously bad about misnaming serial ports. My general rule: As long as it works, the port number doesn't matter.*

Installing a DSL Router

Many home and SOHO users get a DSL connection to share across two or more PCs, so that's the scenario I describe here. Sharing a broadband link is more complex than running a link to a single, standalone computer. I'll point out the steps you can skip if you're just hooking one PC to a DSL line. However, I can pretty much guarantee that as soon as your Significant Other, Progeny Units, or other PC-equipped live-ins see how quickly your system surfs with DSL, you'll be looking into sharing that link.

You can share an Internet link in three basic ways, as follows:

- You can hook the link (such as a DSL terminal adapter) directly to a single PC, then use software running on the PC to share the connection with other PCs on the same local area network. You may already have such software; for example, Windows 98, ME, 2000, and XP all come with software called *Internet Connection Sharing* (*ICS*) that performs this function moderately well.

- You can hook the link into an Ethernet port on an existing network hub or switch, and set up each PC on the network to point to it when going out to the Internet.

- You can buy an integrated device that includes both the terminal adapter and the network hub. In this case, you connect the broadband line to the integrated device, and you connect the PCs to that same device. Sometimes these devices are called *home gateways* if they're targeted for the residential market.

Which way should you go? That depends on what equipment you already have. If you already have a network with an Ethernet hub or switch, then connecting your high-speed link directly to it may be the best choice. If not, a home gateway device is attractive, and that's the method I describe in the procedure that follows.

A direct PC connection is my least favorite alternative because you have to leave the PC that's attached to the broadband link powered up all the time. However, a direct PC connection is less expensive than a home gateway, and it's the method least likely to annoy the technician who's installing your line. ("Hey, buddy, it doesn't say on the work order you're connecting this line to a network—that's gonna cost you extra!")

Editorial Comment

I don't see why you should pay the telco or your ISP any extra money if you're connecting a broadband line to a network. Do you have to pay more for a car if you plan to have several people in your family share it? Do you pay a higher fee for your phone line if four people might use it instead of just one? Charging more for an Internet connection that links to a network is as outrageous to me as that rule in some cities that if you have multiple people sharing a cab, they each have to pay full fare.

Some ISPs even make you turn off the network connection before they'll install your DSL line! I can understand why they might not want to incur the expense of taking network-related support calls if the customer's fee plan doesn't cover them, but I don't understand refusing to even install the line if the network is live. If your ISP pulls this nonsense, see if you can get a different ISP. If you're too far along in the process, go ahead and disable the PC's network connection (you can re-enable it later), but write a letter to the ISP's CEO ASAP.

We now return to your regularly scheduled book.

EQUIPMENT YOU'LL NEED:

➡ *The DSL router (combination terminal adapter and network hub)*

➡ *A serial console cable (usually comes with the router)*

➡ *A cable with modular connectors on both ends to connect the router to the DSL port (also usually comes with the router; if not, you'll have to buy it separately)*

➡ *A PC to program the router (the PC needs to have a free serial port only if you use the console method)*

➡ *PCs with Ethernet cards to connect to the router's built-in hub*

➡ *Ethernet cables to connect your PCs to the router (as many as you have PCs in your network)*

INFORMATION YOU'LL NEED:

➡ *Router programming instructions (usually in the manual or on an installation CD that comes with the router)*

➡ *Router address settings (you'll typically get these from your ISP and/or your DSL installer)*

Here's the procedure for installing a DSL router, and I'm going to take it from the very top, including the provisioning process (which may vary for other countries).

1. Typically, your first move is to call your existing ISP and ask about getting DSL in your area. One of three things will happen:

  • The ISP will say, sure, we'll handle that directly for you (good news, fewer hassles for you).

  • The ISP will say, sure, call Company X, a DSL provider and "partner" with the ISP.

  • The ISP will say, sorry, we don't do DSL, in which case you're going to be looking at a different ISP. Shop around and start over.

2. If you're lucky and the ISP offers DSL and offers to handle your order for you, you'll provide various details to the ISP (address, phone number at your current location, and so on) and you'll choose a level of service if multiple plans are available. (Always ask about free equipment and installation deals.) The ISP places your order with a DSL company.

3. The DSL company orders a new, DSL-quality phone line from the local telco. (Sometimes an existing line can be used.)

4. You wait six weeks or so.

5. The local telco runs a new DSL line to your building and performs initial testing. If the line checks out OK, the telco calls the DSL company and says "It's in, and it's good."

6. You wait a week or so.

7. The DSL company's technician comes to your location, runs the line to the wall you specify, installs a wall jack, and performs additional line tests. The technician also installs a DSL router if you've chosen to receive one as part of the package (if it's free, do it!). If you're supplying your own router, as in this example, the technician merely performs the tests and gives you a piece of paper with a lot of numbers on it. These are the IP addresses you'll need to know to set up your router.

TIP *If you've specified that you want to pull a voice channel off your DSL line, which you can do (much like with ISDN), then the technician will also install a splitter for connecting to a phone or answering machine. The voice channel doesn't interfere with the data channel. Once you verify that the new voice line is working, you may choose to end service for an existing voice line at your location and save yourself some monthly fees.*

8. Wave goodbye to the technician and pull your shiny new DSL router out of the box (Figure 4.8). This box contains both the DSL terminal adapter and a network hub in one enclosure.

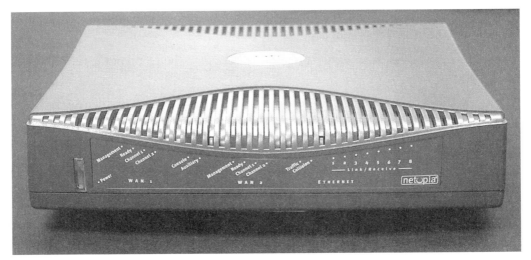

Figure 4.8 *A DSL router*

9. Now you'll have to program the router, which you do from a PC. The first step is to connect a serial cable from a serial port on your PC to the router's Console port (see Figure 4.9).

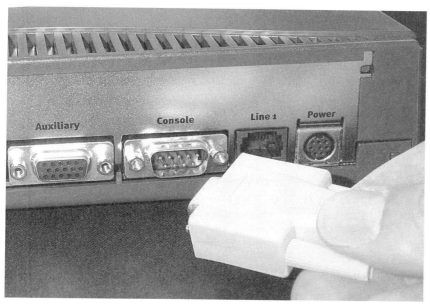

Figure 4.9 *Attaching the console cable*

TIP *You may also be able to program the router simply by connecting your PC's Ethernet card to a port on the router, but this method often requires that you change your PC's network settings, while the console method does not.*

10. Run a simple communications program such as HyperTerminal on your PC and point it to the serial port (usually COM1 or COM2) that you've used for the router connection.

11. Per the router manufacturer's instructions (for example, "point your browser to the router's precoded IP address and enter a password to begin the configuration process"), set the following router characteristics:

- *Wide Area Network* (*WAN*) IP address (this is how the router appears to the outside world)

- *Local Area Network* (*LAN*) IP address (this is how the router appears to the PCs on your network)

- Range of addresses to assign to local PCs (for example, 10.10.10.1 to 10.10.10.255)

- DNS server addresses (usually one primary and one backup; these are the addresses of servers that help your PCs find named computers on the Internet, like www.sybex.com)

The exact items may vary for your network. I'm assuming here that you want the DSL router to automatically assign IP addresses to the PCs in your network, which is usually the easiest way to go. The acronym for this feature is *NAT*, for *network address translation*.

TIP *If this step sounds horribly complicated, it's really not that bad. You'll have a lot of guidance from the router manual or installation CD, and all the numbers will be on the sheet the DSL installer gave you when he blessed your line. But if it all still seems very intimidating, and if you know someone who is familiar with the TCP/IP network protocol, see if you can bribe or blackmail your friend into helping you get set up.*

12. When you're done programming the router, disconnect the console cable from your PC, and from the router's back panel.

13. Connect the router's LINE 1 or LINE port (Figure 4.10) to the DSL port with the communications cable that came with the router (or that you bought separately, if the router didn't come with one).

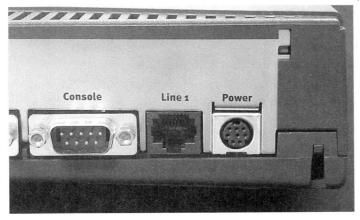

Figure 4.10 *The router's DSL port*

14. Set the router's crossover switch to the NORMAL setting (see Figure 4.11). You'd use the other setting, UPLINK, only if you were connecting your router to another hub. We're going to use the router's built-in hub to connect all the PCs to the DSL line.

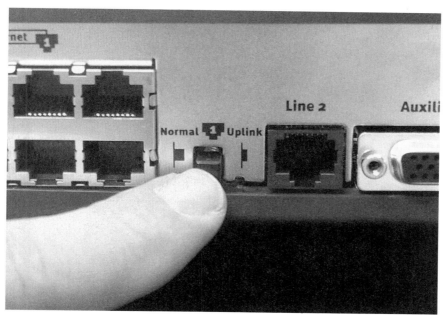

Figure 4.11 *Setting the crossover switch*

15. Run Ethernet cables from the PCs in your network to the Ethernet connections on the back of the router (see Figure 4.12).

16. Connect the router's power supply and verify that the front-panel LEDs look as the router manual says they should.

17. Go around to each PC and change its networking settings per the guidelines provided by your ISP. (If your ISP didn't give you detailed guidelines, call 'em up and demand 'em.) Usually, you'll set the PC's Network Control Panel to automatically get an IP address from the router, and you'll set the PC's default gateway to point to the router's LAN address.

18. Depending on what operating system and version you run on the PCs in your network, you may have to restart the PC so that the new network settings take effect.

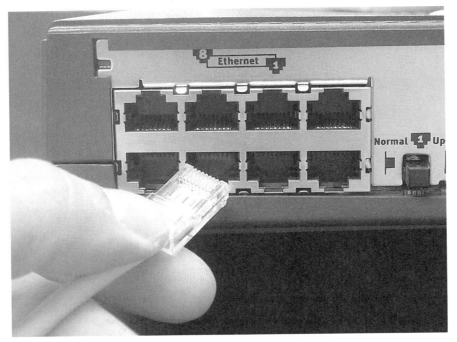

Figure 4.12 *Making Ethernet connections at the router*

19. Test your connection to the Internet.

20. Install firewall software or hardware (see the following warning).

WARNING *If your DSL router doesn't have a built-in firewall, and most low-cost units don't, then you should strongly consider either a separate standalone firewall box (expensive) or firewall software that can run on each PC on your network (much less expensive; look at Zone Labs' ZoneAlarm and Symantec's Norton Personal Firewall). DSL is an "always-on" connection, making your PC(s) much more susceptible to interference from nosy outsiders.*

Considering the Wireless Web

The dream is appealing: instant access to the Internet, cordless, waitless, from anywhere at any time. Alas, the Wireless Web remains frustratingly far from reality. If you want Web access, find a wire someplace. If you can't find one, go wireless in the spirit of the pioneers of the Old West—adventuresome, courageous, and not deterred by periodic setbacks like grizzly bear attacks and dust storms.

I was going to write more about this stuff, but at the present state of the art, it just doesn't work very well and it's really expensive. We can all hope that the various vendors will get their acts together, because the potential is great and the need is clear, but right now I just can't recommend either a satellite or a wireless local loop except in special circumstances.

Satellite

Satellite dishes have always conveyed a certain cachet, the aura of the latest and greatest technology. However, most PC owners I've heard from who've used satellite systems for Internet access tell me that those systems have proved disappointing in practice. Supporting the hypothesis that these systems have a lot of problems, published statistics state that the major retail satellite service vendors lose between a quarter to a half of their user base *every year*, suggesting customer dissatisfaction on a massive scale.

There are several problems with satellites as of the writing of this book:

- Not every home or business is well positioned to point a dish in the right place. You need a fairly clear southern exposure in North America to use most of the commercial systems.

- With current technology, you get good speed in the downstream direction (from the ISP to you) but poor speed in the upstream direction, which requires a dial-up link. If you've become used to DSL and you sit in front of a one-way satellite system for the first time, the *latency* or delay between when you click a link on a Web page and when that linked page starts downloading is maddening. Two-way satellite services purport to alleviate this problem, but they're considerably more expensive as I write this, requiring you to pony up about US$1000 for the hardware.

- Bad weather can disrupt your sessions. This may or may not be a big problem, depending on your area's typical weather patterns and your need for uninterrupted access.

- Satellite access is expensive. Even if you get a deal that includes free hardware (rare), the monthly fee is typically well over twice what you'd pay for DSL or cable modem service. Again, if you're considering satellite, it's probably because you can't get those faster and cheaper technologies, and the satellite companies hire MBA's who know this and price accordingly.

- Satellite, like cable modem, is a shared access service. The more people that sign up, the poorer the performance—at least until your provider launches another satellite.

- The satellite service industry's reputation for customer service is decidedly earthbound, even subterranean.

None of these problems is insurmountable, but taken together, they're fairly discouraging. The brightest rays of light are the newer two-way satellite systems from Hughes and Echostar/Starband that don't require you to use a dial-up analog connection for uploading. If you're thinking about satellite, see if you can negotiate away some of that upfront hardware cost and get a two-way system (maybe offer to provide a quote for the marketing brochures). But if you do, let a professional installer put it in. The two-way systems are fairly complex to install, even for the handy among us, although the one-way systems aren't too difficult.

> **TIP** *If you go satellite, and you hire out the "professional installation," don't let the installer leave the premises until you have demonstrable Internet connectivity. If it doesn't work, you may have to get through various rounds of FPS (finger-pointing syndrome) and it could be weeks before the installer can schedule a return visit.*

Wireless Local Loop

Various companies have popped up to offer a radio-frequency solution to gaining Internet access called *wireless local loop*, or *WLL*. (Another name for this service is *fixed-point wireless*.) The WLL company has a high-speed Internet connection and a network of transmitting cells that beam radio waves to customers, who have special antennas to catch the signal. The antenna connects to a receiver, which in turn connects to an Ethernet adapter in the PC. The customers must connect a regular phone line and modem for upstream communications, just as with one-way satellite service.

The problems here are availability and price. Fewer than a quarter of a million people use WLL in the United States. Even if it's available in your area, whether WLL will actually work for you depends greatly on the presence and position of hills and valleys between you and the transmitting station. For example, Lookout Mountain sits between me and the WLL company in Golden, so I'm out of luck. Even if you can get WLL in your location, it's likely to be fairly expensive, more than any other option except satellite (figure over US$1000 for the installation and over US$125 per month for access). Once availability improves and the price comes down, WLL may be worth considering for the home and SOHO user.

Chapter 5

Printers

f you'd told me 15 years ago, when my embryonic consulting company invested in its first "letter-quality" printer (a thousand-dollar Xerox daisywheel unit that clattered like a machine gun), that in a decade and a half, US$200 would get you a printer that could reproduce a color photograph on glossy paper with stunning fidelity, I would've said *dream on*. Heck, even monochrome inkjet printers didn't exist for PCs at that time (although when the first hit the market, Hewlett-Packard's brilliant ThinkJet, I bought one and threw away my earplugs).

In a similar vein, you can now pick up a "personal laser" printer for less than one-tenth of what that original tank-like HP LaserJet cost, and get far better quality and speed in the bargain (although I doubt any modern laser printer will outlast those indefatigable early models). So upgrading your PC with a faster, better, or more colorful one is an option with many options, even if you're on a budget, as I continually am.

However, the flip side of today's remarkably low costs means that many people approach a printer upgrade with a limited understanding of the tradeoffs and life-cycle costs the different kinds of printer can impose. Don't make a printer upgrade an impulse buy; if you do, you may pick one that's both more expensive and less capable than the advertisements would have you believe.

Intro to Printers

When you think about upgrading a PC system, taking a holistic view can be useful; that is, look at the system as a whole system, rather than just a collection of parts to be improved. Where are the bottlenecks in the activities you perform often? Very often, people have home PCs with fast processors, lots of RAM, speedy disk drives, and a lethargic printer. Hurry up and wait.

Of course, speed isn't everything, and whether you're printing for posterity, for profit, or just for fun, you should also consider beauty. In recent years, printers have gotten prettier even faster than they've gotten faster.

The third big factor to consider is cost, a shifting equation, as we'll see in a minute.

Speed, beauty, and cost: Before we look at each of these variables, we should discuss the four printer categories, and then look at how they stack up in these areas. Those categories are general-purpose inkjet, photo inkjet, laser and laser-like, and niche.

- **Inkjet** printers (see Figure 5.1) work by firing tiny droplets of ink onto the page from a printhead assembly that slides horizontally on a metal bar. They usually have either three colors, now considered old-fashioned, or four colors, which may or may not reside in separate cartridges. (Finding a black-and-white inkjet nowadays isn't easy; they're almost all color units.) Some units will print either color (with a three-color cartridge) or black-and-white (with a black cartridge) but not both at the same time. You have to be a little careful with inkjet printouts because they can smear when the ink's still wet (and even after it dries, depending on ink and paper quality).

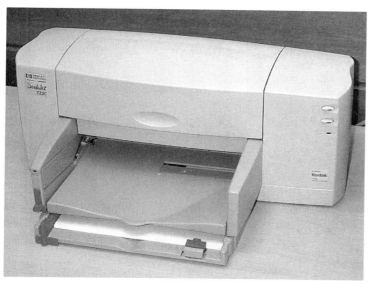

Figure 5.1 *An inkjet printer*

- **Photo inkjet** printers have (usually) six colors of ink for a wider color range, and therefore offer more realistic photographic printing, but they typically don't handle large paper sizes.

- **Laser** (and laser-like units that substitute LEDs [light-emitting diodes] or LCDs [liquid-crystal displays] for the laser as the light source) work by putting a charge on a photo-sensitive drum that picks up charged toner particles and transfers them onto the page via an oppositely-charged corona, after which a high-temperature fuser bonds them to the paper. Laser output doesn't smear and has sharper lines and edges than inkjet printers, but don't look for photo-quality color output here. Figure 5.2 shows a small and inexpensive "personal" laser, and Figure 5.3 shows a bigger "workgroup" laser suitable for sharing on a small network.

Figure 5.2 A "personal" laser printer

Figure 5.3 A "workgroup" laser printer

- **Niche** printers are "none of the above." These include dye sublimation, thermal wax, color laser, dot matrix, and other technologies you're not likely to use for a home or small-office PC unless you find a great deal, because they tend to be expensive. I don't cover these types here because they're fairly rare. Even dot-matrix printers, which stayed alive for years because of their ability to print multi-part forms, are rare today for home or small-office use because most programs can print multi-part forms on inkjet and laser printers.

TIP *Some people like multifunction devices that combine the features of a printer, fax, copier, and scanner (or some subset of those four) in a single device. You can treat the printer part of such devices much like a "regular" laser or inkjet printer, but details of installation and configuration will be different from a single-purpose printer, and different makes and models vary widely in design. While I have a number of friends who use these multifunction devices happily, and they feel they saved money vs. buying separate components, you should consider what will happen if such a device needs service. Can you afford to be without your printer, fax, copier, and scanner all at the same time? If so, a multifunction device could save you some money. Otherwise, you may find that you get better flexibility and performance from "separates," albeit at a somewhat higher cost.*

Now let's return to those big three buying criteria. Speed varies greatly from one category to the next, but basically lasers are fast and inkjets aren't. Another way to say it is that the fastest inkjets are just about on a par with the slowest lasers. There are several reasons for this.

Laser printers typically have their own processor and memory, while inkjets often rely largely or exclusively on the host PC to compose pages. Printers without brains sometimes go by the name *GDI printer*, for *graphical device interface*, the language Windows uses to display and print images; printers with a brain usually communicate with a PC using at least one of two popular languages, PostScript, known for good-looking graphics, and PCL (printer-control language), known for speed.) Moreover, laser printers don't have to worry about color. (Yes, color laser printers are available, but they're a niche category for users who need color but who also need better-looking text and somewhat more speed than inkjets provide. Oh, and for those who have an extra thousand dollars, or two, or three.) Finally, at a basic physical level, laser beams can move faster than printheads.

WARNING *When you compare printer speed ratings, read the fine print. Printers work quickly with text but more slowly with graphics. Also, most inkjets and lasers can print graphics at varying levels of quality and resolution; lower-quality "draft" modes print faster. For multi-page documents, the time to print the first page is usually much slower than to print subsequent pages. Finally, in real life, a printer with more memory can work faster with most documents than one with the minimum amount of RAM. So make sure you're comparing apples to apples when you read that printer A runs at 8 pages per minute and printer B runs at 12; the criteria may be different for those two speeds, and the printers' speeds may be a lot closer than you think.*

Next is cost. Let's take inkjets first. They've become so inexpensive that many retailers basically throw one in when you buy a PC. You can certainly buy expensive inkjets, for example if you need speed, compatibility with the PostScript printing language, or networkability. But most small inkjets for occasional use are so cheap that some of us wonder where the catch is.

Simple: It's the old story of razors and blades. The printers are cheap, but the ink cartridges aren't. In some cases, replacing the ink costs more than the printer costs! (It would be more economical in those cases, if environmentally irresponsible, to just buy a new printer, which comes with ink cartridges; keep the ink, and throw the printer away.) Taking the analysis a little further, inkjets look best on paper that costs significantly more than plain copy paper, and if you want photo quality, you're looking at glossy papers that can run US$2 a sheet! So, the key to analyzing inkjet cost is to look at these consumables and estimate what they'll cost you over the lifetime of the printer. You may well find that buying a more expensive printer that has separate ink cartridge for each of its four colors will save you money in the long run, because you don't have to replace an integrated three-color cartridge just because you printed a lot of blue brochures recently.

If you don't need color, then you may be smart to buy a small laser printer like the nifty Lexmark E210 (US$200!), because lasers have a much lower cost per page than inkjets.

Third is beauty, and although it lives in the beholder's eye, some generalizations about print quality are possible and legitimate. First, when it comes to inkjets, higher resolution (*dots per inch*, or *dpi*) is *usually* better but not always. For example, an inkjet that varies the size of the droplets of ink it sends onto the page will produce better results than one with fixed droplet sizes. A 600dpi printer may look better than a 720dpi or 800dpi printer. Different printer makers have different techniques for getting cleaner edges and better halftones, all of which contribute to the ultimate image quality. Finally, at least on non-glossy papers, inkjet ink tends to spread, bleeding one dot into another; that means lower effective resolution, but skillfully handled, more image realism.

With lasers, resolution is a good guide to print quality. I can't imagine buying a laser with lower than 600dpi resolution, and 1200dpi units are now available in a wide range of prices.

Another aspect of output quality is the printer's ability to render the full spectrum of colors. Inkjets with four cartridges (cyan, magenta, yellow, and black) give ground to photo inkjets with six or more cartridges in this area. With laser printers, the ability to render shades of gray is a function of the printer's maximum resolution (1200dpi is better than 600 here) and software driver (PostScript drivers usually produce nicer output than PCL drivers).

> **TIP** *Many variables affect print quality. If you have time and you want to make the best choice, carry a four- or five-page document file around with you to the computer stores or to friends' houses or offices, and print some samples. Make sure the document is representative of the sort of thing you'll be printing. Then compare the results. (Sort of like taking a sonically demanding CD to the stereo stores as a way of evaluating hi-fi audio gear.) If that sounds like too much work, I sympathize; you can read the better trade rags and take their word on the print quality issue. In particular, PC Magazine does an annual printer roundup that I've found generally fair and accurate.*

Although speed, cost, and beauty are the main factors to consider when upgrading to a newer printer, other factors should figure in to your decision, too. Here are some of the more germane:

• **Paper size capability**: Do you need sizes beyond letter? You may have to pay more for an inkjet that can do legal-size printouts, although many lasers come with both letter and legal trays. If you need tabloid-size printouts (11 × 17), you'll certainly have to pirate the kids' college fund more aggressively.

- **Paper capacity**: Look for two numbers: standard capacity (number of sheets that can fit in the tray), and upgradable capacity (through adding paper trays). If you want a printer that can chug out hundreds of pages at a time without babysitting, this is important; lasers usually offer more capacity than inkjets.

- **Paper weight options**: Most printers can handle 20- to 24-pound weight paper, but can the printer you're considering print card stock? You may want to make your own business cards, for example, or homemade birthday cards.

- **Envelopes:** Some say they can do envelopes, but it's a royal pain and they jam half the time. Don't believe the ads: Try it yourself, or make the salesperson do it (assuming you can find a salesperson at a computer store nowadays).

- **Duplexing**: Want to print on both sides of the page? Can the printer do it? Does the printer make it easy?

- **Duty cycle**: A fancy term for how many pages per month the printer can comfortably handle without excessive wear or failure. Not an issue for casual printing, but if you're printing up long or multicopy documents, it could be something to consider.

- **Frequency of changing consumables**: For inkjets, we're talking ink cartridge capacity; for lasers, toner cartridge capacity. I will go on record as saying that most small inkjets have cartridges that are way too small and require replacement way too often. Your time is valuable.

- **Memory upgradability**: Some printers have no RAM, some have a little, and some have a fair amount. Those that have RAM may run faster with more, especially on multi-page jobs. Some inkjets aren't upgradable because they don't have the circuitry to handle additional RAM. I like to spec enough RAM to hold three pages of printout at full resolution.

Printer Ports

One of the decisions you must make when you upgrade your PC system with a new printer is which port you'll use to connect that printer. Different models of printer offer different ports, and your PC may limit your choices here, too.

Don't take this decision lightly, because choosing a slow port can limit the performance of an otherwise fast new printer. Your choices can include parallel, USB, FireWire, serial, infrared, and network—all of which I will discuss in the following sections.

Parallel

For several years, the parallel port has been the preferred choice of small-printer manufacturers. It's well standardized, the cables come in only two flavors instead of the myriad variations of serial cables, and it shuttles data reasonably quickly. Data travels across a parallel interface via an eight-lane highway, that is, 8 bits at a time. Figure 5.4 shows a typical parallel port connection at the back of a PC, and Figure 5.5 shows a typical parallel cable.

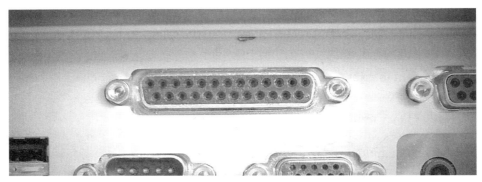

Figure 5.4 *A PC parallel port*

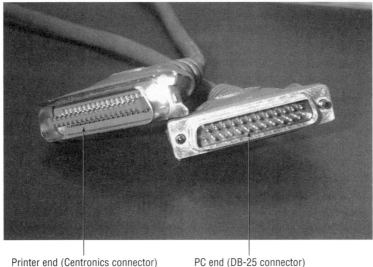

Printer end (Centronics connector)   PC end (DB-25 connector)

Figure 5.5 *A parallel cable*

The printer end of the parallel cable usually has a "Centronics"-style connector, shown in Figure 5.5, with notches for two spring retaining clips to hold the connector in place. The PC end of the cable usually has a "DB-25" connector with 25 pins that fit into the sockets of the PC's parallel port (one row of 13 and one row of 12, the asymmetry giving these connectors a slight "D" shape). The PC end of the cable secures to the PC via two screws.

> **TIP** *Use the shortest parallel cable you can. The best length is 6′; you can go up to 12′ without too many worries, but longer than that and you should get a parallel signal boosting device from your favorite electronics source, such as Data Comm Warehouse.*

So, what are the two cable types? Basically, old-style or *unidirectional* cables work with the first-generation parallel ports; IEEE-1284 or *bi-directional* cables work with second-generation parallel ports that permit not only faster speeds but also more printer-to-PC communication (such as "I'm out of toner"). IEEE-1284 cables cost more, but most modern parallel printers require them to work with full speed and functionality.

You can't tell the cables apart by looking at the connectors, which are identical; you have to look at the printing along the cable jacket for IEEE-1284 or bi-directional. Don't see either, and you've got yourself an old cable that you should probably just retire. The old cables should stay 6′ long or less; the new ones can go up to 12′ or 15′ depending on the signal strength of your PC's port (stick with 12′ to be safe).

> **TIP** *You'll need to set the parallel port type in the BIOS to get the best performance with any given printer. The options are usually compatible, ECP, and EPP. Compatible in this context means the old, slow flavor; ECP (for extended capabilities port) and EPP (for enhanced parallel port) both work with the newer bi-directional standard, although one or the other may work better with any given printer (consult the printer's manual). The procedure for making BIOS settings varies from PC to PC, but basically you type a function key or other key combination at power-on. I've seen lots of fast printers connected to PCs with the slow port setting, needlessly hampering performance.*

The parallel port is slowly yielding to the newer USB port as the PC printer connector of choice. One reason is that most PCs only offer one parallel port, and although you can sometimes make that port do double duty and serve two devices, such arrangements are always a compromise and subject to various annoying limitations (such as not being able to use both devices at once).

Anyway, although most USB printers also offer a parallel port, you can no longer assume its presence. If you want to use the parallel port rather than USB—for example, because your desktop doesn't have a USB port or has one of the flaky, first-generation USB ports—then make sure the printer you want has a parallel connector.

USB (Universal Serial Bus)

The USB is becoming the most popular printer interface for several reasons: it's convenient, reasonably simple, well standardized, fast, shareable, and cheap.

I provide details and photos about USB in Chapter 11. Suffice it to say here that if you're buying a new printer and you have a reasonably modern PC with built-in USB support, the USB interface should work just as well as the parallel interface, and maybe better. USB 2.0, which is just emerging as I write this, is far faster than the parallel port; if your PC and printer support USB 2.0, consider it seriously.

Having said that, you should consider what other USB devices you have or plan to have on the system. If other devices will generate a lot of USB traffic, and your parallel port is free, maybe using that good old parallel port is your fastest solution, because the USB traffic won't compete with printer traffic for the USB bus. Also, it pays to check the magazine reviews. Some printer manufacturers have, umm, *not* done a great job of implementing USB—I have heard horror stories. Even if you're going with USB, consider getting a printer that also offers a parallel connector just in case you're not happy with the USB implementation.

Serial

Few modern printers use a serial interface anymore, and I'm thankful for small mercies. I only mention it because if your PC doesn't have a USB port and if an image scanner, for example, already occupies its sole parallel port, you don't have another easy choice. You should also consider the serial port if, for some reason, you have to locate your printer more than 12 to 15 feet from your PC; good quality serial cables can usually run 100 feet and sometimes longer with no problem.

The downside is speed: the serial interface is slower than parallel or USB, although it's adequate for text-only printing with occasional light graphics. If most of what you print involves graphics (and that includes Web pages), you probably won't be happy with the serial port, and you may want to consider an add-in USB controller such as I discuss in Chapter 11.

> **TIP** *Get the cable from the printer manufacturer. Wiring serial cables used to be something of a black art, because every printer was a bit different. If you buy the cable from the printer maker, you don't have to worry about whether the hardware handshaking wires (the wires that let the printer tell the computer to pause if the printer's memory buffer is full) are connected properly.*

The serial cable just plugs into a free serial (or COM) port on the back of your PC, and into a similar port on the printer. The PC port usually uses a 9-pin connector, but the cable may expect a 25-pin connector; if that's the case, you may be able to use a serial port adapter, such as that shown in Figure 5.6. Be careful, though, for such adapters come in two flavors, "straight-through" and "null modem." Check with the printer manufacturer to see which one you need, and buy accordingly.

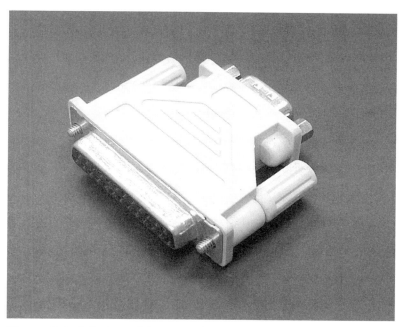

Figure 5.6 *A 9-pin to 25-pin serial port converter*

TIP *Configure the serial port per the printer manufacturer's suggestions. Normally, this means the same speed setting as the printer (use the highest speed it supports), hardware handshaking, 8 data bits, 1 stop bit, and no parity. The meaning of these settings isn't too important here; the main thing is to match your computer's settings (which, in Windows, you normally set via the Device Manager's "Ports" section) with the printer's settings; they have to match, or the two devices can't communicate.*

Infrared

Infrared ports—those little dark-red windows you may have wondered about on your computer's back panel (see Figure 5.7)—appear in just about every laptop you can buy, but in just about none of the desktops. So, if you happen to have a portable computer, and you like the idea of convenient wireless printing, you may want to get a printer with an infrared port. (These also go by the name *IrDA port*, for Infrared Data Association.) The speed of these ports isn't terrible (it ranges between 115Kbps and 4Mbps) as long as you don't do a lot of heavy graphics or really long documents.

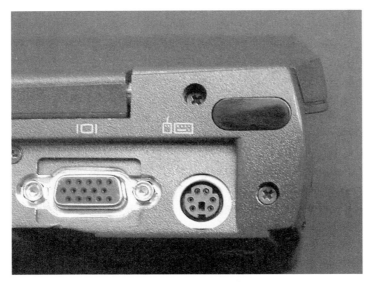

Figure 5.7 *An infrared port on a laptop*

If you already have a printer but it doesn't have an infrared port, you can probably retrofit it with a parallel-to-IrDA device from a vendor such as ACTiSYS. You might go this route, for example, if you want to use the cool feature of some digital cameras to "print" photos directly from the camera to an inkjet printer via the infrared ports. You can also buy infrared port add-on boards for desktop PCs.

So why hasn't infrared taken the world by storm? Several reasons:

- The range is short—typically between 3 and 9 feet, depending on hardware.

- Infrared requires a line-of-sight path, meaning you may have to move devices around to get them to "see" each other.

- Infrared ports are notorious for dropping connections.

An up-and-coming technology named Bluetooth may prove to be a much better vehicle for wireless printing from desktops, laptops, and PDAs (personal digital assistants, like the Palm Pilot). Bluetooth is a radio-frequency standard, so line-of-sight isn't an issue anymore. Also, the distance limitation is about 30 feet, which is a whole lot more practical than 3 feet! Watch the computer magazines for information about Bluetooth as the standard evolves.

Network

If you have a home or small-office network and you want all the PCs on the network to be able to print to a single printer, you have four options for connecting the printer, as follows:

- **Direct network connection**. This means your printer has a network port on its back panel, and you connect the printer directly to a hub or switch via a network cable. Figure 5.8 shows a printer with a built-in RJ-45 Ethernet network port.

- **Standalone print server connection**. You connect your printer's parallel cable to a box called a *print server* (see Figure 5.9), which in turn connects to your network.

Figure 5.8 *A printer's direct network port*

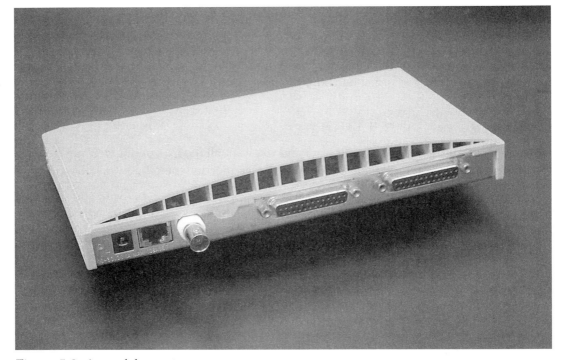

Figure 5.9 *A standalone print server*

- **PC server connection**. If you have a "dedicated" PC acting as a server, you can connect the printer via parallel, serial, or USB link to that server PC and share the printer via the server's built-in resource-sharing utilities.

- **Workstation connection**. You can connect a PC to a workstation in a peer-to-peer network such as Windows Me or 98 or 2000 or XP, using a parallel, serial, USB, or even infrared connection, then share the printer with other workgroup members.

Which is best? I'm always partial to the direct network connection; it costs somewhat more, but you don't have any speed bottlenecks, and you don't have to have any PCs turned on (other than the one you're printing from) in order to print. If the printer you're considering doesn't have a network port, find out if you can add one in, but check the cost: my experience has been that add-in ports are ridiculously overpriced.

Small networks don't generally need a standalone print server, and they have to throttle down network traffic to parallel or USB speeds, but these little boxes work fine for printing mainly text documents, and they give you flexibility in physical placement of printers.

If you have a dedicated PC server, most network operating systems make it easy to share a printer that connects directly to the server via parallel, USB, or serial port, although again you could be giving up some speed depending on the port you choose, and the distance limits of the selected port could constrain where you put the printer.

Finally, if one person's going to be using the printer a lot more than anyone else, consider the workstation connection method.

> **TIP** *Match the network connection to your network. If you use Fast Ethernet at 100Mbps (and there's not much reason anymore to use regular 10Mbps Ethernet), make sure the printer can run at that higher speed. Most printers with Fast Ethernet connections can automatically throttle down to regular Ethernet if they detect that speed on the hub or switch to which they connect; that's a good feature to check for and it doesn't add to the cost.*

Setting up an Inkjet Printer

Installing inkjet printers is easy. You don't have to open your PC's cover, and you don't need many tools. However, people often skip one or two steps and don't get the quality they've paid for.

Printer Hardware

Here's how to set up a new inkjet printer.

EQUIPMENT YOU'LL NEED:

➡ *A screwdriver (if you're connecting a parallel or serial cable)*

INFORMATION YOU'LL NEED:

➡ *Your printer's installation manual*

The procedure is typical, but as always, you should refer to your printer's manual (if available) for exact details. The variety of methods for installing inkjet printers is even wider than for most other types of add-on devices.

1. Remove the bits of tape that printer manufacturers use to make sure the unit doesn't come apart in shipment.

2. Open the unit and remove the plastic tabs holding the printhead assembly in place. You can throw these away.

3. Ink cartridges come separately, so you have to install them yourself. (Note that many cartridges ship with a little piece of plastic over the printhead, and you have to remove this protective film before installing the cartridge.)

4. The procedure is usually straightforward: open a lid at the top of the printer to gain access. Open the cartridge latch, insert the cartridge, and close the latch (see Figure 5.10). It usually snaps into place. You're likely to find instructions specific to your printer inside the cardboard box that contained the cartridge.

5. Set the paper tray for the right size paper (see Figure 5.11). Usually you move one or two sliding tabs in the paper tray to a marked position.

6. Pop some paper in. (If you're going to use fancy glossy paper, take note of whether it should go in shiny-side-up or shiny-side-down; look for an embossed icon in the plastic paper tray that may give you a clue, or check the manual or the packaging the paper came in.) I always fan the edges first, to help prevent jams.

Cartridge latch   Access lid

Cartridge

Figure 5.10 *Installing an ink cartridge*

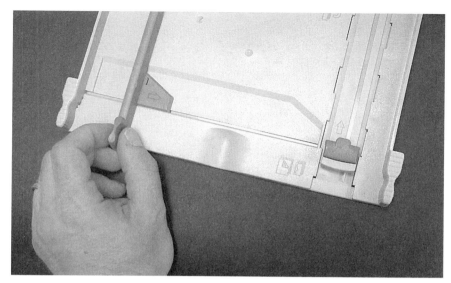

Figure 5.11 *Setting paper size*

7. Plug in the unit's AC power cord.

TIP *You don't normally want to plug a printer into a battery backup unit; plug it into a surge protector if you like, or directly into the wall socket.*

8. Make sure your PC is off.

9. Connect the signal cable (USB, parallel, serial, or network) to the printer (see Figure 5.12), then to the PC. If you use a parallel connection, secure the cable to the printer with the two retaining clips, and secure it to the PC with the screws or knurled knobs provided.

10. Turn on the printer and see if it passes its self-test. Usually it will have an indicator light somewhere that will eventually glow green if everything's OK internally. Some printer models have an LCD panel that will display a message like "Ready" or "OK."

11. Assuming the unit passes its self-test, turn on the PC. If you're running Windows 95 or newer, the operating system will probably detect the device automatically and install the drivers for it. The PC may ask you for your Windows CD-ROM. Alternatively, it may ask for a CD-ROM provided by the printer manufacturer, in which case you should use that. Either way, follow the directions on screen.

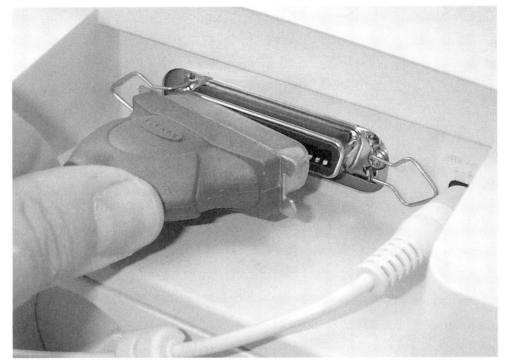

Figure 5.12 *Connecting a parallel cable to a printer*

12. Print a test page and file it away. Normally you'll do this from the PC, via the printer's Properties window; the General tab normally has a Print Test Page button.

13. Configure the printer and align the printheads, as discussed in the next two sections.

Printer Configuration

The software that comes with your printer (or that you install from your operating system's CD-ROM) may let you set various printer-configuration options. For example, with inkjets, the choice of paper can have a dramatic impact on output quality.

Many inkjets let you choose from three paper types: regular copy paper, high-quality inkjet paper (with short fibers for less ink spreading), and glossy photo-quality paper. Whatever you choose, make sure the software setting (see Figure 5.13) matches the type of paper in the printer's tray.

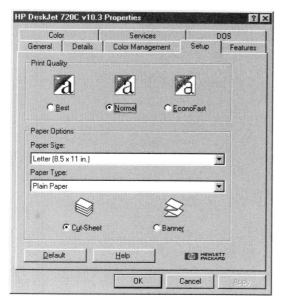

Figure 5.13 *Configuring your inkjet for paper type*

TIP *The cost difference between plain copy paper and high-quality, short-fiber inkjet paper usually isn't very much, but the difference in output quality is noticeable. On the other hand, glossy photo paper is a lot more expensive than short-fiber inkjet paper, and you'll probably only want to use the glossy stuff for special occasions.*

Head Alignment

The final step in setting up your inkjet is to perform a head alignment. This procedure makes sure that the multiple printheads line up exactly right. The way it normally works is as follows:

1. Open the printer's property sheet or run the printer's configuration utility.

2. Choose Align Printheads or a similar command (see Figure 5.14).

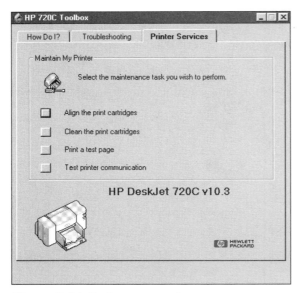

Figure 5.14 *Performing an alignment test*

3. The printer will print a page, which you must then inspect. It will display several numbered or lettered lines; choose the straightest ones.

4. The PC will ask you to enter the letters or numbers corresponding to the best-aligned images.

5. The printer will print another page and you go through the drill again. You may even have to do it a third time, although two usually does it.

6. When you're happy, the printer prints an alignment test page which should look crisp and without any "jaggies."

Installing a Laser Printer

Installing a laser printer has become a fairly easy job; the most complex part of it is installing the toner cartridge. The following sections walk through a typical laser printer setup, provide a few configuration tips, and take a closer look at toner cartridge ins and outs.

Printer Hardware

The procedure for installing a laser printer includes many similar steps to installing an inkjet printer.

EQUIPMENT YOU'LL NEED:

➡ *A screwdriver (if you're connecting a parallel or serial cable)*

INFORMATION YOU'LL NEED:

➡ *Your printer's installation manual*

I'll abbreviate the steps that are redundant and elaborate on the steps that aren't.

1. Remove any pieces of tape on the outside of the printer.

2. Open the unit and remove any plastic tabs the manufacturer installed to prevent components from rattling around during shipment.

3. Install the toner cartridge (see Figure 5.15). Some toner cartridges come with a piece of plastic tape that you must pull out to permit the flow of toner inside the cartridge; other types don't need this step. Usually, you slide pins on the cartridge into corresponding slots inside the printer. Take your time, line everything up, and don't force anything; the toner cartridge should be an easy fit.

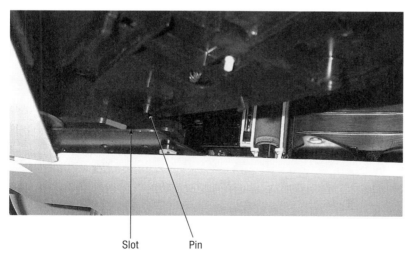

Slot   Pin

Figure 5.15 *Installing a toner cartridge*

4. Install the fuser cleaner pad, if your printer uses one. This is a plastic bar about 9 inches long with a cotton cleaning pad on one side and gripper handles on the other (see Figure 5.16). It normally fits into a slot above the fuser roller.

Figure 5.16 *Installing a fuser cleaning pad*

5. Place the printer in a location where it is at least two inches away from all walls or other possible ventilation impediments. Lasers generate more heat than inkjets, and they need more air. Also, make sure you have enough room for any "straight-through" manual feed operations that you may perform, for example, with card stock or envelopes.

6. Set the paper tray for the right size paper. Usually you move one or two sliding tabs in the paper tray to a marked position.

7. Load some paper in the tray (fan the edges first to help prevent jams). The better quality laser papers will indicate on the packaging which side should be printed first. Find out which side your printer prints on (you may have to perform an experiment by marking a page with an "X" on the top) and make sure you load the paper appropriately.

8. Plug the unit's AC power cord into a wall outlet. Lasers can draw a fair amount of power, so if you can avoid using the same circuit that large household appliances use, so much the better.

TIP *By the way, don't plug your laser printer into a power backup device. Laser printers draw a lot of current and will drain the battery very quickly.*

9. Make sure your PC is off.

10. Connect the signal cable (USB, parallel, serial, or network) to the printer and then to the PC.

11. Turn on the printer and see if it passes its self-test. Lasers usually have an LCD panel that provides power-up status information (see Figure 5.17).

TIP *Some laser printers take a really long time to power up. Give your new unit five minutes before giving up on it and assuming it has a problem.*

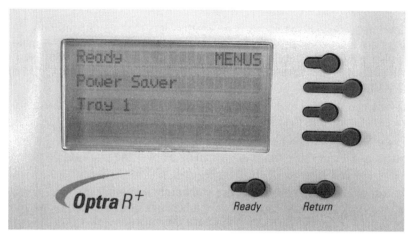

Figure 5.17 *A happy laser's LCD panel*

12. If the unit passes its self-test, turn on the PC, which should automatically detect the printer if you run Windows 95 or higher. Follow the on-screen directions to install the drivers for the printer.

13. Print a test page (in Windows, from the printer's property sheet, which you normally access by choosing command Start➤ Settings➤ Printers, right-clicking the printer of interest, and choosing Properties). and store it in your PC hardware file; it should contain useful details on your printer's make, model, installed options, page count, and so on. If your printer has a separate "configuration" printout page, run that as well, and file it, too.

14. Configure the printer in software, as the following section discusses.

Toner Cartridge Secrets

The great thing about laser printers is that just about every part you might need to replace gets replaced when you install a new toner cartridge! The subject of a certain amount of popular mythology (the issue of "new vs. recycled" cartridges has assumed religious fervor in some circles), toner cartridges are so important to the quality of your printed documents that the issue deserves some quick tips.

- Don't replace the cartridge the minute you see a "Toner Low" message on your printer's LCD panel. That's a very good time to make sure you have a spare cartridge on hand, sure, but you can usually get one or two hundred more pages out of that cartridge by removing it and gently shaking it back and forth and side to side. (Don't go overboard and turn the thing upside down though!) Doing so redistributes the toner and buys you some time.

- Whether you get "new" or "recycled" toner cartridges matters less than you might think, because manufacturers are allowed to sell new cartridges that use recycled parts! The main thing is to find a supplier you trust in case you get a bum cartridge and need to return it. I don't waste time with cartridges that squeak or squeal or produce crummy output, I just return them for a replacement.

- If you have a choice between long-life and regular cartridges, the long-life ones are usually a better deal. You save some time, and the per-page cost is typically less.

- Don't ever move a laser printer with the toner cartridge in it, unless you're just going a few feet. Even a small bump or tilt can cause toner to go spilling all over the place inside the printer, leaving you with a nasty and unhealthy mess to clean up.

- Toner cartridges, like just about all PC equipment, are stubbornly non-biodegradable. If you get a return box for shipping back your used cartridge, take advantage of it. You don't have to pay for the shipping, and returning the old cartridge helps save the environment.

Configuring a Printer

After your laser printer is physically working, you should follow the manufacturer's instructions for configuring it. In Windows, all the settings will live on the printer's property sheet. Laser printer configuration settings can be many and varied, but here are a few tips that may be useful:

- You may be able to choose PostScript or PCL for your printer language. If you print a lot of graphics, you may prefer PostScript, but PCL is usually quicker.

- Make sure the amount of memory indicated on the printer's property sheet matches the amount actually present in the printer. You can usually print a configuration page from the laser printer's LCD panel to verify how much RAM it has.

- Your printer may have an option for downloading fonts or using built-in fonts. The built-in fonts are faster, and most lasers have font sets that match your PC's fonts exactly; however, if you notice problems, choose the download option.

- You may want to set your everyday resolution to a low value, such as 300 or 600dpi, even if your printer can handle more. The reason is speed. Set maximum resolution for final output or documents others will see. (My main laser printer runs at about half speed at 1200dpi compared to 600dpi.)

- Paper type isn't as big a deal with lasers as it is with inkjets, so don't be surprised if you don't see any choice for it.

Maintaining Your Printer

Today's PC printers require very little maintenance, which however is not the same as "no maintenance." The following sections on cleaning, lubrication, and paper will extend your printer's life and reduce the likelihood of problems. The final section on ozone filters applies only to owners of older laser printers and may help extend *your* life as well as your printer's!

Cleaning

The other day I ran across a college Web site on which network administrators had posted some computer equipment maintenance guidelines. The printer maintenance page asserted that staff should clean the laser printers every week. That may be good advice for a school printer that processes thousands of pages a day, but home and SOHO users, relax: Once every three or four months is probably just fine.

EQUIPMENT YOU'LL NEED:
- ➡ *Antistatic wipes*
- ➡ *Isopropyl alcohol*
- ➡ *Cotton swabs*
- ➡ *A lint-free cotton cloth*
- ➡ *A replacement fuser pad (if your printer uses these)*

Here's the typical procedure for cleaning a laser printer:

1. Turn off the printer.

2. Disconnect the power cord.

3. Open the printer. Methods vary, but usually there's some sort of latch toward the top that you can trip to unhinge the upper part of the printer's plastic shell. Some printers have side panels you can open to get at the internals.

4. Clean paper pathways with an antistatic wipe (see Figure 5.18). If you live in a humid climate where static electricity isn't a problem, you can use a regular cleaning cloth, as long as it's lint free.

WARNING *If you see a lot of toner inside the printer, don't inhale deeply and then blow it out. These very fine toner particles are hazardous to your health. Either wipe up the toner with slightly moistened wipes, or vacuum it up with a computer vacuum device equipped with a special toner-catching filter. (I'm not kidding about the filter; regular hand-held vacuum cleaners don't trap the toner well and are liable to blow it right through the bag pores and into the air!) You can also use the computer vacuum cleaner to suck up paper dust.*

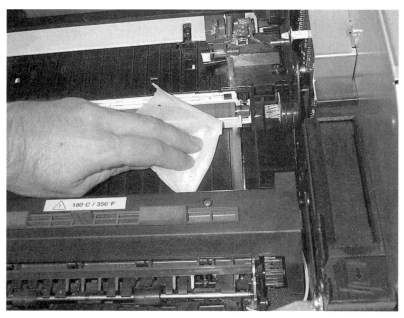

Figure 5.18 *Wiping clean a laser printer's interior*

5. Clean paper feed rollers. You can clean plastic feed rollers with rubbing alcohol and cotton swabs, or (if access permits) an alcohol-moistened cotton cloth. The rubber rollers take a bit stronger medicine; if you can find a solvent called Goof-Off at your local grocery store, you can use it to clean rubber rollers, as long as you're careful not to spill the stuff (it's strong, and it'll bleach any plastic it touches). My preferred technique is to put a couple of drops of Goof-Off on the end of a cotton swab and then scrub away.

6. Replace the fuser cleaning pad. The fuser's the hot part that melts the toner into the page, and it accumulates toner over time. Many laser printers have a cotton cleaning element that sits atop the fuser roller. You get a new fuser pad with a new toner cartridge, but I recommend buying fuser pads separately and replacing them about twice as often as you replace toner. They get too caked up otherwise.

TIP *As a stopgap measure if you don't have a spare fuser pad and your present one is caked up pretty thick, you can break out the old Swiss army knife and scrape the cotton cleaning pad over a trash can, much as you'd scrape the charcoal off a burnt piece of toast.*

Cleaning an inkjet printer is a simpler matter; usually all you need to do is wipe down the slider rail on which the printhead moves, using a lint-free cotton cloth. Make sure the printhead assembly can move freely left and right; if not, lubricate it as described in the following section. There's no need to clean the printheads or ink cartridges; they don't usually last long enough to get dirty enough to clean! But let your manufacturer's manual be your guide.

Lubrication

You normally don't have to worry about lubricating laser printers. If you hear squealing and screeching and groaning, ten to one it's your toner cartridge, and the noise will go away when you replace it. However, if you have an old printer or one that sees a lot of use, you can *sparingly* apply a few drops of light machine oil to the gears and cogs that drive the various drums and rollers (see Figure 5.19). I like to clean the gears first with a cotton swab; otherwise, adding oil can create a sticky goo.

Inkjet printers are a different breed, and they do sometimes require a bit of lubricating. The printhead slides back and forth across a metal rod that must be clean and lightly oiled, or else the printhead will stick slightly as it moves across the page, resulting in poor quality printouts. I suggest you clean the slider rail first as thoroughly as you can, then apply a thin film of light machine oil with a cloth, as shown in Figure 5.20. Don't use a paper towel: they can leave paper fibers behind.

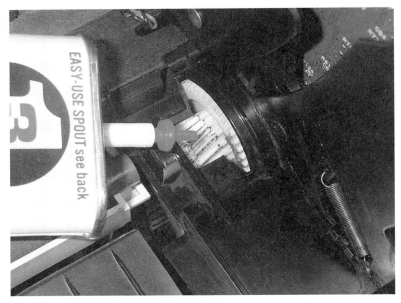

Figure 5.19 Applying machine oil to a laser printer drive train

Figure 5.20 Lubricating an inkjet slider rail

Make sure you get all surfaces of the slider; you'll have to move the printhead back and forth to do so. You'll also discover that as you move the printhead assembly, it scrapes tiny accumulations of oily dust over to the side. Wipe these off, then lube the slider bar again and slide the printhead back and forth; repeat until you don't notice any such scrapings anymore.

You may need to lubricate the printheads if you haven't used your inkjet in a long time. The printer driver probably has a button for cleaning the heads; if not, it'll have one for aligning the cartridges. Either one can help dislodge dried ink.

Paper

Paper maintenance? Well, yes. Let me explain.

Paper jams can be messy, time-consuming to fix, and even damaging to your printer (when you smack it for jamming the fourth page that day). You can dramatically reduce the frequency of paper jams by doing three things:

- Keep paper in its package until you plan to use it. This helps keep the proper level of water content in the paper. Even when I open a ream package, I just tear off the end, pull out what I need, and leave the remaining paper inside the wrapping. I live in a dry climate, and if I leave paper out for a few weeks before I use it, it gets very dry and doesn't feed as well.

- Fan the paper before placing it into the printer tray. This almost eliminates stuck-together pages, a major cause of jams.

- If you print labels, hand-feed them if your printer offers a "straight-through" paper path feed option. Labels can peel off when curled through a printer's normal feed path, especially if the printer is hot.

Another miscellaneous paper tip: Use name-brand papers with low "paper dust" content. You'll be able to tell, by looking inside the printer, which papers are dusty and which are cleaner.

Ozone Filters

You may have an older-model laser printer, which by the way are terrific deals these days. They last just about forever, they cost next to nothing (check eBay for units in your area so you can save on shipping), and most models are plenty fast if you print primarily text documents.

Anyway, if you do pick up a vintage laser, you should check to see if the unit comes with an *ozone filter*. The higher-intensity lasers in older printers create ozone, which is bad for plastic, rubber, and human beings. Ozone filters convert ozone (which is three atoms of oxygen in one molecule, or O_3) to regular oxygen (O_2) and carbon dioxide (CO_2), both of which present no problems for mechanical and human parts.

Trouble is, nobody knows about ozone filters, so nobody knows that they need replacing every year or so. Check your manual, or check the printer manufacturer's Web site, and find out if your printer has an ozone filter. If it does, replace it right away, because the odds are high it's never been done before.

Chapter **6**

Displays

One of these days I'm going to sharpen my pencil and figure out how many different PC's I've seen over the last couple of decades or so. I am sure the figure is definitely in the thousands. And if I were a betting man, which I am, I'd bet you a box of *Krispy Kreme* doughnuts that if you were to run right out and upgrade your display, you'd enjoy the improvement more than just about any other upgrade you could perform. To paraphrase the great English poet John Keats (he's dead, so he won't mind), a display of beauty is a joy forever.

This chapter spells out how you can upgrade to modern monitor technology, and even deploy multiple monitors and monitor calibration to enhance your computing experience. Your eyes will thank you. (Send the doughnuts to me, care of Sybex, Inc., Alameda, California, USA. And please pack the box so I can tell if the publishing staff breaks into it before forwarding it to me.)

Intro to Displays

First, a couple of notes on terminology. A *video adapter* (also known as *video circuit*, *display adapter*, *display controller*, and in the case of a card that fits into an expansion slot, *video card* or *video board*) is the electronic device that sits inside your PC and processes the bits and bytes that define what you see on the screen. The video adapter doesn't have to be an add-in board; it may be integrated with the PC's *motherboard*, or main circuit board, in which case it is said to be *on-board video*. Some video adapters don't do much more than pass along whatever pixels are handed to them, but most modern video adapters perform various acceleration operations (hence another term you may see: *accelerator board*) and offload from the CPU some of the responsibility for drawing pictures. Nearly all video adapters translate the digital pictures they get from the PC into analog signals that typical picture-tube monitors can understand.

Display terminology is a little simpler. First, "display" = "monitor" = "screen." Two main types of displays exist: *CRT* (*cathode ray tube*, or picture tube) and *LCD* (*liquid crystal display*). The big, traditional CRT monitors work by shooting electrons from three electron guns (one each for red, green, and blue) at the inside surface of the glass picture tube, where those electrons excite phosphorescent particles into glowing and appearing as a dot on the display surface. Before the particles cool off, the guns hit 'em again with another barrage of electrons, so the electron guns are constantly redrawing the display many times per second. Incoming analog (wave-type) signals tells the electron guns how hard to shoot.

(By the way, and let me say right up front: It's not smart to open up CRT monitors. When the manufacturers say "no user-serviceable parts inside," that's actually true with monitors, and the innards contain electrical components that can shock you even with the power off.)

LCD panels are cousins of the thin-screen displays you've seen on notebook computers for years now; they're digital and they use tiny light-emitting transistors to create each dot.

The display *system*, which consists of the video adapter and the display, is the afterthought of the modern PC. How many PC ads have you seen with the mice-print disclaimer, "Monitor sold separately."? And how many PCs have you considered buying based on the sans-monitor price, only to put yourself in the position of scrimping on the display in order to fit the computer into your budget? In a similar vein, most home and corporate PC buyers are much more concerned about CPU and memory specs than about the performance and capabilities of the PC's graphics circuitry—making such circuitry a prime candidate for cutting corners in those heavily discounted "home PC" models that otherwise seem so compellingly attractive.

At least up to a point, I'd rather work on an old, slow PC with a big, gorgeous display and fast video card than on a fast, new PC with a small, ugly screen and a bargain-basement video card. Once you get used to a quality display system, you won't ever want to go back. But many of you have become accustomed to your existing display even if it isn't great-looking, so you may not be aware of how really good it can look.

You can boil down the key elements of display system hardware into the major categories of *viewable area, desk area, image quality, adjustability, speed, options,* and *warranty.* The following sections provide some details.

Viewable Area

Size isn't everything, but it does matter for two main reasons.

First is your health—specifically that of your eyes. The smaller the screen's viewable area, the greater the likelihood you'll have tired eyes at the end of the day and need stronger glasses at the end of the decade.

> **TIP** *Note that I said "viewable area." Monitor manufacturers have gotten away for years with defining a monitor's size as the diagonal corner-to-corner measurement before the plastic bezel is placed on the screen! The vendors have now been shamed into printing the viewable size on packaging and spec sheets. If you see the term "nominal size," it means the misleading value.*

Second is usability. Today's PCs and PC operating systems let you have multiple programs running at the same time, which puts pressure on screen real estate. A bigger monitor means you can more easily keep that browser window open along with your e-mail program and appointment calendar.

> **TIP** *Viewable area is a characteristic of both your video adapter and your monitor. You may have a large monitor, but if your video adapter doesn't support higher resolutions, you won't be able to take full advantage of that size.*

Assuming you don't want to consider a flat-screen LCD display (see "Installing a Flat-Panel Monitor" later in this chapter for the pros and cons), consider a 17-inch CRT monitor for everyday use; they've come way down in price in recent years and you can now pick up a very nice unit for well under US$500. If you can get a good deal on a 19-, 20-, or 21-inch CRT monitor, and you spend a lot of time with your computer, that's a good choice too; but make sure you evaluate the cost of putting two 17-inch monitors side by side before you go with a larger screen. Beyond 17-inch, the manufacturing costs go up considerably, and you may be able to get two 17-inch monitors (and about 50 square inches more viewable area) for less than one 21-inch monitor. Another criterion as you consider screen sizes is desk area, as the next section explores.

Desk Area

If size is good when it comes to viewable area, it's bad when it comes to desk area—hence the growing popularity of LCD panel displays at the expense of their bulkier CRT predecessors. I replaced one of my CRTs with an LCD panel during the course of writing this book, and I marveled at the extra work area the switch provided (see Figures 6.1 and 6.2).

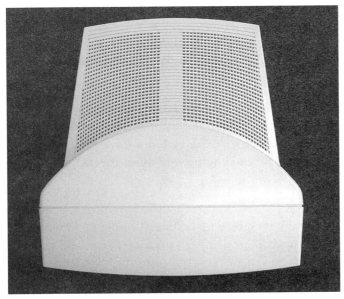

Figure 6.1 *A 15-inch CRT, top view*

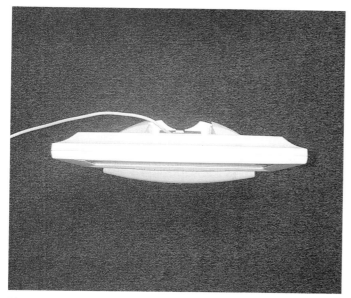

Figure 6.2 *A 15-inch LCD, top view*

You may also want to give some thought to the one-big-CRT vs. two-smaller-CRTs dilemma when considering how much room you want to devote to PC display hardware.

I'm glad to report that many manufacturers are now making "slimmer" versions of their CRT displays. While not anywhere near as thin as LCD panels, these slim CRTs can be half the depth of a typical CRT and yet still cost less than LCD panels. If you have space to spare, you'll get the best bang for your buck with a traditional, bulky CRT.

Image Quality

Some aspects of image quality depend on a combination of video circuitry specs and display specs; other aspects are unique to the monitor.

The two main quality issues that depend on both adapter and monitor are resolution and refresh rate. The maximum *resolution* (that is, how many pixels, or tiny dots of light, the display can handle in the horizontal and vertical dimensions) depends on what the display can handle and what the video card can provide. The *refresh rate*, which affects how flickery the monitor appears (jittery displays contribute to headaches and eyestrain), also requires cooperation between the adapter and monitor.

Both these subjects receive more attention later in this chapter.

As far as monitor-specific quality goes, there are a few things to keep in mind:

- *Glare* is a big issue; non-glare screens are much easier on the eyes (position your monitor accordingly, by the way).

- *Dot pitch* is another monitor spec to watch for: It's a value in millimeters that indicates the distance between adjoining pixels (smaller numbers are better, and anything over 0.32 may not look great).

- Make sure any new monitor you're considering has sharp *focus* at all points on the screen, including the corners.

TIP *CRT monitors use two different designs to help focus the electron beam: shadow mask and aperture grille. Many so-called flat-screen displays use the aperture grille technique, but it results in two very fine, faint horizontal lines appearing on the screen (you can see them most easily against a white background).*

Adjustability

One of the monitors in my office is a lovely, three-year-old, 17-inch monitor with rich colors and excellent detail. However, I have that monitor connected to a little-used server computer, because the image tilts down to the right and the monitor doesn't offer a control to fix that (most newer monitors do). Make sure any monitor upgrade you're considering offers a full suite of adjustments, as well as the *de rigueur* tilt-and-swivel base.

TIP *It's harder on your neck to look up than it is to look down, so your eyes should be about level with the top third of your monitor. A simple height adjustment at your workspace can make a big ergonomic "upgrade," and it's free! Also be aware that experts recommend your eyes be no closer than 18 inches to your screen.*

In bygone days, computer authors had to mention *multisynching* as a key aspect of monitor adjustability. Multisynching is the ability of a monitor to adjust automatically to different resolutions and refresh rates. I don't think I've seen a single-frequency monitor in five years, though, so you're not likely to, either—unless you're looking at a monitor originally designed for an *engineering workstation* (such as machines built by Sun or Apollo or HP).

WARNING *Workstation monitors are often single-frequency units, and they don't use the standard VGA connectors, either. So if you're shopping and you suspect the seller's monitor isn't built for PCs, ask. If it isn't, skip it. Trying to get a workstation monitor to work with PC video adapters is sometimes possible, but it's never worth the hassle.*

Speed

With CRT monitors, speed is primarily a function of the display adapter. Modern operating systems use the display system a great deal, so a quick display adapter can make a PC with a slow CPU feel a lot faster. I've successfully upgraded many slow PCs with fast video cards to squeeze an extra year or two of life out of them. If you play computer games, of course, you want all the speed you can get.

The big problem with speed is that the computer industry hasn't figured out how to measure it in a way that you can easily compare products relative to each other. Video benchmark programs do exist, but they all test different aspects of a video adapter's performance: 2-D vs. 3-D, bitmap rendering vs. line drawing, and so on.

Things have gotten so complex that I just check the Internet for reviews and trust the magazines to tell me which boards are faster than others. Even then, you have to read carefully to make sure the kind of things the magazines are testing relate to the kind of work (or play) you do with your PC. For example, if you're a business user, 2-D performance is likely to be more important than 3-D performance.

With LCD monitors, you have the opposite situation from CRT monitors: Speed is more likely to be a monitor issue than a video card issue—especially with digital video content. Be sure to test an LCD monitor with a video clip before you buy it. Also, do a lot of opening and closing of windows, scrolling in large documents, and so on, to make sure the LCD's slower response won't irritate you.

Options

When choosing a video adapter, you may want to think about multimedia options, as you can often save money by buying some of those options as part of a high-end video adapter instead of as separate add-in cards. Four popular options follow:

- **TV tuner**. This gives your PC the capability to display TV shows in a window on your monitor. Video adapters with a TV tuner can typically connect via cable or antenna.

- **NTSC input**. Some video adapters don't have a TV tuner but they can accept a signal from a TV, or from a VCR, both of which use the NTSC signaling format.

- **NTSC output**. This lets you hook your PC up to a TV instead of (or in addition to) a computer monitor. Businesses sometimes use this capability for meetings or training sessions; big-screen TVs cost a lot less than big-screen computer monitors. You can also send your PC's display signal to a VCR, for example, to make an instructional video. Formerly, to accomplish this, you had to buy a gizmo called a *scan converter* for several hundred dollars. (I know, I bought one, I think it was around the same time I bought a first-generation flatbed image scanner for US$1700. Being an early adopter is an expensive habit....)

- **Multi-monitor support**. Some video cards come with connectors for *two* monitors. Now that modern versions of Windows support multiple-monitor operation, this can be a cool way to upgrade your display system, as I explore further in the later section "Installing Multiple Monitors."

Warranty

Almost nobody fixes PC monitors anymore. (Heck, not too many people fix PCs, period, compared to a decade ago.) A while back, I learned I needed a new "flyback transformer" for one of my PC monitors; when I finally found someone who would do the work, the cost was 80 percent of a new monitor. A model with a five-year warranty is worth a few extra bucks compared to a model with a three-year warranty, because if a monitor breaks, chances are it will break completely and irreparably.

Personally, I don't worry about warranties for video adapters. They're all electronic and my experience is that if they work for 30 days, they'll work for 10 years. The one exception might be those video adapters with on-board TV tuners; those components aren't as reliable as the rest of the circuitry.

Upgrading a Video Adapter

You may want to upgrade your video adapter hardware for one or more of the following reasons:

- You want faster 2-D graphics, also known as "business graphics," for programs such as word processors, photo editors, spreadsheets, and the like.

- You want faster 3-D graphics, most likely for games (unless you're a film special-effects designer working on *Jurassic Park XVII*).

- You want more pixels and more colors than you can display now. (You can probably achieve this goal by simply adding memory to your existing video card, if that's an option, as I discuss in "Adding Memory to a Video Card" later in this chapter.)

- You want higher refresh rates for less eye fatigue.

- You can't quite afford a new PC but you want to wring as much performance out of the box as you can.

The good news is that adding a new video adapter is a fairly painless operation, as PC surgeries go: easier than upgrading a processor or memory, although not quite as easy as adding an external device such as a USB camera. The other good news is that it's an upgrade you can really "feel" in most cases, in the form of faster display response, higher refresh rates, greater resolutions, and deeper color depths. The following sections lay out the essentials; as always, the specific details in the video adapter manual should augment (and, in case of conflict, supercede) what I write here.

Disabling Motherboard Video

If your existing video adapter is an on-board type that's integrated with your motherboard, and if you don't want to use multiple monitors (see "Installing Multiple Monitors," later in this chapter), then you may need to disable the integrated video circuit when you insert an add-in video board. Some (mostly older) PCs get confused to the point of paralysis when faced with two active video devices.

> **TIP** *Unless you know for sure that this is necessary, you might go ahead and try adding the new video board without disabling the on-board video. If it works, you're in a good position to add another monitor later on, if you decide to do so. If it doesn't, you've only lost 10 minutes or so.*

Sometimes all you need to do to disable motherboard video is make a setting via the PC's BIOS setup program, which you activate at startup with keystrokes such as F1 or Alt+Enter or something similar (the exact command will either appear on the screen as your PC starts up, or it is printed in your PC owner's manual). In other cases, you may need to change a switch or jumper setting on the motherboard, in which case you'll have to get guidance from your owner's manual, PC manufacturer's Web site, or tech support line to get the exact procedure. (Motherboards sometimes have *lots* of switches and jumpers, most of which have little or no labeling.)

Adding a Video Card

Your new video card will either use the *Peripheral Component Interconnect (PCI)* bus or the *Advanced Graphics Port (AGP)* bus to connect to your motherboard. The AGP port has the potential to be faster, although whether it turns out to be or not depends largely on the particular adapter you put into it. All other things being equal, if you have a choice, go AGP.

Not all PCs have an AGP slot. Make sure yours does before you run out and buy an AGP video card. Figure 6.3 shows what one looks like; it's quite different from a PCI slot (Figure 6.4). PCI slots are almost always beige or cream-colored. Another clue you can use is that you'll only ever see one AGP slot in a PC, whereas you're likely to see at least two or three PCI slots.

Figure 6.3 *An AGP slot*

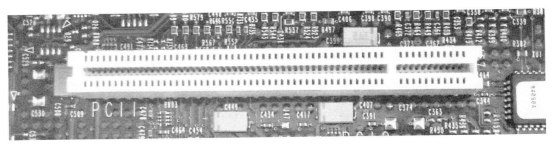

Figure 6.4 *A PCI slot*

Nowadays you have two kinds of AGP slots, referred to as 2X and 4X, with the latter being faster. Generally, video boards that work in 4X AGP slots also work in 2X slots, just more slowly. Figure 6.5 shows a popular video card, the ATI All-in-Wonder Radeon, which also has TV input and output capabilities. The version shown has an AGP connector.

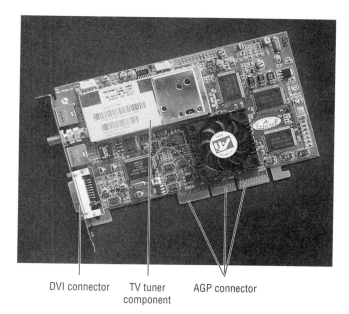

DVI connector   TV tuner   AGP connector
component

Figure 6.5 *A popular video card (AGP version)*

Once you've got these few key things figured out, you can get started.

EQUIPMENT YOU'LL NEED:

➡ *An antistatic wrist strap (optional, but highly recommended)*

➡ *A screwdriver to remove your PC's cover*

➡ *A screwdriver to remove the old video board, if present, and secure the new one (typically Phillips or Torx)*

➡ *An antistatic bag to hold the old video board, if present*

➡ *A new video board*

➡ *A converter cable (if your new card has a DVI connector but no analog connector)*

INFORMATION YOU'LL NEED:

➡ *Whether your video card is PCI or AGP*

➡ *What connectors your video card and monitor use (VGA or DVI)*

Here's the typical procedure for adding a video card to your PC.

1. Remove all jewelry from your hands, wrists, and neck.

2. Disconnect the keyboard, mouse, display, power, and any other connectors from the PC's back panel.

3. Open the PC cover and, if you're adding a video board to a PC that uses motherboard video, locate an unused PCI slot or the AGP slot. If you're replacing an existing plug-in video board, identify it (the back-panel connector with the 15-pin VGA shell is your best clue).

4. Attach the antistatic wrist strap. One end goes on your wrist, the other end on the computer's chassis or silver power supply housing.

5. From the empty slot location you already identified, or from the existing add-in video board location, remove the expansion-slot cover plate (save the screw). Put the cover plate wherever you store old PC parts you may need again later. If you removed an existing video board, put it in an antistatic bag and label it. You can use it later to build a cheap PC for your five-year-old. (Once the kids hit six, they'll want newer technology.)

6. Slide the new video controller into the expansion slot. Line it up first, then press down firmly until the card snaps into place (see Figure 6.6).

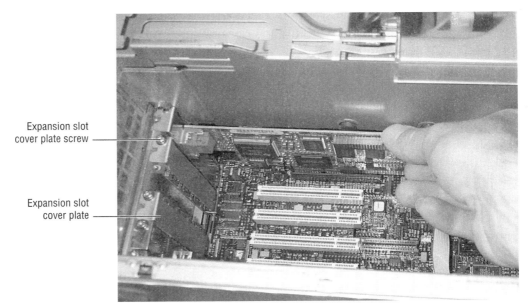

Expansion slot
cover plate screw

Expansion slot
cover plate

Figure 6.6 *Inserting an AGP video board*

7. Replace the slot cover plate screw.

8. Disconnect the antistatic wrist strap.

9. Put the cover back on the PC.

10. Reconnect the keyboard, mouse, display, and any other peripheral cables.

TIP *If you need an adapter to convert between a DVI connector on your new video board and an analog 15-pin VGA connector on your monitor, attach it now.*

11. Power up the PC. Follow the manufacturer's instructions for installing any required software for the card; with most Windows PCs, the computer will automatically detect it and prompt you with directions.

12. This last step is where you'll install the *driver* for the video card, that is, the software that tells your computer how to interact with the controller. With Windows operating systems, you almost always have a choice: You can let Windows choose the driver, which will be Microsoft-certified and will reside on your Windows CD, or you can run a vendor-supplied program (usually on a CD that came with the board) that will install a newer, faster, but typically uncertified driver. It's your call; I usually go with the vendor-supplied driver unless it turns out to cause problems, in which case I go back and install the Microsoft-certified driver.

Adding Memory to a Video Card

If your goal is to enjoy higher resolutions at greater color depths, then you may be able to use your existing video card and simply add memory to it. (Yep, video cards have memory—typically very fast memory.) Many times, a person will buy a video card thinking, "I won't ever need to work beyond 800 × 600," and then they will buy a bigger monitor and all of a sudden need that extra resolution. If you're in that boat, here's what you need to know.

Before you add memory to a video card, you have to find out 1) how much memory your video card has, and 2) how much it's capable of hosting. You can generally get the first bit of information from your operating system (in Windows, you'd go to Device Manager and check out the properties for the display adapter). The second bit of information you can usually glean from the video adapter manufacturer's Web site, or from your user manual if you happen to have it. Some video adapters aren't upgradable, and some of them ship with the maximum complement of memory.

TIP *Certain video adapters, such as Intel's 810 graphics controller (popular in many home PCs), can make use of main system memory and thereby reduce cost. Whether they also run faster seems to depend on the specific implementation; I've seen it go both ways.*

The next thing you have to find out is what kind of video memory your card uses. Again, you can usually get this information from your video card manual, or the manufacturer's Web site; the sections after this one cover the major types you're likely to see. After you've identified the size and type memory you need and you've purchased some, preferably from the video card manufacturer itself, you're ready to perform the upgrade.

EQUIPMENT YOU'LL NEED:

➡ *An antistatic wrist strap (optional, but highly recommended)*

➡ *A screwdriver to remove your PC's cover*

➡ *A screwdriver to remove the video board (typically Phillips or Torx)*

➡ *Stabilant-22 contact enhancement fluid (optional, but recommended; get at an electronics supply house, or a Mercedes or Audi dealer)*

➡ *A flat-bottom paper cup (optional, but handy for holding screws)*

INFORMATION YOU'LL NEED:

➡ *The type of module (VRAM, WRAM, SGRAM, or DDR)*

Follow these basic steps:

1. Disconnect the keyboard, mouse, display, power, and any other connectors.

2. Open the PC cover.

3. Attach the antistatic wrist strap to your wrist and to the PC's metal chassis.

4. Remove the screw holding the video board in place and set it aside where it won't roll away somewhere, such as in a paper cup.

5. Remove the video board by grasping it at the corners and pulling up at alternate corners. Don't grab any components soldered to the board if you can help it.

6. Take the memory module out of its antistatic bag. (If it didn't come in an antistatic bag, or at least a plastic box, consider returning it.) It may be in the same kind of packaging you'd see for computer main memory (see Chapter 2, "Memory," for details), or it may

be in the form of a *daughterboard* that piggybacks onto the main video board, fitting over rows of pins sticking out from the video board.

7. If you have Stabilant-22, apply a thin film of the fluid to the contacts, either along the edge of the module or at the pins where the daughterboard connects to the main board.

8. Plug the memory into the video card. The precise procedure will vary depending on memory type and video card manufacturer, but generally you just line up the pins with the socket and push.

9. Plug the video card back into its slot.

10. Replace the screw holding the video board in place.

11. Remove the antistatic wrist strap.

12. Put the cover back on the PC.

13. Reconnect the keyboard, mouse, display, and any other peripheral cables.

14. Restart the PC.

15. Go to the operating system setup facility for the display (in Windows, this is the Display control panel's Settings tab). You should see new options for resolution, color depth, and refresh rate, made possible by the additional video memory.

VRAM

Video Random Access Memory (VRAM) is faster than regular system memory because it is dual-ported: one port for input (from the computer to the video adapter) and one for output (from the video adapter to the display). Regular RAM can be read from or written to, but not both at once. The dual-ported design allows for faster refresh rates because the display can be reading the VRAM even as the PC is updating the display information. Faster refresh rates are especially important at higher resolutions where these rates tend to sag. The downside is that VRAM costs more than regular dynamic RAM (DRAM).

WRAM

Windows Random Access Memory (WRAM) is the same as VRAM in basic principle, but it is a faster implementation of the concept—anywhere from 30 to 50 percent faster in Windows systems, according to the techie literature. It's also roughly 20 percent cheaper because, among other reasons, it doesn't require as many chips.

SGRAM

Synchronous Graphics Random Access Memory (SGRAM) has become popular for video adapters. Even though it is a single-ported type, SGRAM can be written to or read from two pages at a time, so the net effect is speed comparable to VRAM and WRAM.

DDR

Dual Data Rate (DDR) memory works by taking SDRAM (synchronous dynamic random access memory; see Chapter 2's section of the same name) and doubling the number of data transfers that can take place in a single transfer cycle. DDR is fast enough that it's showing up as primary computer memory in really fast machines, and it's definitely fast enough to work as video memory. Many high-end video adapters, such as the ATI All-in-Wonder Radeon, use DDR.

Setting Up Your Monitor

Setting up your display involves a number of tweaks that you make via your PC's operating system (Windows, Linux, what have you) and some that you make via your monitor's controls. Resolution, color depth, and refresh rate are operating system settings, and are discussed in the following sections. "Third-Party Calibration Utilities," the last discussion in this section, introduces a few monitor calibration utilities to help you tune up your monitor.

Resolution

Resolution is simply how many pixels the display system shows you at one time. Normally you see resolution measured as a horizontal value followed by an "×" and the vertical value, as in 1024×768. Popular PC display system resolutions are 800×600, 1024×768, 1280×1024, and (for those of you with higher discretionary incomes) 1600×1200.

> **TIP** *On a Windows PC, set the resolution via the Settings tab in the Display Control Panel. Windows will usually display a test image to make sure the monitor can support the value you've chosen, and then ask you to click OK if the test image is, in fact, OK. Experiment with the available settings until you find one that works best for you.*

More isn't necessarily better when it comes to resolution. As you increase the resolution, the size of the characters on screen decreases. That's why you wouldn't normally want to set a 15-inch monitor to 1024×768 resolution: Everything gets too small to see! Conversely, if the monitor is large, low resolutions look "chunky" and you're not getting all the sharpness and detail the monitor is capable of displaying. The best advice is to match resolution to screen size, as suggested by the following guidelines:

15-inch monitor: 640 × 480 or 800 × 600

17-inch monitor: 800 × 600 or 1024 × 768

19-inch monitor: 1024 × 768 or 1280 × 1024

21-inch monitor: 1280 × 1024 or 1600 × 1200

Another factor to bear in mind is that your resolution selection affects two other choices: color depth and refresh rate. Specifically, the higher the resolution, the fewer colors you can display (because your video adapter only has so much memory to store all that data) and the lower your maximum refresh rate will be (because your monitor can only draw so many pixels per second).

TIP *If you work with digital video, you'll find that most display adapters can play back video files more smoothly at lower resolutions, all other factors being equal.*

Color Depth

Color depth means how many colors the display system can show at once. It's a characteristic of the video card, but not of a CRT monitor; CRT monitors work with analog signals and can manage as many different gradations of color as the video adapter can throw at them. The more colors your display system can show, the richer the colors on your screen appear, and the more lifelike photographs and movies look.

The color depth value may appear differently in different documents, so the following list should clarify things:

8-bit color means 256 colors at once.

15-bit color, or *high color*, means 16,000 colors at once.

16-bit color, also called *high color*, means 32,000 colors at once.

24-bit color, or *true color*, means 16.7 million colors at once.

32-bit color, also called *true color*, means 4.3 trillion colors at once.

The human eye, at its best, can only see 11 or 12 million colors, so 24-bit color display systems are able to show more colors than you or I can detect. (My wife claims that she has "true-color" eyes while mine are "high-color" on a good day. Unfortunately, biologists back up that assertion: On average, women have better color vision than men.)

If you're running Windows and you tinker with the color depth settings on the Settings tab of the Display control panel, you'll discover that the list of possible color depths changes as you change the resolution. That is, you may be able to display true color at 800 × 600 resolution, but only high color at 1024 × 768 resolution. If you find such a limitation and it bothers you, look into whether you can add memory to your video card.

TIP *For those of you working with digital video, you pay a price for the realism of higher color depths, and that price is speed. All other things being equal, a video clip captured with 8-bit color is likely to run faster than a clip captured with 24-bit color. If your system chokes when trying to play true-color, high-resolution movies, consider upgrading the video card (although at some point you may have to also upgrade the CPU, as well).*

Refresh Rate

One of the more neglected monitor settings, the *refresh rate* is a measure of how rapidly the display "repaints" itself. On a CRT monitor, the phosphorescent coating on the inside of the tube only stays lit for a short time after being zapped by the electron guns. The refresh rate indicates how often the guns revisit each pixel and zap it again to keep it lit. (The refresh rate is not applicable for an LCD panel, which doesn't use electron guns.) Too slow a refresh rate, and you can see the pixels fade before they get re-zapped, a phenomenon we know as *flicker*.

Refresh rate is measured in hertz (Hz), or cycles per second. Here are my own guidelines, in short:

- 60Hz is too slow and will give you headaches.

- 72Hz is way better than 60 but still not flicker-free.

- 80Hz and 85Hz are good, and you're not likely to notice any flicker at all.

- More than 85Hz is probably overkill; set it only if it doesn't limit your resolution options.

- If you can see flicker at 100Hz, you should lay off the coffee.

The higher the resolution, the more limited your options will be when it comes to refresh rate. However, with today's video adapters and monitors (both must support the desired refresh rate), you should have no trouble being able to set a comfortable value at your preferred resolution.

On Windows systems, set the refresh rate on the Settings tab of the Display Control Panel; you may have to click the Advanced button and hunt for the setting, which is sometimes buried moderately deep in the user interface.

TIP *Some adapters are preset at the factory to 60Hz, a value that works with virtually every monitor made in the last decade. If you've never checked your display adapter's refresh rate, do it right now.*

Third-Party Calibration Utilities

You can use monitor calibration utilities to do three things:

- Tune up your present monitor so you don't have to upgrade.
- Evaluate monitors you're thinking about buying.
- Tune up the new monitor you just bought.

I was a little skeptical the first time I used one of these programs. After all, how much can you really adjust a monitor? Nowadays, the answer turns out to be quite a bit.

Monitor Adjustments

On the CRT monitor I'm using to write this book—a NEC MultiSync FE700 17-inch flat screen budget model (book authors don't make a *lot* of money unless they also write diet books on the side)—I have the following adjustments available:

- Brightness
- Contrast
- Left/Right (also called Horizontal Position on many monitors)
- Down/Up (also called Vertical Position)
- Narrow/Wide (also called Horizontal Size)
- Short/Tall (also called Vertical Size)
- Color Temperature
- In/Out Pincushioning
- Left/Right Pincushioning
- Tilt
- Align (Trapezoid)
- Rotate
- Moiré Canceller
- Linearity

Consult your monitor's instruction manual for detailed definitions of these settings, or just play around with them to get a feel for what they do.

You might assume that today's monitors are in fine adjustment when they come out of the box, so you don't need to fool with the adjustments. Do not make that assumption. The monitor manufacturers don't know ahead of time which video card you'll be connecting their monitor to, nor do they know the lighting characteristics of your workspace. Plus, monitors get bumped around in shipment. I don't think I've ever seen a monitor that looked perfect right off the bat.

I've used two utilities that I really like, one free and one not. The free one is the Nokia Monitor Test (NTEST.EXE). You can't get this from Nokia anymore, but search for it on the Internet with a good search engine (I use www.google.com) and you're sure to run across a copy. It includes test screens for geometry, convergence, resolution, moiré, brightness and contrast, readability, color, and screen regulation (see Figure 6.7). In addition, the help file is quite helpful, even if it does mangle the English language a little.

The not-free one is DisplayMate, of which you can get an extremely limited demo version at www.displaymate.com. (The full version runs about US$70 or so at this writing.) DisplayMate is certainly the more powerful of the two, but unless you spend several hours a day in front of your monitor, you'll probably be quite happy with NTEST.

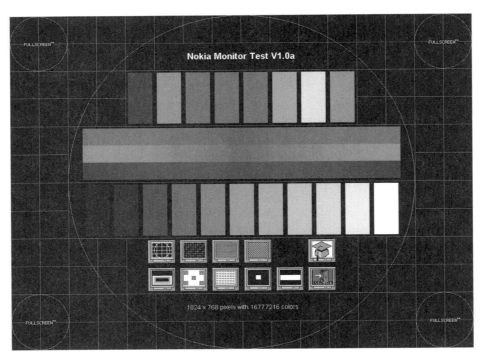

Figure 6.7 *Nokia Monitor Test*

Whichever of these programs you choose, or if you find something else that's even better, you'll be amazed at how the sum of several seemingly subtle adjustments to your display can make your computing experience more aesthetically pleasing. And if you don't have access to either of these programs, by all means at least adjust brightness and contrast according to the following simple procedure:

1. Turn the brightness down until you can no longer see the black background around the perimeter of the image area.

2. Turn the contrast all the way down.

3. Bring the contrast up slowly until the picture looks sharp, clear, and easy on the eyes. Don't increase the contrast too far, or the image will probably go out of focus.

4. Repeat this procedure whenever the room lighting changes.

TIP *Most people set their monitor's brightness too high, causing unnecessary fatigue and poor image clarity.*

Installing Multiple Monitors

One of the great upgrades you can perform if you run Windows 98, ME, 2000, or XP is to add a monitor to your PC for a multiple-monitor setup. All these operating systems can support up to nine (!) monitors, so you can set up a virtual Mission Control in your home office (and get a tan from the radiation at the same time).

The procedure for installing multiple monitors on a typical PC with on-board video is the same as that for adding a new video adapter, discussed earlier in the chapter, with one major exception: You must configure the operating system to use the new monitor. In Windows, that's done on the Settings tab of the Display Control Panel. When you power up your PC after adding a second video adapter and monitor, the Settings tab should show both displays (see Figure 6.8), but you will probably have to check the box labeled "Extend my Windows desktop onto this monitor" before you'll be able to use it.

A few flies can land in the ointment. First and most common, you may discover that the adapter you want to use for your secondary monitor (that is, not the one that shows PC startup messages) doesn't work in that capacity. Many adapters can function only as primary adapters in a multi-monitor setup; the adapter manufacturer should be able to provide this detail.

A second issue you may encounter is that if you're combining motherboard video and add-in video, not all motherboards let you use the integrated video adapter at all. That is, the BIOS detects the add-in adapter, and automatically disables the motherboard display controller. You may or may not be able to work around this problem via the BIOS setup program; you'll have to consult your PC's manual for help here, or call a support tech.

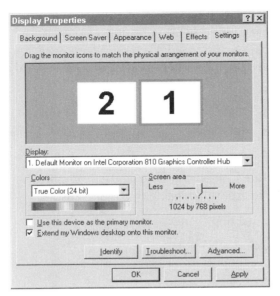

Figure 6.8 *Configuring multiple monitors*

In a related problem, if, after installing a new video adapter but before installing the second monitor, your original display is blank at startup, power everything down and plug your monitor into the new adapter. Chances are your operating system or BIOS is trying to use the new board as the default display.

Installing a Flat-Panel Monitor

With a spate of recent price drops, flat-panel LCD monitors (see Figure 6.9) are becoming very interesting choices for both business and home users. The LCD monitor is a fundamentally different animal than a CRT monitor, and it works like a notebook computer display works: Each dot is actually a transistor that emits a constant light when fed a digital signal.

LCD monitors are thin, light (meaning you won't pull a muscle moving one), and cool, in both senses of the word. They present rock-solid images because they don't use phosphors that need constant refreshing, so you can say goodbye to refresh rate issues. They typically have low-glare, matte surfaces. They also emit less electromagnetic radiation than CRTs, they use less power, and they're perfectly quiet (many CRTs emit a low-level buzz, especially as they age). Finally, because the tiny electronic devices emitting the light are right there at the display surface, you don't have any focusing or convergence problems with these monitors as you may in a traditional CRT, where electron guns throw electrons at a glass tube several inches away and hope they arrive at just the right time and place.

Figure 6.9 *An LCD monitor*

Sounds just about perfect. So what's the downside to these units? The most significant one is price. You can generally buy two comparably sized CRT monitors for the price of one LCD monitor. The next most significant drawback is the fact that these units don't do a very good job with motion: Text blurs when you scroll it, and digital videos don't look nearly as good as they do on a CRT (gamers take note!). This is because of the LCD cells' *latency*, or the time delay between when they receive a signal and when they emit a dot of light. Finally, when LCD panel technology was young, you also had to put up with *jitter*, that is, a pixel that would bounce back and forth between two adjacent locations because the monitor couldn't figure out exactly where it should go. My recent tests suggest that jitter is pretty much a thing of the past, but keep an eye out for it when you're shopping.

The digital nature of LCD monitors is turning out to be a mixed blessing, although the problems are likely to shake out in the next few years. Here's what's going on with cables and connectors for these units. Because the LCD monitor is a digital device, there's a certain inefficiency to the traditional process for getting display data from computer to monitor. The computer starts with a digital image; the video card converts that to an analog signal; then the digital LCD monitor has to convert that analog signal back to digital! (The CRT is perfectly happy accepting the analog signal and, in fact, demands it.) Couldn't things go faster if you just skipped the digital-to-analog-to-digital conversion? You bet. But you need new cables and connectors, and as usual, the computer industry has done its best to make life confusing.

When you buy an LCD, it is likely to have one of three different connectors: the old analog style (see Figure 6.10) that works with just about any graphics card but requires the double signal conversion; a newer digital-only style (called DVI-D, for digital video interface—digital) that will only connect to a graphics card that has the same digital-only connector; and a hybrid connector (called DVI-I, for digital video interface—integrated; see Figure 6.11) that can support either analog or digital signals. So you have to be careful to match up the LCD panel with your graphics card.

Figure 6.10 *A 15-pin analog VGA connector*

Figure 6.11 *A DVI-I connector*

TIP *If your graphics card has a DVI-D connector, but you have a DVI-I cable coming off your LCD panel, you can buy a cable adapter to mate the two.*

Here's what you'll need for the job.

EQUIPMENT YOU'LL NEED:

➡ *A screwdriver to secure video cable connections*

➡ *A DVI-I to analog converter (optional)*

➡ *A DVI-D to DVI-I converter (optional)*

INFORMATION YOU'LL NEED:

➡ *The type of signal connectors (analog, DVI-I, or DVI-D) supported by your monitor and video card*

Assuming your video adapter and LCD monitor support the same connector type, installing the LCD monitor is simplicity itself.

1. Turn off the computer.

2. Disconnect the old monitor.

3. Connect the signal cable to your monitor and to the PC's back panel. (Here's where you may need an adapter, such as the one in Figure 6.12, if your video card and LCD monitor don't support the same connectors.)

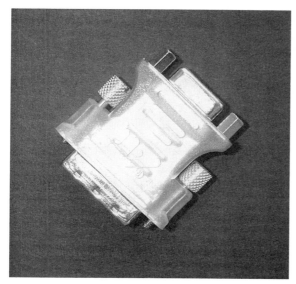

Figure 6.12 *A DVI-I to analog converter*

4. If your LCD monitor has built-in speakers, you have the option to connect your PC's sound output to the LCD monitor's back panel (see Figures 6.13 and 6.14).

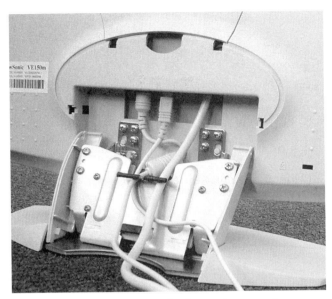

Figure 6.13 *LCD monitor back-panel connections*

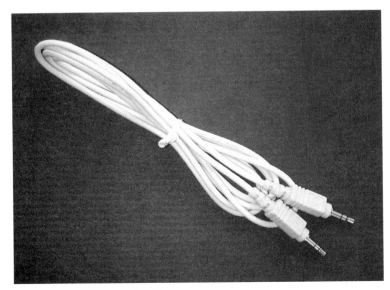

Figure 6.14 *A sound cable*

5. Plug the LCD monitor into an AC outlet.

6. Turn on the computer.

7. Use the front-panel controls to adjust the display.

8. Optionally, install any software that came with the LCD monitor.

You normally don't even have to make any settings in your operating system: Modern LCD panels, like my ViewSonic VE150m, automatically detect the resolution from the incoming signal.

Maintaining Your Monitor

Few people are aware that their CRT monitors will last longer if they would only follow a few simple maintenance tips. Read this section so that you will become one of those few.

- **Dust it**. Dust is the enemy of your monitor. It sneaks in through the vent slots and builds up inside the housing, effectively insulating some of the electrical components inside so they run hotter than they should. Get one of those compressed-air cans and shoot some air down into those vent slots every few months to kick up the dust.

WARNING *I don't recommend that you ever open a monitor case in order to dust it, or for any other reason. One reason is safety: Monitors contain power capacitors that can shock you even when the unit is off and disconnected from the wall outlet. The other reason is that it's just too easy to bump the interior components (technical term: "guts") and throw your monitor out of adjustment, at which point you may be faced with buying a new one.*

- **Leave it on during the day**. Thermal stress in general is bad for electronics, but I have another reason for leaving monitors on from dawn to dusk (or dusk to dawn, if you're a writer): *degaussing*. Every time you turn your monitor on, it degausses, which clears away any internal magnetic fields that may be impairing the accurate delivery of electrons to the screen. You know, you hear the click of a relay and a sort of oscillating humming noise, and the display (if it appears quickly enough) seems to shake and shimmy. Most monitor manufacturers suggest you not degauss the monitor more than once or twice a day.

- **Clean it *carefully***. By which I mean, don't use anything other than mild soap and water unless the manufacturer specifically says it's OK to do so. Depending on the anti-glare coating used by your monitor's manufacturer, an ammonia-based cleaner could ruin it permanently.

WARNING *Don't clean your CRT's surface while the unit is on. Clean it first thing in the morning before you start to use it. Why? Think about what happens when you drive through a cold-water car wash after a long hot summer drive. That cold water can actually crack the hot tube; I've seen it happen.*

LCD monitors don't need dusting because they don't have, or need, ventilation holes. Also, you don't realize any benefit by leaving LCD monitors on during the day, because they don't get hot. You should clean the surface according to the manufacturer's recommendations, but other than that, LCD panels are virtually maintenance-free.

Chapter 7

Networking

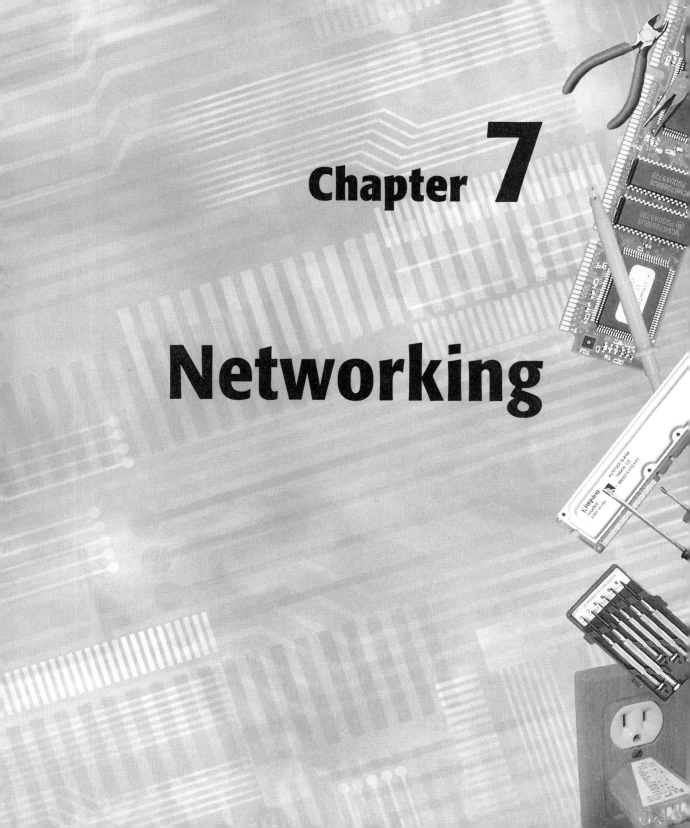

Networks can save money by letting you share expensive devices. They let you share things like printers, broadband Internet connections, tape drives, CD burners, and, well, just about anything you can hook up to a PC.

Beyond device sharing, networks make data sharing easy, too. Yes, you can use diskettes for that purpose, but more and more, we find ourselves working with files that are too large to fit on diskette. Zip and Jaz drives can solve that problem, but if you have to buy a drive for each PC in your home, that can get a little expensive. With a network, you can zap a file from one PC to another faster than any other method.

You can also use a network as a data backup device. That is, Dad can back up his data files to Mom's PC at night. That way, you have some data security even without buying a CD burner, cartridge drive, or tape drive. Finally, many people are getting into multi-player games, and even hosting game parties at their houses. Networks (combined with pizza) make that sort of social event possible.

I can't cover the entire scope of local area networking for home and small-office use in one chapter. (Heck, I wrote a 400-page book about it, and even that wasn't exhaustive.) But what I can do here is introduce you to some networking technologies and make some suggestions to get you going in the right direction. I can also show you how to perform some of the hardware-related tasks that you'll face regardless of your network's software configuration.

Intro to Networking

When you set up a small *local area network*, or *LAN*, you have to make several decisions, including the following:

- Physical connection
- Signaling method
- Network protocol
- Network architecture
- Network software

With a few exceptions, you can make each of these decisions independently of the others. The following sections take a quick look at each one individually.

Physical Connection

You can connect PCs using dedicated cabling, existing phone cabling, wireless radio frequency devices, and power line adapters. So, which of these hardware choices is the best? In the best consultant tradition, my answer is, "It depends," but I'll offer a few opinions in the following sections.

Dedicated Cabling

Dedicated cabling gives the best results, without a doubt. You have to run network cables, though, which can range from being no big deal to a huge pain, depending on the space.

> **TIP** *If you're a renter and you're setting up a home network, you may find your landlord more amenable to the idea of running network cabling than you think; because it's a home improvement, it could be a selling point for the next tenant. Don't just ask for permission; see if the landlord will pay for the installation!*

Normally you'll run cables in a star pattern with a little box (either a hub or a switch) at the center and your PCs at the ends. You should place the hub or switch as centrally as possible to minimize the cable lengths. (If you're just networking two PCs, then you can skip the hub, save a few bucks, and use a *crossover* cable instead of a *straight-through* cable.)

There are different kinds of dedicated cabling, but unless you have unusual needs, the one you want to use is *Unshielded Twisted Pair, Category* 5 (*UTP Cat 5* in the lingo), which looks a lot like phone wire. You might consider coaxial cable if you have really long runs (over 100 meters) or an electrically noisy environment (such as if you're manufacturing Van de Graaf generators in your basement).

As for the hub or switch, I usually recommend that you go with a switch for better speed, although some gamers say that a regular hub works better with multi-user games. The price difference used to be huge, but today it's negligible; you can get a perfectly nice little 8-port switch for under US$100.

For an informal home or small-office network, get an "unmanaged" hub or switch. You don't need the capabilities of a managed device, which can report network statistics or problems to a central monitoring station. If you get a hub for an Ethernet LAN, I recommend a combo type that can handle regular Ethernet (10Mbps) or fast Ethernet (100Mbps). The reason: Many DSL and cable modems use a 10Mbps connection only, and if you have a hub that accepts only 100Mbps connections, you're out of luck when you decide to share that broadband Internet link over your network.

Wireless

Wireless is cool, especially if laying cable would be difficult or costly, but your network will run slower than it would with dedicated cabling (you should expect to see 7–8Mbps in a nominal 11Mbps setup), and wireless network adapters are more expensive than traditional wired adapters. Instead of a hub or a switch, an all-wireless LAN uses a different kind of device, called an *access point*, to connect the PCs and manage traffic; this is called "infrastructure mode." You'd try to position an access point centrally, though, just as you would a hub or switch in a wired network.

You may be able to get away without an access point (using something called "*ad hoc* mode") if your wireless PCs don't need to connect to an existing wired network and the PCs you want to connect are close enough to find each other. Distance is a big issue with wireless systems; with the wireless network I built for this book, for example, no PC can be more than 100m from another PC or from an access point. So, if you have two PCs that are 150m apart, you're probably going to have to install an access point roughly in the middle.

Phone Line

Another possibility is to use existing phone lines to carry network data. Intel, Sonicblue, and 3Com all offer products in this category, and adapters are available for both USB and PCI. The theory is that you can use your phone and your network at the same time; you connect your phone jack to your network card, and then plug in your phone to a separate port on the network card.

However, phone line networking has not taken the world by storm yet, partly because it's somewhat slower than the best wireless products (you're likely to see about 4Mbps with a so-called 10Mbps setup), partly because it doesn't work well if your phone system wiring is marginal (which is often the case), and partly because you don't always have a phone jack where you want to put a computer (if you have to install new wiring, you may as well go with a traditional wired LAN).

Some people really like phone-line networking, but I feel obligated to rain on their parade just a little bit. In my experience, the technology is slow and unreliable unless your home phone wiring is exceptionally clean. I'm betting you'll be happier with a wired LAN or with a radio-frequency wireless setup. Now, that's just my opinion, and if you want to try phone-line networking, go for it, but here's some quick advice: Get a money-back guarantee from your hardware supplier if you can't get it to work in your house, and make sure the system is compatible with either the 10Mbps or, better yet, the 20Mbps *HomePNA* standard (*HomePNA* is short for *Home Phoneline Networking Alliance*). HomePNA has a 1Mbps standard that's as slow as molasses in January.

Power Line

Some companies are even working on using your AC outlets for networking purposes, but I haven't seen anything that works well so far in that category. Power-line networking has one big advantage over phone-line networking in that every room in a house or office has a power outlet, while not every room necessarily has a phone jack. The Web site to watch is `www.homeplug.org`, home of the HomePlug Powerline Alliance.

No matter what hardware you choose for the physical link between your PCs, you'll have to buy devices for your existing computers to connect to the network. These devices are called (logically enough) "network adapters," and they typically plug into an available device slot, a USB port, or a credit-card socket on a laptop. Most budget PCs don't come with networking hardware included (if yours does, though, you're ahead of the game as long as the hardware is what you want).

Signaling Method

The signaling method is the language your network cards use to talk to each other. You really have only three choices if you use dedicated cables: *Token Ring*, *Ethernet*, and *Fast Ethernet*.

Not many folks use Token Ring for small networks anymore, so cross that one off. If you're a speed junkie like me, that's a slam-dunk now that Fast Ethernet is about the same cost as regular Ethernet. Fast Ethernet runs at 100Mbps, ten times faster than regular Ethernet.

If you go wireless, you'll probably want to use a radio frequency spread spectrum standard called *802.11b* (which is an Institute of Electrical and Electronic Engineers standard). This technology is rather sophisticated, in that it can automatically select the best transmission frequencies. Other wireless systems exist, such as "HomeRF," but 802.11b is what you want. HomeRF is inferior to 802.11b in both speed (1.6Mbps maximum as I write this) and range (about 50m).

By the way, in case you're wondering, I should mention that the "Bluetooth" wireless standard that I discuss in Chapter 4, "Communications," isn't really for building networks, but rather for connecting one or two devices (like a Personal Digital Assistant or a printer) to a single PC, in a so-called *PAN* (*personal access network*).

Network Protocol

If you'll let me oversimplify things a little, the network protocol is the language your computer's operating systems use to talk to each other. Your choices in the PC world are basically three: *NetBEUI*, *IPX*, and *TCP/IP*. Don't worry about all the alphabet soup just yet, because I can probably simplify this choice for you in a hurry. If you want to connect to the Internet (and who doesn't these days?), you'll want TCP/IP. The only reason you'd use IPX is if you need to have a Novell network for some reason.

> **TIP** *If you hate the Internet and you never plan to connect to it, and you know you'll never need to connect to remote computers using a router, then you should consider using NetBEUI (pronounced Net-Booie) as your network protocol. It's simple, reliable, and fast. Unfortunately, it doesn't come with Windows XP.*

The TCP/IP protocol (actually, it's a set of protocols) was developed by the U.S. Department of Defense and is extremely flexible. The price of that flexibility, however, is complexity. Each computer in a TCP/IP network has to have its own *IP address*, which is four numbers separated by dots (like *192.168.0.10*), and its own *subnet mask*, which has a similar format (255.255.255.0). You may also have to supply a *default gateway address* and a *DNS server address* if you're connecting to the Internet. (The book *TCP/IP Jumpstart* by Andrew G. Blank contains a lot more detail on all this than I can provide here.)

Managing these addresses can be a bit of a chore, which may qualify as the understatement of the year, but the good news is that, depending on your network setup, you may never need to mess with it. For example:

- If you're connecting to a DSL modem or cable modem, you may use a router that can automatically set up the PCs in your network with IP address and subnet mask information. Your broadband supplier should be able to help you with this setup.

- Even if you don't have a router, more recent versions of Windows (98, ME, XP, 2000) automatically give themselves IP addresses if they can't get them from another computer or router on the network.

Network Architecture

"Architecture" may seem like an odd word to describe a computer network, but all it means in this context is which networking model you want to use. You have two basic choices, *peer-to-peer* and *client/server*.

- In a peer-to-peer network, also called a *workgroup* network, any PC can share resources with any other PC, and you can use any computer to run application programs (word processing, spreadsheet, games, and so on).

- In a client/server network, most or all of the sharing is done by one or more central PCs that you don't use to run your programs; these central PCs are called *dedicated servers*. (Mostly what they're dedicated to is eating up your time and money.)

If you have only a few computers, you don't have serious security needs, and you're watching the dollars, then you should go with peer-to-peer. The latest versions of Windows work well with this model, for example, and I've successfully connected from two to two dozen computers in a single peer-to-peer network.

TIP *The thing you must remember when networking Windows computers in a workgroup is that the workgroup name must be the same on all the PCs or they won't be able to communicate with each other. See the documentation for your version of the operating system to see how to set the workgroup name; normally you get to it via the Network Control Panel or the Network and Dial-Up Connections folder.*

Network Software

Your choices for network software depend on the operating system(s) you're currently using. In some cases, you may be able to get by without buying anything new, as would be the case (for example) if you wanted to run a small peer-to-peer network with Windows 98, ME, 2000, NT, or XP. If you want a client/server type network, however, you're probably looking at buying some additional software, such as Linux, Windows 2000 or XP Server, Novell NetWare, and so on.

Setting up servers in a client/server network is highly product-dependent, so I won't try to discuss the options here beyond saying that it's very smart to enlist the help of someone who's done it before!

Installing a Wired Network

In this example, I'll assume that your job is to network three PCs, two desktops and one laptop, in a peer-to-peer Ethernet network (the most common configuration for a small home or office LAN).

For simplicity's sake, I'll also assume that the computers are all in the same room, so you don't have to run your cables through walls. Run the cables under carpet or inside molding strips, buy cables with the connectors already on the ends, and keep the wires away from any sources of electromagnetic interference.

If your PCs are in different rooms, then you should probably get some help from someone who runs cables through walls for a living. If you have a friend in the phone installation business, she may be able to help you install network cable; it isn't all that different from phone cable, but you should find someone who has a cable tester just to make sure everything's done right—cable problems can be a bear to troubleshoot.

TIP *If you're thinking of building a house, or remodeling your existing one, consider having network wiring run to each room that you plan to put under construction (well, except the smallest ones). Wiring a house while it's being built or remodeled is comparatively cheap, plus it may raise the value of your property. If you do this, think about running cable for audio equipment, as well.*

By the way, I talk about connecting your network to the Internet in Chapter 4. Here, the focus is on getting your PCs to talk to each other.

EQUIPMENT YOU'LL NEED:

➡ *Three Fast Ethernet (100Mbps) network adapters (2 PCI cards for the desktops and 1 PC Card for the laptop)*

➡ *One combo (10/100) Ethernet hub or switch*

➡ *A medium Phillips-head screwdriver (for removing adapter cover plates)*

➡ *A screwdriver appropriate for removing the desktop PCs' covers*

➡ *Three Category 5 UTP cables with RJ-45 connectors at each end, with no cable over 100 meters long (these are "straight-through" cables, not "crossover" cables!)*

➡ *An antistatic wrist strap (optional but recommended)*

The key to success in upgrading standalone PCs to a LAN is to take things one step at a time, and test the equipment at each step when possible. With that in mind, here we go:

1. Shut down the first desktop PC and disconnect its power cord.

2. Disconnect all the cables from the PC's back panel, marking any that you don't think you'll remember.

3. Remove the PC's cover (see Chapter 1, "Read Me First," for details, if you're unfamiliar with this process).

4. Attach the antistatic wrist strap. One end goes on your wrist, the other attaches to the PC's chassis. You're going to be handling electronic components and you don't want to ruin them with static electricity.

5. Locate a free PCI slot. (You can use an ISA slot if that's all you have, but it'll slow you down.) In systems with both PCI and ISA slots, the PCI slots are usually beige or white, and the ISA slots are usually black.

6. Remove the slot cover, if present. This is a little metal plate affixed by a single screw (see Figure 7.1). Save the screw, because you'll use it to secure the network adapter.

7. Remove the first PCI network adapter from its antistatic bag (see Figure 7.2).

8. Insert the adapter into the PCI slot. Line it up and push it in gently the first part of the way to make sure the adapter isn't hanging up on anything, then push it firmly until the card "thuds" into place.

Figure 7.1 Removing a PCI slot cover

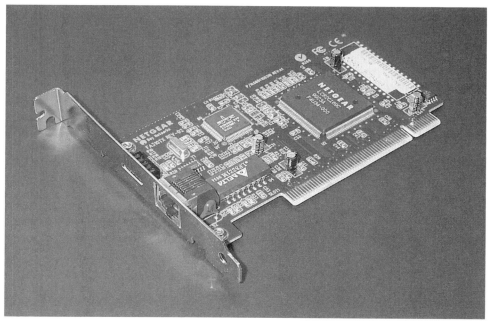

Figure 7.2 A PCI network adapter

TIP *All modern network cards are completely configurable via software. If you have a "vintage" adapter with settings you must adjust with jumpers or switches on the adapter, I recommend that you leave everything at the default setting until your network is up and running successfully.*

9. Secure the adapter with the screw you removed in step 6.

10. Remove the antistatic wrist strap.

11. Replace the PC's cover.

12. Reconnect the cables to the PC's back panel, but don't connect a network cable to the adapter just yet.

13. Reconnect the power cord and turn on the PC.

14. If you have an operating system that supports Plug and Play, as most versions of Windows do, you should see one or more messages informing you that "new hardware has been detected."

Finding Interrupts

You may not have enough resources (interrupts, memory addresses, and so on) for your new PCI device, especially if your PC is an older one or isn't set up properly for Plug and Play. Here are a few things you might try:

- Check your operating system hardware utility (in Windows it's Device Manager) to see if you're loading drivers for any devices that you're not using. If so, disable or remove the unused device or devices, and restart.

- If you disable or remove a device in your operating system but it keeps coming back, like a boomerang, you may have to turn the device off in your BIOS setup program (which you generally get to by pressing a function key, or key combination, at power-on time).

- If the above two tips don't seem to have any effect, tear into the PC and actually remove any PCI or ISA bus circuit boards you're not using.

- Back to the BIOS setup program for a moment: If it's not set for a Plug and Play operating system, but you're running Windows, change the setting so that "Plug and Play OS" reads "yes" and also turn on the "Reset Configuration Data" feature (which lets the operating system juggle system resources in an attempt to find interrupts for everybody). Then, restart.

- If none of these tricks work, but you have a USB port in your PC, then you may want to consider using a USB network adapter instead of a PCI card. It won't be quite as fast, but at least it'll work...

TIP *If you run Windows, it may automatically install the necessary drivers for your new card, but you should read your card manufacturer's documentation as to the exact procedure to follow. Often, the manufacturer provides a newer driver than the one that Windows uses automatically.*

15. If your operating system detects the card (in Windows, it will show up in Device Manager, which you get to via the System Control Panel) and doesn't display any errors (such as yellow or red icons in the Device Manager display), then things are looking good. You can even double-click the icon for the network card to see if Windows thinks it's working properly (see Figure 7.3). If not, then you may have a bad board, or it may not be seated all the way in its slot, in which cases the Windows Troubleshooter won't help you; reseat the board, try it in a different slot, and even try it in a different PC if you have one, to narrow down the possibilities.

TIP *Consider swapping network boards if you have another one, to see if the problem is with the computer or the board. It's very unlikely that two boards would be simultaneously defective!*

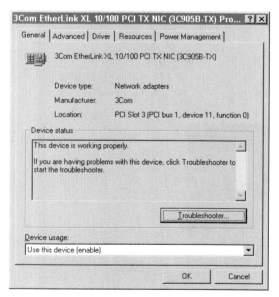

Figure 7.3 *Proof that Windows sees your new network card*

16. If your network adapter comes with a diagnostic test, you should run that at this point as well. The message from your operating system means only that it "sees" the device; it doesn't test the network card's internal functions. You won't be able to perform a full test of the network adapter until it's connected to another computer, but you should be able to perform an "internal" test. Check your card manufacturer's documentation for details. If you have a bad network card, you'll want to know it sooner rather than later.

WARNING *Some PCI boards require a specific version of the PCI bus. For example, I recently ran across a board that required PCI version 2.2, but I was putting the board into a computer that supported only PCI 2.1. The PC could see the card and Windows thought everything was copacetic, but the thing wouldn't work. If a network adapter requires a particular version of PCI, it should say so on the box, the spec sheet, or the Web site. How do you figure out what version of PCI your computer uses? Check the manual if you have it; check the manufacturer's Web site for specs; and, failing that, if you know the chipset on which your PC is based (such as "Intel 440BX"), go visit* `http://developer.intel.com/design/chipsets/linecard.htm`.

17. Repeat steps 1 through 16 for the second desktop PC.

18. Turn on your laptop and let the operating system boot completely, if it's Plug-and-Play compliant.

19. Install the credit-card-sized network adapter into an open PC Card slot (see Figure 7.4). If you're running some flavor of Windows, the operating system should immediately detect the device and tell you if you need to supply a manufacturer's disc.

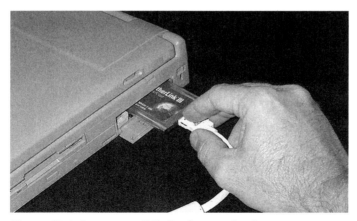

Figure 7.4 *Inserting a PC Card network adapter*

20. Supply a driver diskette or CD as prompted. As with the desktop systems, follow the installation instructions that came with the adapter, especially with regard to whether you should use a Microsoft driver or a manufacturer-supplied driver. You'll probably have to restart your computer once or twice during the process.

21. Check to see whether your operating system sees the new device. (In Windows, you'll see a little icon in the system tray, opposite the Start button, that you can double-click, or you can use the Device Manager method mentioned in step 15.)

22. Run a diagnostic test for the PC Card adapter, if one is available.

23. Configure all three PCs to use the same network protocol (usually this will be TCP/IP). If you have a recent version of Windows, for example, TCP/IP is probably already installed; check the Network Control Panel (Windows 9*x*/ME) or the Network and Dial-Up Connections folder (Windows 2000/XP).

24. Make sure the IP address information is either set automatically for you by the operating system, or manually set so that the subnet mask is the same for all three PCs. You may have to restart your PC after changing the IP address. On Windows PCs, you can check the address in use by running **WINIPCFG** (Windows 9*x* and ME) from the Start ➢ Run dialog box, or **IPCONFIG** (Windows 2000 and XP) from a command window.

TIP *If you don't have a clue about this stuff, you can try starting with 192.168.0.1, 192.168.0.2, and so forth on up to 192.168.0.254; the subnet mask for these addresses is 255.255.255.0. These are addresses that have been set aside expressly for private networks and won't ever duplicate public Internet addresses.*

25. Set all three PCs to use the same workgroup name (this is a peer-to-peer network we're setting up). Again, in Windows, you'd check the Network Control Panel, or the Network Identification tab of the System Control Panel.

26. If you run Windows, make sure each of the three PCs has a unique *computer name* (also called *NetBIOS name*). (In Windows, for example, you'd set this up with the Network Control Panel, or possibly the System Control Panel.) Keep the name to less than 15 characters and don't put any spaces in it.

27. Turn off all the PCs.

28. Unpack your hub or switch (either will work, although I generally prefer switches, which usually move data around a bit more intelligently and quickly) but don't plug it in to an AC power supply just yet. Figure 7.5 shows a typical small switch; Figure 7.6 shows a small hub. You should place the switch or hub as centrally as possible with respect to the three PCs. Generally, with Ethernet and Fast Ethernet, you can't have a cable longer than 100 meters, and if you can use shorter cables, you're wise to do so.

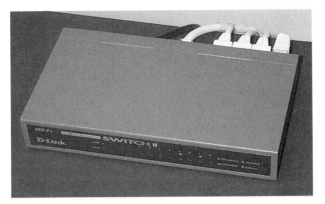

Figure 7.5 *A small network switch*

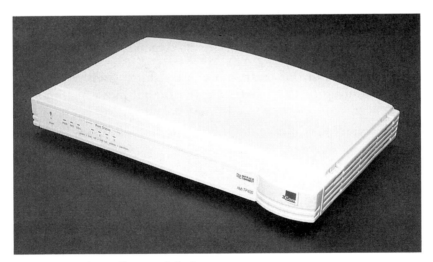

Figure 7.6 *A small network hub*

29. Round up your three Ethernet cables and plug them into available ports on the back of the switch or hub (see Figure 7.7). The cable connectors are like modular phone plugs, but a little wider; they go by the name *RJ-45* (your phone uses RJ-11). If you see a port labeled UPLINK, don't use it before checking your hub's documentation; this is a special port for daisy chaining or "stacking" another hub to create a larger LAN.

TIP *If you plan to run your cables over a false ceiling or through walls, you'll probably need to get Teflon-coated cables for compliance with local fire codes; they're a bit more expensive.*

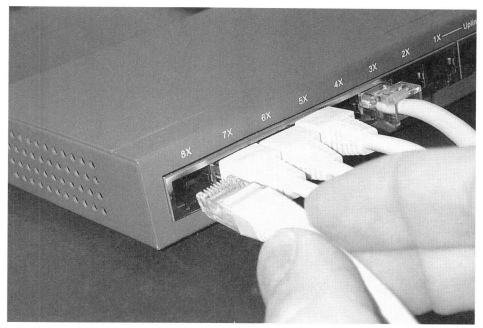

Figure 7.7 *Connecting cables to a switch*

30. Plug the other end of each cable into the network adapters you just installed in the three PCs (see Figure 7.8).

31. Plug in the power for your switch or hub, and turn it on, if it has a switch (most don't nowadays). If it has front-panel lights, make sure they come on the way the device's manual says they should. Usually you'll have one light indicating power, and a bunch of other lights indicating the status of the various network connections; those other lights will probably be dimmed until you turn on the PCs.

32. Turn on the PCs and let them boot normally. As the PCs come online and initialize their new network adapters, you should see additional lights come on at the hub or switch (see Figure 7.9).

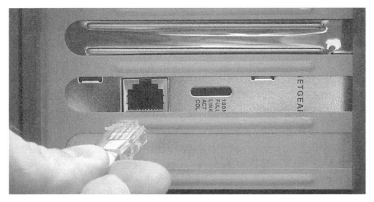

Figure 7.8 *Connecting a cable to a network adapter*

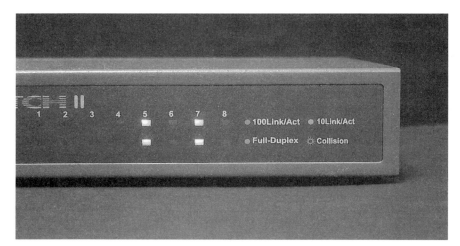

Figure 7.9 *Activity lights mean "live" networked PCs.*

33. See if the PCs can "see" each other, for example, by double-clicking Network Neighborhood (sometimes called "My Network Places") on the Windows desktop and then double-clicking "Computers Near Me." Sometimes you have to give the PCs five minutes or so to find each other. You may also need to restart the switch or hub.

If all has gone well, you're ready to start sharing files, printers, and whatever else you want to share, according to the instructions for your particular operating system. Otherwise, you may have to do some troubleshooting:

• Run your network adapters' diagnostic programs again, now that the network is connected.

- Double-check computer names, workgroup names, and IP addresses.

- Try different ports on your hub or switch; one may be bad.

- Double-check the drivers for your network adapters; contact the manufacturer to see if newer ones are available for download from the Web.

- Try using the **PING** command from a command prompt to see if you've successfully established physical connectivity between PCs (see your operating system documentation for details, but the syntax is basically **PING** followed by the IP address).

- Remember the #1 rule of troubleshooting: *Change only one thing at a time.* Otherwise, you're likely to get hopelessly lost.

If all this fails, find a friend who knows networks and bribe him or her with food, drink, and (in extreme cases) money. For heaven's sake, don't beat your head against a wall! This stuff is easier than it used to be, but it's still complicated, and you're not expected to get everything just right the first time. If you have trouble and you refuse to get help, you will hate your new network instead of love it.

Installing a Wireless Network

The example I'm going to use for installing a wireless network is an 802.11b system from D-Link, which makes good low-cost networking gear, but the general procedure would be very similar with other radio-frequency wireless networks. The photos will show you three different network adapters: a USB device, a PCI adapter, and a PC Card device for a laptop. Instead of a hub, these network adapters will all communicate with a single *Wireless Access Point* (WAP).

EQUIPMENT YOU'LL NEED:

➡ *Three wireless network adapters (one PCI card, one USB adapter, and one PC Card for the laptop)*

➡ *One Wireless Access Point (WAP)*

➡ *A medium Phillips-head screwdriver (for removing the adapter cover plate for PCI adapter installation)*

➡ *A screwdriver appropriate for removing one desktop PC's cover*

➡ *An antistatic wrist strap (optional, but recommended for PCI adapter installation)*

I'll start with the easier network adapter installation and move to the more complex ones. As with installing a wired network, the secret to success is to test as you go. By the way, some of the following steps are condensed versions of similar steps in the previous section, "Installing a Wired Network," so you may want to read that section first to get the hang of things.

1. Turn on your laptop and let the operating system boot completely, if it's Plug-and-Play compliant.

2. Install the drivers for the PC Card wireless adapter, per the manufacturer's instructions. (You shouldn't really have to install drivers first in the classical Plug-and-Play scheme of things, but the reality is that this step is often necessary to avoid problems the first time the PC "sees" the card. Whaddayagonnado.)

3. Install the credit-card-sized network adapter into an open PC Card slot (see Figure 7.10). If you're running some flavor of Windows, the operating system should immediately detect the device and tell you if you need to supply a manufacturer's disc.

4. Supply a driver diskette or CD as prompted. Again, follow the installation instructions that came with the adapter, especially with regard to whether you should use a Microsoft driver or a manufacturer-supplied driver. You'll probably have to restart your computer.

Figure 7.10 *Inserting a PC Card wireless network adapter*

5. Check to see whether your operating system sees the new device; for example, in Windows, look at the system tray.

6. Run a diagnostic test for the PC Card adapter, if one is available. If the device has a power-on LED, check its status to see if the device passed its own power-on self-test.

7. Turn off the laptop.

8. Move to the next PC, where the USB adapter will go. Turn on the PC and let it boot up.

9. Repeat steps 2 through 6 for the USB adapter installation, but instead of sliding a credit-card type device into a laptop slot, connect the USB wireless adapter (see Figure 7.11) to the PC with a standard USB cable.

TIP *Place the USB adapter at least 1m away from any electrical device to minimize the chance of interference. If the device has an antenna, position it per the manufacturer's suggestions (you can move it around later to get the best reception).*

10. Move to the PC where the PCI adapter will go. Make sure it's off and remove the power cord.

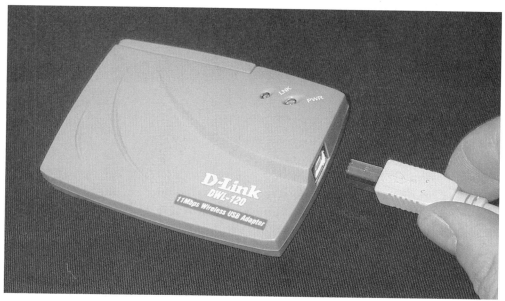

Figure 7.11 *Connecting a USB wireless network adapter*

11. Go through the same basic procedure as described in "Installing a Wired Network," steps 2 through 16, to install the PCI card. Note that this card typically looks quite a bit different from a wired-Ethernet network card; what manufacturers typically do with wireless PCI devices is take a PC Card adapter and put it into a PCI "holder," which fits into the PCI bus (see Figure 7.12). This approach is less expensive for the manufacturer, who basically buys the PCI holder from someone else, and throws it into a box with a notebook PC Card adapter.

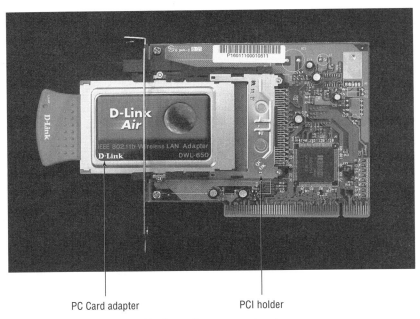

PC Card adapter   PCI holder

Figure 7.12 *A "PCI holder" wireless network adapter*

WARNING *Careful here! PCI holders require more resources (interrupts, and so on) than regular Ethernet cards. When building the wireless network shown in these photos, I discovered that merely removing my old, traditional, wired Ethernet card wasn't enough to free up enough system resources for the PCI holder and its piggybacked PC Card adapter. I had to remove some other devices as well. On a newer PC (the one I used was vintage 1999), you may not bump into this problem, because newer PCs do a better job allocating interrupts on the PCI bus.*

12. Unpack the *Wireless Access Point* (WAP; see Figure 7.13). Now technically, you don't need one of these guys to run an 802.11b network; you can let the computers talk to each other in "ad hoc" mode, which you set using the adapter's configuration utility. However, the access point gives you a lot more range in terms of physical distance. For example, if you can place the WAP roughly in the middle of the PCs you're connecting, the maximum distance of 100m applies to the WAP-to-PC distance, not the PC-to-PC distance. The WAP can also make it a lot easier to connect your network to the Internet, because the WAP typically has a wired-Ethernet port on it that you can hook up directly to a DSL router. And you'll need a WAP to connect your wireless "cell" to a traditional wired network, if one already exists.

13. Plug in the WAP and place it so that it's well within range of the notebook computer, preferably in the same room.

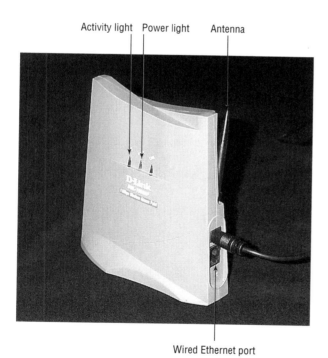

Activity light   Power light   Antenna

Wired Ethernet port

Figure 7.13 *A wireless access point*

14. Run the PC Card adapter's configuration program on the notebook computer. Follow the manufacturer's directions, but it may be as simple as clicking an icon in the taskbar's system tray. Set the PC Card to use "infrastructure" mode (as opposed to "ad hoc" mode) and leave the SSID (Service Set Identity) at its default value. You can think of the SSID as the name of the wireless "cell" to which all three computers will connect; this name must be the same for all computers in the cell.

15. Set your notebook PC's wireless adapter to use an IP address and subnet mask that's compatible with the WAP's default setting. For example, if the WAP manual says it defaults to 192.168.0.1, set your notebook computer's IP address to 192.168.0.2 (and make sure the subnet mask is the same, too, in this example 255.255.255.0). You may have to restart the notebook computer after you make this change. With any luck, your PC Card adapter will show that it has linked to the WAP (see Figure 7.14); if so, skip to step 17.

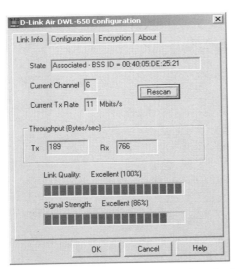

Figure 7.14 *A notebook that's found a WAP*

16. If your PC can't find the WAP automatically, install the WAP configuration program that came in the box onto your notebook PC. Run it, and enter the WAP's hardware address, also called MAC address; it's normally printed on the WAP label somewhere. Once you're connected and running the WAP configuration program, you can change the details as needed: IP address, subnet mask, and SSID.

TIP *Good advice for setting up any network: Leave everything at the factory settings to the extent feasible, get it working, and then change settings later as needed.*

17. Position the WAP roughly in the middle of your three-computer grouping for best reception. Try to minimize the number of intervening walls, ceilings, lead-lined vaults, and so on.

18. Repeat steps 14 and 15 for the other two PCs on your network.

19. See if your PCs can see each other on the network. If not, troubleshoot per the guidelines in the preceding section. If so, you can proceed to share directories and printers (for example, in Windows, by right-clicking them and choosing "Sharing").

20. Play around with the positioning of the WAP and the USB adapter to maximize signal strength. You may want to affix the WAP to the wall; most manufacturers supply screws and anchors for this purpose.

Upgrading from two or more standalone PCs to a networked environment is still a lot more complicated than it should be, but this chapter has introduced you to the necessary steps. Once you do have a network in place, you won't have to do the "sneakernet" thing ever again!

Chapter 8

Power

f you've ever experienced a power failure while working on your PC, smelled that distressingly distinctive electrical smoke that drifts up slowly from a fried PC, put up with intermittent and seemingly random crashes, or just run out of juice on a plane while frantically trying to save that critical file on your notebook computer, then you can appreciate the importance of power to PC operation. This chapter shows you how to upgrade or replace a PC's power supply; add a battery backup unit to a desktop PC; and upgrade a notebook computer's portable battery pack.

This one's certainly not the sexiest chapter in the book, and I'm willing to bet it's not the one you turned to first; but it may be the most important, so I'm glad you found your way here eventually.

Intro to Power

When we discuss PC power, we're really talking about two things: a power source and a power supply. The *power source* is typically either an AC outlet, either with or without a battery backup unit as helpful intermediary, or a notebook computer's portable battery. The *power supply* is the silver metal box inside the PC that takes AC power in and converts it to regulated DC volts that go to the motherboard and to other internal components.

Starting at the source, it's a good idea to make sure any AC outlet into which you plan to connect a computer has been wired correctly by the installing electrician. You can do this simply and cheaply by buying an outlet tester for five bucks from Radio Shack. This little gizmo (see Figure 8.1) plugs into an AC outlet and two or three LED lights report on any wiring problems if they exist. Call an electrician, if you're not one, to fix the problems.

You can improve the power source that your PC sees by installing a battery backup unit with surge suppression (which blocks voltage spikes from getting to your PC) and line filtering (which smoothes out the power curve). I always recommend that you get one that not only provides power to your PC during a brownout, but also includes the suppression and filtering characteristics (cheaper ones don't).

The battery feature of a battery backup unit is what lets you run a desktop PC for a few minutes when the AC power goes away. A battery stores DC power, however, so these units actually contain an AC-to-DC converter for charging the battery, and a DC-to-AC converter for delivering AC power from the DC battery.

Battery backup units are heavy and moderately expensive, in the ballpark of $100 to $200 these days depending on the PC you have and how you've tricked it out with add-in boards, memory, and other options. (Pick one of these units up and you gain an understanding of why electric cars haven't ever become popular, despite their near-zero pollution output.) They typically last three to four years, although newer units let you replace the battery component separately for a small degree of cost savings.

Figure 8.1 *An AC outlet tester*

The power supply is an internal component of your PC whose job is to accept the alternating current provided by an AC outlet, or battery backup unit, and turn it into direct current suitable for your motherboard, hard drives, fans, and so forth. (Typically, PC components need DC voltages of 3.3V, 5V, and 12V.) The transformation of AC to DC involves a fair amount of heat, so power supplies usually come with a built-in fan to dissipate that heat safely and (sometimes) quietly. The power supply is usually a silver box with a yellow label on it, and it's easy to find: It's right where the power cord plugs in to the computer!

Although power supplies in notebook computers are highly reliable and almost always appropriately sized for the computer, power supplies in desktop computers—particularly home computers—are generally cheap, too small, and likely to fail if you start hot-rodding your PC. So this chapter spends some time showing how to upgrade or replace a power supply in a desktop computer. (You probably won't ever have to perform this chore in a notebook.) In fact, that's where I'll begin.

Upgrading or Replacing a Power Supply

Upgrading a power supply can provide more reliable, safer, and quieter operation. The procedures are just about the same whether you're upgrading a working power supply or replacing a dead one. This section discusses everything from minor surgery (adding a Y-adapter) to a complete transplant (replacing the entire power supply).

Adding a Connector

If your only problem with your power supply is that you've run out of connectors to plug new devices into, and if your power supply is hale and hearty (see "How Many Watts?" later in this chapter), a short trip to the local radio and electronics store is all you need. Pick yourself up a Y-adapter (as shown in Figures 8.2 and 8.3) that turns a single power supply connector into two connectors. The installation is so simple that I'm not even going to break it out into a numbered list of steps: Just plug the Y-adapter into an available socket, and you're done.

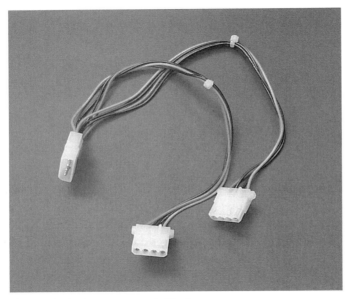

Figure 8.2 *A power supply Y-adapter*

WARNING *Caveat: If you install a Y-adapter and your power supply is already of the 90-pound-weakling variety, you are likely to overheat it and kill it.*

Replacing the Entire Power Supply

Most of the time, when your power supply dies, you just replace it as a whole. (For those like me who watch pennies, and if you suspect that the power supply's fan has died but the power supply itself is still OK, see the section later in this chapter titled "Replacing the Fan Only.")

Figure 8.3 *A Y-adapter in place*

Many of you may want to upgrade the power supply so that it can properly support all the internal devices your PC now has, in which case the procedures in this section will apply also. In either situation, you'll need to take a few preliminary steps, as follows:

- Determine how big a power supply you really need.
- Decide on a single-speed fan or variable-speed fan.
- Decide between a thermally protected unit and an unprotected unit.
- Note the power supply's dimensions.
- Make a few other quality decisions.
- Find a source for your new power supply.

The following sections look at each topic in turn.

How Many Watts?

As I mentioned in this chapter's introduction, many PC manufacturers these days cut corners on the size of the power supply. Systems that should really have a 300-watt power supply come with a 100- or 150-watt unit. That anemic power supply may be fine for supplying power to the PC as it shipped from the factory, but install extra memory, an internal CD-RW drive, internal modem, video card, and network adapter, and a 100-watt power supply is likely to create all sorts of hard-to-diagnose problems—or simply overheat and die.

So how many watts do you really need? My stock answer is to get the most wattage you can in a given size, or *form factor* as the techies like to call "size." A beefier power supply runs cooler (and therefore safer), is better for your PC, is less likely to die under stress, and is more likely to deliver constant, solid volts.

Is this approach wasteful of electricity? Not much. The difference in energy use will amount to just a few cents a month on your electric bill. The reason is that power supplies supply only the amount of power that your system is demanding. A 350-watt power supply doesn't supply 350 watts unless the devices in your PC need that much power.

If you want to get scientific about it, though, you certainly can. I've compiled Table 8.1 from several different sources. If your PC came with detailed power specs, that information will be more accurate for your system than these generic "ballpark" estimates.

Table 8.1 *PC Component Power Requirements*

COMPONENT	POWER DRAW (IN WATTS)
Motherboard without CPU or memory	25
466MHz Celeron CPU	21
600MHz Athlon CPU	46
800MHz Pentium III	24
Main memory, per 64MB	5
IDE hard drive	10
SCSI hard drive	25
CD-ROM drive	20
Network card	5
Faxmodem card	10
Miscellaneous ISA or PCI card	5
Fast video card	25
SCSI controller	25

Here's the procedure for using Table 8.1:

1. Add up the numbers in the Power Draw column for every device in your system. (If you have ISA or PCI cards not listed, count them as 5 watts each, or consult the documentation for the cards to get a more accurate number.)

2. Multiply the result by 2. You want the power supply to have plenty of headroom, and besides, you may add hardware later on.

3. Round up to the nearest standard power supply size. Typical numbers are 100, 200, 300, 350, 400, and 425 watts.

Single Speed versus Variable Speed

If you're like me, you like your computer to be quiet. In fact, if it weren't for the fact that most fanless PC designs tend to melt down (like the old DEC VAXmate), I'd get a PC with no fan at all. (The Macintosh people love to point to the G4 cube, but it's a little pricey and not too easy to work on. Having said that, I love its silent operation and wish it were a PC!)

For this reason, I'm a big fan of power supplies with variable-speed fans. One of the computers I use regularly is an HP Kayak workstation, which has two variable-speed fans. As things heat up, the fans go faster, so you don't have to endure the extra noise unless the computer needs the fan speed.

Variable-speed fans are usually an extra-cost option. But what price do you put on your nerves?

Heat-Sensing versus Non-Heat-Sensing

This one's easy. Don't ever get a power supply that doesn't have a thermal cutoff switch. If you do, you may save a dollar or two, but the power supply won't be able to turn itself off if the fan fails and the temperature soars to dangerous levels. The result is a much higher risk of damage to your PC and of starting a fire.

Dimensions

The typical sizes you'll hear about are AT, ATX, and custom ATX:

- *AT power supplies* typically have one built-in fan, a power cord socket, and an auxiliary power socket (e.g. for a monitor). These guys connect to the motherboard via two 6-pin connectors in line.

- *ATX power supplies* typically have one built-in fan and a power cord socket, but no auxiliary power socket. ATX supplies connect to the motherboard with a single 20-pin connector.

- *Custom power supplies* vary in one respect or another from the AT and ATX standards.

If you're buying your replacement power supply from a Web site, as I do a lot these days, don't just rely on categorizing your power supply as AT or ATX or Dell in order to get a good size match. Get out the ruler and take some measurements. Today's PC manufacturers cram a lot of components into an ever-smaller space, and if your replacement power supply is even an eighth of an inch too big in any dimension, it may not fit properly into the system unit.

The measurements you should take are:

- Length

- Width

- Height

- Distance between mounting screws

- Length of pigtails (at least measure the longest one)

That last one merits a quick comment. The *pigtails* are the wires coming off the power supply leading to the white plastic connectors into which you plug hard drives, CD-ROM drives, and so forth. If you buy a replacement power supply that has shorter pigtails than the old one, you may not have enough length to make the necessary connections. Yes, you can run to the local electronics store and buy some extension cables, but it's probably easier just to check out this specification ahead of time. All the specs should be on the power supply manufacturer's Web site.

Other Quality Issues

Consider the following characteristics, too, when shopping power supplies:

- *EMI/RFI.* That's *electromagnetic interference* and *radio frequency interference*. The quieter your power supply is in this regard, the less likely it is to interfere with your motherboard and add-in circuit boards.

- *Protection circuits.* In addition to thermal protection, you want short-circuit protection and over-current protection.

- *Warranty.* If it's less than five years, *caveat emptor*. The quality may not be where you'd like to see it.

Finding a Replacement Power Supply

So now that you know just what kind of power supply you need, how do you get one? If you have a highly standard, mainstream PC, you can probably just take your old power supply into a computer store (preferably one that has a repair shop) and ask the store techie to match it for you.

On the other hand, power supplies are a low-margin item, so the retail stores typically stock very few models. Also, I've been less than delighted with the quality (and price) of some of the power supplies I've bought in computer stores.

Another option is your PC manufacturer. However, this option may not be an ideal solution either. When I called Hewlett-Packard for a power supply for a little Pavilion home PC I'd recently purchased, the company advised me that I couldn't get just the power supply, I had to take a whole new PC as my only warranty repair option. (This brain-dead tech support policy is becoming common among vendors that market lines of home PCs—one reason I prefer buying "small business" PCs even for home.)

I didn't want the hassle of moving all my circuit boards, disks, and memory over to a new PC, so I said forget about the warranty, I'll *buy* the power supply. (I'm a big spender when the amount is under $50.) Identifying the right part took an hour and lots of phone calls, only to find it was back ordered three months. Adding insult to injury, the replacement unit was the same wimpy 100-watt rating as the original, and I couldn't order a bigger one.

I went out onto the Web and found a unit that met my needs in about ten minutes. It was more powerful, cheaper, and quieter than the original unit, and it arrived the next day. I now buy almost all power supplies over the Internet. If you can find the right model at PC Power & Cooling, that's a good company with an excellent Web site (`www.pcpowercooling.com`). If not, visit your favorite search engine and key in the model of your PC and the phrase "power supply."

Rolling Up Your Sleeves and Getting to Work

Okay, you've identified the power supply specs you need, you've obtained a suitable replacement unit, and you're ready to perform surgery. To give you a word of encouragement: Replacing a power supply is a whole lot easier than replacing a CPU or installing a new hard drive. So let's go.

EQUIPMENT YOU'LL NEED:

➡ *Antistatic wrist strap (optional, but recommended)*

➡ *An appropriate screwdriver to remove your PC's cover*

➡ *An appropriate screwdriver to remove the power supply (usually a Phillips head; may be the same as what you need to open the cover, may not be)*

➡ *A replacement power supply*

➡ *Strong fingers*

Here are the typical steps, although the precise details (such as how many screws the PC uses to secure the power supply) may vary from one PC to another.

1. Disconnect the keyboard, mouse, display, power, and any other connectors.

2. Open the PC cover. The power supply is a silver box with a yellow label on it (see Figure 8.4). (Of course, you have the replacement unit in your hand, so you know what it looks like!)

TIP *As always when you're about to delve inside a PC's case, remove all jewelry from your hands, wrists, and neck.*

Figure 8.4 *A typical power supply*

3. Disconnect the power connector from the motherboard (see Figure 8.5). Typically you'll see a big group of colored wires running from the power supply to a motherboard connector. The connector will probably have a single tab along one of the long sides that you'll have to depress in order to pull the connector loose from the motherboard. Be gentle but firm.

4. Remove the power connectors from all other devices: the diskette drive, any internal hard drives, CD-ROM drives, and Zip drives (see Figure 8.6). Again you'll see the bundles of colored wires leading from the power supply to the devices. Take your time; power connectors are well known for being tight and difficult to remove. (Here's where strong fingers help.) I have good luck working the connectors from side to side while pulling out. However, if you need to, you can prize the connectors loose with a flat-blade screwdriver.

TIP *You may see a special small connector at the motherboard that runs to the power supply and that is labeled "FAN-A" or something similar. Disconnect this connector by pulling it straight out from the motherboard.*

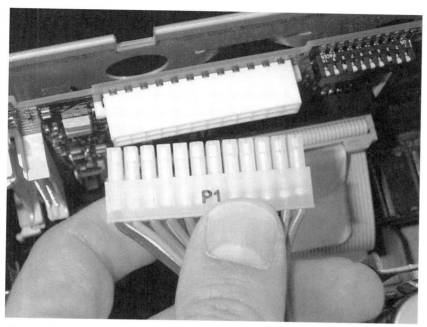

Figure 8.5 *Removing the motherboard connector*

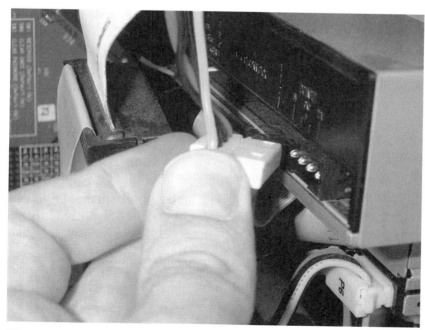

Figure 8.6 *Removing device power connectors*

5. Remove the screws holding the power supply into place (see Figure 8.7) and set them aside. Usually there are four of these, right around the place where the power cord connects to the computer. Some PC designers thoughtfully replaced screws with knurled knobs.

Figure 8.7 *Removing power supply screws*

6. If a grille covers the power supply fan, and the new power supply doesn't come with a new grille, remove the grille and set it aside (see Figure 8.8).

7. If you removed a grille in step 6, install it onto your new power supply.

8. Mount your new power supply on the PC's chassis and secure it with the screws you set aside in step 5.

9. Connect power to the PC's internal devices. This step is the opposite of step 4. A smaller connector (called a Berg connector) goes to the internal diskette drive; the rest of the connectors (called Molex) are the same and connect to all internal storage devices. Reconnect the "FAN-A" connector if present.

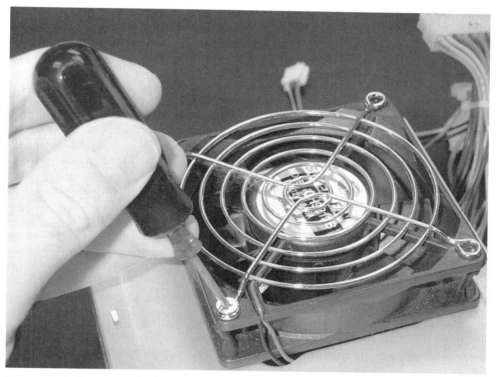

Figure 8.8 *Removing the fan grille*

10. Connect the biggest power connector to the motherboard. This step is the opposite of step 3. Push until the connector is firmly seated; on most PCs you'll hear a click as the tab locks into place.

11. Put the cover back on the PC.

12. Reconnect the keyboard, mouse, display, and any other peripheral cables.

13. Power up the PC and run it for several hours, if possible, to make sure heat buildup isn't a problem with the new unit. Listen for the fan to make sure it's working; if it's not, shut the PC off immediately and either replace the fan or get a different power supply. Make sure the PC can access all internal devices: disk drives, CD-ROM drive, diskette drive, and so on.

Replacing the Fan Only

Nearly all internal power supplies have fans. Often, the power supply fails because its fan fails. When the fan dies, the temperature inside the power supply builds up to a dangerous level, at which point a temperature cutoff switch shuts it down. (If you have a cheapo power supply with no temperature cutoff switch, then the temperature inside the power supply builds up to the point at which something melts.) The symptoms of this problem are a PC that works for awhile, then suddenly shuts down, refusing to power on again until an hour or two later. (You may smell the delicate aroma of vaporizing wire insulation.) When the power supply has cooled sufficiently to reset the temperature switch, you can resume use of the PC—until it heats up again.

In this situation, as long as your PC hasn't experienced too many of these temperature cycles (and "too many" may be as few as two or three), you may be able to restore your PC to health by just replacing the fan component of the power supply. Fans are cheap—you should be able to pick one up for a few dollars at the local computer repair shop. In fact, you can probably get a better (that is, cooler and quieter) fan than the one that came installed with your PC. The only catch is that you may have to do a bit of wire splicing, as the following procedure demonstrates.

TIP *Normally, you're well advised to just replace the whole power supply, fan included. It's not much more money, it's less time, and it's less risk. However, if you find yourself (as I have a few times) in a position where you can't get a replacement power supply quickly, but you can get a replacement fan, here's how to proceed if the computer absolutely positively has to get fixed NOW.*

EQUIPMENT YOU'LL NEED:

→ *An appropriate screwdriver to remove your PC's cover*

→ *An appropriate screwdriver to remove the power supply (usually a Phillips head; may be the same as what you need to open the cover, may not be)*

→ *An appropriate screwdriver to remove the fan (also usually a Phillips head)*

→ *A replacement fan*

→ *Rubber fan mounting plugs (should come with new fan, if needed)*

→ *Wire cutters (may not be necessary)*

→ *A wire stripper (may not be necessary)*

→ *Two small wire nuts (may not be necessary)*

→ *Electrical tape (may not be necessary)*

Don't attempt this job unless you solemnly promise to yourself and your loved ones not to touch anything inside the power supply other than the fan wires. Power supplies contain *capacitors*, whose job it is to store voltages even though the power is off. Short out one of these components with your finger, and you could get a nasty jolt. When you have your equipment together, follow these steps:

1. Follow steps 1 through 6 in the "Replacing the Entire Power Supply" section.

2. If the fan is an external unit, remove the screws holding the fan in place. If rubber mounting plugs hold the fan in place for vibration isolation, snip these guys loose with the wire cutters.

3. Remove any screws holding the plate where the fan connects to the body of the power supply, as shown in Figure 8.9. (You may also have to prise some tabs apart slightly on the plate with a flat-blade screwdriver.)

Figure 8.9 *Removing screws securing the fan plate*

4. Pull off the plate, being careful not to strain the two small wires connecting the fan to the internal circuit board (see Figure 8.10).

5. Look to see if those two small wires connect via a removable connector. If so, you're in luck. Pull the connector away from the circuit board and skip steps 6 through 8.

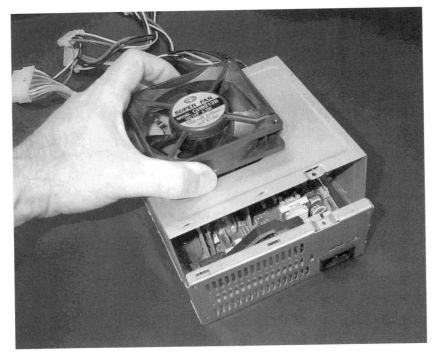

Figure 8.10 *Removing the fan plate*

6. If the two small wires don't use a removable connector, snip 'em with the wire cutters and throw away the old fan.

7. Strip a quarter inch or so of insulation off the wires you just snipped. (The wires coming off the new fan are probably already stripped at the ends.)

8. Matching the red wire to the red wire and black to black, twist the wires together inside a small wire nut (see Figure 8.11). (Yes, you could solder them, but wire nuts work just fine.)

9. Mount the fan to the metal plate, either with the new rubber plugs or with the four screws you removed in step 2.

10. Snap the plate back onto the power supply housing.

11. Reinstall any screws you removed in step 3.

12. Button up the PC and test the system by following steps 7 through 13 in the "Replacing the Entire Power Supply" section.

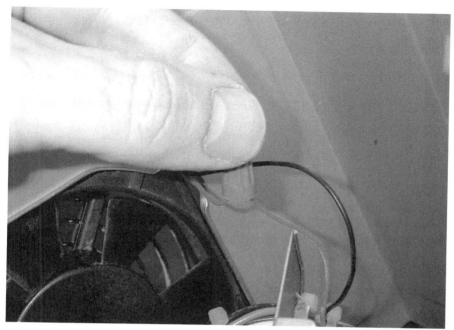

Figure 8.11 *Applying wire nuts to fan wires*

Adding a Battery Backup Unit

I live in Golden, Colorado, where heavy snow, lightning strikes, or suicidal squirrels can interrupt the power. So I've become a religious user of battery backup units. They tide me over for the five or ten minutes I need to save my work and shut down my system properly after a power outage.

Many PC users don't realize the other services that some battery backup units provide. In areas where the line voltage isn't rock solid, the backup unit can provide line voltage stabilization and filtering to smooth out the power curve. Not all backup units provide this function, and it isn't as necessary as it used to be, but it's a plus if it doesn't cost you too much extra.

Battery backup units also typically provide surge protection, which clamps down on voltage spikes that could harm your equipment. Some manufacturers even offer insurance if your PC is damaged by a voltage spike while connected to the manufacturer's backup unit. I've never tried to collect on such insurance, so I don't know how much red tape is involved, but the fact that it's even offered inspires a certain amount of confidence.

This section helps you decide what kind of battery backup unit to get; how big it should be (in rated capacity, not physical dimensions!), and how to install it.

What Kind?

Traditionally, battery backup units fall into two categories: the *uninterruptible power supply*, or *UPS*, and the *standby power supply*, or *SPS*. The UPS always provides power from its battery; when connected to a live AC outlet, the UPS continually recharges the battery. By contrast, the SPS normally provides power from the wall outlet, and switches to the battery if it detects a power cut.

> **TIP** *Whether you use an SPS or UPS is not as much of a concern as it used to be. Conventional wisdom is that the UPS is better because no switchover time is involved, but most modern SPS devices switch over so fast from line to battery power that they'll work just fine (and often at less cost).*

I do suggest that you get a battery backup unit that advertises surge suppression and line filtering. These options don't cost much more, and they can provide valuable protection to your PC and its components.

How Big?

Calculating the right power rating for your battery backup unit is both more complex and more necessary than calculating the right power rating for an internal power supply. With the internal unit, you don't pay much more for higher ratings, so I advise you to get the most power you can get in the given form factor (size). However, with battery backups, you pay significant amounts for higher rated hardware, so you should probably go through the simple math I'm about to describe.

The first step is to figure the rated power draw of your existing system. Usually, you'll connect just the system unit and monitor to the battery backup unit; printers typically draw a lot of power, and you can always resume a print job after you regain AC power. However, make sure you include the monitor in your calculation! It doesn't do you much good if your PC is up and running but you can't interact with it. Today's popular 17-inch monitors use more power than their 15-inch predecessors.

To get the power draw figures, look at the electrical specifications on your PC's or monitor's exterior cover. (These specs usually appear near the power cord connection.) You'll see a figure for either watts or amps. If the rating is in watts, you don't have to do any math. If it's in amps, multiply the amps value by the voltage (for example, 110 in the US) to get watts. (Actually, amps times volts gives you a value called *VA* or *volt-amps*, which isn't exactly the same as watts but is close enough for our purposes here.)

Have you added memory or other devices to your PC since you bought it? If so, the power draw estimate on the PC's cover probably isn't accurate anymore. Flip back to Table 8.1 and add the watt values of any added devices to the watt value for your PC. Finally, add the watt value for your monitor to get a grand total. Multiply that by 1.2 to give yourself a bit of headroom in case you add more devices later on.

The wattage or VA requirement by itself isn't all you need to know. You must also consider how long you need your battery backup unit to provide power. If you think you can save your work and perform an orderly shutdown within five minutes, you can save some money compared to buying a battery backup that will give you 20 minutes. The Electric Power Research Institute (EPRI) in the United States advises that 80 percent of all brownouts in North America last less than five minutes, so battery backup units that offer 15- or 30-minute protection may be overkill; you be the judge.

Also, be aware that most backup devices can supply higher-than-rated wattages for shorter periods of time, up to a point. A unit rated at 450 watts for five minutes might be able to supply 500 watts for three minutes, for example.

Armed with the total wattage figure (padded by at least 20 percent as I suggested above), and the amount of time you think you need to run your PC in a power outage, you're ready to visit the battery manufacturer's Web site, punch those numbers into the model selector, and see what the manufacturer recommends for you. You can also call the manufacturer by phone, but that's a slower process.

Installing the Battery Backup Unit

This is one of the easier jobs you'll ever perform on your PC! No tools required, and no surgery necessary.

1. Charge the battery backup unit. Lots of folks omit this step, but think about it for a minute. If you don't charge the battery, and if it comes from the store in a relatively uncharged condition (as it probably will), then you don't really have any protection. I like to plug the unit in, turn it on, and let it charge up overnight before connecting it to a computer.

2. Turn off your PC and disconnect its power cord from the AC outlet.

3. Plug your PC's power cord into the battery backup unit.

4. Repeat steps 2 and 3 for your monitor.

5. Power up the PC and monitor.

6. Check to make sure everything's working fine. (If you followed step 1, it probably is.) However, don't load any data files; you don't want to create a problem for yourself in step 7.

7. Test the battery backup unit (see Figure 8.12). The simplest way to do this is to just unplug it from the wall outlet, simulating a power cut. Your PC and monitor should continue working fine. The battery backup unit will probably beep at you with an annoyingly loud tone to signal that it has detected a power loss.

Figure 8.12 *Testing a battery backup unit*

8. (Optional) If you run an operating system that the battery backup unit vendor supports, you can connect a serial cable (which also goes by the name "heart beat" cable and which you must usually buy separately) between the unit and a COM port on your PC. Figure 8.13 shows such a serial port connection. The purpose of this is to provide a communication channel whereby the battery backup unit can notify your operating system of a power cut. The operating system can then warn you of the situation (as if you didn't notice that all the lights went out) and, if you don't intervene manually to shut down the computer, perform a shutdown routine to protect your data. Follow the battery backup unit's documentation to install any necessary software onto your PC and to test the serial link; the details vary depending on the operating system you're running.

Serial
link

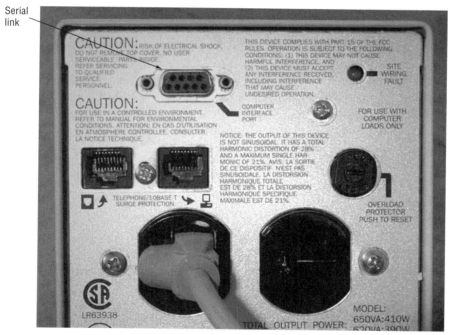

Figure 8.13 *A battery backup serial link*

9. Send in that warranty card. This step may be required for you to cash in on the manufacturer's equipment protection guarantee, should your PC ever sustain power-related damage when connected to the backup unit.

Notebook Power Issues

Notebook computers are a bit of a different animal than desktops when it comes to power issues. First of all, the power source may be AC wall power, but it may also be battery power, meaning that the need for battery backup goes away—the battery backup's already there. Second, given that notebook computers use a lot less power than desktop units, internal power supply failures are less likely on notebooks. I've had over a dozen notebook PCs over the past 15 years, and I've never seen an internal power supply go bad.

The notebook computer power issues that do deserve a few moments of your time are extra batteries, portable battery chargers, and international voltage conversion adapters.

Care and Feeding of Extra Batteries

The best notebook upgrade, next to more RAM and a good carrying case, is an extra battery, and I'll give you two reasons. First, you need one if you ever take long trips. I do a fair amount of work in the New York area, and the 5-hour flight from New York to Denver is a lot to ask of a single battery. Second, notebook batteries often die in a catastrophic and highly inconvenient way when they reach the end of their useful life. It's not at all unusual to have a battery fail so suddenly that your notebook PC gives you the low-power warning about three seconds before the power goes away completely! If that happens, your spare will come in very handy.

You'll normally buy an extra battery through your notebook PC's manufacturer or an authorized reseller. In many cases, you don't have much choice, because the size and shape of notebook PC batteries varies all over the map. If you can't find what you need, try Laptop Express in Denver, Colorado, at 303.312.1922 and www.laptopexpress.com.

If you have an extra battery, here are a few tips:

- Keep it in the proverbial cool, dry place when not in use. Batteries don't like moisture.

- Rotate it with your main battery. Most batteries work better if you run them nearly all the way down from time to time, rather than keeping them fully charged their entire life. Rotating batteries is also a good way to make sure both are still working!

- Keep the warranty info. Some batteries fail very young in life, and you don't want to pay for the manufacturer's defect.

TIP *If you know you won't need the battery, as for example if you're only going to be using your notebook in a hotel room, and if you're anxious to cut back the weight of your carry-on bag, you can probably remove the battery from the notebook and leave it at home. It's a main contributor to your computer's weight. Some notebooks come with a dummy panel that you should install in place of the battery when you do this. The only problem with this approach is that you don't have any protection from power glitches while working.*

On-the-Go Chargers

Your notebook computer came with a power adapter that charges the battery, but you may want to add a charger that will work from another source, such as a vehicle cigarette lighter. These are generally fine in my experience, but don't expect your car's electrical system to charge your notebook's battery while the notebook is powered on.

Sometimes people are tempted to buy quick-charge devices that claim to fully charge your notebook battery in minutes, rather than hours. Such devices are likely to damage your battery and reduce its working lifetime. My recommendation is to stay away from these quick chargers and use the money to buy an extra battery instead.

Voltage Conversion Kits

Nowadays, most notebook AC adapters are capable of handling either North American 110VAC power or European 220VAC power. If yours falls into this category (and the label on the adapter will tell you—see Figure 8.14), then the only thing you need to buy if you're traveling overseas is a physical plug adapter.

Actually, if you're traveling to Europe, you should get a plug adapter *kit* containing several adapters, as shown in Figure 8.15, because different places in Europe use different physical plugs. Europeans traveling to North America have an easier time of it: One adapter fits all plugs.

If your AC adapter is not compatible with the voltage of wall power in the country you're visiting, then you can go one of two directions: Buy a separate AC adapter from your notebook manufacturer, or buy a generic power transformer that will convert from one AC standard to another. I generally recommend the first option, even though it's likely to cost you more dollars. I've bought a few of those generic power transformers, and two of them failed after only a few hours' use. When you buy a power supply from your notebook manufacturer, you're likely to get a higher quality unit. And if you're using your notebook on business, the last thing you want is to have power problems 7000 miles away from your friendly computer store.

Figure 8.14 *A notebook AC adapter label*

Figure 8.15 *Power plug adapters*

Chapter 9

Of Mice and Multimedia

Nobody doesn't like multimedia. Graphics, sound, video—these are all big fun, and a big part of why home computing is well on its way to replacing baseball as the American national pastime. (There's the designated hitter rule, too, of course.) How does one take advantage of all the cool multimedia software that's available? One must add cool hardware, and this chapter shows one a few ways to do just that.

Mice, keyboards, and their relatives may not seem nearly as sexy as multimedia gizmos like webcams and video grabbers. However, when you pay them a wee bit of attention, they're just liable to take off their glasses, let down their hair, and make you wonder what you've been over-looking all this time. You'll also find that upgrading your input devices (as with a graphics tablet, for example) opens up your PC's multimedia possibilities, so that's where this chapter will begin.

Intro to Input Devices

Before you think about delving into games or other multimedia pursuits, you may want to upgrade your input devices so that they're as fast, accurate, and comfortable as they can be. For example, mouse quality may not matter a huge amount if you use the PC primarily to send and receive e-mail, but it's a big factor if you intend on playing fast-action multimedia games. Although at last count there were thirty zillion PC input devices on the market, here I'll focus on mice, trackballs, joysticks, and keyboards.

Mice, Trackballs, and Joysticks

Mice have come a long way since Doug Englebart built his now-famous wooden contraption at Stanford Research Institute back in 1964. However, the mouse you get with a typical home or small office PC is usually an "el cheapo" model that neither works nor feels as good as it could. Given the amount of time you spend using the mouse, it's a prime candidate for a hardware upgrade. To make the best choice, you should know a bit about these high-tech rodents.

First off, mice can be *corded* or *cordless*. You're probably already familiar with corded mice, or you probably wouldn't be reading this book. Cordless mice generally have batteries inside the mouse enclosure and transmit a radio signal to a receiver that connects to your PC's mouse or USB port. Cordless mice are becoming more popular as manufacturers have improved signal range and battery life, although the *sampling rate*—how often the mouse signals its position—is usually less than the best corded USB mice. (Mice that connect to your PC's PS/2 style mouse port typically use a sample rate of 40 to 60Hz, or samples per second; USB mice typically boost that to 125Hz for smoother line drawing and better gaming. You can check your mouse's sample rate with the MouseRate utility, which you can get free from various Internet locations, and if you have a PS/2 style mouse you can boost the rate with the PS2RatePlus utility, also a Web freebie.)

If you categorize mice by their inner workings, you see three types: mechanical, opto-mechanical, and optical.

- *Mechanical* mice use a rolling ball to move two plastic rods, one indicating horizontal movement and the other indicating vertical movement. These mice are rare nowadays but they have the virtue of working on practically any surface. Many people don't realize that you must clean them periodically, as dust builds up on the rods (see Figure 9.1) and the rubber ball gets dusty, too.

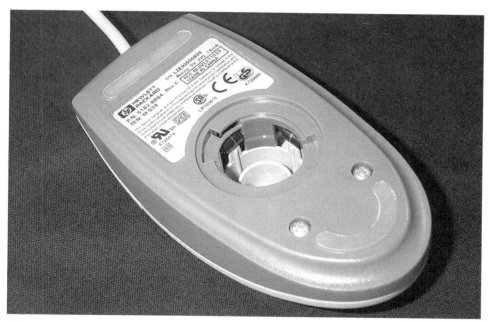

Figure 9.1 *Dust buildup in a mechanical mouse*

- Most modern mice are *opto-mechanical*: A rolling ball moves slotted wheels, and photo-cells watch the direction and speed of those wheels. You have to clean the rolling ball periodically, and blow out dust.

- Purely *optical* mice generally use a camera pointing at the mouse pad (or other surface) to detect motion and direction, and they use a light to illuminate the surface. These don't need much cleaning; an occasional wipe around the light and lens will do.

Yet another way to evaluate mice is by their *resolution*, usually given in dots per inch (dpi). This measurement indicates how many pulses the mouse sends when you move it one inch. Higher resolutions mean you can make smaller mouse movements to move the cursor the same distance on the screen. Beyond 600 or 800dpi, the benefit of additional resolution is debatable for most users.

Mice for PCs generally have two buttons and some have more, whose action you can program with the mouse setup utility. Many mice also have a thumbwheel that sits between the two main buttons and lets you scroll up or down without using a program's scroll bars.

Some folks prefer *trackballs* (see Figure 9.2) to traditional mice. With a trackball device, you move a ball with your thumb or finger instead of moving the mouse over a pad. You can think of a trackball as an upside-down mouse. Personally, I've never been able to adjust to trackballs, but you may want to give one a try, especially if a traditional mouse is uncomfortable to you for some reason, or if you don't have enough room on your desk for a mouse pad.

Figure 9.2 *A typical trackball input device*

Finally, you may want to look at a *joystick* device, especially if you're a game player. Joysticks send X-position, Y-position, and firing button signals to your PC. Early joysticks were analog and were known for occupying a lot of CPU time; newer models are digital, with their own microprocessors, and they bother the PC's CPU much less often. These devices have become pretty sophisticated, and so-called *force-feedback* joysticks even provide tactile resistance at the direction of the game software.

Joysticks typically connect to their own special 15-pin female *game port* on the back of the PC or sound card (see Figure 9.3), a port that you can also use to connect a MIDI (Musical Instrument Digital Interface) device like a synthesizer. I'll have more to say about MIDI devices later in the chapter. You can generally connect either two two-button joysticks or one four-button joystick to a standard PC game port, but check the spec sheet before you buy. Many joysticks have more than four buttons, and the additional ones are usually programmable.

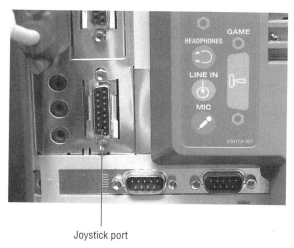

Joystick port

Figure 9.3 *A joystick port*

TIP *Note that force-feedback joysticks tend to use the MIDI-out line to send data to the joystick, so you won't be able to use the joystick and a MIDI musical instrument at the same time. You can't play the electronic tuba while flying a virtual plane anyway, so this should be no great loss.*

Keyboards

Ever write with one of those fancy $150 Mont Blanc rollerball pens? They glide over the page so smoothly that the two-dollar disposable rollerballs you'd been perfectly happy with all your life now seem scratchy, flimsy, and just plain crude. Using a great keyboard is a lot like using one of those fine pens; it's a revelation. (I firmly believe it makes you write better, too.)

I have yet to find the perfect keyboard, which is a matter of taste anyway; but I can tell you about two keyboard characteristics that will probably make you want to throw the flimsy stock one you're probably using right now into the "delete" can along with those scratchy pens: *switch type* and *key layout*.

Switch Type

Just about every keyboard made today uses a membrane mechanism in which the key presses down on a rubber membrane having a metal contact on its lower surface. The pressing key forces this contact down onto another contact, closing a switch and sending a signal to the computer. Some very good keyboards use membrane technology, especially on fine laptop computers such as those made by Toshiba. But most desktop PC keyboards don't execute the membrane technology very pleasingly. The keys feel mushy, indeterminate, and wobbly.

A fine candidate for a keyboard upgrade is the original AT-style 101-key keyboard (see Figure 9.4), originally developed by IBM. This device uses a "buckling spring" that gives you a satisfying, unambiguous click when you type a key. The 101-key classic is practically indestructible and many professional writers think it's the best keyboard you can buy, although some people feel it is a bit noisy. You can still get it, and for less than half the cost of that Mont Blanc pen, from `www.pckeyboard.com` (specify IBM 42H1292 or Unicomp 42H1292X, with the PS/2 style connector).

Figure 9.4 *The oldie but goodie IBM keyboard*

Key Layout

The second criterion to consider when looking at a keyboard upgrade is the key layout—specifically, *straight* versus *articulated* (a fancy word for "bent"). A few years ago, some bright designer noticed that your hands come together at the keyboard at a pronounced angle rather than straight on. Not long after, you could buy "natural" or "ergonomic" keyboards that split the keys into two groups, making an obtuse angle (see Figure 9.5). More expensive articulated keyboards, like the Kinesis Maxim, let you adjust the angle for your personal body, but you can get a fixed-angle keyboard for US$100 or so from Microsoft, if you don't mind mushy keys. Now, if someone would just figure out how to cut one of the IBM 101-key jobs in half and put a hinge in there...

Figure 9.5 *A fixed-angle ergonomic keyboard*

Upgrade Input Devices

This section looks at two input device upgrades: a cordless mouse, and a pressure-sensitive graphics tablet. The first is an upgrade you might consider for convenience (to reduce cord clutter) and comfort (to reduce "cable drag"); the second is an upgrade that brings new capabilities to your PC in terms of creating computer graphics or artwork.

Installing a Cordless Mouse

Walk into my office and you might be able to see the computers underneath all the cords. One of these days I'm going to devote a weekend to making my office fully cordless (except for power), just to see if it can be done. Meanwhile, the mouse is a good place to start, especially since that darned cord hanging off the edge of the desk is always tugging in the opposite direction I want to go.

EQUIPMENT YOU'LL NEED:

➡ *A cordless mouse*

➡ *A cordless mouse base station with a PS/2-to-USB adapter*

➡ *Two AA alkaline batteries (the regular type works fine; you don't need the "ultra" type)*

This example looks at replacing your standard corded mouse with a Logitech "Cordless Mouseman Optical" (shown in Figure 9.6), the first cordless optical mouse I'm aware of and a pretty cool product (I've been using it while writing this book). This device uses fancy circuitry to extend battery life for the always-on LED that illuminates the surface below the mouse. The mouse has four power modes but is never completely off. You'll find that you get better battery life with light-colored mouse pads or surfaces (you don't absolutely have to use a pad with cordless mice, but most users do).

Figure 9.6 *A cordless optical mouse*

1. Turn off your PC.

2. Yank out your old mouse. Unplug it from the (most likely) PS/2 mouse connector on the back of your PC.

3. Plug in the cordless mouse's base station (see Figure 9.7). This is a radio frequency receiver to which your cordless mouse transmits. You can connect it in one of two ways: straight into a PS/2 connector using the supplied adapter (Figure 9.8), or into a USB port without the adapter. Why the option? The manufacturer is hedging its bets that one day, PCs will all use USB mice and the PS/2 port will go away.

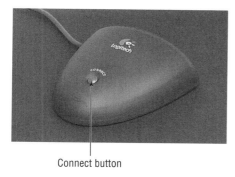

Connect button

Figure 9.7 *The cordless mouse base station*

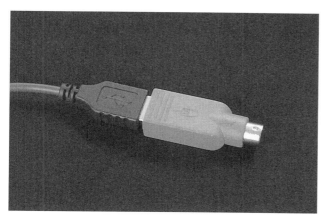

Figure 9.8 *A USB-to-PS/2 adapter*

4. Place the base station where it will be no more than 6 feet away from the mouse.

5. Pop open the mouse's battery cover and insert the batteries (see Figure 9.9). You could use rechargeable batteries, but the manufacturer in this case doesn't recommend it due to their higher cost and the relatively long life of regular batteries in this mouse (around two months in my experience, although the manufacturer says three).

Figure 9.9 *Energizing the new mouse.*

6. Boot the PC.

7. Follow the manufacturer's instructions to install the necessary supporting software. You'll probably have to do without the mouse for this step, but that's not usually a big deal, because you typically just insert a CD-ROM and tap the Enter key several times.

8. Reboot the PC.

9. Establish the communication link between the base station and the mouse by first clicking the Connect button on the base station and then using a pointed object such as a pencil or pen to click the Connect button on the back of the mouse (see Figure 9.10).

TIP *The mouse and base station can work with hundreds of different frequencies, but if you find that the mouse conflicts with another short-range RF device, repeat this step to choose an alternate frequency.*

10. Set up the various mouse options (speed, double-click speed, programmable button, and so forth) via the Control Panel or the mouse setup utility.

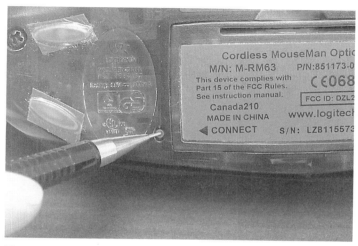

Figure 9.10 *Establishing the communications link*

Cool Mouse Accessories

One of the pleasures of researching a book like this is discovering some slick widget you didn't know about before. Well, while writing this chapter I discovered three, all from one company: www.everglide.com.

First is the "mouse bungee." This is an elegant little stand to hold up your mouse cord so it doesn't drag on your mouse when you move it. (Gravity drag is one reason I started using cordless mice, but with the mouse bungee I may just go back to the cord—and therefore higher sampling rates.)

Second is the Giganta mouse pad. This pad's surface is so much smoother and slicker than the cheap pads we've all been brainwashed to accept, that my mouse hand is noticeably less tired at day's end. (Note that some optical mice prefer a light color pad, some dark; read the reviews and buy accordingly.) Some folks I know, including my intrepid technical editor Jim Kelly, also like pads that use 3M's Precise Mousing Surface.

Third, and even weirder than the mouse bungee, is Mouse Skatez, a slippery tape that you place over your mouse's feet to reduce sliding friction. You can see this in Figure 9.10.

Hey, if you're going to spend time at the PC, you may as well do it in style and comfort. Figure 9.11 shows all three mouse accessories (trust me, the Mouse Skatez are there); the cost is about US$50 for the lot.

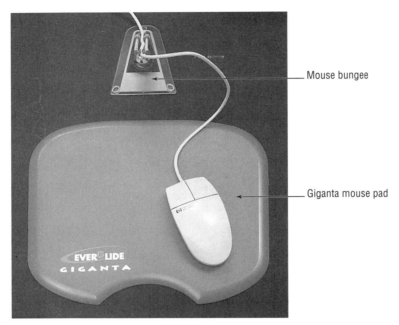

Mouse bungee

Giganta mouse pad

Figure 9.11 *Hip mouse accoutrements*

Installing a Pressure-Sensitive Tablet

Mice and trackballs are great, but a pressure-sensitive tablet does two things for you that those devices just can't do:

- It lets you draw with a pen, which is great if you're an artist or if you occasionally need to do artistic-type drawing or tracing with your PC.

- It lets you push harder to create thicker lines in your drawing program (such as Painter or Photoshop). This benefit is analogous to the advance from harpsichord to piano: All of a sudden, force makes a difference in the final outcome!

Until recently, pressure-sensitive tablets have been out of the average PC user's price range, but products like Wacom's Graphire (see Figure 9.12) have changed that situation dramatically. The Graphire is a pressure-sensitive tablet, pen, and cordless (and battery-less!) mouse in one US$100 package. It connects to your PC via a USB or serial port (the USB option being much more convenient).

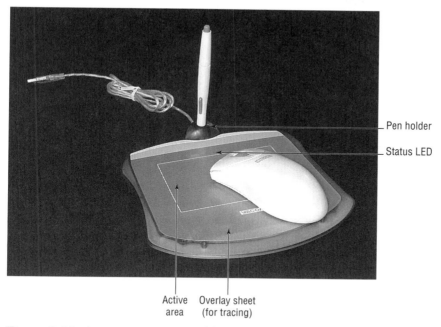

Figure 9.12 *A pressure-sensitive tablet, on a budget*

When you're using the pen, you push down a little to left-click. The switch on the pen's side lets you right-click when you move it one direction, and double-left-click when you move it the other direction. It's very odd at first, but with a little practice you'll get used to it. And, when you don't really need the pen, you can revert to the bundled mouse, which is always on. The pen even comes with an "eraser" that works automatically with many graphics packages, and it's pressure sensitive too: the more you push on the eraser, the more thoroughly your lines disappear.

The procedure for installing this device is almost too simple to print, but here it is:

1. Plug the tablet into an available USB port on the back of your PC or on a USB hub.

2. Install the software per the manufacturer's suggestions and make adjustments to the available settings. For example, most users will prefer to set up the tablet for relative positioning mode, which is the way mice work, instead of absolute positioning mode. You can also set the pen's pressure sensitivity (the tablet can detect 512 levels of pressure).

The Graphire's sample rate is around 50Hz, which is lower than the best corded USB mice and means that (for example) you get more curve nodes when you draw slowly in a paint program than when you draw quickly. Also, the Graphire's fairly small size makes it feel a little cramped if you've ever created computer art on a larger tablet, like the Summagraphics II that I used for a couple of years. So, if you have a few hundred dollars and you do computer art for a living, you may want to look at the Intuos line of tablets, which let you go bigger and which offer more levels of pressure sensitivity. But if you're just dabbling, the Graphire looks and works great, and removes one of the biggest constraints computer artists and artistes have endured— that is, no pressure sensitivity in a "normal" PC input device.

Intro to Multimedia

Multimedia means, technically, "many media," but we use it in the PC biz to mean virtually any content beyond the typed alphanumeric character: still images, moving images, and music. In short, multimedia is what makes PCs fun, and multimedia upgrades are among the most popular.

If your basic hardware setup isn't up to snuff, however, multimedia upgrades can be frustrating. If you haven't taken a look at the other chapters in this book that deal with upgrading memory, hard drives, and display hardware, you'll want to do so before diving into multimedia upgrades. You don't want to turbocharge a car that already has a marginal suspension and engine, and you shouldn't expect to start processing digital video on your PC if it's not in great general health to start with. Multimedia technologies are demanding, and you'll need a quick CPU, plenty of RAM, a fast disk, and a fleet graphics card if you want to get into video processing. On the other hand, if you're mainly interested in still images and music clips, you don't need as much hardware horsepower.

Pictures

Images on your PC can come from many sources:

- You can create your own, with graphics software (a pressure-sensitive tablet is great for artists; see the section "Installing a Pressure-Sensitive Tablet" earlier in this chapter for more information).

- You can scan photographs or other documents using a flatbed scanner, a device that connects to your PC via a USB or SCSI connection. Scanners have come way down in price since my company bought one of the very first units for $1700!

- You can download images from the Internet or receive them from friends in e-mail attachments.

- You can use a digital camera or webcam to take photographs in digital format.

Raw picture quality on the PC boils down to two characteristics, *resolution* (how many dots, or pixels, the image has) and *color depth* (how many different colors it displays). When you look at devices like scanners and cameras, these are the statistics you'll want to consider. For example, an inexpensive webcam device can't create as large a still image as a more expensive unit can. Generally speaking, the higher the resolution and color depth a device can handle, the more expensive it is.

Motion

Most sources of video are analog: TV, VCRs, most camcorders, and so on. However, PCs are digital. Nowadays, a slew of products are available to bridge that gap, at least for the foreseeable future until digital camcorders, TVs, and VCRs become mainstream. What can these products let you do with a PC? Here's a sampling:

- Capture live TV broadcasts and save them on your PC

- Capture home videos from a VCR or camcorder

- Perform digital editing (such as splices, titles, and special effects) in captured video

- Make an analog video (such as a VHS tape) of edited captured video

- Prepare digitized movies for posting on a Web site

This sounds expensive, and it used to be. (Still is, if you want top-of-the-line gear.) However, some high-end PC graphics cards have almost all of these capabilities built in! Even if you have a regular graphics card with no special video capture or playback capabilities, you can retrofit those capabilities with products that cost in the US$100 range. No kidding!

When you start thinking about movies on your PC, the relevant specs are resolution and color depth, just as with still images, and a new one, the *frame rate*. The frame rate is how many images the PC can display in a second. Most users consider 15 frames per second (fps) to be reasonably okay, and 30fps is considered smooth. Just as you might expect, video cards and capture devices that can work at higher resolutions, color depths, and frame rates tend to be more expensive.

Another important factor in computer video is compression. Raw video streams take a huge amount of disk space, but with compression technologies, you can shrink a digital video file to a small fraction of its uncompressed size without giving up too much perceived quality. So when you look at a device like the Dazzle Digital Video Creator or the ATI All-in-Wonder Radeon, find out what compression options it offers. Video compression and decompression is always faster when implemented in hardware than in software, so the better the hardware, the greater the likelihood that your video hardware will be able to keep up with its capture or playback duties without dropping frames.

Music

Music in the PC world comes in a very wide variety of formats, but you can break them all down into two categories, *waveform* and *Musical Instrument Digital Interface* (*MIDI*).

- When you make a recording using a microphone and your PC's sound circuitry, you're creating a waveform audio file. Anything you can hear, you can make into a waveform file. Compression technology can shrink large waveform files down to a small fraction of their original "raw" size, but these files still tend to take up a lot of disk space.

- MIDI files are quite different. A MIDI device, such as a sound card, contains a variety of predefined sounds in its silicon chips. A MIDI music file is a series of instructions specifying which of these predefined sounds should play at what moment (think of a player-piano roll to get the concept). Because MIDI files don't attempt to capture a real-world sound wave, they can be much smaller than waveform audio files. Most computer games use MIDI files for this reason.

Just about all PCs sold today come with some sort of sound circuitry to support the playback and recording of both waveform audio and MIDI, although the quality of that support varies all over the map, so people often look at upgrading it with a plug-in sound card.

Sound Investments

This section looks at two popular PC upgrades in the sound department: beefing up your speaker system, and interfacing your PC with a synthesizer or other digital instrument. The good news about both of these upgrades is that they're not extremely demanding on your computer, so you can perform them even if your system is in the slow-to-medium speed category.

Add Speakers

If you suspect that those tiny, tinny multimedia speakers that came with your PC may be cheating you out of some sonic enjoyment, and you want a higher-fidelity experience when listening to an audio CD in your PC or when playing back your synthesized MIDI masterpiece, the industry now offers dozens of ways to drain your bank account.

The first step up is to go from a two-speaker setup to a three-speaker system (two "satellite" speakers and a subwoofer), and that's what I'm going to discuss here because it's the most popular upgrade. You can move to a three-speaker setup for US$50 and up. If you want bigger and better, and you have a fair amount more discretionary capital (US$200 plus), you can invest in a quadraphonic four-speaker setup, or in a five-speaker surround-sound system typically consisting of four satellites and one subwoofer. Longtime high-end audio supplier Klipsch makes a good example of this type system.

> **TIP** *In the world of speakers, bigger is almost always better, because larger speakers are more efficient than smaller ones. If you check out the spec. sheets, look for the frequency range (you want at least 70Hz to 18KHz, but the wider the better) and total harmonic distortion, or THD (under 1% is good, and the lower the better). Having said that, there's no substitute for actually hearing the speakers you're thinking about buying, and most good computer stores have a kiosk where you can do some comparisons. If you can bring your own audio CD, so much the better.*

You don't need any special equipment to perform this upgrade, so let's get right to it.

1. Turn off the PC.

2. Remove your old speakers. Typically this involves removing one connector at the PC's back panel from the "Line Out" or "Speaker Out" port. If your old speakers are powered, you'll have a power cord to disconnect, too.

3. Unpack your new speaker system. A three-speaker setup (see Figure 9.13) uses two midrange speakers to handle middle and high frequencies, and one subwoofer to handle low frequencies. The subwoofer contains an amplifier for itself and for the satellite speakers, so it can be moderately heavy.

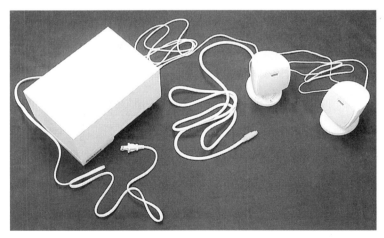

Figure 9.13 *A three-speaker sound setup*

4. Position the satellite speakers on either side of your monitor (see Figure 9.14). First, you should make sure that the speakers are shielded, to avoid interfering with your monitor's image (just about all decent satellite speakers are shielded, but many subwoofers aren't).

5. Place the subwoofer box on the floor, in front of where your legs normally rest, and away from any magnetic disks (see Figure 9.15).

Figure 9.14 Positioning midrange satellite speakers

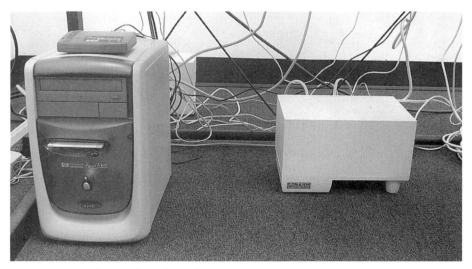

Figure 9.15 Placing the subwoofer

6. Connect the signal cable to your PC (see Figure 9.16). Your PC may have only one speaker output connector, in which case that's the one you must use. If your PC has two outputs, one called "speaker out" (or something similar) and another one called "line out," then use the line out connector. It's unamplified and probably cleaner than the amplified signal (sound card amplifiers are generally neither powerful nor high quality).

Figure 9.16 *Connecting the signal cable to the PC's audio out port*

7. Connect the subwoofer cable to the subwoofer (see Figure 9.17). This generally comes off one of the two satellite speakers and it may be rather thick, because this cable routes not only music to the subwoofer, but also power from the subwoofer to the satellites.

Figure 9.17 *Connecting the subwoofer*

8. Plug in the subwoofer's AC power cord.

9. Set the volume on your new system to its lowest level, if that's obvious, or to the middle of its range, if it's not (see Figure 9.18). You don't want to blow the speakers out the first day you own them.

Figure 9.18 *Set a non-obvious volume dial in the middle for safety*

10. Turn on your PC. Unlike with some other devices, your operating system won't detect the new speaker system, nor does it need to; the signal coming from your PC's sound circuit doesn't change in any way when you change speakers.

11. Pop in a CD and/or fire up your favorite game, and rock out. (As I write this, I'm rediscovering that the Pat Metheny group actually has a bass player.)

Connect a MIDI Keyboard

If you're a closet musician, like me, and you've never experimented with MIDI equipment, I envy you. PCs have become great platforms for composing music. With today's hardware and software, you can set up your own multitrack recording studio with an amazingly small investment.

The great thing about MIDI and PCs is that you don't have to go out and spend much money at first. Simply hook up a MIDI keyboard to your PC, as I show you how to do in this section, and install some simple sequencing software. If you don't have a MIDI keyboard, borrow one from a friend and see if you like it; if you do, buy one—these things have gotten really inexpensive. My little Yamaha synthesizer cost me a couple of hundred dollars and has surprisingly good sound. (Small synthesizers are also good for teaching kids about music if you don't have a "real" piano.) If you enjoy the new compositional opportunities this technology provides, don't be surprised if you find yourself running up your credit card balance by buying interfaces, effects boxes, and new MIDI instruments at the local musician's superstore.

EQUIPMENT YOU'LL NEED:

➡ *A PC-to-MIDI adapter cable, sometimes called a "Y" cable (buy at a musician's store or a large computer store)*

➡ *Two MIDI signal cables (buy at a musician's store), male by male, long enough to reach from PC to keyboard (the usual recommended maximum is 50 feet, but shorter cables are less expensive)*

In this example, I connect a synthesizer to a PC's MIDI/game port, but you don't have to do it this way. You can buy a MIDI interface box that hooks up to a USB port, which may be the way to go if (for example) you want to connect to a laptop PC that has no MIDI/game port. Now, here are the steps.

1. Turn off the PC.

2. Connect the PC-to-MIDI adapter cable (see Figure 9.19) to your PC's MIDI/game port. Only one of the cable connectors will fit (it's the male 15-pin "D"-shaped connector) so you can't do this incorrectly. If you already have a joystick or two connected to the game port, remove it; you'll be able to reconnect it to the joystick connector on the adapter cable.

3. Attach one of the MIDI signal cables to the PC-to-MIDI adapter cable's "Out" connector.

4. Connect the other end of that MIDI cable to the synthesizer's "In" connector (see Figure 9.20).

5. Attach the other MIDI signal cable to the PC-to-MIDI adapter cable's "In" connector.

6. Connect the other end of that MIDI cable to the synthesizer's "Out" connector.

TIP *If you get into more high-end MIDI gear, you'll discover the "Thru" connector, which lets you daisy-chain multiple MIDI instruments together. PCs with typical sound cards don't have a "Thru" connector, but you can get MIDI interfaces that hang off the USB bus that do.*

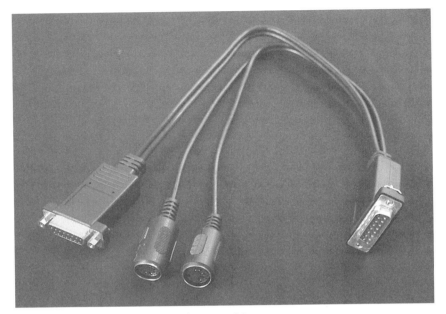

Figure 9.19 *A PC-to-MIDI adapter cable*

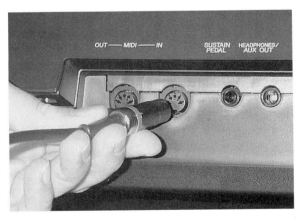

Figure 9.20 *Connecting the PC output to the synthesizer input*

7. If you disconnected a joystick in step 2, reconnect it to the joystick connector on the PC-to-MIDI adapter cable; this is the only connection left to make at this point.

8. Power on and boot up your PC.

9. Turn on your MIDI keyboard (Figure 9.21).

Figure 9.21 *An inexpensive but fun MIDI synthesizer*

10. If you want to play a MIDI file on your synthesizer, instead of from your PC's sound card, you'll have to tell your PC to send the MIDI output signal to the right place. You usually do this in Windows in the Sound folder of the Control Panel; set the "MIDI Playback Device" to your MIDI port, which may appear with an obscure techie name like MPU-401 just to be annoying.

11. To test MIDI output, open Windows Media Player or some other sound playback program, load a MIDI file, and play it. It should play through your synthesizer's built-in speakers or through any external speakers that you've connected to your synthesizer.

WARNING *If the sounds you hear differ from what you hear when you select your sound card's built-in synthesizer and play back a MIDI file through your PC's speakers (for example, if you get violins with one method and a xylophone with the other), then you have a mapping problem. It could be that your synthesizer doesn't support the General MIDI specification, which most PC operating systems presume, and has a different patch list. (The patch list relates MIDI code numbers to instrument sounds.) You may be able to obtain a software map from your synthesizer's manufacturer; it'll take the form of a CFG or IDF file. Otherwise, you'll have to create your own using a tool such as Microsoft's free and downloadable IDFEdit utility. Or just buy a different synthesizer that conforms to General MIDI.*

12. If you want to "capture" MIDI from your synthesizer as you play it, you'll need an extra piece of software called a *sequencer*. Popular ones are Cakewalk and Cubase; you can surf the Web for reviews. You can get a decent little sequencer for US$100 and up. For casual use and experimentation, download a freebie, such as Anvil Studio (www .anvilstudio.com). You'll also probably have to issue a special command at the synthesizer before starting the recording session (it's REC-0 on my little Yamaha keyboard).

Stills and Movies

When it comes to images and movies, some of the more popular PC upgrades are installing a digital camera, connecting a "black box" to capture videos from VCR or camcorder source material, and installing a *webcam*, a small camera that allows you to send video e-mails or grab still images that don't have to be as high quality as those you'd get with a digital camera.

Using a Digital Camera

Digital cameras got a bad rap for their first couple of years due to crummy picture quality and very high cost, but as so often happens, the technology has gotten better and cheaper. In order to get intimately familiar with digital photography so I could comment intelligently on it in this book, we decided to shoot every photograph in the book with a digital camera, the US$400 Kodak DC340 (see Figure 9.22), which connects to the PC via a USB cable. What follows is a condensed summary of what we learned working daily with this technology.

Figure 9.22 *A popular 2-megapixel digital camera*

First, don't get too sucked in to the notion that higher resolutions are better. The difference in quality between a 2-megapixel camera and a 3-megapixel camera just isn't earth-shattering for amateur applications, and the large file sizes of the higher-resolution cameras can be more trouble than it's worth.

Second, if you plan on doing close-up work, use a tripod. These cameras aren't yet fast enough to grab good detail shots from a handheld position, especially in sub-optimal lighting conditions.

Third, plan to buy a *lot* of batteries. I've never seen a device go through batteries as fast as a digital camera; on some days we went through three sets of four AA batteries in one day. On that note, don't waste your money buying the new "premium" or "ultra" alkaline batteries that supposedly give you longer life than the regular kind. The premium batteries cost a lot more and didn't give us a proportionally longer lifetime. Rechargeable batteries are a good idea; you can select NiCd (nickel-cadmium) or NiMH (nickel-metal hydride), but get at least two sets. Also, you can buy AC adapters for most digital cameras (to my way of thinking, this shouldn't be an "extra" but it usually is), which is a good solution to the battery-eating problem if you do studio work in a fixed location.

TIP *When your digital camera has rejected your batteries, don't toss 'em. They probably still have enough juice to run your TV or VCR remote controls.*

Next, experiment with the different settings. These devices work much differently from the film cameras you're used to, so be prepared to set aside most of what you've learned and get familiar with a new set of options and controls. Heck, the film isn't costing you anything, so spend a day just trying out different combinations of exposure, lighting, and sharpness values. Note down your conclusions, because you won't remember them a week later!

Finally, don't get too angry at the quirks of this immature technology. The software that the manufacturer provided for transferring images from the camera onto the PC locked up our Windows 2000 PCs from time to time, and the user interface wasn't very sophisticated either (no right-clicking!). The camera itself had some serious design flaws, like putting the LCD preview panel right where your nose hits it when taking pictures (we were forever cleaning off little grease spots), and using cryptic little hieroglyphics instead of (rather than in addition to) words. Plus, the preview panel for close-ups doesn't match up exactly with the actual photo's cropping points, a problem I've heard from other digicam users.

Quibbles aside, we love our little digital camera. It saved us a huge amount of time, not only because we were able to see our shots instantly and re-shoot right away if we weren't happy with the results, but also because we didn't have to make the trip to the developer and wait an hour for prints after shooting a "roll." The detail we were able to capture in close-ups was as crisp, or crisper, as what you could capture with a professional film camera costing twice as much.

Once the digicam makers iron out the user interface bugs, figure out how to fix the battery life problem, and reduce size, weight, and cost a bit more, digital cameras will be the clear choice for any shutterbug with a PC and a high-quality inkjet printer. These devices are terrific when you don't need to go to film and you need to process images fast, as in our case. But don't throw your film camera away just yet.

Using an External Capture Device

Some of today's more sophisticated graphics controllers come with video capture capabilities built in, but if you don't have one, don't despair. You can buy an external capture device for not a lot of cash, giving you video grabbing ability without even having to crack your PC's case. One of the more popular ones is the Digital Video Creator line from Dazzle; Figure 9.23 shows the DVC-80 model, which connects to your PC via a USB port and captures 352x240 video at 30fps.

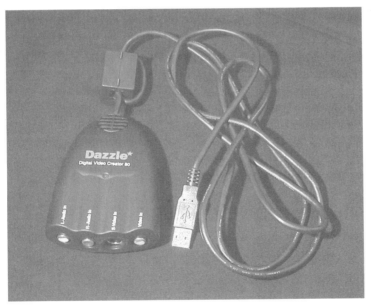

Figure 9.23 *A "black box" video capture device*

These devices are very clever and perform surprisingly well, but be aware that if you want the best possible video capture quality, you'll need to open your PC and install a PCI card. The USB bus is convenient but much slower than the PCI bus. That could all change with USB version 2.0, however!

Installing an external capture device is a simple matter of connecting the box to a USB port and installing the manufacturer's software, so I won't go through that in detail here. Instead, in the steps below, I take you through a typical procedure for capturing video from an analog camcorder (in this case, a Sony Hi-8 model) to a digital file on the PC.

I was doing this sort of thing a decade ago, when it required big, clunky US$20,000 boxes called *scan converters*, and I can tell you that the Dazzle (and its siblings in the market) makes a complex task just about as simple as it can be. The DVC-80 saves to only one format, MPEG-1, but more expensive models from Dazzle and others save to MPEG-2 and include software to convert your movies to DVD and other formats.

EQUIPMENT YOU'LL NEED:

➡ *A camcorder with a tape containing the content you want to digitize*

➡ *An audio cable with two RCA-style plugs on either end (you typically have to buy this separately, grrr)*

➡ *A video cable (either composite, with RCA plugs, or S-video, which is higher quality; again, buy it separately)*

➡ *The DVC-80 box*

Once you get your cables and camcorder together, follow these steps:

1. Connect the video cable to the camcorder's video out connector (Figure 9.24). If your camcorder has an S-video port, use that rather than the composite video.

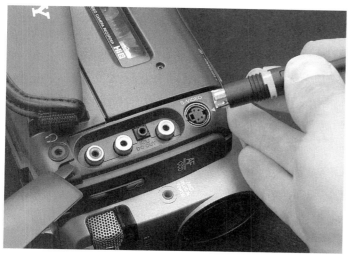

Figure 9.24 *The camcorder video-out connection*

2. Connect the audio cable to the camcorder's audio out connectors (Figure 9.25). There will be two of these, one for the left channel and one for the right.

Figure 9.25 *The camcorder audio-out connection*

3. Attach the other end of the video cable to the Dazzle box's video in connector.

4. Attach the other end of the audio cables to the Dazzle box's audio in connectors (Figure 9.26).

5. Turn on the camcorder. You can run it from the battery, but you should run it from AC power if possible, to ensure the steadiest possible playback.

6. Using the camcorder's preview display (such as an LCD panel), cue the tape to start a few seconds before the point where you want to start recording, and then pause the playback (Figure 9.27).

7. On the PC, open the Dazzle's capture utility and start the recording process. Make sure you have plenty of disk space!

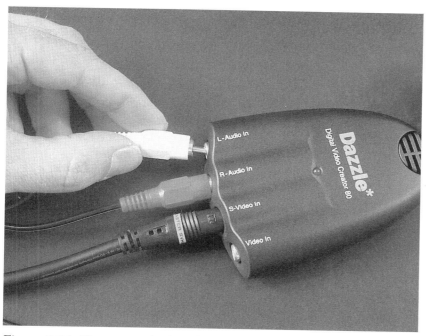

Figure 9.26 *The capture box's audio-in connections*

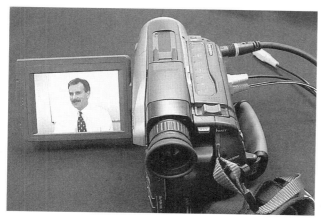

Figure 9.27 *Cueing the tape on the camcorder*

8. On the camcorder, press the pause control again to start playback.

9. Watch the camcorder's preview display and when you get a few seconds past the end of the clip you want, stop the camcorder and stop the recording process at the PC.

10. Play back the clip (say, using Windows Media Player) to make sure you got everything you wanted. You can edit the digital file with whatever digital video editor you have. Devices like the Dazzle DVC come with bundled software, and if you want to get sophisticated, you can buy a professional editing package like Adobe Premiere.

Buying a Webcam

Webcams, also known affectionately as "egg-cams" because of their shape (see Figure 9.28), have become so inexpensive and are so much fun for casual use that sales have really taken flight. A webcam is just a little camera that you can mount on top of your monitor (or wherever else you'd like) to take either still shots or limited-quality movies.

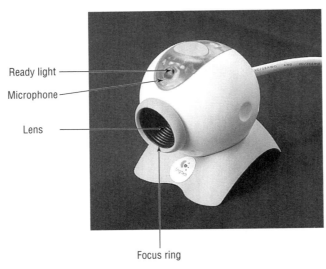

Ready light

Microphone

Lens

Focus ring

Figure 9.28 *A Logitech QuickCam model*

Webcams usually cost much less than digital cameras, and a *whole* lot less than digital camcorders, yet the quality of the stills and movies they create is sufficient for sending the occasional still or video e-mail attachment. You have to spend a few hundred dollars to get a webcam with adequate quality for business teleconferencing, but the US$50 to US$100 webcam isn't designed for that, and as long as you tailor your expectations a bit (don't expect 30fps video!), inexpensive webcams can be very entertaining.

Here's what you need to know before buying a webcam:

- Check the maximum resolution. Typical values are 352x288 and 640x480.

- See if the webcam has a built-in microphone. Those that don't mean you'll spend money on an "extra."

- Some webcams include a motion detection feature (useful for spying on baby- or house-sitters, if you're so inclined).

- Low-end cams use manual focus; more expensive units have autofocus.

- Check still image quality; the "fisheye" effect is a common problem.

- Most webcams need a lot of light to work well. If you're buying one for a dim space, beware.

- See if the webcam works with Microsoft NetMeeting if you plan to do teleconferencing.

- Also, be aware that teleconferencing works poorly with dial-up connections, but better with DSL, cable modem, or other broadband Internet links.

- USB webcams have to compress video fairly severely. Look at a sample video clip and see if it will meet your needs. You may be better off using an analog camcorder and a capture box, if you're after anything above minimum-quality video.

- Ask what format the webcam saves video to. MPEG-1 is smaller and less capable than MPEG-2, and if you work with Windows, you may want *AVI* support (*Audio-Video Interleave*, the most common digital video format on Windows PCs).

Setting up most webcams involves a simple three-step process: install the software, mount the camera (either on your monitor, or on a table, as shown in Figure 9.29), and then connect the cam to a USB port at the back of your PC or on a USB hub. You may want to supplement the manufacturer's mounting hardware with a bit of double-stick foam tape, to reduce camera vibration (and so you don't knock the thing off its perch when you point it in a different direction).

Figure 9.29 *An alternative webcam mounting arrangement*

The procedure for taking still snapshots is usually as simple as pressing the button on top of the egg, but grabbing videos is somewhat more involved. The exact procedure varies, but generally you fire up the webcam's Control Panel to set the video characteristics and start and stop recording.

Chapter 10

BIOS and CPU

Most PC users regard the motherboard (or *system board*, or *main board*, as it is sometimes called) as essentially non-upgradable and non-maintainable, with the sole exception of adding memory (see Chapter 1, "Read Me First"). As this chapter shows, however, two other aspects of the motherboard are ripe for upgrading on many systems: the *BIOS (basic input/output system)* and the *CPU (central processing unit)*. This chapter provides you with an overview of both of these low-level components and tells you how to upgrade them safely and successfully, beginning with the BIOS.

BIOS Overview

The BIOS is simply a chunk of software that directs the PC's startup procedure, performing a few useful preliminary tasks before passing control to the operating system. Unlike most software, the BIOS doesn't load from your hard drive, a CD, or a diskette. Instead, the BIOS loads from a chip on the motherboard. (That makes sense if you think about the fact that when the PC first starts, it doesn't even know about any connected disk drives.)

So what does the BIOS do, exactly? First, it performs a power-on self-test, or POST, to make sure the PC's vital organs are all alive and well. If the POST fails, as (for example) it may if your keyboard isn't connected, the BIOS typically displays a message on the screen with an error code.

Second, the BIOS takes an inventory of motherboard resources, such as how many parallel ports you have, how many serial ports, integrated USB or SCSI controllers, and so forth. Modern Plug and Play BIOS systems will pass this information along to the operating system, so that, say, Windows Me doesn't have to scavenge for all those details itself. (The operating system has plenty of other devices to detect that are separate from the motherboard, such as modems and network cards). Third, the BIOS looks around for possible boot devices. Modern PCs can boot from a variety of devices: a hard drive (most common), a CD-ROM (handy for troubleshooting and system recovery), a diskette (ditto), or even a removable cartridge device such as a Zip or Jaz drive.

Fourth, the BIOS passes control of the PC to the operating system, presuming that the POST passes muster and the BIOS is able to locate a valid boot device.

The BIOS can do lots of other things besides these four. For example, it can enforce some power-on security by demanding a power-on password. It can also perform some power management, spinning down disks and powering off the monitor after a predetermined interval of idle time. The BIOS can do some rudimentary virus detection and prevention, too. You control all these functions from the BIOS setup program (typically accessible with a function-key command at power-on).

Why would you ever want to modify the BIOS software? A few reasons:

- You want to upgrade to a CPU that the present version of the BIOS doesn't support.

- You want to upgrade your operating system to a version that the present BIOS doesn't support. For example, lots of PCs need a BIOS upgrade if you're upgrading from Windows 95/98 to Windows 2000/XP.

- Your current BIOS has a bug, such as the PC restarting instead of powering down when you execute a shutdown command, and the BIOS vendor has fixed this bug in the latest version.

- You want to correct a Plug and Play problem that is preventing your operating system from using a particular motherboard device. Newer versions of the BIOS often work better with Plug and Play operating systems such as Windows Me. (You usually see this problem only when you upgrade to a newer operating system.)

- You want better power management features.

Updating the BIOS

About the only thing you would ever need to do with your PC's BIOS is to update it, a procedure known as *flashing*. Updating the BIOS code isn't as simple as updating an application program on your hard drive, because the BIOS code isn't designed to be modified frequently. Most PCs never have their BIOS flashed; of those that do, the event rarely occurs more than twice or perhaps three times during the PC's usable lifetime.

How to Tell What BIOS You Have

The first step in flashing your BIOS is making sure you need to flash it! That is, you should verify which version you have on your PC before performing an update. If the latest available version is the same as the one you have, then skip it—flashing your BIOS would have no effect (other than, in extremely rare cases, correcting any code blocks that have become corrupted somehow).

- You can usually tell what version of the BIOS you have from your operating system. For example, in Windows, you can run the System Information utility: Use the Search or Find command to locate either `MSINFO.EXE` or `MSINFO32.EXE`, and then double-click it.

- Alternately, you can simply watch for the BIOS version when you power on your PC; the version typically appears in the upper left corner of the screen.

- If neither of those methods works, then you can usually check the BIOS version by entering the BIOS setup program for your PC. The specific commands vary, but you'll usually see an on-screen prompt early in the PC's startup sequence that says something like, "Press F2 for Setup." The BIOS version usually appears front and center when you enter the setup utility.

How to Get the Latest Version of Your BIOS

As soon as you've determined what BIOS version you have, the next step is to get the latest version, if a newer one is available.

EQUIPMENT YOU'LL NEED:

➡ *A computer with a working Internet connection*

INFORMATION YOU'LL NEED:

➡ *The Web address of your PC supplier*

This step is simple to describe, but not always simple to execute. You start at the main Web page of your PC manufacturer and navigate to where the downloadable BIOS code is stored. Click the file that's correct for your PC and specify a convenient download location.

TIP *One tip that may help speed your search is to click the search engine and type in the words* **BIOS** *and* **upgrade***.*

Note that the file will probably be about a megabyte in size, so it may take a few minutes to download over a slow dial-up link.

WARNING *It's very important to verify that the BIOS you download is the correct one for your PC. If you get this wrong, you may not be able to use your PC anymore!*

Power Backup is Essential!

If memory serves, part of the credo of every medical doctor is, "First, do no harm." That's not a bad motto for PC upgraders, either: Make sure you don't make your computer worse off than it was before you started an upgrade operation! This is especially good advice when you're doing something as low-level as flashing the BIOS. You're going to be modifying the very code that tells your PC how to get up in the morning; if you scramble that code somehow, you could end up with an unbootable PC.

The most important step you can take to avoid disaster when flashing the BIOS is to hook up your PC to a battery backup unit. This way, if you experience a loss of AC power during the process, the backup unit will keep the system up and running.

The odds against a power glitch during a BIOS update are astronomical, but it has happened to me, and it was quite a chore to recover. I ended up having to get a replacement BIOS chip overnighted to me! (Thankfully, the chip wasn't soldered to the motherboard.) Most of the time, you could recover by simply reflashing the BIOS, but I'm here to tell you that that's not always an option.

EQUIPMENT YOU'LL NEED:

➡ *A battery backup unit*

If you don't already have a battery backup unit connected to your PC, the procedure is simple:

1. Plug the battery unit into an AC power outlet.

2. Let it charge fully (usually overnight).

3. Plug your PC into the battery unit (see Figure 10.1).

Figure 10.1 A battery backup unit

4. Test the battery by unplugging it while your PC is running. Your PC should continue to run, and the battery will probably sound an annoying alarm.

5. Plug the battery unit back into the AC outlet.

6. (Optional) Connect a serial cable from the battery unit (which has only one serial port) to an available COM port on your PC. Install the battery unit's software onto your PC, following any instructions provided by the battery manufacturer. This step lets the battery alert your operating system about a power cut, so the OS can notify the user (you) to make an orderly shutdown before the battery runs dry.

Keep the Old BIOS on Diskette

When you upgrade your BIOS per the manufacturer's instructions, you may be asked if you'd like to keep a copy of the old BIOS on diskette. *Always say yes to this question*, and pop in a blank, formatted diskette when prompted. (Some flash programs save the old BIOS to your hard drive; the program should let you know if it does so.) When the flash program (which usually has a name like PHLASH.EXE, and which actually performs the BIOS update) has created the diskette with the old BIOS on it, label that diskette and put it somewhere handy. If the updated BIOS creates some problem with your PC—such as a device not working anymore—you can go back to the old BIOS until the BIOS manufacturer comes out with a new version that fixes the problem.

Performing the Update

If you've discovered your BIOS version and you've determined that a newer version exists, it's time to update your PC to the latest version.

EQUIPMENT YOU'LL NEED:

➡ *One boot diskette with no other files on it (see your operating system help files, or your PC manual, for how to create a boot diskette; for example, with Windows 95/98/ME, use the* SYS *command)*

INFORMATION YOU'LL NEED:

➡ *Settings from the previous BIOS*

Here are the typical steps to performing a BIOS upgrade. Note that the specific procedure recommended by the BIOS manufacturer may not match the following steps perfectly, in which case you should follow the manufacturer's procedure.

1. Run your PC's BIOS setup utility and be sure to make a note of all settings. When you upgrade the BIOS, these settings will be reset to their default values. The specific commands to run the BIOS setup utility vary from PC to PC, but generally, you must press a function key (such as F2 or F11) or a combination of keys (such as Ctrl+Alt+Enter) when your PC is first starting up—that is, before Windows or Linux starts to load. Your PC's user manual should tell you how to run the BIOS setup utility; you may also get a clue from the text messages that appear during the initial startup phase.

NOTE *Remember to write legibly and take note of every setting! You'll need to refer to your notes in step 9 to reset everything back to your PC's original configuration.*

2. Insert the boot diskette into your floppy drive.

3. Run the program you downloaded from the PC manufacturer's Web site, either by double-clicking it in your file management program (such as Windows Explorer) or by typing its pathname at a command prompt. The program will move the necessary files onto the boot diskette.

4. When prompted to do so, restart the PC, leaving the boot diskette in the drive.

5. The system will start slower than usual but eventually you should see the BIOS flash program. Answer Yes when asked if you want to proceed.

6. Sit back and watch the program do its thing.

7. Restart the PC and verify that the new BIOS version appears at the upper left corner of the screen.

8. Verify that all your devices work properly.

9. Restart the PC again, enter the BIOS setup program as described in Step 1, and adjust any settings that changed as a result of the upgrade.

CPU Overview

The CPU is the heart, soul, and brain of your PC, all rolled into one. The CPU either directs or touches just about everything that happens in a computer, from opening a file to drawing a picture on the screen. You can think of the CPU as much like the engine of a car: Other subsystems exist, but the CPU (engine) is the one upon which every other system depends.

Car enthusiasts have a saying, "The only substitute for cubic inches is cubic money," meaning that if you want to make a car perform, the approach that provides the most bang for your buck is to get the biggest engine you can. The same is true of a PC's CPU. You can make a PC go faster without replacing the CPU, and in many systems, replacing the CPU isn't even an option. But if you can replace the CPU, it is likely to give you the best speed boost for your money, because the CPU is involved in just about every operation the PC performs—unlike, say, a video adapter, which speeds up only display operations, or a disk controller, which speeds up only disk operations.

Unlike upgrading the BIOS, which is normally a pretty simple procedure, upgrading or replacing a CPU can be touchy. First, not all CPUs work with all motherboards, either physically (in terms of how the CPUs attach to the motherboards) or electrically (in terms of the signaling conventions used by the connectors). Second, once you get a perfect match lined up, the procedure involves a fair amount of surgery. You'll probably have to remove some of your PC's internal components just to get to the CPU. Third, you can usually install a faster CPU than your PC originally came with, but if you do, your choices won't be unlimited and you'll have to change some settings on a motherboard switch. You may even have to update your BIOS first to ensure that it supports the newer, faster CPU you're installing.

Let's take the physical connectors first. Basically, CPUs come in two forms: *socket* and *slot*. The original Pentium, the Pentium III, and the Pentium 4 are all available as socket CPUs, meaning they plug into a square socket on the motherboard, as shown in Figure 10.2. Sockets have two types: PPGA, for plastic pin grid array, and FC-PGA, for flip chip pin grid array. Both have 370 pins (!) and lie flat on the motherboard. The Pentium 4 uses a new connector, Socket W, which has 423 pins.

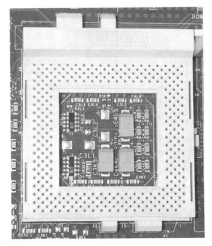

Figure 10.2 *A CPU socket*

The Pentium II and Pentium III are both available as slot CPUs, meaning they plug into a slot on the motherboard that is much like a slot you'd plug a video adapter card or internal modem into. In a slot configuration, as shown in Figure 10.3, the CPU is perpendicular to the plane of the motherboard, instead of parallel to it as in the socket configuration. Several types of slot CPUs exist: "Slot 1" denotes a non-Xeon Intel CPU, "Slot 2" denotes a Xeon Intel CPU, and "Slot A" denotes an AMD CPU (which is physically compatible with a Slot 1 motherboard, but not electrically compatible with it). Within each category are several variations; for example, a Slot 1 CPU may be "SECC" (with gold contacts inside the black plastic housing) or "SECC2" (with gold contacts exposed outside the housing).

CPU slot

Figure 10.3 *A CPU slot*

Because of the physical differences between these CPU packaging types, you may not always be able to upgrade a PC from one type to another. For example, you can't upgrade a Pentium II or Pentium III to a Pentium 4, because the socket pinout (pin arrangement) is different, requiring a Pentium 4-compatible motherboard.

The other relevant characteristics of CPUs are *CPU speed*, *cache size*, and *bus speed*. You should be aware of all three variables if you're trying to match exactly a processor that's already in your PC.

- *CPU speed* is the megahertz rating of the CPU. If you're unsure of your CPU speed, and you have an Intel chip, you can get a processor frequency ID utility at `http://support.intel.com/support/processors/tools/frequencyID`. You can check out the differences between CPU speeds at `http://www.intel.com/procs/perf/icomp/index.htm` and at `http://www.cpuscorecard.com`.

- *Cache size* typically means the size of the chip's level 2 cache, high-speed but expensive memory used to store frequently used instructions as a cost-effective way of speeding up CPU operations. The Pentium II, III, and 4 CPUs can have either 256KB or 512KB caches; the Celeron processors have 128KB caches, which is one reason they typically run slower than their bigger siblings.

- *Bus speed,* specifically *frontside bus speed,* refers to the speed with which the CPU communicates with main memory. Sometimes a given CPU family can work with different frontside bus speeds. For example, the Pentium III CPU can support either a 100MHz frontside bus, or a 133MHz frontside bus. For the curious, the frontside bus is distinct from the communications channel between the CPU and its level two cache, which goes by the moniker (you guessed it) *backside bus.*

Make sure you get the right CPU for your motherboard by checking with your PC vendor or the manufacturer of your motherboard to ensure that your motherboard supports the CPU's slot or socket type, speed, cache size, and bus speed.

Replacing a CPU

Other than replacing an entire motherboard lock, stock, and barrel, replacing a CPU is the most delicate operation you can perform with a PC.

The procedure varies depending on the type of CPU socket or slot that your motherboard uses. Through the years, PC manufacturers have used a number of different socket and slot types. Some are relatively easy to upgrade, some are a little tricky, and some are a major pain in the transistor. The sections that follow lay out the steps for each of the common types, which I have grouped as follows:

- ZIF *(zero insertion force)* socket CPUs

- Non-ZIF socket CPUs

- Slot cartridge CPUs

Before I get into the specific installation procedures, however, a word about CPUs and heat dissipation is in order.

Heat Sinks, Cooling Fans, and Overclocking

Two technologies keep a CPU from frying itself into oblivion: *heat sinks* (finned metal structures that clamp onto a CPU chip and lead heat away from it, like a radiator) and *cooling fans*.

The first point to make is that if you buy a CPU in a retail package, say from Intel, you should normally use whatever came in the box. The CPU manufacturer knows its products better than anyone, and you can be pretty sure that your CPU will perform at or below its rated temperature if you install what the manufacturer gives you.

Second, if you get a CPU that doesn't come with a heat sink or cooling fan—as you may if you buy a CPU from a private party, say on eBay—you can use the same hardware that your original CPU used, as long as you're merely replacing the CPU with another one of the same speed and type. *Don't assume that you can use the same hardware, however, if you're upgrading the CPU type and/or speed!* Faster CPUs use more power than slower ones, and they generate more heat.

A word now about *overclocking*. This is the practice of running a CPU at higher than its rated speed by modifying the timing settings on the motherboard. I am in no position to get all moral and tell readers never to overclock a PC, because I was an overclocker before overclocking was cool. The first PC my consulting company bought was a 6MHz IBM PC/AT, and after it went out of warranty, I overclocked it to 8MHz (don't laugh, it felt fast at the time) by replacing a crystal on the motherboard.

Of course, I saved the original crystal in case my scheme didn't work. But in hindsight, I know that I could have damaged my CPU; I'd have had to buy a new motherboard, which at that time would have cost about $5000. So, my advice about overclocking is as follows:

- It is demonstrably true that most CPUs can run substantially faster than their rated speed.

- The particular CPU that you own may not be one of these faster CPUs, in which case overclocking could damage it. So, you should have enough cash on hand to replace the CPU if things don't work out.

- You will have to invest some time, energy, and money enhancing the cooling hardware if you overclock. (Some die-hard hot-rodders have gone so far as to use water-cooled CPU jackets and circulating pumps! Cool, but if such a gizmo ever leaks, your hardware becomes wetware, leaving you "noware.")

- Other non-CPU motherboard components may not be able to handle overclocking.

- You may experience intermittent hardware problems that you never had before.

- Overclocking is for risk-happy tinkerers. If you want more speed, the least-hassle method is still to upgrade the processor or buy a new PC. If you really want to experiment with overclocking, check out www.overclockers.com.

Replacing a CPU with a ZIF Socket

If you're living right, the CPU you'll replace will use a zero insertion force (ZIF) socket. A ZIF socket has a lever right next to the socket like the one shown in Figure 10.4. Pull the lever, and you reduce tension on the CPU pins so that you can simply lift out the CPU!

Lever—

Figure 10.4 *The lever on a ZIF socket*

EQUIPMENT YOU'LL NEED:

➡ *Appropriate screwdrivers to remove PC cover*

➡ *Needle-nose pliers*

➡ *A flashlight*

➡ *An antistatic wrist strap (optional, but highly recommended)*

➡ *Stabilant-22 contact enhancement fluid (optional, but recommended; get at an electronics supply house, or a Mercedes or Audi dealer)*

INFORMATION YOU'LL NEED:

➡ *The motherboard switch settings (if you're installing a faster CPU)*

Here's the procedure for replacing a ZIF socket CPU:

1. Disconnect the keyboard, mouse, display, power, and any other connectors.

2. Open the PC cover. (If you're not comfortable with this operation, please see Chapter 1.)

3. Remove whatever components (power supply, plastic airflow guides, etc.) may be obscuring access to the CPU.

4. Disconnect whatever cables may be in the way, too. Put a bit of masking tape on them and their respective connectors and then label both with a felt pen so that reconnecting the cables is easy later.

5. If the CPU has a fan that attaches to the motherboard or to a power supply connector, disconnect the fan.

6. Remove the CPU's heat shield (see Figure 10.5). This component dissipates heat from the processor. Typically, a spring-loaded clip holds it into place. Your needle-nose pliers will come in handy at this step.

WARNING *Take great care not to scratch the motherboard when removing the CPU heat shield clip. You may have to use some force to release the clip; one slip and your motherboard is toast.*

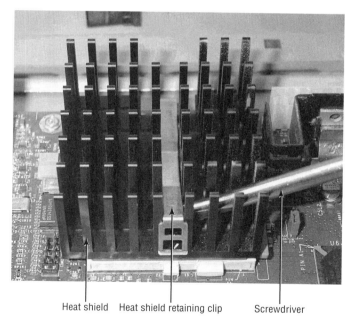

Heat shield   Heat shield retaining clip   Screwdriver

Figure 10.5 *Removing a typical CPU heat shield*

7. Once the heat shield is off, release the CPU by raising the lever right next to the CPU socket (see Figure 10.6), and then remove the CPU.

Figure 10.6 *Releasing the lever on a ZIF socket*

8. Insert the new CPU into the same socket, lining it up carefully so that the corner without a pin fits onto the corner of the socket without a hole. The chip can fit into the socket only one way. Some chips have a notch to indicate the #1 pin location; others have a golden triangle (see Figure 10.7). (The flashlight may be helpful here.) You can optionally dribble some Stabilant-22 into the holes of the CPU socket for contact enhancement, but if you do, use the stuff sparingly—a little goes a long way.

9. Move the lever into its original position (that is, down) to lock the new CPU into place.

10. Reattach the heat shield or attach a new one. If you're installing a faster CPU, you'll probably need a new (and more efficient) heat shield. If one came in the box with the CPU, use it.

Figure 10.7 *Socket CPUs have one corner that is different from the others.*

11. If the heat shield you're using comes with a fan, you may need to plug that fan in to a power source. If the connector is a tiny white plastic female connector, look on the motherboard near the CPU slot for a couple of pins sticking up and a label saying "FAN." If the connector is a larger white plastic male connector with four pins inside a sort of shield, like the power connectors for a hard drive (see Figure 10.8), then you can plug it in to any available plug coming off of the power supply.

12. If your new CPU runs at a different speed from the old one, you'll probably need to change one or more *dual inline package (DIP)* switches on the motherboard (see Figure 10.9). Typically, PC manufacturers place a label inside the cover (as shown in Figure 10.10), on the power supply, or elsewhere inside the box with a legend describing how to set the motherboard switches.

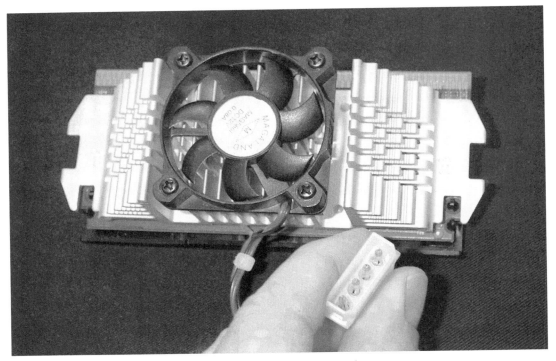

Figure 10.8 *This CPU fan draws power from the power supply.*

DIP switch

Figure 10.9 *A typical motherboard DIP switch*

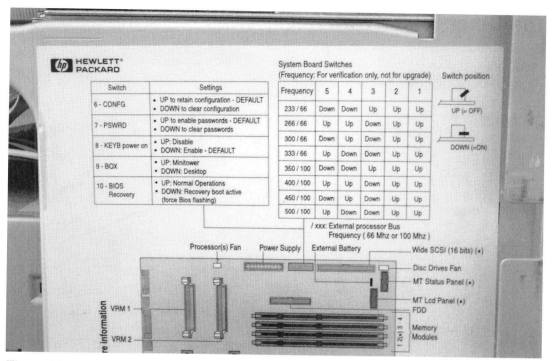

Figure 10.10 *A typical motherboard switch label*

13. Reconnect any cables that you disconnected in step 4. You can remove the bits of masking tape that you used to help you remember what goes where, although it won't hurt anything to leave them in place.

14. Reinstall any components that you removed in step 3.

15. Put the cover back on the PC.

16. Reconnect the keyboard, mouse, display, and any other peripheral cables.

17. Restart the PC and watch for any BIOS errors that may indicate you didn't get the motherboard switch settings just right. If you don't see any such errors, the system should start normally.

The Other Kind ("Fork Required")

If you're unlucky, you have an older socket-type PC that doesn't use a ZIF socket, but that doesn't mean you can't perform the CPU upgrade surgery. Before you proceed, it's time to get out the elbow grease—and to obtain a special piece of hardware called a CPU fork (see Figure 10.11).

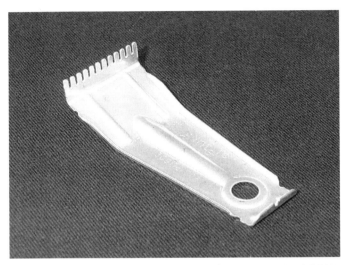

Figure 10.11 *A CPU fork helps pry loose a non-ZIF CPU.*

Using a CPU fork to upgrade an older socket-type PC is a bit tricky and requires both more muscle and more hand-eye coordination than the upgrade described previously.

EQUIPMENT REQUIRED:

➡ *A CPU fork (you can use a small slot screwdriver, but it's not nearly as safe)*

➡ *A deck of playing cards*

➡ *A short length of 2 × 2 wood*

➡ *Stabilant-22 (recommended, but not strictly necessary)*

The procedure is basically the same as laid out in the previous section, with modifications to steps 7 and 8.

To start with, instead of releasing the CPU with the lever in step 7, you must whip out your CPU fork and work it gently but firmly underneath one corner of the CPU, wedging it farther in and slowly prying up as you go.

When you get one corner started, move to the opposite corner and repeat the process; you don't want to bend the CPU pins when you remove the chip, so it's important to work on each of the four corners (see Figure 10.12). That way, you can lift the CPU almost straight out when you've loosened each corner.

Figure 10.12 *Prying a CPU out of its non-ZIF socket*

The installation of the new CPU (step 8 in the previous section) requires some elbow grease, too. The CPU pins fit very snugly into a non-ZIF socket, and if you don't press down really hard, they may not make proper contact. So, two bits of advice when installing a socketed CPU without the benefit of a lever:

- Support the motherboard's socket by placing a deck of playing cards or some other similar expediency directly under the socket. You don't want to flex the motherboard to the point that you crack a circuit trace.

- Press down evenly and slowly but with a lot of pressure. You may find a piece of wood, such as a short length of 2 × 2, helpful here if it's difficult for you to get your fingers down to the CPU.

After you've pressed the CPU down firmly into place, follow steps 10 through 17 in the previous section.

Replacing Slot Cartridge CPUs

Most slot cartridge CPUs install pretty much the same way. The procedure is simpler and easier than a non-ZIF socket CPU installation, and about the same level of difficulty as a ZIF socket installation.

EQUIPMENT YOU'LL NEED

➡ *Screwdrivers as necessary to remove the PC cover*

➡ *A flashlight*

➡ *An antistatic wrist strap (optional, but highly recommended)*

➡ *Stabilant-22 contact enhancement fluid (optional, but recommended; get at an electronics supply house, or a Mercedes or Audi dealer)*

INFORMATION YOU'LL NEED

➡ *The motherboard switch settings (if you're installing a faster CPU)*

Once you have your equipment together, follow these steps:

1. Disconnect the keyboard, mouse, display, power, and any other connectors.

2. Open the PC cover.

3. Remove any components (power supply, plastic airflow guides, etc.) that may be obscuring access to the CPU.

4. Disconnect any cables that are in the way, too. Put a bit of masking tape on them and their respective connectors, and label both cable and connector with a felt pen so that reconnecting the cables is easy later.

5. If the CPU has a fan that attaches to the motherboard or to a power supply connector, disconnect the fan. (You don't have to remove the heat shield or attached fan.)

6. Press the lock tabs holding the CPU into its bracket (see Figure 10.13) to release them.

7. Using a firm but slow rocking motion, work the CPU out of the slot. Grab as much of the CPU as you can; don't just hold it by the heat shield. The CPU has probably never been out of this slot, so it's likely to be seated very snugly into place. Take your time!

Figure 10.13 *Slot CPU lock tabs*

8. Reattach the heat shield or attach a new one. If you're installing a faster CPU, you'll probably need a new (and more efficient) heat shield. If one came in the box with the CPU, use it. You may have to slide the heat shield onto the CPU package by pushing four metal rods through holes in the circuit board (see Figure 10-14), and then attaching a securing clip.

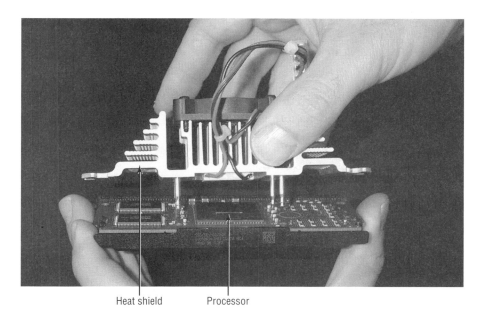

Heat shield   Processor

Figure 10.14 *Connecting a heat shield to a slot processor*

9. Optionally, coat the new CPU's card-edge connectors with a film of Stabilant-22 (see Figure 10.15). I find this step especially helpful in getting the new CPU to seat properly.

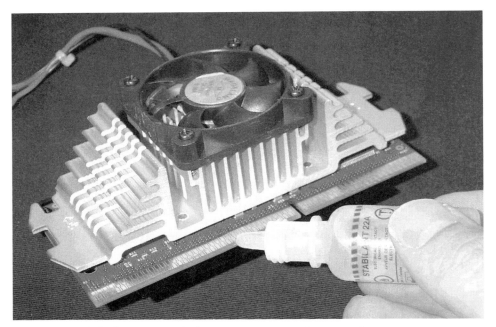

Figure 10.15 *Lubricating and cleaning contacts at the same time*

10. Carefully line up the new CPU with the slot and push down. The clips on the CPU should lock into place inside the mounting bracket.

TIP *Nine out of ten times, when a new slot CPU doesn't work, the reason is that it is not fully seated in its slot. Push down hard.*

11. If the heat shield you're using comes with a fan, you may need to plug that fan into a power source. If the connector is a tiny white female connector, look on the motherboard near the CPU slot for a couple of pins sticking up and a label saying FAN. If the connector is a larger white male connector with four pins inside a sort of shield, like the power connectors for a hard drive, then you can plug it into any available socket coming off of the power supply.

12. If your new CPU runs at a different speed than the old one, you'll probably need to change one or more switches on the motherboard. Typically, there's a label inside the cover, on the power supply, or elsewhere inside the box with a legend describing how to set the motherboard switches.

13. Reconnect any cables that you disconnected in step 4. You can remove the bits of masking tape that you used to help you remember what goes where, although it won't hurt anything to leave them in place.

14. Reinstall any components that you removed in step 3.

15. Put the cover back on the PC.

16. Reconnect the keyboard, mouse, display, and any other peripheral cables.

17. Restart the PC and watch for any BIOS errors that may indicate you didn't get the motherboard switch settings just right. If you don't see any such errors, the system should start normally.

What about if you have a socket-type CPU but your motherboard requires a slot-type CPU? You may want to consider using a slot-to-socket adapter called a *slocket* (or, less melodically, *slotket*), like the one shown in Figure 10.16.

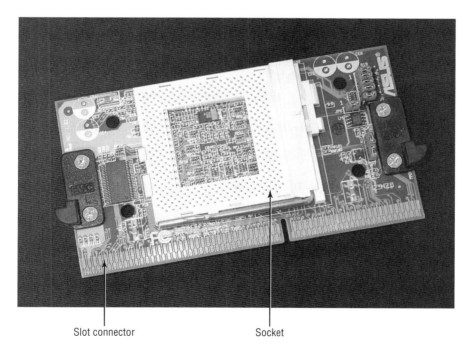

Slot connector   Socket

Figure 10.16 *A slocket adapts a socket CPU to a slot motherboard.*

Be aware that Intel generally recommends against the use of slockets. You're always better off installing the type of CPU (slot or socket) that your motherboard was designed for. But if that's just not an option, then get out on the Web and do some surfing for the keywords *slocket* and *slotket*; you'll find many vendors with products that may work for you.

WARNING *Slockets often don't work on two-CPU systems because of space constraints.*

Adding a CPU

Two circumstances exist in which you'd add a CPU to an existing system, as opposed to replacing one: first, if you've purchased a CPU-less motherboard as part of a motherboard replacement or as part of a new PC construction project; and second, if you have a motherboard (and operating system) capable of running two CPUs and you decide you want to add the second one.

Although the basic procedures are the same as for replacing a CPU (see previous section), here are a few tips you may want to keep in mind if you fall into one of these two special cases.

Adding a CPU to a Bare-Bones Motherboard

The main tip I want to share with you about installing a CPU onto a bare system board is to *support the board properly* before you add the CPU. If you've already mounted the motherboard into the case before installing the CPU, then it should have adequate support. But if not, make sure you support the back of the motherboard before exerting pressure to insert a CPU.

For example, you can lay it on a piece of plywood that has a couple of pieces of cardboard tacked to the top. You don't want the backboard to be so rigid that you damage solder joints, but you don't want the motherboard to flex too much when you press the CPU into its slot, either.

Whenever you're working with a motherboard outside an enclosure, static electricity is even more of a danger than usual, because you don't have a metal chassis to dissipate any static charge that your body may develop. Consider the following suggestions:

- Plan to install the CPU in one sitting. Don't get up in the middle of the work, walk across a carpeted floor, answer the phone, then walk back, sit down, and resume installing the CPU.

- Before you pick up either the CPU or the motherboard, touch something big and metallic, like a file cabinet, to ground yourself.

- Keep the motherboard and the CPU in their antistatic bags until you're ready to do the work.

When adding a CPU, you may also have to add a *VRM*, or *voltage regulator module* (see Figure 10.17). This is a circuit board that plugs into a slot right next to the CPU slot. The VRM is responsible for sensing the voltage that the CPU module needs and for providing that voltage exactly and unwaveringly.

Figure 10.17 *A voltage regulator module*

TIP *Not all VRMs are the same! If you get a VRM in a kit with the CPU, great— it's sure to be the right one. If you get a VRM separately from the CPU, make sure it's compatible with your CPU type! You may need to contact your PC's tech support line to verify this information.*

Filling Out a Dual-CPU System (Windows NT/2000/XP)

Certain PC operating systems, most notably Windows NT and Windows 2000/XP (Professional and Server versions only), can support multiple CPUs running simultaneously, using a technology called *SMP*, for *symmetric multi-processing*. (DOS, Windows 95, 98, and ME do not support SMP—meaning that although these operating systems can run just fine on a PC with two processors, the operating system will use only one of those processors and the other one will remain "idle.") Out of the box, both Windows NT and Windows 2000 Professional can run two CPUs at a time; some OEM versions of these operating systems can support even more than that.

How much of a speed boost do you actually get from adding a second CPU to a Windows NT or 2000 system? Not as much as you'd expect, I'm afraid (although 2000 does a bit better in this regard than NT). My experience has been that you can expect something like 25- to 30 percent better performance all around, and more than that if you run software (such as 3D Studio or Photoshop) that includes optimizations for SMP systems. Without getting too detailed, the basic reason you don't get twice as much speed when you add a second CPU is that the processing workload isn't capable of being perfectly divided between the two processors. For example, many operating system processes *must* execute on the first CPU in a two-CPU system.

The procedure for adding a CPU to a system that already has one varies in three respects from the procedure for replacing an existing CPU:

- You may have to obtain the appropriate voltage regulator module (VRM), as described in the previous section.

- You must make sure the second CPU is identical to the first in every major respect—processor type, speed, frontside bus speed, and L2 cache. (On a high-speed server with four or more CPUs, it is recommended that you buy all four CPUs from the same *batch*, to ensure against timing discrepancies!)

- Install the second CPU before telling your operating system about it. For example, if you change the computer type to multiprocessing in the Windows 2000 Device Manager before a second CPU is physically present in the machine, you won't be able to boot!

Most home PCs don't provide for an additional CPU on the motherboard. However, if you have a business- or workstation-class PC, it's worth a peek in the manual (or inside the case) to see if that computer can host two CPUs. If it can, and if you can get a second processor from eBay or some similar source at a good price, this upgrade can rank very high on the bang-per-buck scale.

Chapter 11

Buses

A computer *bus* is a communication channel between two or more components. Many of the products I've discussed in this book connect to a PC via one of three popular buses: *USB* (*universal serial bus*), *SCSI* (*small computer systems interface*), and *FireWire* (*IEEE-1394*). This chapter takes a closer look at these buses, with an eye to helping you set them up correctly regardless of whether you're configuring a new hard drive, digital camera, or CD burner.

Intro to Buses

To go faster while driving from point A to point B, you can do one of two things: get a faster car, or find a road with fewer traffic signals and a higher speed limit. Similarly, to make a computer go faster, you can do one of two things: make individual components faster, as for example by installing a 10,000-rpm hard drive to replace a 5,400-rpm unit, or make the communications channel between devices faster, for example by using a SCSI channel for hard drives instead of IDE.

A typical PC has multiple communications channels, and some of them are not upgradable. For example, the bus between the CPU and main memory is built into the motherboard, and you can't change it without changing the motherboard. The *PCI* (*peripheral component interconnect*) bus for add-in expansion boards is also part of the motherboard, and is also not upgradable.

By contrast, the USB, SCSI, and FireWire buses may be integrated with your motherboard, too, but these buses *are* upgradable in the sense that you can add a faster, newer bus controller card to your PC and either disable or ignore the motherboard bus. If you don't have integrated USB, SCSI, or FireWire, you can add any or all of these buses via a controller card. These controllers are just circuit boards, like an internal modem or a video card, and they typically plug into a PCI slot inside your PC. However, unlike an internal modem or video card, an add-in controller lets you connect lots of new devices to your computer.

Reasons to Upgrade

Why would you want to upgrade a bus? The main reasons are compatibility and speed. For example, you may have a PC whose integrated USB controller and supporting code is "version 1.0," that is, the very first implementation of USB. Some PC manufacturers started putting USB capability into their PCs before the standard had truly settled out. These PCs don't work well with many new USB devices, so you could add a new USB controller to make those devices function properly.

Here's another example from my own experience. I was upgrading a Pentium II system to a Pentium III running at a higher clock speed. The system passed its power-on tests, but it choked when trying to access the hard drive. After a little research, I discovered that the SCSI bus integrated with the motherboard needed a firmware upgrade in order to work right with the faster, newer CPU. (Firmware is software encoded on a chip; for example, a computer's BIOS is firmware.) Sometimes you can upgrade firmware, and sometimes you can't. In my case, I couldn't. So, I installed a SCSI controller that was firmware-upgradeable, and disabled the on-board SCSI controller. At that point, everything worked like a dream.

You may also consider upgrading a bus controller to enjoy a speed boost. The prime example coming up as I write this is USB 2.0. Although no commercial products for this upgrade to the universal serial bus are yet available, they will be soon, and they'll run as fast as 480MB per second—that is to say, 40 times faster than the fastest USB 1.1 devices! However, to take advantage of USB 2.0, you'll need to upgrade your PC with a new USB host controller.

Reasons to Add

Now, why would you want to add a *new* bus to an existing PC? The reasons here are typically convenience, expandability, and speed.

Convenience takes several forms, but certainly one of them is the ability to add hardware to your computer without ripping into the system unit. Every time you open your PC's cover, you run the risk of unintentionally damaging something. (If you're prone to the occasional expression of temperament, like I am, you also run the risk of intentionally damaging something if you can't get it to work right.) You may also find it convenient to use some modern peripherals with a PC that is getting a little long in the tooth; adding a modern bus controller is a great way to do that.

Expandability has become a big deal in today's world of super-thin hardware profit margins. Many small PCs sold today have only one to three expansion slots. This helps PC manufacturers save money, but it severely limits your expansion options. If you add a bus controller to one of those precious slots, you can effectively make the slot do double- or triple-duty or even more, by supporting multiple peripheral devices that connect to that single controller.

Speed is addictive for PC users, and nowadays the place you're most likely to notice a speed bottleneck is in device input and output (I/O). Processors have gotten so fast that additional speed gains don't necessarily make a computer "feel" faster, but you know right away when your hard drive or CD burner doubles in speed by virtue of being connected to a faster bus. For example, one of the first things I usually do when hot-rodding a PC is to replace the existing IDE hard drive with a higher-performing SCSI drive, requiring that I add a bus controller if the PC doesn't have SCSI built in (and most don't).

USB

It has taken a few years and lots of selling by the computer hardware industry, but the USB is finally coming into its own as a replacement for the older serial and parallel ports that have been the mainstay for peripheral device connection until, well, about now.

The old-style serial port (of which most PCs have two, in the form of male 9-pin connectors) really supports only one device at a time. So, if you have two serial ports, you can have two devices hooked up to your PC via serial ports. The same is true of the faster parallel port (of which most PCs have merely one, in the form of a female 25-pin connector). The parallel port can support multiple devices in theory, but in practice, that doesn't work very well, as anyone who has tried to run an external Zip drive and printer on the same parallel port will attest. You can't run both devices at the same time, and sometimes the parallel cables aren't even fully compatible, so your printer runs slower than it would otherwise.

By contrast, you can hang up to 127 devices (!) off a single USB port, in a *tiered star* arrangement. You have to put hubs in the chain every so often to provide power and ports; the hubs daisy-chain together (the "tiered" part), and the devices you actually use connect to the hubs via cables in a hub-and-spoke arrangement (the "star" part). USB is mainly an external bus, meaning that the devices you connect to the USB controller are external devices (although a few exceptions exist).

In addition, USB devices are generally *hot swappable*, meaning you can add and remove them without powering down the computer. (This last feature is a characteristic of the Plug and Play standard.) Having said that, if you're running some flavor of Windows on your PC, you should issue a "stop" command for any disk or network devices on the USB before physically disconnecting them. You typically stop a USB device using the system tray, which is a little area on the taskbar opposite the Start button.

All those USB devices share a single *interrupt* (input/output channel) on the PC, so interrupt conflicts with other devices are unlikely. USB is really easy to configure in that you don't have to concern yourself with any resource assignments—that is, not just interrupts, but also memory addresses, device IDs, and so on. The bus handles those details behind the scenes. This fact means less finagling with your operating system, and no setting switches or jumpers on the devices themselves.

You can hop down to the local computer store and pick up USB versions of the following kinds of peripherals:

- Speakers

- Monitors

- Keyboards

- Mice
- Joysticks
- CD burners
- Scanners
- Printers
- Modems
- Digital cameras
- MP3 players
- Network connections (such as USB-to-Ethernet)
- Tape drives
- Floppy drives

Not all PC operating systems support USB, but most popular ones do, with the notable exceptions of Windows NT 4.0 and the original version of Windows 95.

Figure 11.1 shows typical USB ports on a PC's back panel, with their tongue-depressor tab. Most PCs have two USB ports.

Figure 11.1 Typical USB ports on a PC

Figure 11.2 shows the cable connector (called an *"A" connector*) that plugs into the USB port.

Figure 11.2 *Cable connector for plugging into a PC*

Figure 11.3 shows a typical USB port on an external USB device—in this case a flatbed scanner.

Figure 11.4 shows the cable connector (called a *"B" connector*) that plugs into that port. Watch out, though; many USB device manufacturers use nonstandard cable connectors, meaning that you have to use their proprietary cables.

Figure 11.3 *Typical USB port on an external device*

Figure 11.4 *Cable connector for plugging into a device*

TIP *Many USB keyboards act as a pass-through in that they have two USB ports, one to connect to the computer (or hub) and another to connect to a USB mouse. That's handy because it saves your having to run the mouse cable all the way down to the PC's back panel (or hub). When USB devices connect in this way, it's called daisy chaining. (Isn't that just precious?)*

One of the big advantages of USB compared to serial and parallel ports is that it's faster, up to 100 times faster than a regular old-style serial port, even though USB is still a serial interface (meaning that bits flow one after another down the wire, like cars on a single-lane highway). The speed depends on the mode; USB can operate in *isochronous* or *asynchronous* mode, but not both at the same time. In isochronous mode, data transfers occur at a fixed, guaranteed level of 12Mbps (megabits per second). Modems, monitors, and speakers often use this mode. In asynchronous mode, data moves at 1.5Mbps, a speed more appropriate for keyboards and mice. Incidentally, you may hear 12Mbps referred to as "full speed," and 1.5Mbps referred to as "low speed."

USB version 1.1 is pretty stable compared to its predecessors. USB version 1.0, which came out in 1996, worked about as well as version 1.0 of anything, which is to say, not very. Version 1.0a made some improvements, but you're really better off with version 1.1 if you want USB to function as intended. (Some of the things that don't work very well in earlier versions are device detection and hot-swappability.)

How do you find out what version your devices support? Check out their specifications, which should be printed on the box or published on the manufacturer's Web site. How about your controller? Here again, check the detailed specs for your PC, and go to the PC builder's Web site if you need to. Theoretically, the controller specification didn't change between versions 1.0 and 1.1, but your PC's BIOS may not support the newer version.

TIP *If your PC specs out to USB version 1.0, or even 1.0a, and you have the latest BIOS (see Chapter 10, "BIOS and CPU"), you may want to consider upgrading to a USB 1.1 controller—especially if it can also support USB 2.0 when peripherals for that bus become available. Adaptec's USB2Connect is such a product, for example; it's a 32-bit PCI card with two external ports and one internal port.*

In the new version of USB, 2.0, the maximum speed is 480Mbps—that is, mighty quick. USB 2.0 is sure to give SCSI and FireWire a run for their money if it lives up to its lofty specifications. However, although the specification was approved in mid-2000, it's getting off to a rather slow start. Ask your local computer store guru occasionally about USB 2.0 devices; when they arrive, the combination of high speed and simple connectivity should be extremely appealing for those of us who can think of other things to do with a nice summer weekend than configure a SCSI device chain.

Installing a USB Host Adapter

Installing a USB host adapter, or controller, is not much different from installing any sort of circuit board. Figure 11.5 shows an add-in USB controller that fits into a standard 32-bit PCI slot and provides two external ports and one internal one. Note that USB doesn't replace the PCI bus, but it works in cooperation with it, just as SCSI and FireWire do.

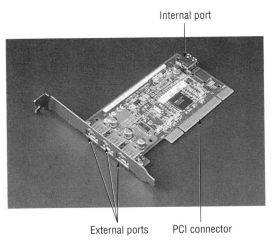

Internal port

External ports   PCI connector

Figure 11.5 *An add-in USB controller*

Before you install a USB host adapter, you should verify that your operating system can handle it. Most do nowadays, but you can download a little utility called Intel USB System Check from, among other places, **www.usb.org**. Assuming your operating system gets a green light from the utility, proceed as follows.

EQUIPMENT YOU'LL NEED:

➡ *An antistatic wrist strap (optional, but recommended)*

➡ *An appropriate screwdriver to remove your PC's cover*

➡ *A screwdriver to secure your host adapter (usually Phillips head)*

➡ *The USB host adapter*

INFORMATION YOU'LL NEED:

➡ *Your PC's user manual (for details of cover removal)*

➡ *Your USB host adapter manual (for details of software installation)*

1. Remove all jewelry from your hands, wrists, and neck.

2. Disconnect the keyboard, mouse, display, power, and any other connectors from the PC's back panel.

3. Open the PC cover and locate an unused PCI slot (see Figure 11.6). PCI slots are usually beige or cream-colored. Check the USB controller manual to see if it needs to sit in a 32-bit slot or a 64-bit slot (the 64-bit slots are longer); most likely, either will do.

4. Remove the expansion slot cover plate, saving the screw. Put the cover plate into the drawer or envelope where you store old PC parts that you may need to reuse someday.

5. Slide the USB controller into the expansion slot. Line it up first, then press down firmly until the card snaps into place. Make sure it's level in the slot (see Figure 11.7).

6. Replace the slot cover screw. (If you're connecting any internal USB devices, you would do so at this point. In this example, I'm assuming that your USB devices are external, which is the more common scenario.)

7. Put the cover back on the PC.

8. Reconnect the keyboard, mouse, display, and any other peripheral cables.

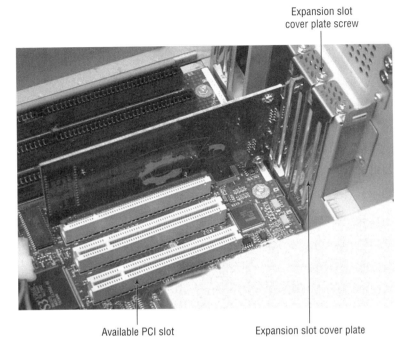

Expansion slot
cover plate screw

Available PCI slot   Expansion slot cover plate

Figure 11.6 *Locating a free expansion slot*

Figure 11.7 *A correctly installed controller*

9. Power up the PC. Follow the manufacturer's instructions for installing any required software for the card; with most Windows PCs, the computer will automatically detect it, and all you need to do is follow the on-screen instructions.

10. Congratulations: You're ready to start attaching USB devices to the card.

TIP *Troubleshooting tip: If Windows has problems finding devices on the bus, try removing the bus host controller in Device Manager and rebooting the PC. That lets Windows redetect the controller and every USB device connected to it.*

Installing a USB Hub

What the heck is a hub? It's a device that you'll probably need to use if you have more than a couple of USB devices on your PC. Hubs provide device connection points, power management, and device detection services. The USB host (either a circuit on the PC's motherboard or an add-in adapter) is the *root hub*.

Basically, think of a hub as analogous to a power strip; it gives you more ports into which you can plug USB devices. Figure 11.8 shows a pretty typical USB hub.

Figure 11.8 *A USB hub*

TIP *Integrated hubs, which are built right into a USB device (such as a monitor), are very handy and reduce clutter. However, when you move to USB 2.0, remember that you'll need new hubs, at which point the integrated hub can be a drawback instead of an advantage.*

When you buy a USB hub, consider whether you want a *bus-powered* or *self-powered* hub. (A self-powered hub comes with its own power supply and plugs into an AC outlet.) I always recommend self-powered hubs for desktop PCs, because they can supply more power to downstream devices: 500mA (milliamps) per port, as opposed to only 100mA for a bus-powered hub. If you're buying a hub that you plan to use with a portable PC, then you may consider a bus-powered hub; but even then, take a look at the current draw of the devices you plan to connect and make sure the hub can handle it.

Installing a USB hub is so simple that I'm not even going to create the usual list of steps. You just connect the new USB hub to an existing hub (or to one of your PC's USB ports) with a cable, and then connect any USB devices to the available ports on the new hub. If you have a self-powered hub, you'll also have to plug it in and perhaps turn it on (some hubs don't have a power switch).

USB Configuration Rules

Most of you won't be hooking up lots of USB devices to your PC, but for those who do, here are the main configuration rules.

- USB devices may not be more than five meters from a hub. As a practical matter, I like to keep the distance to three meters, which is a typical USB cable length; but as always with computer cables, the shorter the better.

- Don't connect one bus-powered hub to another bus-powered hub.

- Bus-powered hubs (as opposed to self-powered hubs, which have their own power supply) can support a maximum of four downstream ports.

- Don't exceed five tiers, where a tier is a layer of devices coming off a hub.

- USB 2.0 uses the same cables as USB 1.1, but different hubs.

- If you mix USB 1.1 and 2.0 devices on the same bus, the bus runs at the speed of the slowest devices (that is, you won't get USB 2.0 speed).

If you're still having USB troubles after following all these rules, you may want to do a bit of cable swapping; there are a lot of substandard USB cables out there.

Measuring USB Power Draw

One of the more common problems with USB devices "disappearing" is power draw. You won't see this problem if you have only one or two devices on the bus, but when you start talking about three or more devices, it's very common.

The basic issue is that when too many devices draw their power from the bus instead of from external power sources (AC adapters), the bus can't handle the current and basically "gives up." The effect you see as a user is that your devices seem to vanish, even though they're still connected.

TIP *If you run a recent version of Windows on your PC, you can probably check the maximum available bus power in the Device Manager (known affectionately to PC pros as "Device Mangler"). You'll find Device Manager in the System control panel, either on its own tab, or as a button on a tab named Hardware. Open the "Universal Serial Bus controllers" node (or similarly named) and double-click the icon labeled "USB Root Hub." It should declare the total power available somewhere on the property sheet; it may even tell you how much power existing USB devices are drawing from the bus, as shown in Figure 11.9.*

My advice is that whenever you get an AC power adapter with a USB device, use it. The less you depend on bus power to run your peripherals, the fewer problems you'll have. If the only USB devices you use are a keyboard, mouse, and one or two very low power-draw items (such as a digital still camera), then don't worry about power draw; it won't be an issue for you.

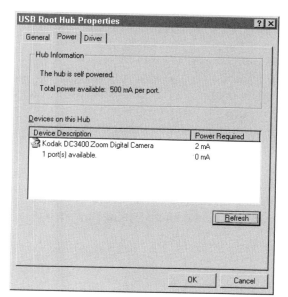

Figure 11.9 *Checking USB power in Windows 2000*

FireWire

FireWire, also known by its formal name of IEEE 1394 (IEEE is the Institute of Electrical and Electronic Engineers), is a very cool upgrade for your PC. Unfortunately, it's much better known in the Macintosh world than the PC world, meaning that (as with most things Mac) its hardware is a bit more expensive than we'd like it to be.

FireWire is very similar to USB in most practical respects. It's a Plug and Play bus with a tiered star design, and supports both asynchronous and isochronous data transfer modes. A single FireWire port supports up to 63 devices on a single bus, and in theory, you can connect up to 1023 buses together! (Don't try this at home. Or if you do, take a picture and send it to me.)

To add to the similarities, FireWire supports hot swapping; you don't have to configure FireWire devices manually (for example, with switches or jumpers) to set their bus IDs; and FireWire is a serial bus (one-lane highway).

In the performance department, however, FireWire leaves USB version 1 in the dust. This bus supports data transfer rates of 100, 200, and even 400Mbps, compared to the 12Mbps ceiling for USB 1.1. FireWire is therefore suitable for high-bandwidth devices, such as hard drives, digital camcorders, stereos, digital TVs, VCRs, DVD players, and video teleconferencing equipment. In fact, although you can also use FireWire for more prosaic applications such as printers, scanners, and hard drives, its focus is on consumer audio/video equipment, and that's where you'll find the widest selection of FireWire gizmos.

The original FireWire spec came out in 1995, and an update occurred in 2000 (the so-called IEEE 1394a-2000 standard, if you really want to know). A revision is in the works as I write this, and IEEE 1394b is expected to offer twice the top speed of today's FireWire devices, that is, 800Mbps. The bad news is that you're likely to see 800Mbps FireWire on Macintosh computers before it gets to the PC platform. FireWire hasn't yet caught fire (sorry) in the PC industry, perhaps due to the slightly more complex setup and maintenance requirements it imposes. To keep up with FireWire, visit www.1394ta.org from time to time.

FireWire connectors (see Figure 11.10) use six pins: Two provide power and ground, and four (in the form of two twisted pairs) provide data and signaling. This is a more expensive arrangement than USB, which is one reason FireWire setups cost more than USB setups. A variant of this connector provides only the four data and signaling pins, meaning that such devices must be self-powered (i.e., plug into an AC outlet).

Installing FireWire

The procedure for installing a FireWire host adapter (such as the one in Figure 11.11) is virtually identical to that described earlier in this chapter under "Installing a USB Host Adapter," so I won't repeat that information here. The same is true of installing a FireWire hub. Remember, FireWire is just about exactly like USB except for the speed factor.

Figure 11.10 *A FireWire cable connector*

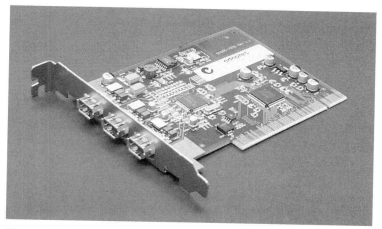

Figure 11.11 *An add-in FireWire controller*

FireWire Configuration Rules

Here are a few rules to keep in mind when configuring a FireWire bus.

- FireWire devices may be no more than 4.5 meters from a hub. This is shorter than for USB and reflects the basic physical truth that the faster a bus can move data, the shorter its cables are probably going to have to be.

- The maximum number of hops (basically, each cable in the data stream counts as a hop) is 16. So, the maximum distance from the controller to the last device in a chain is 72 meters, end-to-end.

- The standard permits connecting devices having different speeds on the same FireWire bus. It's possible to have one device communicating at 400Mbps while another is communicating at (say) 100Mbps, but you must make sure that for the faster device, every device between it and the host adapter is capable of the maximum speed.

As with USB, if you follow the configuration rules and still have connectivity problems, cable quality may be an issue.

SCSI

Even though it's not necessarily fashionable to admit it, I like SCSI even though it's not the newest kid on the block, and here's why:

- It's fast—faster than USB (at least version 1) and (usually) faster than IDE (Integrated Device Electronics, the basis for nearly all PC hard drive interconnections). Windows 2000/XP, in particular, really screams with SCSI hard drives.

- SCSI doesn't bog down as much as other buses do when you hang multiple devices on it, which is one reason SCSI is so popular for servers that must have several hard drives online at once.

- Every time you think it's going to finally succumb to its competitors, it gets better, faster, and easier to set up.

- "SCSI" is fun to say (the pronunciation is "scuzzy").

True, USB 2.0 and FireWire are faster than SCSI. But as I write this, USB 2.0 hasn't really arrived, and FireWire devices are both scarcer and (usually) more expensive than SCSI devices. If you want speed and you want it right now, you should give SCSI a hard look, especially if you can't find FireWire devices that meet your needs at a comparable cost.

One of the reasons SCSI has been able to keep pace with other buses is that it uses a parallel data path instead of a serial path. That is, instead of a single-lane highway, SCSI uses an eight-lane highway (or wider). That's a big advantage when you're looking at moving lots of data. (It's also the main reason SCSI cables are so bulky and expensive.)

So how fast is SCSI? It all depends on which flavor of SCSI you're talking about. Just as with IDE and EIDE interfaces for hard drives, the SCSI bus has evolved over time, getting faster with each successive version. The unfortunate thing about SCSI (and one reason more consumers don't use it) is that the names for these different versions have been maddeningly inconsistent and hard to understand. I'll try to lay out the main variations in the following list:

SCSI-1 is the original spec and nobody uses it anymore. Throughput is 5MBps (note from the capital "B" that this is mega*bytes* per second, not mega*bits* per second, as we use with USB and FireWire discussions—so 5MBps is equal to 40Mbps).

SCSI-2, also known as **Fast SCSI**, has a top speed of 10MBps and is still in moderately widespread use. This flavor uses an 8-bit-wide data path.

Ultra SCSI is another 8-bit-wide specification that tops out at 20MBps, although the "Ultra Wide" variant goes to 16 bits in width and handles 40MBps.

Ultra2 SCSI is an exclusively 16-bit-wide implementation that maxes out at 40MBps in the narrow variant and 80MBps in the wide (16-bit) variant.

Ultra160 SCSI is also 16 bits wide only, and can hit 160MBps. To put that figure into some perspective, it is about the same speed that gossip travels in a small community. Put another way, it's about three times faster than FireWire.

With these various standards come different connectors and cables. You'll normally get proper internal cables when you buy a SCSI host adapter, but if you want to connect one or more external devices, you'll probably have to buy the cable separately. The bad news is that SCSI cables are expensive (remember, they've got more wires in 'em due to that parallel architecture). The good news is that you can usually save a few bucks buying your cables over the Internet. One good source in North America is DataComm Warehouse, accessible via **www.warehouse.com**.

Figure 11.12 shows some common SCSI cable connectors and their designations. (I omit the oldest type of cable, a SCSI-1 cable, because you almost never see it anymore except on old Macintosh systems.)

TIP *Always check your controller manual for details on maximum cable length. Different controllers support different lengths. Go longer than the specified limit, and your bus probably won't work right.*

WARNING *SCSI has its roots in the past, and it is not a Plug and Play bus. So, if you want to add or remove a SCSI device, power your PC down first.*

The basic procedure for setting up a SCSI bus is to first install the host adapter (here you'd follow the same procedure as given earlier in this chapter under "Installing a USB Host Adapter"). Then, set the host adapter's SCSI ID (see the section later in this chapter titled "Setting the Controller's SCSI ID"), connect any SCSI devices (hard drives, scanners, what have you), set the device IDs, and set the bus termination. The details will depend on exactly what you're installing, so I can't prescribe a specific "one size fits all" sequence of detailed steps. For that, you'll have to read the documentation for your SCSI controller and SCSI devices. However, the following sections will give you a lot of helpful hints, starting with what sort of controller you should choose.

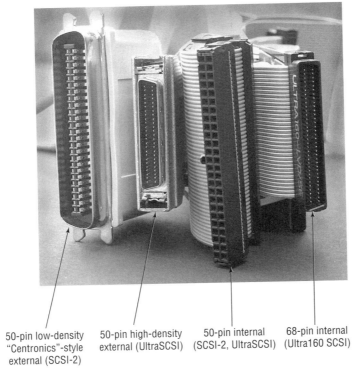

50-pin low-density   50-pin high-density   50-pin internal   68-pin internal
"Centronics"-style   external (UltraSCSI)   (SCSI-2, UltraSCSI)   (Ultra160 SCSI)
external (SCSI-2)

Figure 11.12   *SCSI cable connectors*

Single- and Dual-Channel Controllers

When upgrading a PC to include SCSI support, you should think about how many SCSI devices you'll possibly add to the system. If the answer is one or two, then a single-channel controller should do just fine. As soon as you get to three, however, it's time to think about a dual-channel controller. Such a device is basically two controllers on a single adapter (see Figure 11.13). You get the advantage of greater expandability without sacrificing another slot on your motherboard. Also, a dual-channel controller usually costs a lot less than two single-channel controllers.

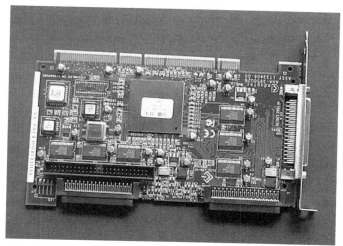

Figure 11.13 *A dual-channel SCSI controller*

Now, if a single channel will support anywhere from 6 to 15 devices, why do I suggest you consider a dual-channel adapter if you may have only three or four devices? The reason is performance. You can usually put two high-speed devices on a single SCSI channel without noticing much performance impact, but more than that and you may be slowing things down. By splitting busy devices across the two channels of a dual-channel controller, you get better speed.

TIP *You can have more than one SCSI controller in a single PC. If you already have one controller and you want to add SCSI devices, adding a second controller lets you divide up the devices between the two controllers for maximum speed.*

Setting the Controller's SCSI ID

Every device on the SCSI bus has to have a unique ID number. Therefore, when you add a SCSI controller to your PC, you have to choose an ID number for it.

The time-honored tradition is that the controller has ID number 7, and that's probably what your controller card comes preconfigured to use, but it's worth checking. I don't recommend you change the controller's SCSI ID if it's already set to the number 7. If it's something else, consider changing it to the number 7. The reason is that whatever device on the SCSI bus has the number 7 ID is the device that gets top priority when accessing the bus. Nearly all systems will run fastest when the controller has top priority.

Device IDs

The big thing here is to make sure no device IDs conflict with each other, or with the controller's ID. Traditionally, the first SCSI hard drive on your system has ID number 0, the second has ID number 1, and so on; I recommend going with tradition unless you have a specific reason not to.

TIP *SCSI IDs do not have to be sequential.*

You typically set the ID on an internal SCSI device using a *jumper*, a tiny plastic block with two holes in it that fit over pins that stick out from the device's main circuit board. Tweezers are a big help when you're setting jumpers. Figure 11.14 shows jumpers on a SCSI hard drive, and Figure 11.15 shows the disk-drive label detailing how to position the jumpers to indicate a particular ID.

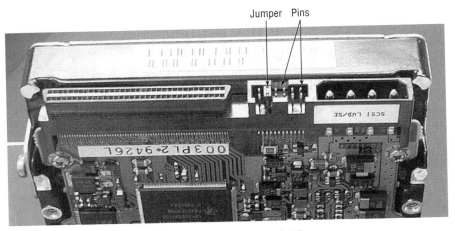

Figure 11.14 *Jumpers dictate an internal device's ID.*

TIP *If you have more jumpers than you need, don't throw away the extras; hang them off unused pins on the connector block. You may need them later if you ever have to reconfigure the device to use a different ID.*

On an external SCSI device, you'll normally set the ID with a switch on the device's back panel. These can vary in form from thumbwheels to DIP (dual inline package) switches; check the manual for the device if the settings aren't obvious.

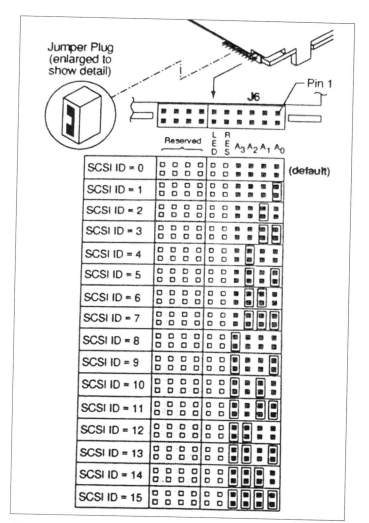

Figure 11.15 *A disk-drive label explains how to set ID jumpers.*

If you want to get fancy, and I say *why not*, you can take advantage of the fact that SCSI is a *prioritized* bus. That is, different ID numbers get priority in the case when two or more devices try to use the bus at the same precise moment. In order from highest priority to least, the ID sequence is 7, 6, 5, 4, 3, 2, 1, 0, 15, 14, 13, 12, 11, 10, 9, 8. (8-bit devices must only use IDs 0 through 7; 16-bit devices may use IDs 0 through 15. Your device manual should state whether it's an 8-bit or 16-bit device.)

So how do you actually use priorities? It's not as obvious as assigning the most-used device to the highest priority. What you actually want to do is put your faster devices, such as hard drives, at low priorities (the first at 0, in an 8-bit system, the second at 1, and so on, working upward) and your slower devices, such as CD drives, at high priorities going down (the first device at 6, the next at 5, and so on, working downward). The reason is that if you give slow devices a low priority, they'll never get to use the bus, because the faster devices freeze them out! Think of the SCSI priority as a handicap: fast devices don't need any help because they're already fast, but slow devices need a boost from a higher SCSI priority ID.

Setting Termination

Next to conflicting device IDs, incorrect *termination* is the leading cause of SCSI problems. Thankfully, terminating the SCSI bus has gotten much easier over the years, although it can still be a bit complex.

The main thing you should remember is that the two ends of the bus chain must be terminated. You can think of terminators (which are really just electrical resistors) as sort of sponges that soak up the leftover signals at the end of the chain so those signals don't reflect back into the chain. (I apologize in advance to any electrical engineers who are horrified at this oversimplification, but I find it a useful concept.)

Termination gets tricky because SCSI is such a flexible bus. The controller can be at one end of the chain but it can also be in the middle of the chain. The latter setup is common, for example, when you have a single internal SCSI device (a hard drive) and one or more external SCSI devices (scanner, CD burner, etc.). The internal device plugs into the controller, and the external devices plug into the controller, too, so the controller's in the middle and must not be terminated. Remove those external devices, however, and the controller is now on the end, and must be terminated.

If you go out today and buy a SCSI controller, you'll probably want an Ultra160 unit to get the best possible speed. And if you only intend to connect that controller to one or more internal devices (say, a hard drive and a CD burner), then termination becomes pretty easy for you! Just use the cable that comes with the controller; it has a terminator built into the end of it (see Figure 11.16). This cable will normally plug into a controller connector called LVD, for *low voltage differential*; LVD channels let you take full advantage of Ultra160's speed potential. Internal LVD SCSI devices come unterminated and you can't terminate them, because they're designed to work with the special terminated cable.

In other situations, you may have to do some terminating yourself (no Schwarzenegger jokes, please). SCSI-2 and Ultra SCSI external devices have many different ways of providing termination. They may have a switch, a jumper, or a special resistor pack (as in Figure 11.17) that you must attach to one of the two SCSI connectors on the back panel of the device. You'll have to check the device's installation manual for the details. Just remember: Always terminate the *ends* of the bus, never the middle.

Cable Terminator

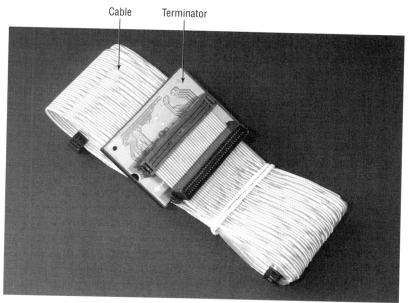

Figure 11.16 *A terminated Ultra160 LVD cable*

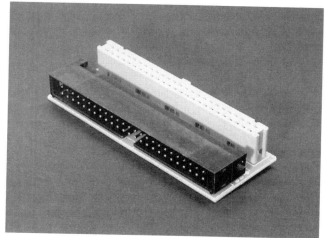

Figure 11.17 *A resistor pack terminator*

I'll end this section with a bit of good news: Most modern SCSI adapters are auto-terminating. That is, they sense whether they're on the end of the device chain or in the middle of it, and set their own termination accordingly. If you have an older adapter, though, you may want to see if it's auto-terminating or if you have to set a switch or jumper by hand.

Other SCSI Settings

You may also bump into the following SCSI settings, although they're less common nowadays than five or ten years ago. You'll normally set these options via your controller's setup program for the controller, and by switches or jumpers for other SCSI devices:

Parity   The SCSI bus uses parity to detect errors. The basic rule nowadays is to make sure all your devices are set to support parity.

Synchronous vs. Asynchronous   Today's high-speed SCSI devices typically use synchronous signaling, but go by the device's manual.

Disconnect/Reconnect   This feature lets a device temporarily disconnect itself from the bus, for example, if it goes offline. If you have two or more SCSI devices attached to a single controller, you should usually enable this feature (it's especially important in Windows 2000). If you have only one SCSI device, such as a high-speed hard drive, you can disable the feature and squeeze a bit more speed out of the system.

Host adapter BIOS   If you plan to use SCSI for the first hard drive on your system, you must make sure to enable the controller's BIOS. Otherwise, the PC won't have any way to access the hard drive in order to boot your operating system. Again, you'll typically make this setting via the host adapter's setup utility. For example, Adaptec cards come with a program called *SCSI Select*, which you activate by pressing Ctrl+A when prompted to do so by the computer during the initial boot process.

Notebook Bus Upgrades

Just about everything in this chapter so far has focused on full-size PCs. Can you upgrade a bus, or add a bus, to a portable PC? Sure, although you're not likely to see the same kind of speed that you would on a full-sized computer. The reason is that most notebooks don't give you a PCI slot into which you can add a bus controller. Instead, you have to use a PC Card ("credit card") slot or, slower still, a parallel port.

Many devices exist on the market to bring SCSI and USB to a portable PC via the PC Card slot. Somewhat fewer let you use your notebook's parallel port as an intermediary for connecting to SCSI and USB devices, but these exist if you hunt for them.

Installing such devices is generally a trivial task: Plug 'em in, follow the instructions for adding any necessary software, and go. You don't even have to crack open the computer's case. Just don't expect top speed: the PC Card interface isn't going to let you run as fast as a PCI slot would, and parallel-port devices only merit your consideration if you're connecting fairly slow peripherals.

Other Buses

To be thorough, I should mention a few other buses you may bump into. You won't be upgrading to these buses, so I won't go into as much detail on them as I did on USB, FireWire, and SCSI.

ISA (Industry Standard Architecture) This bus was the long-time standard for PC expansion cards, but it's a bit rare nowadays to find a new PC that includes any ISA slots. Those that do typically only have one or two. The width of the ISA bus is only 16 bits (really old PCs had an 8-bit ISA bus) and it's slower and more limited than the PCI bus, which most PC motherboards now use for add-in cards.

MCA (Micro Channel Architecture) You may bump into this if you have an old IBM PS/2 computer. Technically, MCA had a lot going for it compared to ISA, including a 32-bit data transfer path, better speed, and better electrical characteristics (less noise). You don't see this one anymore, largely because IBM made it very expensive to develop MCA devices, and PCI came along as a better replacement.

EISA (Extended Industry Standard Architecture) This bus is an improvement on ISA and fairly comparable to MCA in terms of performance. You mostly find EISA in older PC servers. It, too, fell in popularity when PCI came along.

If your PC is based on any of these buses, it's a good candidate for replacement rather than upgrading. You really need the PCI bus to accommodate today's coolest devices, and in my view, trying to update an ISA, MCA, or EISA machine will almost always turn out to be an exercise in frustration. (Don't return this book though; you'll need it when you buy a PCI-based PC!)

Chapter 12

References and Resources

We all realize that the subject of upgrading your PC is too broad to cover completely in 3000 pages, much less 300; although I've tried to hit the high points, occasions are sure to arise when you need more than I've been able to squeeze between these covers. To help you at those times, this section provides some valuable Internet and print references and resources.

Internet References and Resources

The Internet is an excellent and speedy source of information. Unfortunately, it is also an excellent and speedy source of *misinformation*, so it helps to be discriminating about where you get your PC hardware advice. First I'll share a few hardware-oriented Web sites that I've found helpful over the years, and then I'll give you some newsgroups that you may enjoy patronizing.

Web Sites

The following World Wide Web sites contain a wealth of information or are capable of pointing you to a wealth of information. Although I don't vouch for their accuracy, and I disavow any responsibility if you visit one of these sites and read some bad advice that leads to your electrocution and/or death, I can tell you that my experiences with these sites have been generally positive.

FYI, I omit the leading "http://" part of the address name if the site begins with "www," but I include it if the site begins with something else.

```
http://support.intel.com/support/motherboards/identify.htm
```

A site that can help you identify an Intel motherboard.

```
http://support.microsoft.com/support
```

Microsoft's knowledge base used to be a CD-only subscription service, but now it's free and on the Web. If you run any flavor of Windows and get hardware-related error messages, look 'em up in these sites' search facilities.

```
www.amazon.com
```

Still the premier Web bookstore, its best feature is reader reviews, and its second-best feature is that it usually ships a book when it says it'll ship a book. Amazon.com also sells a limited selection of computer hardware these days, and it's very informative to see what other folks have said about a particular piece of gear before you plunk down your cash.

www.anandtech.com

Many informative articles on various hardware topics at this site.

www.bn.com

The Barnes & Noble online bookstore. Not as many reader reviews as Amazon.com, but getting more popular all the time.

www.cnet.com

Lots of links and an excellent search engine that can help you find troubleshooting tips on specific hardware as well as where to get the best online deals.

www.copernic.com

Home of a great freeware program that lets you search the Web with multiple search engines at once. One of the best downloads around.

www.dell.com/outlet

Hard to beat for new computers and related gear. Original factory warranty and great prices for refurbished and overstocked equipment if you don't mind the odd scratch or blemish.

www.ebay.com

A terrific place to get bargains on used (and occasionally new) hardware. Be sure to check out sellers' ratings to see what their track record is like, and consider using an escrow service for big-ticket items. I've used eBay to buy everything from memory to CPU upgrades, and I haven't been disappointed yet.

www.excite.com

A popular Web search site.

www.google.com

My personal favorite all-purpose Web search engine, at least for the time being. Put phrases in double quotes and precede 'em with a plus sign to mandate an exact match.

www.ieee.org

For those of you who like delving into the academic aspects of computing from time to time, this site, the home of the Institute for Electrical and Electronic Engineers, always has some interesting stuff to offer on particular topics. If articles like "Cable Modem Bottlenecks Explained" sound fun to you (they are to me! I admit it!), check it out.

`www.i-sw.com`

My little company, Independent Software, Inc. Stop in, say hello, check out the latest books, and by all means tell me what you thought about this one.

`www.linux.org/hardware`

Good source for details about hardware that's compatible with this up-and-coming operating system. By the way, be cool and pronounce it correctly: LINN-ux.

`www.lycos.com`

One of the Web's main search sites.

`www.microhouse.com`

Home of the famous CD-based MicroHouse Technical Library, including data on motherboards, network interface cards, hard drives, controllers, and peripheral cards.

`www.microsoft.com/hcl`

The home of the famous Hardware Compatibility List, which can help you Windows users figure out if the cool new device you're thinking about buying has Windows drivers that Microsoft's Windows Hardware Quality Lab has tested and blessed.

`www.microwarehouse.com`

One of my favorite online retailers for PC hardware.

`www.motherboardexpress.com`

Good source of system boards, CPUs, all manner of peripherals, system enclosures, power supplies, and so on.

`www.motherboards.com`

Another source of system boards, CPUs, memory, and other upgrades.

`www.northernlight.com`

An intriguing search site that categorizes results, usually intelligently and always bravely.

`www.overclockers.com`

Information for those wishing to push their existing PCs to the limit and occasionally beyond. If you want to find out how to build a water-cooled jacket for your PC's processor so you can run it at twice its rated speed without frying, look no further.

`www.pcconnection.com`

One of my favorite online retailers for PC hardware.

`www.pcguide.com`

Charles Kozierok's PCGuide site is one of the more informative all-around hardware sites on the Web.

`www.seagate.com`

Home of the world's biggest disk drive company and source of diagrams, jumper settings, hardware specs, and some pretty informative white papers, too.

`www.storagereview.com`

A really good site with informative and detailed reviews on a large number of popular hard drives. You know you're at a good Web site when you can easily hyperlink from one review to other related reviews.

`www.sybex.com`

Check out the Sybex site periodically to see what's new in the book list. One of the more respected computer publishers around, and I say that having already cashed my advance check.

`www.yahoo.com`

A goodly chunk of the Web, organized topically.

`www.zdnet.com/pcmag`

A fine source of reliable information, the companion Web site to the venerable PC Magazine print publication. This site offers useful buyer's guides and lots of product reviews.

Newsgroups

Usenet newsgroups are forums where anyone can join, read message threads (that is, sequences of questions and replies), post messages, and perform keyword searches. Generally these messages are in plain text format, although some newsgroups support binary attachments and even binary posts, for example to exchange software. The Usenet is divided into topics of interest, generally at least hinted at by the newsgroup names. (My favorite one of all time is `alt.windows95.crash.crash.crash`.)

To participate in Usenet, you need a *newsreader* program, but that's not a problem because, if you have a PC, you probably already have such a program. For example, Outlook Express comes with most versions of Windows, and it doubles as a newsreader as well as an e-mail program. Free Agent is another newsreader that a lot of people like.

Check with your Internet Service Provider (ISP) for details as to how to configure your newsreader. Normally all you have to do is enter the name of a *news server*, such as `netnews` `.worldnet.att.net` or `news.mindspring.com`, in an account properties dialog box. If your ISP doesn't offer newsgroups, fire it summarily and sign up with one that does.

The single best place to search the entire Usenet is now Google, which purchased deja.com's massive Usenet archive. Search Google's Usenet archives by pointing your Web browser to the following address:

`http://groups.google.com`

Once you get your newsreader set up, here's a list of newsgroups to check out on a rainy day:

`alt.comp.hardware`

`alt.comp.hardware.homebuilt`

`alt.comp.hardware.homedesigned`

`alt.comp.hardware.overclocking`

`alt.comp.hardware.pc-homebuilt`

`alt.comp.periphs.cdr`

`alt.comp.periphs.dcameras`

`alt.comp.periphs.keyboard`

`alt.comp.periphs.videocards.ati`

`alt.comp.periphs.videocards.elsa`

`alt.comp.periphs.videocards.matrox`

`alt.comp.periphs.videocards.nvidia`

`alt.comp.periphs.webcam`

`comp.benchmarks`

`comp.home.automation`

`comp.home.misc`

`comp.laser-printers`

`comp.multimedia`

```
comp.os.linux.hardware

comp.periphs

comp.periphs.printers

comp.periphs.scanners

comp.periphs.scsi

comp.sys.ibm.pc.hardware.cd-rom

comp.sys.ibm.pc.hardware.chips

comp.sys.ibm.pc.hardware.comm

comp.sys.ibm.pc.hardware.misc

comp.sys.ibm.pc.hardware.networking

comp.sys.ibm.pc.hardware.storage

comp.sys.ibm.pc.hardware.systems

comp.sys.ibm.pc.hardware.video

comp.sys.ibm.pc.hardware.misc

comp.sys.intel

comp.sys.laptops

microsoft.public.win2000.hardware

microsoft.public.windowsme.hardware

misc.forsale.computers.monitors

misc.forsale.computers.printers

misc.forsale.computers.storage

redhat.hardware.arch.intel
```

TIP *Messages drop off newsgroups as they age. (Those servers out there in cyber-space have only so much disk space.) So if you run across anything in a newsgroup that you think you'd like to keep for future reference, you should save to disk or print it out, because there's a good chance it'll be gone next time you synchronize the newsgroup.*

Print References and Resources

Although I do a lot of research on the Internet, I've found that there's still a place for old-fashioned magazines and books. Here are some of my favorites.

Magazines

You can't beat magazines for up-to-date information on the latest hardware upgrades. Books are good for background knowledge, but when it's time to buy, scan the recent magazines for reviews and prices.

Business Week
1221 Avenue of The Americas, New York, NY 10020
www.businessweek.com

Huh? Well, for one thing, this magazine has Stephen Wildstrom, one of the better technical writers around. In addition, *BW* performs the occasional computer technology overview, which no other magazine can match for conciseness and general common sense.

Computer Shopper
www.zdnet.com/computershopper

It's huge, but you can find great deals if you're patient. The articles are pretty good, too, if you want something a bit less technical than, say, *PC Magazine*.

Computerworld
500 Old Connecticut Path, Framingham, MA 01701
www.computerworld.com

A venerable periodical. Excellent, especially if your interests include non-PC platforms.

Information Week
600 Community Drive, Manhasset, NY 11030
www.informationweek.com

Very good if you can find the time to read a weekly periodical.

InfoWorld
P.O. Box 1172, Skokie, IL 60076
www.infoworld.com

Essential if you're in the computer industry, covers non-PC platforms and "big iron" too, but its PC articles are opinionated and well-informed.

PC Magazine
One Park Avenue, New York, NY 10016
`www.pcmag.com`

The one rag you'd want if you could only subscribe to one, *PC Magazine* has the best collection of columnists and techies in the business since *Byte* went out of print (R.I.P.). And thankfully the average issue is no longer ten thousand pages.

Books

Here's a smattering of books that, in my judgment, are worth your attention next time you find yourself at a brick-and-mortar bookstore.

The BIOS Companion, Phil Croucher, Advice Press

I met Phil, a.k.a. "Mr. BIOS," several years ago in London when he was getting ready to teach one of my PC networking seminars. I've never met anyone who knows more about the different flavors and species of computer BIOS's, and who can actually explain what all those arcane settings really mean. This book's hard to find, but worth the hunt.

Build Your Own PC, Morris Rosenthal, McGraw-Hill

Don't build a PC from parts to save money, because you probably won't—even if you value your time at zero. If you want to build a PC for fun, however, or to gain a deeper appreciation of how a PC works, then this book provides a good overview of the process along with a number of helpful suggestions along the way.

The Complete PC Upgrade & Maintenance Guide, Mark Minasi, Sybex

Mark and I both taught seminars and made videos for several years with the late great Data-Tech Institute, and I'm still not sure how we managed to avoid ever meeting in person. He's one of a small group of technical writers who has a talent for explaining complex subjects in accessible language. His book's especially good if you have an interest in the evolution of the PC over the years.

The Digital Filmmaking Handbook, Ben Long and Sonja Schenk, Charles River Media

If your interest in upgrading your PC stems from a hidden desire to make and edit movies with your computer, then this book is a good place to start. Don't feel you have to read every chapter though: some are intended for those who plan to make a living with this stuff.

MIDI for the Professional, Paul Lehrman and Tim Tully, Music Sales Corp.

If you're into computer music, this is the best one-volume treatment I've seen.

PC Hardware in a Nutshell, Robert Bruce Thompson et al, O'Reilly

You may not always agree with the positions the authors take in this book, but it's nice to read a hardware book that offers opinions in addition to the dry facts—and the opinions are informed ones. Well executed, and a good complement to the encyclopedic tome from Minasi.

Index

Note to the Reader: Page numbers in **bold** indicate the principle discussion of a topic or the definition of a term. Page numbers in *italic* indicate illustrations.

Numbers

802.1b wireless standard, **147**
4mm tape drives, **43**

A

"A" cable connectors, *254*, **254**
AC outlets, *See also* power
    networking via, 146–147
    notebook adapter kits, 189, *190*
    testing, 168, *169*
accelerator boards, 116
access points, **145–146**, *See also* WAP
access time, **17**
ACTiSYS vendor, 96
"ad hoc mode", **146**
adapters, *See also* networks; video adapters
    AC adapters, 189, *190*
    CPU socket adapters, 245–246, *245*
    defined, **12**, *13–14*
    PC-to-MIDI adapter cables, 211, *212*
    USB host adapters, 256–259, *256*, *258*
    USB-to-PS/2 adapters, 199, *199*
    Y-adapters, 170, *170–171*
AGP (Advanced Graphics Port), *See also* video adapters
    connectors, 124, *125*
    ports, 123–124, *124*
    video boards, 126, *126*
Amazon.com, **276–277**
antistatic bags, 34, *34*
antistatic wrist straps, 28, **28**, 33
aperture grille technique, 120
architectures, network, **148–149**
asynchronous mode, **255**
AT/ATX power supplies, **173–174**
ATI All-in-Wonder Radeon video card, 124, *125*, 130
audio. *See* multimedia
average access time, **40**
AVI (Audio-Video Interleave), 221

B

"B" cable connectors, **254**, 255
backside bus, 232
batteries, *See also* power
    for cordless mice, 200, *200*
    for digital cameras, 214–216, *214*
BEDO (Burst Extended Data Out) memory, **22**
bi-directional cables, **93**
The BIOS Companion (Croucher), **283**
BIOS software, **224–229**
    defined, **224**
    enabling for SCSI controllers, 272
    functions of, 224
    reasons to upgrade, 225
    running setup utility, 19, 229
    setting printer ports, 93
    updating (flashing)
        battery backup units and, 226–228, *227*
        determining need for, 225–226
        downloading latest version, 226
        keeping old BIOS on diskettes, 228
        overview of, 225
        performing updates, 228–229
        warning, 226
    verifying version of, 225–226
Blank, Andrew G., 148
Bluetooth technology, **97**, 147
book resources, **283–284**
boot devices, 224
BRI (Basic Rate Interface), 67
buffered memory, **18**
Build Your Own PC (Rosenthal), **283**
burners, CD, **41**, 58–59, **58–59**
bus speed, **17**, **232**
bus-powered hubs, **260**
buses, **250–273**
    defined, **250**
    EISA buses, 273
    FireWire buses
        connectors, 262, *263*
        defined, **262**

device configuration, 263–264
installing, 262, 263
overview of, 250
speed, 262
versus USBs, 262
ISA buses, 273
MCA buses, 273
notebook bus upgrades, 272–273
PCI buses, 250
reasons to add, 251
reasons to upgrade, 250–251
SCSI buses
assigning device priorities, 269–270
benefits of, 264
cable connectors, 265, 266
cables, 265
Disconnect/Reconnect feature, 272
dual-channel controllers, 266–267, 267
enabling controller BIOS, 272
overview of, 250, 264
parity support, 272
setting controller IDs, 267
setting device IDs, 268–269, 268–269
setting options, 272
setting termination, 270–272, 271
setup, overview, 265–266
single-channel controllers, 266–267
speed, 264–265
versions of, 264–265
warning, 265
USB buses
"A" cable connectors, 254, 254
asynchronous mode, 255
"B" cable connectors, 254, 255
configuring, 252
daisy chaining devices, 252, 255
device configuration, 260
device hot swappability, 252
device support for, 255
devices, listed, 252–253
installing USB host adapters, 256–259,
256, 258
installing USB hubs, 259–260, 259
interrupts, 252
isochronous mode, 255

measuring device power draw, 260–261,
261
overview of, 250
versus parallel ports, 252, 255
ports, 253, 253, 254, 254
versus serial ports, 252, 255
speed, 255
troubleshooting, 259
USB keyboards, 255
version 2.0, 256, 259, 260, 264
versions of, 255–256
Business Week magazine, **282**

C

cable connectors, *See also* adapters; connectors
for network hubs/switches, 156, 157
for SCSI buses, 265, 266
for USB devices, 254, 255–256
cable modem service, **68–69**
cables
data connector cables, 45–46, 45–46,
48–49, 49, 56
dedicated cables, 145
finding online, 265
to inkjet printers, 101, 102
to network adapters, 156–157, 157–158
parallel cables, 92–93, 92
to PC back panels, 8
PC-to-MIDI adapter cables, 211, 212
phone line cables, 146
for SCSI buses, 265
signal cables, 13, 13–14
Ultra 160 LVD cables, 270, 271
USB cables, 8
UTP cables, 145
cache, **40–41**
cache size, CPU, **232**
call waiting, 66
cameras, *See also* multimedia
camcorders, 216–220, 216–219
digital cameras, 214–216, 214
webcams, 220–222, 220, 222
capacitors, **181**
capturing video, 216–219, **216–220**

cartridge drives, **41**
CD-R/CD-RW drives, *See also* storage devices
    defined, **41–42**
    disc media, 59–60
    external/internal drives, 58–59, *58–59*
    upgrading to, 54–58, *56–58*
CD-ROM drives
    using discarded, 58
    overview of, 41, 59
    removing, 54–56, *56*
    warning, 42
Centronics connectors, *92*, **93**
chip speed, **17**
cleaning, *See also* maintenance
    CRT displays, 141–142
    inkjet printers, 109, 111
    laser printers, 109–111, *110*
    LCD displays, 142
    mice, 193, *193*
    tape drives, 62
client/server networks, **148**, 149
color depth display, **131–132**, 204–205
communications, **64–84**
    cable modem service, 68–69
    dial-up modems
        cables, 8
        call waiting and, 66
        installing external modems, 69–74,
            70–73
        installing internal modems, 74–75, *75*
        internal vs. external modems, 65
        multilink modems, 66
        overview of, 64–65
        ports, 9
        speeding up, 65–66
        surge protection, 72, *72*
        voice modems, 66
        warnings, 74, 75
    DSL service
        costs, 68, 76
        installing DSL routers, 77–82, *78–82*
        overview of, 68
        sharing on networks, 75–76
        voice channels, 78
        warning, 82

ISDN service, 67
    overview of, 64
    sharing Internet connections, 76
    wireless services
        overview of, 82–83
        satellite, 83–84
        wireless local loop, 84
The Complete PC Upgrade & Maintenance Guide
    (Minasi), **283**
compressing video files, 205
computer names, **155**
Computer Shopper magazine, **282**
Computerworld magazine, **282**
connectors, *See also* adapters; cable connectors
    AGP connectors, 124, *125*
    Centronics connectors, *92*, 93
    DB-25 connectors, 92, 93
    DVI connectors, *125*, 127, 138, *138*
    for FireWire buses, 262, *263*
    for LCD displays, 137–138, *138*
    LVD connectors, 270, *271*
    PCI connectors, 256
    power connectors, 45, *45*, 49, *50*, *56*
    VGA connectors, 138, *138*
contact enhancer, 27, 29, **29**, 72, 129
contact materials in memory modules, **18**
CPUs, **229–248**
    adding, 246–248, *247*
    backside bus, 232
    cache size, 232
    cooling fans, 233, 237, *238*, 244
    CPU forks, 240, *240*
    defined, **229–230**
    frontside bus speed, 232
    heat sinks/shields, **233**, 235, *235*, 236–237,
        243, *243–244*
    motherboard DIP switches, 237, *238–239*
    overclocking, 233
    overview of, 230–232
    replacing
        non-ZIF socket CPUs, 240–242,
            240–241
        overview of, 230, 232
        slot cartridge CPUs, 242–246, *243–245*
        slot-to-socket adapters and, 245–246,
            245

warnings, 235, 246

    ZIF socket CPUs, 234–239, *234–239*

running two at once, 247–248

slot CPUs, 231, *231*, 232

socket CPUs, 230, *230*, 231, 232

speed, 231–232

CRIMMs (Continuity Rambus Inline Memory Module), 26

Croucher, Phil, 283

CRT displays. *See* displays

D

daisy chaining USB devices, 252, **255**

DAT (Digital Audio Tape) drives, **43**

data communication channel, 17

data connector cables, *45–46*, **45–46**, **48–49**, *49, 56*

DataComm Warehouse, 93, 265

daughterboards, 129

Dazzle's DVC devices, *216–219*, **216–220**

DB-25 connectors, *92*, **93**

DDR (Dual Data Rate) memory, **23**, **130**

dedicated servers, **148**

default gateway addresses, 148

defragmenting hard drives, **61**

degaussing displays, **141**

desk area for displays, *118–119*, **118–119**

Device Manager, 261

dial-up modems. *See* communications

Digital Audio Tape (DAT) drives, **43**

digital cameras, *214*, **214–216**

The Digital Filmmaking Handbook (Long and Schenk), **283**

Digital Linear Tape (DLT) drives, **43**

digital subscriber line. *See* DSL

Digital Video Creator devices, *216–219*, **216–220**

DIMM (Dual Inline Memory Module), 25, **25–26**

DIP (dual inline package) switches, **237**, *238–239*

Direct Memory Access (DMA), 53

Disconnect/Reconnect feature, **272**

disk drives, internal, **12**, *13–14*, *See also* storage devices

diskette drives, 38–39

displays, **116–142**

adjustability, 120

adjusting settings

    color depth, 131–132

    listed, 133

    refresh rate, 119, 132–133

    resolution, 119, 130–131

    speed and, 132

    using third-party utilities, 133–135, *134*

CRT displays

    cleaning, 141–142

    cost, 118

    defined, **116**

    desk area, 118–119, *118*

    leaving on, 141

    opening up, 116, 141

    slim CRTs, 119

    speed, 121

    warnings, 141–142

degaussing, 141

dot pitch, 120

focus, 120

glare, 120

image quality, 117, 119–120

LCD displays

    cleaning, 142

    connectors, 137–138, *138*

    cost, 137

    defined, **116**, **136**, *137*

    desk area, 118–119, *119*

    drawbacks, 137

    installing, 139–141, *139–140*

    speed, 121

multimedia options, 121–122

multiple, installing, 122, 135–136, *136*

multisynching ability, 120

overview of, 116–117

terminology, 116

with TV tuners, 121, 124, *125*

using with VCRs, 121

video adapters

    defined, **116**

disabling motherboard video, 123
speed and, 121
upgrading, overview, 122–123
warranties, 122
video cables/ports, 8–9
video cards
adding memory to, 127–130
defined, **116**
drivers, 127
installing, 125–127, *126*
port connections, 123–124, *124–125*
viewable area, 117–118
warnings, 120, 141–142
warranties, 122
workstation monitors, 120
DLT (Digital Linear Tape) drives, **43**
DMA (Direct Memory Access), 53
DNS server addresses, **80**, 148
dot pitch, **120**
dpi (dots per inch), 90
Drive Copy utility, 52
drivers, **52**, 127
drives, internal disk, **12**, *13–14*, *See also* storage
devices
DSL (digital subscriber line), *See also*
communications
costs, 68, 76
installing DSL routers, 77–82, *78–82*
overview of, 68
sharing on networks, 75–76
voice channels, 78
warning, 82
Dual Data Rate (DDR) memory, **23**, **130**
dual-channel controllers, SCSI, **266–267**, *267*
dust, 7
DVC (Digital Video Creator) devices, *216–219*,
216–220
DVD drives, **42**
DVI connectors, *125*, 127, *138*, **138**
DVI-I to analog converters, 138–139, *139*

E

ECC (Error Correction Code), **17**
ECP (extended capabilities port), 93

EDO (Extended Data Out) memory, **21**
8mm tape drives, **43**
802.1b wireless standard, **147**
EISA (Extended Industry Standard Architecture)
buses, **273**
EMI (electromagnetic interference), 174
Englebart, Doug, 192
EPP (enhanced parallel port), 93
EPRI (Electric Power Research Institute), 185
error-checking memory, 17
Ethernet networks, 147
EverGlide's Giganta mouse pads, **201**, *202*
expansion slots, **12**, *13–14*

F

fans, *See also* power
capacitors and, 181
removing grilles, 178, *179*
replacing, 180–182, *181–183*
single/variable speeds, 173
Fast Ethernet networks, 147
FDISK program, 51
filtering, line, **168**
FireWire buses, *See also* buses
configuring devices, 263–264
connectors, 262, *263*
defined, **262**
installing, 262, *263*
overview of, 250
speed, 262
versus USBs, 262
fixed-point wireless, **84**
flashing. *See* updating BIOS
floppy disk drives, 38–39
form factor, **172**
4mm tape drives, **43**
FPM (Fast Page Mode) memory, **21**
frame rates, **205**
frontside bus speed, **232**

G

game ports, *195*, **195**, *See also* joysticks
gateway addresses, 148

GDI (graphical device interface) printers, **89**
Ghost utility, 52
Giganta mouse pads, **201**, *202*
glare, 120
Goof-Off solvent, 111
graphics tablets, pressure-sensitive, **202–204**, *203*

H

hand tools. *See* PC upgrades
hard drives, *See also* storage devices
    cache, 40–41
    defragmenting, 61
    durability, 40
    IDE drives
        adding, 43–51, *44–50*
        defined, **39**
        upgrading to SCSI, 51–52
        warnings, 48, 49
    mirroring, 52
    overview of, 38–39
    partitioning, 51
    rotational speed, 40
    SCSI drives, **39**
    seek time, 40
heat sensing power supplies, **173**
heat sinks/shields for CPUs, **233**, 235, *235*, 236–237, 243, *243–244*
help. *See* resources; Web site resources
home gateways, **76**
HomePNA (Home Phoneline Networking Alliance), **146**
HomeRF wireless standard, 147
hops, 264
hot swappability, **252**
hubs
    defined, **259**
    installing USB hubs, 259–260, *259*
    in wired networks, 145, **155–158**, *156*

I

ICN (Internet Call Notification) feature, **66**
ICS (Internet Connection Sharing) software, **76**

IDE drives. *See* hard drives
IEEE-1284 cables, **93**
IEEE-1394. *See* FireWire
images. *See* displays; multimedia
Info World magazine, **282**
information. *See* resources; Web site resources
Information Week magazine, **282**
infrared ports, **96–97**
"infrastructure mode", **146**
inkjet printers. *See* printers
input devices, **192–204**, *See also* multimedia
    joysticks
        defined, **194**
        force-feedback joysticks, 194, 195
        MIDI devices and, 195
        ports for, 195, *195*
    keyboards
        ergonomic keyboards, 196–197, *197*
        using great ones, 195
        IBM keyboards, 196, *196*
        key layout, 196–197, *197*
        switches, 195–196, *196*
    mice
        accessories, 201, *202*
        cleaning, 193, *193*
        corded mice, 192
        cordless, installing, 197–200, *198–201*
        cordless mice, 192
        mechanical mice, 193, *193*
        optical mice, 193
        opto-mechanical mice, 193
        overview of, 192, 194
        resolution, 194
        sample rates, 192–193
    overview of, 192, 197
    pressure-sensitive graphics tablets, 202–204, *203*
    trackballs, 194, *194*
installing, *See also* replacing; upgrading
    battery backup units, 185
    CD-R/CD-RW drives, 54–58, *56–58*
    cordless mice, 197–200, *198–201*
    CPUs in CPU-less boards, 246–248, *247*
    DSL routers, 77–82, *78–82*
    external capture devices, 216–220, *216–219*
    external modems, 69–74, *70–73*

FireWire buses, 262, *263*
graphics tablets, 202–204, *203*
inkjet printers, 99–104, *100–104*
internal modems, 74–75, *75*
Jaz drives, 53–54
laser printers, 104–109, *105–107*
LCD displays, 139–141, *139–140*
multiple displays, 122, 135–136, *136*
second CPUs, 247–248
second IDE drives, 43–51, *44–50*
tape drives, 60, *60–61*
USB host adapters, 256–259, *256, 258*
USB hubs, 259–260, *259*
video adapter drivers, 127
Zip drives, 53–54, *53–54*
installing networks. *See* networks
integrated hubs, 259
Intel Web sites, 231–232, 257, 276
internal disk drives, **12**, *13–14*
Internet Call Notification (ICN), **66**
Internet Connection Sharing (ICS), **76**
Internet connections. *See* communications
Internet resources. *See* Web site resources
interrupts, 152, 252
IP addresses, 78, 79, 148, 155
IPX protocol, 147
IrDA (infrared) ports, **96–97**
ISA buses, **273**
ISA slots, 12
ISDN connection services, **67**
isochronous mode, **255**

J

Jaz drives, **41**, 53–54, *See also* storage devices
jeweler screwdrivers, 3, *3*
jewelry, 6, 176
jitter, **137**
joysticks, *See also* input devices
force-feedback joysticks, 194, 195
MIDI devices and, 195
ports for, 195, *195*
jumpers, master/slave, **46**, *47*
jumpers, SCSI device ID, *268–269*, **268–269**

K

Kelly, Jim, 201
keyboards, *See also* input devices
cables, 8
ergonomic keyboards, 196–197, *197*
using great ones, 195
IBM keyboards, 196, *196*
key layout, 196–197, *197*
Kinesis Maxim keyboards, 197
ports, *9*
switches, 195–196, *196*
USB keyboards, 255
Kozierok, Charles, 279

L

LANs. *See* networks
Laptop Express, 188
laptops, *See also* notebook power
infrared ports, 96–97
network adapters, *160*, **160–161**, 162, *162*, 164, *164*
upgrading buses, 272–273
on wired networks, 154–155, *154*
laser printers. *See* printers
latency, **83**, **137**
LCD displays. *See* displays
Lehrman, Paul, 284
line filtering, **168**
load balancing, 45
Logitech cordless mouse, **197–200**, *198–201*
Logitech QuickCam webcam, 220, **220**
Long, Ben, 283
LVD connectors, 270, *271*

M

magazine resources, **282–283**
magnetism, 3
main boards. *See* motherboards
maintenance
cleaning
CRT displays, 141–142
inkjet printers, 109, 111

laser printers, 109–111, *110*
LCD displays, 142
mice, 193, *193*
tape drives, 62
lubricating printers, 111–113, *112*
notebook battery care, 188
master/slave jumpers, **46**, *47*
Mbps/MBps, 265
MCA (Micro Channel Architecture) buses, **273**
memory, **16–35**
adding to video cards, 127–130
buffering, 18
capacity
defined, **17**
warning, 20
what you can add, 19–20
what you have, 19
what you need, 16, 20–21
double-checking specs, 18
error-checking, 17
modules
adding, 27–31, *28–30*
antistatic protection, 28, 33, 34, *34*
contact materials, 18
DIMM packaging, 25–26, *25*
locating in PCs, *13–14*
packaging, 17
pins, 18
removing, 31–35, *33–34*
RIMM packaging, 26, *27*
SIMM packaging, 24–25, *24*
socket locations, 28
warnings, 25, 26
overview of, 16
registering, 17
speed, 17, 21–23
types
BEDO, 22
DDR, 23, 130
EDO, 21
FPM, 21
overview of, 17, 21
RDRAM, 22
SDRAM, 22
SGRAM, 130
SRAM, 23, *23*

VRAM, 129
WRAM, 129
upgradability in printers, 91
voltage, 18
mice, *See also* input devices
accessories, 201, *202*
cables/ports on PC back panel, 8–9
cleaning, 193, *193*
corded mice, 192
cordless, installing, 197–200, *198–201*
cordless mice, 192
mechanical mice, 193, *193*
optical mice, 193
opto-mechanical mice, 193
overview of, 192, 194
resolution, 194
sample rates, 192–193
MicroHouse Technical Library, 278
MIDI (Musical Instrument Digital Interface),
See also multimedia
files, 206
joysticks and, 195
keyboards, 210–214, *212–213*
ports, 195, *195*
MIDI for the Professional (Lehrman and Tully),
284
Minasi, Mark, 283, 284
mirroring hard drives, **52**
modems. *See* communications
monitors. *See* displays
motherboards, **12**, *13–14*, 116, *See also* BIOS;
CPUs
mouse. *See* mice
Mouse Skatez, *201*, **201**
MouseRate utility, 192
MTBF (mean time between failures), 40
multilink modems, **66**
multimedia, **204–222**, *See also* input devices
digital cameras, 214–216, *214*
display options, 121–122
MIDI keyboards, 210–214, *212–213*
motion, 205
music, 206
overview of, 192, 204
pictures, 204–205
speakers, 8–9, 206–210, *207–210*

video capture devices, 216–220, *216–219*
warning, 213
webcams, 220–222, *220, 222*
multiread drives, 59–60
multisynching, display, **120**
My Computer, 19

N

names, computer/workgroup, **155**
NAT (network address translation), **80**
NetBEUI protocol, 147
networks, **144–165**
    installing wired networks
        computer names, 155
        configuring adapters, 152
        connecting cables, 156–157, *157–158*
        desktop PC setup, 150–154, *151, 153*
        equipment needed, 150
        finding interrupts, 152
        hubs, 145, 155–158, *156*
        inserting PCI adapters, 150–152, *151*
        IP addresses, 155
        laptop setup, 154–155, *154*
        network protocols, 155
        overview of, 149–150
        removing PCI slot covers, 150, *151*
        signaling methods, 147
        steps in, 150–158
        switches, 145, 155–158, *156–158*
        and testing, 158
        troubleshooting, 153–154, *153,*
          158–159
        warning, 154
        workgroup names, 155
    installing wireless networks
        Bluetooth and, 147
        desktop PC setup, 161–162, *161–162,*
          164–165
        equipment needed, 159
        overview of, 145–146, 159
        PC Card for laptops, 160–161, *160,*
          162, *162,* 164, *164*
        PCI adapters, 161–162, *162*
        signaling methods, 147
        steps in, 160–165
        USB adapters, 161, *161*
        warning, 162
        Wireless Access Points, 163–165,
          163–164
    LAN IP addresses, 79
    network adapters, 147
    network architectures, 148–149
    network protocols, 147–148
    network software, 149
    overview of, 144
    physical connections
        dedicated cabling, 145
        overview of, 144–145
        phone lines, 146
        power lines, 146–147
        wireless devices, 145–146
    printer port connections, 97–99, *97–98*
    sharing DSL service, 75–76
news servers, 280
newsgroups, **279–281**
newsreader programs, 279–280
Nokia Monitor Test, *134,* **134**
notebook power, *See also* laptops; power
    battery care, 188
    battery chargers, 189
    extra batteries, 188
    overview of, 188
    power supplies, 169
    removing batteries, 189
    voltage conversion kits, 189, *190*
NTSC input/output to/from monitors, **121**

O

optical drives, **41–42**, *See also* CD-R/CD-RW
    drives
optical mice, **193**
overclocking CPUs, **233**, 278
ozone filters for printers, **113–114**

P

paging, 16
PANs (personal access networks), **147**

parallel ports, *See also* ports
    connecting printers to, 8–9, 92–94, *92*
    versus USB buses, 252, 255
    Zip drives for, 54, *54*
parity, 272
parity memory, 17
partitioning hard drives, **51**
PC Card network adapter, *160*, **160–161**, 162, *162*, 164, *164*
PC Hardware in a Nutshell (Thompson), **284**
PC Magazine, **283**
PC upgrades, **2–14**
    hand tools for
        dental mirrors, 5
        electrical tape, 4
        flashlights, 4, *4*
        jar lids, 5
        needle-nose pliers, 4, 5
        nut drivers, 4
        overview of, 2
        "PC toolkits" and, 2
        retrieval spiders, 5, 5
        screwdrivers, 3, *3*
        warning, 3
        wire cutters, 4, 5
        wire ties, 5
    handling internal components, 6–7
    internal components, 12–13, *13–14*
    opening covers
        back panel cables/ports, 8–9
        cover latches/screws, 7, *10*
        overview of, 7
        power screws, 7, *10*
        and replacing, 9, *12*
        steps in, 7–9
PC-to-MIDI adapter cables, 211, *212*
PCI (peripheral component interconnect)
    buses, 250
    connectors, *256*
    network adapters, 150–152, *151*, 161–162, *162*
    slot covers, removing, 150, *151*
    slots, 12, 123, 124, *124*, **257**, *258*
PCL (printer-control language), 89, 90
peer-to-peer networks, **148–149**

personal access networks (PANs), **147**
Phillips screwdrivers, 3, *3*
phone line LAN connections, 146, *See also* communications
photo inkjet printers, 87, **87**
pictures, **204–205**, *See also* displays; multimedia
pigtails, **174**
PING command, 159
pins in memory modules, **18**
PIO (Programmed Input/Output), 53
ports
    connecting printers to
        infrared ports, 96–97
        on networks, 97–99, *97–98*
        overview of, 91
        parallel ports, 92–94, *92*
        serial ports, 94–95, *95*
        USB ports, 93–94
    connecting video cards to, 123–124, *124–125*
    game ports, 195, *195*
    parallel ports
        connecting printers to, 8–9, 92–94, *92*
        versus USB buses, 252, 255
        Zip drives for, 54, *54*
    on PC back panels, *9*
    serial ports
        connecting battery backup units to, 187, *187*
        connecting printers to, 94–95, *95*
        defined, 70–71, *70–71*
        versus USB buses, 252, 255
    USB ports, 93–94, 253, *253*, 254, *254*
POST (power-on self-test), **224**
PostScript language, 89, 90
power, **168–190**
    battery backup units
        automatic PC shutdowns via, 187, *187*
        calculating power ratings, 184–185
        defined, **168**
        installing, 185
        kinds of, 184
        overview of, 183–184
        power time needed, 185
        serial port connections, 187, *187*

testing, 186, *186*
in updating BIOS, 226–228, *227*
warranties, 187
cables/jacks on PC back panel, 8–9
connectors, 45, *45*, 49, 50, 56
measuring draw of USB devices,
260–261, *261*
in notebooks
battery care, 188
battery chargers, 189
extra batteries, 188
overview of, 188
power supplies, 169
removing batteries, 189
voltage conversion kits, 189, *190*
overview of, 168
power sources
AC outlets, networking via, 146–147
AC outlets, testing, 168, *169*
battery backup units, 168, 183–187,
186–187
defined, **168**
power supplies, defined, **12**, *13–14*, **168**,
169, *176*
replacing power supplies
AT/ATX power supplies, 173–174
calculating watts needed, 172–173
EMI/RFI and, 174
equipment needed, 175
finding replacements, 174–175
getting dimensions, 173–174
heat/non-heat sensing units, 173
overview of, 170–171
protection circuits and, 174
reconnecting connectors, 178–179
removing fan grilles, 178, *179*
removing power connectors, 176, *177*
removing power supply screws, 178, *178*
single/variable fan speeds and, 173
steps in, 175–179
warranties and, 174
upgrading power supplies
by adding connectors, 170, *170*
capacitors and, 181
overview of, 169
by replacing, 170–179, *171*, *176–179*

by replacing fans only, 180–182,
181–183
warning, 170
PowerQuest's Partition Magic, **51**
pressure-sensitive graphics tablets,
202–204, *203*
print servers, **97**, *98*
printer-control language (PCL), 89, 90
printers, **86–114**
factors in buying
beauty, 86, 90
cartridge capacity, 91
cost, 86, 89–90
duplexing, 91
duty cycle, 91
envelopes feature, 91
memory upgradability, 91
paper capacity, 91
paper size capability, 90
paper weight options, 91
print quality, 90
resolution, 90
speed, 86, 89
warning, 89
GDI printers, 89
inkjet printers
aligning printheads, 103–104, *104*
cleaning, 109, 111
configuring options, 102–103, *103*
connecting cables, 101, *102*
cost, 89–90
defined, **86–87**, *87*
ink cartridges, 91, 100, *100*
installing, 99–104, *100–104*
lubricating, 111–113, *112*
paper tray setup, 100, *101*
paper type options, 102–103, *103*
print quality, 90
reducing paper jams, 113
speed, 89
laser printers
cleaning, 109–111, *110*
configuring, 108–109
cost, 89, 90
defined, **87**, *88*
fuser cleaning pads, 106, *106*, 111

installing, 104–109, *105–107*
LCD panels, 107, *107*
loading paper, 106
lubricating, 111, *112*
ozone filters, 113–114
print quality, 90
properties sheet, 107
reducing paper jams, 113
speed, 89
toner cartridges, 91, 105, *105*, 108
in multifunction devices, 88
niche printers, 88
overview of, 86
photo inkjet printers, 87, *87*
port connections
infrared ports, 96–97
on networks, 97–99, *97–98*
overview of, 91
parallel ports, 92–94, *92*
serial ports, 94–95, *95*
USB ports, 93–94
processors. *See* CPUs
Promise Technology, Inc., 44, *44*
protection circuits, 174
protocols, network, **147–148**, 155
PS/2 adapters, USB-to-, *199*, **199**
PS2RatePlus utility, 193

Q

QIC (quarter inch cartridge) tape drives, **42–43**

R

RAM. *See* memory
RAW (Read-After-Write) verification, 43
RDRAM (Rambus Dynamic RAM), **22**
refresh rates, 119, **132–133**
registered memory, **17**
removing
CD-ROM drives, 54–56, *56*
fan grilles, 178, *179*
memory modules, 31–35, *33–34*
notebook batteries, 189
PCI slot covers, 150, *151*

replacing, *See also* installing; upgrading
CPUs, **234–246**
non-ZIF socket CPUs, 240–242, *240–241*
overview of, 230, 232
slot cartridge CPUs, 242–246, *243–245*
slot-to-socket adapters and, 245–246, *245*
warnings, 235, 246
ZIF socket CPUs, 234–239, *234–239*
power supplies, **170–179**
AT/ATX power supplies, 173–174
calculating watts needed, 172–173
EMI/RFI and, 174
equipment needed, 175
finding replacements, 174–175
getting dimensions, 173–174
heat/non-heat sensing units, 173
overview of, 170–171
protection circuits and, 174
reconnecting connectors, 178–179
removing fan grilles, 178, *179*
removing power connectors, 176, *177*
removing power supply screws, 178, *178*
single/variable fan speeds and, 173
steps in, 175–179
warranties and, 174
power supply fans, 180–182, *181–183*
resistor pack terminators, 270, *271*
resolution, *See also* displays
defined, **119**, **130–131**
digital cameras and, 215
mice and, 194
multimedia images and, 204–205
printers and, 90
resources, *See also* Web site resources
books, 283–284
magazines, 282–283
newsgroups, 279–281
Web sites, 276–279
RFI (radio frequency interference), 174
RIMM (Rambus Inline Memory Module), **26**, 27
root hubs, **259**
Rosenthal, Morris, 283
rotational speed of hard drives, **40**
routers, DSL, **77–82**, *78–82*

S

sampling rates, **192–193**
satellite services, **83–84**
scan converters, 121, 217
Schenk, Sonja, 283
screens. *See* displays
SCSI buses, **264–272**, *See also* buses
    benefits of, 264
    cable connectors, 265, 266
    cables, 265
    Disconnect/Reconnect feature, 272
    dual-channel controllers, 266–267, *267*
    overview of, 250, 264
    parity support, 272
    settings
        controller IDs, 267
        device IDs, 268–269, *268–269*
        device priorities, 269–270
        enabling controller BIOS, 272
        options, 272
        overview of, 265–266
        termination, 270–272, *271*
    single-channel controllers, 266–267
    speed, 264–265
    versions of, 264–265
    warning, 265
SCSI drives, *See also* storage devices
    defined, **39**
    rotational speed, 40
    tape drives for, *60–61*, **60**
    upgrading IDE drives to, 51–52
    Zip drives for, 54
SDRAM (Synchronous Dynamic RAM), **22**
seek time, **40**
self-powered hubs, **260**
sequencer software, **214**
serial ports, *See also* ports
    connecting battery backup units to, 187, *187*
    connecting printers to, 94–95, *95*
    defined, *70–71*, **70–71**
    versus USB buses, 252, 255
SGRAM (Synchronous Graphics RAM), **130**
sharing, *See also* networks
    DSL service, 75–76
    Internet connections, 76

side rails, *47*, **47**, 48
signal cables, *13–14*, **13**
signaling methods on networks, **147**
SIMM (Single Inline Memory Module), 24,
    24–25
single-channel controllers, SCSI, **266–267**
slave/master jumpers, **46**, 47
slocket adapters, CPU, *245*, **245–246**
slot cartridge CPUs, **242–246**, *243–245*
slot CPUs, *231*, **231**, 232
slot screwdrivers, 3, *3*
slots
    expansion slots, 12, *13–14*
    ISA slots, 12
    PCI slots, 12, 123, 124, *124*, **257**, *258*
    removing PCI slot covers, 150, *151*
SMP (symmetric multi-processing), **248**
SO-RIMM (Small Outline Rambus Inline
    Memory Module), 26
Sony Hi-8 camcorder, *217–219*, **217–220**
sound. *See* multimedia
speaker cables/ports, 8–9
speaker systems, **206–210**, *207–210*
speed
    bus speed, 17, 232
    of cooling fans, 173
    CPU speed, 231–232
    of displays, 121, 132
    of FireWire buses, 262
    hard drive rotational speed, 40
    memory speed, 17
    of printers, 86, 89
    of SCSI buses, 264–265
    speeding up modems, 65–66
    of USB buses, 255
SPS (standby power supply) batteries, **184**
SRAM (Static RAM), 23, **23**
SSID (Service Set Identity), **164**
Stabilant-22 contact enhancer, 27, 29, **29**, 72,
    129
static bags, anti-, 34, *34*
static electricity, 6
static wrist straps, anti-, 28, **28**, 33
storage devices, **38–62**
    adding

CD-R/CD-RW drives, 54–58, *56–58*
Jaz drives, 53–54
second IDE drives, 43–51, *44–50*
tape drives, 60, *60–61*
Zip drives, 53–54, *53–54*
cartridge drives, 41
CD-R/CD-RW optical drives
defined, **41–42**
disc media, 59–60
external/internal drives, 58–59, *58–59*
upgrading CD-ROM drives to, 54–58,
56–58
DVD drives, 42
floppy disk drives, 38–39
hard drives
cache, 40–41
defragmenting, 61
durability, 40
interfaces, 39
mirroring, 52
overview of, 38–39
partitioning, 51
rotational speed, 40
seek time, 40
IDE drives
adding, 43–51, *44–50*
defined, **39**
rotational speed, 40
upgrading to SCSI, 51–52
warnings, 48, 49
Jaz drives, 41, 53–54
maintaining, 61–62
overview of, 38
SCSI drives
defined, **39**
rotational speed, 40
upgrading IDE to, 51–52
tape drives
adding, 60, *60–61*
cleaning, 62
defined, **42–43**
retensioning, 62
warning, 42
Zip drives, 41, 53–54, *53–54*
subnet masks, 148

surge protection, 72, **72**, 168, 183
swapping, 16
switches
DIP switches, 237, *238–239*
in keyboards, 195–196, *196*
on wired networks, 145, 155–158, *156–158*
symmetric multi-processing (SMP), **248**
Synchronous Dynamic RAM (SDRAM), **22**
system boards. *See* motherboards
system trays, **252**

T

tape drives, *See also* storage devices
adding, 60, *60–61*
cleaning, 62
defined, **42–43**
retensioning, 62
TCP/IP Jumpstart (Blank), 148
TCP/IP protocols, 147, **148**
telephone line LAN connections, **146**, *See also*
communications
terminal adapters, 64
termination, SCSI bus, **270–272**, *271*
terminator modules, 26
testing
AC outlets, 168, *169*
battery backup units, 186, *186*
wired networks, 158
THD (total harmonic distortion), 207
Thompson, Robert Bruce, 284
Token Ring networks, 147
toner cartridges, 91, *105*, **105**, 108
tools, hand. *See* PC upgrades
Torx screwdrivers, 3, *3*
trackballs, *194*, **194**
tracks, **40**
Travan tape drives, **42–43**
troubleshooting
USB buses, 259
wired networks, 153–154, *153*, 158–159
Tully, Tim, 284
TV tuners, 121, 124, *125*

U

Ultra 160 LVD cable, **270**, *271*
Ultra ATA drives, **39**, 40
updating BIOS software
 battery backup units and, 226–228, *227*
 determining need for, 225–226
 downloading latest version, 226
 keeping old BIOS on diskettes, 228
 overview of, 225
 performing updates, 228–229
 reasons for, 225
 warning, 226
upgrading, *See also* installing; PC upgrades;
 replacing
 buses, reasons for, 250–251
 IDE hard drives to SCSI, 51–52
 notebook buses, 272–273
 power supplies
  by adding connectors, 170, *170*
  capacitors and, 181
  overview of, 169
  by replacing, 170–179, *171*, *176–179*
  by replacing fans only, 180–182,
   181–183
  warning, 170
 printer memory, 91
 to USB 2.0 buses, 256, 259, 260
 video display adapters, 122–123
UPS (uninterruptible power supply) batteries, **184**
USB buses, **252–261**, *See also* buses
 "A" cable connectors, 254, *254*
 asynchronous mode, 255
 configuring, 252
 versus FireWire buses, 262
 installing USB host adapters, 256–259,
  256, 258
 installing USB hubs, 259–260, *259*
 isochronous mode, 255
 overview of, 250
 versus parallel ports, 252, 255
 ports, 9, 253, *253*, 254, *254*
 versus serial ports, 252, 255
 speed, 255
 troubleshooting, 259

upgrading to 2.0, 256, 259, 260
USB cables, 8
USB devices
 "B" cable connectors, 254, *255*
 CD burners, 58–59
 configuration, 260
 daisy chaining, 252, 255
 hot swappability, 252
 interrupts, 252
 keyboards, 255
 listed, 252–253
 measuring power draw, 260–261, *261*
 printers, 93–94
 support for, 255
 wireless network adapters, 161, *161*
 Zip drives, 54
USB-to-PS/2 adapters, 199, *199*
versions of, 255–256
Usenet newsgroups, **279–281**
UTP (Unshielded Twisted Pair) cable, **145**

V

VA (volt-amps), 185
VCRs, using displays with, 121
VGA connectors, *138*, **138**
video adapters, *See also* displays
 defined, **116**
 disabling motherboard video, 123
 speed and, 121
 upgrading, overview of, 122–123
 video cards
  adding memory to, 127–130
  defined, **116**
  drivers, 127
  installing, 125–127, *126*
  port connections, 123–124, *124–125*
 warranties, 122
video cables/ports, 8–9
video images. *See* multimedia
viewable area, **117–118**
voice channels, DSL, **78**
voice modems, **66**
voltage conversion kits, **189**, *190*

voltage, memory, **18**
VRAM (Video RAM), **129**
VRM (voltage regulator module), 247, **247**

W

Wacom's Graphire, installing, **202–204**, *203*
WAN (Wide Area Network) IP addresses, 79
WAP (Wireless Access Point) devices, 145–146,
 163–164, **163–165**
warranties
 battery backup units, 187
 displays, 122
 power supplies, 174
waveform files, **206**
Web connections. *See* communications
Web site resources, *See also* resources
 Anvil Studio sequencer, 214
 bookstores, 276–277
 CPU overclocking, 233, 278
 CPU speed differences, 232
 DataComm Warehouse cables, 265
 DisplayMate, 134
 DSL services, 68
 FireWire news, 262
 Google, 134, 277, 280
 HomePlug Powerline Alliance, 146
 Intel motherboards, 276
 Intel processors, 231–232
 Intel USB System Check, 257
 jumpers, 46

 Laptop Express, 188
 listed, 276–279
 magazines, 282–283
 memory configurators, 18
 Microsoft, 276, 278
 mouse accessories, 201
 newsgroups, 279–281
 overview of, 276
 PCI versions, 154
 search engines, 277, 278, 279
webcams, *220*, **220–222**, *222*
Wildstrom, Stephen, 282
wireless networks. *See* networks
wireless services, *See also* communications
 overview of, 82–83
 satellite, 83–84
 wireless local loop, 84
workgroup names, **155**
workgroup networks, **148–149**
workstation monitors, 120
WRAM (Windows RAM), **129**

Y

"Y" cable, **211**, *212*
Y-adapters, *170–171*, **170**

Z

Zip drives, **41**, 53–54, *53–54*, *See also* storage
 devices

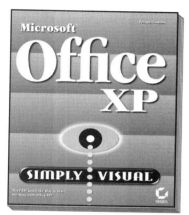
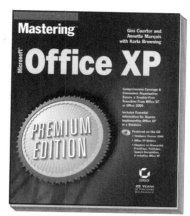
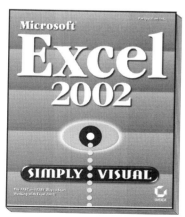